CHRONICLES OF THE FAE PRINCESS

CHRONICLES OF THE FAE PRINCESS

THE HALFLING FAE ACADEMY™ COMPLETE TRILOGY

J.L. HENDRICKS

MICHAEL ANDERLE

DISRUPTIVE IMAGINATION

LMBPN Publishing
PMB 196, 2540 South Maryland Pkwy
Las Vegas, NV 89109

First US edition, May 2020
Version 1.02, March 2022
eBook ISBN: 978-1-64202-923-9
Print ISBN: 978-1-64202-924-6

THE CHRONICLES OF THE FAE PRINCESS TEAM

Thanks to our Beta Readers:

Crystal Wren, Nicole Emens, Micky Cocker, Mary Morris, John Ashmore, Kelly O'Donnell, Larry Omans, Michael Baumann, Daniel Weigert, Rachel Beckman, Theresa Holmes, Jim Caplan

Thanks to our JIT Team:

Angel LaVey
Dave Hicks
Deb Mader
Debi Sateren
Diane L. Smith
Jackey Hankard-Brodie
Jeff Goode
Kathleen Fettig
Micky Cocker
Misty Roa
Paul Westman
Veronica Stephan-Miller

Editor
SkyHunter Editing Team

DEDICATIONS

Dedicated to all you dreamers out there.
Never stifle your imagination,
and never stop going after your dreams!

— J.L. Hendricks

To Family, Friends and
Those Who Love
To Read.
May We All Enjoy Grace
To Live The Life We Are
Called.

— Michael Anderle

PART I

PROLOGUE

Lilliana ducked her head into the biting wind and continued down the sidewalk. Of the many reasons Boston had been the city of choice for her and her husband, the winter weather wasn't one of them. She pulled the collar of her coat close around her neck to keep off some of the chill, then moved nearer to the crowd in front of her.

Warmth radiated off them, but that wasn't what motivated her to get so close she could just about peek over their shoulders and see what their grocery bags had to say about their dinner plans. She was hoping if she crowded them enough, the people swarming the sidewalk and spilling out onto the edges of the street would take the hint and hurry up or allow her to pass.

Either way, she needed to move faster. The hair standing up on the back of her neck and the sensation of eyes scraping down her spine was enough to confirm her suspicions. They'd found her. Which meant they had found her husband and baby daughter as well.

Lilliana had always known this was a possibility. She had never pretended—to herself or to James—that they could simply go about their lives like normal people and forget about her past. Even if those tracking her hadn't ever found them, a part of her would never be able to fully separate herself from who she really was. That reality put her family in danger, and she had done what she could to prepare herself and her husband for it. From early in their relationship, as soon as she had revealed her secret to him, she had taught James how to move around unobserved and remain hidden so they had some chance of staying out of the grasp of her enemies.

They had succeeded for years, but not this time. They'd been too comfortable and stayed in Boston for too long. No home had ever been permanent, no city would ever be the place where Lilliana and James could settle and live out their lives together. Even after their daughter was born, they'd had to keep moving. But the contentment of being a little family had made Boston too much of a temptation. They'd lingered well after they should have moved on. Days had turned to weeks, which had turned to months—months on borrowed time. Now they were paying the price. She had picked up a tail.

A very good one if she had to make an evaluation. Whoever had been sent after her had tracked Lilliana without giving themselves away until only moments ago. She didn't know how long she had been followed or how much they had learned about her life. She couldn't go back home. Her enemies may have been in Boston for long enough to have already identified her home and learned what few routines she and James allowed themselves.

They may know the grocery store he liked to go to or the park they took Ariana to for fresh air. They may know his favorite bakery and the smell of the lemon spritz cookies which lured him there. They may even know that cobbled street she loved and the dips in the old, worn stones she knew so well. They may already know where she and her family lived.

But maybe they didn't. They may have just arrived and had happened to catch her trail early. She might still have a chance to direct them away from her husband and daughter.

But she couldn't go home. Nothing could make her lead them right to the people she loved the most. This was exactly why she had established a safe house in the city, far away from the cozy apartment they'd settled into when they'd moved here.

Finally, the crowd ahead of her dispersed over a wider stretch of sidewalk, some melting into shops or restaurants and others finding their cars. Lilliana rushed forward, weaving between them as fast as she could. The people she pushed past wouldn't have seen anything odd if they looked at her. Nothing stranger than a woman running like hell down the sidewalk occasionally trying to hide behind one of them. She was always careful to make sure her glamours were fully engaged before walking among the human inhabitants of the city. That didn't stop them from expressing some of their famed Boston kindness of spirit, complete with a few creatively woven, expletive-laden sentences hurled her way.

Their attitude didn't matter to Lilliana. She simply had to escape. If she could lose her tail somewhere on the streets, she could buy herself some extra time. She continued to bob and weave her way between people, pushing herself to move as fast as she could without drawing the attention of the police. Not that they could help her. They wouldn't be able to see who was following her. Besides, a wide-eyed woman rambling about mythical creatures and lands which don't exist probably wouldn't do much to help her.

At least the run was warming her up.

Lilliana hazarded a glance over her shoulder, but no one was behind her. Which didn't mean they were gone. She could still feel them watching her, and she had the distinct sensation of not being alone. Out of the corner of her eye, she caught a shimmer in the glass storefront of a nearby boutique. They were there. They'd managed to conceal themselves, even from her.

She ducked down a tight alley and out onto another street, where she turned and headed back in the other direction for several blocks. Returning to the first street, she retraced her steps. The detour delayed some of her progress through the city but would confuse the trail she left. She ran for several more minutes before she felt confident enough to pause at the stop for the bus that would bring her close to her safe house.

The wait was only a matter of a few moments, but it felt like she was standing there for hours. When the bus finally arrived, Lilliana allowed herself to be caught in the crush of people trying to enter and exit at the same time. Eventually, she was shoved inside, where she landed on the only seat left. She had ignored the little old lady behind her and she didn't even care.

Her hand shook as she fished her phone from her pocket, flipped it open, and dialed James. With every ring, she tried to regain her composure. He didn't answer. Then the beep of the voicemail sliced through her. This might have been her last chance to speak to him for a long time, and she wouldn't even get to say goodbye. But she couldn't dwell on her pain. What she had to tell him was too important.

"James." Her voice was husky as she tried to speak loud enough for him to hear her, but not so loud that everyone around her could. "I need you to listen to me very carefully. First, know that I love you and Ariana very, very much. I always will."

She drew in a breath and let it out slowly.

"I've been discovered. Someone has been tracking me. I don't know for how long or if they know anything about you and Ariana yet. You have to get out. Now. As fast as you can. There's a loose floorboard in the bedroom closet. There's a space under there where I've stashed some things just in case this happened. You'll find cash and the documents you'll need. Take all of it. I won't be going back to the house."

Emotion tightened her throat painfully and tears formed in the corners of her eyes, burning as she tried to bring herself to give the next instructions. They were so final. It had to be done, but Lilliana felt like as soon as she said it, she would be tearing herself away from her family completely.

"You need to make sure Ariana has everything she could need. Pack as much as you possibly can. You'll need at least a few days' worth of baby food and formula, diapers, and wipes. And a few changes of clothes. You don't know when you're going to be able to stop or buy new things, so you're going to have to take as much as you'll be able to carry with you. And don't forget Oscar."

The image of the blue stuffed bunny—well-loved even in the brief time he had belonged to her baby daughter—was all the encouragement her tears needed to spill over and sear their way down her cheeks. The other people on the bus could see her, but it didn't matter. None of them knew her. They didn't know what she was facing or what it felt like to leave this message.

"Please take care of yourself and of our daughter. She has to be your focus now. Think only about the two of you and getting as far away as you possibly can. Stay safe. You're not going to be able to contact me anymore. Just know how much I love you. I will think of you every moment we're apart and wish I was there with you. Kiss Ariana for me and don't let her forget me. Sing our song to her and tell her every day how precious she is to me. I love you, James. More than I'll ever be able to tell you. Now, run."

Lilliana closed the phone and shoved it back into her pocket. The bus was close to her stop, and the anxious feeling was building in the pit of her stomach again. As soon as the bus stopped, she stood and joined the stampede to the exit. She hurried down two blocks, turned a corner, and rushed into a seedy, stained, and battered neighborhood. Stopping beside a green metal trashcan which had spilled the contents of the bag forced inside by some dissatisfied, jaded city worker, she retrieved her phone and stared at it for a few seconds. James might call her back. If he did, she wanted to hear his voice and say goodbye.

The phone stayed silent. She drew another breath, snapped it in half, and dumped the useless pieces into the trashcan. The sensation of being watched returned as she kept walking. But there were people staring at her from their apartment windows and watching her progress from their stoops. A group of men took a few steps after her but hung back when she didn't slow down.

Her safe house was on the next block. If she could get inside, she would be out of danger—at least for the moment. She spotted her shortcut up ahead, a dark alley between two apartment buildings. As usual, the alley smelled of heat pumped through an exhaust fan and of trash in the dumpsters pushed up against the brick walls of the buildings. Littered with garbage and detritus from daily downtrodden life, it was hardly a lovely stroll. But it would get her to the safe house faster.

Lilliana was halfway there, slipping between two tightly positioned dumpsters. The end of the alley was so close she saw an opaque puff of breath from someone strolling by on the sidewalk. That was the last image she saw before an explosion tore through the air and ripped the concrete out from under her feet.

CHAPTER ONE

Phillipsburg, Montana – Halfling Fae Academy
Early June

"If you just focus a little harder, you can figure it out," said the halfling fae teenager. Her long, silver braid shimmered in the sunlight as she turned to address the girl standing across from her.

"Oh, because you're doing it *so* perfectly, right?" the other girl spat.

Several inches shorter, and with hair so inky black it had a blue sheen, she was a stark contrast to her fellow fae. Their appearances marked each of their differences, creating a visual of the distance between them.

As with the two boys who stood several yards away, they were from opposing Courts. Court rivalry was the reason they weren't getting along as they paired off to train in the field behind their academy, perfecting their abilities. But it was also why they'd been forced together.

As the most powerful and promising halfling fae of the Elmhurst Academiae Superiorum, the four young fae were required to train together by the headmaster. They were supposed to collaborate, build their skills, and assist each other to reach their full potential. On paper, it had seemed like a good idea.

With their abilities, they could become exceptional. If they worked hard, each of the four had the potential to pursue successful careers. It wasn't lost on Principal Elmhurst that some healthy competition among the four would push them all to do better and reach new goals faster.

But in practice, things weren't working out very smoothly. The two Seelie and two Unseelie were having a tough time cooperating, and the struggle showed when they met to hone their skills and work on new abilities. Principal Elmhurst didn't care about the tension. She had no patience for the politics and deep-rooted conflict between the Seelie and Unseelie Courts—neither of which were excuses she'd accept. The four had reluctantly resigned themselves to spending at least their foreseeable future at the academy together.

"Actually, if you would stop flailing around long enough, I could show you," Luna, the silver-haired Seelie fae, said.

She had always tried to encourage cooperation in the group and had made an effort to be nice to the others, but today Vivi was pushing Luna to her limits. Even Carson, Vivi's fellow Unseelie, put more effort into cooperating and making the most of their forced alliance. Not so much with Vivi. The somewhat embittered wild card of the bunch made no secret of her frustration at being stuck with a pair of inferior Seelie fae.

Vivi was absolutely confident in her belief that she was the best halfling at the academy. She would complete her education there, go on to graduate college, and have no problem at all in obtaining a job at the embassy. It was what she had to do. Her father expected it of her, and he would tolerate nothing less. She wasn't alone in her aspirations to land one of the highly coveted jobs at the embassy. Securing such a position was the only way a halfling could gain admittance into Faerie, and Carson also had his sights set on the same goal.

Though both had the potential to achieve such an impressive accomplishment, the most skilled fae in the academy was actually

Luna. Quieter and more studious, she possessed a better mastery of her magic and tried to help the others—like Vivi—as much as she could. When Vivi would accept it, that is. Far more often, the antagonistic Unseelie pushed away any offer of help. Sometimes this meant choosing to do her own thing and figure it out for herself. And sometimes it meant creating trouble for the group just to make a point and have a laugh.

"We've been at this for hours." Zander, the other Seelie fae, strode toward the girls. "I'm hungry. Let's all take a break and cool off." This was his way of telling the pair to take a step back from each other before they started another fight.

"I'm hungry, too," Luna said. "Let's go to the café. My mom will make us something."

Meeting at Luna's mother's café was one of the few ways the four willingly spent time together when they weren't training. Like everyone but Zander, Luna had a human mother and a fae father. But she didn't know her father, didn't even know his name. She attended the halfling academy on a scholarship, and the only way Nicoletta was able to open the small café near the campus was through the secret support of an unknown investor.

Luna had always suspected that her father had sent the money for her mother to start her business. But Nicoletta had rejected the possibility immediately. She didn't believe he would go to such an extent to help them.

It wasn't that he'd had absolutely nothing to do with Luna. Not wanting to be a full-time father to a halfling child, he had left Nicoletta as soon as he'd found out she was pregnant. But over the years, he had been a part of Luna's life from a distance. Every once in a great while, he would send money for Luna. Usually, these moments of fatherly attention came when she demonstrated a special skill, accomplished a major task, or had done extremely well in a class. She pushed herself to excel for many reasons, but a fundamental part of her drive to do well was for her father. She craved his attention, even though she didn't know him or anything about him.

Nicoletta had refused to divulge even the most basic details to her daughter. She didn't tell Luna her father's name, or where they had met, or anything about their relationship. The only thing she'd revealed was that he was very powerful. Of course, to a human like her mother, Luna was also very powerful, so *that* piece of information didn't mean much.

This was another thing setting her apart from the other three in her group. She was the only one relying on a scholarship to pay for her tuition at the halfling academy. Even Zander had his dues paid by his fae parent. He had been left on his human father's doorstep by his fae mother and had never met her, or had anything to do with her, but she'd seen to it that her son attended the school and received a monthly stipend like the others.

But the café did well for Luna and her mother. Though humans often came by to indulge in Nicoletta's delicious cooking, the spot mostly catered to the fae, which included the halfling students. Few local eateries provided vegetarian menus. Montana was beef country, where restaurants offered heavily meat-based menus, so the fae had limited options when it came to grabbing a bite to eat. Nicoletta's diner ensured that the students at the academy, and any family who visited or lived in the area, had somewhere to rely on for a meal consisting of more than a plate of iceberg lettuce and a handful of meager cucumber slices.

There wouldn't be many halflings or fae in the café. Summer meant most of the students were gone. The summer season was supposed to be spent at home with their families, or on vacation with a fae parent. Usually, the only students who lingered around the campus during breaks were those who needed extra tutoring to hone their skills and abilities, and the orphans surrendered to the academy for training.

Neither case applied to Luna or her group. This summer, Principal Elmhurst had insisted the four halflings stay behind at the academy to give them more opportunity to gel. It was the first time in which students had crossed Courts to work together. These four were a unique unit. Never in the history of the Elmhurst Academiae Superiorum had a group of Halflings succeeded in harnessing the Power of

Five. But the academy board and the principal believed it might be possible with the collaboration of these four, even with the unusual combination of two from the Seelie Court and two from the Unseelie. All they needed to do now was find the right fifth person, and they could accomplish this incredibly rare and amazing feat.

It had been centuries since any group of halflings anywhere had created the Power of Five. Most fae didn't even believe it was possible anymore. But Principal Elmhurst was convinced and had insisted on the four students working closely to try to achieve it. Which had meant foregoing their summer away from the school in favor of spending the weeks working on their skills and learning to deal with each other more effectively.

And while they trained, they also waited. Searches were being performed across various academies around the world to find their fifth member. Though conducted among the most powerful and highly skilled of all the halfling academies, the search was yet to discover anyone who came even close to matching the power required to complete the group.

They arrived at the café and sank onto the benches arranged out front. Vivi groaned and dropped her head back against the bench.

"I'm so tired of working with these Seelie scum," she muttered to Carson.

Vivi and Carson were from the Unseelie Court, while Luna and Zander were from the Seelie Court. Neither fae Court played well with the other. The fae could be nuisances, but the Unseelie seemed to have a bit of evil bred into their souls. Of the two Courts, a human would fare better after meeting a Seelie fae. Most human interactions with the Unseelie ended in disaster or broken hearts.

The lucky humans worked for the different Courts in menial labor positions, or they were used for consensual breeding purposes.

Luna and Zander ignored Vivi, which only made her angrier. She wanted a reaction. She intended to make them just as uncomfortable and frustrated as she was. Her gaze lingered for a brief second on Zander, but she looked away, forcing down the thoughts and feelings which always crept up on her when she glanced at him. She focused instead on utilizing her magic in a new way, a way to at least allow her to have some fun if she was going to be forced to work with the Seelie. A practical joke would bring Luna down a couple of pegs, and that was exactly what Vivi needed.

Zander looked at Vivi, not for the first time curious about the expression in her intense eyes when they flickered over him before she turned away. The possibility that she might like him sometimes flashed through his mind, but just as quickly as it did, he pushed it away. It was impossible. Simply being from the different Courts would stop it. No one ever crossed Courts for romantic relationships, not that he had ever heard of.

"I have an idea," Luna said, pulling them all out of their own thoughts and bringing their attention to her. "We've been having trouble working together to make anything happen. We can't just keep focusing on our individual skills and abilities. If we're going to accomplish the Power of Five, we have to be able to work together. I think we should try to create a Faerie circle of purple pansies. We will have to merge our powers together to make it happen. We'll have to be in harmony, or it could end up just becoming a jungle or some other disaster."

Vivi snorted. "Are you kidding me? That's your big idea? How could you be so childish?"

"We have to start somewhere," Zander said. "So far, all our other attempts have failed. We're stuck together, so we might as well put some effort into making something happen."

"Are you suggesting we sprout up some purple pansies right out here? Right out in the open in front of everyone?" Carson asked.

"No. We need to go somewhere out of the way," said Zander.

"How about the field outside the academy?" Vivi suggested. "Where we *always* practice."

"No. It's not isolated enough. We need to be able to focus completely," Zander said.

A tension simmered within the group as to who truly held the leadership position, but in almost all situations, the Seelie male was the one who rose to the top.

"There's another field on the outskirts of town. It's not too far from here, but no one is ever there," Luna said.

"Perfect. Let's get something to eat and then head that way," Zander said.

After lunch, they made their way toward the field. The two pairs walked along separately, each fae speaking only to their Court-mate.

"How am I supposed to survive the school year living with her?" Luna asked, glancing over her shoulder at Vivi and Carson. Their heads were close together, and the brief snippets of the conversation she caught told her they were also discussing the impending moves that would force the two girls and the two boys to live together.

"It's going to be fine," Zander said.

"That's easy for you to say," Luna said. "Anyone can get along with you. You're going to convert Carson into your best friend by the end of the first night."

Zander let out a short laugh. "I doubt that."

It might have been a bit of a stretch to imagine the two fae guys suddenly bonding and creating a tight friendship within the first few hours of forced cohabitation, but Luna could still believe it was possible. If anyone could make something like that happen, it was Zander. He was the undisputed golden boy of the academy, the type of student every teacher longed for. A parent could fill all the walls in the house with pictures of amazing things, running out of space long before *he* ran out of accomplishments. He led in any activity he chose and achieved straight A's in all his classes with seemingly little effort.

But his grades weren't so unique among the group. With the exception of Vivi, they all maintained A averages in their classes. Only Vivi coasted along just behind them, her report cards cluttered with B's. Not because she wasn't smart enough to score the same high grades and achieve the academic awards as the other three. In fact, she was brilliant. Vivi simply didn't apply herself to any of her work.

She used to work just as hard as the others, but her enthusiasm had faded. She'd given up pushing herself all the time after last Christmas. She'd been excited for weeks about the upcoming ski trip she was going on with her fae father. It had been only the two of them after her mother had died, and the time they spent together had meant so much to her. She would never admit that, of course.

Everyone knew how hard Vivi's father was on her, and the pressure he put on her to excel at everything. She wanted nothing more in the world than for him to show her love and approval. But she couldn't let anyone know that. To an outsider, she appeared to not even care. Giving up on trying for more impressive grades meant he didn't give her the approval she wanted, but it also meant she didn't get hurt as often.

Christmas had been her breaking point. She'd been looking forward to it, had worked hard to make sure there would be plenty for the two of them to talk about, and she'd silently longed for the praise he would give her. Then, exactly two days before he was supposed to arrive at the academy to pick her up, he'd bailed on her.

He had no big excuse, no reason for why he couldn't be with her. Only a terse phone message delivered by someone from the office. It wasn't just that he hadn't come or that they weren't able to go on their skiing trip. Her father punking out on her meant Vivi spent the Christmas holiday at the academy by herself. Her only companions were the unsociable halflings who got off on being alone…or had been abandoned by their fae parent.

Since then, she'd been pissed off and had carried an even bigger chip on her shoulder.

"I don't know which I'm looking forward to less," Carson said. "Being in such close quarters with Zander all the time or the swarms of Seelie girls who will darken my doorstep."

"Don't even try. You know you're going to enjoy every single second of it. You might only date Unseelie girls, but you'll mess around with anyone who has breasts. Zander living with you will just be like a funnel bringing in a constant supply of fresh girls. When he rejects them, you'll be right there to scoop them up and make the most of all their desperation," Vivi said with a laugh.

Carson had the reputation around Elmhurst of being a male slut, and he did his best to live up to it.

They arrived at the field and reluctantly gathered in a loose circle at the center.

"I can put up a shield to keep the humans from seeing what we're doing," Carson volunteered.

It took him only a few moments to create the enchantment that would prevent any wayward human from happening by and seeing them conjuring flowers and creating little bursts of magic. It was a caution they had learned to employ early in their education. Their academy didn't exist in some different realm or in a place inaccessible by anyone other than their kind. They were right smack in the middle of a very human town, which meant always having to be careful and avoid being caught.

When the shield was in place, they started their attempts to conjure the Faerie circle. Every time they got close, Vivi derailed them. Her concentration wasn't there, her mind too far away with her plans to punk Luna.

"Seriously, Vivi," Carson finally snapped. "Unless you want to throw up camp out here and rough it until this thing happens, you need to get yourself together and stop screwing around."

His threat was enough to make her focus, and they made one more attempt. All around them, the Faerie circle formed. It was large and impressive, and the group was briefly excited until they realized the blooms around them were black instead of purple.

"Vivi!" the three shouted at her, but she only responded with a smirk.

Zander cleared the field of the black pansies. "Again," he snapped.

"Who are you to decide what we're going to do?" Vivi asked.

"You're the one who's making this so difficult," he replied angrily. "Shut up and focus."

A few hours later, Luna scanned the large circle of purple pansies that finally surrounded them. She smiled and nodded. "It looks good," she said. "Let's try another one."

Carson and Zander murmured in agreement, but Vivi scowled and backed away from them. With a slight sweep of her hand, she turned all the purple blooms black again and crouched to gather some in a bouquet. She presented them to Zander with a mocking smile. Instead of taking them, the Seelie male snapped his fingers and the flowers disintegrated in her hand.

"Don't be too impressed with yourself because of your little parlor trick," he said to Vivi. "Any of us could change the colors of the flowers. In fact, any of us could create the entire circle on our own. The difficult part of this is creating something with the four of us merging our powers together. It's the combination that matters. We have to be in harmony in order to accomplish tasks together."

The reason they were attempting to obtain the Power of Five was the level of power it would bring them. If a full-blooded group of fae obtained the Power of Five, they could do anything. Bring down planes, build a skyscraper in a day, make an entire neighborhood disappear, really anything they set their minds to. Of course, the fae knew not to mess with humans on such a grand scale.

But for a group of Halflings to obtain the Power of Five meant great respect from the Faerie world. They couldn't do quite as much as a full-blooded Power of Five could, but if records were correct, a halfling Power of Five could do more than any individual fae could.

The Seelie and Unseelie Queens could use them to keep the rebels at bay. The Power of Five could be harnessed to defend the Faerie Courts, or any large group the Courts deemed worthy of protection. They could also be used as a weapon against their enemies.

Vivi didn't want to hear it. She still believed Luna's plan to be woefully childish, and that it offered no real benefit as they worked on their abilities. Creating Faerie circles was something the halflings learned before puberty. A very basic skill, it was a common feature of playtime for the young of their kind. The challenge came when trying to do it as a group. Just the temperaments of such different people working together rendered the task almost impossible.

"It's a huge achievement that we were even able to do this to begin with," Luna said. "We need to keep practicing so we can get better at it."

Zander moved to stand between Luna and Vivi. "Look, we all know these tricks are child's play. The difficulty comes in merging our powers together. That's what the Power of Five is all about. If we can learn to work together in harmony, we will be unstoppable and can do anything we want."

"No," Vivi said. "I'm done. We've been out here for hours, and I've had my fill of silly flowers. I want to leave." Sometimes, she even wondered why they were trying. Sure, if she was one of the Five, she'd get her dream job, or rather her father's dream of what her job should be. But she was beginning to understand that her father would never show her any love. He was using her to advance his own status, exactly like most fae parents did with any of their children.

It wouldn't matter if she was one of the most powerful halfling fae in the world. She still wouldn't be worthy of his love.

CHAPTER TWO

Both sets of students dragged their feet as much as they could when it came to moving in together. The idea of being pushed together to work on their skills while giving up the break all the other students were enjoying was frustrating enough. Having to live in the same small space meant not even enjoying the relief of a break from each other when they were sleeping or relaxing at the end of the day. They were forced to be together, forced to deal with each other from the moment they opened their eyes in the morning until they closed them again at night. And technically even the time in between. The thought was intolerable.

But they could only resist the commands of the principal for so long. Living together was part of being a group. The more time they spent with each other, the better the chances they had of getting along. Even if they never learned to actually like each other, they would learn to cooperate. They could mesh their skills and abilities, increasing their powers to strengthen and improve each other's. None of them had believed that was going to happen, but they hadn't been given a choice. What Principal Elmhurst wanted, she got. It had only been a matter of time before they were ejected from their existing rooms and wedged into new ones with each other.

And that time had come.

Luna surveyed the room. She'd arrived first, which meant it was her choice which bed she wanted to claim for her own. It was an important decision. This would be the only space she'd be able to call hers for the rest of her time at the academy. Two more years. Or until Elmhurst had another idea and moved them again.

Luna considered each of the two beds. They were positioned in opposite corners, which at least provided some semblance of separation between them. It wasn't exactly privacy, but it was something.

Finally, she decided on the bed tucked into the corner next to a window with a view of the grounds beyond the heavy curtains, and it was on the other side of the room from the door to the hallway. It would be less noisy and give her more of a feeling of her own area. She set her trunk on the floor beside the bed and lifted the lid. No sooner had she reached in to take out her pajamas than the door to the room slammed open and stomping footsteps announced the arrival of her reluctant new roommate.

"Who says you get that bed?" Vivi immediately demanded.

"Hello to you, too," Luna said.

"That's the bed I want," the Unseelie fae said. "You're going to have to move to the other one."

Luna scoffed. "No. I was the first one to get here, which means I got to choose the bed I want. This one's mine."

"I don't care if you were the first one here. That's the bed I want," Vivi said, her voice creeping up louder.

"Again, no," Luna said.

Vivi tossed her bag onto the other bed and pushed her trunk up against the side of the bed with her foot. She eyed Luna's trunk, and a vicious smile curled her lips up. Focusing her magic on the clothes stacked inside, she shifted them around until she found what she was looking for.

"Here," she said, "let me help you unpack, roomie."

She lifted the pairs of neatly folded underwear from the trunk and made them float over Luna's head. They unfolded and puffed out in the air, looking like the sails of a ship. Luna let out an infuriated cry.

"Stop that!" She reached up to grab them, but Vivi lifted them higher. "What in Buddha's name is wrong with you?"

"I'm just curious. Has anyone even ever seen these things? I doubt it. Why would you want to show off dingy briefs? I guess this is all the proof I need that you aren't getting any play from anyone."

"Tell me, Vivi. Do you have to distribute numbered tickets for access to yours? Like at a deli counter? Now serving…"

The girls dissolved into a fierce argument, tearing into each other until the door opened again.

"Hey! Stop it, the two of you!" Zander shouted over their voices. "You've only lived together for ten minutes, and you're already on the brink of killing each other. This is ridiculous. At least try to get along. Vivi, put Luna's underwear down. Luna, stop making fun of Vivi. This is a seriously uncomfortable conversation for me, so I'd appreciate it if you just went ahead and cooperated. It's going to be better for everyone if you at least put a little bit of effort into co-existing with each other."

"So, does this mean all is fantastic over at the House of Zander and Carson?" Vivi snipped.

"Why does he get to come first in the title? You know, alphabetical order is the most widely accepted method of categorization in lists, and according to that standard, I would come first, making it the House of Carson and Zander," Carson said, appearing at the door.

No one could tell if he was joking or being serious, but it didn't matter. He strode into the room and approached Vivi. Though he tried not to let it show, his growing feelings for her would be obvious when he looked at her. The last thing the group needed was the additional tension if she rejected his crush on her.

"Vivi, Principal Elmhurst is looking for you. She wants you to go to her office before practice this afternoon," Carson said.

"Why? What's going on?" Vivi asked.

"Do you have a whole lot of time for me to make a list for you?" Luna crossed her arms over her chest.

Zander muffled a laugh and walked across the room to offer his help unpacking. "Be nice," he murmured to her.

"Why?" Luna asked.

"I don't need her to be nice," Vivi said, tossing one last rude comment to them before sweeping out of the room with Carson.

She hated seeing the way Luna associated with Zander. They were so comfortable with each other. He spoke to her easily, and she was able to laugh and smile with him without the uncertainty and uneasiness Vivi felt when she was near him. They didn't seem to have a spark of interest between them, but their close friendship made Vivi seethe with jealousy.

Carson strode beside her as she made her way to the principal's dark, imposing office at the front of the school. He lingered until she knocked on the door and Elmhurst called out for her to come inside. She glanced at Carson for an instant before going in.

"You wanted to see me?" Vivi asked.

"Your father wants you to call him," Principal Elmhurst said, without even a greeting.

"All right. I'll call when I finish practice this afternoon."

"Now. He says it's important that he speak to you as soon as possible," the principal said.

Vivi's heart jumped a little, and she swallowed hard and nodded. Elmhurst directed her to the small alcove at the side of the office containing the only phone available for student use. She picked it up and dialed her father's number. The ringing buzzed in her chest. He let it ring longer than usual, and Vivi knew it was on purpose. Each ring increased her anxiety and reminded her of the control he had over her.

"Hello?" he answered.

"Hi, Dad," she said.

It only took those two words to start his onslaught. "What is wrong with you?" he demanded.

"What do you mean?" she asked.

"I've heard of your antics. I know what you've been doing during the time you should be spending studying at that expensive school. I didn't send you there so you could torment your fellow students and make a fool of yourself. Don't forget who you are and what you are supposed to achieve. Only excellence matters. Your grades are abominable, and I believe I have been extremely understanding and patient with you. No more, Vivi. Do you understand me? I'm tired of hearing about your mistakes and failures. If you don't get your act together, I won't be seeing you at Christmas," he growled angrily.

Her stomach clenched and heat rushed across her cheeks. Last Christmas had been a crushing blow. The promise of going on the trip this year dangled in front of her, pushing her through when she was ready to throw in the towel. Now he was threatening to pull it out from under her again.

"Yes, Dad," she said quietly.

"We will go only if you behave. If going skiing in Switzerland means anything to you, you will figure out what has been happening and leading you down this path, and you will straighten yourself out. Am I understood?" he asked.

"Yes, Dad." This was her chance to defend herself, and she took it. "But you have to understand what I'm going through. They are making me work with those people."

"I know, Vivi. I hate that you have been paired with the Seelie as well, but I also see the value in the experiment."

"You do?" she asked, startled by the declaration. Her father hadn't talked much about the pairing other than acknowledging that she'd have to stay on campus at the academy through the summer.

"Yes. Life isn't always easy, and you won't get the luxury of only working with people you know, understand, and agree with. You will be forced into difficult situations and be in circumstances requiring you to work with people of all kinds. Training starts now. If you are able to work with the Seelie, it will go a long way toward helping you get that embassy job."

"Yes, Dad."

She was still juggling with the feeling of conflict an hour later when she and Carson walked out onto the field to meet with the others. She desperately wanted her father's approval but loathed what she had to do to earn it. The anger he'd spewed at her was shocking. Not that she wasn't accustomed to him being upset with her—it was a fairly standard state of being for her father. But this was intense and immediate, and he'd thrown accusations at her which had come as a surprise.

He had to have a mole at the school. Someone had to be working with him, following her and monitoring her behavior so they could report back to her father. It was unnerving and put her on edge. Trusting those around her wasn't something she regularly concerned herself with, but now she knew she couldn't relax at all. She had no way of knowing who was watching her and what incident would be brought right back to her father.

Her mood was dark as she stalked into the middle of the tall grass. She noticed Luna approaching from the corner of her eye and turned to her suspiciously.

"Is everything all right?" Luna asked.

"Why do you care? And what business is it of yours, anyway?" she yelled directly into Luna's face. "You hate me as much as I hate you. Why would you come up to me acting like you have some sort of compassion for me? There has to be some sort of ulterior motive."

Luna glared at her, but then drew a breath and tried to force the negativity from her voice. "Yeah, there is. We need to get along, especially now that we're roommates, and will be until we graduate. The best roommates are friends, and friends help each other when they're down."

Vivi considered the words for a few seconds, then finally relented with a nod. She did her best to shake off the mood. This was what she needed to be focusing on now. Not her father's anger. Not whoever was keeping tabs on her and making sure he knew about her every action. Not even her distaste at having to live with Luna and the Seelie adding insult to injury by taking the bed she wanted. What Vivi's father said made sense. If she could prove herself able to cooperate and be successful with two Seelie, she'd be a much more attractive candidate for a position at the embassy. With such a role would come success, respect, and the all-important pass to enter Faerie. The embassy was the only way halflings could enter Faerie, and she wasn't about to resign herself to an existence stuck only in the human world.

"Fine," she said. "I'll work with you."

"We'll start where we left off?" Zander asked. "Let's make another of the Faerie circles. Purple pansies, right?"

"Training for your career as a preschool teacher, Zander?" Carson asked.

"You would make for good practice," Zander snapped back.

"I thought we were going to try to work together," Luna said.

They went to work, trying to recapture the circle they had managed to create the previous day. Vivi messed up their flow and concentration the first few times, but only an hour later, they finally succeeded. This represented a tremendous improvement from the day before, and they all felt a little boost while studying the purple pansies surrounding them.

Rather than wiping the circle away and starting again, they decided to continue building on the success they'd already found. Soon the tips of vines pushed up from the grass around the flowers, wriggling and swaying, dancing like thick green snakes as they reached up toward the sky. Almost as suddenly as the creeping plants appeared, they crashed. The group's concentration broke, destroying the focus required to maintain the magic they created, making it disappear.

All four let out growls and cries of exasperation. Seeing their ability to create the Faerie circle together in such a comparatively short amount of time had encouraged them. Which only made the disappointment of having it destroyed more poignant. Carson stalked away, digging his fingers through his hair. Luna closed her eyes, drawing in a few deep breaths to try to dissolve the angry feeling boiling in her belly.

"Crickets!" Vivi shouted. The angry word was the best embodiment of the frustration and disgust she was feeling. The sound crickets made was among the most hated in the world for fae, so using their name as a curse always seemed appropriate. "We have to try again," she said. "That was great. We did it once, which means we can do it again."

"She's right," Zander said with a sigh. "This is what we're supposed to be dealing with. Principal Elmhurst told us it wasn't going to be easy. She said we were going to have to learn to control our abilities and work with each other to meld them so we can accomplish bigger things. It's not just going to happen overnight because we want it to."

"We had it, though," Carson said. "It was right there. We had it."

"Yes," said Luna. "We did it once. It's a start, but it's not enough. Just because we managed to create the circle once and add in a few vines and stuff, it doesn't mean we have this down. We have to keep trying. So, let's just do it again."

"But, without our fifth, how are we going to achieve the true Power of Five?" Vivi asked.

They looked at each other and Carson answered, surprising them all. "If the four of us can get our act together, then when they find the fifth, it will be easy to get him in and get the connection we need."

"Him?" Luna chuckled. "I sure hope he's cuter than either of you."

Vivi snorted and agreed. "It would be nice to have some real eye candy around here."

The tension which had been building now began to break, if only just a tiny crack. It was probably the first time Luna and Vivi agreed on anything. The being who had been watching from a distance smiled and turned to head back to the main campus buildings.

The four kept going, struggling and limping their way back to the point where they were able to resurrect the purple flowers. It took several more tries for them to become more than just shaky, almost translucent suggestions of the pansies.

Finally, the flowers were solid, and the four celebrated their accomplishment for a few seconds. Again, they crafted vines that rose from the ground. This time, the creepers remained. As dusk fell around them, the teenage fae created more dancing vines and guided them to weave in and out of the circle. As the vines moved around, some of them burst into bright, fragrant blooms.

The empty brown field seemed to disappear, giving way to the vibrantly colorful, beautiful scene unfolding around them.

"It looks like *A Midsummer Night's Dream*," Luna murmured, spinning around slowly to take in the gorgeous details.

The magic was stronger now, allowing them to release some of the intense concentration they had maintained while creating the circle. They walked around within it and Zander swept up to Luna dramatically.

He gave a deep, playful bow. "If this is *A Midsummer Night's Dream*, we should be dancing, shouldn't we?" he asked.

Luna laughed and allowed Zander to take her hand and pull her into a dance. As they spun around, an idea came into Vivi's mind.

"You two are adorable," she said. "But I don't think you're close enough. Maybe I can help you with that."

She sent some of the vines out of the flowery growth, and before Luna and Zander could react, they were tangled within them. The vines wrapped tightly around the pair, forcing them up against each other. Vivi sniggered as they both struggled. The vines kept tightening more and more, winding around their bodies until the two fae tumbled to the ground.

"Vivi, stop it," Zander commanded.

"Why?" Vivi asked. "You look like you're enjoying your special moment. Maybe Carson and I should go and let the two of you be alone."

CHAPTER THREE

Vivi was laughing so hard she could barely contain herself. Every time she saw Zander and Luna struggling against the vines or trying to come up with a way to get themselves loose, she just laughed all the harder.

The circle they created was strong enough now and no longer required the constant concentration and precise focus with meager beginnings of a ring of purple pansies. It was still important for all of them to focus their energy and skills on the beautiful surroundings they created, but the prank Vivi played on Zander and Luna meant the group was all but forced to keep concentrating on the vines.

But her sheer amusement at watching the two Seelie fae was enough to keep Vivi concentrating on sustaining the spell. Carson was so stunned at what he was seeing that he kept contributing his own magic without thinking. As for Luna and Zander, neither could help but think about the flowered vines coiling around their bodies and crushing them against each other. Their thoughts simply continued to feed into the Faerie circle, making the magic more powerful. Finally, Vivi decided she'd had enough and released the spell tightening the vines around them.

Luna was most certainly not in the mood for a joke. She clawed her way out of the vines and took three long, furious strides across the field toward the other teenage girl. Vivi smiled smugly, expecting maybe a few tart words, probably nothing more than another simpering speech about how they all needed to get along and trust each other.

But Luna was way past that point. She was furious and wanted to make sure Vivi knew it, but this time, words weren't enough. She stomped up to the other girl and performed one of her favorite Krav Maga moves. The attack was so fast that Vivi barely had the chance to process what was happening before she crashed to the ground, pain exploding within her head.

It took a moment for what happened to sink in. Pain radiated from her face and around her head. She pushed herself up into a sitting position. Warmth trickled down her cheek, and Vivi touched it with her fingertips. She realized it was blood, pouring from her busted lip. The tender swelling around her eye was progressively getting worse. She'd have one hell of a shiner within the next couple of days. Dizziness rolled over her, and Vivi gave up on her initial plan to scramble back to her feet and attack Luna. She simply crouched in the dirt, waiting for the world to stop spinning and for some of the pain to go away.

"Come on. Can somebody use their healing skills to help me?" she demanded. "Carson, you know you're the best. Come help me. Please."

It wasn't merely a platitude spoken in the hopes of receiving help. It was a declaration of the truth. Luna was the smartest and most skilled of the four of them. But when it came to healing, nobody could compete with Carson. He was unquestionably the most talented, and his set of abilities could prove extremely useful one day. It made sense for her to appeal to the other Unseelie fae and to think of him and his abilities first should they find the need for healing.

"Not yet," Carson said.

"Excuse me?" Vivi snapped. "Did you just say 'Not yet?' Can't you see I need help? She smashed my face in."

"I think that might be taking it a little to the extreme side," Luna said with a scoff. "It was a basic kick. If anything, your face got right in the way of my foot. You should be able to avoid an attack better than that."

"Look, this is a prime opportunity for all of us. We're supposed to be working on our skills and improving them. No better way to improve a skill than to put it into practice," Carson said.

"Are you suggesting I give myself a refresher on healing skills by healing myself?" Vivi asked. "Somehow that's supposed to make this whole situation better?"

"I mean, it can't hurt to try your hand at some healing. It might be useful later in life," he said.

"Yeah, the next time a Seelie scum gets the drop on me and attacks me, completely unprovoked," Vivi mumbled.

"You turned the Faerie circle we made against her, so it wrapped around her and Zander and nearly strangled them," Carson pointed out. "I wouldn't really call that an unprovoked attack. Let's be honest, Vivi. We all kind of feel like you got what you deserved."

"Fine," Vivi seethed. "Then I'll do it myself. Just make sure the shield is still in place. The last thing I need right now is some human wandering along and calling an ambulance."

"It's in place," Carson reassured her.

Vivi primed herself, trying to get into the headspace she needed to call her healing skills into use. Her lip was throbbing and stinging where it had split open. She wanted to heal that first and concentrated all her abilities on it. She envisioned the cut in her lip and that she wanted it to be better. Suddenly, her lips started to swell. It wasn't a gentle softening or the type of major swelling caused by eating something she was allergic to. Instead, it felt like air was steadily filling her lips, plumping them up like balloons.

She tried to yell, but her voice was stuck behind her puffed-up lips and came out as a high-pitched squeal. Soon she would look like her head was almost entirely composed of lips. Finally, she figured out how to get the magic under control and her mouth returned to normal size—except for the swelling from the cut, which was still not healed. Vivi kicked the ground and let out an angry groan. She moved on from trying to heal the damage to her lip caused by Luna's sharp kick and concentrated on her blackened eye instead.

A few moments later, both eyes were completely black, the whites and irises obliterated with only two dark voids staring back at the other three teens. They burst into laughter, watching as Vivi tried to reverse the effect as quickly as possible. She became more frustrated with every attempt. Carson, Zander, and Luna watched, chuckling as Vivi changed the color of her skin to a wide variety of shades and patterns, made one eye drastically bigger than the other, and shrunk her lips down to almost nothing. When she had grown a layer of skin that covered her entire face, Carson decided she'd had enough.

"Your healing skills are terrible," he said. "But if you could master a few of those things you just did to yourself and figure out how to do them to other people, they could be really beneficial in combat."

Vivi mumbled something through the skin—probably a scathing remark, but none of them could decipher the words.

"Maybe we could leave her like this for just a little bit longer," Luna suggested. "It's nice not having to listen to her talking."

Zander chuckled, but then shook his head. "No. She's flailed around enough for one evening. Carson, go ahead and help her."

Carson approached Vivi and held onto her shoulders to stop her pacing and spinning in circles—which she'd been doing since the new skin obscured her vision. She seemed to be breathing just fine, which was good, but being unable to see or speak clearly was agitating her.

"You deserved to feel some of this pain before I used my healing magic on you, but if you stand still, I can help you," Carson said.

Vivi thrashed around, making screaming sounds, and Carson moved away. The others laughed, sending seething anger through her. But then something occurred to her. She was livid at them for laughing at her, but her father's voice reverberated through her mind. His words interrupted her raging thoughts. Again, she heard how angry he was at her behavior and how deeply disappointed he was in her grades and performance at school. The threat of not going on the skiing trip for Christmas, not seeing her father at all for the holiday, if she didn't straighten up and start behaving properly, took hold. She had messed up yet again.

Forcing herself to stand still, she breathed in a few times as deeply as she could and then exhaled. She nodded slowly.

"Have you calmed down now?" Carson asked, and she nodded again. "All right. Let's see what we can do about all this."

Vivi stayed as still and quiet as she could while Carson went to work undoing the damage she'd done to herself first before turning his attention to the injuries Luna had inflicted. She really wanted to keep control of herself and not mess up again. She had to remind herself that the behavior was beneath her. She shouldn't allow her anger, frustration, and disappointment to get the better of her.

Vivi wanted to prove she was worthy of her fae heritage, that she had what it took to achieve her lofty goals. But she still had some growing up to do, which meant sometimes she exploded. She had to learn to control herself better and do what needed to be done, even when it was the last thing in the world she wanted to do.

It seemed the others also wished to make sure she understood that.

"You really need to start cooperating," Zander said after Carson had healed her. "None of us are thrilled about this arrangement, but it's important for all of us to be willing to work together. The faster we integrate and start doing what we need to do, the better it's going to be for everyone involved. If we can show Elmhurst we can do this and can possibly achieve the Power of Five, she might get off our backs some, and we'll be taken off lock-down."

Vivi nodded. "I'm just so mad about losing my summer to do *this*. I can't stand it."

"You have some serious anger management issues. You might want to look into getting some help for them," Carson said.

Vivi scoffed at the idea, brushing it off as a joke. But maybe it didn't sound all that ridiculous. She thought it through, considering whether going to see someone about what she was feeling and the way she reacted to things, might help her now as well as in the long run.

Finally, she shook her head. Not willing to admit she had a

problem—or that someone might be able to help her with it—she turned the conversation on Carson and changed the subject.

"So, have any of the Seelie girls who are still on campus stopped by your room to see Zander?" she teased. "Even more importantly, how many times have you taken advantage of that particular situation?"

Carson made an over-dramatic grimace and waved his hands as though he couldn't stand the thought of even the words getting anywhere near him. "I wouldn't touch a Seelie girl with a ten-foot pole."

Vivi let out a short laugh. "Don't even try to act like that now that Zander and Luna are around. I'm sure they've heard just as much about you as I have. They probably know all about you and your bad boy ways under the bleachers with the silly Seelie Court chicks, too."

Carson gave a playboy grin and shrugged. "All right. Maybe that wasn't entirely accurate. I wouldn't *date* a Seelie Court girl, but I have had my share of fun. It doesn't really matter which Court a girl comes from once you get her in the dark and all worked up. Even the prissiest of Seelie girls can put on quite a show if they're given the right encouragement.

"As a matter of fact, according to my own personal research, the Seelie girls can actually be even more fun. I think being with an Unseelie guy seems so forbidden it makes them feel naughty. They want to let go of all their inhibitions and see just how bad they can be. Now, I haven't gotten through the whole population on campus to get total information, but my sample size is pretty impressive. Of course, I'm happy to continue finding more specimens. Purely for scientific research." He winked at Luna.

Carson pressed his hand to his chest, holding it over his heart to show his sincerity, and grinned at the faces cringing back at him.

"Seriously, Carson. You are such a man whore," Zander said.

It was exactly the reaction Carson wanted. His reputation was carefully cultivated over all the time he had spent at the academy. He didn't want anyone, especially the three others standing in front of him, to know it was all merely a cover. For as much as he was considered the sex god of campus, Carson actually had no experience at all.

In fact, he was a virgin, and he couldn't handle anyone finding out the truth. He was sixteen—the age when he should be having sex with every girl who was willing, no matter what Court she was from. But he simply wasn't ready. He was embarrassed to admit it, so he just didn't. He preferred that everyone believe he went through the girls in school like popcorn rather than knowing he hadn't gotten anywhere with any of them.

The sky had grown dark while Vivi had struggled with healing herself, and the group decided to return to campus. Zander and Luna strode off with Vivi and Carson lingering behind. Carson watched Vivi track Zander's movements as they left the field, then nudged her with his elbow.

"Are you ever going to act on your crush on Zander?" he asked.

Vivi threw him a scowl. "I don't have a crush on Zander."

Carson smiled and nodded, knowing he'd gotten to her. Which, of course, meant he was completely right.

***

The next day Carson was sitting outside under one of the large trees dotting the grounds of the academy when Zander walked up and threw himself onto the grass beside him. Carson closed the textbook he'd been studying and stared at the Seelie boy.

"It's summer," Zander said. "What are you reading?"

"We're stuck here at the school, so it's hardly summer. It might be according to the calendar, but as long as I'm sleeping in that dorm room and wandering around the campus all day, every day, it's still the school year. I figured I'd get a head start on the reading list for when the semester starts again," said Carson.

"It's not like you need help with your grades. You already have all A's," Zander pointed out.

"It's just going to get more competitive from here on out," Carson said. "Getting a job at the embassy starts here. Only the best will get into the right colleges and establish the connections to land one of the positions. That's all I want, and I'm not settling for anything less. So

I'm going to get ahead no matter how many days I have to spend studying or how many people I have to stomp on to climb my way up."

"That's a cheery thought. But along that line, I came to find you to ask if you think we're ready for controlling the wind," Zander said.

Carson's eyes widened and he grinned. "That would be awesome. Yes. We should totally find the girls and do that this afternoon. No more of this purple pansy nonsense. Let's control some wind!"

He put up his hand for a high-five, but Zander left him hanging, eyeing the palm suspiciously. "Um. I'm good," he said.

Carson waited another few seconds, then his shoulders sagged. He held his hand up, still persisting. "Come on," he said. "I thought we were doing the whole team spirit thing and trying to get our lives back."

Zander finally relented. "All right." In an effort to be friendly with his new roommate and encourage harmony among the group, he sighed and reached up to smack his palm against Carson's.

At the last second, Carson pulled his hand away. "Too slow!"

A group of people who were sauntering past laughed at him and Zander shook his head, wondering why he even bothered. An Unseelie was always going to be an Unseelie. No point in trying to make a connection with them.

Carson was still laughing when Luna and Vivi arrived. They were walking a few feet apart, creating a clear delineation between them while still moving casually along together.

"What's everybody laughing about?" Luna asked as she approached. She caught Zander's taut features and her expression dropped. "Oh. Everybody except Zander, I mean."

"Are we going to do this, or what?" Zander asked, standing up and stalking away from them.

The other three exchanged glances and followed as he made his way toward the field.

CHAPTER FOUR

Shanghai, China

"That thing has eyes, Mia," Becky gasped. "It has *eyes.*"

Mia laughed at her best friend's reaction. "It's not like they can see you. Look," she pointed out, happily using the wooden skewer stuck through the fried eel to dangle the creature in Becky's face. "Deep-fried, see?"

Becky grimaced and tried to duck out of the way. "I thought you were supposed to be a good influence on me," she said.

Mia scoffed. "Why would you think that?" Her brow furrowed and she scrunched her nose.

"You're the older one," Becky pointed out.

"We're both sixteen." Chuckling, Mia shook her head in exasperation at her best friend.

"Yeah, but you'll be seventeen in October, so that makes you my elder. You should be the responsible one," Becky whined.

Mia rolled her eyes. There's no way Becky would say something like that if they weren't in Shanghai. They would both start their junior year in the fall, and the slightly younger girl would never put herself a step under anyone.

It was merely a ploy to stop Mia from teasing her with the freaky-looking street food. She tucked the skewer back into the tall wooden display and looped her arm through Becky's. "Let's go see if we can find something you actually want to try," she said.

They made their way farther into the bustling night market. When they had planned their trip here, Mia had envisioned Shanghai being cooler than the summer weather back home. Instead, the temperature earlier in the day had soared over ninety degrees, and the high humidity made the air thick and steamy. Once the sun had set, the humidity had finally eased and the temperature fell, making it far more comfortable to roam around the vibrant market.

Or at least not as sticky.

The atmosphere was invigorating. Music played, and layers of voices added to the sounds and smells, creating the backdrop for hundreds of people weaving around the stalls and tiny shops. Their energy fed off each other in an almost dizzying experience, unlike anything Mia or Becky had ever seen.

Coming to a new country for the first time had been a culture shock, but somehow being in the market made them feel like part of something bigger. They were among the throng of people, each trying to take it all in. As chaotic and intense as it was, it was also unifying somehow.

Children picked out treats from carts peddling elaborate hand-crafted sweets. Mysterious smells, some enticing, some strange, lured people to stalls offering an overwhelming array of food, from the creepy speared creatures to adorable buns crafted to look like little animals.

Women ogled gorgeous fabrics and tried on clothes, while others scoured tightly packed displays of trinkets and collectibles. All around them, languages mixed, bouncing back and forth. People who didn't understand a word of what each other were saying still communicated and laughed. Nearby, an old woman grinned as she clutched a young tourist's hand, and Mia's heart warmed. It was a reminder that ultimately, they were all the same.

She had no way of knowing she was about to discover it wasn't true. Moving among the crowds, she was different.

"How about one of those?" Becky asked, pointing to a nearby stall.

Mia studied the bamboo basket filled with steamed buns in the shape of panda bears. She smiled and nodded. Using some of the words their instructor taught them leading up to the trip, they each ordered a bear.

Mia's teeth sank into the soft dough and found the sweet chocolate paste inside. "Good choice," she said, nodding.

They continued on their stroll, nibbling their way through the buns. Becky stared at hers for a second, then grinned at Mia. "Can you imagine if your dad was here?" she asked.

Mia chuckled. "He would have eaten everything by now," she said. "He would have just started at the first stall and made his way through, trying something at each one."

"How far do you think he would have made it before we needed to roll him back to the hotel?" Becky snickered.

"Halfway down the street," Mia said. "Then he'd just come back tomorrow to try the rest."

A hint of sadness lay behind the amusement. She felt homesick and missed her father. This was the longest time she had ever been away from him. Her mother died when she was only a baby, and Mia had no memories of her. All she had ever known was it being only the two of them.

The sad feeling didn't last for long, though. She caught Becky staring across the street at Brad, who hesitated at a nearby stand trying to build up his courage to eat a fried scorpion. Another of the high schoolers in China for the Wushu tournament, Brad was also Becky's secret crush. Mia knew her best friend had been studying the form of Chinese Kung Fu long before she met Brad. But that didn't mean he wasn't a bonus.

"Go talk to him," Mia urged.

Becky shook her head. Her attention shifted from Brad to the remainder of the bun in her hand, but then drifted back to him. "I can't," she whispered.

"Why not? He's right there. Like,"—she counted out an estimation—"nine steps away."

Becky sighed. "What do I do? Just walk up to him and be like 'Hi, Brad' or what?" She spoke as if it was the most absurd concept she'd ever heard.

Mia blinked. "Yes," she said. "That's exactly what you're supposed to do."

"I can't do that!" Becky gasped.

"Why not?"

"Because it's *Brad.* He doesn't even know I exist." She threw her hands in the air in exasperation.

"You kicked him in the face when he was standing too close behind you at practice two weeks ago. Then you traveled in the same group with him to *China.* Pretty sure he knows you exist." Mia laughed at her friend's silliness.

Becky groaned and covered her eyes with one hand. "Oh, Buddha. I was trying to erase that whole kicking-him thing from my memory," she said. "Thanks for reminding me."

Mia pressed her hand to Becky's back and turned her toward the group of guys all daring each other to eat the scorpions.

"Look at them. They're all having fun and taking in the new experience. Go join them."

"I'm not eating a scorpion," Becky said firmly.

"You don't have to. Just go talk to him. Tell him he did a good job at practice this morning or something. You know if you don't, you'll regret it." The older of the two girls cast a knowing look at the boys in front of them.

Becky took a resolute breath and crossed the street toward the group. Mia lingered in place so she could watch. Becky approached the stall beside the one where the boys gathered, and she pretended to inspect the items on display. She shifted sideways a few inches, paused, then crept over a few more. This continued until she bounced into Brad. He stumbled slightly, then turned around to face Becky. His wide grin elicited one from Becky, and just like that, the other guys were forgotten.

"My work here is done," Mia murmured.

They still had plenty of time before they were due back at the hotel for lights out. Which meant Mia could do some exploring of the market on her own. Becky would catch up with her eventually.

Mia continued along the same road, browsing the numerous items for sale. Soon the tightly packed stalls thinned out, many replaced by permanent shop buildings. The boisterous crowds had lessened. Mia moved more slowly through this area so she could peek through shop windows and get a glimpse of what was inside.

One particular shop intrigued her. The building appeared to be ancient, and something about it caught her attention. She had taken a step toward it when the door opened and the time-worn face of an old woman appeared. She beckoned to Mia with her outstretched hand.

"Come inside," the woman called out. Mia hesitated, and the woman beckoned again. "No afraid. Come," she said in broken English.

Mia allowed her curiosity to guide her. She walked across the street as the old woman disappeared through the door. A heady, spicy scent wafted out at her when Mia opened the door and slipped into the shop. Inside was a concentrated version of the market. Shelves towering nearly to the ceiling held exquisite teapots, cups, ornate boxes, and other objects. Tables laden with even more curios were arranged with narrow passages between them.

She inhaled the competing aromas that confirmed this was a tea shop, but something about the place wasn't quite like the others they had already visited on their tour. A few steps into the shop, she realized the old woman wasn't in the room.

"Hello?" she called.

Rich silks hung from the walls, draped casually to create different segments in the shop. Mia made her way through the first section and passed lush peacock-blue fabric trimmed with gold tassels, into a second area. This part of the shop was somewhat calmer than the first, but with so much going on, it was impossible to decide where to look first.

"Here," the woman called from farther in the shop.

Mia followed the sound of her voice and finally ducked through the purple drapes hanging over the entrance to the last room. The old woman sat on a cushion on the floor beside a low table.

"Your shop is amazing," Mia said.

The old woman gestured to the cushion across from her. "Join me."

Mia lowered herself onto the cushion and studied the traditional tea service laid out in front of them. An intoxicating smell rose up from the pot.

"I'm Mia," she said.

"I know."

"How do you know?"

The woman offered a wise smile as she filled Mia's cup. "I wait for you come. You call me Grandmother." She touched the edge of the cup. "Here. Drink."

"What do you mean you've been waiting for me?" Mia asked.

The encounter felt strange and part of her wanted to leave, but something else was keeping her there. As odd as the interaction was, it was also intriguing. She wanted to know more.

"Drink," Grandmother said again. "Unique in all China."

Mia picked up the cup and brought it to her lips. The strong, spicy scent filled her lungs before she even took a sip. The flavor rushed over her tongue and burned in her throat, but as soon as it was gone from her mouth, she wanted more.

She drained the cup, and Grandmother filled it again. The second went down well, but her head started to swim. Squeezing her eyes closed, Mia waited for the feeling to pass. When she opened her eyes, Grandmother was gone.

"Hello?" she called. "Grandmother?" The shop was silent. Mia carefully set the cup back on the table and stood. She wobbled a bit before righting herself. "Thanks for the tea," she called. "I have to get back and meet up with the rest of my group. Goodnight."

A tingling sensation crept through her body until it felt like her fingertips should be glowing. The shop was different now as she made her way out. Everything was familiar, but she noticed colors and patterns which hadn't been there before. She told herself it had to be the smells of the herbs and teas getting to her. Fresh air would clear her head.

Mia stumbled through the tea shop door and back out onto the street. The air felt cooler as she drew it deep into her lungs. Letting it out slowly, she waited for the effects to wear off. A flicker of movement to one side caught her attention.

She squinted in the direction of the movement and thought she saw the flash of something black scramble over the edge of a nearby building and disappear onto the roof. A growl sounded behind, and she whipped around. Something glowed in the shadowy space between two nearby buildings. The eyes grew bigger as the thing closed in on her, and long, spindly fingers snaked out to creep across the front of the shop.

Fantastic, she thought. *Trust me to get myself drugged in a foreign country. Everybody else will be competing, and I'll become a public service announcement.* The way everything looked, like a Pink Floyd video, with scary shadows which couldn't be real, Mia suspected that the tea had to have been laced with something. But she couldn't figure it out. All she wanted to do was find Becky and get back to the hotel.

Their coach had warned them many times not to separate. She should have listened to him instead of leaving Becky to flirt with Brad.

She tried shutting her eyes again, but this time the creature didn't disappear when she opened them. It was coming closer and soon strode out of the gap. It appeared almost human, but with disproportionately long arms, legs, and fingers. Long hair hung around a face with huge glowing eyes. Fear gripped Mia, and she ran back toward the crowd. Hallucination or not, she simply wanted to get away from it.

The creature followed close behind her, moving along the front of the buildings. No one else seemed to notice it. Ahead of her, dark purple smoke streamed from either side of the street, joining together to create a mass that blocked her way. The cloud turned solid and writhed, suddenly turning to reveal the massive face of a snake, with sharp, gruesome teeth.

Mia stumbled backward away from the snake, then turned to run in the opposite direction. The creature with the glowing eyes took a step toward her, and she made her choice. She rushed full speed toward the snake, only for it to become a puff of smoke when she got close. The busy part of the night market wasn't far ahead. If she could just get there quickly, she could find Becky, return to the hotel, and sleep this off.

The creature was closing in on her, and still no one noticed. A narrow area forced her to slow down, and she felt fingertips trace her spine. An instant later, a woman grabbed her wrist and yanked her behind an empty stall.

The woman pushed her to the ground and stood to look back toward the creature. She was armed with a strange-looking weapon which she pointed at the monster. No one gasped or screamed. Mia had expected a reaction to a woman brandishing a weapon—something resembling a crossbow strung with a long dagger—at the edge of a crowded market. Yet no pandemonium ensued.

"Crickets. He's gone," the woman said. She crouched beside Mia and searched her face. "Are you all right?"

"You could see that thing?" Mia asked.

The woman studied Mia, her expression strange. "Of course. I've been after it for a long time. Troublesome creatures, boggarts."

"*Boggart?*" Mia asked. "What is that? Why couldn't anyone else see it?"

"Did you hit your head? Humans can't see boggarts. Or any of what they think of as mythological creatures, for that matter. Makes it easier to do my job, I suppose." She shrugged.

Mia's head was reeling. She didn't understand what this woman meant when she'd said humans couldn't see the creature which Mia had just clearly seen and been chased by. And what other creatures? That tea must have been seriously strong.

"What job?" she asked.

The woman extended a hand with a friendly grin.

"I'm Cassia, the best bounty hunter of the fae."

CHAPTER FIVE

The girl stared at Cassia for a few seconds, blinking as if that was going to change what she was seeing. Perhaps she believed if she did it enough times, her eyelashes would brush away the words and she could simply replace them with ones she liked better.

"Are you all right?" Cassia asked.

"Tea," the girl responded.

"Tea?"

She nodded.

"I drank some," she rubbed her temples and wished she was in Kansas again.

"That's lovely," Cassia replied, unsure of why the girl felt the need to share that.

"Mia?" someone called from outside the stall where they were still hiding. "Where are you?"

The girl's eyes widened, and she shot to her feet. "Becky!" she called out and scrambled around the side of the stall and back out into the street.

"What happened to you?" Becky asked.

Cassia rose up enough to watch their interaction. The new girl looked Mia over and grabbed her hands, holding her arms out to her sides to examine her further. Mia gave her a few seconds, then wrenched her hands away.

"Don't worry," Mia reassured the other girl. "All in one piece. Physically, at least."

Becky stared quizzically at her. "What do you mean?"

Mia shook her head, then glanced back toward Cassia for a brief second. Becky followed her gaze but didn't acknowledge Cassia's presence.

"I think that old woman slipped something into my tea," said Mia.

"What old woman?" Becky asked.

Mia turned slightly to look at the stall. She shook her head, then rolled her eyes as she glanced back at her friend. "Not her," she said. "The old woman at the tea shop."

"Not who? Who are you talking about?" Becky's brows furrowed and she nibbled on her lower lip, wondering what in the world had gotten into her best friend.

Cassia leaned against the side of the stall, knowing Becky couldn't see her. No human was supposed to be able to. Yet when Mia glanced back again, this time almost turning all the way around to face her, it was obvious she was looking directly at Cassia. Mia glanced back at Becky, then closed her eyes tightly and squeezed the bridge of her nose.

Looping her arm with Becky's, she steered her back in the direction of the night market. "I think it's time to head back to the hotel," Mia said. "A good night's sleep sounds like exactly what I need right now."

As they headed down the street, Cassia moved out from behind the stall to watch their progress. The thought of the boggart popped back into her mind. She'd been searching for the creature for too long to just let it go so easily. This wasn't a game of hide and seek they were playing to amuse themselves. The boggart was a nasty, vile creature that had already proven itself to be dangerous to the children of the area. Finding him would ensure the young ones were protected.

Cassia retraced her steps to where she had last seen the boggart and resumed her search. Her tracking skills were strong and precise, the very reason behind her reputation as the best bounty hunter of her kind. Those abilities immediately drew her farther along the street, but she had gone only a few steps when she felt something on her shoulder. It was a cool, gentle touch as if the wind itself had formed a hand to stop her. But the grip wasn't that of the wind. Cassia knew it was her father.

For thirty-four years, the ghostly touch had been there to guide her. Cassia would rather have his earthly presence be there with her, but the transcended form brought her great comfort and helped her along her way, nonetheless. Flynn Tarran had been the greatest bounty hunter of his time, perhaps the greatest to have ever lived. It was that skill and devotion which had earned him the coveted role of protecting the fae princess.

And that devotion had cost him his life. He'd laid down his life to defend the princess, but in the end, it wasn't enough. The princess had been murdered, and Cassia was left with only the lingering of her father's spirit and the duty to take up his mission and carry it on. It was a duty she struggled to take seriously.

The stories her father had told her of the princess and the threats to her life had always been fantastical and had kept Cassia up long past when she should have been asleep. But she never actually believed them. Not until his death had she realized the significance of the responsibility that was placed at her feet. It didn't matter what she believed, she had her assignment.

Her secret assignment.

Cassia would much rather stick to what she knew. She liked chasing the tangible threats, the creatures she understood, had seen, and even gone after countless times before. That's what she wanted to do now. The urge to track down the boggart and dig him out of whatever hiding place he'd found was strong. She wanted to leave the brightness of the night market behind her and delve into the shadows where she was more comfortable.

But the touch on her shoulder stopped her. He didn't often interfere with what she was doing. Usually his spirit watched over her from a distance, giving her a sense of being guarded rather than herded. Occasionally, as he would when he'd been alive, he encouraged her to take another path. It could be as soft as a brush of cool air on her cheek or a map unfolding in front of her. It could also be as unmistakable as this nudge, stopping her from going any farther along the empty portion of the street, turning her back toward the market instead.

She had to follow Mia.

There were too many questions left unanswered.

The two girls had already disappeared far down the street and into the market, and Cassia hurried after them. The same skills that had brought her to the boggart had put her on Mia's trail. None of the humans she pushed her way past could see her, but they would be able to feel her. This meant Cassia couldn't simply shove through with abandon. As much as the frustrating moments—when chatty women stopped, blocking the path to scrutinize a piece of fabric, or men paused to try the next snack—inspired her to elbow them out of the way, she held back.

She had seen before what could happen if she let herself run free. The chaos and fighting that might break out among the humans simply weren't worth the time saved. Finally, Cassia caught sight of Mia. The same thing that stood out to her about the girl before was bold and impossible to overlook in the crowd. Wavy red hair hung past her shoulders, swept into swirls and tangles after running from the boggart and pushing through the crowd.

It was that feature, along with her scent, which made her impossible. Her scent was human. Cassia knew it well. Over fifty years of training with her father before his death had instructed her to easily differentiate between species simply by their scent. But it was her hair that truly stood out. To have so easily seen both Cassia and the boggart, Mia should have been fae. But the dramatic flash of fiery hair eliminated that possibility.

None in either the Seelie or Unseelie Court had naturally red hair. Those of the Seelie Court, like Cassia, had silver hair, while the Unseelie Court was marked by hair so dark and inky it appeared almost blue in the right light.

This knowledge spurred Cassia's curiosity as she continued to follow Mia and Becky as they wove their way through the city. Mia was human by scent and by appearance, and yet she possessed the ability to see what only those of the mythical realm could see.

Could Mia possibly be another creature? She wanted to know who this intriguing girl was and what it was about her that was so important. Something about her was special, or Cassia's father wouldn't have guided her to follow Mia.

After a long trek through the city, Mia and Becky finally stopped outside a hotel. They chatted with several other people who looked to be about their age. A familiarity existed among them and in the way they spoke. This wasn't an accidental encounter or people meeting for the first time. Aware that none of the others could see her, though Mia might, Cassia stayed back. She crept close to the hotel and inched along until she was able to wait in the shadows for the two girls to enter the hotel.

They paused in front of the elevator, and Cassia slipped into the stairwell. She rushed up to the second floor and peeked through the narrow window to check if they'd come out onto this level. Several seconds passed without the elevator opening, so she ran up to the next floor and the next.

On the fourth level, she finally caught sight of them. They strolled along the hallway until they reached a door. After a few words, Becky took out a key and opened the door.

When Mia paused and glanced her way, Cassia retreated from the doorway. When she checked again, the red-haired girl was no longer in the hallway.

Cassia hesitated in the stairwell. She had nothing left to do here tonight. Mia was staying inside, which would make it easier to keep an eye on her. So Cassia had time to go back for the boggart.

The crowds in the night market had begun to thin as she made her way back through. She could sense the boggart, but the trail was weak. It must be old, a route the creature had taken in recent days or weeks, but not tonight. Cassia focused harder and found another trail, but this one faded within mere moments of following it.

Her aggravation began to build as she found the fifth old trail that led her to nothing. The boggart could be anywhere. These things were fast and crafty. Their glamour could make them blend in with any humans, but the fae could always see past it. Even if she couldn't see a boggart, Cassia would never miss one. Their rank scent was like a sewer.

This would all have been so much easier if not for that one little boy. Only eight years old, he'd believed the mysterious creature that had taken up residence in the attic of his home could be a friend. Naming it would have been meant to connect them, but that was the last thing anyone should do when encountering a boggart. Giving one of these beings a name took them from mischievous to truly nasty and cruel. This one left the house destroyed and the little boy hurt and barely hanging on in its wake.

But the creature hadn't stopped there. As Cassia continued to scour the city for the boggart's trail, she thought of the others who had fallen victim to it. No one knew if the creature went after toddlers and babies because a child had named it, but going after the most vulnerable only made it more reprehensible. Cassia was unfailing in her determination to find the boggart and stop it from making any more of the little children sick. So far, no one who had been stricken by the illness had died, but she wasn't willing to test it. If the boggart was using a potion to make these children ill, it could make the concoction stronger and worsen the effect.

Then, she caught the trail again. This one was fresher, and Cassia felt a surge of optimism. She rushed after it, her hands tingling to reach for any of the daggers hidden among her leather clothes or the crossbow on her back. This thing had to be stopped.

She rushed along the narrow alleys and streets, blocking out everything around her so she could think only of tracking the boggart. Suddenly she skidded to a stop. Her feet were at the base of a sewer and the trail was gone.

CHAPTER SIX

Mia was shaking Becky awake a full hour before they had to leave the hotel. She knew her best friend well enough to know that mornings were not her favorite time of day by a long shot. Becky would fight against waking up with everything in her. Which meant Mia would need at least four rounds of shaking her and telling her they had to get ready before Becky eventually dragged herself out of her bedding cocoon.

"Come on," she insisted on her fifth shake. "We have to get breakfast before the competition."

Becky made a few indistinct grumbling sounds and rolled her head to the other side but didn't open her eyes. It was time for more extreme measures. Mia jumped onto the edge of the bed beside Becky and wrenched the blankets away from her. That did it. Becky's eyes opened and she gave Mia an angry, if blurry, stare.

"What are you doing?" she mumbled.

"Getting you up so we can go get breakfast. Come on. Carb loading time!" Mia announced.

Becky reached down, feeling around for the blanket, but Mia held it out of her reach.

"I thought you were supposed to carb load the night before you did something," Becky muttered.

"Well, we're doing it the morning of. We'll throw some protein in too. Get up."

Becky finally accepted she was beaten. Resigned to the morning which had come far too early for her liking, she slid off the side of the bed and dragged herself over to the bathroom. By the time she was dressed and mostly conscious, they were heading out of the room only three minutes later than Mia had planned. She decided to take that as a victory.

Everyone participating in the Wushu competition seemed to have the same idea and the hotel restaurant was packed nearly full. The hostess grabbed two menus and led them to a tiny table against the wall. It was sticky and sprinkled with crumbs, evidence of the people who had eaten there before them. The hostess tried to shoo them back to the front of the restaurant so the table could be cleaned before they sat, but Mia shook her head.

"No, no. It's fine," she said. "We'll just sit down."

She wasn't about to give up the spot and risk someone else swooping in and taking it out from under them. Her stomach was rumbling after an hour spent dedicated to waking up her friend, and the effort of the competition also loomed ahead of her.

Becky had perked up by the time they ordered. She was back to babbling about the boys at the night market when Mia spotted something strange from the corner of her eye. At first, she thought it was merely someone moving oddly between the tables. When she turned to look at it, she realized it wasn't one of the teenagers swarming the restaurant. The creature was yellow and scaly. It maneuvered between the tables without effort, floating through the air like a ghost. No one else in the restaurant was looking at it. The only reactions seemed to be wrinkled noses and contorted facial expressions when the spectral figure moved past the tables.

As soon as it came within a few feet of their table, Mia understood the reactions. The strong, disgusting smell of decay and putrid, rotting meat filled her nostrils. Becky put down her fork and shook her head, probably trying to get the odor out of her nose. "What's that smell?" she asked, wrinkling her nose.

"I think it's that," Mia said, nodding toward the scaly yellow ghost.

"What?" Becky asked.

Mia gestured with her eyes. "That," she said.

Becky glanced over her shoulder, her gaze focused on the space the creature filled, but she didn't react.

"What am I looking at? Samuel? I mean, he has some post-practice odor problems sometimes, but it's never been at this level." Becky giggled.

"You don't see that?" Mia asked incredulously. She thought she must still be hallucinating from the tea she drank the night before. *Note to self, never drink tea offered by an old lady again.*

Cassia had arrived at the hotel before the sun came up so she could continue following Mia, still trying to figure out who she was. So as not to cause any panic, she put on her human glamour before entering Mia's hotel.

This brought her to the back corner of the restaurant, where she tucked into a massive breakfast and watched the two girls. Almost immediately, she spotted exactly what she was waiting for—the sluagh came into the restaurant, and Mia could clearly see it.

"How does she see that?" Cassia muttered through a bite of syrup-soaked pancakes.

"Excuse me?" the girl at the next table asked her.

Cassia glanced at her and shook her head. "Nothing," she said, swallowing.

The girl turned away, and Cassia looked back at Mia. The sluagh was moving around the restaurant as though it was looking for mischief, but no one could see it.

No one but Mia.

It was confirmation of the strangeness Cassia thought she'd experienced the night before outside the market. She'd told herself she might have imagined it or that it wasn't what she thought. But this was unmistakable.

Somehow, someway, Mia wasn't fully human.

A few minutes later, the girls finished their breakfast, paid, and headed out of the restaurant. Cassia did the same, waiting in the lobby of the hotel until they came back down, now dressed for the competition. She fell into step behind them and followed them through the city. Her glamours helped her blend in with the groups of teenagers, but they wouldn't do any good if Mia turned to look at her. Mia would immediately recognize her. Cassia thanked the Faerie gods the girl didn't see her.

Instead, the two girls hurried off, their heads bent toward each other as they chatted. As they walked along the sidewalk, they passed beneath the plane trees that lined the streets of Shanghai. Cassia caught sight of fluttering movements between the branches. Anyone else looking at the trees might think the shaking leaves and swaying branches could be the wind. Cassia knew better. The branches were bouncing too much to just be the soft sway of the warm breeze. It was wood nymphs.

The mischievous little creatures danced and played between the branches, watching the world go by beneath them. One caught sight of Mia and Becky and scrambled to the end of a low-hanging branch. Followed by one of his friends, the nymph reached down and tugged at their hair with his long fingers. The other joined in, forcing the girls to stop. Becky brushed at her hair, obviously thinking it was nothing more than the branches catching in her flyaway strands, but Mia looked up. She saw the bright, buggy eyes of the little wood nymph looking down at her while the other played in Becky's hair as though it were a sandbox. She let out a cry and Becky turned to face her.

"What? What's wrong?" Becky asked.

"What are you?" Mia demanded, waving at the nymphs who easily avoided her hands.

Cassia laughed. It was funny to see the playful creatures interacting with the humans who couldn't see them as they tried hopelessly to figure out what was happening. Knowing Mia saw them made it even funnier.

"Mia, who are you talking to?" Becky glanced around but didn't see anyone close enough for Mia to be speaking to.

Mia approached the base of the tree and was preparing to climb when the screech of tires stopped her. Cassia saw the near-accident happen before Mia did. It took the laughter right out of her mouth and tightened her heart in her chest.

A taxi driving erratically came far too close to a moped overloaded with four men and a haphazard stack of boxes. The moped was swerving under its uneven load and overcorrected when the taxi nearly hit it, which sent it careening toward Becky. The girl jumped away just in time. Cassia hurried to the trees, knowing Mia was too distracted to notice her.

"You stop that," she whispered up to the nymphs. "Leave them alone and stop causing trouble."

Tearing her hair away from the fingers of the little brown creature tugging on her, Mia ran for Becky. Her friend sagged back against Mia, her hand pressed to her chest. The men on the moped skidded to a stop a few feet away and stared back at the girls as if debating whether to return and apologize. Mia shot them a glare, dismissing them with her hand.

"Are you all right?" she asked Becky.

Becky stared at her for a long second, then nodded. "I think so. They came out of nowhere. I was so busy trying to get my hair untangled from the tree, I almost didn't get a chance to get out of the way."

Mia nodded. "I saw." She reached down and scooped their bags up from where they had dropped them. "Let's go."

With everything Cassia had witnessed so far, she was still stumped as to who the red-headed girl was. *She couldn't be a halfling, could she?* Cassia knew that all halflings bore the coloring of their Court, even if they had very little fae ancestry within their human DNA, they still looked like they belonged with either their inky-black hair or their striking silver tresses.

Cassia considered for a moment that Mia might possibly be

another supernatural creature gifted with the ability of sight. Being able to see past fae glamours was something most supernatural creatures could do, even their various halflings could do it.

But that didn't feel right to the bounty hunter. The girl was out in daylight, so she couldn't be a vampire, dhampir perhaps, but her coloring was too flush. Dhampirs always had a look of the dead with their dark eyes and pale skin. Mia had bright eyes and a nice pink hue to her complexion.

Then she considered the possibility of a shifter. And immediately ruled that out as well. Shifters always smelled of their race. Cassia didn't know of any shifter race who could hide their scent and appear as purely human.

Maybe she was a witch, or at least a halfling witch with very little magical ability? There had to be some reason this girl was left out in the wild without a supernatural protector, at the very least. None of the various races would allow a known halfling—half human and half supernatural—to be with full-blooded humans unless the child had zero skills.

It was rare, but sometimes when a supernatural mated with a human, the resulting child could be born with no powers, but the supernatural elements of DNA were almost always dominant. A child would have some sort of power. Cassia had seen too many offspring of human/supernatural pairings to believe this girl had been passed over as not having anything worthy of her race's notice.

Mia must have been a pure accident that her supernatural parent didn't even know about. It happened, but it was rare. As a bounty hunter, it was Cassia's responsibility to discover *what* Mia was and send her to the appropriate halfling academy.

She decided to continue following the girl, not only because it was her job, but also because her father had nudged her along this path.

As they continued through Shanghai, Mia looked around, her gaze flitting back and forth as though on edge. The girl was probably hoping nothing else unexplainable would appear on the streets. She wasn't so lucky.

Not two blocks later, Mia stopped in her tracks.

Ahead of Cassia, a bogan stood glaring at Mia. These were even nastier than boggarts. Generally, a bogan was a hired henchman. This particular one used a glamour that made him look like a plain Chinese man, but she saw the creature for what it really was, and from Mia's frozen stature, so could she.

Cassia prepared to eliminate him, trying to figure out how to do it without causing a scene. But the bogan made a grab for Mia's arm, trying to pull her into the alleyway the girls were passing.

Mia screamed, "Monster."

Cassia's heart lurched, and before she could make a move, Mia surged forward. In a frenzy of movement, she wrestled the bogan down to the ground then flipped him over onto his stomach, wrenching his arms behind his back so he was immobile. An older man came out of a shop beside her and shouted something.

Cassia caught a few words of it—he saw the creature Mia was holding on the ground simply as a punk. Switching to English, he offered to handle the man for the girls. Mia nodded and moved aside to let him yank the man up. The shop owner told the girls to go, and they didn't hesitate. It took only a few seconds for them to disappear in the crowd.

As they ran away, Cassia heard Becky say they would be late to the Wushu Competition. Cassia knew exactly where they were headed and decided to take the bogan in, collect the bounty, and join up with the girls once she was done.

With a quick shift of her glamour, Cassia appeared as a human police officer. She rushed forward and took control of the bogan, rattling off what little Chinese she had picked up what she hoped sounded like an official cop spiel about arresting him. As she dragged him down the street, Cassia held the creature close. The little monster would know what she was. He would be able to see past the cop image and know she was fae.

He leaned his head back so he could hiss into her ear. "I'll split the job with you." His breath was hot and disgusting against her neck.

"What job?" she asked.

She knew what he meant, but she needed more information. He

had to know Cassia was a bounty hunter. She was the best the fae had, so most fae would know who she was on sight. His statement told her that a bounty was out on Mia's head. But Cassia knew if it was a legitimate bounty, she would know about it already and likely be after it herself.

That implied a criminal element to the bounty, and Mia might be in danger. It worried Cassia, but she didn't have time to interrogate the bogan about it now. She needed to get rid of him and return to Mia as fast as possible.

It felt like it took far too long, but eventually she found a secure place and opened a portal to Forasaon prison to turn the bogan over. Not all fae could portal into the prison, only those who had been magically *keyed* into the system were allowed access. But even still, there were other precautions in place to stop anyone who found a way past the *lock*.

Her bounty struggled against her grip. The giant ogres stationed at the portal where they landed would be intimidating to anyone who wasn't as accustomed to them as Cassia was. She shoved the bogan toward them and they studied it with distaste.

"What is this?" one asked.

She scoffed. "Losing your touch?" she taunted. "It's a bogan."

"I know," the ogre growled. "But there is no bounty on its head."

Fan, the head jailer, came toward them. "Hello, Cassandra. What are you up to today?" he asked.

"I caught this thing in Shanghai, attacking two human girls in broad daylight." She hated being called Cassandra, and it wasn't even her real name. Cassia stood for Cassia. It wasn't a nickname or a shortened version of her name. But that never stopped Fan from teasing her.

"Thank you for handling that," the jailer said, "but since there is no bounty on its head, there is no pay for bringing him in."

Cassia let out a stream of profanities and stomped away, going back toward the portal to Shanghai.

"She's probably already dead by now!" the bogan shouted the moment before Cassia touched the portal.

She turned around sharply and took a step toward him. "What did you say?" she asked through gritted teeth.

"The girl. There's no use rushing back to her. She's probably already dead by now. My partner will have taken care of her." The bogan had dropped his disguise, and his large beady eyes now revealed his mirth. He was happy.

Fan grabbed the bogan by his throat, turned him around, and lifted him so Cassia was glaring directly into his eyes. "What do you mean by that?" she demanded.

The bogan cackled. "You have no idea what you're dealing with."

Fan's eyes sliced over to Cassia. "What's he talking about?"

Cassia shook her head. Now wasn't the time to explain. She headed through the portal back to Shanghai so she could find the girls.

CHAPTER SEVEN

Mia figured their arrival at the Wushu competition would go one of two ways. Master Chen was going to be angry when she and Becky got there, or he was already so angry they would simply vaporize before they made it all the way onto the competition floor. Either way, she was choosing to see it as a chance to boost her adrenaline before the competition began. Optimism, the power of positive thinking, and all those other things she'd seen splashed across motivational banners in her high school.

The truth was, Master Chen was really a kind person. Originally from Hong Kong, the elderly man had a peaceful, calm presence, and very rarely became upset. When his temper did get the best of him, though, it was time to duck and cover. Fortunately, they had only seen that happen twice in the ten years they'd been training with him. Unfortunately, Becky and Mia had just done the one thing guaranteed to push him over the edge. They were late.

Promptness and punctuality were extremely important character traits for Master Chen. He saw them as a demonstration of commitment and discipline. Being late to something, especially a competition like this, was a display of disrespect, which would never be tolerated. Being late meant doing laps. One mile for every minute of lateness.

That was going to be a lot of running to do after completing the first stage of the competition. Mia hoped for some understanding and compassion, considering the circumstances.

It didn't start well.

"Mia, Becky, what is this?" Master Chen shouted as he came across the room toward them.

"I'm sorry." Mia started to explain.

"You are no longer permitted to explore the city. Unless you are here at the competition, practicing with the others, or at an activity with the team, you are to be in your hotel room. Do you understand me?" he said.

"We couldn't help it," Becky replied, on the brink of tears.

"You must take responsibility for yourself and what you do." He stared them down.

"She's right," Mia said. "We were—attacked."

"Attacked?" Master Chen asked.

"Yes. On our walk here. Someone came after us, and I defended us. I managed to subdue him until help came."

"She was amazing," Becky added. "Took him right down before anyone got hurt."

He nodded slowly. "I am proud of you for how you handled yourself in that situation, Mia. That was very dangerous and could have gone much worse. Be that as it may, you were still late, and that has impacted everyone in this competition. You will do laps after the competition. You should have scheduled extra time in your walk for unexpected events," he said before he returned to the group.

Mia watched him for a few seconds, then turned to Becky. "Clearly."

Becky still appeared shaken up by the encounter but she managed a laugh. "I guess that went as well as we could hope."

Mia nodded. "Let's go get ready. You'll be going up in the first group."

Mia slung her arm around Becky's shoulders as they headed for the first event. She decided to take the punishment in stride. As her best friend had said, that had gone fairly well. They were going to have to do laps, but since a special group dinner was set for later that night with the team, Master Chen probably wouldn't make them do as many as technically warranted.

Several minutes later, Mia stood on the sidelines watching Becky. The team had broken up into groups to wander around the large competition floor and watch the competitors. This first day of the competition was taolu. The series of movements required tremendous control and connection with the body. It was an art as well as a show of strength and agility. Becky was competing in the category for sixteen and over, and her skill was obvious. Even in the first minutes of the competition, it was clear she was one of the best there.

Mia was proud as she watched Becky go through the movements and sequences of the taolu. Deep concentration etched her face, but her expression also showed how much she loved what she was doing. Wushu had become an important part of her life, as it had for Mia. It gave her a sense of strength and ability, and she was proud to work her way through the levels.

At the end of her demonstration, Becky surprised and delighted onlookers with an exquisitely executed double backflip. She landed effortlessly facing the judges, bowed, and left the mat with an air of confidence, as though it was no big deal.

Mia wasn't buying it. Becky would be bursting at the seams with excitement over her performance. As soon as she reached her, Becky threw her arms around Mia and squealed. Mia hugged her back, indulging in a few seconds of bouncing up and down in celebration.

"That was amazing," Mia exclaimed.

"Really?" Becky asked, glancing back at the judges even though their faces were totally expressionless.

"Yeah. I think you have a really good chance of winning your age division. There haven't been any other competitors even close to you," Mia reassured her.

Becky's face glowed. She squeezed Mia's hands and looked into her eyes. "Are you ready? It's going to be your turn soon."

A swirl of excitement, nervousness, and anticipation filled Mia's belly, but she nodded. She had the skill to handle it. As his best student back in Pasadena, Master Chen had insisted Mia should compete in the adult division for this competition. He believed in her and had told her repeatedly that if she simply kept a level head and focused, if she reminded herself that she had it in her, she could do very well.

Mia was ready to face the challenge. Confronting the strange creature on the street had given her a boost, and she carried that feeling of power with her onto the mat. When she had first arrived, she had been shaken, then watching the competitors perform their taolus, she began to relax and accept that some part of her knew she was stronger than she thought possible.

Even though she was freaked out by what she'd seen since the night before, something in her subconscious told her not to worry, that she controlled her destiny and had more than enough power to overcome anything or anyone.

She figured it was all the Wushu training she'd done over the past ten years. Master Chen had drilled into them the power of mind over matter, so her subconscious must have already been working to calm her and help her to overcome the freakiness of the past sixteen hours.

With a deep breath and the knowledge that she could perform her moves in her sleep, she strode onto the mat.

With Becky and Master Chen watching, she performed her taolu carefully. She lost herself in the movements, ignoring everything else around her, until she finished in a flurry of applause.

There were no winners on the first day of the competition. That day was only for the taolu and would be followed by two days of hand-to-hand bouts before finals on the fourth day determined the winners of the different categories. Mia and Becky still felt confident in the day's success as they were leaving the venue, bolstered by Master Chen reducing their punishment to only running two miles. Mia took his leniency as a victory.

The group dinner was a special event they had all been looking forward to since before they even left for Shanghai. They had the unique privilege of eating in a monastery that had existed for centuries. Though the monastery and the grounds were essentially a tourist stop now, drawing in huge crowds coming to marvel at the beauty of the structure and the sheer awe of experiencing something so old, the dinner was different. It required a special invitation, and a lot had gone into securing the invite. But Master Chen had managed it. They would be welcomed into the amazing space after visiting hours had ended and would be given the opportunity to see it in a way few did.

They were all excited as they hurried back to the hotel to take showers and dress for the night. Everyone had brought along a special outfit for the dinner, and there was plenty of chatting, giggling, and twirling as the girls revealed their chosen looks.

Mia slipped into the dress she had selected and tucked her feet into the moderate heels she'd convinced her father to buy for her. Now she hoped she'd be able to manage walking in them on the uneven streets. The girls styled their hair and helped each other with their makeup, putting far more time into preparing for this than they had anything else since arriving in Shanghai. Both knew this was a once-in-a-lifetime experience they would always remember, and they wanted to look good in their memories.

They rushed down to the meeting spot in front of the hotel, arriving seconds before Master Chen. Mia was relieved. She didn't want to fathom trying to run laps in her dress and heels after dinner.

Becky held Mia behind as the rest of the group began to walk off. "Do you mind if we sit with the guys?" she whispered.

Mia knew Becky wasn't talking about just any *guys*. She was talking about a *guy*, the one guy in particular who Becky hadn't been able to get off her mind for months.

"That's fine," Mia said. "I'm just looking forward to the experience."

Cassia watched Mia and Becky giggle as they linked arms and tucked their heads close together, whispering to each other and following close behind the other kids. She fell into step behind them. She had to keep a close eye on Mia after what happened that morning, but she didn't want the girl to notice her. Their stroll through the city was pleasantly uneventful. Cassia was hoping they were done with attacks for the day. Seeing Mia alive after the bogan's declaration at the prison was a relief, and she hoped they could skate through the rest of the day without another incident.

All seemed to be working in her favor. They arrived at the ancient monastery, and Cassia hid in the shadows as the group walked reverently inside. When they were safely within the confines of the structure, Cassia decided it was time for some boggart hunting. That nasty creature was still in Shanghai somewhere, and she was determined to eliminate him.

However, the bogan's promise of a partner waiting for Mia was still weighing heavily on her mind. The possibility of those two related creatures working together was strong. If she could find the boggart and remove him, it would eliminate the danger.

As she crossed the courtyard, something caught her eye. A woman walked along the edge of the grounds. Cassia sighed. Maybe this wasn't going to be the smooth night she had hoped for after all.

CHAPTER EIGHT

Something wasn't right about the little Chinese woman wandering through the monastery grounds. Cassia knew it instantly, and it wasn't because the woman's glamour wasn't working well, or because her dark wig was askew.

Being a fae bounty hunter might give her an edge, but she ventured to guess a good percentage of people who caught a glimpse of this woman would immediately recognize something was a bit off.

The woman, standing so serenely looking out over the grounds and occasionally snapping pictures, just didn't fit the scene. For one, it was after visiting hours, and she was the only one seemingly wandering the grounds. A small woman like her walking around alone in the dark was unusual and would likely arouse suspicion. Even odder, though, was that the frail-looking woman was using an analog camera, an older one. Most tourists these days whipped out cell phones with selfie sticks and snapped digital pictures. Even the older generations had digital cameras to capture their memories when they decided to play tourist. But here was this woman, occasionally raising her ancient camera and snapping a picture in the dark.

Completely in the dark. As in, nothing changed when the little old woman pressed the button. She was walking around taking pictures in the dark, but the camera had no flash. Either she was the world's worst tourist photographer, or she wasn't taking pictures at all.

Cassia squinted, and the magical façade of an old Chinese woman disappeared. Instead, the monstrous visage was something that would send the entire monastery running and screaming for their lives—a redcap.

A particularly nasty creature without the flattering touch of her glamour, she was far less unassuming. She was three feet of bearded, razor-toothed trouble. Cassia needed to make sure this thing didn't get anywhere near Mia. Stepping lightly, but quickly, she closed the gap between herself and the redcap.

Cassia skidded to a halt a few feet away from the creature. The redcap spun around to face her and bared her sharp teeth. Her deep-set red eyes seemed to paralyze Cassia by simply making contact with her own. The camera dropped to the ground, bouncing with a clatter, exposing it as merely a shell made of plastic. Long, sharp talons stretched from fingers that reached out to Cassia, threatening to rip her skin from her bones and shred them, making her easier to swallow. Eating their victims, especially if they could do it alive, was one of the less appealing characteristics of redcaps. Which was saying a lot considering that even the females were bearded and horrible enough to be frequently sought-after assassins.

The redcap's long, thin, scraggly beard blew away from her face on the breeze, curling back up around her shoulder and mixing with the thick, unkempt hair, topped with a cheap wig of long black locks. With her façade now gone, the redcap raced toward Cassia, using her shocking speed to gain an immediate advantage. Leaping into the air, her mouth opening wide, saliva dripping from sharpened teeth that looked like millions of yellow nails, she bore down on Cassia.

Instinct kicked in, and Cassia lifted a leg and shifted her weight forward. She kicked the creature in the face as it fell and sent her skidding away in shock. She had expected easy prey, and while a fight was not a deterrent, it required a slightly different approach. Pulling herself into a malleable defensive fighting position, Cassia prepared for the next attack.

She was ready for just about anything from a redcap who was capable of viciousness and randomness of attack at equal levels. What she did not prepare for was the broken, shrill voice of the creature as she slinked back a few steps on what could be best described as hooves somewhat resembling feet. It had toes, it had a heel, but it clomped and stomped on the ground like a particularly aggressive, but very short buffalo.

"Cassia, what a pleasure," the words leaked out of her more than they were spoken, eyes sparkling with recognition.

Vowels were elongated and the voice broke between letters, making it sound like it came from somewhere beyond her body, a dimension of darkness far away. A dimension where monsters lurked and waited, never needing to speak because their anger was always present and filled the space around them like a whirlwind of malice.

"Trust me, the pleasure is all yours," Cassia responded, trying to shake off the nerves accompanying her encounter with one of the most despicable creatures in any universe.

Her knuckles cracked in anticipation, and she scanned the redcap, looking for any potential weak spots. Maybe the knees, maybe the collarbone, but probably not those teeth. Those teeth were capable of so much more than a mere bite. So much more than just death.

"Are you really going to try to take me in?" the redcap asked in a condescending tone. "Many have tried before."

"We have your partner," Cassia said. "Forasaon is waiting to make it a complete set."

A mirthless sound that resembled a laugh escaped the redcap's grimy mouth. "That won't be happening. But I appreciate you coming up to say hello. It saves me the need to seek out another morsel to tide me over until my next meal."

"I've heard I'm a bit salty," Cassia quipped.

Keep talking, that was the key, and it would give Cassia more time to form a plan. The more she kept the nasty thing off guard, the less time she had to worry about those teeth biting into her skin and ripping her apart.

"No bother. You're just the appetizer. That girl is the main course.

I want her friend to watch while I devour her bones. I want her to hear her screams while I rip her skin off. I want her to see her eyes while she begs for me to end her life. And then," the redcap smiled, its hundreds of sharp, randomly sized, pointed teeth scraping together as she did so, "I'll have her for dessert."

"That's a lovely menu you've got planned out for yourself," Cassia said. "Too bad you're not going to have much of an appetite when I'm finished with you. You know, once you have your stomach kicked in and all your teeth missing."

The redcap roared and pounced again, this time swiping at Cassia's legs with her long talons. Cassia jumped to avoid them then delivered a kick that missed the creature's head by inches. Continuing her spin to avoid having her back to the creature meant planting her feet, but doing so gave the redcap something to aim for. Blinding pain shot through her as the long, sharp talons pierced her leg, pulling at her with an iron grip and surprising strength.

Falling on her back was the last thing Cassia wanted, but the best she could do was to straighten her body before she landed in a seated position. Bouncing hard on her rear, she used her free foot to kick at the face of the creature. A blow connected and sent her head snapping backward, and her grip loosened. Another connected with the mouth and Cassia heard several teeth crunch under her foot.

The creature leapt in a rage, and Cassia rolled in time for it to miss her. She scrambled to her feet and swung a fist into the redcap that buried deep in her stomach and crumpled her to the ground. A flurry of kicks to the downed monster sent her rolling away, but Cassia wasn't planning on letting her foe escape.

Cassia jumped after her, narrowly avoided a swipe of the talons, only to find her face smashed in by a sweeping hoof-foot. Her vision exploded in stars and lights that danced and obscured the real world. She rolled away as far as possible to give herself space to recover, which was when she saw the blood all over the ground. And on her shirt. Her nose was broken, and a cut above her eye was gushing. These injuries—combined with the tears in her leg—meant she was experiencing a cacophony of pain. And she was seriously pissed off.

As the stars faded from her vision, she focused again on the creature now crawling toward her, but half of what she saw was colored red. The taste of iron filled her mouth and ignited a new sense of purpose in her. She had to try to control herself. Her father had always said, "Anger without discipline is suicide, but anger with discipline is revenge."

She waited until the last second, lying prone on the ground and pretending to be semi-conscious. The redcap got within a few feet of her and a long, gray tongue swept around her mouth, broken teeth falling out and littering the ground around her. Her arms raised as she prepared to bring her talons down and rip into Cassia's body, when Cassia jumped up, ramming her palm into the creature's nose and spinning into a kick to the knee. The creature slumped, a sound of shock mixing with a roar of pain at what had to be a shattered knee. The thought of her knives ran through Cassia's mind, but she shook it off. Alive. She wanted it alive.

The redcap lifted her face toward Cassia and bared her bloody, stained teeth. Taking a moment to aim, Cassia strode forward and thrust a kick from the center of her body, using every bit of strength she had in her to plant her foot in the creature's jaw. The kick was perfectly placed, just low enough, at just the right angle, with just the right power, to knock the brain out for a little nap. The redcap splayed on the ground, her arms loose noodles with sharp pointy ends.

Breathing through her mouth, and wiping globs of drying blood from her nose, Cassia tied up the redcap and sat beside her, taking a moment to wipe the blood from her face and take stock of her handiwork. She had captured a redcap *alive*. Fan was going to hate that. Or love it. It was hard to tell with him sometimes.

"What in the living Hades did you get yourself into this time, Cassia?" Fan boomed.

Well. That eliminated the 'love it' possibility.

"I caught this one outside the monastery. She was pretending to be human and stalking two human girls," said Cassia. "I think she is the partner the bogan was talking about earlier."

Fan studied the redcap, then gave Cassia an almost-approving nod. "I'm surprised you were able to bring her in—especially alive."

Cassia couldn't help but be offended by the comment. "What's that supposed to mean? I'm a bounty hunter. Bringing all forms of nasty creatures to you is kind of my thing. It's what I do," she pointed out.

"That might be true, but this is different. *This one* has a very large bounty on her head. Her list of crimes is extensive. Mostly murder," Fan said.

"And you know every single one of them," the redcap spat. She had come to right after Cassia had brought her through the portal. The ogres held her down while Fan inspected her.

"What does that mean?" Cassia asked.

Fan eyed the creature with disgust. "She likes to leave just enough bones behind to make sure that we can identify her victims," he grumbled. "It's her calling card."

The creature's smile grew more maniacal, and Cassia felt her stomach turn. This was a serial killer who took great pleasure in making sure everyone knew what she had done. Her cockiness didn't just show she had no remorse and very much enjoyed every horrific murder, but that she believed she would do it again. There wasn't a bit of her entitled, self-absorbed mind that believed she had been stopped.

"That's just lovely," Cassia commented. "You can go right ahead and stuff her under a rock somewhere and pay me my bounty."

"Late for something?" Fan asked flippantly.

"It's never too soon to get the Hades out of here." Cassia suppressed the shiver threatening to surge up her spine. Had she known how awful the redcap truly was, she would have killed it when she'd had the chance.

Behind Fan, the ogre guards watched Cassia and Fan's exchange. It was obvious they were amused by the back and forth, their shoulders shaking as they tried to cover up their laughter. Faylynne barely tolerated them referring to him as Fan without exploding. They knew it wouldn't do them any good for him to catch them laughing at him.

"You sure know how to charm, Cassia," Fan said.

"Does my eagerness to get out of the depths of despair and get back to doing something productive offend you?" She arched an eyebrow.

The ogres were quickly losing their resolve to show respect to the lead jailer, and their growing chuckles were audible.

"Maybe it wouldn't be as bad if you hung around and carried on a real conversation for once." Fan's half-smile unnerved her.

A touch of something suggestive echoed in his voice, but Cassia would shut that down fast. She couldn't stand Fan. At least, she didn't think she could. She did not have the mental space to handle an awkward flirtatious conversation right then. Behind Fan, one of the ogres rolled his eyes at the comment.

"You're right, Fan. Why don't you go find me someone I can do that with?" The snark was beginning to return, and Cassia was ready to put the redcap out of her mind.

"There are times when I really want to snap you in two, you know that?" Fan asked.

Cassia glared at him and at the redcap, then back again. "If I keep collecting these death threats, I'm going to develop a punch card system. I have to say that hers was a lot more creative."

That was all it took. The ogre trying his hardest to hold back his laughter let it out, and the deep sound made the building rumble around them.

Once Cassia was back at her hotel and cleaned up, she focused on who Mia really was. To send a bogan after a human wasn't unheard of. It was possible a fae, or some other creature, had taken a liking to Mia and now wanted her as a trophy. But to send a redcap? Especially one so vicious? This was personal.

Some fae lord or someone else really high up had it in for Mia. No, she wasn't a human. The girl had to be the descendant of an important fae. *Why else would there be so much muscle after the teenager?* Cassia went through everything she had learned about Mia and came to the conclusion that, if not for her red hair, the girl appeared to be a halfling fae. She hadn't demonstrated any real power, other than seeing past glamours and an uncanny ability to fight.

So why wasn't Mia back in the States in one of the halfling fae academies? She may not gain entry to the Elmhurst Academiae Superiorum, but she would deserve a spot in one of the lower level academies, at the very least. If nothing more than to learn how to protect herself from the various monsters of their world.

No, she must be a halfling. Maybe she was a distant relative of a witch and somewhere else along the line a powerful fae was mixed in? She couldn't be sure, a red-headed halfling was a first for Cassia.

All halflings attended special schools in their home countries to learn about their abilities and how to master them. Then, the leaders of their different races would choose the most promising candidates to work for them on Earth.

The fae rarely allowed halflings on Faerie, but sometimes it happened. However, most of their organizations on Earth were staffed by halflings. The halflings were more loyal to their fae family than the humans who worked for the fae.

Mia deserved a spot in an academy, and Cassia was going to find a way to take the girl there.

CHAPTER NINE

Phillipsburg, Montana

"We're here so much we might as well just pitch tents and start living off the land," Vivi snipped, as they made their way into the field again.

Carson rolled his eyes at her. "What would you know about living off the land? That doesn't mean you call a waiter over to bring you a drink while you're lying on the beach during a vacation, you know."

Vivi glared at him. She was tired of his jokes and of the way he seemed to want to push her until she cracked. There were times when she thought of him as a close friend and other times when he made her want to pop his head like a pimple. She wondered what it was about him and why he felt the need to tease and make fun of her.

"You're right. Why don't we just go back to the school and ask Elmhurst if we can practice controlling the wind in the banquet hall? I bet it would be a lot of fun to see the peas swirling around the ceiling," Zander said sarcastically. "Maybe the kitchen wants to make lemon meringue pie for dessert, and we can provide the air."

"Maybe we should get a little bit of atmosphere going here." Luna tried to diffuse the tension. "If it didn't just look like the same giant field we keep coming to, it might be more interesting."

"What do you suggest, Little Miss Sunshine? If you're thinking about making another circle of purple pansies, you can just keep it to yourself. I don't want to see another one of those ridiculous flowers for as long as I can possibly avoid it." Vivi rolled her eyes.

"All right, that's enough. I'm not interested in wasting any more time standing around here bickering. The whole reason we're stuck here at the school this summer rather than being able to be off living our lives is that we can't get along. I don't know about any of you, but I'm seriously done with having this be my entire existence. I'd like to see something other than the two miles around the school at some point before graduation," Zander said.

"I don't take saying this about a Seelie lightly, but he's right," Carson said. "If we ever want to get our lives back and not tempt Elmhurst to force us to do everything in tandem, we have to start gelling better. So, let's stop trying to one-up each other and start working together."

"Listen to that." Luna laughed. "I think you're having a good influence on him, Zander."

Carson chuckled. "Maybe I'm the good influence, did you ever think of that?"

Zander gave him an unconvinced look. "How do you figure?"

"I saw the look in your eyes when you were checking out my...textbook," Carson said.

The four laughed, some of the tension lifting away from them.

Luna performed a few quick lunges and rocked her neck back and forth to loosen the muscles. At five feet, eight inches, Luna was particularly tall for a fae girl. But her height had served her well. Growing up in a rough neighborhood hadn't exactly given her the opportunity to be delicate and demure. She'd had to learn to take care of herself and had trained in Taekwondo from a very young age.

Continuing with her martial arts study had resulted in her taking Krav Maga as her PE class. Half the time, she had her face buried in a book, trying to absorb everything she possibly could about magic, and the other half she was learning to kick butt and defend herself. It was a valuable combination that made a meaningful contribution to the group. Of course, it had also given her the skill to bash Vivi's face in after her nasty practical joke.

It was something she was going to have to learn to balance. Like the other three in the group, learning to understand her abilities and utilize them to their highest potential was how she would help elevate their skills.

"What are you doing?" Vivi asked.

"Stretching," Luna said.

"Does doing magic frequently require stretching ahead of time? I must have missed that little tidbit in health class," the smaller girl quipped. But she spoke with a smile, and Luna grinned back.

She was under no illusions that this meant the two of them were friends. At any given time, Vivi could go right back to tormenting her. It was the Unseelie way. They were what they were.

"I don't know what I might have to be preparing myself for," Luna teased.

"I think Vivi is willing to call a truce for today," Carson said. "What do you say, Viv? You'll avoid the temptation to bounce Luna around like she's in the tumble cycle of the dryer?"

"Fine," Vivi said. "No practical jokes today."

"I'm just going to note that you did say today," Luna pointed out.

The other fae girl nodded and shrugged. "I reserve the right to change my mind and resume the hilarity at any given point beyond today."

Carson shook his head and chuckled. Sometimes he just couldn't get enough of Vivi. He was attracted to her, and his feelings were growing progressively stronger, but she was way too much to handle. It was far easier to stay friends and occasionally tease her for the fun of watching her get flustered.

"All right. Let's do this thing," Zander said.

All it takes is focusing tremendously hard on something and wanting it to happen badly enough for it to occur to you just how infrequently something really crosses your mind. That's what all the young fae were thinking as they stood in the field, anticipating the wind. From stiff gusts to gentle breezes, the wind wasn't ever really something any of them had given a tremendous amount of thought to. When it was there, it was; when it wasn't, it wasn't.

Occasionally, on a particularly hot day, each of the teens had hoped for something to break up the stillness in the air and give them a little bit of cooling relief. And in the bitter cold of the Montana winter, there was always the hope of avoiding one of the stinging spirals of air carrying ice crystals and snow. But the wind itself wasn't a strong enough contender for their attention.

Until now. Then it was the only thing any of them could think about. Today was about learning to rein in their abilities and use them to control the movement and intensity of the wind. Doing that as a group was already daunting enough. Now was not the time to try to actually conjure the wind as well. They agreed to wait for some natural breezes and maybe one day build up to creating it. Maybe.

They had already talked about how they were going to harness the power of the wind and what they were going to do with it once they had it under their control. After the purple pansy circle debacle, they knew working together from the beginning was essential to achieving any type of success. They were ready, but the wind refused to cooperate.

The four had been standing there waiting for almost half an hour when a gust finally built up in the trees along the edge of the field. The branches rustled, and the grass around them was flattened. They braced themselves, and when the wind grew stronger, they put their plan in motion.

They focused on every aspect of the wind. How it felt on their skin, what it sounded like in their ears, even what it smelled like as it whipped up the dampness from the trees and the summer-warmed dirt beneath the grass. Finally, they were ready and concentrated their abilities on harnessing the wind in an effort to pass it around among themselves.

Nothing happened. It should have been fairly easy. They should have been able to take hold of the breeze, draw it down, and pass it around like a ball. They had all seen other students doing something similar before. Of course, they were older and weren't being required to work together. The wind quieted and they all expelled the breaths they realized they'd been holding.

"Let's just try again," Zander said. "It's fine that it didn't work the first time. We just need to work on it a little. Are you ready?"

The other three nodded, and they went back to waiting for another breeze.

For the next several hours they went through the cycle of waiting for the wind, attempting to gain control of it, then dealing with the inevitable screw up and having to move on. Unlike during their first practice sessions in the field when trying to create the Faerie Circle, this time they couldn't point directly at Vivi and blame her lack of concentration for them not being able to accomplish what they set out to do. There were a few times when she'd been distracted or frustrated and the effort had failed, but the others had done the same as well.

Zander kept pushing them right into the next attempt. A few times, he tried to scrap all the plans they made and create a completely new approach. They'd only been working together for a short time, but the other three young fae were already accustomed to him. As intense as his icy blue eyes and silvery Seelie hair was, Zander was focused almost to a fault. He would rather drive himself into the ground than let up for even an instant and threaten the future he saw for himself. Even more than any of the others, his sights were focused on obtaining the elusive pass into Faerie. But he was acutely aware that only one percent of halflings ever achieved such a status.

He didn't allow the knowledge to deter or intimidate him. Instead, it pushed and motivated him to constantly work harder and accomplish new levels of success and esteem within the academy. It also put him in the position of being de facto leader of the little gang Principal Elmhurst had constructed. He resented being yoked together with them and having to associate so closely with Unseelie on a daily basis, but he took the assignment as an opportunity to showcase himself and hone his skills even more.

As far as Zander was concerned, they could accomplish the Power of Five on their own, despite only being four. Not technically having enough people to accomplish the power wasn't a deterrent for him. Instead, he figured each of them just needed to work a little harder to make up for the open spot in the group.

Finally, they started to get the hang of controlling and manipulating the wind. But that didn't mean it was going well. The wind seemed to be manipulating them right back.

"Vivi, I thought we agreed," Carson said.

The dark-haired girl shook her head, making the fading light of the afternoon shimmer on the bluish sheen of her glossy strands. She held up her hands innocently.

"That one is not me. I said I wasn't going to do anything today, and I didn't," she protested.

They both turned to watch Luna tumbling around in the air.

"Well, you have to admit it's a little convenient, considering that crack about the dryer and the whole underwear incident," Carson pointed out.

A few minutes earlier, one of their attempts to control the wind went sideways and Luna was sucked up into the air. Now she was trapped in a current, spinning and rolling around as gusts came from both sides of the field and collided.

"Can we just stop with conversation about who did this and get me down?" Luna shrieked.

The three fae went to work, trying to regain control of the wind. They didn't want to just suddenly take away the wind and risk injuring Luna if she crashed to the ground. Instead, they needed to gradually release the power of the wind so she could ease back down. It took several minutes, but finally, they managed to lower Luna onto the ground with only a small thump and a grunt of frustration.

She pushed to her feet, brushing herself off and glaring at the others around her. "Well, that was delightful," she muttered.

She tried to take a step, and the world spun around her. She stumbled a little, twirled, and dropped back to the ground. Zander rushed to her side, kneeling and lifting her head.

"Are you all right?" he asked. "What happened?"

Luna managed a smile and shook her head, which only made the swirling worse. She groaned and pressed the heel of her hand to the center of her forehead and squeezed her eyes closed. "I'm fine. Just dizzy. That was a bit on the intense side," she said.

"Just think, though. Now you are fully prepared in the event you ever decide to go into astronaut training," Carson said. "You've already got that spinning around thing down pat."

"Thanks for that," Luna said. "Way to see the silver lining."

After a few more minutes of sitting and trying to let her head assimilate to being still again, Luna was able to climb to her feet.

"Feeling better?" Zander asked. Luna nodded. "Good. You up for going for another round?"

"Of course, she is," Vivi said. "She's always up for everything, aren't you, Luna? She has to be the best at everything. Wouldn't want her grades to slip or Principal Elmhurst to get disappointed in her and risk her scholarship."

Luna glared at the smaller fae, her arms crossed over her chest. "Oh. There's Vivi. Things around here were just getting too pleasant, and I knew that couldn't be happening with her here. But, never fear, I found her."

"Vivi, you promised," Carson said. "Luna, stop provoking her."

"Who put you in charge?" Vivi asked.

"I didn't provoke her. She was just born like that," Luna argued.

"The wind is picking up," Zander told them. He'd checked out of their petty bickering partway through the attempts to lower Luna to the ground and was done dealing with them for the day. He was going to figure this out and make the group successful if he had to drag the other three behind him the entire way. "This time, let's just try to stop it halfway across the field, change its direction, and send it back the other way. We've done it before. That will be our reset point."

Two days later, that was still their reset point. All four sat in the middle of the field, exhausted from pushing themselves as hard as they could from the time they woke up until they went to bed. As it had been for the last two days, a picnic basket lay tipped over a few yards away. They'd packed it before leaving the academy so they wouldn't have to take a long break in the middle of the day to go back and eat lunch. Both days they ended up having to hunt down various elements of their meal after the wind picked up the basket and sent it flying around the field, making it rain down wax-paper wrapped sandwiches and pieces of fruit.

They all looked a bit worse for wear after their battle against the wind these past days. Vivi sat with her legs sprawled in front of her, her black hair sticking up from her head at drastic angles, as though she had stuck her finger in an electrical socket. In reality, she had just been hit directly in the face with a massive blast of wind, right after trying to toss it to Carson and not moving fast enough.

Zander had long, shallow scratches along his arm and one side of his face from twigs broken off from some of the trees in the woods. They had come along with a particularly intense stream of wind and he didn't move out of the way fast enough. Carson was streaked with dirt and grass stains from being picked up and thrown several feet, then skidding across the ground.

But they'd done it. The wind had chewed them up and spat them out over the long hours they spent in the field, but finally their powers merged, and they'd mastered the skills. Once they'd figured it out, it seemed almost ridiculous that it had taken so much effort. Simple wind control was a skill halflings learned when they were thirteen or fourteen. These four had learned it when they were twelve, demonstrating their exceptional skill and ability. But it wasn't just the ability to control the wind they'd needed in this situation. They were still learning to collaborate and utilize their powers as a unit rather than individuals. Doing that with a skill far more advanced than just conjuring up some flowers took considerably more control and effort. Once they'd realized that and began to truly apply themselves toward combining their powers rather than just exerting their own skills, it became much easier.

Now their bodies were sore, and their minds felt wrung out and exhausted from the exertion. It was still fairly early in the evening, but none of them had any energy left.

"Can I interest anybody in dinner at the cafe to celebrate?" Luna asked.

"Absolutely," Zander said.

"I'm starving," Carson agreed.

"At least you got to eat most of your lunch," Vivi added. "My sandwich got blown into the woods and was stolen by a squirrel."

"I offered you part of mine," Carson argued.

"Your chickpea version of tuna fish isn't something I'm getting anywhere near. I've never even eaten tuna, and I can tell you that yours is so wrong," Vivi countered.

"I think it's delicious, Carson," Luna offered.

"Thank you," Carson said. "The cooks at the academy think so, too. That's why they make it for me."

"They make it for you because you're spoiled," Zander said.

They all dragged themselves to their feet and brushed away remnants of grass and dirt.

"Let's go back to the dorms and clean up, then we'll go get something to eat. Mom made her more than meat meatloaf today, with mashed potatoes and mushroom gravy on the side."

Luna's announcement was enough to fuel all of them to hurry back to the academy. Even though the prospect of long, hot showers was extremely appealing, the dinner waiting for them outweighed it. They met up in front of the dorm and headed to the restaurant, ready to relax.

CHAPTER TEN

Shanghai, China

The next few days saw Cassia keeping a close eye on Mia. When Cassia returned to the monastery after dumping the redcap off with Fan, she was relieved to see the girl was still safe and there weren't any other creatures going after her.

While she had taken care of the immediate threat to the girl, Cassia knew that more would come. Only she still didn't know why or what to do with the girl. A tiny voice in the back of her mind told her to leave the teen to her own devices. Cassia had saved her twice, and the girl needed to figure out how to protect herself.

On the other hand, Cassia reminded herself that her father wanted her to follow the girl for a reason. No regular halfling would have such powerful enemies. Maybe it had to do with her fae parentage?

Cassia kept enough distance to ensure that Mia wouldn't see her, but she had noticed the girl looking at her a few times with a curious stare. No matter what glamour Cassia used, Mia seemed to recognize her but had never approached her. And Cassia had no need to speak to Mia, not until the final day of the Wushu Championships.

Mia had just bowed to the judges after trouncing her opponent and smiled brightly at Becky. When the halfling's entire body stiffened and her eyes bulged, Cassia knew something was wrong. She followed the direction of Mia's stare and recognized the figure glaring at Cassia's new charge. At that very moment, she knew without a doubt that she would be ensuring the girl's safety forever.

The Unseelie fae bounty hunter who had Mia in his sights began to stalk toward his prey. Cassia wasn't sure how Mia knew she was in danger, but from the look of fear on her face, she was all too aware. It was time to make Mia disappear.

In order to do that, Cassia would have to use mind-warping. She hated to use it on innocent humans, but she had to extract Mia without sending up any red flags.

Quickly changing her glamour to that of a middle-aged red-headed woman, she made her way to Mia and her friend. "Mia, darling!" Cassia pulled the girl into a hug and whispered into her ear. "Follow my lead if you want to get out of here alive and leave your friends safe."

"What? Who?" Mia didn't know what was going on, but she did recognize the person hugging her. It was that fae bounty hunter she'd met almost a week ago in the night market. The same one who had been following her all week.

The girl had never made Mia feel worried for her safety. In fact, whenever she had seen the fae, she had felt safer, as though the woman was her personal bodyguard. When she looked over the bounty hunter's shoulder, she spotted the man with the pointy ears glaring daggers at her and knew that she was in danger. But she couldn't leave her friends in the lurch either. If Becky thought Mia was in danger, she'd insist on going with her.

And Master Chen would never allow Mia to leave without him. He *was* responsible for her safety while they were in China, after all. She might be able to escape for a few hours without any trouble, but with everything she'd seen the past week, danger was following her. Her greatest wish was to finish the competition and go home, leaving the monsters behind in China.

At least she'd had part of her wish granted.

Now, she wasn't sure what to do. Her teenage self wanted to scream "Monster!" and run for cover. But that small soft voice in the back of her mind screamed for her to trust the woman hugging her and save her friends.

When Cassia pulled back, she winked. "Mia, I'm so glad I was able to see your final performance. Your father will be so proud."

Mia frowned, wondering if the bounty hunter knew her father. She was about to ask when Cassia grabbed her hand and squeezed it.

"Master Chen?" Cassia looked to the Asian man who stood calmly as he watched the interchange between the two women.

He bowed slightly. "I am."

"My name is Cassandra Jennings. I'm Mia's Aunt." She put her hand out, and Master Chen shook it.

His brow furrowed. "Excuse me, but I thought Mia's only family was her father?"

Still holding the man's hand, Cassia looked into his eyes and initiated her magic. "Mia's father is my brother. I live and work in Asia, so we rarely see each other. But James has given me permission to take Mia for a couple of weeks. I have paperwork for you." She pulled out a blank piece of paper and handed it to Master Chen, who studied it.

He nodded and smiled at Mia. "Well, Mia, it looks like your Chinese holiday gets to continue. I'm very happy for you." His stilted voice worried Mia, and she looked between her Wushu Master and the woman standing next to her.

Becky had been quiet during this exchange, but in her confusion, she spoke up. "But I know you don't have any other family."

Cassia turned to the young girl and took her hand. "You've probably just forgotten all about me. I haven't seen Mia in several years. My work has kept me here in China. But we've met before, Becky. Four years ago, at Christmas."

Becky's eyes glossed over, and she swayed just enough to grab

Mia's attention. When Mia put her hand on her friend's arm, she felt power surging through the girl.

"Oh, that's right. Yes, I just forgot." Becky's monotone voice had Mia even more concerned.

"What are you doing?" Mia whispered, glaring at Cassia.

"I'll explain when we get out of here, but you're in imminent danger. You must leave with me now." Cassia smiled and let Becky's hand go.

Mia was confused and scared. Should she go with Cassandra? Or should she stay with her friends and hope whatever that other monster wanted, Master Chen could take care of her and Becky. After all, the entire team was adept at fighting, even though Mia was the only one with real-world experience fighting creatures. She was confident they'd win out.

"No, I'm not leaving with you. I don't even know who you are." Mia looked at the bounty hunter and at Master Chen. "I've never seen her before we arrived in China."

Master Chen only smiled and nodded. "Of course, you want to leave with your aunt now. I understand. Enjoy your holiday, and we will all see you when you return home at the end of the summer."

Becky hugged her best friend as though she really thought all was well and they'd part company only to meet up again later this summer.

"What's going on?" Mia studied her friend and instructor. "They aren't even here with us, are they?" She noted the glossy eyes and vacant stares on them both and shivered.

"It's for their own safety. Trust me, you don't want to deal with what's waiting to grab you here. It's much better for everyone in this stadium if we go outside. Now." Cassia pulled Mia with her, and Mia stumbled for a few steps before looking back at the scary man eyeing her.

Mia bit her lip, righted herself, and joined Cassia in their hasty retreat. "You had better tell me everything, and I mean all of it, the second we get outside." Not sure if she made the right choice, Mia went willingly with the fae.

Cassia wanted nothing more than to find a discreet place to create a portal and take Mia away from China. But she had to get far enough from the other bounty hunters to create a safe portal—one they wouldn't be able to trace. Not all fae could trace a portal, but enough of the bounty hunters were able to, and she had to assume the one following them could too.

With Mia in tow, Cassia wove through the throng milling about outside of the conference center and went several blocks before turning down an alley. While the sun hadn't set yet, it was late enough in the day that the shadows were long and helped to cover their movement.

Once Mia no longer felt the oppression of the person hunting them, she came to a stop and glared at Cassandra. "All right, who are you? I remember you from the other night at the market, and I've noticed you following me around the city this week. What's going on?"

Cassia sighed and scanned the area around them. "This really isn't the best place to have this conversation."

"I don't care. I demand to know what's happening. I'm not going anywhere with you until you explain what happened back there." Mia put her fisted hands on her hips and stood her ground.

This wasn't the way Cassia wanted to do this. But with their safety at risk, she had to. She placed a hand on the wall next to them and thought of where she wanted to go.

Underneath her palm, a shimmering portal of blues and purples swirled out from her hand and created a space that was large enough for a person to walk through.

Mia stared in astonishment at the anomaly in front of her. "What?" She shook her head and rubbed her eyes. "What is that?" She pointed to the wall and took a few steps back.

"Don't worry, it's completely safe. And my name is Cassia, not Cassandra." She shook her head and thought of Fan for a moment before refocusing on the current situation. She shouldn't have used Fan's teasing name for her. Later on, she'd have to evaluate why *that* name came to mind instead of the many other aliases she used.

Mia blinked. "But what *is* it?"

Smirking, Cassia pulled her hand back and the swirling colors coalesced into a doorway of sorts. "It's a portal. The fae use it for traveling between our two worlds as well as to transport ourselves all around Earth. Come, follow me and I'll explain it all once we are in a safer location." She held her hand out for Mia to take.

The teenager shook her head. No way was she going to walk inside a wall. Who knew what was on the other side?

"I promise it's much safer than standing here and waiting for Narco or one of his henchmen to find us." She nodded in the direction they had come from.

"You'll tell me all once we get through that thing?" Mia gulped and steeled herself for the impossible. Of course, she'd read sci-fi novels and even watched movies where portals had been used for travel. But she had never ever believed it was real. If this *was* real, how many other things were real? She now knew monsters existed. What else would she see?

CHAPTER ELEVEN

Shanghai, China

Cassia wanted to believe that she'd gotten them away from danger. After the run-in with the fake old lady tourist on the grounds of the monastery, she wanted to tell herself they were going to be safe now. It made it easier to whisk Mia away when she could convince herself the danger was past. But that wasn't the case.

As they moved through the city, she sensed someone following them. It wasn't another of the creatures or even one of the bounties she'd been trying to track down when she stumbled upon this mysterious girl. It was someone much more dangerous.

She grabbed Mia's arm and pulled her into a narrow alleyway, crouching behind a stack of rough wooden crates and boxes. She held up a finger to her lips to keep Mia quiet.

"What's wrong?" Mia asked.

Cassia shook her head, insisting the girl not speak anymore. She didn't want to take a chance on Mia being heard by the person pursuing them. Footsteps came into the alley and Cassia pushed back against the cold, damp stone wall of the building beside her. She put an arm over Mia to crush her back so both of them were fully concealed behind the boxes. It wouldn't take much to find them.

In retrospect, she should have gone for a more concealed hiding spot than behind a bunch of crates built from slats which anyone could see between if they crouched low enough.

It wouldn't have mattered where she portaled to, the hunter following them had to have had the ability to trace portals since he was already on their trail. Knowing this, Cassia was even more grateful she hadn't portaled to somewhere she *thought* would be safe.

It was much better to try and lose them in a large city such as Shanghai, before portaling around the world to a safer spot. No need to burn any of her secure hideouts yet.

They needed to get off the street and out of sight as fast as possible. With any luck, they had confused their pursuer, and he'd go back to trying to scout them out among the crowd.

Cassia held her breath. It was pointless, but it made her feel better. It was a habit from when she was a little girl. If she was hiding like a child playing hide-and-seek with her father, or when she grew older and began finding herself in sticky situations, she would hold her breath, She had almost believed the act of drawing in air and letting it out again was what made her visible. Or that the little bit of movement would give the person on the verge of finding her the advantage.

The footsteps came closer and stopped. Cassia hazarded a peek through the slats in front of her and scanned the visible portion of the person's legs. They told her enough. Seconds stretched on and felt like hours before they stepped back and walked out of the alley. She rose for a second, just long enough to catch sight of the full person before he disappeared around the corner and onto the street.

"That's what I was afraid of," she muttered.

"What?" Mia asked. "What's going on? Who was that?"

"We need to get you somewhere safe," Cassia replied.

She sat on her heels, her head resting against the wall while she considered their options. They had to find somewhere secure where she could protect Mia and keep her out of the wrong hands until she figured out what to do with her.

A thought flashed into her mind and she stood, reaching down to help Mia to her feet. "I know where. Come on. We need to hurry."

The fae led Mia along the alley in the opposite direction from where they'd come. Squeezing between the buildings and scrambling over low walls and trash cans would make their way more challenging, but it would keep them off the street where they would be easily found.

"Cassia, what's going on? Who was that person following us?" Mia demanded.

"His name is Narco. He's a bounty hunter," said Cassia.

"Like you?"

"Not exactly. He normally works for the Queen of the Unseelie Court. Let's just say he doesn't follow the rules very well."

"What does that mean?" Mia asked.

"He's a bad guy. Like, a seriously bad guy. By all standards, even Unseelie fae. If he has set his sights on you, it's dangerous, and we need to stay far ahead of him." Cassia stopped at an intersection of garbage cans and overthrown boxes of expired produce. She waved a hand in front of her nose and looked for the best way through.

"How do you know about him?" Mia worked to keep up with Cassia as they headed who knew where. Her face scrunched in disgust as she passed the stench of the overturned trash.

Once they were down the next street, Cassia inhaled deeply and let the breath out slowly, trying to calm the trembling of her heart in her chest, while clearing her sinuses of the offending odor. She stood on her toes to look over a low wall then pulled herself up to balance on the top. There were a few loops of old barbed wire, but she used one boot to flatten it so she could help Mia up and over it.

"I've had dealings with him in the past. It's a fun game for him to find out what bounties other hunters are looking for, use the tracing and work they've already done, and swoop in to make the claim himself. But that's just obnoxious more than anything. Narco is dark and won't hesitate to destroy whatever is standing in his path if he thinks it will make it easier for him to accomplish what he wants. I have reason to believe he is the one that killed my father."

Mia drew in a sharp breath and went quiet.

They continued through the city toward the outskirts. Cassia knew of a place to stash Mia for a little while, at least until she could figure out what to do with her.

There had to be something more about her. She must be very special. There were too many people after Mia, too much interest in her. She wasn't displaying special powers, but that didn't mean anything. Depending on who and what she was, Mia might not have total control over her abilities yet. In a way, that could make it even more dangerous.

They were silent for the remainder of the journey, and finally their destination lay in front of them. The abandoned apartment complex was tiny, featuring only eight units.

"What is this place?" Mia asked.

"It used to be an apartment complex. Well, I guess it still is, but no one lives here anymore. It was condemned a few years back and everyone was forced to move out. It's been on my radar for a little while. I meant to come here and check it out when I was searching for the boggart we ran into at the market, but I never got around to it."

She didn't mention that the main reason she hadn't gotten around to pursuing her instincts about the complex was that she was so focused on following Mia and trying to keep her safe.

"And you think we'll be safe here?" Mia asked, eyeing the sagging building and overgrown patch of grass around it suspiciously.

"It's shelter," Cassia replied. "And that look on your face underscores why I chose it. No one is going to think of somewhere like this when searching for you. We'll lay low for a while and then decide where to go from there."

Mia still looked confused and concerned, a twisted blend of emotions flowing through her vibrant eyes. Cassia couldn't blame her. Everything she'd been through already was a lot for anyone to handle, much less a teenage girl. A slight shudder went through the young halfling as they continued.

They walked over the cracked sidewalk, crushing blades of grass that had forced their way up through the concrete. Cassia made a conscious effort to avoid the tiny flowers sprouting in places. She didn't like the idea of destroying something so delicate and beautiful. It was an odd thought, but she tried not to dwell on it too much.

Two thick pieces of wood were nailed crossways over the front door of the first of the two buildings, preventing them from opening it. Cassia could have broken through one of the windows but didn't want to call more attention to them as they prowled around.

They made their way around to the back of the building. Here, the door that accessed the breezeway at the front of the building was open, possibly smashed in by a kick or two. It hung away from the doorframe, hinges rusted and decayed.

Cassia stuck her head into the room and listened for any signs that someone else had chosen the spot as their own place of refuge. When the building remained silent, she slipped inside. Mia followed behind her. The air was dusty and unpleasant, but they couldn't expect anything else in a place abandoned and closed up years ago. The building was set up with four apartments, one on either side of the hall on two floors. Cassia tested the first door, but it wouldn't budge. The second was crushed, the middle nearly split in two. She eyed the metal steps that led up to the next floor.

"Let's try up there," she suggested. "If there's nothing better, we'll try our luck with building number two."

They climbed the stairs and tried the first apartment. The door resisted, but Mia stopped her.

"Can't you just use your magic to open it?" she asked.

"It's kind of bad form, but I guess whoever locked it in the first place probably doesn't care if we're in there," Cassia replied. "We could go back to the one on the bottom floor, but I'd feel better with us up here. Being off the ground always feels more secure."

She used her magic to release the lock and opened the door to the apartment. Dank air rushed out at them, but the windows allowed enough light inside for them to see the room. It was overflowing with dirty mattresses, discarded clothes, and trash. Cassia slammed the door shut and shook her head. They moved over to the second apartment and found much of the same.

"On second thought, let's not jump straight to the first option. Let's check out what's behind door number two," Cassia said.

They made their way to the second building and up to the second floor. After scouring the first three apartments, they found the door to the fourth standing partially open. Cassia went inside first. It was cluttered like the others, but not as much. But they'd wasted enough time, and this was probably as good as they were going to get. They entered the apartment and closed the door behind them.

"Home sweet home," Mia murmured.

"Not forever," Cassia promised. "Just for now."

"And then?" Mia asked.

"And then, well, it won't be," Cassia replied. She studied a hallway across the room. "Should we explore the rest of it?"

Mia nodded. "Why not?"

They picked their way through the living room and into the hallway, where a familiar, sickening odor wafted to Cassia. The farther inside they walked, the stronger the smell became. She cringed. Eight apartments and she'd had the bad luck to choose this one. Or the good luck, depending on how she decided to look at it.

The stench was almost palpable and forced Cassia and Mia to wrinkle their noses in disgust. Covering her face with one arm, Cassia opened the door to the bedroom, and the handle turned easily in her hand. The door swung open slowly, hinges creaking, halting only when it hit a stopper that made an audible springy sound. Everything beyond a few feet into the room was masked in pitch darkness. There should have been a window in there somewhere, but it must have been covered by a thick curtain which blotted out the light.

"Nope, nothing creepy about this at all," Mia said under her breath.

"I know that smell," Cassia said. She'd smelled it countless times before. She had been right about her suspicions.

"Ick?" Mia asked.

"Not exactly. Come on, the boggart's in here, I smell it," Cassia said, her voice just above a whisper. Reluctantly, Mia followed. Cassia reached for a battle knife on her belt and pulled it from its sheath. Just before they entered the complete darkness, she made eye contact with Mia and waved the knife in the air. "Want one?"

"Why would I need one?" Mia asked, her eyes snapping toward a dark corner of the room. Something had moved. Perhaps it was a mouse or another small rodent, or maybe it was just the rattling of the stuff piled everywhere or falling over.

"This boggart has hurt little children. He's a mean and nasty creature, and the reason I'm in China to begin with," Cassia said, dashing Mia's hope.

"Thanks, but I don't need a knife to protect myself," Mia said, feeling her way into the room with one hand on the wall, the other lightly brushing against Cassia to make sure she was still there.

The smell of mildew was almost overwhelming, burrowing deep into their lungs and bringing them to the verge of coughing every time they inhaled. This complex must have suffered badly from the flooding a few months back, and the summer heat and wet carpet would have combined to create the perfect environment for mold. Furniture and possessions, haphazardly thrown together, stacked against the walls, relayed a sense that at one time, someone had left this room with hopes of coming back for their belongings.

Now a boggart lived there. The nasty little thing had moved in and would not be happy about their intrusion. Cassia held an arm in front of Mia, stopping her progress just at the corner of the wall Mia was holding ended and where the main part of the bedroom likely began.

"Do you hear it?" Cassia asked.

Mia heard a low grumbling sound, like an angry animal mumbling to itself.

Taking a huge risk, Cassia flung herself into the room, crashing through stacks of stuff to where she hoped the window would be. When she felt the drape under her hand, she gave it a hard yank, but only part of it fell. It was enough to let in some sunlight, though, and give the room a sickly cast.

Just a few feet away, she saw it.

Three feet high, the creature stood with its arms hanging at its sides. The light from outside just barely illuminated its outline, but even in the darkness, she could see the ugly human-like form it had taken. Hair sprouted in spirals from the sides of its head, leaving the top bald like a clown. It wore what appeared to be overalls, stained and dirty, and its eyes glowed a deep orange. It stared past Mia to Cassia. Its mouth was a black hole which seemed to wriggle and writhe as if it were made of thousands of ants.

"He is not happy," Cassia muttered. "I've never seen that particular look on one. I'm not sure if I should be encouraged by the gross makeover or not."

Suddenly, the thing sniffed deeply three times, its head following the scent like a blind dog looking for a treat. Then it halted, and its eyes bored a hole into Mia. Even though the mouth shifted and moved, it appeared to curl into a smile. It had smelled her, and its eyes widened, impossibly large, taking up most of its face. Still, it made no sound other than the breathy grumbling.

Mia expected to be scared at this moment, standing in the dark, staring at a malevolent boggart with orange eyes, but instead, she straightened up. Her body filled with adrenaline, and her mind went blank of any thoughts other than action. She had two choices: run or fight. She had chosen.

"I got this," she heard herself say as if her voice came from far away. Cassia raised her hand in protest, but it was too late. Mia was already moving toward the boggart.

It screamed.

Not the scream of a fearful beast, but the scream of one who is unbelievably angry. Mia and Cassia had invaded its space and had dared to make eye contact with it. Now it wanted blood, and Mia knew it was something she should do herself. A part of her that she didn't even know existed screamed at her to take down this beast and prove her worth to the bounty hunter.

The boggart launched itself at her, its mouth widening to become an endless black hole of violence. Without a second thought, Mia sidestepped just as the boggart reached her, and she punched it in the jaw. It crumpled to the ground at her feet and she punted it almost across the room. The creature crashed through a soggy table and into a bookshelf that fell apart, sending cracked moldy books across the floor and temporarily burying it.

Mia dove after it, and Cassia stepped back. She had intended to join in the fight, but frankly, it seemed like Mia had it handled. She winced as the girl performed a roundhouse kick that sent the boggart across the room where it landed. The small man-like creature stood and shook its head—probably to get rid of the dizziness. The grumbling grew louder, and it charged again, its stocky legs—like those of a toddler who did weighted squats—churned and allowed it to move unnaturally fast.

The boggart swiped at Mia, who dodged it before it flung itself at her waist. She ducked and it sailed over her into a glass table, shattering it and sending shards all over the room. The creature got to its feet, unaffected by the little nicks and cuts all over its body. Then it dove again, but this time Mia caught it mid-air with a kick directly to the face. Its head snapped back while its body continued moving forward, then it landed with a heavy thud.

When the boggart didn't move again for a few seconds, Mia turned to Cassia. "So, what now?" she asked, a smile on her face as if she had just done a particularly demanding gardening job and was ready for the next chore.

"Now," Cassia said, unraveling a rope from one of the many pockets of goodies on her belt, "We tie it up. Here," she said, tossing Mia some of the length. "You get the legs. I'll get the arms. Then, we can carry it...him out of here." She studied the creature and noted the Adam's apple in the boggart's throat and said, "Yup, it's a him."

"On it," Mia said, grabbing the rope. She was surprised at herself.

Cassia stared at the boggart. They'd moved him into the living room away from the destruction, but that was as far as her plan went. She'd been chasing after him for so long, and now he was suddenly at her mercy. At least, at Mia's mercy.

Cassia was happy to go along with it. She was impressed by the mysterious young woman's ability to take down the creature, but now that she had him, she wasn't sure what she should do next. This little guy could pad her finances even more, and he was technically her assignment. Bringing him in would open her up for another bounty, or allow her to focus more on Mia and keeping her safe.

"What's wrong?" Mia asked. "Was I too hard on him?"

Mia moved toward the boggart as though she was going to comfort the smelly little being, but Cassia shook her head, rushing to stop her. "No. That was fine. You were amazing, actually. I was just thinking about what to do with him. I can't take you with me to turn him in. But I also don't want to leave you here alone."

Cassia looked down at the boggart again as it grunted and shifted. Leaving Mia alone was a terrible idea. No telling what else could be lurking around here. But she didn't have many options when it came to handing the boggart in. She released a long breath, debating with herself about what she should do.

CHAPTER TWELVE

Montana

The Beyond Meat meatloaf Luna's mother made was just as delicious as they all expected it to be. Meatloaf and mashed potatoes may have been a heavy meal for a summer evening, but they didn't care. All four of the young fae were famished after working so hard, and a filling, comforting meal was exactly what they needed.

As soon as the plates hit the table in front of them, they dove into their very large portions. The diner might not be like other restaurants in the area because of the menu, but one thing it shared with other Montana eating spots was the plates were always piled high, and customers went home satisfied. If the meatloaf and mashed potatoes weren't going to be enough for the teens, the large basket of homemade yeast rolls and butter sprinkled with coarse salt would top them off.

And if in the extreme circumstance that they ate it all and still needed something to push them over the edge, Nicoletta was always good for a slab of home-baked cake or one of her famous pies. Luna was secretly dreaming of a couple of slices of cherry pineapple pie even as she filled herself with mashed potatoes and mushroom gravy.

"If there's one good thing I can say about being stuck in this place all summer, it's that at least I get to regularly gorge myself on your mother's food," Carson said. His fork made it into his mouth before it closed after the last words.

Luna smiled. She was proud of her mother and enjoyed it when the others at the academy acknowledged her. Only a few students were there on scholarship, and the vast majority were extremely prosperous, if not wealthy. Many of them saw a separation between her and the other students. While they received their monthly stipends and were able to look forward to luxurious vacations and other indulgences, she and her mother lived a far simpler life.

Sometimes Nicoletta slipped Luna spending money and also made sure she received the money her father sent, but it wasn't nearly as much as what the others were given. Luna wasn't ashamed. The life they lived now was a major step up from the challenging, often rough neighborhood where they had lived before she'd entered the academy.

Vivi reached her fork across the table and quickly filled it with a scoop of Zander's mashed potatoes, raising her eyebrows and laughing around the bite when he protested. The momentary lapse in tension and anger between the two Courts brought the realization to Luna's mind. She picked up her third yeast roll and coated it heavily with butter. As she sank her teeth into the rich, fluffy bread, she was thankful for the millionth time for her athletic build and fast metabolism.

"You know what I just realized? The summer is already half over, and we have barely done anything together as a team," she said.

"What do you call all those hours we just spent trying to master being in control of the wind?" Vivi asked. "And the ridiculous purple pansy circles from last week?"

"Work," said Luna. "That's all just us working together because we have to in order to improve our skills. It's not really about us getting to know each other better or making any real connection. Principal Elmhurst wants us to gel and become a team, rather than four individuals. That's not going to happen if all we ever do together is practice our skills and occasionally sit down for a meal."

"Luna's right," Zander said. "If we're ever going to really come together and make a cohesive team, we have to actually spend time together. Doing something away from campus and finding out about one another in an unstructured environment would be good for us."

"Wow. You Seelie fae really do enjoy all the warm and fuzzy moments, don't you?" Vivi said.

Luna rolled her eyes. "Are you ever going to let up? You know, you're not the only one whose life was disrupted by Elmhurst deciding the four of us are her best chance at bringing glory to the academy. Did it ever occur to you that you are just as much of an interference in our lives as we are in yours? The least you could do is put a little bit of effort into not having all these walls up. I'm not asking you to have a slumber party with me or paint each other's nails while we dream about our futures. I'm just asking you to tolerate me for a little while and see if you can actually learn something about me, and about Zander, too. And, while I know this is a revolutionary concept, maybe you could let us find out a little something about you too."

Vivi looked a little taken aback by Luna's intensity, but a smile flickered briefly on her lips. "I mean, we are already kind of stuck in a perpetual slumber party."

Luna offered a hint of a smile in return. "And if I whip out the sparkly nail polish and ask you to create a dream journal with me, you are more than welcome to tell me I've gone way too far."

"Deal," the dark-haired fae said.

"Awesome," Carson said. "Look at all this progress. So, what are we going to do?"

"Let's do something fun. How about mini golf? Or is there anything playing at the movies any of you would like to see?" Luna suggested.

"There's really not that much to do around Phillipsburg," Carson said. "I've done the mini-golf so many times I could probably be blindfolded and still get a hole-in-one at every hole."

"And there's nothing good at the theater. They only show a couple of movies at a time, and I'm not interested in either one of them," Zander said.

"I wish we could go somewhere else. Somewhere interesting where none of us have been before," Luna said. "I'm so tired of being around Philipsburg, Montana. There has to be something more out there we could do."

"Well, we could, if we had a portal," Carson said.

"None of us have the power to open a portal," Zander replied.

"No halflings do," Luna said.

"Why don't we try combining our power to open one?" Vivi asked.

The rest of the group quieted and stared at her. The waitress came by and cleared away their dinner plates. They waited while another server came up with huge slices of cherry pineapple pie, a massive bowl of almond ice cream to put on top, and spoons.

Three sets of eyes stared back at Vivi as though she were crazy, but she didn't back down. She just let them keep on staring as she used her spoon to scoop up some of the ice cream and drop it on top of her pie.

Finally, Carson spoke. "You think we could do that?" he asked.

"I've never heard of a halfling being able to open a portal," Zander said.

"Neither have I," Luna said.

"It takes too much power. It's just not possible," Carson added.

"That's the thing. I'm not suggesting that just one of us go wandering out into the field and create a portal to send us on an adventure. One halfling can't do that. But the four most powerful halflings this academy has ever seen might be able to do it."

Zander thought about the proposition for a few seconds. It sounded ridiculous. But the prospect of combining their skills into a power far exceeding what they possessed individually and using that to create a portal was intriguing. There was no guarantee it would work, but now that the idea was in his head, he didn't want to just let it go.

"We should try it," he said.

The other three turned their attention to him now.

"Really?" Vivi asked.

He nodded and attacked his plate of pie. The crust and filling were still warm, making the vanilla almond milk ice cream melt into a sweet pool around it.

"It's not like we have anything better to do. If we manage to make one, it will be ridiculously amazing, and we'll be able to go wherever we want. And if we don't, at least it's something we did that isn't what Elmhurst would be expecting," he said.

The others laughed and agreed. They finished their dessert and went to thank Luna's mother. She happily offered hugs to them all, and they complied. Luna noticed their casual response and how they pretended to be put-off by the hug, but all three willingly curled into her affectionate arms and even rested their heads on her shoulder for a moment, savoring the attention. Did any of them ever receive the affection and acknowledgment they wanted from their own parents?

When they left the diner, they returned to what they had begun to think of as *their* field. It offered them the ideal combination of an isolated, yet easily accessible location with adequate space and separation from the rest of campus. There were still a few signs of the aftermath of their wind experiments in the form of branches, trees, and leaves scattered across the grass.

"Do you think we should go ahead and put up a protective shield this time?" Carson asked.

They had purposely not put up the shield when working with the wind out of worry it would block too much of the air currents from coming in. It had put them at risk of being caught by any humans who happened by, and they'd seen at least one elderly man wander past at the edge of the field when Luna had been tumbling around in mid-air.

He'd looked right at the group but hadn't said anything, nor did he react in any way. Either he couldn't see far enough to know what was happening, or he'd just figured he had lost his marbles years ago, and it was really just showing up now.

But this was different. Manipulating the wind was one thing. Playing with the possibility of portals was another thing entirely. A portal could be an exceptional tool, providing immediate transportation from one place to another. It could allow them to travel easily and access places they'd never be able to go otherwise. But it could also be extremely dangerous. If not made correctly, a portal could send them somewhere they didn't want to go and not allow for a way back. They might even enter the portal and never emerge.

They were willing to take on the risk, but they weren't going to do it out in the open. The last thing they needed was to have to explain to Principal Elmhurst that a wayward human had been drawn in by the fun of watching them do magic and had ended up tumbling through a portal never to be seen again. That would not bode well for the future of their education or their chances of securing one of the coveted spots at the embassy. Generally speaking, fae who allowed humans to be harmed or lost through magic weren't looked upon kindly. That type of exposure threatened their entire world.

"Go ahead," Zander said. "Make it big. Encompass the whole field if you can. I think we should start small and try to create a portal that brings us just from one end of the field to the other. If we can get that down, we'll move on to a longer trip."

As soon as Carson had the protective shield in place, they gathered at one end of the field. They readied themselves for the challenge, all concentrating hard on the creation of the portal. They focused intensely for as long as they could keep it up, but nothing happened.

"Maybe we're thinking about different places," Luna suggested. "I've heard portals have to be created with a very specific place in mind. If the person creating it isn't focused hard enough on that specific place, the magic can't do what they want it to do."

"Are you saying the magic gets confused?" Vivi said. "Or lost?"

"All right. Everyone look across the field. Do you see that big stick with the two pieces coming off it in the shape of a Y? If you look directly through that Y, you'll see a patch of grass that looks a little different than the rest of the grass. It's thicker or something. Focus on that. Concentrate on that being the spot where we want our portal to go," Zander told them.

They regrouped and tried again. A few minutes later, it still hadn't happened.

"See, I never heard that the person had to concentrate so hard on the exact spot they wanted to go to," Carson said. "It doesn't make sense. What if they're creating a portal that goes somewhere they've never been before? They can't exactly focus completely on that place if they don't really know where they're going."

"Then what do you know about portals?" Luna asked, slightly frustrated to have her theory questioned.

"It's not necessarily about pinpointing the exact place you want to end up when you go through the portal," Carson explained. "It's about your intention and your needs."

"Well, I *intend* for this to work so we can be the first halflings to make a portal," Vivi said.

"And I *need* to have something impressive to add to my resume," Zander said.

Carson nodded, his hands planted on his hips. "Very funny. Both of you. I'm serious, though. I knew someone who knew someone—"

"Who knew someone who knew someone who had a cousin whose neighbor's sister's cat—" Vivi said.

"They created a portal," Carson said, pushing right past her sarcasm. "And it worked. But they said it took having very clear intentions and knowing why they needed the portal for it to happen."

"It wouldn't hurt to try," Luna said. "I guess our intentions are to use our powers together to create a portal we can use to get away from the academy every now and then."

"And we need it because we don't want to be trapped here all the time," Vivi added.

"And because it would help us to mesh better and become a stronger team," Zander offered.

"All right. Let's try it," Carson said.

They positioned themselves at the end of the protective dome again and focused their powers. Combining their energy and concentration, they envisioned the portal forming at their feet and connecting them to the other side of the field. As the intensity of their shared magic grew stronger, they reached out and held each other's hands. The physical connection linked their abilities even more and they felt the power strengthening.

Suddenly a loud popping sounded, and purple smoke billowed up from the ground. It filled the dome of the protective shield and obliterated their vision for several seconds. Luna coughed and swiped at the smoke, trying to clear as much of it as she could.

"Well, that didn't go as planned," she said.

"Yeah. Which one of you *intended* for the field to explode in purple smoke?" Vivi asked. "Because I definitely didn't *need* that to happen."

"It's taking revenge for all the purple flowers we made," Carson said. "It just couldn't take it anymore."

"Let's get this smoke out and try again," Vivi said.

They tried to wave away the smoke, but it didn't work. A spell to clear it helped some, but eventually they had to remove the protective dome for a few seconds to let the smoke dissipate before putting the shield back up. If anyone happened by at that moment, they would see a puff of purple smoke suddenly appear, but no source for it. Fortunately, the smoke seemed to disappear quickly once beyond the protective shield. It could easily be explained away as being from a campfire or stupid kids playing with fireworks, as such things so frequently were.

"Look," Carson said, pointing at the ground at his feet.

Luna came to stand beside him and studied the grass, which dipped down several inches in a perfect circle, as though a large stamp had crushed it. "We dented the ground," she said.

"Maybe it's the beginning of a portal," Carson said. "Like we almost got it, but it didn't quite get all the way through."

Zander stood to the other side of Carson and tilted his head, looking down at the impression. "Nope. I think we just dented the ground."

"Then let's crank up the shield and try it again," Vivi said.

She didn't have the same frustration and aggravation this time as she had when they'd practiced the Faerie circle or the wind control. The possibility of being able to combine with the others to create the first halfling-produced portal fueled her. She was bound and determined to make this happen. This wasn't just about being able to collaborate with the others and please Principal Elmhurst. Vivi also wanted that achievement for herself. If she was going to have to be part of this foursome, she was going to make fae history.

"Let's go," Zander said.

The handsome Seelie boy was just as driven to succeed in this, compelled to create something incredible that would make him stand out. He was convinced that if the four of them were able to create a portal together, it would solidify his chances of securing a pass to Faerie. But it wasn't just the job and prestige he was after.

If Zander was able to receive that pass and enter the fae realm, he could seek out the fae mother who had left him on his father's doorstep so many years ago. He would finally have the chance to confront her about abandoning him at birth and ask her how she'd been able to do it so easily. He'd never understood how a mother could leave her newborn baby and only think of him again when it was time for him to go to school.

The effect of their combined magic happened much more quickly this time. But it didn't create a portal. Vivi let out a scream as a blast of magic sent her flying across the field to what they'd intended to be the endpoint of the portal. She was quickly followed by the other three, then all four were sent back. They tumbled to the ground and lay there, groaning.

"Crickets!" Carson shouted.

"Well, at least this time, we actually went somewhere," Zander said. "It wasn't exactly through a portal, but it was something."

"It was something, all right," Luna said.

"Come on. Let's try again," Zander said, pulling himself up off the ground.

They focused their minds, concentrating as hard as they could on combining their magic to create the portal. Energy buzzed in the air. Something was changing. None of the four acknowledged it. They didn't want to get too excited, didn't want to be too hopeful that something was finally going to work. Instead, they moved closer to each other and held hands more tightly. A rush of magic and energy flowed through their connected palms. It was happening. The world was responding to their magic, changing according to their will.

Above them, the sky rumbled. They looked at each other, confused and curious, and in the next instant, rain began to pour from the dome around them.

That was not their will.

Gasping, they let go of their hands and stared in shock at the protective shield. Beyond it, the sky was still, and not a single drop of rain fell. Inside, the four fae looked like drowned rats and were already standing in mud. Vivi's hair hung in her eyes, and her shoulders sagged under her wet clothes. She glared at the other three and lifted a finger.

"One. More. Time."

CHAPTER THIRTEEN

Shanghai, China

"What do you mean, *take him in?*" Mia asked.

"You know that I'm a bounty hunter," Cassia said. "Well, this creature isn't just some smelly little interloper who's angry at us for storming his abode. Actually, that's exactly what he is, but that's not the point. This boggart is why I came to China in the first place. I've been tracking him for quite a while."

"Why?" Mia asked.

"How much do you know about boggarts?" the fae bounty hunter asked.

"Including that they smell horrible and are really nasty when they fight?"

"Yes," Cassia replied.

"Then I know they smell horrible and are really nasty when they fight," Mia said.

Cassia laughed. "I guess that's a start. These creatures are spirits of a sort. They inhabit homes and can be extremely mischievous. A lot of times they aren't harmful, just more annoying than anything. But sometimes they can become dangerous. When they live in a home and are relatively peaceful, their smell isn't as bad. It has almost an earthy quality to it. Not necessarily something anyone would want to convert into a scented candle and advertise as the next big trend in home fragrance, but not overtly offensive."

"Then what happened to this one to make it smell so horrible? It's like somebody dipped him into the sewer and then rolled him around in the trash like they were breading fried chicken."

"That is a truly awful visual," Cassia said. "But not an entirely inaccurate analysis. Boggarts develop their distinctly horrible smell if they're given a name. Giving one of these creatures a name also causes it to get more intense and more dangerous. Before, they might play practical jokes and be a nuisance to the family who lives in the house. But after being given a name, these spirits become evil. They can hurt people and cause tremendous difficulties for anyone who stands in their way.

"Of course, it's a natural instinct to name things. People do it all the time. They themselves have a name. They name their children, their pets. Some people even name their house plants. That's the challenge with boggarts. When someone realizes there's something in their home, it's the normal inclination to want to familiarize yourself with it. Giving it a name helps to make it more personal and create a relationship. This is especially true for the families who have had the same boggart in their home for years. It's particularly challenging when there are children in the house."

"Children name everything," Mia said.

"Yes," Cassia said. "It's just something they do. Unfortunately, that's what happened with this boggart. There was a young boy living in the home he had decided to inhabit. He was mischievous and almost playful. The boy decided the boggart might be his friend and would be happy to have a name like everyone else. Of course, that made all Hades break loose. He's had a bounty out ever since. And that's what I've been chasing."

"Is this the same one from the market the night we first saw each other?" Mia asked. It was really sinking in at that moment that she had witnessed something extraordinary at the night market. That night she thought it was just the extremely strong tea the elderly woman had given her. Now she realized she had the innate power to see beyond the plane humans could perceive.

Those crowds milling through the streets and stuffing the intersections at the night market had no idea of the dangerous creature that lurked among them. They couldn't see what she saw, or what the bounty hunter saw. The two of them were the only ones to witness the boggart slithering along the sides of the buildings like a giant snake.

"Yes," Cassia said.

"So, what happens now? Or what's supposed to happen?"

"Now that I have him, I'm supposed to bring him into the Faerie prison and turn him over to the head jailer."

"What will happen to him then?" Mia asked.

Cassia shrugged. "I really don't know for sure. All I'm there for is to turn him over to the authorities so I can collect on the bounty. What happens to him after that is his problem and something he earned."

"But you can't bring me with you to drop him off?" Mia asked.

Cassia shook her head adamantly. "No. That wouldn't be possible. You see, Forasaon isn't an ordinary prison. It's in Faerie. Access to Faerie is restricted. Only halflings with very specific positions are ever allowed in. I can't just bring you. But I also can't leave you alone here."

"Why not?"

"Because it could be dangerous. We managed to take down this boggart, but there are seven other apartments. As we just proved, they might seem empty, but may not be empty at all. We have no way of knowing what could be wandering around in them. I can't leave you alone and potentially vulnerable to really dangerous creatures."

"But you deserve to bring this guy in and collect your bounty. You've been working so hard to track him, and now you finally have him," Mia pointed out.

"I think technically you're the one who actually took him down," Cassia said.

Mia let out a short laugh. "Maybe, but I'm sure if I hadn't jumped in, you could have managed him just fine on your own."

Cassia chuckled. "Probably. But I am really impressed by your fighting skills. You can really hold your own out there."

"Well, up until very recently, holding my own out there meant not getting myself destroyed on the mat during my Wushu competitions."

"The skills are in your blood," the bounty hunter replied. "It's part of your fae heritage. Though you are much stronger and more skilled than I ever could have imagined."

"Thank you. I'm also a big girl. I promise you can leave me here alone and bring the boggart in. Nothing is going to happen to me. I highly doubt this dude had any neighbors. The stench alone is enough to drive them out. You go ahead. Do your thing." Mia waved Cassia off. "I'll just hang around here and wait for you to get back."

"Are you sure?" Cassia asked. "I can stay with you. We can just keep him tied up for a little while longer until you feel more comfortable."

"Honestly, I don't think anything's going to make me a whole lot more comfortable. And I'm certainly not going to be more comfortable hanging around in an abandoned apartment with a tied-up creature that tried very hard to wipe me off the face of the planet," Mia said.

Cassia thought about it. As much as she didn't want to leave Mia alone in the apartment, she really hated the idea of the boggart escaping and running off again, leaving her unable to collect her bounty. It was not one of her career aspirations to dedicate the rest of her life to finding this one creature. She could just quickly take him to Forasaon, make sure the credits were applied to her account, and return.

"It won't take long," she told the halfling. "Just stay here. I'll be back as fast as I can."

"I'll be fine," Mia reassured her.

The moment Cassia crossed through the portal, Mia began pacing, wondering what in the heck she had gotten herself into. She was of fae descent? How was that even possible? Her dad was human, no doubt about that. But her mother....

Hauling an unconscious boggart into the prison wasn't exactly Cassia's idea of a fun activity. But at least it wasn't nearly as hard as some of the other bounties she'd dragged through the portal over the years. He was small compared to a lot of the other creatures she brought in, which helped with navigating herself and his hairy little body into the reception area of the prison.

Cassia dropped him at her feet, flattened her hands on the desk, and stared at Fan. He was wrapped up in a conversation with one of his goons and didn't look her way until the ogre cleared his throat and not-so-subtly nodded in her direction. Fan turned and his eyes widened. A smile curled his lips, and if lips could walk, that would be a swagger.

"Cassia. You just can't get enough of me, can you?" he asked.

"I reached that point quite a while ago, Fan. But, alas, it's part of my job," she replied.

The ogres behind Fan chortled and turned their backs to muffle the sound. Cassia was sure their boss wouldn't be too happy knowing they were laughing at him.

But Fan didn't pay any attention to them. He was just staring at her, his mind drifting to the feeling that built up in his stomach every time he laid eyes on the beautiful fae. "Why do you have to be like that?" he asked. "I'm just trying to be friendly."

"Well, here's the thing. I'm in a little bit of a hurry, and I'd like to be on my way," Cassia replied.

He narrowed his eyes as he studied her, trying to figure her out—which he did almost every time they interacted. "Then why are you here?"

Cassia blinked a few times. It was like Fan had forgotten where he was and what his job was. "You're the head jailer of Forasaon, Fan," she pointed out. "And I'm a bounty hunter. I think the reason I've come is pretty self-explanatory."

"Don't call me Fan," he said. "You know I hate that."

She did. But she never gave it much thought when she was at the prison trying to get her job done. Everybody called him Fan. That probably made it one of those 'two wrongs don't make a right' and 'if everybody else jumped off a cliff, would you go along with them?' situations, but it was what it was.

"I'm sorry. You're the head jailer of Forasaon, *Faylynne*. And I'm a bounty hunter. I'm here to turn in my assignment and collect my bounty," she said.

"Your assignment?" he asked.

Cassia pointed at her feet. Fan walked around and looked down at the boggart. He was still mostly unconscious, but occasionally muttered and thrashed around. The ties were too tight for him to escape, and every time he struggled, he eventually gave up and sagged against the floor again.

"You finally snagged the boggart you've been after, I see," Fan said.

"Yeah. This thing dragged me to China and all over Shanghai, causing trouble."

"How did you finally manage to get it?"

"Invaded his apartment," she said. "Accidentally, actually."

"Ah," Fan said with a short laugh. "Only you would manage something like that."

Cassia wasn't sure what that was supposed to mean. It sounded like the jailer thought he was being funny, but it came across awkwardly, as though he was questioning her skills.

"You mean only the best bounty hunter of our time could manage to bring in a boggart? Is that meant as an insult?"

He muttered for a few seconds, attempting to retract the comment, but never quite finding the right words. "I mean..." he started again, but Cassia shook her head.

She was done talking. She had to get back through the portal to China and the apartment. Mia shouldn't be left alone for this long.

"This has been lots of fun, but I really do need to be on my way," she said. "If you'll go ahead and send my credits for the bounty to my account, I would appreciate it."

"Sure," Fan said hesitantly. "Let me just get this guy into a cell and I'll be right back to handle everything."

"Put him in a cell? He's practically unconscious. What is he possibly going to do in the forty-five seconds it's going to take you to give me my money?" she asked.

"Just hold on. It's protocol. We need to secure the inmate before any other business can proceed," he said.

Cassia was fairly certain he was making that up. There were plenty of times when she'd brought assignments into the prison in a similar condition to the boggart's and she'd seen no rush to get them stashed away.

Fan and his goons were just as likely to leave them on the floor until they had handled their business because it was just easier that way. Now suddenly, Fan wanted to keep everything organized to the point of carrying away a totally incapacitated boggart.

He scooped the boggart up with one arm and carried it toward the cells. The ogres leaned toward each other, whispering and laughing. Cassia rolled her eyes when she caught them digging their elbows into each other's ribs and she glared at them.

"I'm glad you're finding this so hilarious, but I really do need to get going. What is with your boss today?" she asked.

"Same thing as always," one of them said.

"Which is?"

The ogres laughed again. Cassia felt like she was the butt of an inside joke, and she hated it. Before she could ask them again, Fan came back into the room. He smiled at her.

"So, how have things been? I bet you're happy to have that boggart off your back, huh?"

Cassia narrowed her eyes at the jailer. "Things have been busy. I really am in a hurry, though. I have to get back. If you could settle my account, I'll be on my way."

"Speaking of your account, the claim for the redcap you brought in the other day was paid to your account. You are officially a very rich female." He put his hands on his hips and smiled at her. "What are you going to do with all that money? Any big plans?"

"Right now, my big plan is to get my money and get back to what I was doing before I got the boggart," she said.

"You're always in so much of a hurry when you come here," Fan said.

If Cassia didn't know any better—or at least she hoped she knew better—she would have thought the jailer was pouting.

"This isn't a social call, Fan." She held her hands up. "Excuse me, Faylynne. I'm here to do my job. I'm a bounty hunter. This is what I do. People tell me who the bad guys are. I go find them. When I do, I bring them in here to you so you can do whatever it is you do with them. You pay me for it. Then I go back and do it all again. We've been through this a lot of times over the years," she said.

She turned and moved toward the portal, but Fan approached her.

"What else do you do?" he asked. "I mean, other than finding the bad guys and bringing them in here to me. There have to be other things you do in your downtime."

Cassia let out a long sigh. "I don't have downtime, Fan. This is my life. It's all I was ever meant to do. It's all I do. If I'm not tracking a bounty, I'm sleeping. Sometimes eating. There's not a whole lot of kicking-back-to-relax time in my world."

Cassia started to leave again, but Fan took another step toward her. He didn't want her to go. Not yet. These times when she brought in her bounty assignments were the only times he got to see her, and it wasn't nearly enough for him. He wanted to be closer to her, but he didn't know how.

"But there is," he said. "I mean, there could be. With the money you just earned from the redcap, you don't have to worry about finding any more bounties for a long time. You could just take some time to do other things."

Cassia shook her head. "There's not really anything else I want to do."

That wasn't entirely true. Her focus was on Mia now, but she still didn't know what she was supposed to do with the girl. All Cassia knew was that she needed to get back to the apartment as fast as possible. She'd already taken too much time squaring off with the head jailer. She approached the portal for the third time, and for the third time, Fan stopped her.

"What about your claim for the boggart?" he asked. "Don't you want to wait until it's credited? It's a much smaller one than the redcap, so it won't take as long."

Cassia shook her head. "I really don't have time. Just credit it to my account."

She made her way to the portal, but when she attempted to activate it, nothing happened. She tried again, and still, it wouldn't allow her through. Fan stared back at her when she turned to him. He was behind this. The head jailer was the only one who could turn off access to the portal to prevent anyone from leaving. She couldn't go anywhere.

CHAPTER FOURTEEN

Shanghai, China

Mia stood around in the apartment for a few moments after Cassia left, trying to decide what to do. She was still attempting to wrap her head around it all. Her reality had shifted completely, going from what she thought was a normal life to something decidedly not normal.

At least, not normal to *her*. To Cassia and the creatures chasing them, this was just life. And apparently, it was for her now as well. That was a lot to try to take in, and Mia decided she needed to sit for a few minutes.

The combination of the fight against the boggart and the weighty pressure of everything she'd learned over the last few days had exhausted her, and she felt like all the energy inside her had drained out. She had no way of knowing what was coming next, and she needed to take a break before it all came down on her again.

But maybe it wouldn't. Maybe capturing the boggart was all they'd have to deal with before Cassia took her home. The bounty hunter would come back, having turned the creature in, and they could move on without any more difficulty. Mia knew the chances of that were small, but she let it buoy her spirits as she searched around the apartment for somewhere to relax.

It wasn't the most welcoming environment now that the fight with the boggart had left it in tatters. It hadn't really been the most welcoming environment before. But now the stacks of boxes and discarded items were thrown around, some broken, and the contents of others spilled out across the floor.

She thought she'd noticed some scurrying movements in what had tumbled out of one box, but she didn't want to put too much thought into it. She could handle a spider or even an ambitious mouse who decided to call the apartment home. But now was not the time for her to discover a species of micro-creatures with the same attitude problem as the boggart.

Even if something tiny and strange was lurking around in the apartment with her, Mia could probably handle it. What she'd learned about herself in the last few days was confusing and disorienting, but what really stood out was the empowerment. She had discovered one thing for sure. Monsters were real and she could see them.

That meant she wasn't losing her mind or hallucinating when she'd thought she'd seen the creature at the night market, or in the restaurant at breakfast. She hadn't imagined things when she'd seen the tiny monsters in the tree that caught her hair and annoyed Becky into almost getting hit by a moped. Those monsters were really there, and not only could she see them, but she could fight them. And win.

This gave Mia confidence in herself and in her abilities. She could trust herself to know what was going on around her and to defend herself when she needed to.

Her only real concern now...was her father. Becky and Master Chen should be good for a little while, but her father's mind hadn't been messed with. Mia wasn't sure if that was a good thing or a bad thing. She'd have to remember to ask Cassia what they were going to do about informing him.

Although, if the boggart was at the center of the creatures

attacking her, then maybe she could go home as planned and wouldn't have to keep hiding out in disgusting, moldy apartments.

As she picked her way through the apartment, trying to find somewhere at least halfway clean where she could make a little nest to relax, she thought she heard something. Wondering if it might just be things falling over in response to her moving around, she paused. Staying as still as she could, Mia listened to the building around her. She heard it again, this time louder. It wasn't in the apartment with her, but out somewhere in the rest of the building.

Curious, she crept through the debris and out into the hallway between the two apartments. The noise came from the hallway toward the front of the complex. Although she knew the dangers, Mia decided to have a look anyway. After fighting the boggart earlier today, and handing it a beating at that, she felt like she might be ready for harder challenges.

As she crept down the hallway, she hyped herself up, thinking of the training she received and the fight from earlier in the day. Even Cassia seemed impressed by her ability. Maybe this 'fighting bad guys' stuff wasn't so hard after all. She had told Cassia she could handle herself, and she'd proved it once already. If this was something that needed her to use her training, she could prove it again, too.

Light pooled from the edge of the entryway, and Mia slowed down. It was hard to see, but she could tell that someone was there—or possibly more than one person. Hiding in the late afternoon shadows as best she could, gave her the element of surprise as well as the ability to turn back if she thought the fight would be too much for her.

A faint murmuring sound, like two people having a hushed conversation, floated back to her, and she strained to hear it. She could only catch snippets of sound and not a language she knew. Maybe it was just two foreign people, hanging out at an abandoned apartment complex. Where a boggart was. She was close now, close enough to see shapes fairly clearly.

Two men stood there in the entry to the complex. At least it looked like two men. Only she wasn't sure they were human at all.

One of them—the shorter one—was nearly translucent in the light and had a wide hunched troll-like frame. He nearly shimmered when he moved around, and the light played off of him. It was transfixing in its own way, but a smell wafted from him that reminded her of the boggart, although admittedly, it wasn't as bad. But just barely.

It was more like the smell of rotting meat, or a dead animal on the side of a back road in the middle of summer. It was terrible for sure, but terrible was relative when talking about the boggart whose stench had made her want to rip her own nose off.

The translucent creature seemed to walk on air. It reminded Mia of how she moved in her dreams sometimes, where she had the sense of being underwater, even when she wasn't. Whatever the creature was, it was sniffing the air, as if it sensed something.

The taller one, a thin man with tufts of platinum blond—practically silver—hair sticking out from under his red baseball cap, was striking in appearance. He had an attractive jaw and deep blue eyes and full lips. She imagined he must be a leader of some kind. People who looked like him weren't often yes-men or assistants. Tall, good looking men with blond hair like that often ended up running whatever business they were in, if only because people naturally gravitated to them.

He was beautiful, until suddenly he wasn't. For a split second, it was as if he had been replaced by a short, fuzzy brown creature. The red baseball cap was still there, but the eyes, so sharp and almond-shaped, had turned large, round, and wild. His nose had grown and was pointed, and his lips had thinned enough to bare his sharp jagged teeth. Then the image of him returned to normal, as if it was a blip in an old movie where someone had replaced a frame. When she was back to seeing the attractive man, she found it hard to remember that the other image had ever been there at all.

But it was. She'd seen it. And she knew what that meant. These two weren't just troublemakers hanging out at an abandoned apartment complex, they were the real deal. The pair might be a little more difficult to fight than a boggart, especially considering there were two of them and one of her. Perhaps she should just go back to the apartment and wait for Cassia to return.

Mia tried to take a step backward, but the men turned with their noses in the air as if sniffing her out. Now their eyes were aimed in her direction, and she turned to run. Her feet took her quickly to the only place she could think of—the apartment where she had fought the boggart.

She flung the door open and slammed it shut. After flipping the lock, she moved back into the shadowed room. Figuring it would be easier to fight in a room she had some knowledge of rather than a hallway, she shifted to the same spot where the boggart had stood. They would come down the hallway, break open the door, rush into the living room and, then...what exactly?

She'd beat the crap out of them, that's what.

Her Wushu training prepared her for various styles of martial arts, but it did nothing to equip her to fight a being who didn't appear the same when you looked at him twice in rapid succession and really missed out on the whole troll ghost thing. Still, she was confident in her abilities at hand-to-hand, and if she could get them one-on-one, she might be able to do some serious damage in short order.

The face-shifting one should be easy. Find a weak spot and hit it hard. Repeatedly. That was something she was good at, and as long as she could keep her cool, she could ramp up the violence fast enough. Being a young girl would work to her advantage. They wouldn't expect someone like her to fight the way she could, so she would at least mop the floor with the one on the right before he even realized what was going on.

Of course, the one on the left looked translucent, like someone had formed air and given it a sheen. How the heck was she supposed to fight a ghost? Would the rules regarding ghosts in the stories of her childhood apply to this thing? Maybe, just maybe if she couldn't touch it, it couldn't touch her. It was worth a shot. Either way, she was going to have to figure it out quickly because just then, the door to the apartment banged open and splinters went flying down the hall and across her vision.

Nothing could have prepared her for the creature coming around the corner. For a flash of a second, it was the tall, good-looking man, but instantly it switched, and the creature it truly was bared its teeth. Saliva dripped from its mouth and puddled on the ground.

Something brown dipped in red liquid hung on its head in place of the red baseball cap. As it scanned Mia, its wide round eyes focused only on her. They were yellow with black slits like a cat's, and they appeared to see more than just an easy target in her. The thing wanted to hurt her, to rip her to shreds.

Instinctively, she knew it would attack her with fury and use her as a trophy. She realized with horror what the creature was…a redcap. She'd read some scary fairy tales a few years back about fae and their various monsters. The thing licking its pointy teeth and staring at her like she was its next meal, looked exactly like what she'd read about.

Suddenly, she wished Cassia hadn't left her there all alone.

Redcaps were notorious for vile, evil behavior in literature, and this one seemed particularly nasty. Or maybe since it was her first experience with one, she just thought it was extra evil.

All elements of the handsome man she'd seen earlier had faded away, leaving a short hairy monster with a long beard and human skin standing in front of her. It would leap to attack soon, and she would have to respond. As a matter of fact, why wait?

She never was one to wait for an attack on the mat, so why wait here?

Without another thought, Mia slammed her fist into its pointed nose, and it howled as it flew backward.

Rather than chase after it, to try and ground and pound, Mia pivoted to the side and just narrowly avoided a book thrown by the spectral creature. It was nearly invisible, only its glowing eyes were easy to see, and it seemed to be concentrating hard on reaching for a book on the ground nearby. Mia ran to it, kicking out sideways to connect with its body, but she went right through it. Landing awkwardly, she turned around and found herself being punched, albeit somewhat weakly, in the gut.

For a moment, the two of them stared at each other, as if neither knew what to do next, then the redcap came flying into Mia's vision. Gnashing its teeth, it narrowly missed her, and she ducked and rolled away to another side of the room. Grabbing a chair, she tossed it as hard as she could, smashing it over the thing's back. Then she had to duck as the ghost creature threw a lamp at her.

Thinking quickly, she picked the lamp up and tossed it at the redcap, hitting it in the back of the head as it tried to stand. It howled and fell to its knees, shaking off the effects of the blow as best it could. Running to the redcap, Mia kicked it hard in the ribs, and it lashed out, swinging its arm at her in an effort to create some distance while inflicting damage. Its claws left a long scratch on her leg.

Mia jumped back, wincing in pain as blood trickled down her leg, pooling in her sock. It could have been much worse, but thankfully she'd avoided the full brunt of the attack. As the redcap ran at her again, its terrifying face switching between the glamour and the real monster underneath, she grabbed a chair from beside her.

The old metal seat would have been just as at home at a church banquet as a pro wrestling show, and now she swung it like a baseball bat, the seat connecting with the side of the monster's head and sending it crumpling to the ground.

Mia lifted the chair high and slammed it into the redcap a few more times, making sure to hit it as hard as possible on the legs, hoping to slow its progress. Satisfied that she had done some decent damage, she tried to run, but something caught her ankle.

Mia looked into the face of the translucent creature, who was focusing all of its energy on wrapping itself around her leg and holding her in place. She tried to kick it, but it did no good. The thing held her just long enough for the redcap to stand again, tackle her, and force her to the ground.

When the translucent creature lost its grip, Mia rolled as far away as possible. Slowly, the redcap stood up, showing little in the way of damage, and she knew this was going to be much more of a fight than she'd assumed it would be.

The redcap was strong and fast, and it was obviously trained in some fashion. But Mia's experience had taught her that no matter how well-trained a fighter is, they are never prepared for one thing. Chaos. It was time to bring a little confusion to the fight.

"Okay, now that we have met each other," she said, with a confidence in her voice that she hoped didn't sound false, "I think we should lay down some ground rules."

The redcap growled deeply in response, and the ghost creature peeked around its shoulder. The ghost held an iron and was busy winding up for a toss. Better make this quick.

"First ground rule: don't get mad when I kick your butt to kingdom come."

CHAPTER FIFTEEN

The steam iron flew over Mia's head, narrowly missing her and crashing into the window behind her. The glass shattered, sending the appliance outside and an idea into Mia's head. Between the fact that she was still inexperienced at fighting for her life and that one of them was a freakin' ghost thing, she decided her best plan of action was to try to escape.

This would require two things: a way out and some distance between them. She had no idea what lay beyond the apartment complex and the area surrounding it seemed like it had been abandoned for a while, but it had to be better than being locked in a room with two malevolent monsters.

She ducked behind a couch as an ironing board sailed over her head and she checked it off the list of items the ghost thing could grab. The creature didn't seem hindered by the shape of an object, only weight, and the iron had looked particularly difficult for it to wield. While the appliance had crashed through the window, it had flown at an arc that would have required a lot of force behind it. For the most part, if she could avoid being trapped by that thing, she could ignore it. Its primary job was distraction.

That left the redcap. His teeth were sharp and vicious, and his claws were even more terrifying. So far, Mia had avoided any major damage, but she was going to have to go hand to hand with it, and she might not be so lucky for much longer. Her training had taught her how to absorb impact and take damage, but nothing in it had prepared her for a bearded goblin-thing that seemed intent on actually devouring her. After beating her to within an inch of her life, obviously.

Mia popped up from behind the couch, grabbed the bottom of it, and flipped it, then tossed it in the direction of the two creatures. The redcap tried to bat it away, and the ghost simply let it fall through him. Oddly enough, the pair of them were never more than a few feet apart, but right now wasn't the best time to figure out if their proximity meant something. If she could just survive the fight and gain the upper hand, she could get out of there and figure out a theory for their interpersonal relationship later.

Moving closer to the living room was Mia's priority. She dove and rolled in that direction, her plan depending on the giant glass windows in the room. The redcap was on her quickly, and it tackled her to the ground. She thrust her knee into his stomach and flipped him over her head, rolling aside to avoid a vase the ghost tossed at her head. The stubby creature—having shed his glamour as a tall, attractive man—crawled toward her, and she planted a foot in its nose. This didn't seem to deter it, so she repeated the action twice more. With each kick, the redcap seemed to slow down.

Taking the opportunity, Mia bolted for the wall of the living room, then dove behind a table as the redcap tossed a chair at her. It bounced off the wall a foot from the huge window. It was now or never.

She stood, curling her fingers at it as she beckoned the thing to try again. Enraged, the redcap grabbed another chair, a heavier one this time, and flung it at her hard. She ducked and it crashed through the window, landing on the ground outside. Before she could do anything else, the creature was on her again, and they both tumbled to the side as they struggled with each other.

Sharp teeth ripped down Mia's arm, and she elbowed the redcap in the nose to get it off her. The creature scrambled to its feet as she checked her wound. The injury was superficial, but a stream of blood was trickling down her hand and dripping on the carpeted floor. Rather than making her afraid, it angered her.

Instead of taking her chance with the window, Mia charged, barreling into the redcap and knocking it back into the wall, creating a crater in the plasterboard. She punched its head repeatedly, more brawling than using the techniques she'd learned, and she mentally scolded herself for it.

Moving back just a step, she used a roundhouse kick to drive the back of its skull into the wall. The redcap moaned as it slumped to the floor, and Mia spun around and went in search of the ghost creature. It had disappeared. Now was her chance, and she knew it, so she barreled for the window. No time to worry about the landing, she just needed to jump.

As she approached the window, she caught sight of the grassy hill outside. If she built enough momentum, the fall wouldn't be too bad, and she would land about one and a half stories down. She increased her speed and tried to judge how best to dive through the broken glass —she would have to go out like a missile, as if she was diving off a board into a swimming pool.

But the potential landing for a dive like that could be ugly, so she had to make sure to tuck and roll and land as flat on her back as she could, taking the force spread out over her body rather than in one place. All this ran through her mind in the span of a second, and suddenly she was at the window. Without hesitation, she elongated herself into a projectile, cleared the window arms first, and performed a swan dive outside.

She spun in the air and landed with a dull thud on the still damp grass. Having closed her eyes after making the flip, Mia opened them again, looking up into the gray-blue sky. She marveled that she wasn't hurt. A little out of breath, maybe, but otherwise, she felt fine. Chalking it up to luck and good conditioning, she hopped to her feet. She didn't know exactly where she would go, but it had to be somewhere and quick. Shadows were moving in the apartment above, and soon enough, they would be coming after her.

Mia frantically looked for a place to hide. Somewhere not easily visible from the window and which might help to put some distance between her and the two creatures. If she ran across the open field behind the complex, it would take her to a side street, but she would be easily seen and caught.

The complex itself seemed like the best bet in which to lose them, and she could run back inside and get out of sight faster. Then she could duck between the buildings and get to the other side.

The last thing she wanted, outside of being eaten for dinner by the redcap, was to go somewhere Cassia wouldn't be able to find her. She needed to be close enough that when Cassia came back and saw the chaos caused by the fight, she would know Mia was nearby and could reach her.

Just as Mia crossed into the hallway between the apartments in the building, she heard the redcap shouting near the window. Either they'd seen her and were coming, or they had missed her and were now searching.

Either way, she needed to hide. Darting between the apartments, she made her way to a second building. The doors of the two apartments she passed were locked solid, so she kept moving until she reached the other side of the building. There she stopped, her back pressed to the mildewed stonework façade, to catch her breath.

She strained to hear—while calming her breathing so as to not be conspicuous—she thought she could just make out the voice of the redcap back at the first building. It was grumbling, as if it was angry and cursing itself, and she had a problem. It was getting closer.

Mia closed her eyes for a second to steel herself. Up ahead was a dead-end road and a store that appeared as abandoned as the apartments. If she could get inside without them noticing her, she could hide and wait for Cassia. Undoubtedly, when the bounty hunter showed up, there would be a ruckus as she took the redcap to task. Mia could come out then and help, but staying alive and safe were her top priorities now.

The store was about two hundred yards away, and in a sprint, it would still take her close to a minute to get there. If she was lucky, they wouldn't see her at all, and a door would be unlocked or a window open. If not, she would have to break in and hope they didn't notice. If she was really unlucky, the fistfight would resume. The cut on her leg and the bite on her arm were draining her far more than the fall. Something about the creature's scratch and bite seemed to affect her more.

Taking a deep breath, Mia tried to push everything else out of her mind. It wasn't a blind terror but a focused mission. Her training had given her a lot of practice in katas to be performed in high-pressure situations, and while she'd been able to use precious few of them in the fight in the apartment, if she was caught out in the open, it would be easier. Consoling herself that she had a plan for every eventuality, she took off, barreling across the large open area between the apartments and the store. Behind her, in the distance, she heard the howl of the redcap.

No!

Still, it seemed pretty far away, and unless it could outrun her, she was going to make it to the store first. Maybe she could find some weapons inside or lock the creatures out somehow. It was worth the shot. Her legs churned until the muscles in her thighs burned and her lungs felt like they were being squeezed. She reached the store at such a speed she didn't have time to fully stop, and she ended up sliding on her heels into the wall next to the door. She yanked on the handle, but it refused to budge. The lock was old and rusted, just an old padlock, probably thrown on in desperation when the area had flooded. A good kick might knock it open.

Mia hazarded a glance behind her. The redcap and the ghost were halfway there already. They knew where she was going, so her best chance was to get in and get ready for them. The fight wasn't over, but maybe she'd find something in there to hit back with. She kicked at the lock, and it broke easily under her foot. She dashed inside, slammed the door shut and flung a file cabinet to the ground to block it from opening. They were almost to the building now, and she stacked a couple of chairs on the file cabinet then backed away.

She had no clue if somewhere in the building another door had been left unlocked, or if there were windows that could be broken into or were broken already. All she could hope was they would try to come through the main door. She waited for the inevitable crash, squinting in the dim light as she searched for a weapon.

When her eyes adjusted, she inspected the room, which appeared to be a small abandoned hardware store. Most of the shelves were empty, but a few things still sat on shelves or hung from the walls. She dashed to the back of the store, just as the front door shook with the first attempt by the redcap to gain access. She vaulted over a counter where an empty register sat, cash drawer still open, then entered the backroom.

A desk sat in the middle of the room, covered with water-stained paper and various office equipment, including an ancient ruined computer. She scanned the room until she found something near a poster of some swimsuit model.

Jackpot.

A sledgehammer lay on the ground, likely forgotten in an attempt to remodel and fix the building before it was deemed unsalvageable. Lifting it, she felt like the mythical Thor, and she smiled for the first time since the beginning of the battle with the redcap. Hefting it to her shoulder, she strode out of the room.

The door was caving in, falling backward, and the ghost figure had already walked through the wall and was trying to grab the chairs and fling them away. Occasionally he would grasp one leg and move the chair a bit, but not enough. Every time he failed, he would curse and thrash, but it didn't matter. The redcap was almost in.

The door cracked open, and a piece of wood fell off. The redcap peered inside and made eye contact with Mia. It roared and charged again, this time sending the filing cabinet skidding off to the side, and the chairs flying in all directions.

Mia braced herself. She only had one good swing with the sledge-hammer, after which it would be faster and more effective to use her hand-to-hand skills. The redcap bore down on her, and rather than swinging for its head, she aimed a little lower, concentrating on hitting center mass.

With a swing resembling a golfer teeing-off more than anything else, she brought the sledgehammer down in an arc the redcap couldn't see in the darkness. The weapon connected with the monster's stomach, lifting it off the ground and into the air. The creature landed with a thud on one of the shelves.

A shrill cry came from the ghost creature, who inexplicably ducked behind the door as Mia made her way to the redcap. It tried to stand but she laid a kick into its ribs, further attacking the area she'd injured with the sledgehammer. It rolled on its back and coughed up a bubble of blood that stained its shirt.

It wobbled as it tried to get to its feet again, and it almost managed to stand, but Mia hit it with a series of blows to the face and stomach. It fell backward, and she put her hands on her knees to catch her breath. The legs of the beast twitched, and she stood to hit it again, but the shrill scream came from behind her. The ghost creature was flying at her, its hands clenched around the blade of a table saw. She ducked just in time for it to miss her and it dropped the blade. Screaming unintelligible curses, the ghost thing swooped to pick it up again, a desperate madness in its eyes.

Rather than trying to avoid it, she turned and ran for the back of the store, near the now-defunct electric exit sign. The door there may be locked, but it was probably a lock like the one she'd broken already.

If she hit it with full steam, she had a chance at getting outside, and possibly to escape. Running as hard as she could with whatever energy remained in her body, she kicked at the door and it flew open, sending her sprawling onto the cold floor of what was once the back storage room of the store.

CHAPTER SIXTEEN

"What in blazes is wrong with this thing?" Cassia asked, kicking at the wall where the portal should be. She had done everything she needed to do and now had to get back to Mia before all Hades broke loose. Not that she knew of any specific evil about to break loose, but knowing her luck, something was happening, and she wasn't there to handle it. She had a nagging feeling that she may have made a mistake by bringing the boggart in.

They paid well, though.

Still, enough was enough, it was time to get back to Mia and figure out what to do next. If Cassia could just get this stupid portal to work... Above the area where the portal normally opened up, a wooden sign in bright letters said, THANK YOU FOR VISITING. It had always bugged her. This was a jail. The only people ever going through that portal had to be there, either because it was their job, or because they were a prisoner. No visitors ever came through.

It was a stupid freaking sign.

Despite this being a stone wall, Cassia was determined if the portal didn't open soon, that sign was getting knocked down, kicked into pieces and turned into firewood. From behind her, Fan was chuckling, which at first made her more frustrated.

Then, as the realization dawned on her, Cassia's spine stiffened and she spun around to give him a deadly glare. His chuckling stopped abruptly, and he appeared to swallow hard. She marched over to him and slammed her hands on his desk.

Fan jumped a little, but the smile hadn't left his face. Either he was too stupid to know how angry she was, or he was too cocky. Cassia was leaning toward stupid because if it was cocky, he was going to end up with a broken nose.

"What is wrong with the portal?" Cassia asked, her voice level and low. She was trying to keep control of herself, but not only was the anger rising to nuclear levels, panic was starting to have a parade in her stomach. Something was going on with Mia, she just knew it, and she needed to get back there right this minute.

"Nothing. It works just fine."

"Then why isn't it opening for me?" Cassia asked, enunciating her consonants heavily. Her t's especially screamed a tremendous amount of a warning to the listener who should have known she meant business.

Unfortunately, the listener was Fan, who seemed unfazed and continued smiling like a goon, tapping his pen on the desk. "Maybe you didn't ask it nicely enough," he said.

There was a moment where Cassia stood in place, trying to make sure she was processing the words correctly. If this empty-headed, dumb-faced jackanape—

"He's so bad at this." One of the ogres from behind the desk was speaking to a second ogre, both holding mugs of steaming coffee and casually discussing the entertainment of the moment in their loudest possible voices.

Ogres were not known for their ability to keep their voices down, which made them such good jailers. When an ogre yells that it was lights out, people on the other side of the town would begin to turn off their lights. Then there was the effect their voices had on the movement of the earth.

Humans usually confuse the deep baritone yell of an ogre with an earthquake. They don't actually cause earthquakes, but some of the

4.0 quakes were really only the earth transmitting the vibrations resulting from groups of ogres yelling or partying.

"Yeah, even *I* would be better at getting a date than Fan. I bet she doesn't even know he has it bad for her. Ha, ha." The second ogre was blatantly making eye contact with Cassia as if she were a cartoon he was watching rather than a living being.

"That's true," said the first ogre. "And you haven't had a date in... how long?"

The words were reverberating as loud as rumbles of thunder, and Fan's face turned a shade of red Cassia had never seen before. Ducking his head, Fan held out one finger to Cassia and spun his chair around.

"Been down here too long," said the second ogre, unaware that Fan was now looking at him. Or not understanding what it meant. "He forgot how to hit on women. No smoothness."

"Hey." Fan spoke with enough bass in his voice to stop their conversation, though he still sounded defeated. "We can hear you."

The ogres stared back at Fan, then looked to Cassia. Their big dumb eyes blinked a few times, and they slowly nodded. "So, did you hear about the...uhh...new keys?" asked one of them, not so subtly changing the subject.

"No. What keys? I thought we were talking about Fan and the pretty lady."

"Oh crickets," mumbled Fan, and he spun back around to Cassia.

"It's fine," Cassia held up her hand. Poor guy. She thought he was just an idiot, or a dingleberry, but he was just an awkward guy who liked a girl who wasn't interested. It was sweet.

"Just open the portal, please."

Without another word—and with his head in his hand—Fan pushed a button on his desk and the portal sprang to life. Cassia looked back one last time before walking through.

He *was* cute, though.

The last thing she heard before going through the portal was one of the ogres saying, "Boy, you sure screwed that one up, Fan."

Cassia shook her head, laughter bubbling up in spite of herself as she entered the apartment from the portal.

The laughter stopped abruptly.

The apartment was in shambles. Mia wasn't going to be in there—Cassia could tell by the silence—but she searched anyway. She called out for the girl but received no response. The living room was empty, and so was the bedroom. Mia was nowhere to be found, and it worried the snot out of Cassia.

She clung briefly to hopeful thoughts: Mia may have just fallen asleep, or maybe she'd climbed out the window, or—the best-case scenario—she was simply exploring the complex. When Cassia spotted the splintered door, she held back a string of expletives. Her instincts had been right—Mia was in trouble.

The outside was strangely quiet, and Cassia was torn on what to do next. She could either go wandering around outside or she could try to gather some clues. She turned and studied the room again. It was a mess, but what was different from last time?

It appeared that Mia had been lounging around at some point. There was a spot cleared off on what had at one time been a pretty nice couch. The seats were still a little indented where the girl must have been sitting, and the pillow resting against the arm meant she'd likely been lying on the couch.

Moving over to the porch door, Cassia confirmed it was locked. That made sense. Even if Mia had gone out there and then came back, she would likely have locked it behind her. Make sure the only way in and out of the room was the main door or the portal. That's what Cassia would have done too.

Still curious, Cassia unlocked the heavy metal latch and opened the door to the patio. The hinges squealed as it opened, years of rusted and moldy metal fighting to stay closed forever. That gave her a clue. Mia wouldn't have come out on the patio for fear of making too much noise. No one likes the sound of metal grinding together, and opening the patio door would have been far too loud for someone who was alone and afraid.

Shutting the door and locking it, out of habit if nothing else,

Cassia went back to the couch. Part of her wanted to sit on the couch the way she thought Mia would have, trying to see from her point of view. It was a compulsion she couldn't fight, no matter how silly it seemed, and eventually she gave in, sitting on the couch and turning sideways.

Ahead of her was the wall, empty except for a dent where the boggart had caused some damage. To her left was the patio door which she had already ruled out. To the right was an empty TV stand, the television gone long enough for a layer of dust to collect on the surface, leaving no trace of it ever having been there. Above the TV stand was a cheap long mirror. It reflected the light from the patio during the daytime, she supposed, helping brighten the room without the need for flipping switches.

Switches. Where were the switches? Some of the lights outside the building were on, probably just solar-powered emergency lights, but if the city had at any point taken over the complex intending on using it, the electricity cabling might still run to the building. Maybe Mia had thought the same thing and had gone to turn on a light? Cassia stood and looked around for the switch, finding it on the wall near the door. Flipping it did nothing.

Something wasn't right. Cassia had been gone a good while, and if Mia got a bug in her and wanted to go exploring, she would have returned by now. It was possible she'd gone wandering and gotten lost or hurt herself. Or worse. Something had hurt *her*.

The splintered door worried Cassia. She didn't want to jump to conclusions that someone—or some*thing*—had broken into the apartment, but what else could the broken door mean?

Convinced there was nothing else she could find in this apartment, Cassia decided to search the others in the building. Grabbing a pen from a jar beside the kitchen sink, she held her breath to avoid inhaling the fetid stench from the refrigerator as she ripped one of the grocery lists off its door. She wrote a note to Mia and set it on the couch. If the girl came back and somehow missed her, at least she would know Cassia was looking for her.

Closing what was left of the door quietly behind her, Cassia approached the apartment across the hall. The door was locked and seemed like it hadn't been opened in a very long time. Which meant she'd have to search the other buildings as well as the surrounding area. Most likely, if Mia was still nearby, she would be in one of the other apartments, probably searching through stuff on a damp and disappointing treasure hunt.

Unless something had gotten to her. Cassia shuddered at the thought. The people pursuing Mia seemed like they meant business. What if they'd found her while Cassia was busy being hit on by a shy prison warden? How would she live with herself knowing she'd left that girl in a dangerous situation, and allowed her to be captured? Cassia had the strong feeling if Mia had been taken, she wouldn't remain alive for long. Something about the people chasing her didn't feel like they were the kidnapping-and-keeping-safe kind.

Guilt was wracking her brain as she reached the bottom floor of the building. She tried to shake it away and focus, searching for footprints or any other sign that Mia had gone off in a specific direction. Or a sign of a struggle.

Two buildings were up ahead, the one on the left backed up to an empty yard, and beyond was a street lined with apartments. The building on the right was attached to the office for the complex, with a long winding driveway leading from the main road.

Cassia approached the buildings, not making a decision either way yet, trying to focus on the surroundings and what clues there may be.

A faint noise, like something falling over, echoed from the area of the office. Cassia stopped, her head snapping in that direction as she listened. The hum of the city was distant but constant, and it was hard to pick up individual sounds nearby unless they were loud.

The sound didn't repeat itself, but now Cassia had to know what had caused it. She headed right toward the office and snuck around to the front of the building.

The door was open—just slightly—and Cassia gently pulled it. It swung open without much sound, a pretty good indication of fairly regular use. That only made her worry more. Whoever was using the office could have spotted Mia and done something to her. There didn't seem to be anyone inside at the moment though, but Cassia poked her head in to check.

The office was empty, save for a desk with a few magazines and newspapers on it. The smiling faces of celebrities on the pages creeped Cassia out, and she turned them over before moving deeper into the office. Something was plugged into the wall here, and as she listened, she heard water running in the next room. It was faint, the sound a leaky toilet makes rather than a sink that's been left to drip.

She opened the door and scanned the room. A nightlight plugged into the wall glowed a bright blue, and sure enough, the water ran in the commode. Someone was here, often enough that electricity was turned on in this building. But who? And did they do something to Mia?

Cassia shut the door quietly and turned around, and almost shrieked loudly. A rat—at least the size of a small dog—ran across the room, knocking over a near-empty trash can, sending crumpled paper to the floor. Exhaling slowly, Cassia realized these must have been the sounds she'd heard—just a rat rummaging round in an empty complex.

Where in Hades was Mia? There were two buildings left to search, then Cassia would double back to the first apartment. Maybe the girl would be there waiting for her. Or she would find Mia picking through abandoned possessions in one of the buildings.

"Come on, Mia," Cassia said under her breath. "Make a noise."

CHAPTER SEVENTEEN

Mia didn't really have time to worry about smashing onto the dirty floor. She scrambled across it until she got her feet under her, then headed deeper into the room. She heard the redcap and ghost creature following close behind her. Only seconds after she dove behind a stack of empty cardboard boxes, the door smashed open.

Her body trembled, her heart pounding in her chest so hard she could hear it in her ears and feel the blood pulsing on the sides of her neck. This wasn't good decision making. As soon as she'd heard that strange sound in the apartment, she should have just blocked the door and found the farthest corner to wait it out until Cassia came back.

But, no. She had to go investigate and see what it could be. Because, of course she did. That's what had recently been getting her into these sorts of situations. It's exactly what had happened the night she and Becky had gone out with the other students to explore the market in Shanghai. The area, congested with other people and alive with the sights, sounds, and smells of all the vendors and shops hadn't been enough for her. She had to go farther, deeper, to drift away from the established path and see what she could find for herself.

That was how she'd ended up in the tea shop with the overpowering smell and the mysterious old woman who'd plied her with powerful tea and searched her eyes deeply, as though she were wondering about something just beyond Mia's awareness.

It was the reason Mia had been there to see the boggart for the first time and watch in awe as it maneuvered around the people, unseen and unnoticed. But it was also how she'd met the bounty hunter who had saved Mia and was now guiding her as she learned more about herself.

For that reason, Mia couldn't completely regret how events had unfolded in China. No, they weren't what she'd expected when she had packed her bag and boarded that plane. She had just meant to come here and compete against other students who were as passionate about the same martial arts as she was. She'd even hoped to demonstrate her skill and ability well enough to come out on top.

She couldn't have imagined that coming here would completely change her life. But she had to keep fighting. Her life might be in turmoil and she might not fully understand what was going on around her, but it was *her* life. Hers to toss aside and give over to the creatures pursuing her so viciously, or hers to save. Mia knew which one she was going to try.

The redcap crossed the room, kicking boxes and crates as he stalked past them. Mia clamped a hand over her mouth to silence her gasps and cries of fear. She needed to stay as quiet as she possibly could and not give away her location. If she could wait for them to go to the other side of the room, she would have a chance to slip past them and get away.

They were moving in her direction and Mia looked around, trying to identify her next hiding spot. A stack of wooden pallets sat nearby, similar to the ones she and Cassia had hidden behind in the alley before coming to the apartment. It seemed like the perfect spot. It had worked for them then, so she may as well see if it would work for her now.

As soon as the redcap turned to look at the ghost, she sprinted toward the pallets. Her feet skidded in the dirt and dust that had built up on the smooth cement, and she almost crashed to the ground. She went with the momentum, rolling as she would to avoid a blow, then braced herself for impact with the wood. Her mind raced, hoping she wouldn't hit them, hoping by some twist of fate she'd slip around them and nothing would fall on her.

Suddenly, she realized the movement across the floor had stopped. Her body had squeezed perfectly into a small space between the pallets and a stack of discarded plastic milk crates, leaving everything still standing.

A breath shuddered from her lungs and she squeezed her eyes closed tightly, giving herself a moment to calm down. It couldn't last for long. She had to keep moving. The creatures were getting angrier the more they moved around the room, and soon enough, they would abandon their delicate search technique and simply trash the room.

Pressing her back against the wall, Mia shuffled sideways to ease behind the stacks to a unit of metal shelves. She rolled onto her belly and slithered across the empty bottom shelf. Abandoned products created a wall that blocked nearly the entire shelf from view. Spider webs stuck to her skin, and a thick layer of dust and dirt tickled at her nose. She could taste the filth in her throat as she breathed, but it didn't matter. There were far worse things ahead of her if she let these guys get their hands on her.

Mia slipped off the shelf onto the floor and hopped to the balls of her feet to scramble further. Ahead of her, a faint light glowed at the bottom corner of one of the cardboard boxes. It wasn't the light filtering from the main room of the floor. She followed it as it snaked across the floor and disappeared beneath the far wall.

It took a few seconds for it to sink in—she'd progressed all the way around the room and had found the door leading out the back of the building. Her heart jumped. All she had to do was get through that door, and then she could make a run for it. She would return to the apartment building and hide.

The space in front of the door had little to conceal her. She had to make a choice. Either she could try to slip out and possibly take much more time to escape, or she could burst out of hiding and go full speed until she was back at the apartment.

That tactic had the chance of disorienting her pursuers, so they didn't immediately come after her, giving her a little bit of a head start to find the most concealed path toward the apartment building. She thought about everything her Wushu master taught her. It wasn't just about the actual movements or the katas. It wasn't about physical strength, agility, and stamina.

What she needed now was everything else he had instilled in her over the years of training under him. His strictness and expectation of excellence had been challenging when going through the same movements for the thousandth time or running laps for being late. But they had taught her determination. They'd given her drive and strength. They'd imbued her with a sense of trust and faith in herself, and accountability for her actions. He'd taught her to believe in what she knew within herself and to not question it. Hesitation could be disastrous.

Mia knew what she had to do. Priming her muscles and steadying her mind, she burst from her crouching position. Her body shot toward the light gleaming from under the door. She put her hands out in front of her and shoved with all her strength.

Her palms hit the door before she'd even considered the possibility of it being locked. The weight and speed of her impact broke through the boards crossed over what turned out to be double doors leading out onto a cement porch. She grabbed the metal banister tightly and pushed back just in time to stop herself from tumbling over.

She had already thrown herself out a window that day. Such a maneuver would be unnecessary, especially when a set of cement steps that led to the ground provided a much more controlled and less dangerous route. Mia was so focused on not falling as she made her way down that she didn't pay sufficient attention to her surroundings. It wasn't until she'd left the stairs and was running that she spotted the fence in front of her.

She had expected the back area to be open, probably with a loading dock, but a huge fence loomed only a few yards from her. Mia ran around the side of the store and sprinted down the narrow alley between another fence and the building. Halfway to the front, she hit another fence. She grabbed it, shaking it frantically. She hadn't seen the massive chain-link barrier when she'd run toward the store earlier. Now she was trapped, a cage at the back of the store keeping her from going any farther.

Mia stuck her foot into the fence and tried to scramble up, but sharp points on the metal cut into her hands. Above her were coils of razor wire. There was no way she could get over and to the other side. Her only chance was to run back inside. She jumped to the ground and raced up the alley. But before she reached the other end, the two creatures came around the corner.

Their eyes burned into her as they approached. The redcap rubbed his hands together, a sickening smile on his lips as he moved toward her. "Have you finished your little escape now? I built up quite an appetite coming after you. But that's fine. It only means I'm going to enjoy my dinner all the more," he said.

"No." The ghost stopped the redcap's advance. "You can't do that. We have to capture her alive."

"You saw what I've been through trying to catch her. She wasn't supposed to be this difficult. Look at her. Who is she to make it so hard on us? I will savor every bite of her," the redcap said.

"You can't," the ghost insisted. "She has to be kept alive. You know that. We were sent to capture her, not destroy her. Our employer wants her captured alive."

The redcap narrowed his eyes at the ghost and took an angry step toward him. Mia continued to scan the alley for any way she might be able to get out. She pushed on the fence, yanking at the corners in the hope of finding a piece that was broken and could fold out of the way. But it was secure.

As the redcap faced off against the ghost, Mia formed a plan to get around them. If she could slip past while they were distracted by each other, she might be able to get back into the store. She pressed her spine against the brick wall of the building and started easing her way back down the alley.

"I know what our employer wants of us," the redcap growled. "But the agreement was to bring her in alive if it was within our power. She is to be stopped first. That is the most important thing."

"Yes, she's to be stopped, but bringing her in alive is what he wants. There would be little good in announcing we've found her and had the chance to bring her in, only that we couldn't because there was nothing left of her. She's right here in front of us. Trapped like a little mouse in a cage. We must capture her and bring her in alive," the ghost demanded.

The bricks behind her scraped Mia's hands as she kept them flattened against the wall and moved slowly but consistently along the building. Just a few more yards to the corner, and she could break free and run for the door. Once inside, she could push as many boxes and crates into their path as possible to slow their progress and make a run for the apartment.

Cassia was coming. She had to be. The bounty hunter had already been gone for so long. It couldn't be too much longer before she returned. When she did, they could battle these things together.

"You know, you're right," the redcap said to his companion. "I've been so selfish thinking only of my own needs. I can't just destroy her now and have nothing to bring back. We'll earn our pay, and the favor of our employer, by bringing this thing back to him to do whatever he wants with her."

The sinister note deepened in his voice and Mia squeezed her eyes closed, swallowing hard as she tried to will her legs to keep moving. Cassia had told Mia how impressed she was by her, that she was brave and a good fighter. Mia wasn't feeling it at that moment, but she had to try to channel it. While the two arrogant creatures in front of her were arguing, she had to do everything she could to escape. Just a few more steps now.

"What do you mean?" the ghost asked.

"You said she would be no good if we found her only to have nothing left because she was killed and eaten before we could bring her back. That is absolutely true. But I'm still hungry, and she seems so delicious. Our employer asked us to bring her back alive but didn't say anything about her being intact." He turned sharply to Mia, making her scream and push herself hard against the bricks. "She could easily stay alive, even if she were missing an arm or a leg."

Mia lashed out, burying her foot in the redcap's stomach. He grunted and stumbled back, and the ghost was pulled along with him as if something had blown him out of the way. Mia didn't stay in place long enough to think about it too much.

She sprinted toward the end of the alley, but the redcap surged in front of her. She screamed again and ran the other way, not knowing what to do next, but desperate to stay out of his grasp. Mia whipped around and pressed her back against the wall again.

He was coming toward her, and she pushed back harder against the bricks, wishing more than anything she had a safe place to go. It didn't matter where. She just needed a place, any place where she'd be safe, where these monsters wouldn't be able to follow her. Somewhere they couldn't find her.

The wall behind her began to give way, and Mia's first thought was that the bricks were crumbling. She couldn't find her feet as they dissolved behind her and the redcap let out a chilling scream. His hand dipped into his coat and reappeared, gripping a gun. The blast exploding from it tore another scream from Mia's throat just as the wall vanished and she fell back.

She didn't hit the ground. She just kept falling. When she opened her eyes, the space around her looked like some strange vortex. Colors and shapes swirled and merged around her, making her dizzy as they spun faster and faster.

Mia had gone down the rabbit hole. It was all she could think. She'd somehow ended up in a confusing, nonsensical dream and didn't know when she would wake up. That's what it had to be. A dream.

CHAPTER EIGHTEEN

Phillipsburg, Montana

"There's a reason it's called the Power of Five." Carson climbed to his feet yet again. "It's because it needs five people."

He groaned and tried to stretch the pain and tension out of his muscles. It was somehow even harder being tossed around by the failed portal over and over than it had been with the wind. It was almost as though the magic they were using kept getting more offended that the four young fae were trying to do something so beyond what their abilities should be able to manage. In retribution, it was building up their hopes and making them think they had accomplished their goal.

At the very last second, their dreams would be dashed when yet again they'd be picked up and either thrown across the field or unceremoniously lifted and dumped onto the ground. At least the sudden thunderstorms had only happened two more times. Any more frequently and their dome might have turned into a swimming pool.

Then they would have to attempt a water portal, which was

infinitely more difficult. Vivi might be up for it, though. Much to the surprise—and pleasure—of the other three, the dark-haired Unseelie girl had maintained her commitment to good behavior even through all their spectacular failures. She'd continued to push them to the next effort and offer suggestions for how to make it the successful one. They had gone past the flowers and the wind to find a challenge that had captured her attention and had brought her focus to its sharpest point. She wasn't willing to let go.

"That's just a suggestion," Zander said.

"No, I think that's actually how it works. If it wasn't, they would call it the Power-of-however-many-people-you-happen-to-have-around-you-at-the-moment-and-can't-figure-out-how-to-make-the-spell-work," Luna said.

"Come on. We can figure out how to do this. How many times has Principal Elmhurst said we are the most powerful halflings she's ever worked with? She's been drilling it into our heads all summer long that we are the ones who can make this incredible thing happen. If she has that much faith in us, why can't we do it on our own?" Zander asked.

"Because she has also spent the entire summer looking for another person to add to our group so that we can have five," Carson pointed out. "We actually do need that other person."

"I'm with Zander," Vivi said. "We can't just give up. Not yet."

Luna and Carson exchanged glances then looked at Zander.

"Let's go, then," their de facto leader said.

"This was all your idea, I want to remind you," Carson said to Luna.

"My idea was for the four of us to do something fun together to help us get to know each other better and take some time away from all the work. It's not my fault we ended up right back in this field doing more work," she replied.

Zander laughed and opened his soaking wet arms. "What are you talking about? This is fun. I'm having fun. Vivi, aren't you having fun?"

"No."

"See? Vivi is having fun. This isn't work. It's a means to an end. We figure out how to open the portal, and we can go anywhere we want and do all kinds of fun things together."

"That was inspiring," Carson said flatly.

They all walked to the end of the dome again and prepared for yet another attempt. It went on that way for another three hours until finally Carson glared at Zander through another pouring rainstorm and shook his head.

"I'm done," he said. "It's late and I'm hungry. Time for a break."

"We've been at this long enough, Zander," Luna said.

Her voice didn't have the same edge as Carson's. Instead, she appealed to him through the softness in her tone, the friendship between them coming through the words. She knew his intensity, his drive to be the best he could possibly be, then push through that and be even better.

But she also knew he didn't know when it was too much. He didn't know when he needed to stop and give himself time to rest. When he was committed to something, it was all he could think about. He would push himself into the ground if it was what it took to accomplish the next goal he set for himself.

That's where the three of them came in. Zander hated for them to try to control him, especially Carson and Vivi. But they were his protection from himself. They stood between him and his own destruction. At least, he hoped they did.

"All right," he finally said. "It's late. We'll try again another time."

"Here, Luna, let me help you dry off."

The voice was so unexpected that at first, Luna wasn't sure she'd actually heard it. When she turned, Vivi was standing a few feet away, looking at her expectantly. She had actually been the one to offer to help her.

Luna and Zander glanced at each other in shock but didn't say anything. It was unlike Vivi to volunteer to do anything for anyone else. Offering to do something for a Seelie—and Luna especially—was totally out of the realm of their understanding of the girl. They didn't want to make a big deal out of it and possibly spook her.

Instead, Luna nodded. "Sure," she said. "Thank you."

Vivi nodded in return and gestured behind Luna. "Back up a little. Spread your arms out."

Luna did what she asked but did her best to ready herself for anything. There was still a considerable part of her that was convinced she was being set up. Any second now, Vivi could turn on her and make this into another of her humiliating practical jokes. It would just be worse because Luna had actually set herself up for it.

But that's not what happened. Luna spread her arms out and closed her eyes, and Vivi used her magic to sweep warm air over the Seelie girl until her clothes were dry. She told Luna to turn around and did the same until her silvery hair hung smooth. Luna faced her with a soft smile on her lips.

Before either of the girls could say anything, Carson approached Vivi and threw an arm around her shoulders. "That's my girl," he said.

Vivi's face darkened and she shoved him away, turning to sneer at him.

Luna immediately snickered. "There's the Vivi I know and love to hate," she said.

Everyone laughed, including Vivi. "Come on," she said. "Let's go back to campus. I'm sure the kitchen will have something for us."

***

All four had agreed to get an early start. They met up at the entrance to their dormitory just as the sun was rising in the East in order to catch the first bus of the day. The little field on the outskirts of town was a nice change of pace for them, plus none of the remaining students would be able to watch their failed attempts at obtaining the power of five, so it was the perfect place to practice.

The stop was a few blocks away from the academy. Now, as they made their way to the academy entrance, they walked closer together than they ever had before, possibly a result of trying so hard to make the portal together.

As they strode past the large ivy-covered brick wall surrounding the grounds of the school, Carson paused. He'd spotted something strange about the wall but wasn't entirely sure what it could be. He reached out and flattened his hand on Zander's chest to stop him.

"What are you doing?" Zander asked. But the agitation in his voice dampened when he saw the other boy's eyes focused on the wall ahead of them.

"Look at that," said Carson. "What's going on with that wall?"

Luna and Vivi paused and followed the guys' gaze to the wall. Right beside the towering black gate leading onto the grounds of the school, a portion of the wall looked strange. The thick covering of ivy looked like it was bending in toward the bricks and liquefying at the edges. Beyond the leaves, the bricks had faded into one mass and had begun to swirl.

"Is that a portal?" Luna asked. She moved in front of Vivi and Carson, curiosity drawing her closer to the wall. It looked like a portal was opening on the wall, but that didn't make any sense.

"Could we have—" Carson started, but Zander shook his head sharply to stop him.

"No way. We didn't accidentally make a portal all the way over here from the field," he said. "And the next morning at that."

"It would be awesome if we did, though," Carson said.

Sparks sprang out of the wall, and the four gasped and backed away. In the next second, they were running toward it. This was bizarre. They reached the wall just as the portal opened in front of them.

Something was coming at them fast, and they jumped out of the way just in time to avoid colliding with a terrified-looking girl falling through the portal. She stumbled a few steps and smashed unceremoniously onto the ground.

In the next instant, a shot rang out, and a blazing bullet hit the ground next to Zander's foot. He bent to reach for it, but Luna grabbed his shirt to stop him.

"Don't touch it. It's hot," she said.

They turned their attention back to the wall, where the portal was now closing. When it had fully sealed, the girl lifted her head from the ground and stared around frantically. Her emerald eyes were wild with fear and she scrambled to her feet, jumping away from the four teens as she stared at each one of them in turn.

"Who are you?" she demanded. "Who are you?"

She struck a fighting pose that looked like she seriously knew what she was doing and the four exchanged glances, trying to understand what was happening. The girl whipped around to look at the wall, searching the ivy and staring at the bricks as though she was afraid something was there.

The wall was solid again, but she stared at it like she didn't believe it. She was waiting for something to come after her, even though the portal had closed almost as soon as she'd fallen through it. There wasn't time for anything to follow her except the bullet. She spun around again and resumed her aggressive pose.

The four young fae had no idea what to think. They were shocked. None of them had ever seen a human go through a portal and had certainly never seen one open on the wall like that.

It wasn't even within the grounds, just out on the sidewalk where any of the humans could have seen. Fortunately, it was so early in the morning that no one was walking past, but it could have been disastrous if someone had seen her ungraceful and unexpected arrival.

The only experiences the students had with portals were the ones specifically created in certain areas inside the campus buildings that were put there purposefully and for express reasons. Only specific people from the academy were allowed to use them, and they went to places on exacting records.

To ensure they were kept secure and no one misused them, these portals were always guarded by a group of full fae. Usually the headmistress was among those closely monitoring the portals and every instance of their use.

Something told the four fae that Principal Elmhurst didn't know about this particular portal and wasn't anticipating the arrival of the frightened human. They couldn't just keep standing there staring at the girl and wondering how she had shown up.

Vivi took a step closer. "Who are you?" she asked.

Zander moved ahead of Luna, using his arm to push her back. He stood in front of the group, squaring off against the strange human girl. He was prepared to fight if he had to, prepared to put himself between the intruder and his team so they would be safe.

It should have been a reassuring gesture to them. He meant it as a show of unity. Instead, it got under Vivi's skin after she'd spent all day and night trying to cooperate and to make their group more cohesive.

She pushed to the head of the group, stalking out in front of Zander. It offended her that he would think not only that she would need to be protected, but that *he* was the one who should be providing that protection. That's not how this was going to go. Zander didn't need to protect her, or the others. He wasn't their leader. That was a role Vivi wanted for herself.

Mia's eyes met those of the girl in front of her. Her hair was so dark it stood out in stark contrast to the sunshine around her and seemed to glisten almost blue in the sunlight. Her eyes pierced Mia's, and the intensity in that stare was alarming.

But it didn't intimidate Mia into trying to get away or softening the strength of her stance. She didn't know who these people were or where she was. If it came down to it, she was going to defend herself.

Fury rushed through her veins, and her hands twitched. "Who are *you?*" she demanded.

They needed to come up with an explanation and fast. They were standing in front of Mia, acting like *she* was the threat and that they were entitled to information about her. But *she* was the one who had spent her day being hounded by monsters and had just fallen down the rabbit hole with bullets chasing her.

It had been a seriously rough day, and she'd had enough. It was time for something to go right for Mia, even if that only meant these people explaining to her where she was and who they were. They could figure out where to go from there then.

Luna studied the girl, taking note of the torn clothes and bloody injuries all over her body. Her red hair was a mess and her eyes were wide with fear or possibly shock and had luggage so big Vivi's entire wardrobe would fit in them. For a brief moment, she pitied the frightened human who looked to have been in a war.

Mia stared at each of the four standing in front of her in turn. They looked like they were about her age, but there was something strange about them. She couldn't quite place it, couldn't quite figure out what it was that was making her feel so odd facing off against them. The group didn't look fully cohesive. Instead, it looked like two sets of two. A boy and a girl each, two were all silver and ice blue, and the others were dark. The contrast was intense, but so was the clear connection among them. There were tension and conflict, but there was also a sense of togetherness, a clear delineation of *them*, and *her*.

Silence fell over them and they stood there unmoving. Their postures were tight, their gazes flickering between each other. The five were stiff, on guard, none knowing what to do next.

CHAPTER NINETEEN

China

Cassia closed the door to the apartment behind her, keeping her concentration on any sounds she might pick up. For a second, she thought she heard something slamming, but it was pretty far off. Most likely on the streets nearby, and not within the complex.

She went over to the first apartment building, just like she and Mia had when they'd first arrived at the complex. They hadn't entered the first apartment then. It had been locked and Cassia hadn't bothered with it, and instead had just moved on to the next building.

It had appeared to bother Mia when she had realized the fae could simply force the door open if she wanted to. Maybe the halfling had given into that curiosity and come over here to figure out her own way into the locked apartment.

Cassia approached the first door and reached for the handle. It was still locked, with no signs of anyone entering recently. She used her magic to release the lock anyway. Finding Mia was critical. Cassia couldn't just skip over a place because it didn't make sense. She had to look everywhere. When the lock was disengaged, she reached for the knob again.

The door opened under her hand and she was surprised to find a light on in the hallway, illuminating the kitchen and living room. It was strange to see electricity working in a place like this, and it sent an eerie shiver along her spine.

The living room was empty, but there was a fresh smell to it, and the carpet had been replaced recently. It looked cared for, and if she hadn't already seen the rooms of the other buildings, she would have assumed this was a new apartment, ready to rent.

"Well, crickets," she muttered. "If I'd just unlocked the door, I could have found this place. Of course, this might actually be creepier than the abandoned places, so maybe I was right."

As hopeful as she was upon finding a clean, empty room and seeing a light on, hopeful that Mia was hiding in there, the place turned up empty too. Cassia stood in the kitchen and tried to think. This inexplicably perfect apartment aside, the rest of the building still looked dilapidated. Where could Mia have gone?

If she was looking for adventure, she would have found it in the other rooms and would likely still be there by now. If she was looking for a cleaner place to stay, she would have ended up in this apartment —if she had found a way in. So, where was she?

Cassia walked to the screen door leading to the porch of the upper floor apartment and stared out over the grounds surrounding the building. The complex looked dark and foreboding. There was something sinister to it that she couldn't put her finger on.

She was just about to turn away when something caught her eye. Cassia spun back around to look out again and spotted a glinting in the dim light. It looked like glass—quite a lot of it—spread out behind the apartment. She could just see it from the porch because it was higher up and sat on a bit of a hill above the other building.

There was a field beside the building, then a street with a small shop. The shop appeared abandoned too, only there was something wrong, something different about the store, and when Cassia understood what it was, she took off running, cursing herself for not seeing it before. The shop door was cracked open.

She bolted out of the apartment without bothering to lock it and ran down the stairs. She leapt off the third step from the bottom, landed in mid-stride, then raced for the shop.

Cassia ran faster than she had in quite some time, spurred on by the need to protect the young girl. From inside the store, she heard crashing sounds and something screeching. Whatever was going on in there was not good, and she had a sinking feeling it involved Mia.

Mia had proved she could handle herself in a tough fight, and she'd impressed Cassia with the way she'd dealt with the boggart. But Cassia didn't know what was inside the store with the girl, and the bounty hunters who were after her certainly hadn't seemed like they were going to be an easy fight.

Cassia was deeply worried that Mia was in the kind of trouble that could prove fatal. She kept running as hard as she could, past the other apartment building and through the field toward the store.

She slammed into the side of the building rather than slow down for the door. Figuring anyone inside might be confused and take their concentration off Mia for a moment, Cassia rammed into the wall, then flung the door open for a second before ducking her head in.

It was dark inside, so she allowed her eyes to adjust for a moment, and eventually shapes within the shop began to form. The room was unoccupied, but the shelves were destroyed. In the middle of the store, a sledgehammer lay on the ground, and everything had that chaotic appearance she recognized quite well. It was the scene of a fight, for sure.

Cassia ran into the room and listened to see if she could hear anything. There didn't seem to be anything close, and she was about to go to the door and look outside when a sound chilled her heart and made her stop cold in her tracks.

A gunshot echoed all around her. It was close, somewhere outside of the building. Across from Cassia was a door to a backroom, and she sprinted for it. She flung it open and ran inside, pushing away a desk as she raced for another door which led outside.

The air was thick with smoke as she entered a passage that led to another alley along the other side of the building. The sound of shouting echoed from around the corner, and of a voice, a female voice. The girl screamed.

Cassia sprinted to the corner and rounded it just in time to see Mia with a portal behind her, sucking her inside. The girl was bent at the waist and was falling. In front of her stood a redcap, its glamour gone, and beside him was a short, nearly transparent troll. A sluagh.

The redcap held a gun, which was smoking, and as Mia disappeared through the portal, he fired several more rounds at her. The bullets all seemed to miss, bouncing off the wall behind the portal and leaving black marks on the concrete.

The sluagh screamed in frustration, and the pair began an argument Cassia couldn't quite hear. It wasn't clear if *they* had opened the portal or if someone else had, but they seemed upset that Mia had gone through it. It didn't matter. They'd fired a gun at Mia, which was all Cassia needed to know.

"I told you," the redcap said to the sluagh. "I needed her to…hey, who are you?"

Instead of bothering with words, Cassia flung herself at the redcap fast enough to land an elbow on its chin and send it barreling backward, the gun skittering off into a dark corner of the alley. The sluagh raced off, undoubtedly to find something to throw at her.

She'd dealt with them before, and they'd been more annoying than harmful. Often, sluaghs tied themselves to someone to feed off their energy and could only use what their host could spare. Considering the redcap was now most certainly missing some teeth and looked like Mia had already put the hurt on him as well, Cassia figured the sluagh wasn't going to be much trouble.

The redcap began to stand, getting to its stubby feet so it could run at her. Dropping low, Cassia swept her legs out, swiping the redcap at the knees and bringing it down to the ground on its back. She jumped on top of it and drove her fist into its stomach. The gun the redcap had dropped was too far away, and every time he reached for it, Cassia slammed her fist into the monster's armpit.

"Where did she go?" Cassia screamed, pounding the redcap in the face with rapid-fire rights and lefts.

"I don't know," it yelled. "I didn't open the portal!"

Cassia didn't believe him and continued punching him in the head. He started to weaken and looked as if he was about to fall unconscious when Cassia noticed something ahead of her. It was the sluagh, and it was picking up the gun.

"Leave or die," it trilled at her.

"You first," she said, grabbing the redcap by the chin and back of the head. As the sluagh raised the gun toward her, she twisted violently, snapping the neck of the redcap, killing it instantly.

There was a slight pop, and the gun dropped to the ground, the sluagh that had held it no longer there. Cassia had been right, it had tied itself to the life force of the redcap, and since that was the case, it couldn't be called back. No one would know what happened here.

She stood slowly, eyeing the wall. It didn't seem possible. Mia couldn't have done that. Not a halfling, not one who didn't know she had fae blood at all.

Cassia approached the wall and lifted her hands to it. Resting her palms against the brick, she felt for the power of the portal. Even though it was closed, the energy would still linger there. Not many fae had the ability to detect the remaining magic of a closed portal, and it was one of the things about Cassia that made her such an incredible bounty hunter.

The special ability didn't stop with just being able to feel for the portal. Once she found it, she could re-open it and follow the trails. She'd done it many times before when in pursuit of criminals. Being able to chase them even when they opened their own portals and closed them the instant they went through meant it was harder to completely avoid her. It was the reason that the majority of fae who had the ability ended up becoming bounty hunters.

Cassia found the center of the portal's power and focused her magic on it, opening it back up. This could be extremely dangerous. She knew that. It was always a risk to go through an unknown portal, but she didn't have the option of hesitating or thinking too much about it.

Whatever danger *she* might be facing, Mia faced even more. Wherever the portal brought Cassia, she was better equipped to manage it than the young halfling. Cassia had to find her and make sure she was safe.

Taking a breath, she jumped through the portal. She was accustomed to traveling this way and barely noticed the swirls of color and twisting feeling that came as she moved through it. An instant later, she landed on a sidewalk in front of four startled teenage halfling fae. It took a second for her to recognize that Mia was standing beside her.

Mia gasped. "You're here."

"I am," she said. "Where's here?"

She looked around and saw the gate to the side of them. It bore a name that she knew very well. Elmhurst Academy. A smile came to her lips. She didn't know how this had happened, but she was glad it had. She turned her attention back to the four sets of eyes staring at her and Mia.

They didn't seem nearly as pleased as she was that she and Mia were there. All four of the halflings were clearly on edge, ready to challenge her new ward in an instant. She positioned herself slightly in front of Mia just in case they decided to get jumpy before she could figure this out. She had to be prepared to keep them away from Mia.

Zander, Carson, Luna, and Vivi couldn't believe what they were seeing. It was shocking enough to see the portal form on the wall and spit out a human girl and a bullet. They weren't at all prepared to see the portal open again and a full fae woman saunter through.

This fae moved with absolute confidence, striding out onto the sidewalk like she owned the portal. She was beautiful, if dressed fiercely and armed to the teeth. This wasn't the parent of one of the students at the academy.

They studied her, evaluating every detail to try and understand who this fae woman might be. The leather jacket over black pants and heavy black boots set her apart from most of the other fae women they encountered on a regular basis. They could see the outline of weapons under her clothes and instinctively knew there were others. When someone who looked like that had one weapon, most of the time, they had a lot of them.

Strength and power radiated off her. She was either a bounty hunter or someone of great power. They didn't know what to take from that. If she was a bounty hunter, was it possible she was chasing down this human girl? That didn't make sense. Fae bounty hunters rarely pursued humans. She would have had to commit truly horrific crimes in order for that to happen, and they doubted that.

"Who are you?" the fae woman asked. "What are you doing here?"

"What do you mean what are we doing here?" Vivi asked defensively. "This is our school. We're the ones wondering what you two are doing here."

"She came through a portal in the wall," said Zander. "Actually, she fell through the portal. A gunshot followed her."

"It almost hit Zander," Luna said. "It followed right after her, and if she hadn't just fallen on her face when she made it through, it could have hit her."

"What's going on? Making a portal here is really stupid. There are humans around here. If it wasn't so early in the morning, she could have gotten caught falling out on the sidewalk," Carson said.

"She probably didn't even fall. She probably got thrown," Vivi said. "How would someone like her know how to use a portal otherwise?"

"We were on our way back to town and saw the portal forming. She hit the ground right in front of us and got up threatening us," Zander added.

Mia struggled to control herself through the fury coursing through her. She turned to Cassia, who was looking her up and down like she expected to find a grave injury she had missed in their first exchange.

"Are you all right?" the bounty hunter asked. Mia had more injuries than when Cassia had left the girl alone in the apartment complex. But nothing looked too bad. No obvious broken bones, since she was standing in a fighting stance. She also seemed to be fairly coherent, but all the blood did bother Cassia.

Mia shook her head adamantly. "No, I'm not all right. Are you hearing what just happened? What the heck is going on? How did I end up here? And where is here, anyway?"

Cassia smiled at her and took a few steps closer to the large gate. She gestured to a plaque on the stone beside the iron. "You're right where you need to be."

CHAPTER TWENTY

Luna, Vivi, Carson, and Zander were stunned by the declaration. They stared at Cassia in shock and surprise. Did she seriously just say this strange girl was where she was meant to be? What was that supposed to mean?

Vivi looked at the other three, waiting for one of them to say something. Especially Zander. He fancied himself the leader of their group, no matter how the others might feel about that particular issue. This would be the ideal situation for him to use some of those leadership aspirations to figure out what the heck was going on.

When he didn't, she moved forward. "You've got to be kidding me," she said, her arms flying up in the air before falling down by her sides. "Not only is this girl showing up out of some bizarre portal that showed up in the wall of *our* school, but now you're just waltzing in here, too? It's not enough for her to get chased by a bullet that could have hit any of us. Now you're saying this is where she belongs? You are severely mistaken. She doesn't belong here. We don't want her here. And while we're on the topic, who do you think you are, deciding something like that?"

The other three stared at her. The rude, mean outburst was a little more the speed they typically expected from Vivi. But coming in the face of strangers showing up and confronting them seemed both appropriate and out of character somehow. She wanted to exert her dominance and didn't like new people coming around, especially humans. But she wasn't just speaking for herself. That fit had been about all four of them. In her own way, she was defending them.

Zander understood her hesitation, but he was willing to be more open. There had to be a reason this girl had shown up here, and the woman was ready to not only protect her but had declared she was meant to be here. He looked at the girl again.

The suddenness of her arrival combined with her immediately going into fighting mode meant they hadn't had much of an opportunity to really look at her. The first thing he noticed about her was her eyes. Bright, vibrant green, and incredibly wide, they caught his attention even with the fear in them. From there, he saw the tangles of coppery red hair billowing down around her shoulders. It looked like she'd experienced something pretty difficult in the time before she'd come through the portal, but that's not what mattered.

It was the color. Naturally red hair wasn't the mark of a fae. It didn't exist among their kind. It was what had set her apart and made them immediately assume she was human. Of course, it was possible she did that intentionally. It could be her version of glamour. He knew plenty of fae and halflings who assumed a variety of different features when they used their glamour. None of the four of them had taken enough time or paid enough attention into looking beyond any glamour she might be using.

He leaned in a little and squinted at her. "Is she a halfling?" he asked. "This academy is only for halflings."

The girl turned slightly, and he realized she wasn't using glamour. Red was the natural color of her hair.

"Look at her," Carson snapped. "Of course she's not."

"When was the last time you heard of a student showing up through a portal in the wall around the grounds?" Vivi asked.

"But she did use the portal," Luna pointed out. "Have you ever known a human girl who could do something like that?"

"Again," Vivi snapped. "I think someone threw her. She pissed off the wrong fae, and they picked her up and tossed her through. Followed it up with shooting at her, hoping it would finish her off before she got where she was going."

"Vivi," Carson said, almost in warning.

"What? You heard the shot and you saw the bullet. Do you have a better explanation? I don't know about you, but I don't know of a lot of people who shoot at people when they want to give them a friendly goodbye," she said.

"That doesn't mean she did anything wrong," Luna said. "You saw how frightened she was. Maybe she didn't even know the people who shot at her."

"But how did she know how to use the portal?" Zander asked. "It's not like they have them just sitting around out in the human world with a sign explaining how to use them."

The woman stood with her arms crossed tightly over her chest, watching in disgust as the four young halflings argued over the girl. Zander finally pulled his attention away from the bickering to look at her. "Who are you?" he asked.

She tightened her arms over her chest and cocked her hip at him. "The daughter of the greatest bounty hunter ever known and protector of what could be."

Mia peered at Cassia out of the corner of her eye, but the four teens clearly understood the cryptic message. Immediately silent, they moved in a little tighter together. They exchanged glances and looked back and forth between themselves and the two who came through the portal. They communicated their questions and concerns to each other without having to say a word. Their eyes established Zander as their speaker, and he looked at the fae woman again.

"Who is this girl? Did she open that portal?" Zander asked.

The leather-clad woman straightened her spine and faced off with him. "Her name is Mia. She is being pursued by some very dangerous people for reasons we don't know, including bounty hunters, redcaps, and others. Today was a particularly difficult and treacherous day for her. I am acting as her guide and her protector, and I took her to a place where I thought she would be safe. It turned out not to be so.

There was already a boggart there, but Mia held her own against it. She fought him and enabled me to capture him without further incident. Unfortunately, that creature wasn't the only danger we faced. A redcap and a sluagh also appeared. As you can imagine, we weren't interested in spending much quality time with them," she said.

"Are you going to tell us she defeated those, too?" Vivi asked sarcastically.

Cassia's eyes moved over to the dark-haired girl. "Is there a reason you refuse to believe that?"

"Because it doesn't make sense. Human girls don't go around getting chased by fae bounty hunters and creatures like redcaps. It just doesn't happen. If it did, there would be chaos all over the place. Even if she did manage to cause enough trouble for herself that some of those creatures might be after her, she wouldn't be able to fight them." Vivi cocked a hip and looked disdainfully at Mia.

Cassia nodded slowly and looked at the others again. "The truth is, those creatures did come after her. We were able to avoid them but got split up when we reached the portal. She came through first and the redcap pursuing her shot at her. I followed after and ensured the portal was closed. It's really that simple."

"That still doesn't explain everything," Zander said. "Why would you say this is where she needs to be?"

"Because she does. She belongs here just as much as any of you. Mia is a halfling," Cassia said.

"She can't be." Vivi snapped. "Look at her hair. There are no fae with red hair."

The others continued to question her, not knowing that in the huge academy building beyond the wall, someone else knew something was happening just beyond the grounds and was going to make it known.

Principal Elmhurst strode down one of the large corridors of the school, heading for the library. She walked the same route several times a day and had done so for the vast majority of her life. It was so familiar to her, she barely thought about it. She didn't count the steps or try to figure out where she was in the walk. She didn't pay attention to what she saw on either side of her.

This academy was in her blood just as it had been for the generations before her. The entirety was imprinted on her mind, and at any given moment, she could describe the sprawling building, every room and nook, every piece of art, and every accolade. That was why she rarely ever acknowledged the gargoyles positioned in the corridor on either side of the entrance to the library.

The gargoyles weren't exactly the most pleasant features of the academy. They weren't all bad. Much of their negative attitudes came from being victims of their circumstances. Neither could leave their post, forced to remain exactly where they were so they could guard the library and as much of the academy as they could see.

One thing they actually enjoyed doing was reporting on the students as much as possible. Whenever Elmhurst came by, they had some little tidbit to tell her about misbehavior among the students, classes being skipped, cheating, or anything they could possibly come up with to cause difficulty for them.

Not that the principal blamed the creatures. Life wasn't easy for them, and the students were rarely compassionate about it. These gargoyles were often the recipient of incessant teasing and had been used for several practical jokes. More than half of which were orchestrated by Vivi.

"Headmistress," one said as she passed him. "You are awake and walking the school very early this morning."

"Hello, Steve. Yes, I had trouble sleeping and thought I could come for a book," Elmhurst said.

The gargoyle cringed at the sound of his name. It was one of the most challenging parts of his life and a tremendous contributor to his bad attitude. It was the same for the statue on the other side of the door. Steve and his partner, Dan, had the names bestowed on them by the first Elmhurst to run the academy.

The gargoyles had taken their place at the library when that

Elmhurst established the academy, and he'd given them names he'd thought were unique and interesting. Unheard of at the time, Dan and Steve were compelling monikers the creatures could be proud of. Of course, as time changed, so did the perception of their names.

Those titles became average and mundane, and being a gargoyle burdened with one of them they became even more miserable. They had no way to change their names or even what people called them. They were as stuck with the names as they were with their posts outside the library. It left them hating the students and wanting to cause as much difficulty for them as they possibly could.

Which was exactly what they wanted to do that day.

"I'm glad you did," Steve said. "I have something to tell you."

"Don't you always?" Elmhurst asked dismissively.

Most of the professors and other staff went to great lengths to ignore the gargoyles and not engage them in conversation. They tired of hearing the snippets of gossip and having to think of even more issues with the students. At least Principal Elmhurst acknowledged them. She thought that was enough for the morning.

"It's important," Steve insisted.

"It is," Dan said. "We thought you needed to know immediately."

"It can't wait until later?" Elmhurst asked. "I really do want to get this book. The day starts very soon, you know."

"Sure, it can wait. I'm sure it is not truly a concern that there are strange portals appearing on the grounds," Steve said.

That made the headmistress stop. "What do you mean strange portals on the academy grounds?"

"Not exactly on the grounds themselves, but very close. In the wall. Two opened just moments ago near the front gate. There are people gathered there, Headmistress."

"Thank you, Steve," she said and hurried out of the corridor and to the front door of the academy.

She rushed down the long path to the front gate, wondering what was going on and worrying about who might be involved. The gargoyles had the ability to perceive things happening around the academy. It allowed them to keep the buildings and the grounds safer. But they didn't know everything.

They couldn't tell her who created the portal or who was there. The principal was concerned that humans might have seen the portals form, not to mention whoever came through them. That could have devastating consequences for the academy.

There was also fear that whoever created the portal was trying to come onto the grounds and cause harm to the students. Enchantments prevented unapproved portals being formed within the grounds but having two form in the wall near the school was far too close for her comfort.

As she approached the heavy gate, movement flickered beyond the bars. It was brief, not enough to see the person's face, and Elmhurst moved faster. Finally, she reached the gate and opened it. Six people turned to look at her as she rushed down the sidewalk toward them. She withheld a gasp when she saw that four of them were who she referred to as the Scooby gang, the four halflings who had so much promise.

"Zander, Luna, Carson, Vivi, what are you doing?" she demanded as she approached. "What's going on?"

"We didn't have anything to do with this," Zander said. "We were heading to the practice field when we saw a portal open in the wall. Then this girl fell through. We've been trying to figure it out ever since."

There was something strange about the answer. She didn't want to think it was insincere, but it didn't seem to have the weight of all the information and details it should have. She turned to the other two to question them about them coming through the portal so close to her grounds and was shocked to see Cassia's face staring back at her.

"Did you do this?" she asked.

"The portal was a necessity," Cassia told her. "There was a very dangerous situation, and utilizing a portal was the only way to escape it."

"Where were you when you created it?" Elmhurst asked.

"China. Outside Shanghai," said Cassia.

"And what was the purpose of coming here? Surely there was another place to take this girl where she would be safe." Elmhurst gave Mia a cursory glance.

"Coming here wasn't the intention," Cassia said. "It was an unintended consequence, but it is where we needed to be."

"She already told us that," Vivi quipped bitterly.

"Mia, this is Principal Elmhurst. She is the headmistress of this academy. Her family established it many generations ago as a place for halfling fae to come and be trained in their skills. That's why I brought you here. Principal, this is Mia. I take full responsibility for her coming here today and for the way she arrived. But this is where she needs to be. She needs to be in your academy. Mia's a halfling who was just discovered."

CHAPTER TWENTY-ONE

Principal Elmhurst stared at the young girl who had made such an unexpected arrival at the academy. She looked so afraid, and yet there was also a strength about her, a confidence that radiated from her even through her confusion. This wasn't cockiness from the way she was raised or arrogance that came from ongoing praise for her skills. This was real and deeply ingrained within her. It was the type of strength that ran through her veins as a part of her blood. She was fascinating, and the principal still didn't know what to think of her.

The same couldn't be said about the Scooby gang. Zander, Carson, Vivi, and Luna had strong opinions about her arrival and the assertion from Cassia that this girl needed to stay.

"Again, trying to insist on this girl staying here," Vivi said. "That's ridiculous. I don't know who you think you are, but you can't just walk up to an institution like this and demand that any wayward halfling you came upon is good enough to be among us."

Vivi had heard the cryptic, almost threatening message from the woman when questioned about her identity, but it didn't impress her as much as it had the others. In Vivi's life, she had become accustomed to people thinking they were far more important than they really were. Any number of fae could claim to be whatever they wanted, and it was up to the people they spoke to to choose to believe them or not.

Vivi learned early on to believe no one. Too many times, she had watched this play out as people tried to persuade and impress her father, seeking to create a more powerful image for themselves through association with her family. It never worked.

"Honestly, Headmistress Elmhurst, you can't possibly be considering allowing this girl to join the academy when you know nothing about her," Carson said.

"You know nothing about her either," the fae woman who had come through the portal commented.

"It doesn't take much to know she can't possibly be good enough for Elmhurst Halfling Academy. This isn't a place just anyone can attend. It's extremely exclusive and difficult to get into." The Unseelie boy crossed his arms over his chest and huffed.

"I'm well aware of that," the woman said.

"Then you are also aware of the extensive prerequisites and aggressive learning environment," Luna said. "There are many other schools this girl could attend. She could go to one of the basic schools and accomplish the levels for halflings who aren't particularly skilled."

She delivered the comment as if she thought she was being kind. Luna believed she was being helpful, guiding this new halfling into a more appropriate situation than Elmhurst. The basic schools were the ones attended by halflings who didn't show much promise in academics or in their magical skills, or those who couldn't afford the heavy price that came with an education at Elmhurst. This was an academy only for those halflings who showed tremendous potential in their magic and control of their skills, or those from exorbitantly wealthy families who showed promise in other ways.

Students who went through the basic schools rarely amounted to much. They would get proper training in what little skills they did have and develop them as much as they could. After school, few would move on to college. Instead, they would go into service for wealthy fae families, or take menial jobs, like accounting, at one of the corporations.

"Luna's right," Zander offered. "The basic schools could be the perfect pace for her. If she's only just now discovering she's a halfling, she can't possibly have the understanding of her skills and abilities necessary to keep up here. At this point, she's probably too old to catch up. Going to one of those schools will help to make the most of what she does have and give her a path after graduation. She could get a steady job at one of the corporations and be just fine."

"Don't build her up too much," Vivi snarled. "She wouldn't even be good enough to work as a janitor for my uncle's company."

"I don't know," Luna said, trying to be as gentle as she could and not completely smash the hopes, dreams, and self-esteem of the new halfling. "That's not necessarily true. Maybe she could be a janitor."

Vivi tossed another scathing look in Mia's direction and rolled her eyes. "I doubt it. Maybe a bit lower. An accountant, perhaps. I mean, it's a stretch, but if she really applied herself, she might be able to squeeze out enough intellect and skill to manage that type of position."

In her mind, a janitor was a better position than an accountant, and Vivi had trouble imagining how someone who got all the way into her late teens without knowing she was a halfling would ever have the skills and abilities to take on any role. She would only end up embarrassing herself and causing difficulty for the company who employed her.

Mia narrowed her eyes at the dark-haired girl.

Vivi's hands clenched and her chest tightened uncomfortably. This new girl was beautiful, and it made Vivi's skin crawl. She disliked being around anyone she thought was prettier than her, and the envy this caused often turned those girls into targets for Vivi's unpleasant jokes.

"That's enough," Principal Elmhurst finally said. "I don't believe any of you were asked for your opinion. For people who are acting so proud of the academy they attend, you aren't putting much effort into being kind and welcoming ambassadors. I will say I understand your concerns and have heard what you had to say about Mia. But you must understand that when it comes to who is admitted into the Elmhurst Academy, the decision lies squarely and solely with me. I don't take into account the opinions of young students when determining who will be given the opportunity for an education here. This is only more Court politics, and I won't stand for it. You know that."

"Yes, Principal Elmhurst," all four of the Scooby gang replied solemnly.

The principal gave a nod and smiled at them. "Good. Now, the four of you should be getting to practice. From what I've seen, you still have a long way to go. I will speak with Mia and Cassia in my office."

The name struck Zander hard. He looked at Carson, Luna, and Vivi, who were having the same reaction. They had known the beautiful woman who'd come through the portal after Mia was powerful in some way. She even introduced herself as the daughter of the greatest of their time, and her clothing suggested she was a bounty hunter. But none of them had known just how accurate her comment was.

They hadn't heard her name yet, and now that they had, they were all struck that they were able to meet the legendary bounty hunter. She truly was the daughter of the greatest of their time, and her presence exuded the same type of confidence, telling them she was as exceptional at her job as her father had been.

Cassia gave them all a long and knowing stare before turning to follow Principal Elmhurst through the gate and up the path toward the school. The building loomed in front of them, stately and impressive. It had the strength that came from being established and secure but still felt exciting and full of possibilities. Every student who came through the halls and every new skill discovered created more potential and renewed the commitment to excellence that led to the Elmhurst family establishing the school so long ago.

Principal Elmhurst led them through the huge arched doors into the building. They followed her along the quiet corridors in silence.

Mia thought about the four teenagers she'd just met. Actually, she hadn't met them at all. Nobody had offered their names; they'd only demanded to know who she was and why she was there. They had made it abundantly clear she wasn't welcome, and that they didn't believe she belonged among them.

Mia didn't know why that bothered her so much. She didn't know what this place was or what made the four other young halflings they'd just encountered so special. Yet, the insinuation that she wasn't as good as they were and therefore shouldn't be allowed to be a part of their school was deeply insulting. It wasn't just the feeling of being left out or made fun of. It cut deeper in a way she didn't really understand.

Finally, they arrived at an impressive dark wooden door. Principal Elmhurst swept her hand in front of her and the door unlatched, swinging open to allow them inside. Mia and Cassia followed, both looking around to take in as much of the rich, beautiful surroundings as they could while the headmistress led them to another door. Everything around them was in deep shades of blue and purple, with occasional accents of white. Large display cases lined either side of the lobby or reception area of the office. Deeply inset lights glowed on trophies, insignia, and other awards on the shelves.

They went through the second door into the main office. Principal Elmhurst took the tall wingback chair behind an elaborately carved wooden desk and gestured to the two chairs across from her.

"Please, sit," she invited.

Cassia and Mia settled into the seats and looked across the desk at the headmistress expectantly. Her eyes swept across them, evaluating them and trying to decide how to proceed. She was calm, any anxiety that had built within her after finding out about the portals opening had long dissipated. Now she was just curious.

It was unusual for anyone to show up at the academy unannounced. The last term had ended several weeks before and the new one would not begin for several more. Existing students wouldn't return to the campus until a few days before classes began again, and the newest students would only arrive a few days before that. Mia was unusual, and Principal Elmhurst needed to know more about her.

"Tell me again how you came to arrive through the portal," she said.

Cassia and Mia exchanged glances. Mia noticed the changes Cassia made to the story about her arrival and didn't know if she wanted to keep up that story or tell how it actually happened. She chose to stay quiet and allow the bounty hunter to make the explanations. Cassia seemed more secure in what was happening, and Mia was prepared to follow along.

Cassia gave the same explanation to Principal Elmhurst as she had to the two boys and two girls earlier. She'd changed the details slightly, but significantly. It wasn't lost on the young halfling that Cassia had avoided telling any of them how the portal had come to be in the first place.

She skirted around the issue, seamlessly going from the creatures pursuing Mia to them entering the portal in order to stay safe. Mia was curious about this, wondering at the meaning behind the changes made to the story. But she stayed quiet. Cassia knew what she was doing. At least, Mia hoped she did.

"Do you understand just how dangerous it was for that portal to open out onto the sidewalk in front of our school?" Principal Elmhurst asked.

"Yes," the bounty hunter said. "I apologize for that. It wasn't our intention at all to put the academy or any of the students at risk. As I said, we traveled through the portal to avoid extreme danger. It brought us here, which I believe is exactly the place we needed to be."

"So, it was a portal of need rather than one of direction," the head-mistress said. It wasn't really a question, but a statement, an acknowledgment of her understanding.

Cassia replied. "Yes. I believe it was."

The principal nodded slowly and turned her attention to Mia. "Would you please step outside for a moment? I'd like to speak to your guardian."

Mia looked at Cassia, who nodded. "Go ahead and just wait right outside. We'll come for you soon," she said.

Mia exited the office and closed the door behind her. When her footsteps faded away, Cassia turned back to Principal Elmhurst.

"This is unprecedented, Cassia," the headmistress said.

"I know," she said. "It is highly unusual, and I apologize for any inconvenience or discomfort we've caused. But I'm telling you, she needs to be here. The portal wouldn't have brought us to this place if it wasn't where she was supposed to be. You know that. She needs to be among her own kind and learn the skills and abilities she's missed out on. This is where she's going to be safest and be able to make the most of herself."

"You understand this is not an ordinary school. While they could have chosen their words more diplomatically, Zander, Carson, Luna, and Vivi were right when they talked about the other halfling schools. This is an extremely prestigious academy. We turn away students every year."

"I understand that. That's why I'm asking you to recognize that she needs to be here," Cassia implored.

"The deadline is past for any scholarships that would be able to defray the cost of tuition and accommodations while she's here. I won't mince words when I tell you the quality of the education and facilities of this academy come at a premium price," Elmhurst said matter-of-factly.

"I'm well aware of the expense of attending this academy," Cassia said. "I'm prepared to cover it. I will pay Mia's fees and send her a monthly stipend."

The cost of attending the academy was high, but Cassia knew she could manage it. With all of the extra bounties she had brought in recently, she had more money than ever before. Especially after the amount she'd earned from capturing the brutal serial killer redcap. Just as Fan had told her at the prison when she'd brought in the boggart, she was a very rich female. She had little need for so much money. Her living expenses rarely amounted to much, and though she'd enjoy having a little padding in her account to ensure she could cover anything that came up, other than her penchant for anime, she could think of no better use for the money than to support and protect Mia. She could always buy the red sailor moon costume next year. The bounty from the redcap alone was enough to pay tuition, room, and board for the remainder of Mia's high school career, and that was what Cassia intended to do with it.

"Even if you are capable of paying the cost, I'm concerned about her ability to fit in with the rest of the students," Elmhurst admitted. "These are exceptionally talented and powerful halflings. They've been learning skills and sharpening their ability to use them their entire lives. I'm worried having just found out about her fae heritage will mean that Mia will be too far behind in her skills. I have no doubt she would probably be just fine in the academics portion of her education, but what about her magic? She is fully untrained, and according to you, didn't even know she was fae until a few days ago. I'm concerned she will quickly fall behind in such an advanced and aggressive program. She can't expect the other students to slow down to accommodate her, or the professors to take extra time to teach down to her. The goal of this academy is to produce the strongest halflings possible."

"I understand that," Cassia said. She couldn't help the smirk which came to her lips. "But I assure you Mia will be fine."

"How can you be sure of that?" the headmistress asked.

Cassia considered how to respond. She had to be careful with her words and not reveal too much too soon. Just as she had with the Scooby gang and the first time she told the story to Principal Elmhurst, she didn't go into full detail about the portal.

She didn't want to tell anyone yet that Mia had been the one to open her own portal to come here. It was an incredible feat, one that made Cassia believe her young ward was going to be very powerful. But in order to assume that power and make the absolute most of her skills and abilities, she needed the right tutelage. Having the highest quality education available to her would ensure she could rise to what was innately within her.

"I've witnessed it myself," she told the principal. "I have experienced moments of her power and seen her use skills she didn't know she had. I've watched her fight various creatures, even a redcap, and survive. Well before she knew the truth about herself, she could perceive magical creatures and didn't panic. She handled them with confidence and grace. She's courageous and unafraid to defend herself and those around her. She is the one who defeated and captured a boggart I just brought in to Forasaon. If you need assurance of her abilities, you are more than welcome to speak with Faylynne, the head jailer there. He will confirm I brought a boggart in and tell you of the condition it was in upon arrival. Mia definitely has exceptional talents. She is just untrained and doesn't know what all she can do yet."

Cassia knew if the principal heard from Fan how thoroughly defeated the boggart was when she'd brought him into the prison, Elmhurst would have to believe in Mia's skill.

"I don't think that is necessary. I will take your word for it," Elmhurst said.

"Thank you," Cassia said, smiling.

"But," the principal continued, "I will only accept her for one semester. She'll be expected to assimilate with the other students and to the school environment as any other student. She will have the same standards and expectations as everyone else. I will ensure there are others available to help bring her up to speed, but she will need to apply herself and demonstrate that she does, in fact, belong among our students. One semester, Cassia. If she does not prove herself, she will need to be transferred to one of the basic academies at the end of the semester."

Cassia nodded. "I understand. She won't disappoint you."

<hr>

Before Cassia left, she took Mia aside and spoke to her. "Mia, I need you to stay here and learn as much as you can about your newfound abilities."

"But why? Why can't I go home and find a tutor there?" Mia knew her voice sounded whiney, but she missed her dad already and wanted to go back to a place that felt familiar. With all of the new revelations since that night in the Chinese night market, she craved normalcy. Staying at an academy where she wasn't wanted, wasn't going to help her feel any better about who she'd become.

"There isn't anyone who can tutor you. This place is safe and is the only academy that can help you to uncover all your potential. You need to work hard and stay under the radar as much as possible. If no one knows you're here, then you'll be safe." The bounty hunter still wasn't sure what was so special about this halfling, but there had to be something considering all of the attention she had received lately.

"What about my father? He'll worry about me and call the police. He knows he doesn't have a sister in China." While Master Chen and Becky's memories had been messed with, no one had said anything to her father—that she was aware of. He would worry a great deal about her if she didn't show up when she was supposed to.

"Don't worry about your father. I'll come up with a cover story to keep you safe."

Mia waved her hands. "No, I don't want you messing with my dad's memories. That can't be good for him, can it?" While she didn't know anything about magic, she couldn't believe that messing with the memories of humans was safe. Her dad had to be human, he would have told her who she was if *he* was the fae parent.

While she hadn't had much time to think about it, her mother had to be the fae parent. Was her mom even dead? Or did she disappear on her husband and daughter right after Mia was born?

Cassia took Mia by the shoulders. "Listen to me. You are in real danger. That danger will follow you around. Do you want anything bad to happen to your dad or Becky? Or anyone else you care about?"

She hadn't thought that far ahead. Mia shook her head. "No, I don't want them to have to deal with what I've seen this past week."

"Then stay here and let me talk to your dad. What's your address? I promise I won't hurt him. He'll just think you're in China still, training." Cassia would have to come up with a better story, but it was enough of a start that by the time she reached Mia's dad, she'd have a better one to convince him of.

Mia nodded. "All right, but if you hurt my dad, I swear you'll regret it."

The intense emotion behind Mia's words and the stony stare impressed Cassia.

"As I said, you're right where you need to be." Cassia turned and left the school.

CHAPTER TWENTY-TWO

With so few students around, and a desire to keep them all together, Mia was given a room near Luna and Vivi. As in, right beside them. To say Vivi didn't take it well would be an understatement.

Every night was an adventure in whatever torment and torture Vivi was going to plot for Mia, who, for the most part, didn't react. She kept her cool and tried to accept the practical jokes as the kind of ribbing that should be expected any time teenagers were left to their own devices. Especially when someone new entered their social circles. It still bothered her though, and while she wouldn't let Vivi know, a few weeks into the relentless mocking and tricks, Mia was about done with it.

Vivi, for her part, decided she was going to have fun with Mia. If she could get the new girl to quit and leave the academy, then great, but if not, she was going to enjoy knocking the pretty smile off her face at every possible opportunity. The hot water trick was especially diabolical, she thought.

One morning when Mia went into the shower, Vivi snuck behind her and placed a hex on the water heater. Using an incantation, she raised and lowered the temperature of the water at random intervals, going from ice cold to scalding hot in a matter of seconds, causing Mia to leave the shower, her skin beet red, and shampoo still in her hair.

Vivi laughed for days at the look on her face, the towel wrapped around her haphazardly, as Mia stomped out of the shower and into her room. She had glared at Vivi, but she'd lacked proof she had anything to do with it.

Then, there were the missing pens. That took more planning but was worth the aggravation. Every chance she got, Vivi would cast a vanishing spell on the pen Mia was using. At first, she would stop what she was doing and look around her desk or start digging through her bag for her lost pen, but eventually, she just started bringing whole canisters of pens with her to the library where she was receiving tutoring in advance of the semester. If Vivi made one disappear, she would just grab another. One time, Vivi made the entire canister disappear, but Mia just reached into her bag and pulled out another can and a new bag of pens. She opened the bag, dumped the pens inside the can then bore a hole through Vivi with an icy stare.

But nothing could compare to the knockout punch Vivi planned for this day. It had been a solid week without doing anything to her, and it was absolute torture, but it was imperative for Mia to think Vivi had given up. She needed to get comfortable and trust that things were normal again in order for this trick to work in all of its multiple parts.

When Vivi arrived early for lunch, she scouted out the best possible seat, directly in the middle of the cafeteria, and sat so she could watch people come out of the line and head to their seats. Mia had been sitting at the same table—the farthest away from the line— every day, so she would most certainly come by where Vivi sat. Vivi had brought an apple and a bottled water with her for lunch rather than going through the line to make sure she had plenty of time to wait for Mia.

But Mia was taking her time, and Vivi was getting anxious. The cafeteria was filling up, and some people were sitting near Mia's regular seat, meaning she might choose somewhere else and blow the whole plan apart. Vivi was about to move a little farther down when Mia came out and approached her usual spot with her tray in her hand.

Normally, she walked with her eyes somewhat downcast, but today she seemed more confident, like she was in a really good mood. That was only going to make this trick all the more delicious.

As Mia got closer, Vivi put her plan into action, using a conjuring spell she'd learned just for the occasion. Suddenly, in Mia's path, just under the foot that was coming down, a banana peel appeared. The trick was cheesy, but that was the point. Who actually slipped on banana peels?

Mia did.

Her leg slid out from under her and shot up in the air, and the rest of her body went airborne. The tray flew out of her hands, and a second spell hit it just in time. As Mia crashed to the ground, the empty platter bounced off her head, the food still floating above her.

Struggling to sit up, Mia glared at Vivi, who smiled and waved. Then she pointed up, and Mia followed the direction of her finger to see the food still hovering. Just when Mia's expression shifted as she figured out what was about to happen, Vivi released the spell and the warm, wet pasta and marinara sauce dropped on the new girl's face. The sauce stained her clothes and colored her hair.

For a moment, the only sound in the room was the laughter of the kids who had witnessed what had happened. Mia sat in the mess, allowing the humiliation and shame to wash over her before she slowly got to her feet and stared Vivi dead in the eyes.

The other girl stood, shrugging as Mia picked up her tray. She aimed it at Vivi and swung her hand, ready to hurl it. Seeing it coming, Vivi began a spell to stop her, but Mia thrust out her free hand, fingers curled into a fist as if she had punched the air in front of her.

Vivi flew across the room, crashing into the wall and sliding down. Mia had done something, but even *she* didn't know what. It was powerful though, and Vivi moaned at the pain in her back from hitting the wall. Mia took off for her room, leaving the mess of food on the floor as Vivi tried to stand.

"What are you looking at?" she yelled at the tables full of other students who were now looking at her wide-eyed. No one had ever stopped Vivi mid-trick before. Not with magic like that. No one had ever publicly humiliated her by slamming her against a wall either. Fury built up inside her as she too stormed off to her room, leaving the full cafeteria free to gossip and laugh.

Vivi was still stinging from the embarrassment of the prank gone wrong the next day when Principal Elmhurst appeared in their dorm to get Mia.

"You have a visitor," the principal said.

Mia suspected her visitor would be Cassia. The bounty hunter was the only person who knew where she was. But it still made her smile when the headmistress led her to the courtyard at the back of the school and she spotted the fae woman looking out over a low stone wall at the grounds surrounding the building. Mia came to stand beside her and followed her gaze to see what had captured her attention.

The courtyard was mostly contained between two sections of the academy building, but a gap in the architecture allowed them to see out beyond the campus onto the rolling grounds behind the school. From this perspective, it appeared as though the grounds went on forever. Ahead of them, the early morning fog blanketed a hedge maze making it look eerie against the rest of the picturesque landscape.

"We went into the maze earlier this week," Mia said.

"Is it as confusing as it looks from up here?" the bounty hunter asked.

"No," Mia said, shaking her head. "It's worse. It changes while you're in it to test your memory and thought. And probably something about magic. I don't know."

Cassia laughed. "I'm glad it's been so valuable to be here."

"I was just distracted by Carson. He got frustrated in the first ten seconds we were in there and ended up just blasting a hole in the hedge to get out."

"How did that go for him?" Cassia asked.

"Not well. The hedge swallowed him and held him for about an hour. Then he had to deal with Principal Elmhurst. It wasn't a good day for him. But I liked the maze," Mia said.

"That's good. So, you probably know why I came here today."

Mia didn't look at her. She didn't want to see the expression in Cassia's eyes and know what she was going to say before it came out. If it was going to be bad, Mia preferred to hang on to her ignorance for as long as possible.

She nodded. "You went to talk to my father again?" Mia's whispered words sounded pained.

Mia had spoken to Cassia after she went to see her dad, and Cassia had assured her he was okay. Whenever they'd emailed each other, he had seemed fine, but Mia still worried about her dad and his safety. And about how the memory invasion would affect him long term.

Their cover story had been that Mia had received an offer to stay in China to study under a Wushu Master of some renown. Because she had done so well, no one questioned the story. Mia's dad was so proud of his daughter and knew it was an honor, so even though he missed her, he'd let her stay.

Cassia had promised she would handle it, but Mia worried that hurting the people she loved would become just another part of her challenges as she struggled to wrap her head around the truth about herself.

Now the bounty hunter was finally back to tell her exactly what happened.

"Yes," Cassia said.

"How is he?" Mia asked. "Was he worried about me?"

"He has no reason to be worried," she admitted. "He truly believes the cover story. He looks forward to your weekly emails, so keep them up. What's important is that he's doing just fine and isn't concerned about you right now."

"I'm glad to hear he's doing well." And she was, but she really did miss him. It had been just the two of them her entire life. Or at least for as long as she could remember. Her mom had been around for her first few months, but she'd died before Mia was a year old. Her dad was all she had as far as family went.

Becky was her best friend. They told each other everything. Mia really wished she could tell Becky the truth. She'd know exactly how to handle Vivi and the other students who were treating her so horribly.

"I didn't give him any sort of timeline or anything, so he isn't expecting you back anytime soon. I modified his memories, so he believes you called him yourself to tell him the good news. That way, he can spread the word to friends and family, so they aren't wondering where you are."

Mia drew in a breath. "There is no other family. It's just the two of us. Always has been."

Cassia nodded. "I know how that feels." She gave Mia a quick hug around the shoulders, then rubbed her back encouragingly. "But he's very happy for you. He says you are amazingly talented, and he knows you're going to get really far. I think part of him was hoping something like that would happen for you while you were in China."

"Really?"

Cassia nodded. "He's extremely proud of you, Mia. He thinks you're incredible."

"I think he's pretty great, too." Mia hung her head. "I don't want to upset him. I know it's going to be hard for us to be apart."

"It will. I know you'll miss him and he's going to miss you. Which reminds me, you're going to need to call him at weird hours and send emails home, as if you're still training in China. You should do the same for your friends from the competition and your old instructor. I manipulated their memories the same way I did your father's, so they think you're back in China getting trained as well. It's important to maintain a consistent story for all of them."

"Yeah, I figured as much. I've been sending them emails late at night mostly because that's the only time I can do it," Mia said.

Her voice trembled slightly. She was still getting accustomed to the new life she had been thrown into without any warning. Before she'd left for China for the Wushu competition, her thoughts of the world had been pretty much limited to Pasadena.

She thought of little other than school and training and had never imagined anything beyond that. Going to Shanghai for the competition was the biggest thrill of her life, something she had looked forward to and planned for months. It was so much bigger than anything she'd experienced, and she believed she would go back to Pasadena carrying those memories and never have anything to compare them to.

Then suddenly, everything changed. It was that fast. She went from knowing her life and who she was to all she ever believed suddenly shifting and coming under question. Her life was completely different now, and it would never be the same again. It was exciting but frightening and disorienting at the same time. She missed her father, Becky, and her other friends, and had moments when she felt isolated and alone.

"I know this is hard for you," Cassia said. "But you need to remind yourself that this is where you're supposed to be. You are fae, Mia. That is who you are. The abilities and skills within you are yours. They've been there since the moment you were born, just waiting for you to discover them. Now that you have, you owe it to yourself to learn more about them and make yourself the most you can possibly be."

"I know," Mia said softly. "I'm trying."

"And you're doing well." When Mia only nodded, Cassia took hold of her chin and turned the younger girl's face toward her so she could meet her bright green eyes. "You also need to remember why we came here in the first place. There are people after you, Mia. I still haven't figured out why, but you're being pursued by very dangerous creatures. You need to learn to defend yourself. I know you have tremendous skill in your martial arts, and you are a powerful fighter. I've seen that for myself. But that will only carry you so far. There will come a time when you'll need to face off against those who don't want to just use their hands or weapons to battle. When that time comes, you need to be able to fight on their terms."

"I will," Mia assured her.

Cassia nodded. "Good. Now, I'm going to be away for a while. I have another assignment in San Diego. Principal Elmhurst knows how to get in touch with me if there is an emergency. Everything is taken care of for you, and I've created a fae account for you. There's money in there, and I'll send you more each month."

"You don't have to do that," Mia said.

Cassia nodded again, staring directly into the younger woman's eyes. "I want to. I want what's best for you. Now, come on. Walk me out."

They were headed through the building again when the headmistress appeared. "Cassia, you're leaving already?" she asked.

"Yes. I have to be in San Diego for another assignment tonight, so I have to find a place where I can create a portal," Cassia replied.

"You can use one of the school portals," Elmhurst offered. "We don't have one to San Diego, but there's one that will bring you to a transportation depot where you can move on. Do you have everything you need?"

Cassia patted the bag hanging over one hip and nodded. "Yes. And thank you. That will be very helpful." She knew the school was guarded against unapproved portals, which was just one more reason Mia's portal was so strange. Even though it was on the outside of the school's fence, it still shouldn't have worked. The fae magic behind the blocking spell was just as powerful as the one going in and out of Forasaon. It shouldn't have worked.

At the very least, Mia should have been sent right back to where she'd started, or at the worst, lost in the void.

"Oh, headmistress. One more thing. You might want to check the spell protecting the academy from unauthorized portals. Especially where we opened one." Cassia shrugged. It wasn't like Mia did it on purpose or even knew where she was headed. But still, the portal shouldn't have worked, and she worried they might have left a rift in the wall. Possibly allowing someone else to take advantage of what Mia had done.

Principal Elmhurst smirked. "Did it the second I had Mia settled."

She shook her head. "I don't know how you opened it there, but everything is fine. There wasn't even a dent in the spell protecting the school. In fact, if it weren't for the gargoyles, I never would have known a portal opened."

Cassia raised her eyebrows. "You have gargoyles?"

"Of course. The library has two stationed outside, and they are in tune with the entire campus, and even parts of town." Elmhurst stood tall, as though she was proud of the security protections she had. Not many schools had gargoyles. Certainly, none had any as in tune as Steve and Dan.

Cassia whispered in Mia's ear, "Make sure you befriend the gargoyles. They will help to keep you safe."

Mia nodded. She wasn't sure what she was supposed to do with gargoyles, but if they were important, she'd find a way.

They proceeded through the corridors until they reached a large octagonal room. Fae stood guard at the door but moved out of the way when Elmhurst approached. Inside, more fae were positioned at the junctures of the walls to provide full protection of the room. The principal brought Cassia up to one of the walls and gestured toward it.

"Whenever you're ready. Have a good journey. I'll see you when you return."

"Thank you," Cassia said again.

When the principal left, Cassia turned to the wall and conjured the portal. Mia watched in fascination as the swirling vortex appeared. Cassia said goodbye and waved as she entered the portal and disappeared. The wall closed behind her, leaving Mia staring at nothing but a blank expanse.

Finally, she turned and left the room. She was a few strides down the hallway when Luna and Zander turned the corner.

"Hi, Mia," Luna said. "Are you all right? You look upset."

"No," Mia said, shaking her head. "Not upset. Just..." she glanced briefly over her shoulder, "will we learn how to make portals?"

Luna and Zander glanced at each other, then turned to Mia. "No. We can't do that."

"Why not?" Mia asked.

"We're halflings. No halfling can create a portal," Zander replied.

Mia started to say something, then stopped. She wanted to keep her secret skill to herself, and Cassia must have had a very good reason to take the credit for opening the portal. Mia still didn't fully understand how she'd made the portal appear, or why it had brought her here to the academy. Instinct told her not to share that information until she learned more.

That was the day she started frequenting the library on her own. Foregoing spending time with the others in the mornings, she immediately went to the library by herself and pored over the huge volumes. Scanning their thick pages and complex language, she looked up everything she could find on both portals and what halflings were capable of doing.

As she searched, she tried to find any information that might be available on her mother. Mia needed to know who she was and what had happened to her.

If only she could call her dad and ask him. She couldn't risk it, but he had to know who her mother was, didn't he?

CHAPTER TWENTY-THREE

The rest of the summer, just a few weeks, seemed to be an exercise in frustration for Mia. The headmaster assigned two girls to help her try to catch up on some of the more basic skills and tasks. It hadn't really worked all that well. No matter what the girls tried to teach Mia, it just never seemed to take. Even small, easy spells eluded her.

A lesson in conjuring, in which the girls had showed her how to produce a flower, had gone nowhere. Flower conjuring was something little halfling girls learned before they could write. They'd frolic in the fields creating flowers to play in as tiny children, graduating to Faerie circles when they were only slightly older. But Mia struggled to produce anything.

Frustration built every day that Mia couldn't figure it out. The girls would show her how, she seemed to understand it, then she would try it and...nothing. Nothing would happen at all. It was in those moments she would doubt her abilities and wonder if she were in the right place. Then she would go back to her room, and Vivi would have laid out some trick, and Mia, without thinking, would defend herself.

One day, Vivi tried to trap her inside a room by removing the doorknob and locking the door. Mia realized too late that Vivi had tricked her into entering the room by telling her the headmistress wanted to see her there. When Mia turned around to leave, the doorknob was missing.

"Very funny, Vivi," she said, her face pressed against the door. "Let me out."

"Let yourself out, Mia. It's just a simple conjuring spell. Just conjure a doorknob and come on out."

"Vivi, you know I am having trouble with conjuring. Just let me out, will you?"

"Sorry, Mia, I have a lunch date with Luna. I have to go. Bye," she said, lowering the volume of her voice to make it sound like she was running away. She stomped her feet lighter and lighter to make it more realistic.

Mia wasn't convinced.

"I know you're still there, Vivi." Silence greeted her, but Mia could swear she heard the faintest of snickering. "I swear if I can get out of here and you are still standing there—"

What, exactly? She didn't know how to do any spells to attack yet, and she certainly couldn't promise to return the favor of a practical joke. All she could do, so far, was defend herself, and she could only do that in very specific circumstances, and only when she wasn't thinking about it. If she concentrated on trying to defend herself, her mouth would go dry and she wouldn't be able to think clearly, and then nothing would happen.

Mia let out a groan of frustration and tried to think of something else. It wasn't long before she leaned back against a bookshelf and closed her eyes. As she drifted off to sleep, her mind wandered to all the different ways she would exact revenge if she could control her own abilities. After some time passed, though Mia wasn't sure how long, a loud banging sound startled her awake.

The door flew open, and Mia, struggling to figure out where she was and what was going on, threw her hands up in the air to defend herself. Tables soared into the air and slammed against the walls.

Books zoomed off the shelves and clattered into the center of the room, and Mia herself seemed to lift off the ground, defying gravity for just a moment, before she settled back onto her feet. She dropped into a stance from her Wushu training, prepared to fight.

Standing across from her were Luna, Vivi and Principal Elmhurst.

"I do apologize for startling you," Principal Elmhurst said primly. The barest trace of a smile crossed her lips. "I trust this sort of incident will not be happening again," she said, glancing at Vivi before facing Mia, who was still breathing heavily, her heart racing. "But if it does, I will be sure to knock."

Principal Elmhurst turned and left the room. Vivi followed, her face contorted in anger and frustration. Luna, on the other hand, stood there, her mouth agape, blinking every so often, until a giant grin broke out across her face.

"Crickets, that was awesome," she finally said.

"I was surprised. I had to defend myself," Mia muttered, dropping the fighting stance and sitting back down on the floor.

"Remind me never to fight you then," Luna said, sitting down cross-legged in front of her.

Mia stared at her quizzically for a moment. "I guess you need the room," Mia said, "I'll clean up in a minute and leave you to it, I just need a second to calm down."

"Oh, I don't need the room," Luna said.

"Then what?" Mia asked, trying to extract an answer out of Luna.

It took a moment for Luna to realize the words bouncing around in her head weren't coming out of her mouth, and she laughed. "Oh, sorry. I just...I don't see people around here who can defend themselves quite like that. What you just did was really cool."

"It was?" Mia's brows furrowed in confusion.

"Yes, very cool," Luna said, and Mia risked a smile. Luna didn't seem like the type to play practical jokes, and Mia was willing to open up a little around her. "Stuff like that, kids our age can't do. I know Principal Elmhurst was shocked, I could see it on her face. The levitating thing, that was sick."

Mia was grinning now. Getting compliments from Cassia was

cool, but receiving them from her peers at the academy was something else entirely. Especially after so much failure at the simple stuff.

"So, do you want to practice sometime? I know a bunch of Krav Maga and Tai Kwon Do stuff I'd love to work on, and the stance you took, was it Wushu?" Excitement filled Luna's voice as she rattled on.

Mia nodded excitedly. "Yes, it was. I've trained for a long time."

"Then come on, we have a great gym that's outfitted with everything we could possibly need." Luna stood abruptly. She held out a hand for Mia, who took it, and they walked out together.

When they arrived at the gym, they wasted no time in getting right into the heart of self-defense practice. Considering this was all martial art and no magical abilities, Mia felt far more comfortable, and Luna was easy to have fun with. Playful katas turned into full-on attack scenarios, and they began to bond over their shared love of martial arts.

Several days later, Principal Elmhurst sat in her office, looking at the pictures of Zander, Vivi, Carson, and Luna spread out across her desk. She'd been sitting like that all morning, contemplating the group she'd created and all they had accomplished together.

But there was still a gap, still a place open in the collaboration. Filling that place would bring their number from four to the elusive five, giving them the opportunity to accomplish even higher feats of skill and power.

They had the potential. She knew they did. These four young halflings were the most incredible she'd ever encountered. All the years she'd spent teaching and guiding halflings, she had never seen power and skills as exceptional as her Scooby gang possessed. They were phenomenal in their talent and could be even better. The Power of Five wasn't fantasy or an abstract concept. It was very real, and *this* could be the time it finally happened within her academy.

But choosing the fifth member of the group was a major decision. She couldn't take it lightly. Selecting the wrong fifth could hold back the other four and prevent them from ever accomplishing what they were truly capable of. The biggest problem was she would never really know. There would be no way to tell if they failed because they'd never had the ability to begin with, or if they were simply being dragged down by a member who didn't fit the position.

The search for the fifth member was exhausting. The team she sent out had scoured every academy, every training ground. They explored the chance it was a younger halfling, though the potential of that being true was next to nothing. They investigated older halflings with more training. But they hadn't found anyone who could begin to match what these four could do. None seemed right to her and she rejected them as soon as the team gave their suggestions.

But things might be different now. She reached in front of her to pick up the photograph set at the top of the desk. It was a shot taken on the grounds of the academy, with the student standing just beyond the hedge maze. Her long red hair glittered in the sunlight as Mia had glanced over her shoulder at someone or something not in the frame.

When she first appeared through the inexplicable portal just beyond the grounds, Principal Elmhurst never would have imagined Mia could be everything Cassia promised. The possibility of Mia taking the fifth spot hadn't crossed her mind. She was concerned the young woman wouldn't be able to keep up, but her opinion was different now.

After watching her train with the others and seeing how she handled Vivi, it was obvious that the legendary bounty hunter who had accompanied the halfling here hadn't been exaggerating her abilities. Mia was still new and required training, but the talent and ability built into her were astounding.

Principal Elmhurst set down the picture and called in her assistant, asking for the four as well as Mia to come to the office. Gathering the pictures, she stashed them away in a drawer so they wouldn't be seen, and then she waited. It only took a few minutes for them to trickle in, and as soon as she saw the five of them standing there together in front of her, she knew she was making the right decision. There was no way to really explain it—nothing that would make sense—but she felt it deep inside her.

There was no reason to skate around the issue or try to present it gently. She folded her hands on her desk and looked into the faces of each of the young fae in front of her.

"I have decided that Mia is the fifth member of your group," she announced.

Disappointment, frustration, hesitation, and anger flickered across the faces of the original four. Some emotions showed up in greater intensity on some faces more than others. While Luna stared back at her with more concern and hesitation, Vivi was visibly infuriated.

That was nothing Principal Elmhurst didn't expect. Vivi hadn't wanted to be a part of the group as it was. There wasn't anyone they could present as the fifth member who she would accept willingly and happily. This was something she simply had to deal with, regardless of her feelings. Which didn't mean Vivi was going down without a fight.

"First, we had to deal with her coming here and getting shoved into our academy. Then, we had to have her live next door to us and be a part of our training. We had to play with her and try to teach her baby skills. We might as well be helping with her teething, and now you want to force her into the fifth position of our group?" Vivi demanded.

"Yes, I do," Elmhurst said. "She is the right one for the position."

"I don't know," Mia started.

"See? She doesn't think she can do it, either," Carson said.

"I didn't say that," Mia argued.

"But it's true," Vivi said. "There's no way she can hold her own in this group. She's not going to be any sort of real contribution. We're supposed to be getting stronger and magnifying each other's skills. How are we supposed to do that with somebody who doesn't even know what they're doing?"

"I am worried her lack of training and relative disconnect from her abilities could drag us down," Zander said, trying to remain as dignified and diplomatic as possible.

"Well then, in that case, I suppose it is most fortunate that I am the one who makes the decisions around here and not you," Principal

Elmhurst said. "The matter is settled. As of now, Mia is your fifth and will be a part of all your training and efforts. As for you, Luna and Vivi, tonight the two of you will move into the larger room down the hall from your current dorm room. With Mia."

Vivi couldn't believe this was happening. It was too much. Being forced to interact with the strange halfling was one thing, but now Elmhurst had dropped Mia in their laps and was making them babysit. Vivi had to work with her, live with her, and rely on her to help them achieve their aspirations.

Vivi wasn't going to take it easily.

As they moved rooms, Vivi figured she had one really good prank left up her sleeve. One that would make Mia so embarrassed that at the very least, she would always know her position in the pecking order of their group was at the bottom. She seethed at the idea that Mia seemed incapable of using her abilities except when it came to defending herself—and specifically against Vivi. It was so unfair that Mia was so terrible except when she was the subject of a prank, so Vivi had to get creative and think of a way to attack her where her defensive abilities wouldn't kick in.

It finally dawned on Vivi after the three girls finished their short move down the hall. The pranks so far had worked for the most part, Mia was simply more capable of fighting back when she became really angry or distressed. What if the prank itself didn't make her upset, but rather it was the humiliation brought on by things she couldn't change?

The idea began formulating in her mind later that night when she went to bed. The next day, while Luna and Mia were busy practicing, she prepared the room for her master plan.

The prank was pretty simple, really, but diabolical. First, she filled a large blanket with enchanted fake bugs. They were tiny little things, smaller than ants, and they were made mostly of liquid so they would squish when hit and would evaporate within a few hours. But they were great for playing jokes on people squeamish about bugs, and if you had a creative mind, like Vivi, they provided many other opportunities. Like covering them in itching powder.

She emptied several cans of itching powder into the blanket with the fake bugs, then enchanted them to wake up and begin crawling all over the first person they came into contact with when they were released. Then she enchanted the blanket to hang just under the ceiling of the room. Now all she had to do was wait for Mia to return, let the blanket drop, and wait for the bugs to fall on her. Then Vivi would trip the fire alarm so everyone would go outside, including a very itchy Mia. The effect would be gloriously funny, and Vivi had a camera ready to capture pictures of the experience.

When she heard the sounds of voices coming down the hall, Vivi stood on the far end of the room—away from the door and far away from the blanket—and waited. Soon, Mia stood outside the door talking to Luna, and Vivi waited anxiously for her to enter.

"I'm going to grab a quick bite to eat and I'll meet you in the library, okay?" Luna asked. Vivi hated that they had become so close. Rarely was there a day when the two of them didn't practice katas together and bore the group to tears with talk of Grandmaster Old Fart or Sensei Older Fart.

"Yeah, I'll meet you there in about ten," Mia said cheerfully and opened the door. Her eyes immediately went to Vivi in the corner of the room. It was like she knew something was up but didn't know what. "Hi—" she started to say.

Vivi began whispering the words to make the blanket drop from the ceiling onto Mia, but Luna burst in unexpectedly. This was even better than Vivi hoped. Luna had it coming, too.

"Hey, I just thought...wait, what the heck?" Luna exclaimed.

The blanket was falling, but Mia grabbed Luna and thrust her hand in the air. A wave of energy burst out of her hand and circled them in an umbrella-like shape. It was a shield, and it was blocking all of the fake bugs from landing on them. Even worse, they were bouncing off the shield and going everywhere.

Including onto Vivi.

Vivi screamed as the bugs swarmed around her, and she began shouting the spell that would de-animate them again, but in her panic and itchiness, she missed words. She kept trying to say it, but more would jump on her, and she would cry out and have to start over. Under the shield, Luna opened her eyes, and both she and Mia were cackling with laughter. The plan had backfired, and Vivi was receiving a taste of her own very itchy medicine.

Mia and Luna backed out of the room, collapsing against a wall in laughter, waiting until the chaos and mild cursing from inside their room stopped. Eventually, all was silent, and they snuck a peek inside. Vivi sat in the middle of the floor, wearing a tank top and gym shorts, covered from head to toe in some kind of cream. It was also in her hair, and while it seemed like it must have covered every inch of her, she was still scratching random places and unable to sit still.

"How did you do it?" she spat, her hands finding other spots where the itching was driving her insane.

"Do what?" Mia asked. She knew what she was being asked, but since she had absolutely no idea how she did it, and Vivi deserved every bit of this frustration, playing dumb only made it funnier.

"How can you be so terrible and do that?" she exclaimed, jumping to her feet and scratching at the thousands of bite marks on her legs. Vivi had used a cream she'd bought for the occasion, one that was supposed to counteract the itching immediately, but either it was a lie, or she had over powdered the little bugs, because she felt like she needed to tear her skin off to finally not itch anymore.

"How can you be so terrible to try to do this?" Mia asked. "You brought this on yourself, Vivi."

Hatred boiled in Vivi's heart. Sheer loathing colored her vision and made her shake with rage. She had to get out of the room, but leaving would expose her to the rest of the school in all her cream-covered glory. Exactly the humiliation she had planned for Mia.

"Who are you?" she finally spat, moving to within inches of Mia's face.

Mia smiled. "I'm your roommate. And you had better get used to it. No more pranks."

Vivi growled and brushed past her, grabbing a handful of clothes out of her drawer and heading as fast as she could to the shower.

CHAPTER TWENTY-FOUR

After the incident with the bug-filled enchanted blanket gone wrong, none of the newly minted group of five was particularly excited when Zander called for their first practice together. It wasn't something he was looking forward to either. But it had to be done.

Principal Elmhurst had made herself extremely clear when she'd established Mia as their fifth member. Nothing was going to change her mind or sway her into not forcing them to work with Mia. They'd already given up their entire summer, and now the weekends, fall break, and holidays all loomed large ahead of them. There was absolutely no question in any of their minds that their headmistress would take away the privilege of them leaving campus during any of those breaks if they hadn't accomplished the goals she had in mind for them.

That wasn't something Zander wanted to deal with. He was more than ready to take his leave of the academy for a while. As much as he enjoyed the challenge of trying to accomplish the Power of Five and honing his skills even further, the stress and tension were just too much for him. He needed to get away, which meant they had to make Principal Elmhurst happy, so she'd be satisfied with allowing them to be apart. If they could prove they'd managed to mesh well enough, she might relent on her never-ending quest to find ways to force them together.

Today was the beginning. It was their first opportunity to really work together in the context of being a unit. Though they had to help Mia at some point, or at least stand by while she attempted to learn skills, this was the first time they'd be actively participating in working with her.

Instead of merely trying to help her pick up on the most basic abilities—which even the youngest of the halflings knew—they'd be expected to combine their skills with hers and elevate them to a new plane of effectiveness.

It was daunting, to say the least. Today he'd decided against going to the field. Instead, he'd reserved one of the practice fields behind the academy. It reminded him of the earliest days with the four of them working together, when they'd barely been able to exist within the same space. In those days, they hadn't ventured far away from the academy and had preferred to do all of their practicing right there on the field. It was time to return there now, time to go back to the beginning and build again. There may be a point in the future when they would introduce Mia to the private haven they'd found at the other field, but not now. She hadn't earned her way up to that yet.

There was little joy and excitement among them as the five trickled out onto the field and gathered in a loose circle in the center. Carson and Vivi looked at the others accusingly, as if blaming Luna, Zander, and Mia for Elmhurst making the momentous decision. Luna and Zander studied Mia out of the corners of their eyes, questioning her presence there, and wondering just how much she was going to delay their success. Mia had no one to glare at. She was alone in her own seething about the situation—solitary in her discomfort and uncertainty.

The others were paired off. The two guys lived with each other and had a camaraderie, even if they did everything to try to both deny and push back against it. There were glimmers of a friendship forming between them, and it was obvious either one of them would choose the other over Mia. The girls were more challenging in their relationship, but even *they* had a history of knowing each other and having lived together before being thrust together with Mia.

But it was more than that. They had their Court loyalties as well. The two Seelie were bonded together by being Seelie, and the two Unseelie were bonded together for the same reason. Their Courts defined and identified them, and they were largely untrusting of the other.

Mia didn't even have that. She couldn't show any loyalty to her Court or connect with the others, because she didn't know to which Court she belonged. Despite all her investigation and exploring at the library, she hadn't found anything leading to who her mother might be.

If she could find just that one detail, she would be able to align herself with either the Seelie or the Unseelie. It didn't really matter to her which one it was. From everything she'd heard, there should be a part of her that hoped she'd find herself as a part of the Seelie fae. In truth, she would have accepted either, just to know where she belonged. It would give her an anchor here, a stronger link to prove this was what she was supposed to be doing.

Hopefully, that day would come soon.

"Let's go ahead and get started," Zander said.

"Hold on. Let me put up a protective barrier," said Carson.

"But we're right on campus. You've never put up a protective barrier when we are practicing in the fields on the school grounds," Luna said.

"Let's just call it extenuating circumstances," Carson said.

"Yeah, like he's worried Mia is going to screw something up, so he's trying to contain the damage," Vivi snapped.

Mia rolled her eyes. "When are you going to get over this?"

"What do you mean?" the Unseelie girl said angrily. "Get over what?"

"That I'm here. That I'm part of your group, and you have to work with me," said Mia.

"Why should we have to get over it?" Vivi asked. "We've been here.

This has been our school for years. You just showed up, and all of a sudden, you're Principal Elmhurst's darling. You have her practically eating out of your hand, giving you all sorts of special accommodations and putting you in a group you have no business being a part of."

"What special accommodations is she giving me? If anything, I have to work ten times harder than anyone else and am expected to excel beyond everyone else just to prove I deserve to breathe the same air you do while I'm inside these gates. As for her putting me in this group, I had nothing to do with that. Trust me when I say that I don't want to be here one bit more than you want me here. I don't understand what this group even is or what we're supposed to be doing, or what the point of me being chosen for it is. All I know is my life got thrown up in the air and scattered around just a few days before I came here. I'm still trying to work my way through it, and the four of you acting like this isn't going to help me get there."

"You act like you're the only one who thinks you have had any challenges in your life," Carson said. "It doesn't make you special that you've been through hard times. It makes you just like any of us."

"I never said it made me special. And I'm sure the four of you have faced challenges in your lives. Everyone does. But try to think for a second what it's been like for me. Every one of you grew up knowing you were half-fae, didn't you? From the very beginning of your life, it was a part of you, something you used to identify yourself. You knew what life was going to hold for you and how that identity would impact your future. I don't have that. I grew up not knowing the fae world existed, much less that I was a part of it. My life went from absolutely normal to something I didn't recognize in a matter of minutes. I'm having to figure out who I am and how my life turned out the way it did while playing catch up to people I'm constantly reminded are the most talented and skilled of their time. So, excuse me if I'm not thrilled about the truly underwhelming welcome wagon you rolled out for me. I'm not going to fall all over myself for you. I'll do my best, and I'll apply myself as much as I possibly can. But that's all I can do, and I'm not dealing with any more nonsense from any of you. I'm not a pushover, and I'm not going to take your crap."

"Crickets," Luna said.

Mia's eyes snapped to her and narrowed. "Is that supposed to be some sort of commentary on what I had to say and your reaction to it?"

Luna shook her head. "Actually, no. I was talking about the word. You should have said, 'I'm not going to take your crickets.' It's the word we use in place of any of those other words you could use. Fae hate the sound of crickets, so it makes sense. If you're going to be here and be one of us, you should at least know that."

The words could have come across as condescending, or even aggressive. Instead, Mia sensed a softness to them, as if Luna was breaking through her resistance for a moment to reach out to her.

The red-headed halfling offered a hint of a smile back. "I never understood why people always loved the sound of crickets and I detested it. I just thought I was strange," she said.

"Not strange. Just fae," Zander said. "Can we get started now?"

"Can I first ask what it is we are supposed to be doing? What is this elusive Power of Five?" Mia had heard the term a few times, but no one had ever explained it to her. She hadn't thought to look it up in her research because she was more focused on learning who her mother was, and what her own abilities were.

Zander nodded. "I guess that makes sense. It might help you if you understood it." He went into the explanation about how if they could merge their powers together, they could be unstoppable. They would achieve something even full-blooded fae rarely did.

With wide eyes and a headache from the absurdity of it all, Mia listened and absorbed the information. It did sound like something she should do. If she could manage this power with them, then no one would be able to tell her she didn't belong there. She was going to prove to herself and everyone else that she *did* belong at the academy.

Mia didn't know how much good the conversation had done, but it felt like they'd reached an understanding, or at least taken a few steps closer to each other. But it didn't mean it would last. She and Luna had started to cooperate while helping her hone her fighting skills, but Elmhurst establishing her as the fifth member of their group and forcing them to live together had driven a wedge in their relationship.

It was entirely possible that the moment they'd just experienced was fully isolated and wouldn't come back. She would just take it for what it was and keep focusing on herself and building her own skills. At least then, she'd be living up to what she'd promised Cassia.

Mia didn't know it, but Cassia was there at the school at that very moment. The bounty hunter had quickly resolved the assignment in San Diego but hadn't told Mia she was returning to the Academy. She didn't want to put too much pressure on the halfling or give her any expectations. Instead, she wanted to check in on her almost anonymously. By coming unannounced, she could see how the girl was fitting in with the others and if her skills and abilities were improving.

Cassia was standing out on one of the massive balconies surrounding the top of the academy and was staring out over the practice field to watch the group work together. It wasn't the first time she had been back. As far as Mia knew, Cassia had left her in the care of the academy, but the bounty hunter had actually returned a few times over the last weeks of the summer to check in.

Not wanting anyone to notice she was there, Cassia retreated back inside the academy. She headed down one of the corridors and entered the front of the library. The gargoyles glared down at her and she almost walked past.

But she hesitated, then turned to the statues. "You know Mia?" she asked Steve. "The new halfling with red hair and green eyes?"

"Of course, the one Principal Elmhurst has taken such a liking to," the gargoyle said.

"I wouldn't say she's taken a liking to her," Dan said from the other side of the library door. "She's only made her a part of the group because she sees something in her."

"Something she's trying to find out for herself," Steve said. "She sure comes to the library a lot."

"I need you to keep an eye on her," Cassia said. "Make sure she's doing what she needs to do and is safe."

"Why would we do that? We have so many other students to worry about, and we report to Principal Elmhurst and the staff, not a bounty hunter," Steve said in a growl.

"I've noticed her many times, and I'm curious about her. I can watch out for her for you," Dan said.

"Thank you. I appreciate it," said Cassia.

Cassia wasn't the only person secretly watching the interactions of the five young halflings. Principal Elmhurst stood at a vantage point only *she* could access and which provided a view of the field. Even if one of them turned and looked directly at her, they wouldn't be able to see her. Her magic was too strong for them, and at this distance, it would be too challenging to counteract a cloaking spell anyway.

Watching them from this distance meant they didn't realize they were under scrutiny. They were more authentic that way. Without them realizing she was observing them, she could truly watch how they interacted with one another and see if she'd made the right choice. There was really no going back on it now. She'd made the decision, and they were starting to work together. Either this succeeded or it didn't, and all she could do was wait and find out.

As of right now, it didn't seem to be working out quite as well as any of them hoped, but Principal Elmhurst wasn't going to lose faith so quickly. It took time for fae to learn to work together with others and combine their powers with one goal in mind. It would be harder for a halfling without much training and who didn't truly know how much she could do. That was proving true for Mia.

Principal Elmhurst watched as each of the four demonstrated how to conjure a cluster of flowers, then they stood together and created a Faerie Circle. She smiled, remembering how much difficulty they'd had with that very thing just a few weeks ago. Now it went smoothly, the circle appearing around them within moments of beginning to focus.

Not so much for Mia. When she joined the squad, nothing seemed to happen. They tried several times, only to drop hands and start shouting at each other for a few seconds before trying again. Elmhurst finally laughed and turned away, returning to her office to continue other work while the five figured each other and themselves out.

On the practice field, Zander was trying for at least the tenth time to explain to Mia how to conjure the flowers properly. Carson was busy watching girls who had shown up early for the semester jogging around the field. Luna looked exhausted. Any second, Vivi was going to explode.

"I think I have it this time," said Mia.

She concentrated hard and did exactly as he instructed. Finally, a few purple blooms dotted the grass at her feet. She gasped and glanced up at the handsome silver-haired boy who grinned back at her in approval.

"There you go. Good job," he said. "Are you ready to try the circle again?"

"Absolutely."

They spread out again and held hands. Mia concentrated as hard as she could, remembering what she'd done before to produce those few flowers. Eventually, a handful of purple pansies appeared around the group, gradually forming a circle. Then they began to generate faster and faster. None of the group knew what to do.

The flowers continued to grow and multiply and were eventually joined by a tangle of vines. The magic was moving too fast for them to react. Soon, the entire protective dome was filled with the flowers and vines, forcing the five halflings against the walls of the dome.

"Vivi, stop it," Luna commanded.

"I'm not doing this," Vivi snarled, wrestling herself out of the grasp of a vine before letting out a howl when another blast of purple pansies formed beside her face, crushing her cheek against the dome.

"Somebody do something. I can barely breathe," Zander said from somewhere in the thick overgrowth.

"Carson, get rid of the dome," said Vivi.

"I can't." Carson's words were muffled by a vine around his neck and by the flowers filling his mouth.

Luna forced away some of the flowers long enough to make the dome disappear. They all fell to the ground and the explosion of flowers and vines spread out across the field, multiplying every second. The few halflings standing on the field and on the track around it screamed when the pansies began to move toward them. They ran, trying to escape them as fast as they could before they got sucked in too.

Luna, Zander, Carson, and Vivi tried to stop them. They blasted out their individual powers, then combined their magic in an effort to stop the flowers from growing and to kill the ones already spreading. They did everything they could to control the magic, but nothing they tried worked. No matter how hard they tried to stop the flowers and vines from spreading, they kept failing.

CHAPTER TWENTY-FIVE

Principal Elmhurst walked away from her work and returned to watching the group of five just in time to see the massive explosion of purple pansies take over the protective dome and nearly suffocate all five of them. How long should she wait before stepping in?

In all honesty, it should have terrified her. It would've been upsetting for any of her students to be taken over by a sudden and seemingly invincible garden of pansies. But it was different with the Scooby gang. Not only was it frightening to watch them be overwhelmed, their apparent inability to fight back was a bit of a concern.

These were her four strongest and most impressive students, plus a wild card who had quickly proved herself to be powerful and strong in her own right. It made sense that they'd done something as ridiculous as create an overwhelming flower garden that threatened to kill them all. It was a little more disconcerting that they didn't seem to be able to figure out how to keep it at bay. Yet, she hadn't panicked. There would be time for that later if it became absolutely necessary.

For now, they'd already progressed by making the protective dome disappear so they weren't all killed right there in the middle of the practice field. Being out in the open gave them more space and made more opportunity for them to defeat what they had created. She would give it a little time. They would probably figure something out. The Scooby gang was nothing if not resourceful, and she had faith in them. They would eventually figure out a way to get the flowers and vines back under control and stop that from happening again soon. She just wanted to see how long it would take for it to happen, and what they would do to make it work.

It was fascinating to watch.

Down on the practice field, Mia was overwhelmed and terrified by what was happening around her. *She* had made it happen, but she didn't know how or what to do to stop it. She watched in horror as more and more purple pansies grew thicker and thicker, vines snaking around, winding their way through the grass of the practice field. Some of the vines were as thick as her leg now, and the pansies had grown until the blooms were as big as dinner plates. It was a fantastic idea for a surrealist painting, but in actual practice, it was not nearly as whimsical and fun.

She stared around frantically to try to find the four others. When they were stuck inside the practice dome, there were a few moments when she'd been afraid the plants had already taken Zander. He was crushed at the bottom, his face flat on the ground and the flowers and vines growing over him as though they were trying to smash him into the soil so they could use him as plant food. This was all getting to be a little bit too *Little Shop of Horrors* for Mia, but she didn't know what to do to make it go away.

Not that it seemed to matter to Vivi. The small Unseelie halfling seemed to be taking this entire experience as a personal insult directly from Mia. She flailed and kicked at the flowers, occasionally sending out a blast of magic to try to make them wither away. All the while, she glared at Mia as though Mia had made this all happen specifically for the purpose of causing trouble for Vivi.

"Make it go away," Vivi shouted at last.

"I can't!" Mia yelled.

"You made it, you can make it stop," Zander said. "Just concentrate."

"Carson made the dome shield thing around us, and he couldn't make it go away," Mia tossed back.

"That's because I was too busy being choked to death by these ridiculous flowers you made," said Carson. "Now, make them stop before they completely take over the field and head for the academy building. I don't think you want to have to explain to the headmistress why her corridors are now one big giant greenhouse."

"At this point, I really wouldn't care," Mia said.

She stared around again, horrified by the sheer extent of what was happening. They were only flowers and vines. Just plants. Yet they were some of the scariest things she'd ever seen in her life. In a lot of ways, she would rather face off against another boggart then be standing there being swallowed alive by a glorified flower bed. She let out a scream, then whipped around to face the wider part of the field.

"Go away! All of you, go away!"

In the next instant, all the flowers and vines were gone. They vanished just as suddenly and unexpectedly as they had appeared. The field went back to nothing but an expanse of green grass. The track was visible again without any of the blooms or vines to cover it up. Everything had gone right back to the way it was, as if she had never conjured any of it.

Inside the academy building, pride surged through Cassia. She stood in the corridor in front of the library, leaning against the wall next to Steve, the gargoyle. On the wall in front of them was a small temporary portal. She hadn't created it for any transportation purpose. There was no place she intended to go, and Principal Elmhurst wouldn't be happy with her if she found out that Cassia had created a portal out in the corridor this way, available for anyone to use or accidentally fall into. However, the portal was just for her to look through.

The enchantments on the school made it impossible for her to create a portal leading outside the building. But for some reason, she had zero problems creating her mini viewscreen.

Almost like a tiny television, the portal swirled in front of her with shades of blue and purple around the edges of an image showing the five halflings on the field. She had watched nervously as the flowers continued to grow and expand, threatening not only the five but also all the other students outside and the buildings themselves if they hadn't regained control. Cassia had witnessed things like this before. It was all too easy for young fae who weren't trained and weren't familiar with their own skills and abilities to suddenly have spurts of power. Of course, they weren't usually this powerful.

Most of the time, when a young person of Cassia's kind—especially a halfling—experienced a sudden burst in the intensity of their power, it was only mild. Sometimes it might cause a little damage or a minor injury. But Mia wasn't just any fae. She was most definitely not just any halfling. Her abilities were incredibly strong already, which meant when she experienced the sudden surge in her skill, it was tremendously powerful. It was also almost impossible to get back under control because she didn't know how to handle it.

Cassia didn't get a whole lot of time to sit around and watch TV, but this was the most entertaining show she'd seen in a long time. It was a thrill when Mia finally found her own voice and took hold of the skills and abilities born into her and commanded them to do as she wanted. She didn't know what she was doing, of course. It wasn't an intentional act or a sign of any new abilities. Instead, it was an act of fear, desperation, and anger. But that was enough. It was enough to show her she had it in her.

"There you go," she said. "That's my girl."

"You were right in asking us to keep an eye on her," Steve said. "She's definitely special."

He sounded afraid, but Cassia wasn't sure what was causing that fear. It might have been watching the explosion of flowers, but she suspected it was much more likely a fear of Mia. The extent of her potential was clear to those who knew what to recognize. This frightened Steve, but excited Dan.

"Keep watching out for her," Cassia said. "It's only going to be more important from now on."

The gargoyles agreed. They knew just how special Mia was. And now that she had seen her powers come to life, she would be more open to developing them further. This was a changing point and opening that would allow her to grow and strengthen at a much more accelerated pace. It would be a lot for everyone in the academy to handle, but they had no choice.

The dichotomy of emotions experienced by the gargoyles outside the library was reflected on the practice field below. The Scooby gang stared at Mia in wonder, a slight hint of fear and worry flickering through them. This confirmed that *she* was the one who had brought about not only the extreme growth of the flowers, but also their instantaneous and inexplicable disappearance.

None of them were capable of doing it. Each of them had tried, all of them had done everything they could to harness the magic and bring it back under control. But they had been unsuccessful. It had taken Mia, the strange and untrained girl who they still didn't trust, to end it.

Witnessing her magic had stunned them, and the enormity of it was not lost. It had to have taken a lot of power to create that circle then make it vanish so quickly. They had clearly underestimated Mia. They had discounted her without a second thought, ready to see her get shipped off to one of the basic schools at the end of the semester. Now that had changed, and they were forced to see her in a different light. Forced to reevaluate what she might be capable of and what that meant for them as a group.

But it wasn't all excitement. Inside the building, Principal Elmhurst watched in shock and concern. Not for the first time, she worried about who Mia might actually be and what would happen if anyone discovered her there. It made her worry about the safety of this unusual but astonishing halfling, and she began considering various ways to protect the girl. Elmhurst had to guard Mia, to keep her safe from the creatures and bounty hunters pursuing her.

The principal had already added a few protections around the grounds before she spoke with a few of her most trusted staff members, ensuring they kept an eagle eye on anyone new, or any possible threats to the school or students.

But beyond that, Principal Elmhurst had to continue to help Mia remain safe from herself. Which meant learning to harness and control her powers. She was obviously gifted, and that gift could offer a tremendous range of benefits. But it could also be extremely risky. She was naturally very dangerous, the most important thing was to help Mia finally get control. That way she wouldn't hurt herself or others with what she could do.

Deeper in the academy, Cassia said goodbye to the gargoyles and strode to the portal room again. The fae guards moved out of the way when she approached, but she barely registered them. Her mind was elsewhere. She was thinking about Mia and the extraordinary gift it was to have found her.

All the moving parts and tiny choices which had led to her being in that night market in Shanghai at exactly the right time. If anything had gone differently, even one small misdirection, she may never have been there, and Mia would have disappeared into the market, never to be discovered.

But that didn't happen. They had found each other as perhaps they were meant to. Cassia was able to put the young girl on this path and guide her into what she could become. It was a long shot. From the beginning, when she recognized that Mia was special, she'd had no real expectation.

That was completely different now. A voice from long ago echoed in her mind and a slight smile came to her lips. She approached one of the smooth walls of the octagonal room and conjured her portal.

As she walked through it, she whispered, "My father might have been right after all."

PART II

CHAPTER TWENTY-SIX

Mia had heard about it so many times, but being there in person proved exhilarating. Even though the trip through the portal to the Vampire Academy was controlled, the glitz and glamor of the city even seeped into the basketball-like gym they were in now.

When she had first heard they would be attending a meet, Mia hadn't been interested. If an event didn't have something to do with martial arts or with practicing her newfound abilities and trying to harness them, she wasn't inclined to focus on it. But when her friends had mentioned they would be traveling through a portal to Las Vegas, Mia had changed her mind.

Before she'd made the trip through the portal, she'd been given precious little information about the nature of the meet. Now she sat with the Scooby Gang in the back row, near the top of the cavernous auditorium, looking down at the court in confusion. It appeared to be a regulation basketball court, but with gray mats surrounding the hoops and padding around each one.

"So, who are we rooting for?" she asked. She was peering down the row when it dawned on her that they all wore shirts bearing their school's logo, and Zander was waving a foam finger with it embla-zoned on the side.

"That has to be a joke," Carson said, his voice a shocked monotone. "Tell me that was a joke."

Mia was quick to reply, "Of course, it was." She faced the court to hide her embarrassment. "I know it's our school, but I've never heard of this game before."

"You've never heard of slamball?" Vivi asked, her voice mocking.

"No. Sorry."

"It's all right. You're new," Luna said, interrupting before things became hairy. Vivi was a few seconds and another lilt in her voice away from Mia delivering a chop to her throat, and Luna must have noticed.

"Yeah. Let up, Vivi." Zander scooted a little closer to Mia. Now flanked on either side by him and Luna, she felt a little less alone, but still very much confused.

"So." Luna drew in a deep breath. "Slamball is kind of like an offi-cial fae sport, right? All of the different academies have a team, though unlike human slamball, which I think is a pretty under-the-radar sport to them anyway, this version allows for more…creative play."

"Yeah, for one, when we say full contact, we mean *full contact*," Carson piped up from the other side of the bench. His eyes, however, never left the empty court. Mia suspected he was going to explode from excitement the second their team took the field.

"Right," said Zander. "We are allowed to use some of our abilities while on the court. For instance, the vampires who are playing against us today, they are super-fast and super strong, and they will use that to their advantage. Also, some of them can fly a bit, or at least hover. See those gray things by the hoops on either side?"

Mia nodded. *Did he say fly?*

"Those are trampolines. The player with the ball can jump on one of those to try to dunk the ball or to get a better angle for a jump shot. They have to look out though," Zander said.

"Why?"

"Because of the full-contact," Luna said. "Slamball can be pretty brutal, and if you are mid-air, you don't have a whole lot of protection. Sailing through the air against a guy who can hover means he has the ability to wait on you and either steal the ball or just flatten you. And flattening people is encouraged."

"Even with students?" Mia asked.

Zander bobbed his head. "Perhaps even more with students," he said. "School pride is on the line. There are fouls you can get if you check someone in the back or something, but hitting them from the front or side—as long as it's not a kick or a punch or something—is fine. Each team has twelve people since it's an academic league, and they can substitute in or out at any time. Which is good since people get carted off hurt all the time."

"So, we are playing against vampires?" Mia asked. The rules of the game were interesting and all, but the idea that actual vampires were going to be on the court and that she was going to see them play a game was fascinating.

"Not the sparkly kind, sorry," Zander said, grinning. "These vampires are really meatheads who happen to be of the undead-drink-blood variety. Some of them are actually dhampirs, though."

"What's a dhampir?" Mia asked, feeling a bit like a four-year-old asking very basic questions in the back seat of a car like "Why is the sky blue?"

"Half-vampire," Luna said. "Sort of like us halflings. They aren't quite as gifted as the vampires when it comes to magical abilities, but they are still super strong and really fast. Plus, they don't fall for the traps like full vampires tend to. Vampires are really adept at wooing people, and at casting wicked spells and stuff that make people do their bidding. Dhampirs aren't subject to it, and many of them are resentful of vampires. Many of them will turn into a full vampire when they die as a human but otherwise live mostly ordinary lives. A number of dhampirs end up becoming vampire hunters, which is helpful for policing them since otherwise, vampires would just try to get away with anything and everything."

"Never trust a vampire," Zander said, lowering his voice. "I know that might seem a little bigoted of me, but seriously, those things are evil when they set their mind to it, and they do more often than not. Really powerful vampires can even woo dhampirs, and that makes them especially dangerous. Thankfully, you don't see those in any of the academies, and it takes so long to get that good you never see it in students. Even still, you want to keep an eye open around them. They have silver tongues and will do anything to get what they want whenever they want it."

So much information was coming at Mia that she sat in silence for a few minutes. It was the first month of her junior year, and her studies were already overwhelming. Being a part of the social life of a fae was exciting, but draining too. She didn't know what was expected of her in certain situations, and it all seemed so formal that she hadn't quite gotten the hang of it yet.

The hierarchies and social graces of the fae world were still so new that she hadn't learned much of any of them, and now vampire students were being thrown into the mix too. After a while, Zander stood to get something from the concession stand and asked if they wanted anything. After taking an enthusiastic and optimistic order from Carson, everyone else settled on a fountain drink.

"Need help carrying all that?" Mia asked.

"I would like that," he said, and his eyes met hers for a brief moment before they darted away.

Mia descended the long staircase to the main lobby floor and decided to ask a few more questions about the world she was now learning about. It was less embarrassing to choose one of them and limit Vivi's mocking, and Zander seemed to be an appealing prospect.

"So, there's *our* school and the Vampire Academy. What other schools compete in slamball?" she asked. They rounded a corner and headed down a hallway toward the outer rim of the building where she assumed the bathrooms and food would be.

"Well, our league is pretty small. There are eight teams, two from each of the four schools. Each team is supposed to be split evenly in terms of talent, but most of the time there ends up being an A team and a B team. Today's game is pretty important because it's our A team against the vampires' A team. They have gone undefeated so far this year, including beating our B team, and we only have one loss so far."

"Who did we lose to?" Mia asked as they turned the corner and found the line for concessions. The smell of hot dogs wafted up to her, and she became aware of the intensity of her hunger and of how long it had been since she had a hotdog at a game of any type. Today, she would rectify this obvious miscarriage of justice.

"The stinkin' shifters."

"Shifters?"

Zander nodded as he read the list above the window where uniformed kids around their age stood taking orders.

"Like werewolves?"

"Yes, and others. It's really hard to get a bead on one of them when they shift mid-match. Plus, they are ridiculously strong. One of our gunners broke his arm in a game against them last year, and he never played again."

"A gunner is a position on the team, right?" she asked.

"Yes," Zander said, turning his bright smile toward her. "See, you're getting it. The gunner is the main shot-taker. Sometimes you have two on the court at once if you really want to press, but most of the time, our team plays with one gunner and two stoppers, who do the defense work. He got absolutely creamed during the game last year, and it shattered some bones in his arm. Took him forever to be able to do simple spells again, and his parents forbade him from playing on the team again this year."

"That's awful," Mia said as they finally reached the window. By this point, her stomach was rumbling, and her desire for a hot dog had turned into a need for a much more elaborate meal. If she wasn't careful, her eyes would make decisions for her stomach that would rival Carson's long list. The girl at the window had disappeared into the kitchen area, which was populated by a group of large men, their skin covered in tattoos.

"So, there are the shifters," Zander continued. "And then us, the vampires and then the witches."

"Witches?"

"Yes, and they aren't normally that competitive, but they can play spoiler a lot. Last year their A team beat the shifters' A team in the last game of the year and gave us homefield advantage in the playoffs. We beat the pants off the shifters in that game, in no small part, I think because of the crowd. It was insane."

The girl at the counter reappeared, her expression weary, as though she would rather be anywhere else in the world. Zander gave her the orders, and Mia chimed in to add a hot dog, a soda, and, at last, a small curly-fry order to the mix.

"We only have one size," the girl at the counter said, her tone impatient. The line behind them seemed to have grown to epic proportions, and snap decisions were required.

"That's fine," Zander said. "I'll help you eat them."

"Order up," the girl said, and fries seemed to materialize above her shoulder as a hairy hand curved around her to sit them on the tray.

Another person came up with a caddy bearing four of their drinks and sat Mia's in front of her. She popped in a straw and carried all the drinks while Zander grabbed the tray as they moved away from the ordering window and went to pay.

As she tried to balance the drinks on the register area to reach into her pocket for her cash, Zander waved her off. "I got it, don't worry."

Mia blushed and grabbed the drinks again, almost spilling hers on her shirt. Which would have completed her embarrassment for the day and given Vivi all the ammunition she would need for a lifetime of torturous barbs.

"Do you play slamball?" Mia asked as they headed for the hallway that would lead them back to their seating area.

"I've thought about it," Zander said. "But frankly, we don't have time. I am far more focused on making our group the best it can be, and with us getting our fifth member late and you not really knowing anything about our world, it kind of puts everything else on the backburner."

"Oh," Mia said, keeping her eyes on the floor as they walked.

Zander must have realized what he had said because he stopped in the hallway. "Hey, that came out wrong. Look, it's not your fault you don't know anything yet, and it's not your fault I don't play slamball. Honestly, even if I had all the time in the world, I probably wouldn't anyway. I'm terrible at shooting baskets, and gunners are the leaders of the team. If I wasn't a gunner, I would be unhappy on the team, and if I *was* the gunner, everyone else would be unhappy, you know?"

Mia couldn't help but laugh a little. Zander grinned.

"Sorry, I didn't mean for it to sound like I blamed you. C'mon. Let's get this stuff up to our seats before the game starts. I think you're really going to like it once it gets going. It's super-fast-paced and a little chaotic, so not knowing what's going on is kind of the natural state of the audience sometimes. Are we good?" he asked.

Mia nodded, but she didn't look at him. She knew his apology was sincere and that he didn't want her to feel bad, but at the same time, she did worry about things like that. What if she was the reason the group hadn't advanced as far in their studies and practice as they should have?

What if *she* was the one holding them back? She wouldn't be able to shake that feeling until she caught up, and with so much to learn, it seemed impossible to get there.

All around them, music filled the air and, what sounded like air horns started blaring in every direction. The crowd erupted in cheers, and the lights dimmed, spotlights dancing all around the arena as Mia and Zander strode through the hall.

"Too late!" he said, a smile stretching across his face as he picked up the pace and began to half-jog to the entrance of the seating area. Mia took after him, doing everything in her power not to spill the drinks, taking extra care with Vivi's bright-red punch, which was sure to find Mia's white shirt if so much as a drop was spilled.

As they rounded the corner and stared up at the steps to find their seats, Mia sensed eyes turning in her direction. Some of the people in the stands who were cheering and smiling, met her gaze and their expressions faltered, their voices dropping. As she headed up the stairs behind Zander, she was all too aware that she was now the center of attention for many people. Very unwanted attention.

CHAPTER TWENTY-SEVEN

Mia sat in her spot between Zander and Luna and tried to focus on what was happening on the court. Music filled the stadium again as an announcer came over the speakers and introduced each member of the starting roster of the vampire team.

The vampires appeared impossibly frail, and Mia had to remind herself they possessed incredible strength regardless of their body type, and that their thin and lanky appearance was a way of luring people in. It was a glamour in a certain way, but more physical than a spell. As each member of the team made it to the sidelines, the tension on the visitor's side of the arena kept building.

When the music changed, and the school song played over the loudspeakers, the noise became deafening. The Scooby Gang surged to their feet, cheering for their classmates while their entire half of the arena joined them. Carson and Zander sang along at the tops of their voices, and Mia glanced at Luna, who was singing to herself and smiling.

Mia wanted to relax, and she allowed herself to enjoy the game, but every now and then, even while their team was entering the court, a student would look at her. Sometimes multiple faces turned, coupled with conspiratorial whispers and the occasional finger pointed in her direction.

Principal Elmhurst had tried to keep Mia and her powers a secret, which had turned out to be a miserable failure. As with any school where teenagers collected, gossip lurked in every corner of every hallway and at every lunch table. Word about Mia had spread through the academy, and now she was a secondary source of entertainment for many of the fae students at the game.

It angered her that everyone seemed to know her business, and now they were concentrating on finding ways to talk about her without making it obvious. She shifted on the bench, and Luna seemed to notice her discomfort. A quick scan of the crowd revealed a few heads turning, with some sniggering to be heard in the distance, even over the blaring speakers.

"Don't worry about them." Luna turned to Mia. "They're just jealous because you got into the coolest gang in the school."

Luna's smile was disarming, and despite herself, Mia relaxed. She didn't want to hide anymore. She didn't even want to strangle them. Well, not all of them. Maybe the original student who had spread information they shouldn't have, whoever was making sure everyone knew about Mia. She'd love to plant her fist through the face of that person and make sure the next time they went gossiping, they did it with broken teeth.

In reality, though, it could be anyone. Lots of people had been around the group and had seen her do things beyond her level of ability, both good and bad. If a teacher was spreading gossip, it would be snuffed out soon enough, and they might be fired for it.

If a student was responsible, then Principal Elmhurst had better hope she found them before Mia did. Expulsion would be a hell of a lot better than any number of the terrible things Mia could do to them without breaking so much as a sweat.

Below them, the game began and, despite the protective screen between the crowd and the court, Mia was quick to learn it wasn't the only barrier. At one point, a fae gunner bounced up for a dunk and was hit by what appeared to be a lightning strike coming from a defender's fingers. A whistle blew the game to a halt, and the fae player landed halfway on the trampoline, his lower half bouncing up and curving over his torso before he hit the floor of the court hard.

"Oh, come on," Carson shouted at the court and surged to his feet, looking for all the world as though he was going to throw his chili-cheese fries at the referee. But he sat with a thud and stuffed a handful of fries into his mouth when the officials convened. Over the loud-speaker, the announcer informed the crowd of a penalty shot as the referees broke up, and the offending vampire earned a foul against him.

"How is that allowed?" Mia asked aghast. She would have assumed a lightning strike went a bit beyond a simple body check.

"Well, they aren't, technically," Zander said.

"It's a foul on the vampire defender," Luna piped up.

"He should be ejected," Carson snapped, the last word yelled at the court as he popped another fry in his mouth.

"Every player gets three personal fouls. It's kind of easy to get a foul called on you with the trampolines, but vampires don't worry about that as much because they can just float and don't need the bounce as much. They still technically have to bounce for a point to score, and they can't hover over them defensively, but they can control their ascent and descent much better," Luna said. "That vampire there just got themselves their first personal foul, but he probably thinks it was worth it. Lightning strikes like that are not expressly forbidden, you just catch a foul for it since it's considered part of their powers."

"It's like if one of us was able to do a force-push and knock one of them across the court, out of the way," Zander explained. "If the student is strong enough, they could pull it off and only get a penalty for it, but it's kind of a cheap way to play."

"I would think shooting someone with lightning is pretty cheap," Mia said.

"Extremely cheap. Low class," Carson muttered and sipped his drink. The straw gurgled as he reached the bottom, and he stared at the cup as if it had emptied itself by magic. "Great. What else can go wrong?"

On the court, the fae player was removed and replaced with a different one, who was allowed to take a penalty shot. As the referee blew the whistle, the fae raced for the first trampoline and bounced off, twirled to one side to avoid the outstretched arm of the defender, and dunked the ball hard. A roar rose from the crowd as the fae score went up by three, and their team tied with the vampires.

"Wait, what is there to stop fans from interfering with the game if vampires have the ability to shoot lighting?" Mia asked as the fae team took a time out.

"There's a protective shield around the court," Carson explained. "Really strong stuff. Keeps the magic in, and outside magic out. It also tempers spells, so witches can't just hex someone to death, and it allows the referees to police the game since they are granted extra power."

"Has anyone ever gotten hurt? I mean, worse than the guy who got hit by lightning?"

"Oh yeah," Zander said. "Especially in the professional leagues. People get knocked around a good bit, and the magic they use in the majors is less tempered by the judges since they are usually highly trained and exceptionally good athletes and spell casters. A couple of seasons ago, a witch was paralyzed when she got checked by a different witch due to a spell that was stronger than the poor witch expected it would be. It was big news. A bunch more regulations went into effect then, including in the Academic League. Hence the transparent plastic walls on the side to protect crowd members from errant blasts."

The more the rules were explained to her, the more Mia seemed to understand them, and she realized it was a mixture of hockey and traditional basketball. Maybe with a little bit of magic thrown in, but it gave it a pizzazz she was sure made it rather unique. The game picked up again, and the frenzied pace became dizzying. It was all Mia could do to keep up.

As the game neared the end of the first quarter, the score was tied, and the Fae Academy had held their own regardless of being down their best player. Despite her basic knowledge of how slamball worked and the pressure of the attention of people in the stands, Mia enjoyed the game and was becoming invested. She loved being part of something with her team. The quarter wore on, and she received fewer stares as students focused on the game. More unifying cheers rose, and she joined the crowd in trying to rally her team.

At one point, Carson cheered with such passion for a check by a fae player on the vampire who had shot the lightning earlier, his remaining fries had soared into the air and missed landing in Vivi's hair by an inch.

Mia was somewhat disappointed when the fries missed Vivi since it would have been a great way to even things out should Mia not make it through the night without a cola stain. Instead, Vivi shuffled away from Carson, moving so close to Zander that he shifted too, and his legs came into contact with Mia's.

As the quarter ended and a small break was called, Carson stood and left for the restrooms—he had finished off his soda so fast that he had ended up drinking half of Vivi's too. Vivi took the opportunity to go as well, leaving Mia with Zander and Luna.

"How do you like it so far?" Luna asked.

"It's really fun," Mia responded, her enthusiasm perhaps a bit more passionate than she had intended. "I really like it. It's like a few sports slapped together with that wizard game. What was that called? Quid-something."

Luna held up a hand, closed her eyes, and clutched the bridge of her nose with the thumb and forefinger of her free hand. "Stop. Stop right there. No."

"What?"

"I know exactly what you're going to say, and no, it is nothing like that. I mean, yes, the witches do whip out broomsticks occasionally, and there is a lot of throwing a ball through a hoop, but that's where the similarities end," Luna said.

"Well, there *is* a lot of magic involved," Zander said, but Luna shot him a glare, and he fell silent.

"Is it the movies you don't like?" Mia asked, unsure of Luna's reaction. "The books are really good if you didn't."

"No."

Zander laughed, and Mia turned to look at him. Luna was almost fuming, which was very unlike her, and Mia hoped she hadn't ticked off her new friend. She needed all the friends she could get in order to counteract Vivi and a school full of gossips.

"She hates that series. Don't let her get started on it," Zander said. "If you do, she'll talk your ear off about its 'simplistic and harmful representation of the magical community.' Right Luna?"

Luna didn't say anything, but her lips were pursed together in a tight line, and she turned to face the court. "Sorry, I was just notic—" Mia said.

"It's fine," Luna interrupted her. "It *is* kind of like that game. Just don't tell anyone I said that, okay?"

Mia broke into a large grin and nodded. "You got it."

Amiable conversation filled the time as the trio waited for Vivi and Carson. When they had returned, the whistle had blown to start the second quarter. Carson was carrying an entire drink caddy, and the expression on Vivi's face confirmed all four drinks were for him.

They stood so the pair could return to their places. Zander glanced at his friend and asked, "Staying hydrated, are we?"

"I don't want to have to get up again," Carson said. He fell silent, and the group focused on the game, their cheering wild and loud as the fae academy scored a point.

The game went back and forth, but the vampires always seemed to grab a lead and hold on to it, forcing the fae team to catch up. Every time the fae side gained a measure of momentum, a vampire player would body check one of the fae so hard they would need to be replaced for a short period.

Much like every game ever, the referees were the subject of the most criticism, at least on the visitors' side of the arena. There was a suspicion of bias toward the home team, that fouls weren't being called on vampires, not only not at the rate they deserved, but also not at the same rate they were called on fae.

It was enough that Mia sat there, elbows on her knees, and a few fingernails in her mouth as the final minutes of the game came closer to reality. The fae team was down by six points when a fae player managed to score a three-point shot before a fae defender stole the ball and made a two-point shot of his own. Before they knew it, they were down by a single point, and the vampire team took a time out with just over a minute to go.

"They're going to wind the clock down," Zander said through gritted teeth. "Man, we're going to lose."

Sure enough, when the whistle blew, the vampire team began to pass the ball back and forth, winding down precious seconds from the clock. It seemed like they would do it forever when a fae burst into the air, flying high off a bounce, and dive-bombed a gunner who was catching the pass. The ball shot loose, and a fae player grabbed it. He sped off for the hoop, bounced it high, and dunked it, tying the game.

"If we can hold them off, the game will go to overtime," Luna explained over the madness of the crowd's reaction.

The whistle blew as the vampire team received the ball, sinking a two-point shot with ease, and they abandoned all hope. But, with a mere three seconds remaining on the clock, the fae team snatched the ball.

As the whistle blew, the fae guard tossed it to the gunner who took one step and jumped, and using his own side's trampoline to boost his height, he tossed the ball at the opposing hoop.

The ball appeared to soar through the air in slow motion and landed on the rim, circling it as the crowd held their breath. The ball hit the rim, and as it began to spin, the buzzer sounded, signaling time expired.

Mia rocked on her seat, her nails in her mouth as she chewed them and wished with her heart that the ball would fall in.

As though pushed from Mia's direction, the ball dove through the hoop, and the crowd went insane. Amidst the crazed cheers, the blaring music, and the announcer calling the game for the fae, Mia embraced Luna and turned to Zander.

The smile he beamed at her contained more than happiness. It held a question. Everyone seemed so sure that no magic could penetrate the court, and yet—

Mia smiled back at him as celebrations broke out in the auditorium.

CHAPTER TWENTY-EIGHT

Cinder felt like she was going to burst with excitement as she zoomed back to the academy ahead of the other students. Being a pixie had its advantages, and it allowed her a quick escape and fast travel through the portals on account of being so small she could not be seen.

A trained eye could spot a pixie, but Cinder made it more difficult by floating and swirling like a piece of dust unless she was in a hurry. Anything to blend in and make herself invisible so she could go where she wanted, whenever she wanted.

Not that her techniques worked all the time. Cinder's magic had a bad habit of backfiring and causing small fires. Enough of a reputation had built by now that whenever a fire broke out—even if in the kitchen and caused by the cooks—Cinder would be blamed. Which was so unfair. Though she couldn't deny that she *was* responsible, at most, half the time.

But today was special. Dan and Steve, the gargoyles of the Fae Academy with the odd names, had tasked her with a job of great importance. She was to follow the new student, Mia, into the portal and keep an eye on her while the halfling attended a game of slamball.

Considering that Cinder remained inside the academy most of the time, the prospect of heading to a different place and being around so many people had been exhilarating. She had accepted the job without hesitation and had zoomed her way through the portal as the last of the students had left for Las Vegas.

Now she headed back, excited, overstimulated, and bursting at the seams with pride at a job well done. Dan was her friend, much more so than Steve, and she was proud that he trusted her with an important mission, and prouder still that she had executed it so well.

With so much to tell him, she began to rehearse her report well before she made it through the portal. She had to keep track of all the information after all, so a little practice couldn't hurt.

As she entered the library, listening to the sounds of the first of the students making their way out of the portal and back home, she made a beeline for Dan, still talking herself through the practice run of her report. By the time she reached him, a minute or so earlier than she had expected, she was still babbling. The gargoyle cocked his eyebrow and waited for her to take a breath. It took a few moments.

"Cinder," he said, interrupting as she drew a deep, nervous breath in preparation. "Start from the beginning, little one."

"Oh." The pixie gave a tiny squeak.

Steve rolled his deep-set eyes. He had never trusted her, that much Cinder knew, but he also seemed to dislike anything he interpreted as silly, and Cinder was nothing if not a little silly.

"For the love of all that is fae, can you get her to calm down?" Steve snapped.

Cinder went still. She had been darting around and between the gargoyles, landing on their heads, and diving off, all while continuing to talk. "Fine," she said, grabbing the chain of a lamppost beside the library's entrance to hold herself still. "See? I can be still. I can stop."

"Good. That's wonderful, Cinder. Please tell us what you found out," Dan said, his deep baritone voice bouncing off the columns of the library and against the entrance hall where the gargoyles stood, locked in place.

"Oh, Dan, it was so exciting! The fae team was getting beaten pretty badly by those dastardly vampires, and then one of them shot lightning." She inhaled while at the same time gasped to create an ear-piercing sound that made Steve roll his eyes again. "There was a lot of back and forth and then, you'll never believe it, the game got all tied up! Then one of the vampires scored, and I was so sad, and I wanted so badly to punch his nose, but then a fae player threw the ball blindly in the air, and it went in! With no time left! It was incredible, and everyone cheered and there were people kissing each other, and I was so happy!"

She sighed and fell silent, having gotten the most pressing details of her mission out, and settled onto a nearby bench, her eyes twinkling lights in the dark.

"That's great, Cinder. However, we sent you there on a mission," Dan said.

"Oh! The halfling, Mia," she exclaimed. "Yes, yes, I watched her like a hawk," she said, placing her fists over her narrowed eyes, as though they were a pair of binoculars.

"And? We haven't got all day," said Steve.

"What else are we going to do?" Dan responded to him. "Play checkers? We're gargoyles, St—"

"Ooh, I didn't tell you about the snacks." Cinder interrupted them, overcome with the need to reveal more information. "They have the greatest-smelling food there and drinks so big I could fly down the straw and bathe in them if I wanted to. Not that I did. Or would. Never crossed my mind, actually. I am just saying I could if I wanted to. Which I don't."

"Cinder, plea—" Dan began to speak.

"Then there was all of that portal business. Do you know when you go through a portal, it takes a few moments to get your sense of balance back? I didn't know that. Not one of their portals anyway. I went through and,"—she made a sound with her lips similar to the noise a plastic container of food makes when the lid is popped off—"there I was, a floating pixie lost in the big cold world of Las Vegas, and I couldn't tell which way was north if I'd had a compass stuck up my—"

"Cinder! The girl!" Steve yelled, and Cinder stopped cold. Her face scrunched up, and she dropped her fists to her sides, her expression resembling either an angry baby or an evil flower.

Steve remained unaffected.

"The girl is fine," Cinder said, in a tone so dead, Steve had no doubt how much Cinder detested him at that moment.

"Fine" was a decent word for it too, she thought. Something kept her from describing Mia as "good" per se, but she couldn't put her finger on it. Since the moment she had first seen the girl, something had stuck out to Cinder and drawn her attention, even before the gargoyles had asked her to follow the halfling. There was something *elegant* about her.

Cinder couldn't quite work it out, but something about Mia spoke of royalty, and only one story had made sense. If the bloodline of Princess Violet was within Mia, it had to be diluted. By multiple generations, by the mixing with human blood, or a combination of the two, there was a distinct dilution in Mia, if it were true. In the two thousand years since Princess Violet had died, so much had changed that Cinder wondered if it was worth noting, or even possible. For now, she kept that secret to herself. No need to cause a ruckus, especially when that particular ruckus could get someone killed.

Even a pixie.

So she didn't mention it to Steve or Dan, or anyone else. Not yet, anyway.

Just before she began to recount the rest of the night's events, a student strode out of the library and turned toward the gargoyles. The boy laughed, his tone filled with derision as he walked up to Dan. "Hey, gargoyle, where would you find the definition for the word 'cretin'?"

Before Dan could dignify such a ridiculous question with a response, the boy smacked the side of the gargoyle and guffawed, which to Cinder sounded like the braying of a constipated goat.

"In a mirror!" the student answered his own question and fell into another fit of uncontrolled mocking laughter.

Rage built up within Cinder, and before she knew what she was doing, she was conjuring a spell in her mind. No one spoke to Dan like that, not in front of her. Not when she wasn't around to hear it either, for that matter. Dan looked out for her and had always been a friend, even when she was too difficult for others to handle. Plus, he had trusted her with a very important mission, one she hadn't finished telling him about yet.

The funny thing about Cinder and her spells was her reaction to them. While her spells were tame and more useful for mischief than any form of battle, she loved using them to wreak havoc on the lives of those who annoyed her. The downside to her powers was that it caused her to sneeze.

Her sneeze was the only way to discharge her magic and activate whatever spell she cast. She had to sneeze. It had infuriated her for a long time that such an involuntary action was the only thing separating her from her already-limited power, but she had grown accustomed to it.

The only problems she experienced these days were those unfortunate times when she was about to sneeze, and it wouldn't come. Which had caused several embarrassing near-spells. Conversely, her sudden sneezes had resulted in a few ill-fated, accidental spells. One of which Steve was still mad about. The academy staff had yet to remove all of the cake crumbs from his ears.

The sneeze was coming, and she knew it might be difficult to do what she wanted originally, so she changed plans. Things moved so fast in her mind that sometimes she didn't have time to settle on one thought before another came barging in, demanding to be heard.

The sneeze exploded from her nose with all the cannon-fire sound of a mouse's squeak, and the boy, who was now attempting to climb onto Dan's back, found himself hovering a few inches above the gargoyle.

"Hey, wait a minute. What's going on here?" he exclaimed, as he floated higher until he was suspended at least ten feet above the ground. His body began to turn in slow cartwheels, so his head was occasionally upside down and staring at Dan and Steve in horror and confusion. "You aren't supposed to use magic against us! I am a student!" he yelled, his face growing redder and more flustered as the blood rushed to his head. He resembled a horribly ugly balloon with its helium running dry, now spinning hopelessly to its final resting place on the ground. But Cinder wasn't moving him down anywhere close.

"It's not us," Dan growled at him. His voice was low and eternally repulsed, but Cinder knew the differences. This was as happy as his voice ever became. He was at least mildly amused.

"Serves you right, though," Steve chimed in.

"Let me down, you miserable relics! My father will hear about this, I swear," the boy screamed as he spun in slow-motion, his pudgy stomach now exposed as his shirt collected around his neck.

"I should hope so," Dan said, and the faintest noise that could be mistaken for a chuckle escaped him.

Cinder flew up to the boy, hovered behind him, and began to push him gently. Her pixie-dust was going to wear off soon, and when it did, she wanted him in a very specific place. A crowd of other students had filed into the hallway and were watching with interest as he floated farther and farther away, heading to a fountain long since filled with murky, filthy, moss-covered, water. It mostly existed to catch rainwater from the edge of the library roof, and now he was hovering over it.

With the slightest touch, Cinder pushed him once more as the dust ran out, and he dropped headlong into the disgusting water. Laughter erupted from the students watching the spectacle, and Cinder flew around Dan in excitement. The boy fumed as he crawled out of the fountain and ran off, embarrassed and angry.

"As you were saying..." Dan said, and Cinder giggled. "But this time, leave out the game."

"Right, so there was someone there that was worrying. Mia didn't seem to notice him at all, but he was certainly watching her. He tried to make it look like he wasn't, but as soon as I saw him, I knew he was up to no good. I followed him around, and I heard him say something to a vampire about enchanting students to keep an eye on the new halfling."

"Do you know who he was?" Dan asked.

"No, but he seemed pretty good at whatever it is he does. He ended up enchanting two of the students to keep an eye on her and report back to him."

"Who?" Steve asked, interested now.

It filled Cinder with immense pride that her spying skills had not only garnered so much information, but that Steve seemed impressed. "One of them was Marcus," she said and hesitated.

"And the other?" Dan asked.

She twisted the hem of her dress before answering. She hated this. "Hazel," she said at last. "I'm sure she has no idea she's doing something bad. She's such a nice girl, and I like her a lot."

Mirthless laughter rumbled from both Dan and Steve. Steve's was also derisive, and Cinder put her hands on her hips. To make matters worse, her nose started itching.

"How silly of you. You should know better, Cinder," Steve said, his tone mocking. "Half-humans are mostly worthless trash. They are mean, deceptive and rude, and giving them an ounce of your emotional attachment is unworthy of a pixie, or any other true fae. They are like those mean girl-people from that human film. Always looking for a way to hurt others."

"Now, you see here," Cinder said, waggling her finger at the pair. "First off, how do you know so much about human-world things when you never leave the Academy Library entrance? And second, I'd rather spend a day with a sweet half-human who has flaws, like Hazel, than an old, grumpy gargoyle like you, Steve."

"You're right," Dan said, sobering up. "Absolutely right. Humans and halflings can be much more than what we give them credit for. Specifically, this Mia. Cinder, I have another task for you."

"Another mission?" she said with an awed sigh. All her anger had disappeared, and she was vibrating with excitement.

"Yes. I want you to get close to Mia," Dan said. "Befriend her like you did Hazel. If things are going to go as I fear, she will need your help."

CHAPTER TWENTY-NINE

"Okay, remember, try *not* to kill each other. Right, Mia?" Zander grinned at Mia. She returned the smile, and the group tightened up their circle.

They were practicing a simple spell to start, using their power to create a basic shield around them, a dome, impenetrable as long as they all focused. It was a rather easy spell, and something many of the students could do, albeit to varying degrees of strength or length of time. But Mia seemed to have trouble with it.

When it came to powers involving throwing, levitating, or growing things, she learned fast. They were all action-based, and one movement would feed into another. But her defensive skills remained far behind. It was as though she became bored and lost interest, or somehow the spell would become an active one, and things would get weird.

Like now.

As soon as the dome was above them, slowly fading inward, like a contact lens that appeared out of thin air, Mia's side began to discolor. No one noticed at first, until Carson glanced her way. He always kept an eye on Mia, watching for situations such as these. Zander gave her a lot of rope, enough to hang herself with, which would be fine if it weren't for the rest of them swinging by her side when she screwed up.

Carson waited only a moment until a yellow lightning bolt shot across her fifth of the shell. "Hey, Zander?" he said, almost beneath his breath.

Mia, whose eyes had been closed until then, opened one and looked around. The moment she saw the lightning, she squeezed them shut.

"Yes, Carson?"

"Uh, I think Mia might be doing it again."

"Doing what, exactly, Carson?"

Zander's eyes were also shut, but not tightly. His lids were calm and relaxed, as was the rest of his body, and he exuded peace and confidence. This was a spell he could handle, and he firmly believed everyone else in his group could manage it, as long as he had enough faith in them.

Unfortunately, Carson was not so positive. "She's about to kill us all, for one," he said.

Zander's sigh was heavy. As he opened his eyes, Mia lost all control. Lightning shot up the side of her dome, zig-zagging in various patterns and ending up striking the ground over and over.

He watched the lightning and turned his attention to Mia. Her eyes were shut tight, and she seemed to be biting her tongue as she concentrated. The problem was when she tried to focus too hard, she made her powers—as chaotic as they were—stronger.

A bolt escaped the directional push she was sending them, shooting off the other side of the dome, and headed for the center. When the lightning reached the middle of the shield, it soared away, aiming at Vivi.

Zander cried out and ran to her, diving at her and pushing her out of the way at the last second. The bolt landed in the grass where she had been standing and destroyed it, lighting some of it on fire.

"Get off of me," yelled Vivi, who had fallen beyond the circle with Zander, into a wide puddle of mud.

Carson glared at her. "He just saved your lif—"

"And ruined my sweater! Get off," she yelled.

Zander stood, wiping mud off his own clothes and glanced at Mia, who was sitting on the ground, covering her eyes with her hands. He couldn't tell for sure, but she appeared to be crying.

"What was that, Mia?" he said, trying to control his anger and focus on how awful Mia must be feeling. Though, with as much as Vivi tortured her, perhaps she didn't feel quite that sorry.

"I don't know," Mia said, deep in her hands. Though her voice was muffled, her disappointment and despair were clear. He knelt close beside her and lowered his voice to a whisper so the others couldn't hear.

"Did you target Vivi on purpose?" he asked.

She lifted her face from her hands, and her makeup was streaked with tears. She looked deep into his eyes. He didn't need to hear her say it, but she was going to anyway. "No. I didn't."

Zander nodded and stood, turning to the group. "All right, so maybe I jinxed us before we started that time," he said. No one laughed at his joke. "How about we all just go on home and get some rest tonight and see each other for class tomorrow? Maybe some of us can cool off a bit."

His last comment was directed at Vivi, who was still fuming, though Luna had managed to get most of the mud off her clothes and from her hair. "If I see her again tonight, I am not responsible for what I do," Vivi said and stomped off.

By the time Mia had returned to the room, showered and dressed, Vivi was lying in her own bed, her sleeping mask emblazoned with "Princess" covering her eyes, and her headphones in. Luna appeared to be sound asleep, but Mia wouldn't get much rest that night. Not until the sun was almost over the horizon, and the new day was beginning.

It was mid-afternoon, and history class would be in full swing by now. Mia, who had overslept and was going to be ten minutes late for her first class of the day, was hurrying to the history room.

Vivi had hidden her alarm clock, and Luna had gone on her morning run before class, so it was by sheer luck that Mia had happened to wake up before the school day was over at all. She barreled into the class and glared at Vivi from across the room, but Vivi was beaming a megawatt smile at her.

"So nice of you to join us. Won't you please sit?" asked Professor Metabo.

Professor Metabo was a kindly old man, short and squat with tufts of white hair sticking out from random places on his head. He often tried to comb them into something resembling a normal haircut, but it was no use, and he was apparently far too prideful to shave it off.

His beard, on the other hand, appeared to be trying to compensate for the lack on top of his head. Long and yellowish-white, it was braided from his chest to his feet. The braid swept the floor between his legs enough that he often stepped on it. Mia took her normal seat beside Luna and opened her book, checking her friend's page and matching it.

"Now, who can tell me what the originals were for?" the professor said, pointing at a slide of a handful of artifacts on the screen above him. They looked like pottery from the ancient Egyptian era, and indeed one of them appeared to have a hieroglyph carved along the bottom border. Vivi raised her hand high and had almost fallen out of her chair before the professor pointed at her.

"They were gifts from fae to humans to store magical power," she said with confidence before turning to glare at Mia again and flicking her hair.

Mia wondered if she could conjure those lightning bolts by herself right there and then.

"Yes, yes, exactly right," the professor said, interrupting Mia's train of thought. "The Egyptians were a fascinating people. They worshiped all kinds of things, and among them were fae. Yes, it's true. Many of the hieroglyphs have been misinterpreted to be about fictional gods created by fanatical priests, but in fact, many were fae creatures who, for their creativity and worship, gifted the Egyptians with power that would not be seen anywhere else on the planet."

"What kind of powers did the fae gift the Egyptians with?" Carson asked from the other side of the room.

Mia couldn't tell if he was genuinely interested or simply trying to get the professor to go off on a tangent as he often did, but either way, she was fascinated. It made so much sense. Of course, the Egyptians had received help from the fae, there was no other way to do anything they did.

"Well, I am glad you asked that, Carson. Very keen question. So, what we know is the ancient fae gifted the powers of glamouring, and we know what that is, don't we?"

The class, in a depressed monotone, muttered that they did. Professor Metabo seemed to take that as an affirmative, but apparently believed he should explain it just in case.

"Right, of course, glamouring is the act of changing a person's appearance, isn't it? That would be useful in battle, or espionage, or in the act of getting people to do your will based on one of their many gods, yes? They also used the power to create, and this is very important. The ancient Egyptians were capable of some very powerful magic of creation, thanks to the ancient fae. This included the ability to create monsters, which is where we have the basis for many stories of revenge of the Pharaohs. Indeed, many of the pyramids themselves were cursed to contain some of these monsters to protect the dead housed inside.

"Speaking of the pyramids, do we know how they were built?" The professor smiled with glee as he awaited a response from anyone in the class.

Another general agreement was shared by the class, but this time it was more of a collective shrug. Most of the students paid very little attention in history class, and others were too sleepy from early classes and late lunches to care.

"The fae, of course!" Professor Metabo announced. "This is why no one has been able to recreate the ability to build a pyramid using tools available at the time. The fae helped them do so in exchange for the use of the pyramids. In ancient times, those pyramids would have stored raw magic, much the same way a nuclear plant stores energy. Both the humans and the fae would have benefited from this, and it truly altered the course of history for both."

Later, he assigned the class a reading portion, which Mia blew through in her voracious desire for knowledge of the fae world. She had long wondered how the early Egyptians could have created such wonders, and a secret pleasure of hers had been watching silly TV shows where they insisted aliens were the true masterminds. If only she could tell those people that the fae were responsible. Her mind reeled from all the stories she had believed she knew about human history and how many would have much simpler explanations if fae were involved.

Her mind wandered to other creatures she understood to be mythical. How many of them were real? The question gnawed at her until class ended, and she joined Carson, Luna, and Zander in the hallway. Vivi, thankfully, went in another direction, heading for the restroom, leaving Mia to join them without the temptation to rip someone's face off.

"Morning, sleepyhead," Zander teased.

"Vivi stole my alarm clock," she said, defending herself.

"We know," said Luna. "She told us right before class. I almost skipped it to come wake you up, but I really love all the history stuff."

"Me too!" Mia said, her response more enthusiastic than she had intended. "Especially since it's all new to me."

"Fae have been in secret contact with humans for a long time. It didn't end well for the ones who had open contact, like with the Egyptians. We will get to all that later in the course," Zander said, "But it isn't pretty."

"Can I ask you guys a question, but promise you won't make fun of me?"

"Yes," said both Zander and Luna.

"No," Carson said and chortled. "Kidding. Yes, go ahead."

"Werewolves."

They fell into silence as they walked, and Zander raised an eyebrow. "What about them?"

"Are they real?" Mia asked.

"Not anymore," Luna said.

"Get out," Mia said, elated to be learning this new information. "What do you mean, 'Not anymore?'"

"Well, wolf shifters are real," Carson said. He didn't mention it much to the group, but shifters were kind of his thing. He studied them intensively and enjoyed the lore in his spare time. "Werewolves, not so much. They were actually a problem at one time."

"Why?" Mia asked. Even Zander and Luna seemed interested. They may have known a version of the long story, but Carson was the expert.

Heat rose in his cheeks as he realized he was being put on the spot. "Well, you see, if a wolf shifter bites a human during a full moon, it creates a werewolf who is controlled by the chaos of the cycle of the moon. Which, of course, means the person has trouble figuring it out, and goes on rampages, and often ends up becoming a huge problem for everyone. So, it's been a law for a long time now that shifters cannot create werewolves."

"What happens if they do, though?" asked Mia, rapt with attention.

"There are hunters who have the job of finding and eliminating illegal fae and other creatures: Bounty hunters." Carson's eyes met Mia's, and the dawning realization clicked in her mind. "It happens every once in a while, that a shifter will turn someone into a werewolf, and it may take some time to find out. That's when someone gets called in to not only hunt down the werewolf and eliminate it but to do the detective work of finding out who turned them and eliminate them too."

"Eliminating them, meaning killing them?" Zander asked.

"Yeah. Kaput. Doneskis. Pushing up daisies. The thing is, werewolves are unpredictable and are stupidly strong. They aren't easy to hunt down since they look like a human most of the time, and when they are a wolf, they are so hard to catch and fight that it sometimes takes a team to get them." Carson scanned the group and spotted Vivi approaching.

"I had no idea," Mia said, her voice no more than a whisper.

"So? Practice later?" Carson said, changing the subject as Vivi reached the group.

"Yeah, I guess so, if everyone is rested and ready. How about you, Vivi?" said Zander.

"I'm fine as long as no one tries to murder me with lightning again," she said.

"I can't make any promises, other than next time, I might not miss," Mia retorted.

Vivi's jaw dropped while both Zander and Carson burst into laughter. Luna took Mia by the hand and led her away. Better to get to the next class than end on any other note than that one.

CHAPTER THIRTY

"I think I'm just really tired," Mia said.

"Has that been your excuse the entire semester?" Vivi asked. "Because it seems to me this isn't a whole lot different than every other time we've tried to accomplish anything."

Mia shot her an angry glare, but it wasn't as if the dark-haired girl was inaccurate. They practiced constantly, shoving sessions in between regular classes and spending their evenings, and well into the night, trying to use their powers together.

But no matter how hard they tried or how often they practiced, they still hadn't accomplished their goal. Something always managed to go wrong, and more often than not, it linked right back to Mia.

Not that she didn't have the gifts of the other members of her group. In fact, they were learning this halfling's abilities were nothing short of astonishing, even beyond those of the four she worked with. But it wasn't the level of her abilities that mattered. The others possessed far more skill. They had trained and learned their entire lives, readying themselves for their education, and for using their magic as they grew older. She hadn't had that opportunity, and it was showing.

That night they stood on the soccer field behind the main academy building, trying again to combine their magic to create a stronger power. The Power of Five loomed over all of them, the potential of achieving something amazing, something no one would expect from young halflings. They all wanted it, but the flashes sparking from Mia's fingertips and the sudden gusts of wind that knocked them around didn't bode well.

"Just try again," Zander said. "It's not going to do any good standing around complaining. We need to keep trying."

"And you think *that's* going to do any good?" Vivi snapped.

Anger surged inside Mia. She was furious at Vivi for the way she constantly ground into her, occasionally giving her only enough of a break to make her think their relationship might start smoothing out, only to snap back. Mia was always left a little off balance and unsure of herself.

She was angry at the forces keeping her from knowing who she truly was, that were putting her through the struggles she was facing now. And she was angry at herself for being unable to catch on the way she wanted to.

She had never struggled this much before. She had always been good at what she did, building skills and mastering abilities with ease. It was exactly that way with her Wushu training. She had excelled almost from the first moment she had begun her training. She was accustomed to being the best.

And then she had come to the academy.

Her anger grew stronger, and the sky went dark. Heavy clouds rolled in from all directions until they covered the moon and stars. All light disappeared. A deafening crash of thunder split the air, accompanied by impossibly bright lightning. It looked like the entire world had caught fire in a second.

When her eyes recovered from the flash, she saw that the whole world hadn't caught fire. Unfortunately, several trees surrounding the soccer field were burning. Lit by the lightning, the trees blazed, flames jumping onto other branches, the fire spreading around the edge of the field.

In the next instant, the clouds broke open, and torrential rain fell on the soccer field. Mia checked the academy building—maybe it was contained, like in the dome in the field at the edge of town. But the rain was also pouring down on the building.

Perfect. This time, she had managed to create a catastrophe that affected not only their practice field but the entire school as well. The Scooby Gang shouted and ran around, flailing as they screamed at Mia to stop the rain which was coming so fast the ground couldn't absorb it.

Puddles had already formed, and the water became deeper with every passing second. Mia tried to stop it, but her efforts only made the rain come down harder.

The others ducked their heads, trying to find a spot away from the deluge so they could breathe. Mia heard them sputtering and gasping. She concentrated as hard as she could, and the rain stopped.

Zander stared at her, his hair hanging in his face, water dripping from his nose and ears. "Well." He gestured toward the edge of the field. "Here's a silver lining. At least the rain was hard enough to stop the fire on the trees from spreading out to the rest of the grounds and to the building."

Mia smiled, but Vivi quickly wiped it away. "Silver lining? You see that as a silver lining? Oh, fantastic, the useless one almost drowned us all, but she didn't actually burn the entire place down, so yay!"

Mia turned to say something to Vivi but fell silent. Professor Elmhurst was hurrying across the field toward them. Mia straightened her spine and tightened her shoulders. She hadn't been aware that the headmistress would be watching their disastrous practice session.

Not that it should have come as any surprise. The principal had become increasingly invested in the team's progress. It was like the harder a time Mia had, the more Elmhurst focused on pushing them to the next level.

"Well, that was quite the display."

This was perfect. Not only did Vivi have to endure the frustration of being a part of these disasters, but now she faced the humiliation of knowing Elmhurst had been watching. The headmistress studied each student, taking in their sopping clothes and the hair stuck to their heads.

"I need to have a talk with you," Elmhurst said. "I've been watching your practices, and I can see that Mia's skills are out of control. You have the ability, Mia. You just aren't focusing enough to make it happen. You haven't gotten control of those abilities. You haven't put them at your own disposal. But I'm telling you, it doesn't have to be that way. You can do anything you put your mind to."

Vivi scoffed and rolled her eyes before she could hold back the reaction out of respect for Elmhurst. But Vivi hated these special after-school pep-talks. More than that, she hated being unable to escape them, or the halfling they were directed toward.

Mia was an absolute pain, but unfortunately, she was also the only chance they had of attaining the Power of Five. Without Mia, they were going nowhere. At least, nowhere big. Nowhere that mattered.

Which wasn't good enough for Vivi. She wanted to be recognized as the very best fae of either Court. It didn't interest her to only be the best Unseelie halfling. She wanted to be known as the best halfling ever born, maybe even on par with mature fae in power and skill.

It had been a dream, something Vivi had always thought about but hadn't believed could ever happen. Not until Mia came around. Now that Vivi had seen some of what the halfling could do, she believed she was witnessing the possibility unfolding in front of her.

This halfling had the chance, too. But that only made Vivi more driven and confident. Mia couldn't be the only halfling to possess so much power. It didn't make any sense. Vivi had to have more abilities and skill than Mia did. The other girl hadn't even grown up with training, so she couldn't possibly be better than Vivi.

"Maybe she'll never be able to control it," Vivi said.

Elmhurst shook her head. "No. That's not the case. She has to keep working on it. Remember, she hasn't been to school among fae since she was little the way the four of you have. Young fae learn their control the same way people learn language. They're exposed to it, and it just becomes a part of them naturally. Mia didn't have that chance, so now she has to work to gain, and maintain, that control. That's why you're going to work on it with her."

"Us?" Vivi asked incredulously.

"What do you mean?" Luna asked. "How can we help Mia learn to control her abilities?"

Elmhurst turned to Mia again. "I want you to concentrate on something small. Just a small enchantment, something you feel comfortable doing. Now, the rest of you will help her learn how to focus. That's the problem. Not that you don't have the abilities or even that you don't have the control. You simply haven't learned to master it yet. I believe you lack focus, and that's why your powers keep going haywire like they do. I've watched many of your practices, and it always seems to go the same way. You seem to have it and are doing well, then everything just—"

"Goes funky?" Mia asked.

Elmhurst laughed. "That's one way to put it. But you can get it. You can learn to find that focus and maintain it so you can sustain the power. It may not be easy. But you can do it."

Mia nodded. Vivi rolled her eyes again when the other halfling girl drew a deep breath as though preparing herself for the challenge ahead.

"She's not asking you to use your mind to pick up the building and turn it around," Vivi pointed out. "Just something easy."

"How about wind?" Carson asked. "You really seemed to get that the last time we worked with it. At least, for a while."

"Perfect," the headmistress said. "Nothing extreme. Just pick up a nice wind and keep it going. The rest of you distract her."

Mia faced the field and closed her eyes. Vivi shouted her name, and Mia whipped around to glare at her through narrowed eyes.

"What?" Vivi asked. "We *are* supposed to distract you, aren't we?"

"Vivi's right," Professor Elmhurst said. "She's not going to learn to focus if she doesn't have to fight distractions. Everybody, try to break her concentration. Mia, you have to try to block it out. Fight the frustration. Don't let it get to you or stop you from doing what you need to do."

Vivi couldn't help but smile. This was fantastic. Usually, she was hassled for doing anything that might distract the others or keep them from being able to use their abilities. Now, Professor Elmhurst was telling her to do exactly that. She could heckle and aggravate Mia, and no one could say anything to her.

It took some time, but finally, Mia began to get the hang of things. Even as Vivi and the group were doing their best to distract her and break her focus, she managed to take hold of her abilities and keep them under her command.

She created a light wind and kept it flowing over the practice field for five minutes, before discharging it smoothly. Nothing bad happened. No rain burst from the sky, and none of the trees flared up, either.

Satisfied at the progress, the headmistress strode away. Mia turned to the group with a triumphant smile, and Luna grinned at her. Zander offered his congratulations, and Carson also appeared somewhat impressed. Vivi wanted no part in the little congratulatory party, but the others wouldn't allow her to go inside.

Now that Mia had more concentration and focus, they wanted to try again. For the next three hours, they attempted all of the spells they had done before. Faerie circles burst from the grass, they played with wind, and she was able to create a small, concentrated storm which she could pass from person to person without risk of drowning.

Finally, the group was tired and ready to call it a night. Mia was gaining control, and they were excited to keep pushing and discover what she could accomplish.

"Why don't we meet up early tomorrow?" Mia asked. "Right after classes."

"Sounds good," Luna replied. "Let's meet up outside the library."

Since two of their group had the last class of their day at the library, it was the most central location to meet. All five agreed and returned to the academy building to get something to eat and get some rest.

CHAPTER THIRTY-ONE

"I don't know. Do you really think that has anything to do with it?" Mia asked, leaning against the wall.

"Absolutely. She has a major complex about being in the Unseelie Court. Having a half-brother in the Seelie Court just drives her crazy," Luna said.

"But he's only a baby. How could she be that offended by a baby?"

"He's a baby now, which means he's super adorable and everybody is falling all over themselves for him. But he's going to get older, and when he does, being in the Seelie Court will become a thing for him. It's already embarrassing enough for her to be a halfling. But to be a halfling with a human father who now has children with two different fae women, one Seelie and one Unseelie, just feels like a complete scandal to her."

"Is it a scandal?" Mia asked.

Luna laughed and shook her head. "Not really. There are a few people here at the academy with half-siblings or step-siblings. Some even have half-siblings who are full human, and some have half-siblings who are full fae. There are some people who have terribly strict rules about the Courts and what is and isn't okay, but there are a lot more halfling families like that than there are regular mother, father, half-kids."

Mia shuddered. "I know what you meant, but 'half-kids' is not a visual I needed."

Luna chuckled. The two halfling fae girls were standing outside the library waiting for the group. They had finished class a few minutes early and had been standing there for a while.

Their conversation had led to a girl in one of their classes, a particularly strange halfling called Sage. She wasn't strange like Vivi, but more a theatrical, melodramatic type of strange. That day she had disrupted class with a long-winded, repetitive speech about oppression that left everyone in the class wondering who exactly she believed was being oppressed. Her words turned back on themselves so many times she had ended up contradicting herself in at least three ways.

Above the two girls, Dan and Steve were listening to their chat. They had been eavesdropping since the pair had arrived, but hadn't said anything. The two gargoyles were doing their best to keep their distance from Mia.

Since their conversation with Cassia, they hadn't spoken much to Mia but had done their best to keep an eye on her as promised. They preferred to watch over her and ensure she was doing fine, but without making it obvious to her, or to anyone else. The gargoyles didn't want any of the students or the faculty to suspect that they liked Mia. They didn't want anyone to think they had any interest in her. That would accomplish nothing but put a big target on her back.

Everyone would wonder why the two curmudgeonly gargoyles were fond of the new halfling. Which might make them look closer at Mia and try to figure her out. Steve and Dan definitely didn't want that. It would put Mia at risk and upset Cassia.

Besides, it would hurt the gargoyles' rep if anyone at the academy discovered they might possibly be nice, or that they actually liked anyone. That would ruin how people saw them. All the students believed the gargoyles were mean spies for the faculty, which was how Dan and Steve preferred it.

Vivi was in a particularly good mood as she approached the library a few minutes later. At least, Vivi's version of a good mood. The practicing in the soccer field the night before and Mia's disaster had inspired a new prank, and Vivi had spent all day mastering it.

Although the near-drowning in Mia's massive storm had made Vivi miserable and ticked off, tossing the smaller storms around later had been more amusing. Which had given her the idea to drop a storm cloud over the heads of the two nasty-spirited gargoyles perched outside the library. But she wasn't simply going to stop at that. As soon as the rain started, she was going to create a bubble around each of them so it would fill with water and drown them.

Her plan sounded far more dastardly than it really was. They weren't going to drown. A little water wasn't going to kill them. It couldn't. Steve and Dan weren't really alive. They were merely animated statues. Since they didn't breathe, they could remain underwater for as long as she wanted, and it wouldn't be a problem. At least, it wouldn't be a problem for them *physically*. But it would certainly aggravate them.

One thing Vivi had learned about the gargoyles early on in her time at the academy was that Dan and Steve hated water. Being permanently attached to their posts outside the library meant constant exposure to the elements. No matter what was going on with the weather, they were out there in it.

They were rained and snowed on throughout the year, and they could do nothing about it, not even shake to get the droplets or snowflakes off. After countless years spent on campus, the two hated anything other than sunshine.

Vivi positioned herself at the perfect spot so she could watch without anyone, particularly Mia and Luna, seeing her. She conjured the storm cloud and positioned it right above the gargoyles. The dark cloud grumbled and broke open, sending a deluge of water down on the statues and the surrounding area of the building.

On the other side of the statues, Luna and Mia glanced up at the sudden rumble of the storm and ran inside to get out of the cold rain.

"Where did that come from?" Mia brushed away the water still clinging to her clothes. "It was sunny just a minute ago."

"I have no idea," Luna replied. "That came out of nowhere."

Out of the corner of her eye, something caught Mia's attention. She glanced out the windows across the library and waved at Luna to get her attention. "Look at that," she said.

They went to the window and peered outside. There was no sign of the rain. Beyond the glass, the day was bright and sunny.

"What's going on?" Luna asked.

"I don't know." Mia shook her head. "Let's go find out."

They hurried to the other door of the library and ran out around the corner of the building to where it was still sunny. A distinct line marked the sky where the clear weather ended, and the storm began. And Vivi was standing behind a column and laughing gleefully.

Mia turned her attention to Dan and Steve. Water was collecting around them in a bubble. The gargoyles were gurgling and shouting, struggling as much as they could without being able to move. They were drowning, and a surge of fear tightened Mia's chest. Terrified for their safety, she ran across the yard toward the rain. She didn't have time to think about anything. Without considering what she was doing, she waved her hand at the gargoyles.

With a loud popping sound, the invisible bubble surrounding the gargoyles burst, and all the water gushed down. Vivi was perfectly positioned for the entire wave to splash onto her. Her scream was high-pitched, and she raised her arms, but she wasn't fast enough to stop herself from being soaked from head to toe.

Carson and Zander approached Mia with Luna in tow, just as the water fell onto Vivi. Mia was still shaking with worry and wrapped up in her effort to save the gargoyles, but the boys instantly burst into laughter. The amusement helped break Mia from her thoughts, and she saw how hilarious Vivi looked, standing there sagging and dripping like a drowned rat.

Vivi released an angry, exasperated sound, somewhere between a growl and roar, stomped her foot, and whipped around to march off to the dorms.

"You better run," Dan shouted after her.

"Watch your back, Vivi. We're going to get even!" Steve added.

They were spitting mad, but at least they were safe. Mia rushed to the pair and stared up at them. "Are you all right?" she asked. "Dan? Steve? Are you okay?"

"We're fine," Dan said flatly, his gaze following Vivi until she disappeared from view.

"I'm so glad," Mia said. "I was so worried you were going to drown."

The gargoyles looked down at her for a few seconds, staring as though they believed she was going to say something else.

"Oh. You really did?" Steve's eyes were wide, apparently surprised by the sentiment.

"Of course. You were completely underwater," she said.

"That's really nice. But we can't actually drown. We can't die. Vivi might be many different kinds of horrible, but she hasn't been murderous...yet. She just wanted to torment us," Dan said.

"Oh, well...I guess you didn't need to be rescued, then." Mia was embarrassed by her frantic reaction, trying to save the lives of beings who weren't actually alive to begin with. But the gargoyles' expressions were almost tender.

"No. Thank you," Steve said. "However, we can't stand water, and Vivi knows that, which is why she did it. She wanted to watch us be miserable. Who knows how long she would have kept it going if you weren't there to stop her? We're very grateful. And we absolutely owe you a favor."

Luna, Zander, and Carson gasped and exchanged amazed glances. They rushed toward the gargoyles, eyes wide.

"I have never heard of the gargoyles granting favors," Luna said to Mia.

Carson went right up to the statues. "Hey, if I knew you were going to be giving out favors, I would have stopped everyone from playing pranks on the two of you guys a long time ago."

The gargoyles promptly spat water at him. Mia joined in as everyone burst out laughing. Carson wiped the water from his eyes, and they walked around to the back of the library on their way to the practice field.

Mia stopped halfway there. "Wait. If the gargoyles aren't alive, and can't move, how is it they can talk and spit water?"

Luna shrugged and looked at the group. No one was offering up an explanation, so she did. "It's magic. Who knows how they do what they do, they just do it."

Mia's brows furrowed in confusion. "I don't know if I'll ever get used to this new life."

The gang laughed with her, and they continued their trek to the practice field, short one member.

"Do you guys actually think Vivi is going to show for practice?" Luna asked.

"I doubt it," Mia replied. "She's bitter enough about having to practice with me in the first place. She's not going to do it after being humiliated like that."

"But there's no point in us going out to the field and practicing without her. You can't exactly accomplish the Power of Five with only four people," Carson said.

"That didn't stop Professor Elmhurst from trying to get the four of us to do it," Zander pointed out.

"True. But that's not the point now. We're supposed to be combining with Mia. We need Vivi if we're going to practice," Luna said.

"Just give her some time to cool off. She'll get over it. Why don't we all take the afternoon to catch up on some schoolwork, then we'll have dinner and see how she is after that," Mia suggested.

"Sounds good," Carson said. "I'll bring her down to the practice field after dinner. I'll be more convincing than the three of you."

CHAPTER THIRTY-TWO

"This is ridiculous, you know?" Vivi asked as she and Carson walked from the main academy building toward the practice field. "I don't need you to be my babysitter."

"I'm not your babysitter," Carson said. "I'm your escort."

She laughed mirthlessly and rolled her eyes. "Because that is just so much better. I also don't need you as my escort. I'm a big girl. I can get to practice on my own."

"Oh, really? So, if I hadn't come up to your dorm room and found you sitting on your bed pouting in your sweatpants, you still would have come?" he asked.

"I was not pouting. I was studying."

"Right. Whatever you were doing, if I hadn't shown up, you're telling me you would have willingly, and under your own volition, taken off those sweatpants, put regular clothes back on, and come down to the practice field to meet up with the rest of us?"

Vivi flashed him a glare. "Shut up."

The pair turned to go past the library, taking the fastest route down to the practice field, and they figured the other three were probably already there waiting for them. As they approached the library, a chorus of angry words was hurled her away. The gargoyles were shouting at her, yelling, and spouting what she could only assume they believed to be insulting curses.

The years they had spent stuck in one place had taken some of the modern edge from their insults.

"You dastardly buffoon!"

"You blunderbuss!"

"Cow-handed cabbage head!"

"Fop-doodle!"

"Fribble!"

"Ginger-snap!"

"Rattlecap!"

Vivi stalked toward them, glaring up at the statues. "You're slipping into rhyme, you idiots," she snapped.

Dan squirted water at her, and when she cried out and jumped away, Steve followed suit. They both followed up with a bigger squirt, soaking her shirt and the front of her skirt.

She growled angrily at them. "I can't believe you did that! I already had to change my uniform once today, thanks to the two of you!" she snarled.

"Thanks to the two of us?" Dan asked incredulously.

"You're going to blame *us* for that?" Steve asked.

"I ended up soaked," Vivi shouted.

"Because you thought it would be funny to put a bubble around us and have a storm fill it up."

"You can't even take a joke. That's why no one around here likes you. You are nothing but miserable chunks of worthless stone."

"At least we have being stone as an excuse," Dan shot back.

Letting out another angry, exasperated cry, Vivi lashed out at them, freezing them into place with a blast of magic. Instantly, they couldn't move what little bit they could or talk. The two gargoyles had been able to move their heads around before, but now they were totally stuck. And bits of ice hung from their stone bodies. Steve had a three-inch icicle suspended from his nose. While tiny, razor-sharp icicles dangled from Dan's eyebrows.

The only thing they could do was move their eyes around in their frozen faces. A furious shout from behind Vivi made her whip around. Mia was running toward her, with Luna and Zander close behind. Apparently, they hadn't had as much of a head start down to the practice field as she expected.

Mia couldn't believe what she was seeing. Actually, she could, and that just made it worse. Vivi had been tormenting the gargoyles again, and she had *frozen* them. Ticked off that the bitter Unseelie was hurting them again, Mia stormed up to Vivi and confronted her. "What is wrong with you?" she demanded.

"Excuse me?" Vivi narrowed her eyes.

"Don't try that. Don't act like you don't know exactly what I'm talking about. What amuses you so much about tormenting Dan and Steve? Is it just because they're easy targets? They can't defend themselves, so you bully them because it's fun? Or is it because they can't really do anything back to you, which is the only reason you would be brave enough to be as nasty to them as you are?"

"Watch your mouth," Vivi said through gritted teeth.

"Or what? What are you going to do to me?" Mia stabbed a finger at the gargoyles. "Look what you did to them. What is it, Vivi? They were so much of a threat to you because they could move their heads and speak? That's all they had, and you took it from them just out of spite. How could you do something like that? You've always been mean, but how could you do something so horrible to creatures who have literally never done anything to you?"

Vivi shook her head, and Mia was surprised at the shame flashing across her eyes. Vivi stared up at the statues before turning to Mia. "I didn't mean to. Really. I know you don't believe me, but I didn't mean to freeze them. I was angry, and it just happened."

"Have you ever done something like this before?" Zander asked. "How long is it going to take to wear off?"

Vivi shrugged, her expression growing more helpless. "I don't know. I wouldn't even know how long it would take for a spell to wear off when used against a gargoyle. It might not last as long as it would for a living being. It might last longer. I don't know."

In the next instant, the librarian rushed from the building and stalked toward them.

"What is going on out here?" she asked.

"It's me," Vivi said. "I got angry at the gargoyles and froze them."

The librarian's mouth fell open, and she glared at Vivi for a few seconds before she was able to bring herself to speak. "Fix it. Fix it right now. Reverse the spell," she demanded.

Vivi turned to the gargoyles and focused on them. She muttered a few words and shot her hand toward them, but nothing happened. "I can't."

"What do you mean you can't? You did it, now reverse it," the librarian said.

"I know I did it, but I can't reverse it. I tried. For some strange reason, I can't make it reverse."

"You need to figure something out."

Vivi shifted uncomfortably, looking between the ground and the statues. The energy around the group was anxious and on edge, all waiting for something to happen.

"I don't know what to do," Vivi said, sounding worried. "I didn't mean for this to happen. Really, I didn't. I'm sorry. If I knew what to do to fix it, I would. Honestly. I just don't know what to do."

It was the first time Mia had seen the girl feel bad about anything. Her head hung, and she appeared to be truly remorseful. But Mia couldn't bring herself to care how the other fae girl was feeling. All she could think about was the gargoyles. Her heart was breaking. She knew how much they were suffering and how horrible this would be for them.

Her eyes slid up and down Dan's face, and she wished he would be free of Vivi's spell and able to move off the pedestal he had been standing on for so long. No sooner had the thought flitted through her mind, than the air snapped loudly and the gargoyle fell forward off his pedestal and onto the ground.

The earth shook at the impact, and Dan blinked. A second later, he began to move. It wasn't smooth, controlled movements like a human, but Dan wasn't a human. He was a statue. And now, though, he was a statue who could move and talk.

The librarian and the Scooby Gang slid their eyes over to Mia, before shifting their attention to Steve. The group dissolved into questions and chattering.

"Aren't you going to move, Steve?" Luna's voice rose over the rest of the noise. "Come on. Just like he did. Just get down."

"Can't you do it?" Vivi asked, actually sounding hopeful. "Dan did. Try it. Maybe you can, too."

Professor Elmhurst looked around. A large crowd of students fanned out, gathering in the library yard. They all stared in shock and surprise at Dan lying on the ground and were all talking over each other.

There were so many voices and words that Mia couldn't pick any out specifically. It was beginning to overwhelm her, and she couldn't imagine what it would be like for the gargoyles. Steve hadn't responded to their questions, or to his companion who had toppled from the pedestal. He wasn't speaking or moving, which meant he was still frozen. If he wasn't, he would have at least said something.

Dan pleaded with her. "Please, Mia. Help him. Do whatever you did for me. Help Steve get down too."

"Mia, what happened here?" Elmhurst asked.

"I don't know." Mia shook her head. "I was worried about them, and the next second, Dan was off his pedestal."

"Do it again," Dan said. "Whatever it is you did when you were worried about me, do it again."

"I can't. I don't know what I did. I don't know how I did it."

"Please," Dan said again.

Mia looked at Elmhurst desperately, and the headmistress gave a weary sigh. "I don't know if this is a good idea. The gargoyles have been at their post since the very beginning of the academy. This is where they belong. But I'll help you."

Mia heaved a sigh of relief. "Thank you."

Elmhurst gave her a few instructions, helping her to refocus on the magic within her and turn it onto the remaining frozen statue. But nothing was happening. She repeated the process several times, but Steve stayed firmly in place.

A few failed attempts later, Steve had turned cotton-candy pink. He still couldn't move or speak, but he looked lovely. The next attempt removed the coloration from him, but still did nothing to get him off his pedestal. The next covered him with a variety of brightly colored feathers. The poor gargoyle seemed better off before she had started messing with him. Finally, she made one more attempt. A slight cracking sound preceded the gargoyle loosening from his place, turning sharply, and falling backward.

The crowd around her gasped, and a few students grabbed her shoulders to shake her. She was sure it was meant as an encouragement, but it was merely another layer of being overwhelmed.

"That's amazing!" someone exclaimed behind her.

"Did you see that?"

"Could they always do that?"

"How did she do that?"

"What does this mean?" Zander asked.

"Dan, Steve," Elmhurst said, pointing at each of the gargoyles to make sure they were paying attention to her. "No matter what just happened, you are to remember that you are still gargoyles. You have a duty."

"Are we?" Dan asked. He shifted, and the movement made him rise up off the ground a few inches. He gasped and glanced at Steve.

The other statue performed the same movement and rose up, too. "We can fly." Steve gasped.

Dan hit the ground and bounced up. Steve followed close behind him. A second later, the stone on their backs made a cracking sound, and their large wings opened, spreading out to the sides so they could fly higher. They made gleeful sounds and soared up higher into the air, swooping and flying in circles.

Mia couldn't imagine what it was like for them. For their entire existence, they had been stuck in place, standing on the same pedestals. They could move their heads and speak, but never anything else. Now they could not only move, but they could also fly.

She watched them happily, thrilled at the sight of them trying different formations and playing with each other in midair.

"Everyone. It's getting late. Everyone back to your dorms," the headmistress announced loudly. The crowd grumbled in protest, but she didn't relent. "Now. Back to your dorms. Except for you five."

She made eye contact with Mia, before studying the other four. They waited while the crowd slowly dissipated. Some students moved on without question, but others lingered. They tried to stay for as long as possible, watching the gargoyles, eyes flickering over the headmistress, and the five students she had pulled aside.

Their curious expressions said they wanted to know what was going on and wanted to be the one to take the juicy gossip back to the other students. But Elmhurst had nothing but patience. She waited until the last students decided there was no subtle way for them to stay any longer, and they left dragging their feet and grumbling as they went. When they were alone, Elmhurst turned her attention to the group.

"I'm sorry, Professor," Mia said. "I really don't know how—"

Elmhurst cut Mia off. "Stop. You just saw what Mia was capable of doing. That was astonishing. I want the five of you to try her magic. Everything she has. Don't let limits on your imagination stop you. Try everything you can think of. But be careful about it. That is my only stipulation. You may try whatever you want to, but you need to be careful not to hurt others or yourselves or cause any massive structural damage to the historic buildings of the academy." She turned away, but only took a few steps before turning back to them. "And maybe you should leave manipulating the weather alone until Mia has more control. Just a suggestion."

She began to turn away again, but Mia approached her. "Professor?"

"Yes, Mia."

"Um..." The request sounded ridiculous now after the magical carte blanche they had just been given. "I'm really worried about my upcoming paper that's due on Egyptian artifact history. I want to go to the library to look up some books on the subject. I know it's late, but can I just pop in there?"

"No. It's far too late. You need to return to your dorms. But you can call up the history back in your room." Without any further explanation, Elmhurst walked away, leaving nothing but the sound of the gargoyles still cheering and laughing with glee as they flew around.

Mia could only imagine they would keep flying until their wings gave out on them. If that was possible. If they weren't really alive, maybe they never became tired. It was possible they would just fly forever.

CHAPTER THIRTY-THREE

The five hurried to the dorm. Usually, they would go their separate ways when they reached the common area, the boys to the room they shared, and the three girls into the other wing to their room.

That's not how it went that night. Instead of parting when they entered the common area, all five headed to the girls' room. Carson and Zander followed without question. It was simply understood they weren't done for the night. They may not be able to go out onto the practice field to try their usual experiments, or even attempt anything new, but that didn't mean they couldn't discuss the gargoyle's reanimation and delve deeper into the challenge presented to them by Elmhurst.

Having the guys in their dorm room was strictly against the rules, but Vivi, Luna, and Mia weren't worried about getting into trouble because of their visitors. They didn't have any other roommates or anyone to disturb, and they didn't think anyone else in the dorm would feel compelled to rat them out simply because the boys were in their room for a few hours.

Even if someone did, the chances of angering Elmhurst were slim to none. After what she experienced that night, Principal Elmhurst seemed almost stunned. She was probably not thinking about rules and discipline at the moment. The five could get away with just about anything.

As long as it didn't hurt anyone, or involve structural damage or weather.

"That was really incredible. I mean, *really* incredible," Carson said when they entered the room. "I don't think I've ever seen anything like that."

"What? Vivi, or Mia?" Luna asked.

Carson thought about his answer for a second. At last, he gave a shrug. "I mean…both. I've never seen anyone freeze animated statues, and I've definitely never seen anyone then free those statues and let them move when they were never able to before. Do you think they could have had something to do with each other?"

"What do you mean?" Zander asked. He dropped onto Luna's bed and stared at the Unseelie boy, who reclined on a bean-bag chair in the middle of the floor.

"Think about it," Carson said. "Those gargoyles were never able to move before. They've been there literally since the library was built. And by there, I mean, right there. On those pedestals. They've never been anywhere else and have never moved other than shifting their heads around and speaking. Do you honestly think that in all the hundreds of years this place has been standing, no one else has ever had a bleeding-heart moment and tried to free them off their pedestals?"

"Hey!" Mia exclaimed. "I'm not a bleeding heart."

"Sorry. I didn't mean that in a bad way."

"Yes, you did," Vivi muttered.

"What I mean,"—Carson pressed on, talking over Vivi—"is that this couldn't have been the first time someone tried to set them free. Even if it wasn't because they cared about them. It's just one of those things. There are creatures standing there talking to you, but they can't go anywhere. Normal teenage curiosity? Someone is going to want to see if they can get them down."

"Or just to be rebellious," Luna added.

"Exactly. But they've never moved. In all this time, no one has been able to move them. Then Vivi freezes them, and they can't do anything but roll their eyes around in that creepy way." He demonstrated, rolling his eyes around for a few seconds until he realized they were staring at him. "Anyway. She can't figure out how to unfreeze them, but then, not only does Mia unfreeze them, she manages to get them totally off their pedestals and flying around. What if they couldn't have done it without each other?"

"I think you are thinking way too much about this," Zander said. "I don't think Vivi and Mia have some sort of unholy alliance we don't know about."

Carson sighed dramatically. "Mia, what do you think?"

Up until this point, Mia hadn't been paying too much attention to the conversation. Instead, she was sifting through her notes and trying to figure out how she was going to get her paper finished. She looked up at the four sets of eyes staring back at her.

"Oh. I was just thinking about..." She hesitated. "What did Elmhurst mean when she said I could call up the history in my dorm room?"

Vivi laughed and tossed herself backward onto her pillows. "So stupid," she muttered.

Apparently, all the remorse and humanity she had discovered outside the library had remained there. Vivi had already reverted to her mean-girl persona. But it didn't matter to Mia all that much. She had learned an important lesson about Vivi that night.

From the experience outside the library, Mia had learned the angry Unseelie fae girl did have a heart and a conscience. That part of her character didn't come out often, but it was there. Mia had seen it, and she had been a part of it surfacing.

She hoped she could coax that side of Vivi to come out again, and maybe eventually remain as her permanent personality. Holding out that hope meant Vivi's attitude didn't bother Mia any longer.

Dismissing Vivi's obvious need for attention, Mia turned her focus on the other three. "What did she mean?" she asked. "Is this a book-delivery situation? I can call the library and let them know what I want, and they will bring it to me? That seems a little counterintuitive. If it's too late for me to be in the library, it's too late for people to be working in there."

"It's not book delivery," Luna said. "She didn't say you could call up the books. She said you could call up the history."

Mia blinked at her. "That didn't tell me anything."

"She meant you could actually access the information and experience it." Zander offered more of an explanation.

"Not helpful."

"Look," Carson said. "You're not in your little human high school anymore. You don't have to study just by reading books or going online. The fae study in a different way. Well, some do. It takes power and skill, but we have that."

Mia rotated her hand as though recoiling a rope. "I'm going to have to ask you to go back to the beginning and pick me up there because I've missed everything that has to do with this explanation."

"You can call up images from the past," Luna explained. "You don't have to just read the words and try to get everything from that. You can actually experience what the books have to say. Like a movie. All you need is a book, and you can enchant it to spill its secrets. More information than the book even contains in print will come to life, and you can watch it."

"Do I need to remind you that I can't even enchant a storm without setting things on fire and almost drowning people?" Mia asked.

Luna laughed. "You'll be fine. We'll help you. Here, let me show you."

The beautiful fae girl rifled through the books on the shelf against the wall and pulled one out. She lay it on the floor and spoke the words of a spell over it. A few seconds later, a glow appeared, emanating from the spine of the book. The light spread, creating a screen, where an image appeared. It reminded Mia of the few times her father convinced her to watch Star Trek with him when she was younger. Or Star Wars. One of them.

Luna had chosen a book on the rainforest, and Mia watched as an image of the jungle came to life and started moving. It was as though she was traveling through it, looking at the plants and animals around her. Every so often, the image would stop and zoom in on a specific animal or a lush plant. Words appeared beside it, providing descriptions and facts.

They all watched for a few minutes before Luna ended the enchantment and closed the book. "See?" she said. "Easy."

"Let me try." Carson scoured the bookshelf. "You have really boring books, you know that? Let me see. This one."

He pulled out a book and set it on the spot Luna's book had occupied. He opened it and performed the same enchantment. As with Luna's spell, the light appeared and created a screen.

A second later, it revealed a loud, violent battle. It was like watching a TV show about a war. It became more intense and violent, and the boys were drawn into it, engrossed by the action. After a few minutes, Luna snapped the book shut. The pages continued to glow until Carson spoke the enchantment to close the image and reluctantly tucked the book back onto the shelf.

"Ready to give it a try?" Luna asked Mia.

Mia nodded. "Sure." She picked up her textbook and opened it to an image. She followed Luna's example carefully, and after a moment, a light started glowing, and a scene appeared in front of her. It lasted only a few seconds before bursting into a ball of flame and disappearing.

"What in Hades' name was that?" asked Carson.

"I have never seen something like that happen before," Luna said.

"Me, neither," Zander added.

"Let me try again." Mia shook her head to clear her mind, flipped the page, and performed the enchantment. This image lasted a few seconds longer before also bursting into a bright fiery ball.

"I think that's probably your clue to just give up," Vivi said. "Maybe you can get into the library early in the morning."

"No. I'm not giving up that easy. I'm going to try again," Mia insisted.

This time, the fervor of her concentration resulted in the entire textbook exploding. The energy shooting from the book sent Mia tumbling backward into the wall. As she fell, she sighed, wishing she could see real artifacts and learn more about them.

In the next instant, a portal formed behind her, and she fell through.

The others didn't hesitate. One right after the next, Luna, Zander, Carson, and Vivi, dove into the portal to follow her. Mia toppled to the floor, grunting as she bounced and landed on her back.

She pulled herself up to her hands and knees and shook her head. "I seriously have to stop doing that," she muttered.

The Scooby Gang fell in a tangled heap to the floor beside her, and Mia scrambled out of the way to avoid being crushed.

"You are going to have to do some fancy explaining about why you don't have a textbook anymore," Carson said with a loud groan.

Vivi climbed to her feet and looked around. "I think she could probably find another one."

For the first time, Mia studied her surroundings. "This is definitely not what I was expecting," she murmured. "Elmhurst is not going to be amused."

They were standing inside the school's library.

CHAPTER THIRTY-FOUR

"How?" Zander shook his head and stared at Mia. "Did *you* create that portal?"

Dazed, Mia stared wide-eyed at her friends. She tried to speak, but nothing would come out. When she winced, she also nodded.

"Did you know you could do this?" Luna whispered.

Mia bit her lower lip, not sure what she should say. Cassia and Mia had both decided to keep her portal-creation ability confidential, but now it wouldn't stay a secret much longer. Vivi would be spreading the news all over campus well before the first class started.

Other than Zander's confused look, the rest didn't seem too surprised. It was almost as though they had expected this to happen. Well, maybe not *this*, but with all of the craziness since she had arrived, the Scooby Gang had moved past immediate disbelief and into the realm of possibilities.

"I can't believe she managed to end up at the library," Vivi said with a hint of awe in her voice.

"Maybe that's exactly where she wanted to be," Luna suggested. "She did tell Elmhurst earlier that she wanted to come here and get a couple books to use while she works on her paper on Egyptian artifacts."

"Maybe *she's* in the same room with both of you, and you should talk to her rather than to each other." Mia glared at the two girls.

"You're right," Luna said. "Is this where you wanted to go?"

Mia hesitated. "I don't know."

"See?" Vivi snapped.

"How did you get here anyway? I mean, a portal, obviously, but how did you conjure it so fast?" Zander asked.

"It was the same as when I first came here. To the academy, I mean. When that happened, I was up against a wall and wished I could be somewhere safe and away from the guy coming after me. The portal showed up behind me, and I fell through."

"Yeah, quickly followed by a bullet that nearly took Zander out," Vivi added.

"Now, that's a bit of an exaggeration," Carson pointed out. "But that's still really interesting. What were you wishing for this time?"

"To be able to actually see artifacts so I can learn about them." Mia's admission sounded far more ridiculous when it came out of her mouth than it had when it was still in her brain.

"And that made the portal bring you here? To the school library?" Vivi asked. "Because it's just bursting at the seams with authentic Egyptian artifacts," she said sarcastically.

"I don't know. How am I supposed to know? And besides, where else would the portal bring me?" Mia asked.

"Uh, Egypt?" Vivi suggested.

"I want to see Egyptian artifacts, not actual Egypt. The portal probably brought me here so I could find a book on Egypt and use that to call up the information. Or have one of you call up the information so I can actually read it before it blows up."

"You're just saying that because you're afraid," Vivi accused.

"What?" Mia asked.

"You're afraid. You're afraid to try to create a portal to go to Egypt."

"I'm not afraid," Mia scoffed.

"Then do it. I dare you to try to open a portal to Egypt," Vivi said.

"This must be the most absurd conversation I have ever had. Well, no. There are a couple of other ones I've had recently that may actually rank higher. Finding out I'm a fae halfling hits right up there on the top of the list. But this one is still pretty absurd." Mia gave Vivi a sardonic look. She narrowed her eyes at Vivi. "I'm not going to try to open a portal to Egypt, and not because I'm afraid to. I have absolutely no desire to go there, no matter how good of a grade it may get me on my paper."

"How about Paris?" Luna asked.

"Yes," Vivi said the second the words were out of Luna's mouth.

"Paris?" Mia asked. "Are there a whole lot of Egyptian artifacts banging around in France?"

"Actually, yes," Luna said. "We could go to the Louvre."

"Yes," Vivi said again. She clapped her hands. "To Paris. But I don't really care about going to the Louvre with you people."

"Why would we go to the Louvre? Are a bunch of paintings going to help me any more than the books?"

"I don't think she's talking about the paintings. I think Luna is suggesting the new Egyptian display. If we get there, we could see the artifacts and the Egyptian art we need to learn about. Seeing and touching those things firsthand would give us the upper hand over the rest of the class," Zander said. "Our papers will be much better because we'll have firsthand knowledge of the artifacts."

"Pretty sure you're not allowed to touch things in the Louvre," Mia pointed out.

Carson snorted. "You can if no one notices you're there. Plus, it's the Louvre. In Paris. Do you need a reason to go?"

"So, is that a yes?" Luna asked.

"Yes!" Vivi interjected. "Yes, Paris. Yes, shopping. Oh, and the Louvre so you four can poke around old pyramid stuff." She waved at them as though she were dismissing servants.

Mia sighed. "Your resounding support is touching. All right. You talked me into it. Let's try this."

The group cheered, but they had no way of knowing they weren't the only ones in the library celebrating. A few rows away, concealed within the stacks, were Hazel and Marcus. They had hidden in the library before closing and had been there ever since, waiting to meet their vampire contact.

They would never have imagined they'd see a portal open, nor had they been prepared for the five halflings to spill out of it. They listened in on the entire conversation and were now brimming with excitement, eager to report something really juicy for once.

Mia walked around the library until she found a surface that would be good for the creation of their portal. The end of the bookshelf was smooth wood and made her feel like even if they didn't get through the portal all the way to Paris, having the surface inside the library meant they were less likely to fall out in the middle of the yard next to the building. She didn't know if that was the case, but it made her feel better thinking it.

"Right here. This is the perfect spot," she told them.

The others stood back and watched as Mia tried to conjure the portal. Nothing happened. No matter how hard she wished to be in the Louvre, it didn't work. She switched to the magic she had used with the group to create the portal, but the bookshelf remained unchanged.

Mia remembered what Elmhurst told her, and she forced herself to focus. She cleared her mind of everything around her and concentrated only on the portal she needed. She thought about the moments in the past when she had created a portal merely based on what she needed, and she directed all that focus onto the bookshelf.

And, again, nothing happened.

"What is it that you aren't doing?" Vivi asked. "You've been able to do this twice before. There has to be something you did during those times you aren't doing now."

"Are you suggesting I throw myself up against a wall and wish the portal into existence?" Mia asked.

"Couldn't hurt."

"No," Zander said. "No one is going to throw themselves against anything. I don't think this is Mia's fault. There are enchantments on the campus to prevent students from just moving around through portals however they want to. Maybe they are stopping her from being able to create a portal that sends us so far away."

The group nodded, and Mia understood now why she had portaled to the library instead of somewhere with real Egyptian artifacts. And why she had originally portaled *outside* the academy instead of inside the gates.

"But the enchantments were designed to stop the power of one fae. Let's try combining all our power together to create the portal. The enchantments might not be able to withstand that," Luna suggested.

Mia nodded. "Sounds good to me. But let's get on with it. I don't want to be lingering around here if Elmhurst decides she wants some midnight reading material."

"Uh." Vivi glanced at the ancient clock hanging on the wall near them. "It's closer to two a.m. now."

Everyone stared wide-eyed at the clock on the wall. They had been in the library for a while and had taken so much time with all of Mia's attempts and their argument over how best to create a portal that no one realized it was so late.

The five gathered together and held hands. It took a few moments for the portal to appear on the bookshelf. For all their lofty goals, it was only the size of a quarter. They all tilted their heads to look at it.

"Well," Mia said. "That's...something."

Carson leaned closer to the bookshelf and spat into the tiny portal. "I hope that makes it all the way," he said.

The girls groaned, disgusted by the Unseelie, but Zander stifled his laugh behind his hand. Mia thought about the other end of the portal. If it really was in the Louvre, someone might have just been hit with a ball of spit that came out of nowhere. Definitely not what anyone expected on a nice visit to a museum.

"We need to focus," Mia said. "There's no way we're squishing ourselves through that. It needs more power to get bigger."

They grabbed each other's hands again and took a few minutes to calm down. When they gathered all their focus, they directed their combined power at the portal. Finally, the portal began to stretch. It was almost gruesome the way it pulled, contorted, and opened. When it settled into a large enough size, they allowed themselves to relax.

"Ready?" Zander asked. He began to walk forward, but Mia stopped him.

"No. I go first." Mia released Luna and Zander's hands and entered first.

She was the one who had landed them in this situation, so she was going to be the one to test what might happen. Her hope was the portal connected to Paris, France, but for all Mia knew, it could connect to Kansas. Or to nothing.

Mia didn't think she would ever get used to traveling through a portal. She remembered the way Cassia had walked so smoothly and easily out of the portal onto the sidewalk outside the academy when they had first arrived.

It was nothing for her, as simple as walking through a door. One of these days, maybe Mia would feel that confident and go through as easily. She hoped that came sooner rather than later. Hanging around with these four, it seemed she would likely be moving through portals pretty often.

Mia didn't realize she had her eyes squeezed shut until she hit the floor and didn't see anything around her. As she opened her eyes, the rest of the group burst out of the portal.

"You guys didn't really get the point of me going through first, did you?" she asked.

"What were you planning to do when you got through safely? Stick your head back through and yell at us?" Vivi answered.

"Carson, I think I found your spit," Luna said, her voice revealing her disgust.

Mia stood and scanned the area around them. They definitely weren't in the library anymore. The floor beneath her was made of several shades of wood, and the tall dark-red walls held ornate frames with paintings on either side of them.

"Are we really here? Did we make it? There isn't some museum wing of the academy I don't know about, is it?" Mia asked.

"This is it," Carson said. "I've been here before. I recognize this exhibit."

Vivi looked like she could barely contain herself. She was so excited they actually did it, she didn't think she could hold it in. She threw a shield up around them and squealed, jumping up and down a few times.

"What's with the shield?" Mia asked.

Vivi paused her celebration to stare at Mia. "We are in one of the most famous museums in the world. Do you know who comes to famous museums? People. A lot of them. We can't just wander around unprotected. It's essential for us to keep our gifts secret from the humans."

"That makes sense."

"Good. Can I go back to my celebration now?"

Mia swept her hand in front of her, gesturing for the other girl to continue. Vivi jumped up and down again, and the group started talking over each other.

"I can't believe we made it," Zander said.

"I can," Mia said.

"Elmhurst did say Mia was capable of incredible things. That's enough to get through the enchantments preventing portals going off-campus," Luna said.

"With some help," Carson added.

"Well, we made it to the museum, but we're not where we needed to go. We still need to get to the Egyptian exhibit," Zander said.

"Do you know how to get there, Carson?" Mia asked.

"Absolutely. This way. Vivi, keep the shield up. We don't have the credentials to be in here, and Security might want to check our tickets."

They meandered through the different wings and exhibits of the museum and finally arrived at the entrance to the Egyptian display. Seeing it made Mia's heart jump with excitement. This was big. They hadn't simply hopped across the campus, or to a nearby area. They had gone off-campus and had traveled to a different country almost halfway around the world. It was astonishing, something young halflings shouldn't be capable of doing.

And it would help her get an awesome grade on her paper.

CHAPTER THIRTY-FIVE

"This place is huge," Mia said as they entered the first room.

"I've never seen anything like it," Luna agreed.

"What did you think it was going to be like?" Vivi asked. "One room with a fake pyramid wall and a sarcophagus?"

"Have you ever been here, Vivi?" Zander asked.

She set her jaw, but her cheeks flushed with color at being called out. "No," she admitted matter-of-factly. "I have not."

"Then you didn't know what it was supposed to look like either, did you? So how did you expect them to know?"

Vivi crossed her arms over her chest and flipped her hair as she turned from the group and walked the few feet away the shield would allow.

"This place is enormous," Carson told them. "The Egyptian exhibit covers two floors and has dozens of rooms. It's probably the biggest place any of us have ever been."

"Then we should spread out. It's too much space to cover in a short time, and we're not going to be able to be here all day. It was late when we left the campus, and we're going to have to get some sleep before class tomorrow. Or is it today?"

Vivi thought for a moment and calculated the time difference. If they left their library at two in the morning, it was ten a.m. in Paris. Which meant the museum was open for business. "We should just divide up and go to different areas of the exhibit, gather all the information we can, and meet back up later," she proposed.

"It would be really easy to get lost," Luna said. "It's so spread out, and only Carson has ever even been here."

"Then we should stick together," Mia suggested. "The last thing we need is for one of us to wander off and the rest of us to not be able to find them when we need to leave. I am not interested in this turning into a *From the Mixed-Up Files of Mrs. Basil E. Frankweiler* situation."

The other four stared at her blankly.

"A what?" Zander finally said.

"I guess halflings who go to fae schools don't have the same reading curriculum as human children," Mia said.

They all shook their heads.

"Let's agree to stick together," Zander said. "We'll explore the same rooms and then move on together."

They began to walk toward the first display, but Mia stopped them again. "Wait. There's one thing we haven't thought about yet. How are we going to get back to campus?"

"It will be easy," Vivi said. "We got here, so we can get home."

Mia threw her arms up in the air. "Just like that. No problem."

"Let's just start looking around," Carson said. "We can worry about getting home later."

They moved farther into the exhibit and explored the massive array of items on display. It only took a few seconds of searching to find some of the items their teacher had spoken about during the lecture.

"Look at this." Mia pointed at an elaborate necklace on a cushion under a square glass protective case. Recessed lighting illuminated the piece in surroundings darkened to protect the ancient artifacts. "Didn't the professor tell us about this necklace?"

"It looks like the right one," Luna agreed. "It's really beautiful. So much more impressive in person than it was in the picture."

She glanced up and gave a little gasp. Luna rushed to another display and pointed at a statue of an Egyptian couple holding hands in front of what appeared to be a doorway.

"She showed us a picture of this." She smiled and gazed back at the statue. "It's adorable. They look so happy."

"Really? I think they look miserable," Vivi said with a derisive snort.

"You would," Mia fired back. But guilt washed over her when a look of longing flashed across Vivi's face as she glanced at Zander. Mia tried to push on, glossing over the uncomfortable moment. "Do you see anything else?"

They continued to wander around the first room, taking in all the amazing artifacts. Several of the pieces had been in their teacher's lecture, but others were stunning surprises. Mia tried to take note of everything, wishing she had brought along a notebook and pen. She had so much to remember, and she didn't want to miss anything.

"This is really amazing," Vivi said as she moved slowly around a display pedestal with an urn taken from the burial chamber of a pyramid. "You know, any of these could be charmed or enchanted to do different things. They just look like old things dug up from tombs or found in temples. But they could actually be magical objects. It's really exciting to think about."

Luna shook her head as she joined the other girl beside the display and looked inside at the urn. "That's doubtful. Some of these items have been here in the museum for decades. Someone would have triggered the magic inside them if there was any. They wouldn't just be sitting around here without anyone noticing the enchantment."

"Like Dan and Steve?" Carson pointed out. "They've been sitting on those pedestals outside the library for hundreds of years, and no one ever knew they could fly. *They* didn't even know they could fly. They didn't even know that they could move off their pedestals. And I daresay far more people with magical awareness and abilities have walked by those two gargoyles in the time they've been there than have come here to brush up on their Egyptian culture awareness."

Luna shrugged, apparently unconvinced. She headed over to another display within the limitations of the shield and peered in.

Mia came up beside her and examined the tiny sarcophagus. "Even still. I wish I could find something with magic. Can you imagine how awesome that would be? To find something that's just been sitting around here in the museum all this time and discover its secrets?"

"It really would," Luna replied. "Just think. Humans all think they know everything about the past. They've dug so deep into history and think they have this understanding of all the people and events from long ago. I mean, look around you. Thousands of artifacts and pieces of history from a millennia ago, and each one of them has a little note next to it explaining exactly what it is."

"Exactly what people *think* it is," Mia clarified.

"Precisely. And most of those notes are probably wrong. So many of these things had different meanings, different purposes, but those real legacies were lost with time. I don't think there's any magic left in these things because they would have been found by now, but so many of them were probably once enchanted. Humans don't even consider there being a different story behind the objects they find."

"Hey," Mia said. "Let's be a little gentler to humans. Remember, some of us thought we were human up until very recently."

Luna shook her head. "Oh, I don't mean any insult. We're all halflings, Mia. Each one of us has a human parent. I don't mean anything spiteful about humans. I'm only saying it's so interesting to see signs of our world in the context of human understanding. They don't know what they're seeing. They have no idea the amazing potential. And even if someone told them, they wouldn't believe it."

Mia nodded. "I know I never would have. It's amazing how much my perspective of the world has changed in only a couple of months. This sounds ridiculous, but thinking about the possibility of any of the objects around here being enchanted makes me feel...proud. I don't know if that's exactly the right word, but to know the secrets makes me feel more connected to who I really am."

"That's lovely, and I'm honored to be here for this very special episode of 'Mia the Super Fae,' but we really need to get a move on," Vivi said. "We've only made our way through one room, and there's about a billion left to go. If we want to have any hope at all of finding everything we need for our papers, we need to keep going."

"We're not going to be able to cover enough space if we have to all stay within the shield," Carson pointed out.

"If we all agree to stay in the same room, we could probably move around without it," Mia said.

"If we all stay in the same place," Luna emphasized.

Everyone turned to stare at Vivi, who rolled her eyes. "I got it. I'll stay in the same room as everyone else. Does someone also want to put me on a leash to make sure I don't get too far away?"

"It may not be too terrible of an idea," Mia muttered.

"All right, that's enough. Vivi, put down the shield. Everybody, you have to act like you belong here, and that nothing is wrong. If you look like you are supposed to be here and are completely comfortable, you're much less likely to call attention and be questioned. Stay aware of where everyone is, and we will move from place to place together. Agreed?" Zander made eye contact with each of the other four.

The others murmured their agreement and moved together into an out-of-the-way corner of the Egyptian wing. Vivi released the shield, making them visible to everyone in the museum. It was still fairly early in the morning, and the museum had only just opened. But a handful of people were already meandering around the Egyptian exhibits. It was important to stay under the radar and not be noticed by the humans there.

If any of them had seen the five teenagers appear out of nowhere, it could have caused serious problems for them. As it was, Mia was already concerned about the possibility of security cameras catching them popping into existence from thin air. At least if the security team did witness that, the halflings had the upper hand. They would be able to disappear before security could cause any issues for them. It's not like they were likely to be seen wandering down the streets of Paris after leaving the museum.

Freed from the restraints of the shield, the group broke apart. They wandered to different parts of the exhibit, each exploring the artifacts and pieces of the collection that caught their attention the most. It gave them the opportunity to search more deeply and find the things that spoke the most to them. Mia still held out hope for finding something special among the ancient objects, to find a glimmer of magic that had gone unnoticed. They quickly lost themselves in the exploration, and time slipped by.

CHAPTER THIRTY-SIX

It was just after two in the morning, and Hazel and Marcus were still hunkering down in the library, buzzing with excitement over what they had witnessed. They moved from behind the stacks from where they had listened to the five talk to a cluster of lower shelves near the bookshelf where the group disappeared.

Luna, Carson, Vivi, Zander, and Mia, had gone through the portal they had created only moments before, but Marcus and Hazel were filled with anticipation. They felt like they were going to burst when they finally heard a soft whooshing sound across the library.

Hazel's heart jumped, and she looked at Marcus, her eyebrows lifting, but she couldn't bring herself to say anything through the excitement.

"He's here," Marcus said, giving voice to her anticipation.

The pair hopped to their feet and rushed out into the open so the vampire they'd eagerly been awaiting would see them. They didn't want to leave him waiting or force him to look for them. He was far too powerful and impressive to be lowered to that. Finally, he turned a corner and strode toward them.

Hazel had always been curious about how José had managed to enter the school. With all of the protections put in place—he shouldn't have been able to get in, but he had. She figured someone else on campus had helped him. She and Marcus couldn't be the only ones he had forced to help him.

"Good evening, José," Hazel managed to say. It felt strange to say it since it was technically morning, but it was the only way she could think of to greet him.

"Hello, Hazel," José said. "Marcus. What do you have to report to me?"

The students exchanged glances, eager to reveal everything to him. They finally let everything spill out, from the conversation they heard, to watching the five create the portal and go to the Louvre. Their voices overlapped, and they repeated themselves a few times, but José followed along. His expression barely changed, but he nodded every now and again. A slight widening of his eyes was enough to tell them he was intrigued by the information. When they finished, both fell silent, breathless.

José thought about everything for several seconds. "Did they see you?" he asked.

Both students shook their heads adamantly.

"No," Marcus said. "We were well hidden the entire time. We only came out after they went through the portal."

"And no one else knows you were here? No one knows your connection to me?"

"No," Hazel assured him. "We haven't said a word to anyone."

He nodded again. "You've done well. Narco will be pleased. I will get in touch with him and let him know what you told me. I will be in touch when there is more to do."

José strode away from Hazel and Marcus, wanting to contact Narco as soon as possible. This information would be valuable to him, and he would want to be able to act on it quickly.

Narco had been waiting to hear the information José had received from the two students in his service. Now his search had gone from nothing to moving fast in one conversation.

"And you are positive the girl is part of the five?" Narco asked.

"Yes," José told him. "Marcus and Hazel assured me it was the five who have been assigned to work together. They are always in each other's company, and any time they are performing any magic, it's all of them. They wouldn't be able to open the portal without her. Their magic isn't strong enough, but hers gives them what they need to be able to accomplish these feats."

"Thank you, José."

Narco ended the conversation and immediately reached out to the others in his service. He formed a team of his followers and sent them to Paris to find the group of five. He didn't care about the other four. They were inconsequential to him beyond their proximity to Mia.

It was Mia that Narco was really interested in. After watching her at the competition and monitoring her at the academy, he was becoming more confident that he had finally found the one he had dedicated himself to seeking out for so many years.

But he didn't want to act with too much haste. That had happened before, and the results were aggravating at best. Though he was certain Mia was the one he wanted, Narco needed to make absolutely sure this time. He had to confirm she truly was the girl he was seeking out, the one he wanted to destroy.

He had already killed a dozen fae girls in Faerie because he had believed they were the one. Those girls had died because he had acted far too quickly. As soon as he had a suspicion that he had found her, Narco would cut the girl down, only to discover later that he had been mistaken.

Not that the lives themselves bothered him. He felt no guilt about the people he had killed. What mattered to him was that even after those deaths, the one he was seeking was still out there. Now the bodies were stacking up, and people would notice.

With every new girl he killed, the chances of someone becoming suspicious and finding a way to link him to the deaths grew higher. He was afraid someone would find out what he was up to, and he couldn't allow that to happen. He wasn't the only one who would be interested in finding her, but the others had different motivations. Narco wanted to be the one to find her first.

If he was right this time, he had finally found the many-generations-past descendant of the long-lost third princess. Which would also mean "Mia" was not her true name. If she was the descendant of the princess, this girl would also be the daughter of the fae woman Narco had killed in Boston seventeen years ago.

At the time, Narco had believed her husband to also be fae. The man had disappeared so quickly and without a trace that Narco had been convinced he had gone to Faerie. It was the only thing that made sense. A mere human could never have outsmarted him.

That's what had led to the deaths of the dozen in Faerie. Narco had spent seventeen years searching the land to find the girl who had slipped through his fingers. He had destroyed anyone he had believed to be her. But something had changed.

He'd heard of a mysterious girl in China, a halfling who lived among humans, unaware of who she was. He had decided to check her out in case she was the one he sought. As unlikely as it seemed, he couldn't afford to let any chance pass him by; the consequences would be too dire.

If this girl was of the princess' line, despite her bloodline being as diluted as it would be by now, she could still cause serious problems for the Unseelie Court. The more he thought about it, the more he realized her having been sired by a human man did make sense.

It infuriated the fae hunter that he hadn't thought of it sooner, and he had focused his attention even more. Of course, he wasn't fully to blame. Narco might have come to the realization of Mia's parentage sooner if Flynn Terran hadn't sent him on a wild goose chase for the princess's line through the Seelie Court for the past forty years.

If Narco hadn't spent so much time searching for the descendant of the princess's line in the Seelie Court, she would never have had the opportunity to have a daughter and further extend the line.

Flynn had led him to believe the woman he sought had returned to Faerie. She was hiding there as she lived her life. It wasn't until he had killed Flynn that Narco had discovered she was on Earth. The woman he had sought was an offspring of the dead royal line, and he had finally located her in Boston. By that time, she'd borne a child. After her death, all that was left was to destroy the child, the last remaining member of the line. But the child had disappeared. Her father had whisked her away before Narco could hunt her down and kill her.

However, now Narco believed he could finally finish what he had started so long ago. He needed to confirm that Mia was the right girl, and once he did, he could kill her. He was eager to finally be done so he could stop this stupid assignment that had hung over him for so long, and move on to greener pastures. This had dominated his life for decades, and Narco was so ready to have it behind him. He was tired of chasing down ghosts and children.

Narco's team was at the Louvre, monitoring Mia's movements, but he was too on edge to wait around for them to send back any information about her. He had started this, and it would be him who would bring it to an end.

He made sure everything was properly in place here before readying himself to go to Paris. Armed with the tools he believed he may need, he opened a portal to Paris and walked through.

He arrived outside the museum, not wanting to call any unwanted attention to himself by appearing out of thin air in front of unsuspecting humans. He blended seamlessly into the groups of tourists and visitors and slipped into the museum. His magic enabled him to pass the ticket desk without paying admission, and he continued into the massive space with confidence and purpose.

Looking like he belonged was everything. People didn't question those who behaved as though they were doing exactly what they were meant to be doing. Purpose was tremendously convincing.

When he was far enough into the museum that fewer humans were watching him closely, he paused to focus on his surroundings. Calling on his tracker skills, he sought out the five students. The skill brought him to the Egyptian area of the museum and the seemingly never-ending corridors, rooms, and displays. They had already spent a few hours there, but they hadn't covered it all. He still had time.

CHAPTER THIRTY-SEVEN

It didn't take long after arriving in the Egyptian section of the museum for Narco to find the five students. They were trying their best to blend in with the people wandering around the museum, and it appeared to be working for the humans around them.

Several adults moved around the students without acknowledging their presence. The five may as well be a part of the exhibit itself. The only ones who paid any attention to them at all were a few younger people who were at the museum with their parents or for school visits.

That made sense. It had nothing to do with their magic, or there being anything different about them. Like all humans, the young people were drawn by the beauty of the five halflings. Fae were aston-ishingly attractive to humans, and even when mixed with human parentage, their beauty shone through. The teenage humans drawn to the group of five would have no idea why.

Narco caught sight of Mia and felt a bump of excitement. Of course, it wasn't the first time he had seen her. The last time he'd been this close to her was at the slamball competition in Las Vegas. At the time, he had been less certain of her identity, but the information he had collected since made him feel more confident that he had found the one he'd been after.

Across the room, the fae bounty hunter spotted a member of the team he had sent ahead to the museum. He made eye contact with the man and acknowledged him. Narco wanted his team to know he was there. It would ensure they were ready for whatever may happen. But he didn't want to interact with them too much.

The more they interacted, the more attention would be drawn to them. He didn't want the five halflings to become aware of anyone following them through the exhibit. If they did, the quest could be ruined.

Narco slipped into the room with the halflings so he could follow them. They were gathered around a pedestal, engrossed by the vase it held.

It had taken most of the time they had spent in the first room for the sheer awe of portaling to the Louvre and the enormity of the Egyptian exhibit to lessen slightly. When it did, the five remembered they should be taking notes for their projects. Their phones coming to mind, they took them out and started snapping pictures.

After a few hours of scouring the exhibit, they had gathered an impressive assortment of photographs and stories to use for their papers. The time difference meant that in Paris, it was approaching lunchtime, but for the students, it was the very wee hours of the morning. They were all starting to feel it. Their eyelids were sagging, their bodies feeling heavier as they went from display to display.

They knew they had more information about the artifacts than they would ever be able to fit into their papers, but they didn't want to stop. Having the opportunity to be in the museum was something they knew they shouldn't have. They shouldn't have been able to create the portal or to get to this incredible place. That pushed them to keep going. None of them wanted to waste a single bit of this opportunity. They didn't want to stop until they had read all the information on Egypt and her magical past.

At the edge of one room, watching the five students exploring the exhibit in the next, Narco had reached the edge of his patience. For the last hour, he followed the group through the displays and observed their reactions to the artifacts.

At first, he'd been excited to be in such close proximity to Mia, knowing that soon he would have what he had wanted for seventeen years. But he had to bide his time, to be patient so he could confirm her identity and find just the right moment to eliminate her.

Narco was so bored that he was ready to simply kill them all and get it over with. They were wasting his time. This entire experience was wasting his time. He had believed from the beginning that a descendant of the long-lost princess would be strong and even forbidding in her power. Which was the reason she had to be removed.

Now that he was this close and watching her, every second aggravated him more. She was nothing like he thought. He had expected the royal to have skill and knowledge, but she didn't appear to have much power at all.

In fact, none of them did. From the snippets of conversations he caught as he followed them, they were intrigued by the possibility of magical artifacts tucked among the countless items in the wing. One of the girls, a lovely Seelie who seemed confident and controlled beyond her years, didn't believe such items would be in the exhibit.

The other girl, the dark-haired Unseelie who glared at the other girls with daggers in her eyes more often than not, was convinced there were. They talked about the artifacts and the excitement of what it would mean to find one. And they promptly walked right past two.

Narco couldn't believe they were so unobservant. They should have recognized the magic contained within the two pieces. While they may have looked mundane to any of the other visitors to the museum, five students who supposedly possessed more magic and power than any halflings ever had should be able to recognize the difference.

One of the magical artifacts was a bracelet. The other was a water jug. He recognized the magic instantly but wasn't sure of its purpose. Closer inspection told Narco that if humans put water inside the jug, it would never run dry. Such a thing would be indescribably valuable for humans who often struggled to find enough clean, safe water to drink.

Mia had been feeling the creeping sensation of eyes on the back of her neck for a while. She tried to ignore it. They were in a strange place, doing something all five knew they shouldn't be doing, and becoming more tired by the minute. Which was enough to put her on edge.

But after moving through three rooms, the sensation didn't go away, and she became more concerned. Someone was watching them. Not in the curious way people tend to do when in museums and starting to blend the other visitors into the exhibits. This was pointed, purposeful watching that made her skin crawl and the hair on her arms stand on end.

She scanned the room, trying to find the person giving her the strange feeling. Three men stood out from the crowd. She had seen them in several of the other rooms the group had been through. Others had, too, of course, but something was odd about the way they moved around the exhibit.

They weren't paying attention to any of the displays. Instead, they strolled around in a very methodical, systematic way, their eyes occasionally flickering to one of the plaques or objects in front of them, but still tracking her movements. Though they didn't directly interact with each other, something about the way they moved around told her the three were connected.

Mia followed the others to the next display, separated sharply from them, and went to another corner of the room. The three men shifted their positions to keep watching her. The longer she studied them, the stronger the strange feeling they inspired got.

They didn't look like the other people visiting the museum. In fact, they didn't look all that human. It took only a short time for her to realize that was because they weren't. They were using glamours. But she could see past them and knew these three men were fae.

She returned to the group as fast as possible and moved with them around the edge of the room until they were farther from the men.

"What was that all about?" Vivi asked.

Mia gave a subtle shake of her head and guided them from the room and into the next.

"What's going on?" Zander asked. "Mia? Is something wrong?"

Mia leaned in, and the other four gathered close around her. "Did you see those three men in the other room?"

"What three men?" Luna asked.

"There are three men who have been following us through the exhibit." She glanced over her shoulder as the first man entered the room, trying to look casual. Mia tipped her head slightly toward him. "That's one of them."

Carson's attention snapped back to her. "He's fae."

Mia nodded. "So are the other two." Within seconds, the other two men filtered into the room. "There they are."

The halflings stiffened, concerned expressions crossing their faces.

"Who are they?" Vivi asked.

Mia shook her head. "I don't know. Any of you recognize them? Are they from the school?"

The thought hadn't occurred to her until that moment, but the possibility reassured her slightly. Maybe these men were from the academy. They all knew they weren't supposed to create portals on campus, and they definitely weren't supposed to make ones that sent them off-campus. Going to a different country when they should have been in their dorms asleep for hours was totally out of the question.

It was possible that opening the portal had triggered an alarm that automatically sent the fae adults to monitor the situation and ensure they returned safely. Only, if that was the case, it would have made sense for the men to have approached them rather than merely following them.

"No," Zander said. "I don't think so."

"I don't recognize them," Carson added.

The two girls made affirming sounds, removing any hope Mia had for an easy explanation. "Whoever they are, it can't be good that they're following us," she pointed out.

"You're right," Zander agreed. "We need to get out of here."

CHAPTER THIRTY-EIGHT

Almost as though they could sense that the halflings had caught on to them, the three fae men moved closer to them. The five left the room, moving through the corridors as fast as they could without running.

"Okay, so we need to get out of here fast. Mia, can you open a portal?" Zander urged.

"I don't know. Where should we go?" Mia asked.

"Freaking anywhere but here would be good," Carson said, picking up the speed a little. The group rounded a corner and found a little space where no one could see them.

"Okay, here goes." Mia tried to focus on creating a portal. Seconds ticked by with nothing happening, and Vivi poked her head around the corner.

"They're almost here, we have to hurry!" she exclaimed.

"I'm trying," Mia said, exasperated. "It's just not worki—"

Suddenly, a dark hole appeared in front of her. It was only a couple of feet tall and so skinny they would have to turn sideways to get through it, but it was there. Without another word, Luna, Zander, and Carson jumped through.

"They're here." Vivi ran into Mia's back, pushing her and falling with her through the portal.

They landed hard on cement, and Mia batted at Vivi in frustration. "Get off of me," she said, pushing Vivi away.

"I saved your skinny butt, Mia. Those guys were right behind me," Vivi retorted.

Zander slid between them as they stood. "Hey, no time for this right now. We have to keep moving," he said.

Two girls realized he was right and nodded, and the group ran through the room. It was a long, high-ceilinged basement full of Egyptian artifacts not on display at the moment. Whether the relics were for specific displays not currently being used or they weren't deemed important enough, the halflings couldn't tell. They ducked through various aisles of items, all seemingly packed there with no rhyme or reason, when they ran past a large, ornate mirror. Everyone rushed by except for Vivi—something made her stop and call out to her friends.

"What is it?" Carson said, panting as he made it back to her. The rest of the halflings were arriving too, and in the distance, people were murmuring. The fae were in the room, and the halflings needed to hurry.

"This mirror. Look at it," Vivi said.

"It's just an old mirror—oh!" Carson noticed it too.

Soon it dawned on everyone else, and they looked at each other before turning toward the voices on their tail. The mirror showed the reflection of the room, but not of them.

Luna reached out to touch the mirror, and her hand sank into the surface. She studied the spot where her arm had disappeared. She glanced over her shoulder at the others and shoved her head into the mirror. All she saw was utter blackness, but it seemed safe.

She walked through and turned. Luna could see through the mirror to her friends as if the world was cut out of the darkness. She poked her head back out, and everyone jumped. "Come on. It's safe!"

One by one, they each stepped through, with Zander going last. Just as he was about to follow, he heard the footsteps of the fae just beyond him. He leapt into the mirror and spun in time to see the fae man run into view.

The fae stopped, confused, and stared around him. "I swear I heard them right here," he muttered.

His gaze passed over the mirror, and everyone held their breath, but he didn't seem to notice anything about it. Instead, he turned and made a portal, which he entered and disappeared through.

Zander left the mirror first, checking the area, and waving his friends out. When the last of them were out, Luna bent to the tag on the side of the mirror and jotted the information in her notebook.

"There's another room back this way."

Carson appeared unconcerned about the details of the mirror, or his future grade. As usual, he was a bit more mission-focused. The group followed him into the next room and stopped when they saw what was inside.

"Really, Carson?" The hair rose on Vivi's arms as she stared at the figures before her. "You had to pick the room with the mummies?"

"Hey, I'm just trying to get us as far away from the fae as I can." He raised his hands almost as if in surrender, but Carson would never surrender. The smirk that accompanied his hands did nothing to settle Vivi.

Three sarcophagi were standing against the wall, their ornate carvings and decorations casting dark and ominous shadows in the dimly lit room. They towered above Vivi, and in spite of herself, she reached out to touch one. She shuddered and snatched her hand away, backpedaling until she bumped into Luna, and they both jumped.

Luna's eyes were wide and round as she stared at the sarcophagi in fascination and horror. "Someone's body is inside that thing," Luna whispered.

"Three someones' bodies are inside all three of these things," Vivi whispered in reply.

"Do you think they could be—" Luna began to ask.

"Zombies?" Vivi finished. They looked at each other and nodded slowly before focusing on the sarcophagi. There was a change in the air as panic began to take hold of them, in the absence of reason.

Mia decided to be that reason. "Zombies aren't real, though," she said. "They are made up, like in movies. It's always just a dude in liquid latex and fake blood, mumbling 'Braaiiinnnss,'" she said, rolling her eyes back in her head and holding her arms out stiffly in front of her while doing a mock shuffle-step toward them.

"Zombies are real," came a voice behind Mia. She turned to see Carson, his back pressed against the wall as he too stared at the sarcophagi. "Everything is real. Remember our talk about werewolves?"

Mia nodded, seeming thoughtful, and suddenly her eyes lit up with a combination of horror and interest. In the last few months, she had seen so many things that should fill her nightmares for the rest of her life, but for some reason coming upon yet another monster which she had believed was entirely movie magic, and finding out it was real, only made her more interested.

"So, do they eat brains? Are they brought back by a shaman? Or a virus? Or, oh, what was the other one… Right! Vampires from another planet?" she asked, going through every origin-story given to her by late-night movie marathons.

"No," Zander began, somewhat confused.

"They are rare." Carson was a little braver now that he was instructing rather than reacting. Zander might fancy himself the leader of their group, but to Carson, no one was more equipped to handle danger than him. And zombies absolutely qualified as danger. Imparting his knowledge would ensure everyone was on the same page. "They are made rarer by only being able to be revived for forty-eight hours. Then the body stops, and they go dead forever after that."

"That doesn't sound too bad," Mia said.

"Except that they can infect a human with their disease. If they do, that human can then infect other people. They can still only survive for two days, but in those two days, they can cause absolute havoc."

During Carson's explanation, Vivi had wandered off. Suddenly, her ear-splitting scream pierced the air, and everyone's heads snapped to the sound. Vivi was at the end of the room, back against the wall, holding her chest and pointing at one of the sarcophagi. The group headed toward her, but they weren't the only ones.

Nearby, Narco heard the scream too and came running.

"Vivi, it's only me," said Luna, coming around from behind the sarcophagi.

"I saw it move," Vivi shouted.

"Yeah, that was me," Luna continued, trying to calm Vivi. She glanced over her shoulder at the group for help as they approached.

"What happened?" Zander was spooked too, but more so, he was angry that Luna would take this opportunity to play a prank on Vivi. Luna usually showed more self-control than to do something like that.

"I walked around the back of the sarcophagi, just to see if it had been opened. Sometimes they are empty, you know? So I did, and I guess I must have bumped it, and it moved a little. Then—oh no."

"What?" Carson asked. "Did you break something?"

"No. Not that, look." Luna pointed out of the room and back the way they had come. A man was running toward them at full speed from way across the room, and he wasn't bothering to be quiet about it.

Mia backed up against one of the sarcophagi and sensed that the solidity of the stone wasn't there. She turned, surprised she had created a new portal. "Guys, look! I made a new portal, come on!"

They all shook their heads, confusing Mia immensely. The man was gaining on them, and though they couldn't see his face, they knew he knew they were there. They had to get out quickly.

"No way," Zander said, staring at the man before turning to Mia. Everyone else was scattering, searching for a place to hide. "A portal like that likely takes people to the Underworld. Osiris is not a being you want to be a subject of, trust me. Come on," he said, pulling her behind the sarcophagi and squeezing her close to him, so that they were tightly pushed together behind it. He wrapped his arms around her protectively as they hid. He whispered in her ear, and unlike Vivi and Luna, now was the first time the hair on her arms raised. "If we leave it active, maybe he goes into it thinking we did. Try to keep it open. Focus."

She did and held her breath as the man ran toward them. He didn't even slow down as he saw the portal and raced for it. At the last moment, as he dove in, his eyes slid across the room to Vivi, and he reached out, but it was too late. He was through.

Mia closed the portal, and they all exhaled.

Hidden only a few feet away, Narco watched, having been beaten to them by one of his own henchmen. He hid below a display of pottery and cursed silently as the group ran from the room.

CHAPTER THIRTY-NINE

Narco couldn't believe what he had witnessed. These halflings shouldn't be a match for his men. They should be easy pickings, ready to be snatched up the instant he gave the command.

Instead, he had watched from his hiding place as Mia led the group in tricking his man. This may be more of a challenge than he anticipated. Just because they hadn't recognized the magical artifacts didn't necessarily mean this was going to be smooth and simple. The group seemed to be able to interact with each other in a way that boosted their effectiveness.

Narco remembered what José had relayed to him from the two students at the halfling academy. The five were being heavily trained, groomed by Elmhurst to magnify their power into something extraordinary. Working together made them stronger and helped them think better.

Which meant he needed them to not be together. If Narco could separate Mia from her friends, he would be able to do with her whatever he pleased. He thought for a few seconds about how he could lure her away from them, and an idea came to him.

Following the group, he waited until the halflings entered a more isolated section and created a portal. He intended to close the portal as soon as Mia tumbled through it, but the entire group moved around it without stopping.

Aggravated, Narco chased after them. He ducked through rooms and wove through the corridors, wanting to cut off their progress. Using his tracker skills, he was able to tell the direction they were going and chose another place to create a portal. He made another, setting it into the floor so she only needed to step on the edge, and it would suck her away from the other four. Again, she avoided it and directed the others to stay away.

Frustration and anger built inside Narco as he continued to pursue the halflings. He watched them pause when Mia turned her attention to a wall in front of her. The wall shimmered slightly as though a portal was about to open, but it didn't. They were trying to escape the Louvre through a portal. Narco couldn't let that happen.

Without wasting the time to try again, Mia and the Scooby Gang raced off. Staying in one place for too long made it more likely the men would find them.

"Come on, Mia, you can do this," Zander said. "Just concentrate. You've done it before."

"I know," she said.

They turned into another corridor, and Mia saw the wall to one side begin to shimmer as a portal appeared. It spread down the wall as though chasing them, spilling onto the floor, and moving close to their feet. Mia grabbed Luna's arm and yanked her to the side.

"What is it?" Luna asked.

"Another portal. Someone's trying to trap us."

They veered around the portal and rushed into the next room. If they weren't being chased and didn't need to get out of the museum fast, she would have stopped here and spent some time exploring the incredible space. The temple room was nothing short of breathtaking.

She could almost believe they were in a true temple, taken right from a pyramid in Egypt. She wanted to stay and take it all in, but the awareness of being followed, and the threat of the strange portals appearing at their every turn, kept her feet moving.

The group ducked behind one of the massive stone pillars and waited until two women who were more invested in their whispered gossip than in the exhibit, moved out of the way.

"Together this time," Mia urged. "Come on. I can't do this myself. We need to work together to get out of here, just like we did to get here."

"We need to do this fast. We can't risk any humans seeing us do this," Vivi added.

"Back to our room, okay?" Mia said.

The rest of the group nodded and huddled together. They held hands and put as much focus as they could into creating the portal. Mia tried not to let the failed attempts weigh on her.

Finally, a portal opened in the pillar, and they sprang through without hesitation. A few seconds later, Mia landed on her face on something soft.

Having learned from experience, she rolled out of the way fast, so the others didn't crush her. She opened her eyes and realized they had landed on her bed. It was dark, but she recognized the dorm room.

Relieved and happier to see the room than she ever thought she would be, she jumped to her feet and waited for the others to right themselves. "We made it!" she gushed.

"Yeah, but we shouldn't have," Zander said.

Mia's smile disappeared, and she narrowed her eyes. "Wow. Way to just take all the zip out of the situation."

"We just had the crickets scared out of us being chased down by unidentified fae in a museum," Vivi pointed out. "I don't think there's a whole lot of zip to be had in that."

"I meant in us being able to make the portal to get back here," Mia snapped. "We were scared and under a lot of pressure, and we still managed to do it. We got back here. Don't you think that warrants at least a few seconds of feeling good about ourselves?"

"Maybe, but like I said, it shouldn't have happened," Zander said. "It shouldn't have worked."

"Then why did you go along with it?" Carson asked.

"Hope, fear, and the realization that we really had no other options for getting back here?" Zander said. "Unless the four of you wanted to figure out a way to hop a flight, the only way to get back to campus was going to be through a portal."

"Wait, why shouldn't it have worked?" Mia asked. "We got there through a portal."

"That was already impressive enough, but it didn't mean the reverse would be possible. It was one thing for us to be able to get a portal opened to the outside world when we were in the library. The campus already has portals in some places and the room where authorized people can create their own. They are heavily controlled, but they are there. Counteracting the security mechanisms isn't easy, but not unfathomable. But getting back into campus—that's not good."

"What do you mean?" Mia asked.

"I'm concerned we did something to damage the enchantments around campus. They may be down, or we may have created a tear in the protections put in place to guard the academy," Zander said.

"Don't worry. You didn't create a tear in the defenses."

The five gasped and jumped closer together at the sound of the voice and the sudden bright illumination when the room light flicked on. Professor Elmhurst was perched on the end of Vivi's bed, but she stood as the five turned to her. She walked toward them slowly, and Mia's anxiety increased with each measured step. She would have preferred the headmistress stalk across the room with intensity, or even run at them.

Which would have made the Elmhurst's mood more easily readable. Her slow walk made them feel like they were being stalked, as if she was measuring them up and trying to decide exactly how severe her reaction should be.

"Professor," Zander said.

She held up a hand to silence him, her eyes closing briefly as if she didn't want to hear the sound of his voice. "Like I said, you didn't put a tear in the protections for the campus, but that is the only thing you don't have to worry about. Imagine my surprise when, after two in the morning, I heard something knocking on my bedroom window. And who do you think it could be?"

Mia knew immediately and swallowed hard. "Dan and Steve."

The headmistress nodded. "Dan and Steve. The gargoyles Mia so benevolently released from the positions they have held for centuries and who are now flying around campus, peering into windows and scaring everyone. But they didn't want to just come by for a visit. They weren't interested in showing off their flying skills or getting directions to the other buildings. No. They wanted to come by and let me know in person that an unauthorized portal opened in the library. As you could probably guess, I was pretty shocked by that news. After all, there are very specific places on campus where portals are permitted, and the library certainly isn't one of them."

Her words were as slow as her steps. There was little emotion in what she was saying, and it was unnerving.

"But I couldn't imagine why the gargoyles would make something like that up. For all their faults, they are devoted to the academy and have always wanted the best for it. So, I got dressed, and I went down to the library to examine it. There was evidence of a portal, but no one was there. Dan and Steve didn't know who did it, so we searched the campus. We checked every person, every classroom, and every dorm room. And who did we discover was missing?"

"Us," Luna murmured.

"How could you do this?" Professor Elmhurst demanded, the anger suddenly bursting from her. "I gave you very specific instructions to return to your dorms. I told you not to go to the library, even when you asked to go to collect sources for your artifact papers. Did I not? I told you to return to your rooms and call up the information. But that wasn't good enough for you. You had to defy me and break the rules by not only leaving your room and going to the library directly against my instructions but then by creating an illegal portal. How could you do that? Do you realize how much trouble you could have caused? How much danger you could have put the entire campus in because of your stupid stunt? Zander is absolutely right. You shouldn't have been able to get back on campus. You should have been stuck. And while you didn't damage the defenses as far as we've been able to tell, you did find a loophole for getting out of campus. That is a very serious situation. And a betrayal of my trust."

CHAPTER FORTY

"If I may." Carson stepped forward. It was so formal, so unlike the rest of them at this moment, all terrified and upset at Elmhurst's anger, that it actually broke the tension, causing Vivi, Luna, and Zander, to laugh.

"If you may what?" Elmhurst said through gritted teeth. She hated being interrupted, especially when she was on a good roll of lecturing, and Carson was the last of the group she expected to be cheeky. Yet, here he was, his hands behind his back, chin up and legs apart, like some TV show lawyer, ready to defend his friend against a murder charge.

"If I may have a few words, Principal. It seems like there may be a great misunderstanding that could be solved if we only took a moment, collected our thoughts, and I was able to speak on behalf of my friends."

Mia stood with her mouth gaping. She had never seen this side of Carson before, and she was taken aback. Not only was he putting himself between the group and Elmhurst, possibly incurring her wrath directly, but he was handling himself like a leader.

Not for the first time, Mia had noticed the brewing rivalry between Carson and Zander on that front, but for now, Zander was letting Carson have this chance, probably to give him enough rope to hang himself with.

Elmhurst straightened, holding her head high and stoically, with only her parted lips indicating that she, too, was taken aback. She eyed him for a moment and appeared to decide to let him talk, closing her mouth tightly so that her lips almost disappeared in a grimace. She nodded, and Carson smiled.

"Earlier when you spoke to us, you were discussing our need to push ourselves. This is a point that was very much on our minds as we proceeded through this evening," he said.

Even his voice had changed in timbre, dropping a hair lower. Either he was mimicking something he had seen on TV, or he possessed a natural inclination for the role of an attorney, but either way, his charm seemed to be working. Elmhurst hadn't expelled them yet.

Yet.

"Continue," Elmhurst said primly.

Carson cleared his throat and glanced at the group, winking as he did so. "Well, it's very simple, isn't it? You told us to try using our magic, to work together and push beyond the constraints we thought possible, as long as we didn't hurt anyone else or cause any more weather patterns to change. My question to you, Principal, is this; was there an unexpected weather anomaly this evening?"

"No." The words came out cold and judging. Carson was making a point, but he was being a jerk about it, and Elmhurst wasn't exactly enjoying the performance.

"And was anyone hurt?" Carson continued, throwing his hands to his sides as if to show off that the group stood before her, unharmed.

"Not that I know of," she said, her voice like a river of ice. It would seem safe if you didn't know how cruel and dangerous it could be.

"Then, aside from a minor infraction of the rules, this is a non-issue. Punishable by, say, a stern talking to, or at worst, an evening of detention. Certainly, considering the admittedly open-ended instructions you gave us, we are not fully to blame here."

"Oh, there is blame for you. All of you," she said.

Zander approached the principal. "Perhaps, but this is my group," he said, putting emphasis on the word 'my.' Carson fumed beside him but said nothing. "I led them during this trip, so if any punishment was to be laid down, it should be on me, not them."

"No, Zander," Mia said. "If anyone is to blame, it's me. I caused it all to happen."

"Enough," Elmhurst snapped. "If there is one of you to punish, then there would be punishment for all. Where did you go?"

"The Louvre," Luna blurted out.

She had been quiet until now, and everyone in the group spun to stare at her. She looked as surprised as they did. They hadn't discussed if they were going to be honest about where they went, but now there was no turning back. Collectively though, they all knew that certain elements of their trip needed to be kept a secret.

"The Louvre?" the principal said. "Why?"

"To gather notes on the Egyptian artifacts," Vivi offered. "Luna has a bunch of notes, don't you, Luna?"

Luna turned to her, her eyes wide and sparkling as if she didn't comprehend Vivi's words. Suddenly it dawned on Luna, and she rummaged through her bag, grabbing her cell phone.

She offered it to Elmhurst, who took it and began to flip through the images. "I also took notes in an app. We saw a lot of items that might have been fae-enchanted, and some that certainly were. It was a very illuminating trip," Luna said.

Elmhurst stared at Luna through narrowed eyes before she returned to studying the pictures. She seemed satisfied after a few images and returned the phone. Placing one finger on her lips, Elmhurst appeared to be thinking about something very deeply, and the group held their breath as they waited. Not even Carson, in his newfound confidence as the lawyer for the group, dared interrupt her.

"I want to make this absolutely clear," she said, eyeing all five of them. "What you did is in clear violation of school rules, but, as Carson so smugly pointed out, it does seem to be justified based on the instructions I, as the school principal, gave you. So, in lieu of punishment, you are all hereby on notice. Any further transgressions against the rules will be met with a harsh penalty. Do I make myself clear?"

The group nodded in relief. Even Vivi seemed pleased. Carson beamed as though he'd just won the Slamball World Championship MVP award.

"Also," Elmhurst continued. "There are to be no other portals created to anywhere on Earth, whatsoever. Do I make myself clear? Not without prior, *direct* permission to open one from me. This is non-negotiable. Are we understood?"

The group nodded.

"Good. I will see you all at breakfast," Elmhurst said, sweeping from the room.

They waited a few moments for her to get away down the hall before they burst out into celebratory cheers.

Unbeknownst to the halflings, Elmhurst hurried away with a grin spreading across her face. Mia was obviously the catalyst for the portal creation. She had been right to put Mia in the group. Now all she needed to do was help the girl to develop her powers, and her team would have no problem obtaining the Power of Five.

It was all she could do to keep from questioning them more on the *how* of it all. She'd allow them to keep their secrets, for now. But she would keep a closer eye on them when they practiced.

Her only real concern was keeping the kids safe. Elmhurst had an idea of who Mia was, but she couldn't risk researching the girl's background. Someone had chased her from China and that someone most likely knew where she was and who she was.

But if they didn't know for sure, Elmhurst wasn't going to help them out with any part of it. For now, she would help Mia become stronger and keep her safe.

Narco plugged his camera into the laptop and pressed the Okay button to initiate the transfer of the file. It wouldn't be very long now until it was fully uploaded, and he could post it to every video-streaming site he could sign up for. All anonymous, of course. Then it would simply be a matter of allowing the video of Mia opening a portal and the kids going through it to make the rounds of the school.

Once everyone saw it, Mia would be in the crosshairs of Elmhurst, which would see her expelled. Expelled meant vulnerable, and that would mean Narco could end this stupid assignment once and for all. Years of wasted time, effort, and energy would be over, and Narco could return to doing real work, not hunting down children.

It had to be her. Mia was the one. A halfling, especially one so new to her studies and her life, should not be able to open a portal at all, let alone one that took them out of the school despite all the protections the academy had in place.

Going as far as the Louvre was more impressive. The kids he had assigned to watch her had said that the portals had taken all five of the halflings to open. Yet, according to the video that was now half uploaded, Mia had opened them all on her own. And she'd been capable of closing it and creating a block so that he couldn't follow or track them at all.

It ticked him off more than a swarm of crickets on a hot summer night. To be bested by anyone, even the most powerful of fae, made him boil with rage, but for a child, a young girl who barely knew what fae were, was beyond humiliating. She was infuriating him by merely existing, and the fact that he had to resort to having other children work for him to keep her under watch, was making him wish he could simply go directly to killing her.

But that presented a problem too. She was never without someone else from her little group, and while a young, confused halfling having trouble adjusting to her new life was a much easier kill to get away with, if he killed another member of the group, the death would raise suspicion and possibly blow his cover.

Narco had to get her alone, one way or another, and excluding her from the group through embarrassment and harassment was his only way. He smiled as the video finished uploading. It wasn't as fun as getting rid of her in person, but a move like this was at least progress. One more step toward a better assignment.

The sooner he completed this age-old assignment, the sooner he could move on to something better that would help him to climb the fae social-ladder. Being stuck in this one job for so many decades had hurt his prospects, and he was done being passed over by younger and less-experienced hunters. It was time to show the world why he was the best bounty hunter the fae had ever seen.

Turning on a VPN to hide his IP address, Narco created the profiles to post under. He listed himself as a student of the academy and loaded the video. Laughter began to overtake him, and he chuckled as he posted them and copied the links to send to his spies. It would be soon now, soon the entire school would see the video and turn on her.

There would be demands for punishment, demands for her expulsion, which would make it easier for him to eliminate her. Without the protections of the academy, she was a nobody. A simple halfling who wouldn't be missed at all by anyone of importance.

The line of the long-lost princess would truly be terminated, and his assignment would be completed. He may even take a break somewhere, a vacation away from children and halflings and stupid, petty, boring, humans.

This video was the key to the beginning of her end, and now, all he had to do was sit back and wait. Narco closed the page and returned to the image of Mia. He stood and stretched, unbuttoning the top button of his shirt and removing his tie. A glass of scotch was in order for this celebration, and he pulled the bottle off a shelf.

"Salut, little one," he said, toasting the image on the screen. "I will see you soon."

CHAPTER FORTY-ONE

It was like the gargoyles had spent the entire day waiting for the very last bits of sunlight to disappear. Once she thought about it, Elmhurst realized that was exactly what the pair were doing. Now that they could get off their pedestals, all day would have become a tense waiting game for them.

They used to just sit at their posts miserably, knowing it was all they had in their entire existence. They had been crafted to sit there and had remained stuck in place for as long as the academy had stood. Hundreds of years, constantly turning seasons, merciless weather, and countless students had defined a life that hadn't truly been a life. Dan and Steve were simply animated statues with nothing else to look forward to.

Every day, all they could do was watch the students who would come close enough to the library for the gargoyles to see them and overhear gossip of what was happening on campus. Their only fulfillment and purpose had been in reporting to the professors, or to the headmistress, anything they discovered about rule-breaking or misbehavior.

Not anymore. When Mia released them, she had changed everything. It wasn't intentional. The young halfling was powerful, but there was no way for her to have known such a thing was even possible. Yet the compassion and desperate hope she had felt for the two gargoyles had somehow done what nobody had ever thought of. And in doing so, she had changed their reality forever.

Professor Elmhurst didn't know how to respond to their transformation, or what those changes meant for Dan and Steve. It was possible the effect of the release was only temporary. They could land back on their pedestals and be attached to them again. They could be free for a day, only to discover the effect gone when they tried to fly away the next night.

So far, that hadn't happened. But they weren't completely free. The gargoyles had limitations to their ability to leave their posts, and they complied without objection.

Every night, as soon as the last of the sun's rays disappeared beyond the horizon, they were released from their pedestals and free to fly around. They took to the skies and soared around campus, peering into windows and exploring hidden corners they never knew existed. But the moment the first light of morning returned to the sky, they had to be back in their places.

At first, it appeared they were merely doing what she asked and not forgetting their duty to be in their places and guard the library. But it didn't take long for Elmhurst to wonder if there was something more going on. Dan and Steve were committed to the academy, but at the same time, this was their first taste of freedom. She had expected them to remain away from their positions, at least a few times, for longer than she required them to, or even just not return one morning.

She had to admit, she was a little bit afraid they may not return from one of their adventures. She worried they would have so much fun flying around the campus that they would decide they wanted to see more, and would venture out into the world.

So, one day she asked them and was surprised to learn it wasn't only their loyalty and their promise to her that brought them back to their positions outside the library each morning. Every night, when they took off from their spots and flew off wherever their whims took them, they knew they were on borrowed time.

As morning drew closer, the desire to go back to the library became stronger. It was an innate need, a drive to return to their places before the sun rose, and by the time the very first rays of light touched the sky, they were back on their spots where they were meant to be.

But despite that time restraint, they were happy. Neither of them expressed any real ambition of touring the world or discovering what else existed beyond the academy. They were very happy to fly around the school grounds and occasionally go a little farther into the nearby town.

They never went too far. They just flew out over the houses and peered down at the streets, enjoying all the amazing sights which neither had ever seen. Each time they flew out, Elmhurst was concerned someone would see them, and something terrible would happen to the gargoyles. But every morning, there they were, sitting on their time-honored places, watching the students, murmuring between themselves and waiting for the night to come.

That's where they were when Hazel whipped around in search of Sariah. The older girl, a senior at the academy, had spent most of the morning so far tormenting Hazel. Before breakfast, as Hazel headed toward the dining hall with a sweet, attractive boy named Lucas, Sariah had taunted and teased her about everything from her hair to her clothes. At breakfast, the older student had knocked a container of salt into Hazel's food, pretending it was an accident, though she muttered a nasty comment which only Hazel heard.

After breakfast, Sariah had made it a point to get close enough to Hazel in the hall and trip the younger girl, almost sending her toppling down the stairs. At the last moment, Lucas had run up and grabbed her arm, stopping her from falling.

He hadn't seen Sariah, and Hazel didn't mention it, but her face burned with embarrassment and anger. Going to class was her only reprieve. She didn't have to be near the older girl or wait for the next horrible thing she was going to say. Hazel hoped to make it last the rest of the day if she could manage to navigate the grounds effectively enough to stay out of her way.

Unfortunately, that break only lasted an hour. Sariah caught up with Hazel outside the library and immediately started laying into her again. No matter how hard the younger girl tried to avoid her, the senior chased after her. Sariah used a spell to make the frog-shaped brooch she wore on her sweater come to life and hop into Hazel's face. An enchantment swirled her thick hair around Hazel's head, obscuring her vision.

"Why are you doing this?" Hazel cried out. "Why can't you just leave me alone?"

"What's wrong? I thought you liked attention," Sariah snapped. "You really seem to be lapping it up when Lucas gives it to you."

"What? What are you talking about?"

From a few yards away, Mia heard the commotion and glanced up as Sariah swiped her hand angrily in the air in front of Hazel. In that instant, Hazel was lifted off her feet and flipped over, so she dangled high above Sariah.

Hazel's skirt flipped inside out and hung down to her shoulders, exposing her tights to everyone. Fortunately, they were black and thick because of the cold weather, and no one could see through them. But Mia knew Hazel would be humiliated. She raced toward the two girls.

"Don't play dumb," Sariah was saying. "You follow him around like a little puppy. Anyone within fifty feet of you can see it. Smell it, too. It's pathetic."

Now Mia knew what this was about. It was no big secret around campus that Sariah had a huge crush on Lucas. According to Luna and Vivi, it had been going on for years. Only on Sariah's side, though. Lucas barely even knew she existed. Not so much with Hazel.

Over the last couple of months, Lucas seemed to have taken a liking to Hazel, giving her as much attention as he could. He didn't do anything over the top, but Mia had seen the way he smiled at Hazel, and he always seemed to be there to walk with her between classes or to study alongside her during breaks.

Not that Hazel took notice at all. She didn't appear to realize he was there other than to greet him or engage in normal conversations. Either she simply didn't share the attraction, or there was something else on her mind, and she was too wrapped up in it to think about him. Which drove Sariah insane. It was bad enough for the boy she liked to be interested in a younger halfling. But to have that other girl not care pushed Sariah over the edge.

Of course, Mia couldn't imagine what would happen if Hazel did notice his attention and decided to act on it. She would probably be even worse off than hanging upside down with her tights out for everyone on campus to see, her face progressively growing redder by the second.

"Sariah, stop it!" Lucas shouted, running from around the side of the library. "Why do you keep doing this?"

"Oh, Lucas, don't worry about it. I'm just playing with her. It's all in good fun. Isn't it, Hazel?" Sariah teased. The spell was holding Hazel by one ankle, and Sariah used it to yank the girl higher and bounce her around a few times.

"She obviously doesn't think it's fun," Lucas pointed out. "Just put her down."

"You want me to put her down?" There was something sinister in Sariah's voice. "You're right. She's probably been up there long enough. I wouldn't want all that information she just put in there during class to fall out of her ears. That would be a tragedy, wouldn't it?" She picked Hazel up higher. "I guess I should just put her back on the ground."

Hazel suddenly dropped a few feet, screaming as she tried to curl into a ball to protect herself when she hit the ground.

"Sariah, don't you dare!" Mia shouted as she reached them. "Don't you even think about dropping her."

Sariah made a disgusted sound and rolled her eyes, lifting Hazel up again. "You've got to be kidding me. Someone else rushing to her defense? What's with this girl?"

"Put her down," Mia commanded. "Gently."

"Why should I?" Sariah demanded.

"Because I'm telling you to. You're going to turn Hazel back over and set her on her feet. Then you're going to apologize."

Mia felt the sting of anger climbing up the back of her neck. She hated seeing the way some of the older halflings tormented the younger ones. Bullying was something she couldn't deal with. It cut too deep, and the pain lasted too long.

Vivi was already difficult enough to deal with on a regular basis. She was mean and liked to upset people, but most of her pranks were relatively harmless. She didn't go this far. Sariah was just being cruel, and Mia wasn't going to stand for it.

"Come on, Sariah. You've had your fun," Lucas said. "There's no reason to keep doing this. Just put her down and go on with your day."

Mia wanted to tell him to stop, that him defending Hazel was only making it worse. Instead, Mia moved closer and positioned herself between Lucas and Sariah. "Now, Sariah," she said.

The senior halfling merely laughed and bobbed Hazel a little more. Mia was officially done. She reached out with one hand to take control of the spell holding Hazel in the air and sent out a blast of magic with the other hand. The spell hit Sariah and flung her across the quad, where she bounced across the ground as though Mia was skipping stones. Hazel remained in the air but hung still now. Mia carefully manipulated the magic to start lowering the other girl to the ground.

Hazel tried to push her skirt back into place but was having difficulty since she was still upside down. She looked down at Mia in amazement.

"Wow," Lucas said, shocked. "That was incredible."

"I've never seen a student do something like that," Hazel told her.

"Like what?"

"You just reversed Sariah's enchantment. The only halflings I've ever known who were able to do something like that are much older, well after college. Full fae can do it, but it takes an unbelievably strong halfling to do it." Lucas whistled and smiled up at Hazel before turning to Mia.

Mia drew in a breath and released it slowly. Add it to the list. Another thing she wasn't supposed to be able to do but had done without even realizing it.

Sweat beaded Mia's brow as she tried to maintain the magic holding Hazel in place.

CHAPTER FORTY-TWO

Before she realized what was happening, Mia began to lose control of Hazel. She was trying to maintain hold of the girl while also lowering her carefully. Mia hadn't been able to flip her back over, and now Hazel was starting to fall.

Before the poor girl's head smacked into the concrete with the force of her entire weight falling from several feet above, Cinder rushed over from her hiding place and sneezed. The spell left Hazel hanging inches above the ground, still upside-down. Mia's and Cinder's eyes met, and a smile stretched so far across the pixie's face that her cheeks hurt. Mia returned the smile as best she could despite her surprise and gave Cinder a little wave.

"Hey, uh, thanks and all, but can I get the rest of the way down now?" Hazel asked. "The blood that rushed to my head is getting rather uncomfortable."

"Oh, yeah, sorry," Mia said, and made a beckoning motion as if she was asking Hazel to come to her, and the girl spun so that she was vertical again.

"Thanks." Hazel grinned. "By the way, who are you?" Mia asked Cinder, who flashed a smile.

"Cinder," the little pixie said. "And you are quite welcome. Just glad you didn't catch on fire."

"Yeah," Mia said, and paused for a beat. "Wait, what?" She lowered Hazel to the ground.

The moment both her feet were solidly on terra firma, Hazel gathered her things, hurrying off in embarrassment.

"Bye. Thank you," she called over her shoulder, the last vowel stretching out as she ran.

"Bye." Mia waved at Hazel but didn't take her eyes off Cinder.

"That was really sweet of you," Cinder said to Mia.

"Thanks, but what in Faerie are you?" she asked so fast that both the acknowledgment and the question sounded like one multi-syllable word.

"I'm a pixie," Cinder said matter-of-factly.

"I thought pixies were a food."

"It's like a fairy. Only better."

"Oh, so like Tink!"

Cinder folded her arms, and her bottom lip protruded for a moment before she realized she had merely proved Mia's point. She thrust her arms against her sides before planting them on her hips and folded them again as she ran the gamut of stances meant to say she was upset, but she couldn't find one that didn't make her look like a cartoon.

"Cinder," she said. "Not Tink."

"Thank you for keeping her from falling on her head," Mia said, oblivious to being corrected. Somewhere in her mind, she had just stepped off a ledge and was flying above London.

"Oh, well, you're welcome."

"Want to come have some tacos? I was heading to the cafeteria, and I'd love to introduce you to everybody," Mia said.

Cinder nearly vibrated with excitement, and the light naturally emanating from her body grew momentarily in size and brightness, making Mia raise her hand to her eyes against the glare.

"I'd love to," Cinder exclaimed and zoomed around Mia's head.

"Well, come on then," Mia said and started walking away.

Over the next few days, Mia and Cinder became inseparable. Wherever Mia went, the little light of Cinder shone beside her shoulder, and the group became used to her rather easily. Except for Vivi, that is.

Vivi hated the little pixie, if for no other reason than for her immediate and close friendship with Mia. The ease with which the little imp had ingratiated herself with the rest of the group irked Vivi too. It wasn't long before Mia and Luna invited the tiny fairy to stay with the three of them in their room, which Vivi voted against, but was overruled. The pixie moved in, and Vivi was just going to have to get used to it.

Getting used to it wasn't as hard as Vivi expected, though. While on the one hand, there was always a small fire to be put out, quite literally as Cinder's magic was rather combustible, on the other hand, the pixie also tried to earn her keep by cleaning their shared space.

Once Vivi realized she would never have to clean their bathroom again if Cinder was there, she backed off on the list of pranks she had been putting together to make the pixie's life a living hell on wings. Besides, Cinder was becoming quite good at putting out her own fires, so when one happened, she was usually already on top of it. Three hundred years of practice gave her a wealth of experience with them.

Cinder wasn't the only one getting chummy with Mia, though. Much to the little pixie's irritation, Hazel started hanging around too. Knowing what she knew of Hazel, Cinder was immediately suspicious but kept her opinions to herself.

One day, Mia turned to the little pixie and asked her a question to help shed light on what Mia had been thinking. "When you look at people," Mia said as Cinder made her tiny little bed and lit a candle nearby with a sneeze that almost set the table on fire too. "Do you see colors around them?"

"Colors?" the little pixie asked. "Like an aura?"

"Yeah, like an aura."

"No." The pixie cocked her head to one side. "Do you?"

"Not with everyone." Mia dropped her voice to a fraction above a whisper. "Just with Hazel, actually. There's this glow around her, and it's a weird color. It's hard to put it into words, but Hazel strikes me as a good person, but her aura—something is off about it. It makes me uncomfortable."

"Oh?"

"Yeah. But no one else sees it. Not even you. I asked Luna and Zander, and they had no idea what I was even talking about."

Cinder kept her mouth shut, but she knew why. Halflings weren't supposed to be able to see auras. Only full fae should be able to see them. She had been arguing with herself over what to say and what not to say to Mia. If she was right, Mia was in even more danger, but there wouldn't be anything Cinder could do about it.

And if she was wrong, Mia would worry over nothing.

However, the halfling needed to know how much danger she was in. But, Cinder reminded herself that if Mia knew, she'd most likely tell her friends. She still wasn't sure Vivi could be trusted or if Carson could keep a secret this big.

No, she would continue to keep an eye out for Mia and look for more signs to tell her if the halfling was related to whom she guessed. The pixie hated keeping this from the girl who was quickly becoming her friend, but it was for Mia's safety. Cinder would simply have to keep telling herself this.

"Have you talked to any of your instructors about it?" Cinder asked, sitting on her bed. Mia dropped onto hers.

Cinder's bed was on the nightstand between Mia's and Luna's beds, and the whiff of air from the mattress blew a gust at the pixie that almost knocked her over.

"Yes, but they didn't see it either. I asked her how she was feeling, and she said she was fine, so I thought maybe I was just seeing things."

"Or maybe it's a leftover enchantment? From Sariah?" Cinder offered.

"Maybe."

"Maybe it's something only you can see because you are the one who broke the spell? Maybe there is something lingering there Sariah has to let go of before it will disappear?"

"I don't know, but I aim to find out one way or the other," Mia said before standing. "At any rate, I need to get to class. We get our grades back today from the Egyptian Artifact papers. See you in a while."

Mia stuffed her books in her bag, slung it over her arm, and headed to class. When she arrived, the rest of her group was standing outside the door, chatting before going in.

"Mia, late again," Vivi said snidely as Mia approached.

"She's not late yet. There's still at least two minutes before the bell," Carson said. Vivi stuck her tongue out at him and folded her arms.

"Enough of that," Zander admonished.

"I still can't get over the fact we were being chased." Luna stared at Zander and Carson with a mixture of worry and hope. She hoped one of them would alleviate her fear that their safety was in question, even here in the school.

"Well, I didn't recognize them, so my guess is it was just some fae who didn't like kids using portals," said Carson.

"I don't think that was it." Zander ran his hand through his hair and looked at Mia. "Did you recognize any of them?"

"No," she responded, before falling silent. Was that accurate? "I don't know, actually. One of them looked familiar, but I didn't get a good look at him this time. It was as if I'd caught a glimpse of someone I had seen before." She shook her head. "But it wasn't the guy who went through that portal to the Underworld." Mia had wondered if it was the fae hunter who she and Cassia had seen in Shanghai. She would never forget his face. If only she could get a better look at him.

"If that's where he went," Vivi interjected. There was a moment of silence as they all envisioned the myriad horrors that would have befallen them had they not realized what it was and went through. Or if where he had ended up going was somewhere worse.

"I almost forgot to tell you guys. I did some more research on that," Luna announced. "I am pretty sure Zander was right, and that portal goes to the Underworld."

"Why?" Carson said.

"Well, the more I looked into portals attached to sarcophagi, the more I noticed there seemed to be two types: one for fae and one for humans. The one for fae would be a two-way door, and they rarely ever used them because not only could they get into the Underworld, but other things could get out. But humans only had a one-way door."

"But the thing chasing us—it was a fae," Zander said.

"True, but I think it still works like a human door regardless of who goes through. So as long as no one makes another fae portal to the Underworld they can get to, whoever it was is probably stuck there," she said.

"Man, I hope so," Carson said.

"But you said there was more than one of them down there with us," Zander said, addressing Mia. "The guy that went through the portal and someone else? Or two more people?"

"I think so," Mia said. It was hard to remember all of the details of the evening. It had all happened so fast, and she was worried maybe she had seen something that hadn't been there. Or maybe she had dreamed about it so much since then that she had added memories. Which could be why the man had looked familiar.

Only, she knew it wasn't a dream, and deep down, she knew she had really seen it. No matter how much she tried to question herself, she knew it was true. She had seen that man before, and he had been with them in the storage room of the Louvre. If he was capable of making a portal, maybe he had already let the first man out.

"I don't think we should tell anybody about the sarcophagus. The research we did on the mirror should be enough to cover any suspicion from the detail in our papers," Zander said. "If there was someone else down there with us, I suspect they would have tried to follow us, realized they couldn't and either given up or would have tried again by now, don't you think?"

There was a general murmur of agreement.

"What if they fail us because they think we cheated somehow?" Luna asked. "It's not like the mirror stuff was in any of the books we were assigned or on any of the artifacts they brought in for us to see. There's no way for us to have known about it without seeing it with our own eyes, or stumbling onto it in the Library. Don't you think that sounds pretty far-fetched?"

The bell rang above them, and Zander shrugged, turning toward the open door of the classroom. "I guess we will cross that bridge if we come to it."

It turned out they had no need for concern. Just a few minutes into class, they were all beaming at each other as their papers were handed back to them with perfect scores. All five had a note from the teacher saying how impressed he was at the level of detail and of their discovery of the mirror. Thanks to Cinder, they had uncovered plenty of information about the mirror in the library to craft flawless papers. That tip had been enough for Vivi to lay off complaining about Cinder's impossibly loud snores for an entire day.

They left the classroom, gathered in the hall, and headed for the cafeteria.

"I think this calls for celebratory pizza," Carson said.

"Doesn't everything call for celebratory pizza with you?" Vivi quipped.

"Yes, but this also calls for celebratory pizza. The only problem is there's nowhere around that makes a good one," Carson said. "Why don't we open a port—"

"No," Zander, Mia, Luna and Vivi, all said in unison. The laughter that broke out was a release, but there was still tension in the air. The more Mia thought about it, the more she was sure of what she had seen, and though no one had followed them into the school, she didn't feel like they were safe yet. Something wasn't right.

CHAPTER FORTY-THREE

Thanksgiving used to be one of Mia's favorite times of the year. It didn't beat either Christmas or Halloween, which wrestled back and forth for the top spot on the list as her absolute favorite holiday, but it was a strong contender.

It ticked off all the boxes. There was beautiful fall weather that let her stuff herself into stretch pants and her favorite sweatshirts and sweaters. There was an abundance of amazing smells, from the burning leaves outside to the spices and food inside. There was time with her father, and watching favorite movies all night. There was a week of leftovers they had said they would turn into all sorts of interesting and innovative foods, which they had ended up eating directly from the containers.

At least, that's what the holiday used to be for her. Not this year. Mia was going to have to get accustomed to her new normal as a fae halfling at the Elmhurst Academy, and that meant looking ahead to a day without any of those boxes ticked. Starting with the fall weather.

Back home, there would be the possibility of some flurries, maybe a dusting of snow on the local foothills, but for the most part, she would get to enjoy the last of the year's pretty leaves and crisp, clean air. Getting up early wasn't her favorite thing, but during the fall, she made it more appealing by wrapping up in her much-loved blanket and standing out on the porch with a steaming cup of coffee or hot tea.

It was going to take a whole lot more than her threadbare pink chenille blanket to ward off the cold, and the winds, of the Montana Thanksgiving. The end of the previous week had brought a massive snowfall, and the snow had kept piling up over the following two days until the students were trapped by several feet. From the window of their dorm, it looked like they were stuck in a huge snow globe, which someone kept jiggling.

Not that it made a huge difference to many of the students. For the most part, the academy closed down for the Thanksgiving holiday. The majority of the students went home to celebrate with their human families, and to enjoy some time away from campus and all their academic pressures as finals loomed before Christmas.

Mia knew that wasn't going to be her. As much as she missed her father and wished she was in her favorite sweatpants awaiting her first heaped plate of mashed potatoes, stuffing, and green bean casserole, she wasn't going to be seeing him this year. As far as he was aware, she was still in Shanghai, learning under a master and wouldn't be able to make the trip back to the United States for the holiday.

Mia imagined this would hurt his feelings and knew he missed her, but her father would also be so proud of her. Seeing her excel in her martial arts meant a lot to him, and he would willingly give up that time with her if it meant she was able to pursue her dream. Part of her wondered if he would be as proud, knowing where she was and what she was studying. She hoped he would be.

Carson dropped onto the wooden bench of the table in the dining hall beside Mia. He crossed his arms on the table, sighed, and dropped his head onto them. It was a dramatic display, but one she had seen from Zander the day before, so she knew what it meant. "Your parents?" she asked.

He nodded and lifted his head. "They called to wish me a Happy Thanksgiving."

"But they aren't having you come home?" Mia finished for him.

"Nope," he said.

He dropped his head onto his arms again, and Mia rubbed his back to comfort him. The five were all sitting around the table, none of them sprung from the academy for the holiday by their parents. Both Carson and Zander had received calls from their human parents, but neither was summoned home, which had disappointed both of them.

"Did you think any of us were going to get out of here?" Vivi reached into the basket in front of her and pulled out a biscuit.

"You make it sound like prison," Mia said.

Vivi shrugged and scanned the dining hall. "It's starting to feel like it. Even if our parents had called us out for the holiday, I doubt Elmhurst would have let us go. She's kept us back for every other break."

"She didn't say she was going to do that this time," Carson pointed out.

"Does it make any difference?" Vivi snapped. "We're all stuck here."

The Unseelie halfling was taking staying at the school over Thanksgiving the hardest. That surprised Mia. Vivi's human parent was her mother, and since she had died, Vivi had no human connections.

Full fae didn't celebrate Thanksgiving. It was purely an American human holiday, which meant fae had no reason to see the break as special in any way. Vivi's father would be living his normal life, working every moment, and would see no point in complicating things by having his daughter home, just for the sake of a break from school.

The only one who didn't seem deflated by the thought of spending Thanksgiving at the academy was Luna. Considering it was only her and her mother, and her mother was human, they always celebrated Thanksgiving. And since she was close by, Luna didn't need to leave school in order to visit her. Staying on campus was easier. But that didn't mean she wasn't going to help the others enjoy their holiday as well.

"Come on, guys. I know you're disappointed about having to be here, but the holiday isn't ruined. We can still celebrate Thanksgiving," she chirped.

"Is your mom making dinner again this year?" Zander asked. His voice held a little bit of a lift as he asked the question, as though the thought may make the week easier.

"Of course, she is."

"What dinner?" Mia asked.

Luna turned to her with a smile. "There are always some students left at the academy over Thanksgiving, and my mother can't stand the thought of people being alone for holidays. Even fae who don't celebrate it. So she started a tradition of hosting a huge Thanksgiving dinner at the diner for the students who didn't leave the academy. It's all vegan, complete with tofurkey and all the trimmings. Anything you can think of for a traditional Thanksgiving dinner, she makes it. It's a really wonderful night. I hope you'll come."

"Absolutely. I will," Mia said. "Thank you. I was having a hard time thinking about celebrating this holiday without my father, but it will definitely be easier if I can spend it with you guys."

"I just hope the snow lets up by then," Zander said. "It would be hard to get to the diner with it like this."

"I'm sure it will," Mia said.

She was wrong. They woke up Thanksgiving morning to a fresh three inches of snow on top of what had already fallen. Luna was in the dining hall before the others arrived, staring at the table and looking disappointed.

Mia sat across from her. "Good morning," she said. "Happy Thanksgiving."

Luna looked up at her with sadness in her eyes. "It should be. But with this snow, how are we possibly going to get to the diner to have dinner? I'm not going to be able to see my mother for the holiday, and we're not going to get to eat all the amazing food together." She sighed and looked at the table again.

"That's not necessarily true," Mia offered. "There's another way we can get there."

"What do you mean?" she asked.

"I know what she means," Carson said from across the table. Their eyes met, and she gave a little nod.

"So do I," someone said from behind Mia.

Mia turned to find Principal Elmhurst standing close behind her. "Oh. Good morning, Professor. Happy Thanksgiving."

"Happy Thanksgiving to you, too, Mia. I hope you aren't talking about making a portal to go to the diner."

"Honestly, I was considering it," Mia admitted.

"You know you can't do that. We've been over this. You are not permitted to make any portals that take you off-campus to anywhere on Earth. That includes Nicolette's diner," Elmhurst said.

"But it's the perfect solution," Mia argued. "I've already proven I can make a safe and reliable portal. And those brought me a whole lot farther than just into town to the diner. But I don't have to be the one to do it. You could open a portal for us in the secure room so you would know exactly where it was and where it would get us. It would be the easiest way to get us all there safely and on time for dinner. We wouldn't have to deal with the snow on the way there or on the way back, either."

"Yes, Mia. I could open a portal very easily, and it would be a fast way to get everyone directly to the diner." The five young halflings grinned at each other, but Elmhurst shot down their growing happiness by shaking her head. "But I'm not going to do that. Luna's mother has several human workers, and there may be human customers at the diner today. There's no way we can risk having them see us coming through a portal. It would be disastrous. I'm very sorry, but a portal is just not an option."

Luna sagged against the table again. "So, dinner is out."

"I didn't say that. We can still get there. It will just take some organization and a little bit of adjustment. But I'll take care of that."

Luna grinned, and Mia's heart soared. It may not be what Mia was used to, but she was going to get Thanksgiving, and she was excited about it.

That afternoon, a bus appeared in front of the school, with another one right behind it. All bundled-up, the students shuffled down the snowy steps and into the cushioned seats inside, eager for the dinner that awaited them.

For many of them, this was a rare and unusual treat. Most students who stayed behind at the academy during Thanksgiving were like Vivi. They only had contact with their fae parent, and so they didn't celebrate the holiday. Several had never celebrated it until Luna's mother started throwing the dinner when Luna entered the academy. Despite not having a full grasp of what the holiday meant, or why they were celebrating, the fae students loved the spread of delicious food and the fun of all being together.

When the students were all on board, Mia noticed Elmhurst walk up to the front wheels of the first bus and say something while sweeping her hand over the tire. She repeated the process on the other front tire and moved on to do the same for both front tires of the other bus. When she returned, the headmistress flashed a smile at the students.

"That will take care of the snow for us," she said.

"What was it?" Mia asked.

"Just a little bit of magic. I can't do anything that will drastically change the snow, or the humans will notice. But that enchantment will pack the snow down just enough to make it safe and easy for the buses to get through on the way there and back," Elmhurst answered.

When they arrived at the diner, platters of food had already filled several tables Nicollette had pushed together and draped with a crisp white cloth. Candles burned along the center of the table, and though the place-settings were the dishes used by the diner every day, they managed to look elegant. Luna ran to hug her mother, and several of the students followed suit, thanking the smiling woman for all she did for them.

Warmth spread through Mia's chest as Nicollette hugged her and welcomed her to the dinner. It felt like the holiday should. They sat and started passing the platters and bowls around, filling their plates with the vast array of dishes prepared for them.

They dug in, and for the next half hour, the diner was filled with the sound of chewing, glasses clinking, and dozens of conversations bubbling among the halflings. When everyone had eaten at least one round of food, Nicollette stood at the end of the table and clinked a knife against a glass. Everyone looked up at her, and she smiled, raising her glass to them.

"Happy Thanksgiving, everyone. I am so glad you were able to join me for the holiday. I'd like to further our holiday celebration by going around the table and sharing what we each are thankful for."

They went around the table, and Mia smiled as she listened to each of the students talk about the things in their lives they were thankful for. A few students giggled, but for the most part, it was a heartwarming way to find out more about each other. Just listening to them share these little glimpses into their minds made her feel closer to them, even though she hadn't met some of them before that day.

When her turn came up, Mia looked around the table, and at her group spread out on either side of her. So many emotions churned through her that she didn't know where to start describing them. But she did know exactly how thankful she was and what was making her feel that way.

"I haven't been a part of Elmhurst Academy as long as the rest of you. I haven't been a part of this world as long as the rest of you have. But it's been an amazing journey. I've learned so much about myself and my history and what I can become. Not just about being a halfling, but about me as a person. I know there is no way that would have happened if it wasn't for the people who have brought me—sometimes kicking and screaming—this far. They were asked to do this, whether they liked it or not. And the 'or not' was a good portion of the time, I know. But they were there anyway. That's why I want to say that this year, I am thankful for all the friends I've made at Elmhurst Academy. Including you, Vivi."

Vivi's gaze snapped to Mia, and her mouth fell open. She blinked a few times, processing what she had just heard. Mia opened her arms and pulled Vivi into a hug. As Mia squeezed her close, Vivi sniffled, fighting back tears.

"No one has ever been thankful for me before," Vivi whispered.

"I am," Mia whispered in reply. She didn't know if it would change anything, but she was glad for the moment she had shared with the Unseelie girl.

"I know we're thankful for you, Mia."

Mia turned to the door of the diner, where Steve and Dan were standing. Gasping, she stared around the restaurant, worried the gargoyles would be seen by the humans.

"Don't worry," Elmhurst said from the head of the table. "When they told me they were planning on coming as soon as they were released from their pedestals at sunset, I made some preparations. Nicollette sent the human staff home early, and once the human diners who were here left, I put up a block to prevent any others from coming."

"We wanted to be a part of your holiday celebration," Dan said.

"It's the first time we've gotten a chance to do anything for Thanksgiving other than watch people leave," Steve told Mia.

"Well, I'm happy to see both of you," Mia replied. She crossed the diner and gave each statue a kiss on the cheek.

The crowd spent nearly two more hours in the diner, finishing their dinner and tucking into massive sweet-potato pies, pumpkin pies, and chocolate cakes. When they were all finished and sufficiently stuffed, they piled into the buses to head back to the academy. Dan and Steve soared high above them but didn't return to the library. As the five went to the dorm, the gargoyles followed close behind.

"What are you going to do now?" Dan asked before they went inside.

Mia turned to them. "We were thinking about watching some movies. Maybe playing some games."

"Mom sent me back with lots of leftovers, so as soon as we have room, we'll eat some more," Luna said.

Mia smiled at the gargoyles as they exchanged glances. "Do you want to join us?"

Dan grinned. He seemed a little star-struck by Mia, while Steve maintained some distance. Even with his reticence, he appeared reluctant to end the evening there, eager to spend more time with the students.

"Sure!" Dan finally agreed.

The gargoyles entered the dorm for the first time and followed the five halflings to the girls' room. The guys left but returned a few minutes later, having changed into their sweats. The girls took turns going into the bathroom to change, and soon they were all comfortable and ready for a night of hanging out and enjoying the holiday together.

They stayed up all night playing board games and cards, watching movies, sharing stories, and eating their way through as many of the leftovers as they could stuff inside themselves. They didn't even think about going to bed until the gargoyles announced they needed to leave so they could return to their spots in time for the sun to go up.

Dan watched as Mia crawled under her covers and rested her head on the pillow. She sighed as her eyes closed, and he felt more secure leaving. Ever since they had gained their freedom, they had been watching over Mia more closely but hadn't noticed anything out of the ordinary.

They truly enjoyed their time away from the library, and they wanted to make sure the time they spent did some good in addition to being fun. For now, Mia seemed safe and content, so the gargoyles slipped out of the window and returned to the library. They touched down on their pedestals with mere seconds to spare before the first bits of sunlight came across the sky.

CHAPTER FORTY-FOUR

The weekend after Thanksgiving was going to be insane this year, and Vivi was ready for it. Starting on Sunday, the slamball championships was to be held over three full days of late-November mayhem, and since the Halfling Academy was hosting this year, there were no classes the entire week.

Even though it meant the students were drafted via random lottery to perform various tasks, like helping with parking, janitorial duties, ushering, and concessions, it was worth it to get the break from class and experience the insanity of all the different academies descending on Montana to liven the place up.

Vivi had yet to be assigned any duties and was more excited than she otherwise would have been at the prospect of being able to enjoy the games without any responsibilities, unlike the others. Luna and Carson had both been drafted into ushering for the heads of the academies, and Zander and Mia were assigned cleanup duties.

Vivi might be assigned to work one of the refreshments stands or some other job, but for the moment, she was free, and she felt like rubbing it in everyone's faces while she still could. This included Amanda and Uri, two Unseelie girls she used to hang out with.

Amanda and Uri were as inseparable as two peas in a pod. Though they came from very different cultures, the two of them had bonded immediately at the academy and were known for their loyalty to their little clique of friends, which at least theoretically included Vivi. Both were wearing the blue-and-gold aprons assigned to the cleanup crew, and Vivi was dying to tease them about it.

"Hey ladies," Vivi said as she approached them. "If I spill my drink everywhere, can I ask specifically for you two to come clean it up, or is it random?"

"Very funny," Uri said as she turned to her, away from whatever deep conversation the two of them were giggling through before Vivi arrived. "What did you end up with?"

"Nothing. I get to watch the games and throw my trash on the ground and go back to the dorm to watch TV while you push a broom around."

"Unless you get drafted for bathroom duty," Amanda said, a smirk crossing her tiny, scrunched-up face. Vivi thought she looked like a constipated chihuahua.

"Yuck. Don't even put that out into the world, Amanda," Vivi said.

"Why don't you ask her?" Amanda said to Uri, who stared back, eyes wide, and shook her head sharply. "Come on, it would be great."

"Ask me what?" Vivi said, suddenly intrigued.

"Fine," Uri said begrudgingly. "We have this plan, and we want to know if you think it's vicious enough. We're on cleanup crew with Zander and, ugh, *Mia*." She said Mia's name as if it physically pained her. "And we were going to do something really cool."

"It's so great," Amanda butted in. "We're going to build this big mess of trash, and then when she goes to clean it up, I'm going to enchant the mustard bottles while Uri goes behind the refreshment counter and—"

"Absolutely not," Vivi said, leaving both of them with their jaws open, though Amanda's was still bouncing up and down a bit.

"Why in the Underworld not?" Uri demanded.

"Look, she may be weird, and she may not really belong here, but..." Vivi closed her eyes as she tried to force the words to come out. She nearly lost the battle. "But she is my friend. Crickets, I can't believe I said that. It's true, though, and if anyone is going to mess with her, it will be me. If I catch wind of either of you doing anything to her, you'll catch it back tenfold from me. Got it?"

"Yeah," Uri said, straightening and holding her hand out to Amanda, who took it. "We got it. See ya around, Vivi."

Vivi waited until they went around a corner before she kicked the wall, hard. What the heck was she doing? On what planet did she stand up for Mia, of all people? She was leaning against the wall when she happened to notice the clock.

Only a few hours remained before the big orientation in the auditorium, and she wanted to get dressed for the occasion. When she arrived at her room, her heart sank. A note was taped to the door, with the official stamp of the academy on the front and her name written across it in the scrawling print of none other than Elmhurst.

Vivi, I noticed you were not yet assigned a duty for the championships. We are low on both bathroom attendants and assistants for the VIP's. Considering your recent grades, and the impressive way you have handled the changes to your team, I have chosen to give you the VIP assistant duty. Do not make me regret it.

-Elmhurst

Vivi smiled so wide it nearly split her face in two. Having the week off would have been nice, but being able to sit in the VIP section and only worry about fetching drinks on occasion? That was worth bragging about.

As they walked out to the fields together, the group shared the details of their various duties and times. Thankfully, they all had the first couple of matches off and planned on sitting together to watch them.

Mia gasped as they approached the soccer fields, which had been enclosed using some fairly powerful magic to create two large stadiums. The covering shimmered in the sunlight, and while it was possible to see through, it was impenetrable by weather—an incredibly strong version of the domes the group created to practice in.

"This is incredible," Mia said as they entered the first stadium via a portal arranged specifically for the games.

"It's really cool. I'd love to know who is casting the spell, but they keep it a pretty closely guarded secret, for obvious reasons," Zander said.

"It has to be at least one representative from each school, though, all working together. We know that," Carson said.

"Why?" Mia asked.

"So that if one of them decides to sabotage the games because their team is losing, the others can hold it together and hold that person accountable," Luna informed her.

"So, there are four people, then?" Mia asked.

"Eight," Vivi interjected. "One for each team participating."

"Wait, I thought there were only eight teams total, two from each elite academy? Is everyone in the playoffs?" Mia asked.

"No, that's just our league. Our league is the Premier League, where the elite schools have A and B teams. There is another league for the other levels of academies. Overall, there are a total of fifteen academies in the US and Canada, and they participate in two leagues. The Premier League and the Banner League. The Banner League is older, and consists of all the original schools from before the Elite schools were created. Most of the lower academies come from the Banner League and end up placing fifth through eighth and filling out the playoffs, and the rest end their season," Luna explained.

"There is only one elite school for each species; Fae, Shifter, Vampire, and Witches. Obviously, we are the Fae Academy, and each elite school has an A and B team. Does that make sense?" Zander asked.

Mia nodded, and she tried to work it out as they entered the lower concourse of the stadium. The magic was more than merely the dome over the fields, it was also enchanting large sections of seating around the grounds, climbing high and angling in.

Each section of seating, lower, upper, and VIP, was separated not by concrete but by magic. They floated in place, and the VIP seating actually moved, driven by a spellcaster in each pod of seats to go where the VIP's told them to. Occasionally, one would dip down between two lower concourse seating areas, and fly back above the playing field to get a better viewing angle as the casters showed the guests all the positions possible for the day's game.

The grounds itself was covered in its own protective, though almost invisible, dome. While the shield over the fields shimmered in the sun and snow, the dome over the stadium was ethereal and intangible. It was as though it were made of the thinnest of smoke, and you could only see it if you screwed up your eyes just right, like attempting to look through the holes in a fence made of gossamer.

They climbed to their seats, up in the nosebleed section, via a complicated portal-to-stairs system. They found their places near the front. Once settled in, Mia figured she could learn a little more about what exactly was going on without feeling like a complete moron, but to her disappointment, Vivi sat between her and Zander, and Carson was on the other side between her and Luna. If she was going to find anything out, it was going to be through the wide eyes and excitable temperament of Carson, or the cutting sarcasm and dismissive attitude of Vivi.

"I know the championships are played out over three days, but I am still a little confused as to how it works," she said, loudly enough in Zander's direction that she hoped he would hear over the crowd and the loud music blaring through the arena.

Instead, Vivi turned, and to Mia's surprise, didn't look at her as if she had just asked if she could eat soup with a knife. "It's a series of brackets," Vivi said, raising her voice over the noise as they began to perform a stomping-and-clapping routine to music that was a well-known slamball tradition. "Our A team made it in as the second-place team, so we play the seventh-ranked team first. That's Shilo Academy, one of the lower shifter academies from Sonoma County, California. We played them last year, but we were third place, and they were sixth, and they stayed in it to the last few minutes. It was embarrassing, but we finally won. We got knocked out by the Shifters' Premier League team in the semi-finals, and people say it was because our team was so shaken by how hard it was to beat the Shilo Shifters."

"But they were in second to last place this year, and we were second place, so it should be an easier game, right?" Mia said.

This time it was Carson who chimed in mid-stomp-and-clap. "If we don't do better this year, heads are going to roll. Their main gunner graduated last year, and they've been spectacularly bad all season. They only placed seventh because their schedule was almost all B level teams. Even those games they barely won. We should mop the floor with them."

"Remember last year, though," Vivi said, and Carson grimaced.

"I don't want to," he said.

"Our A team is actually the favorite to win the championship this year," Vivi continued. "We only lost one game, and that's to the first-place team, the witches' A team. There was a lot of weird stuff happening in that game, and one of the referees was placed on suspension, but nobody knows why. The rumor is that one of the teachers paid them off to call fouls on us, but no one will say. We are on the opposite side of the bracket as them, so if we can make the finals, it will likely be against them. It's really rare for any of the non-elite teams to make the final four, and the witches are likely to sweep their bracket."

"Then we get revenge," Carson said. He sipped a drink Mia wasn't sure she had seen him buy, and they stood for the playing of the Fae Academy Anthem. The game was about to begin.

CHAPTER FORTY-FIVE

"Do you mind if I sit with you guys?" came a voice from behind them, and Mia turned to Hazel, who held a tray of nachos and her ticket, with an expression of hopeful hesitation on her face.

"Yeah, come on," Mia said, and beside her, Cinder muttered something under her breath, but no one else heard it.

The seats were general admission in the upper decks, and the group reluctantly scooted closer together to create the space for Hazel. She was rather small anyway, so it wasn't much room, but it did make everything a little tighter, and it put more space between Mia and Vivi. Though Vivi had been acting a little better recently, keeping a bit of distance was probably a good idea, as far as Mia thought.

Unfortunately for Hazel, Vivi wasn't a fan, and she rolled her eyes and made a face when Hazel sat, as though she had been forced to smell Carson's gym socks.

Sitting between Vivi and Mia wasn't exactly Hazel's preferred scenario, and despite Zander moving over a fair bit, Vivi barely scooted to give her space. She squeezed in anyway. "So, do you have a favorite on the team?" Hazel said as she wiggled into the spot, looking from Mia to Vivi.

"No," Vivi said curtly.

"I'm still really new to the sport," Mia explained. "So, I really don't know much. I think the gunner position is cool, but I don't know any of the players or anything like that."

"The team captain is pretty dreamy." Hazel sighed. It took both Vivi and Mia aback, and they glanced at each other, trying to suppress a laugh.

"Dreamy?" Vivi asked snidely.

"Thorison Granger. He's really, really good," Hazel continued, as Vivi rolled her eyes again.

"You should know," Carson muttered, and Mia shot a questioning look at him. "What? Her dad is a former pro-player. Now he's the academy scout."

"Is that true?" Mia asked, twisting to look at her new friend, who went red in the cheeks and appeared shocked to be called out so bluntly.

"Yes," she said. "He is. I guess I see more of the players than most people do because of it."

"How much more?" Vivi leered, and it took a second for Hazel to understand the implication.

"Not *that* much," she exclaimed as the meaning dawned on her, and a bubble of giggles built into full laughter and rolled through the entire group. Eventually, even Hazel laughed.

As far as the gang was concerned, having Hazel around could be useful, if for nothing else other than her family connections, but to Mia, she was something more. She seemed nice, and aside from her gang chosen to be her friends, Hazel seemed like someone she might organically be friends with, and it meant a lot to her to have someone like that. Besides, Hazel was younger and small, and it felt good to have a little-sister type person after the journey to get to the academy left her feeling like *she* was the little sister.

"It's really coming down out there," Zander said, looking up. The dome's roof was mostly transparent, and when they took their eyes off the field of play, where the game was beginning, a look around showed the grounds of the school being absolutely hammered by snow. It piled up in great drifts and blew around so thick it was difficult to see more than a few feet beyond the protection of the dome. Even the tall, imposing spires of the school were mostly covered by the snow. Silently, Mia thanked every deity imaginable for the portals that would get them where they needed to go.

Luna had explained to her earlier that during times of major snowfall, Elmhurst created portals that took the students from one building to another, so they didn't have to walk in a blizzard. These were semi-permanent pathways that were closed when not needed.

Mia hoped it would give her more of an opportunity to learn how to better use them without making a fool of herself each time. If she kept falling through the portals, she was never going to feel like she belonged.

The game was mostly uneventful, and as the buzzer finally sounded, the score was lopsided in favor of the Fae Academy. The Archers, the A team, dominated the entire game and even played the last few minutes with bench players.

Many in the crowd left early, but the gang stayed back until the very end, Carson munching on various snacks. Eventually, Hazel said her goodbyes and left the group, who sat in the nosebleeds chatting away. The next game was going to be in an hour or so, so they had a little time before they had to leave.

"I know what we should do," Cinder said, interrupting an argument about trampoline vs. hovering-flight strategy between Luna and Zander. "We should have a bonfire!"

"During a blizzard? Are you nuts?" Vivi asked.

"Seriously? You guys can create a shield big enough for all of us to stay safe from the storm and have the bonfire inside, dum-dum."

Vivi's face ran through a range of emotions, beginning with shock and rolling through indignation and into anger rather quickly. "Listen here you little fleck of fairy light, I could—"

"All right, all right," Zander said, interrupting Vivi. "Enough of that. I actually agree with Cinder."

"What?" Carson and Vivi reacted with varying degrees of disbelief.

Carson's words were rather garbled by the number of chocolate candies in his mouth at that moment.

"It could be a good test for Mia, actually. To see if she can create a shield on her own and hold it. It's something all of us can do, and it's important she gets it right because you never know when you will need it."

"That's fair," Carson eventually agreed. "But if we are going to have a bonfire, we are going to need something to roast over it."

"S'mores," Cinder said. "You guys bring the s'mores stuff, and I'll bring the fire. I'm really good at fire." She laughed at herself as the group got the joke and joined in.

"It's agreed then," Zander said. "We can use portals to get back to our rooms and fetch supplies and then use the portal to get back here and just do the bonfire right outside the dome. Come on, let's get going."

Zipping to the dorms, Zander and Carson grabbed the graham crackers, a favorite of both boys, while Luna dug into her stash of chocolate, and Vivi and Mia searched for marshmallows. It ended with both girls sneaking down to the empty kitchens and nicking the first bag they saw.

"You think anyone will notice?" Mia asked as they ran giggling to their room.

"Nah, not with the games. Come on, I need a coat. I still don't trust you not to turn us into snowmen."

Mia shook her head and laughed off the mild insult. For once, Vivi seemed to be having fun *with* Mia and not *at* her. Besides, Vivi was probably right. They had at least a fifty-fifty shot of all being buried in several feet of snow.

Mia tried to calm her nerves about it with the excitement of the upcoming s'more feast, but it lurked in the corner of her mind until they reached the portal and walked through, into the safe area outside the two stadiums. That's when the nerves went into overdrive.

"I don't know if this is a great idea," Mia said slowly. "What if I get it wrong and somehow ruin the games or something?"

"Don't flatter yourself," Vivi said. "The domes over each stadium and the big one we're in right now are impenetrable. It's fortified with the magic of eight leaders of the various academies, and they have backup-security protecting it beyond that. The stadiums will be fine. I'm far more worried about turning into a popsicle."

"She's going to do fine." Zander smiled at Mia. "Let's get out there."

Following his lead, the group of five, plus Cinder, safely tucked inside Mia's coat to prevent her from blowing away, exited the protection of the main bubble. The cold hit them instantly, and they rushed to a section of the courtyard where they could build a fire and turned to Mia. There was no going back now.

"Mia, you have to do it now," Luna shouted over the sound of snow pelting them.

The blizzard-like conditions were disorienting, and the snow seemed to be piling up as Mia watched it. They already had to take giant, high steps to move, and in only a few more hours, the snow was bound to be over their heads.

Mia tried to focus, closing her eyes and holding her palms out to her sides. It was a position she had seen Vivi and Luna take, and they both said it helped them, while Zander and Carson said it made them look like weird statues. Mia figured she would rather resemble a statue than fail, so she put herself in position and focused on the idea of a dome around them.

The wind seemed to settle, and the snow wasn't falling as hard. Mia smiled as she thought of how impressive it would be to have built the dome on the first try, and the heat from the sudden bonfire, wood collected by Carson and Zander with fire provided by Cinder, began to warm her skin. She raised her hands higher and opened her eyes.

Suddenly she wasn't in control anymore. Her smile faltered. The dome, purple-hazed and pulsing like a living being, had swallowed them and seemed to thin. Holes began to open around it in various places, including one in the center above the fire. A large block of snow fell in and landed on the wood, extinguishing the flames.

There was a moment of absolute silence as the dome disappeared, and they all stared at the snow mound that was once a fire.

Luna started laughing first. Then Zander. Then Vivi. Finally,

Carson joined in, despite the stick he held out, the marshmallow long lost in the white snow. Soon enough, Mia began to laugh too.

"All right, so that didn't work. Try it again, before we all freeze to death," Zander said.

At that moment, the two gargoyles landed heavily on either side of the group. Dan stood tall, sniffed the wind, and stuck out a stone tongue to catch some of the fluffy flakes falling from above.

"You should poke holes in your dome," Dan said. "So the smoke can escape. You can't see it, but even the ones over the stadium have some holes poked in, just on the sides."

"But with fire," Steve interrupted. "You will need your holes at the top because the smoke needs to escape. A little bit of snow getting inside won't hurt you."

"They're right," Luna offered. "Give it another shot, Mia."

Mia closed her eyes again and tried to focus, letting the concept of the small holes at the top swirl in her mind. She felt it begin to form, and the wind and snow slowed down. Soon, it felt warmer again as the fire sparked to life once more. Slowly, she opened one eye and stared around her.

The smoke was rising to the top of her dome and escaping through tiny holes. The fire roared in front of them and was so warm Carson was taking off his coat. Marshmallows on sticks were being passed around, and the gargoyles looked on in smug satisfaction before flying off to wherever it was they felt like going for the evening.

The group spent an hour roasting marshmallows and making s'mores, chatting about the night's win and their predictions for the bracket of teams. Mia listened with interest, but something was bugging her. The snow was piling up at the top of the dome, and she was worried that when she released it, it would dump on them all. She couldn't create a portal either, so she needed to figure out another way to move the snow first.

Various ideas were running through her head when something caught her eye. Just outside the dome, between them in the courtyard and the shield covering the soccer fields and makeshift magic stadiums, someone stood in the snow and watched them. His eyes were piercing and menacing, and he was looking into their dome with great excitement.

Only he wasn't looking at the group, or the fire, or the s'mores. Not even at Cinder, the magic fairy who zipped around, creating more sparks when the fire grew low. His eyes were locked on Mia's. And she remembered where she had seen him before. *Twice* before.

First in China at her Wushu competition, then in Paris. She hadn't been sure it was Narco since she didn't get a good look at him, but now she knew it had to be him. He was the one who had chased them through the Louvre. Just before someone else ended up in the Underworld. Her eyes were locked on Narco.

CHAPTER FORTY-SIX

The sight of the fae standing right outside the dome made Mia's skin crawl and her stomach flip. Fear tingled along the back of her neck and made her breath catch in her chest as she remembered barely escaping from him in the museum. That had been one of the most terrifying experiences of her life.

In many ways, it was more frightening than the day she had to run from the monsters chasing her moments before she had tumbled through the portal and landed at the academy. Perhaps more than that, she hadn't understood then what was chasing her. The reality of who and what she was hadn't sunk in, and she hadn't known the full extent of the world she belonged to. She didn't know enough to be terrified.

But now, she did. She knew the dangerous fae with cold eyes posed an incredible danger for her. Finding them in the museum wasn't a fluke. It wasn't the first time he had come after her. Of course, the first time, she hadn't understood what she was seeing, or that he had any connection to her at the time. She still didn't understand why he was chasing her. But with him only a few feet away from her now, this time, the fae's presence made her feel sick.

Mia pushed away the fear, replacing it with defiance and anger. He had no right to make her feel that way, no right to threaten her and her friends. Especially here. The academy was where they were meant to feel safe and secure. Coming this close to them was going too far.

She had to do something. She refused to let him get to any of the others, or to her. Some of her fear seeped through her anger, but she held strong to the resistance and turned it into a sense of strength and focus. She glanced at Zander, catching his eye and gesturing with hers toward the menacing fae.

He stiffened when he saw the man from the museum and gave her a knowing nod. The look traveled to Carson and to Vivi, finally reaching Luna. They all knew he was there and what his presence meant.

"I'm going to go ahead and remove the shield now," Mia announced, trying not to reveal in her voice any of the edgy emotions she felt. "Is everybody ready?"

The students all agreed and braced themselves for the snow to come in on them. Mia knew they didn't need to prepare. At least, she hoped they didn't. She had something else in mind. Bringing all her focus in again, she cleared her mind, centered herself, and concentrated on her plan.

On either side of her, the group lined up, creating a wall between the academy and the hunter. Mia sent a blast of magic to the dome, at the same instant disintegrating the shield and forcing the snow away from her as hard as she could.

Just as she hoped, the pile of snow that had collected on the top of the dome, sped toward the tall fae. Before he had a chance to move out of the way, it dumped down on him. The heavy white snow buried him, concealing him within the mound. Mia didn't allow herself even a second of relief.

"Go!" she shouted to the others. "Get to the school."

Knowing the fae bounty hunter was digging himself out and wouldn't be held under the snow for long, they raced to the school. They had to get away as fast as they could, to be as far from the spot as possible before he got out so he couldn't catch up with them.

Not everyone left. Steve and Dan stayed where they were, watching the mound of snow. They wanted to monitor the stalker's progress and know when he freed himself. The students needed to be out of the way, but someone had to know when he escaped the snow.

They couldn't just let him roam free without anyone knowing where he was. The gargoyles had no reason to fear him. Even so, the sight of him made them uncomfortable and angry.

That also gave them the pleasure of seeing him scramble his way out of the snow, which was great fun in itself. They glided low to the ground, wanting to keep their feet out of the snow as they watched.

It took a while, but finally, his hands emerged from the top of the mound, pushing and clamoring in the snow until he could pull the rest of his body out. Soaking wet, with clumps of snow clinging to him, the fae looked comical and infuriated at the same time. He didn't notice Dan and Steve watching.

He had been seen, and he had no time to waste. He had to escape. He had paid a great sum of money to guarantee a way in and out of the campus, and now was not the time to be caught. He could return again as long as his secret passage was kept secret. Furious and frustrated, he ran toward the trees, scanning the area to ensure no one had seen him leave.

Dan and Steve watched the fae leave the campus grounds, and as soon as he was outside, he created a portal. In an instant, he was gone. The gargoyles returned to the school as fast as they could, heading directly for the headmistress.

The group of five halflings was already in her office when the gargoyles reached the window and peered inside. Mia spotted them and gestured until Elmhurst opened the window and let them in.

"Did you see him, Dan, Steve? Did you see the fae watching our kids?" the headmistress asked when they flew inside.

The gargoyles nodded.

"Yes," Dan said. "We watched him escape from the snow. He left the grounds and used a portal to leave."

Professor Elmhurst thought for a second before rushing to her desk. She reached into her drawer, pulling out what appeared to be a small, parchment-bound book. As she flipped it open, she glanced at the gargoyles.

"Dan, Steve, I need you to do something for me."

"What do you need?" Steve asked.

Both were poised to help, ready to do whatever they could for the headmistress, and for the five halflings.

"Fly around campus and gather up the professors. Get all of the staff. Direct them to the meeting hall. Make sure they understand it is of the gravest of importance. Tell any students you see to go to their dorms and wait there until a professor comes to speak with them," she told them. "Please, hurry."

"Yes, Professor," Dan said.

"Right away," Steve added.

They burst from the window and soared off across campus. Both felt a tremendous sense of purpose and drive. They had spent their entire existence at the library, wishing they could have some impact, that they could actually do something.

Spying on the students and passing along information to any adult who happened by was the most they were ever able to accomplish. It wasn't much, and it rarely had any real effect. Now, they had their chance. It was finally time to truly serve the academy they loved.

"What are you going to do, Professor?" Mia asked.

"If he came onto the campus once, he will do it again. Only next time, he'll be better prepared. He won't want to be denied again. The academy needs to be protected. I'm going to put the school on warning. From now until Christmas break, the campus will be under strict control. Student movements will be limited to the dining hall and the dorms. Unnecessary extra-curricular activities are suspended until further notice."

"But Professor Elmhurst. The championship!" Carson argued.

Zander shifted uncomfortably, not wanting to say anything, his expression strained.

"Yes, Carson. The Championship will continue. The other schools have come to Elmhurst for the games, and we're not going to disappoint them. With additional security, we will continue with the competition as planned."

"Additional security?" Luna asked.

Elmhurst studied the book again. "I'm also going to call in extra full-fae adults to act as additional guards for the campus. Mia, that includes Cassia."

"Cassia?" Mia asked, stunned to hear her guardian's name. It had been a long time since she had seen her, and Mia was surprised to learn that the headmistress held her in such high regard that she would reach out in such dire circumstances.

"Yes. She has been keeping up with you from a distance, monitoring your progress here among the other halflings. She hasn't wanted to interfere. I've been keeping her informed. As a precaution, I reached out to several fae to be ready to come and guard the school if needed. She joined that number after the incident at the museum. She volunteered to come whenever I need her," Elmhurst told her.

"Does she know? I mean, will she..." Mia was not sure what she was trying to ask. She hated the idea of putting Cassia at risk but was also confident that the strong, powerful woman could hold her own.

"She is one of our best bounty hunters. She won't have any trouble protecting herself, or you."

Mia nodded. "When will she get here?"

"I'll reach out to her today. I don't know when she'll be able to come, but hopefully, it will be soon. I want the academy protected as soon as possible."

Mia went to bed that night with a sense of foreboding pressing in around her. The other girls fell asleep more easily, but she lay awake, listening for the occasional sound of Dan and Steve peeking into the window to check on her.

And Carson and Zander were right outside. They had moved their bedding into the hallway and were camping there to be ready if something happened. It was reassuring to know they were there, but at the same time, she wished they would return to their own room. If they did, it would be more normal, and she wouldn't have to feel as on edge.

The next morning, Elmhurst came to the room, moments after the sun rose. Mia heard the boys groaning, their blankets moving across the floor before the door opened. She was already up and dressed, having given up sleeping almost an hour before.

"Mia, Cassia is here," the headmistress announced.

Mia rushed to follow her out of the dorm and across campus back to her office. As soon as she arrived, Cassia ran to meet her and gathered her into a tight hug. "Are you all right?" she asked.

Mia nodded. "I'm fine. Really."

Cassia forced a laugh through her worry. "Adding that 'really' makes me not believe you. You know that, right?"

Mia laughed. "I'm glad you're here."

"I am, too. I wish it wasn't for this reason, but I've missed you. I'm glad I could come. I want to know how everything has been going," Cassia said.

"Go down to the dining hall for breakfast," Elmhurst told them. "I'll be gathering the whole school together later this morning to introduce the additional guards and announce the rules."

Cassia and Mia sat beside each other at one of the long tables at the dining hall and dove into plates overflowing with French toast dripping with maple syrup, fruit salad, roasted potatoes, and plant-based bacon. Hot cups of coffee continuously refilled themselves as long as they drank. They would do so until either the fae or the halfling no longer wanted any, then the cups would drain. It was a favorite feature of the school for Mia, who found not having to get up for a refill an unimaginable luxury.

"I've been keeping up with you through the headmistress," Cassia said to Mia. "But I want to hear from your perspective how things are going."

Mia nodded as she pulled apart a piece of bacon and swirled it in a pool of maple syrup on her plate. "It's actually going really well. Most of it, anyway," she said.

"Most of it?" Cassia asked.

"Yeah. I just…I mean, I guess I thought a halfling academy would be less—"

"Like your old high school?" her guardian asked.

Mia chuckled. "Exactly. I guess I figured since it was full of a bunch of other people who didn't exactly fit in, there would be more of a sense of unity and less bullying."

"Not so much, huh?"

"Not so much." They laughed together. "It's not too bad. I can handle it."

"And the other four?" Cassia asked. "How is the Power of Five coming?"

"We're working on it constantly. We've accomplished some pretty amazing things. At least, I think they're amazing. But I still think everything's amazing. However, other students and even teachers have told us that the things we're able to do are a big deal."

"That's fantastic. I'm so proud of you."

Mia smiled. "Thanks."

"Your father would be really proud of you, too."

Mia's head dropped slightly. "I miss him."

"I know you do," Cassia told her. "I knew it wasn't going to be easy for you to be here and not be able to see him. But you know it's for the best."

"I do understand that, of course. But it still doesn't make it easier. Especially with the holidays. Thanksgiving was hard enough, and it was really nice. We all got together and went to the diner, where Luna's mother had made us a wonderful meal. Then we just hung out for the night. It was almost like being with family."

"They *are* your family," Cassia said, but Mia shook her head.

"No, they're not. Not really."

"Well, I'd like to think I'm part of your family. At least in a way. So I think you should come home with me for Christmas."

Mia's eyes lit up, and her heart lifted. "Really?"

"Absolutely."

"What do you look so happy about?" Vivi asked as the other four halflings came into the dining hall and joined them at their table.

"Cassia just invited me to join her for Christmas," Mia told her.

"That's wonderful," Luna said.

"It can't be for the whole break," Cassia said cautiously. "I would have to bring you back here December twenty-sixth. I'll have to go back to work, and I can't take you with me."

"Oh." Mia shrugged. "That's all right. It's better than having to stay here on campus by myself for the holidays."

"Why don't you come home with me after that?" Luna asked. "You can come stay with me and my mom through the New Year. It would be fun."

"Do you think that's all right?" Mia asked Cassia.

"That's a really sweet offer, Luna. Mia, I'll give you permission to stay with her, but only if Elmhurst says it's safe for you, and for Luna. Now…" Cassia sat taller in her chair and looked each of the five in the eyes. "Tell me everything you know about this fae who's been trailing you. I want to know what he looks like, everywhere you think you've seen him, and what exactly he's been doing."

For the next forty-five minutes, they discussed the mysterious fae and what they have all noticed so far.

Cassia grimaced. "Are you sure it's Narco? Is there any video of the guy?"

The five glanced at each other and shrugged.

"Wait." Luna put a finger up. "The Louvre. It might have video of him. Whoever posted those videos of us online had to have been the fae who's been following us, right? And most likely, he's on camera as well."

"Great idea. I'll look into the video myself and see if I can confirm his identity. I do know most of the bad guys, after all." Cassia laughed, but it wasn't a joyful sound. She was worried about who it might be. And if it was Narco, she knew Mia was in real danger.

Despite the lingering darkness on the edge of her consciousness, the tension building on campus as the new rules locked things down, and the new guards appearing, Mia was beginning to feel happy again.

CHAPTER FORTY-SEVEN

Mia didn't know if she could handle the tension. Anxiety coursed through her. Cold sweat coated her palms, and her shirt was damp and clammy against her skin under her coat. Her pulse pounded in her temples, and she could barely hear anything else around her other than the rush of the blood in her ears.

The feeling kept building, stronger and stronger until she thought she might pass out from not being able to breathe. Beside her, Luna appeared pale and slightly dizzy. She didn't even look at Carson on her other side. His reaction would be just as intense. But she couldn't do anything other than wait.

Finally, it happened. The buzzer splintered the air, and all the tension broke into screams and cheers. Mia jumped to her feet and threw her arms in the air, laughing and hopping up and down. She turned to Luna, who shrieked and grabbed her up in a tight hug. They'd done it. Elmhurst Academy had won the slamball championship.

Sheer delight filled Mia as the stands around her erupted in a celebration so deafening, she didn't hear Zander's voice behind her. But she felt his hands on her shoulders, and when she looked up at him, he was grinning and saying something.

Everyone was beyond thrilled, buzzing with excitement over the exhilarating final game of the competition. It had come right down to the last seconds, the schools of both teams sitting on the very edges of their seats as they waited for the last points to be scored and the final buzzer to determine the champions.

Now the air around them sparkled with green, gold, and silver confetti, enchanted by one of the teachers to fall endlessly from the ceiling. The confetti disappeared as soon as it reached the ground, creating a never-ending cascade of shimmer around the students.

What made it all the better was that nothing had gone wrong. There had been no other threats, no sign of the bad guy, or any of his men since he had left through the portal. The extra fae guards had monitored the campus, and the rules stayed in place to keep the students safe, but everything had remained calm throughout the rest of the competition.

Even the students from the visiting schools had fallen into the pattern of the new rules, and it didn't seem to change their daily life too much. Being required to go from the dorms to meals, to approved activities, and back to their dorms, had also forced them to spend more time together. So, in a lot of ways, the restrictions strengthened friendships and gave students time to get to know each other better.

Not that Mia ever forgot what was going on. She had never pushed the mysterious fae, or his mission, out of her head. He was always lurking there in the corner of her mind, hovering at the edges of her thoughts. Seeing Cassia every day was wonderful, but it was also a reminder of the trouble. If Mia wasn't in danger, her guardian wouldn't be nearby. And part of Mia was always on guard, ready to act if she needed to.

But today she was setting her worries aside and allowing herself to be excited. With as involved as she had ended up becoming in the slamball competition, she felt like she had followed the game her entire life. Though she had only recently learned about it and started watching, she was definitely a fan now.

Sometimes, after watching a game, she would toy with the idea of taking up the sport herself. It had been so long since she had practiced her Wushu—which used to take up most of her life—that she missed having something to devote herself to that way. Her magic was different.

Her power was something she had been born with that she merely needed to rediscover and develop, like an advanced form of walking. Practicing and mastering a sport was different, and the thrill of competition never grew old.

Of course, she would never ever share those thoughts with the others. Mia couldn't risk Vivi hearing it during one of her bouts of sour mood and turning it into yet another opportunity to taunt and humiliate her. Things were definitely better between the two girls since Thanksgiving, and for the most part, Vivi was still standing up for her and being as friendly as Vivi was capable of being. But a few flickers of the bristly Unseelie girl still remained.

Mia didn't have any time or energy to actually pursue anything other than her magic. If she had, she would have been at least trying to maintain her Wushu skills. At least until everything was settled, and they had achieved the Power of Five, she was simply going to have to channel her overachieving, competitive spirit into honing her fae abilities.

Today, though, was all about enjoying the rush of the win and celebrating with her friends. Soon the semester would be over, and they would all break for the holidays. The visiting schools would leave, and everything would settle back into their normal routine. She wanted to savor as much of the fun before that as she possibly could.

"That was amazing!" Carson exclaimed as they bounded down the stands and out into the crowd. "Did you see that final play? I had no idea which way it was going to go."

"Seriously. That was bordering on miraculous. I've never seen playing like that," Zander agreed.

"It must be something in the snow," Mia said. "It's all just *magical.*"

She did a happy twirl, but Vivi only glared at her.

"You do realize you're in Montana. It's *always* snowing in the winter in Montana. Of everything on this campus, the frozen crystals that never stop falling are the least magical thing," she said.

Mia couldn't help herself. She tilted her head in Vivi's direction and stuck her tongue out at her playfully. To Vivi's credit, she smiled.

Luna linked arms with Mia and Zander, looking at both with a wide grin.

"So, what are we going to do now? We have to do something," she said. "We have to celebrate!" Carson agreed. "We should have a party!"

"I think that sounds like a fantastic idea."

The five turned to Elmhurst, who stood behind them, smiling wider than they had seen since the first time they were able to combine their magic successfully. A few pieces of confetti sparkled in her hair, and she held an Elmhurst Academy pennant in one hand.

"Really? Awesome! Mia, you can make a dome like last time. Where's Cinder?" Carson started looking around for the little pixie, but Elmhurst rested a hand on his shoulder to stop him.

"Like I said, a party sounds like a fantastic idea. But let's give Mia a break this time. I'll have the teachers create the party dome for us." She paused and leaned a little closer as though sharing a secret with the five. "And we'll see what they can conjure up."

The halflings exchanged glances and grinned. A surprise was coming their way. Elmhurst told them to join the other students for lunch, and they would find out later what was up her sleeve. The five hurried to the dining hall, excited to talk more about the thrilling win and to wait for Elmhurst's big reveal.

They managed all the way through lunch, spent an hour afterward lingering in the dining hall talking with the other students, and another hour in the common area of the dorm working their way through a board game they'd been trying to finish for more than a week.

They gave up on the game because they couldn't concentrate, and decided to go outside and talk to Steve and Dan. As much as all but Mia hadn't expected they would feel this way, they all found themselves missing the gargoyles during the daylight hours. The group had become so used to spending time with them as soon as the sun had set that now it seemed strange and quiet when they weren't there. It made knowing they were stuck on the pedestals even sadder.

Though that day, it might have been good for them.

"I didn't know they had to sleep," Mia said, staring up at the statues.

"I didn't, either," Carson said.

Both gargoyles stood in their usual positions on the pedestals, but their heads were hanging, and their eyes were closed. If she didn't know they couldn't die, Mia would have been extremely worried about them. Suddenly, Steve cut loose a jagged snore as Dan released a whistling exhale.

"I don't think they really *need* to, necessarily," Luna said. "It's more like they've gotten into the habit of it. Remember, they've never been able to move before. Maybe now that they can fly, they get tired."

"I wouldn't think their stamina would be very good after a few centuries of not moving more than turning their heads," Zander pointed out. "They've been doing really well, considering."

"Look!" Vivi exclaimed.

Mia turned to the Unseelie girl, who was pointing excitedly toward the fields at the back of the school. Her voice was loud enough to disturb the gargoyles, and Dan lifted his head.

"What's going on?" he asked, his voice groggy.

"She's doing it!" Vivi said. "Elmhurst is setting up a party."

"What kind of party?" Steve asked.

It almost sounded like he was still asleep, muttering something in a dream.

"I guess you two sleepyheads haven't heard yet," Mia said. "Elmhurst Academy won the slamball championship!"

"Yeah, and we suggested there should be a celebration, so Elmhurst is setting up a party," Carson said.

"She's doing that just because you suggested it?" Dan asked.

"Well, probably mostly because if she didn't, we were going to have Mia set up another dome," Carson said.

"Ah. She wants to cut down on her liability."

Mia gasped as though offended, but she knew the gargoyle was kidding. "You should come to the party when it's set up," she said. "Celebrate with us."

"Maybe we will," Dan said.

Which meant that they would. His aloof act wasn't fooling her. Waving at the statues, the five halflings rushed to the field to watch the progress of the party setup. The headmistress looked at them as if she wanted to scold them for not waiting for the announcement, but she was also excited. She and a number of the other teachers moved around a dome several times larger than the one Mia had made right after Thanksgiving.

It was much more impressive than hers, not only in size but also in the fact it wasn't overflowing with snow. Instead, it expelled the snow off the top and threw it so it fell several yards away from the edges of the dome. Inside, the adults conjured games and carnival rides, and the smell of fair foods wafted toward them.

"Almost ready," Elmhurst promised them. "Just a few more finishing touches to go."

CHAPTER FORTY-EIGHT

The party was like nothing any of them could have imagined. Even if the five halflings had tried to come up with what they thought Principal Elmhurst and the other teachers would create for them to celebrate the win, their ideas would have fallen far short of what they saw when they finally got to go inside.

It felt like it took forever for them to finish setting up the party. The five halflings roamed around the outer edge of the massive dome, watching everything the teachers were conjuring, thanks to the ingenuity of Zander. As they walked, he *moved* the snow out of their way, giving them enough space to stroll comfortably along the dome.

It seemed that when they noticed what they were sure was going to be the most amazing detail, something across the space would catch their attention, and they went running to see that instead. The result was not being sure of everything inside, and being excited to finally get a chance to explore.

In the last few minutes of their preparation, the teachers enchanted the dome to go from absolutely clear to bright shades of blue, red, purple, green, and gold. It almost resembled a circus tent, and the new opaque quality meant they didn't get to see everything going on inside. Elmhurst's voice boomed out around the campus, amplified by her magic. She invited everyone to come down to the field and enjoy the celebration. Mia and the other halflings were the first in line at what they assumed would be the entrance and, oblivious to the cold, waited eagerly for the grand reveal.

They were excited when the swarm of students came through the academy portals to join them. It wasn't only students from Elmhurst. Many of the kids from the visiting schools had decided to stay a little longer and joined them as well. It created an even more exciting atmosphere that turned from merely a celebration of the Elmhurst win to a unifying celebration of their entire time together.

The groundskeepers were working overtime to push the snow back to make room for all of the students to stand outside the circus dome. Mia watched in wonder as the snow flowed backward in an arcing waterfall, taking the white puffy bits of frozen water away from them and farther out toward the trees. Though the snow was still falling, at least it wasn't covering their legs while they waited.

Instead, the snow barely touched the ground before it was whisked away in a magical wonderland.

The horizon was starting to tint with the colors of sunset when Elmhurst finally appeared at the edge of the dome and came through it to talk to them. She grinned broadly and held out her arms, presenting the dome. Mia expected some big speech similar to the one's teachers were so prone to make in any situation they thought could be a teaching moment.

Instead, she just said one word. "Enjoy!"

The entrance to the dome appeared, and the colors of the sides faded away to reveal the carnival inside. Everyone rushed forward and spread out to cover the huge space inside the dome and discover all the surprises waiting for them. The five ran directly for the Ferris wheel in the center of the dome.

Instead of the usual plain buckets to ride in, this wheel had cars shaped like various creatures and vehicles. The first one that came around resembled an enormous old-fashioned hot-air balloon. The girls hopped into it, and the ride operator closed the door behind them.

As they rose into the air, the two boys climbed into the next bucket, which was shaped like a dancing elephant. The one behind that was a miniaturized version of a locomotive with a whale and a tiny pirate ship across the center of the wheel.

"I'm trying to figure out the theme of this Ferris Wheel," Mia said with a laugh.

Luna and Vivi studied the wheel.

"Well," Luna said. "Looks to me like the theme ended up being a bunch of adult fae with their own ideas, and it exploded into nonsense."

"That is the most perfect party theme I've ever heard of," Mia said.

"Hey, look. There's Hazel." Vivi pointed over the side of the hot-air balloon.

Mia turned from where she was leaning against the side and looked down at the young halfling. Hazel didn't seem to be as wrapped up in the fun of the party as everyone else. Instead, she wandered aimlessly, looking around and watching others walk by.

Marcus came up to her and muttered something that made Hazel's face go dark. The hot-air balloon was climbing higher up on the wheel, making it harder to see what was happening between them, but her posture appeared defensive. She began to move away, but Marcus grabbed her arm.

"What's going on there?" Mia asked.

Luna shook her head. "I don't know, but it doesn't look pleasant."

Hazel pulled away from him, and they exchanged a few more words before another boy approached. Mia realized it was Lucas. He moved partway between Marcus and Hazel and held up a hand to Marcus.

"Looks like Lucas has it all settled." Vivi had a hint of mischief in her voice.

"I hope Sariah doesn't see," Luna said. "The last thing we need is more of that."

"Hopefully, even Sariah wouldn't want to ruin the party by acting like that again," Mia said.

"And if she does, you'll set her straight, huh?" Luna said, nudging Mia playfully.

"If I have to."

Below them, Lucas said something to Hazel, and the pair walked across the dome.

"Where are they going?" Vivi asked, turning around to watch them as their hot air balloon reached the top of the wheel.

"Feeling nosy today, Vivi?" Luna asked.

"Just curious," Vivi said.

She leaned far over the side of the balloon. "They're getting cotton candy."

The guys laughed at the report.

"So scandalous!" Carson yelled.

Vivi leaned farther, and Mia's heart jumped into her throat. She grabbed Vivi by the back of her shirt to tug her into the basket.

"What are you doing?" Vivi asked, shaking free of Mia's grip.

"You were going to fall," Mia said. "I was just stopping you."

Vivi snorted. "Are you serious? Elmhurst and the teachers made this thing. Do you really think they'd let it be dangerous?"

When Mia didn't know what to say, Vivi shot her a teasing look and swung her leg over the side of the basket. Mia gasped as the other girl dropped out of sight. She rushed to the edge and looked over, only to see the Unseelie halfling floating a few inches below. Vivi hovered there for a few seconds, grabbed hold of the edge and climbed back in.

"What was that all about?" Mia asked.

"Halfling baby-proofing," Carson yelled between cupped hands over his mouth.

"They just want to make sure the students don't get hurt," Luna told her. "Whenever there is something like this, they put safeguards in place to stop any of us from ending up injured. Not that there has ever been anything quite like this before. But once we did have a zip-line and somebody unhooked their harness."

"Somebody being Carson?" Mia asked.

"Well," Carson replied, sounding extra huffy. "I'd be offended if it wasn't the truth."

"How is Carson hearing all of our conversations?" Mia squinted at the boys in their own ride. It wasn't far from them, but it shouldn't have been close enough for him to listen to everything they said. Especially since he had to yell back at them in order for them to hear him.

Carson's face split with a joyful grin. "Magic, my dear. Magic." He flitted his hands in the air like a human magician, and a colorful scarf flew from his fingers.

Luna giggled. "He's got this spell he likes to use for eavesdropping. He can hear us as though he's right here with us, but we can't hear him."

Mia nodded. "Huh, not a very good spell if he had to yell for us to hear him."

"Hey, I heard that," Carson shouted. "I'm still working out the kinks."

They all enjoyed a laugh. Mia narrowed her eyes and tilted her head. "If the teachers can just make it so you can't fall like that, why bother to have the buckets for the Ferris Wheel at all? Why not just have the teachers float you around in circles for a while?" she asked.

Vivi rolled her eyes and stared out over the party again. "See, that is how everybody knows you were raised among the humans," Vivi pointed out.

They laughed and spent the remainder of the ride scoping out what they wanted to do next. By the time they landed, they knew they were making a beeline for the row of food booths set up along one side of the dome. With so many options, it was difficult to decide what they wanted to try. Mia studied the booths suspiciously.

"What's wrong?" Carson asked, reaching out to accept a giant soft pretzel from one of the attendants.

"Is it even real?" Mia asked. "I mean, you saw them. Elmhurst and the other teachers just kind of poofed all this stuff into being."

"Poofed? Is that the technical term?" Vivi asked. "I've gone all these years calling it magic."

"Be quiet, Vivi," Luna said. "Eat your candy apple."

Even if Vivi had wanted to respond, the lure of the apple she had chosen was too much, and she sank her teeth into it happily.

"The food is real," Zander assured Mia. "It was brought in from somewhere, not just…poofed into existence."

"That's a relief. I think," Mia said.

"And you sound like an idiot saying poofed by the way." Carson hooted with laughter.

"There you are." Cassia came up to them with a large cardboard container of nachos in one hand. "I've been looking for you. Have you tried the nachos? They're amazing." Cassia picked up one of the nachos, loaded it with the gooey cheese sauce, and stuffed it in her mouth.

Mia chuckled and reached for one. She took a bite and groaned. "Ohhhh, that *is* good," she said. She reached for another. "Have you been enjoying the party?"

"I have. I'm technically supposed to be guarding, but I think that includes going down the giant inflatable slide and eating as much as I can get my hands on," Cassia told her.

"I agree," Mia said.

Cassia slid her eyes over to Vivi. "And from that giant inflatable slide, I saw something interesting."

Vivi glanced at her innocently. "What?"

"Let's just agree to keep hands, feet, torso, and head, inside all rides from now on."

Vivi nodded and turned away, going back to eating her apple as the others laughed.

"What are you doing next?" Mia asked.

"I have to keep wandering around, making sure everything is fine. Enjoy the rest of the celebration. I'll catch up with you tomorrow."

They hugged, and Mia snagged one more chip before her guardian walked away. Mia headed for the booth for her own container of nachos, intending to share them with the others, so she still had room for as many of the other treats as she could fit in her stomach.

CHAPTER FORTY-NINE

"So, I have to ask you," Zander said, a while later, as they waited for their turns on the giant inflatable slide.

"What's that?" Mia asked.

The line in front of them moved up, and she followed. She and Zander were the only two of the five who had decided to do the slide. The others had headed for the hall of mirrors, instead. Which had never been Mia's favorite activity at a carnival. It was disorienting, and she hated that feeling.

Of course, she probably wouldn't feel as much that way now as she used to. Ever since finding Cassia, her entire life had become about being somewhat disoriented and having to try to find her way. Maybe now it would be more amusing to her.

"Was it you?" Zander said.

She threw him a strange look over her shoulder. "Is this some sort of live-action game of *Clue* I wasn't told about?"

"No."

"Good." Mia followed the progress of the line again. "Because if it was, you would be a terrible player."

Zander laughed. "Well, thanks for that. No, I mean, did you have any hand in us winning the slamball championship?"

"What do you mean?"

"You know what I'm talking about. Elmhurst really needed the morale boost of winning. Then they managed to pull it off in a game like that. Did you have something to do with that?"

"No. Are you kidding?" Mia shook her head.

Zander leaned closer. "You can tell me. I wouldn't tell anybody."

Mia made an exasperated sound and turned to glare at him as the line stopped moving. "I didn't do anything, Zander. I didn't use my skills at the game, period. I never have, and never would."

"That's not really true."

"What do you mean?"

"I know you used your skills at the game in Las Vegas. The one we watched against the vampires," Zander said.

Mia was confused. She remembered the game, but she couldn't figure out what he meant. "What are you talking about? I barely even knew what slamball was when we were watching that game. How would I use any powers to affect it?"

"What I'm wondering is how you were able to penetrate the enchantments put around the court to prevent people from doing things like that," he said.

"Things like what?" Mia asked, exasperated. Zander appeared convinced, but the whole situation was a blank to her. "All I did was watch the game. I didn't use any of my skills to do anything."

"You seriously didn't mean to manipulate the game against the vampires in Las Vegas?" he asked.

She shook her head. "No, I didn't."

"And you didn't have anything to do with us winning the Championship?" he continued.

This shake of her head was more adamant. "No. I have no idea how a game would even be influenced. I didn't do anything. At least, I don't think I did. You're freaking me out a little. I would certainly hope I would know if I did something like that."

His eyes narrowed, and he stared at her. It didn't seem like he was searching her to see if she was telling the truth. It was more like he was going back through his own memories of the game they watched in Las Vegas, and then the competition that unfolded here at Elmhurst. His mind flipped through all the games and those moments he believed she had manipulated.

Finally, he gave a slight, resigned shrug. "The game was incredible, but it was neck-and-neck the entire time. It's not like any completely miraculous points were scored, though. I guess if you were really going to affect the game, you wouldn't let it go that far and make it so close. Especially with Carson right on the edge like he was through that whole final."

"Do you really think he had a betting pool going?" Mia asked.

"Where did you hear that?"

"I overheard some of the girls in the bathroom talking about it earlier." Mia's nose scrunched, and in her mind, she went over what she had overheard. She was confident the girls had been talking about their Carson.

Zander shook his head, and they climbed a little farther up the tower supporting the slide. They were almost at the top now, and Mia looked around the carnival in search of the others. She didn't see them near the hall of mirrors, so she assumed they were still inside.

"No, I don't think so. Carson wouldn't do something like that. He's too straight-laced to get into wagers. Getting caught doing something like that wouldn't look good on his applications when he's trying to get into college or work for the Embassy in New York. Besides, I'm fairly certain Vivi started spreading that rumor just so people would show up at our dorm in the middle of the night to irritate us," he told her.

"That sounds like Vivi."

It was Mia's turn to descend the slide, and Zander watched her take her place in front of the opening. She appeared nervous, and he laughed.

"Go on, Mia," he said. "You have battled far more difficult adversaries than a giant puffy slide."

She smiled and dropped onto the green-and-orange striped

surface. His mind ran over their conversation as he listened to her squeal with delight on her way down. He had been almost positive she had done something to help the school win the final game. Not that she would have interfered enough to have gotten in the way of the game actually being played.

She could have changed things up a little to give their home team a leg up against the visitors, but Mia was steadfast in her denial, and he wanted to believe her. She did seem clueless about her influence over the game in Las Vegas and determined to deny she had anything to do with these games, either.

Of course, her denial didn't necessarily mean she didn't do it. Just because she hadn't purposely created an enchantment, or used a spell, didn't mean she hadn't had some influence over the outcome of the game.

As she hit the bottom of the slide and he positioned himself, Zander made a mental note to test the impressive halfling's power of persuasion. On several occasions, she had appeared to be achieving things, or causing things to happen, without willfully doing it, but merely because she had wanted it to happen. Desire could be a very strong power, and he wanted to know how much she could do simply by the force of desiring it to happen.

Desiring something to happen and making it come to be through that desire was a full-fae gift. Halflings had to say certain words or perform specific enchantments in order for anything to happen. Halflings couldn't simply wish these things to be. They weren't genies or djinn. He wanted to know how much control she had over this ability, and how much she might be able to do even when she didn't have that control.

"Go ahead." The attendant perched at the top of the slide waved him through.

Zander grabbed onto the pole at the entrance to the slide and used it to propel himself at a faster speed than Mia had. Mia was waiting for him at the bottom when he landed on the cushion at the end of the slide.

"I think the others may have gotten lost in there. Let's go find them," Mia said.

He agreed, and they walked across the carnival. A few seconds later, Dan and Steve swooped over to them.

"This is fantastic," Steve said. "They should leave this up all the time."

"I don't think anything would ever get done around here if they left this up all the time," Mia said with a laugh. She studied the statues more closely and realized Dan's face was sticky. "Did you eat cotton candy?"

He nodded. "I've never had it before. It's not like we need to eat, but I'm enjoying trying things."

At Thanksgiving dinner, she had watched them delight in the new textures and flavors of the food, not even registering that they had never eaten those things before. Or anything, for all she knew. It was odd to think about them existing for so long, yet having such limited experience. Being freed from their pedestals had suddenly introduced them to a whole new reality and a world of possibilities. It wasn't just about being able to fly, or seeing more of the academy than they ever had. They were learning new things about themselves and finding out what it was like to really live.

In so many ways, Mia felt like she could understand that. To her, coming to the academy. Just that quickly, an entirely new side of her life had opened up, and she had discovered what it was like to really live as her true self.

That sentiment took on somewhat of a dark turn a few minutes later when she, Zander, and the gargoyles entered the hall of mirrors in search of the other three. Mia could have waited outside, but she was determined to experiment and see if the changes in her life had also changed the way she saw the house of mirrors.

Now she was realizing that was far too optimistic a hope. She was just as freaked out and uncomfortable walking through the narrow corridors of mirrors as she ever had been. Maybe even more.

It was reassuring to have Zander close behind her, but soon he took a turn, and she lost his many reflections. She whipped around, but she couldn't see anyone. It was only her and the dozens of reflections of her face appearing around her. Every direction she looked, there were more of her.

Mia's breath grew shallow and fast, and she struggled to calm it down. Her head was growing woozy, and she moved more quickly in hopes of finding anyone. She didn't want to yell out for them. The familiar sensation of being watched scraped along her skin, but if she shouted, she would only be giving herself up.

She ran along the hallways and took every turn she could find. Finally, she burst into an octagonal room that reminded her of the portal room inside the academy. Dan and Steve stood in front of one of the mirrored panels, making faces at each other. They hadn't quite gotten control of their stone features enough to dramatically change their expressions, but even the slight shifts and their tongues sticking out were funny.

"There she is," Zander said a second later when the other four streamed out of a hallway toward her.

"Are you okay, Mia?" Luna asked.

Mia tried to shake off the discomfort. "I thought I might like these places now, but I definitely don't. They're still just as weird."

"What don't you like about them?" Carson asked. "It's just mirrors. You look in a mirror every day."

"Yes, *a* mirror. Just one at a time. Not a hundred. It's just creepy. I feel like I'm staring at myself. No matter what I do, I'm right there, staring back. It's like I'm being forced to confront myself and everything I've ever done. I can't get away from it. I have to look at it and think about who I am and who I'm supposed to be, what I've done or should have done. Or maybe shouldn't have done. What I'll eventually have to do. It's all right here, and it won't leave me alone." A shiver slithered down Mia's spine.

"Poetic," Vivi said.

Mia hadn't meant to pour all that out, but the words wouldn't stop. She wrapped her arms around herself. "Maybe that's why I've never been good at poetry," she quipped, trying to dispel some of the tension. "Maybe poets just have to be in really uncomfortable situations *all* the time."

"I think that's pretty much the consensus for most of them." Zander grinned at her and reached for her hand. "Come on. We'll get you out of here."

He guided her through the corridors with Luna close behind, as though they were creating a protective barrier. They had already gone through most of the maze looking for her and had discovered the way out, so it was easy to get to the exit.

Mia instantly felt better when they left the small structure and returned to the real world. She drew a deep breath and stared up at the top of the dome. The teachers hadn't put the colored panels back after opening the party. Instead, they had created something from a dream.

The reimagined sky was full of bright stars and pillows of snowy white clouds. Snow was still falling, but when it came close to the dome, it was blown away, never reaching the holes in the dome that vented the smoke from the fire pit and the cooking booths.

"I need to learn how to do something like that," she said.

"Like what?" Vivi asked.

Mia pointed up. "Look at the snow. It's not getting in or gathering on the top of the dome at all. I want to be able to do that. You know, for future needs." She chuckled as the others nodded.

"Can you imagine what we could make if we keep getting stronger?" Carson asked. "With the Power of Five, we could make a dome like this on an even bigger scale. We could make it large enough to cover the entire campus. Or even the whole town."

Luna giggled. "Perfect. Just what we would need. A town in a bubble."

"It could have its uses," Mia said. "But I don't think we're ready for that, yet."

"Not yet," Zander said. "But I know what I'm ready for."

"What?" Vivi asked.

"More food," the guys said in unison and headed back toward the booths.

The girls groaned and laughed. They felt like they had eaten their weight in carnival food already, but the guys were bottomless pits. They followed the boys to the food and sampled a few bites of each thing they received before making their way over to a cluster of games.

Dan and Steve were determined to try their luck at a couple of the games of chance. The first few times, they didn't get anywhere, and Mia could see they were becoming frustrated. She remembered what Zander had said about her being able to use her skills to manipulate the slamball game and ensure the winner. What if she might be able to do the same to nudge the outcome of one of these games a little so the gargoyles could have the fun of winning?

Before she could do anything, the ball Steve had thrown went right into the basket he was aiming for. He released a thrilled *whoop* a moment before Dan's water gun propelled a little duck right to the top of a tower to hit a bell. She smiled. She wasn't going to have to try to intervene after all. She was walking up to congratulate them when, from the corner of her eye, she caught Zander staring at her. She didn't turn to look back at him.

The next day, after all the non-Elmhurst students were gone, Cassia called Mia and her friends into Elmhurst's office. "I was able to find the video from the Louvre. Someone had erased it, but they didn't think to erase the off-site back-ups." She chuckled. "I expected better of him."

"Of who?" Mia's brow furrowed and stared at Cassia expectantly.

"Narco. He's the fae who's been trailing you."

Mia nodded and wrapped her arms around her torso. She had known it was Narco, but she had hoped she was wrong.

"Who is he?" Zander, acting as the leader of their group, stood with a worried expression on his face.

Cassia glanced at the headmistress, who nodded. "He's one of the best bounty hunters the Unseelie Court has." She looked at Vivi and Carson, whose expressions were blank. "You two haven't heard of him?"

Vivi thought it over for a moment. "Yeah, I guess I have, but why would he be following us? Or be after Mia? It doesn't make any sense."

"Yeah, if he's this big-shot bounty hunter, why is he interested in halfling students?" Carson scratched his head.

The bounty hunter in the room crossed her arms over her chest and glared out the window. "That's exactly what I want to find out."

CHAPTER FIFTY

Everyone was still talking about the party two weeks later when the semester ended. The visiting schools had left the day after the carnival to return to their own campuses for the end of the semester, and the academy felt too quiet.

Even though the other students had only been on campus with them for the duration of the championships, the halflings had grown used to having so many more people around, and the fun of making new friends. It was a letdown to have them all gone and be made to wait even longer for Christmas break. Every day, classes dragged on, and the teachers seemed to pile more work on the students as if wanting to fill up every possible second they had available.

As soon as the semester ended, they would be on their way and would have two blissful weeks without school.

A few students had grumbled that the teachers seemed to be making up for creating the championship party. As if they didn't want it to look like they were going soft and could be persuaded into fun and frolic from now on.

Not that Mia ever made the mistake of thinking that was a possibility. She and the other five were very familiar with how intense the teachers could be. This was especially true when the teachers had a lot to accomplish in a short time, or when they believed the students weren't applying themselves enough.

But finally, the days had gone by, and the wait was over. It was the last day of the semester, and everyone was going off in different directions for their break. Carson and Zander had already left. Their parents had picked them up early so they could head out of town to spend the holiday with their human families.

Zander had laughed as he told her many of his cousins didn't know he was half-fae. Sometimes he would mess with them, using little enchantments or small spells to play pranks. When she said she didn't think he was the type to play pranks and asked if it was allowed for them to use magic when they were among the humans, Zander had just winked at her and walked away.

That wink had made Mia's cheeks burn, and her fingertips tingle, but she didn't allow herself to think about it too much. Luna was waiting with Mia until Cassia was ready to leave. Many of the other guards were already gone, having left campus when the visiting schools had departed.

Cassia and a few others had decided to stay and provide continued security until the semester ended. That day she was just finishing up, making her rounds, checking over the campus with Elmhurst to ensure the school was secure and ready to be mostly closed down for the holidays. There would still be a few people around, but not enough to keep watch over the entire campus.

"I bet my mother has already started making gingerbread," Luna said wistfully. "She bakes up about a million gingerbread men. And women, and children, and animals, and occasionally even Halloween shapes and turkeys, if she's made too much dough and is tired of using the same cookie cutters. We have so much fun decorating them."

"That sounds like fun," Mia replied. "I've never made gingerbread before."

"What? I'll be sure to save you some when you come to my house after Christmas," she said. "We'll have a great time."

Mia smiled at her as Vivi came into the common area, lugging several bags.

"Are you moving out?" Luna asked with a laugh.

"Not that lucky. No, I'm just never sure what's actually going to happen when I go home for a break. So I would rather be prepared with everything I might need than to go into it blind," Vivi said.

"You're still going skiing with your father, right?" Mia asked.

"That's the plan. I talked to him yesterday, and he was still saying he'll be here this afternoon to pick me up and head for the slopes."

She wasn't letting it show, and definitely wouldn't say anything about it, but Vivi was excited to finally be going on her skiing trip with her father. As he had said he would, he had continued to check in on Vivi, her progress, and her behavior.

Principal Elmhurst hadn't hesitated to tell him how impressed she was with Vivi's progress and her cooperation with the others in the group. The headmistress knew how the fae man felt about his daughter associating with Seelie halflings, but she had emphasized how well they were working together and the advancements Vivi was making.

She had agreed not to give any details about the group's excursion to the museum or creating the portal. Her offer to give them the freedom to experiment and push the limitations of their abilities still stood, which meant hiding some of the realities of their activities from people on the outside. Even parents.

Vivi's father was so pleased by what he had heard that he'd reinstated their skiing trip and had even sent Vivi money to buy a new wardrobe to bring with her. It appeared she had taken full advantage of that perk.

Mia laughed when almost immediately, one of the staff came into the room to inform Vivi that her father had arrived. Vivi groaned and stood, grabbing her luggage again to haul it away.

"Merry Christmas, Vivi," Luna and Mia said in unison.

Vivi rolled her eyes and glanced at them with a slight smile. "Merry Christmas, guys. I'll see you in a couple weeks."

"Have fun skiing," Mia said.

Luna didn't have any reason to rush away from campus since she was staying at home in town with her mother. With a hug and a promise to meet the day after Christmas, they parted ways.

It felt strange to be away from the other four for an entire week. Mia loved spending time with Cassia, and though she missed her father, she and her guardian began to create new Christmas traditions together.

One of her favorites was staying up late into the night drinking peppermint hot chocolate and watching movies in the matching gaudy holiday-pajamas Cassia had picked out for them. But despite all the fun, Mia was excited to stay with Luna for the week after Christmas and was even looking forward to returning to campus.

Vivi arrived two days before classes started again, and Luna and Mia went to meet up with her. They were outside the library, visiting with Dan and Steve the next day when Carson and Zander ran toward them.

Finally back together, the group of five exchanged hugs and high fives, laughing and grinning as they talked about their breaks. Their voices overlapped, and they grew louder and louder as if they had saved up everything they would have said to each other during the break and were letting it all out.

"I know it's only been two weeks, but I feel so out of practice," Carson admitted.

"You didn't use any magic over Christmas?" Luna asked.

He shook his head. "My mom and step-dad were watching me pretty closely. They know I'm getting more powerful and are worried I'll do something as a prank that could end up hurting someone or causing trouble."

"I did a few enchantments and spells, but it's good to be back together. It feels like so long since we've tried to combine our magic to do anything big," Luna agreed.

"Want to try something?" Mia asked. "Just to get back in the groove?"

"Do you think it's safe?" Zander asked. "With the guards gone, Elmhurst might have more rules and restrictions she may want to have us follow this semester."

"So, let's go talk to her and find out," Vivi suggested.

They said goodbye to the gargoyles, promising to see them later, and went to the headmistress's office. She greeted the happy excited-to-be-back-and-ready-for-the-next-semester group of students.

"We were wondering..." Mia spoke slowly. "If we could start practicing together again. As strange as it sounds, we realized we missed each other, and we want to start working on the Power of Five again."

"But we didn't know if that was safe or if anything may have happened while we were gone," Luna said.

The headmistress shook her head. "Thank you for asking. That shows a level of maturity you wouldn't have exhibited earlier in the school year. There has been no sign of Narco or any of his associates. The campus is secure. For now, you can consider it safe and return to your normal practice. But be cautious. Be aware of your surroundings, and don't hesitate to tell me if you see anything strange. Other than that, get back to work."

The five halflings smiled at each other and hurried outside to practice. As they rushed to the fields behind the academy building, Hazel stepped out from around the corner. No one but Dan and Steve had paid her much attention, but she had been back on campus for almost a week.

As soon as the academy had allowed students back into the dorms, she had returned and settled in, not knowing when Mia would return. She wanted to be ready and not miss anything.

CHAPTER FIFTY-ONE

Hazel was still watching Mia, though she didn't want to. Spying on her made Hazel feel guilty. Mia had never done anything to her, and she had actually gone out of her way to help Hazel. She'd been there for Hazel when Sariah had tormented her and had even welcomed her to sit with the group of five during the slamball championship.

Hazel felt terrible about betraying Mia's trust the way she was. She wanted to find some way to tell the other girl what was going on, but she couldn't. José wouldn't permit it. The control the vampire had over her wouldn't allow her to reveal what was going on, so she could do nothing to let Mia know.

It was becoming harder and harder on her the longer the spying dragged out. She talked to Marcus about it, telling him how the situation was making her feel and what she was going through, but it didn't make any difference. Marcus seemed fine with it.

In fact, he was more than fine with it. He was very happy with his situation. His loyalty to his vampire master was going to ensure that Marcus got everything he ever wanted. As long as he did what José told him to, he would be accepted into the best college. The day after graduation, he would be hired for a cushy job that he could hang onto throughout his adulthood and just keep advancing. It was everything most of the halflings could ever ask for, and it was being handed right to him.

Of course, this wasn't merely a magnanimous response from the vampire to his servant. He would want Marcus placed in a high position as a reward to him for his loyalty and his work, but that wasn't the only benefit. A job like that would also give him the ideal opportunity to continue spying for as long as José wanted him to.

Hazel didn't want it. She didn't want any of it. She set herself to find out how the vampire was controlling her, and how she could release herself from that control.

She had been going to the library every night for a couple of weeks when the gargoyles began to take notice. Steve and Dan descended from their pedestals and glided around the sides of the building, peering into the windows until they were able to see what she was doing. Hazel sat by herself at the table farthest back, only one small green lamp glowing in the corner, illuminating her book. Despite bad lighting and their distance, Dan was able to see what she was reading.

"Why would this halfling be reading about vampire thralls?" he asked. "Not just about vampire thralls, but about how to get over them?"

"It's probably something for one of her classes," Steve suggested. "She's writing a paper or doing a project."

Dan shook his head. "She wouldn't have to come here so many times for something like that. And even if she did, why doesn't she have anything with her? She's not taking any notes or writing anything. She's just reading. There's something going on. I think she might be what Cinder warned us about."

Steve moved away from the window, and Dan glanced up at him. "What are you doing?" Dan asked.

"I'm going to fly around some more," Steve replied. "Are you coming?"

"No," Dan said. "I'm going to stick around here. I want to keep an eye on Hazel and find out what she's up to."

"All right, I'll check and see if there's anything out here that might explain what's going on," Steve said.

He flew off, and Dan returned to watching Hazel. A few minutes later, she pulled her phone from her pocket and checked it. Seemingly startled by the time, she stuffed it back into her pocket, scooped her book off the table, and hurried through the library.

Dan glided along the side of the building again, monitoring her movements through the windows to see where she was going. He briefly thought she might be leaving, but instead, she went to the front of the library and into a dark corner. No one else was in the library at this hour; Elmhurst left it open for later hours during the second half of the school year, but few students actually took advantage of it until closer to mid-terms.

But Hazel seemed to be there for a purpose. She sat on a high-backed chair and stared around nervously for a few seconds, as though waiting for someone. Finally, Marcus joined her. He said something to her, and she nodded before standing and following him outside.

Dan followed them discretely into the shadows of a nearby building, where they stood close to each other to talk. Both kept looking back toward the library as if they thought someone else might be inside.

"What is so important that you needed to talk to me tonight?" Marcus demanded.

"We need to talk about what's going on with José," Hazel replied in a conspiratorial whisper.

Marcus rolled his eyes. "Not this again, Hazel."

"Hear me out, Marcus. Listen to me. José has us under his control. We are under the effect of a vampire thrall, and that is what's making us do all these things for him. I read all about it. But we can get out of it. It doesn't have to be this way," she insisted. "We just need help."

"I don't want out. Why don't you understand that?" Marcus snapped. "This is good for me. Working for José is going to open up the world for me. I want that. I don't want help getting away from him. I want the promises of a bright future. I want to know when I get out of this place, I'll be able to get into college and have a job waiting for me. I want the assurance of a good life. Those are all things José is offering me that would have been totally out of reach for me earlier this year."

"It doesn't have to be through him, Marcus. I know you want a good future, but this isn't the only way."

"What would *you* know about it?" Marcus demanded. "It's not as if what he could offer really matters to you that much. Those things were never out of your reach to begin with."

Hazel knew it was true. She'd always had the promise of a bright future. Her father would see to that. "It might be different for me, but that still doesn't mean we have to keep going like this. What if what he's asking of us keeps getting worse? What are his limits? What are yours? The longer we stay under his thrall, the stronger and more intense it will get. I don't want to end up in an even more frightening situation than we're already in. Besides, don't you have any feelings about Mia?"

"What do you mean, feelings about Mia?" Marcus asked. "What kind of feelings should I have about her?"

"She hasn't done anything wrong. Not to either of us. In fact, she's been really nice. She's protected me and tried to be my friend. There's been nothing to show that she deserves this," Hazel said.

"It's not for us to decide what she deserves. This is up to José, and this is what he wants."

"But that's just it. Why? Why does he want it? He's never given us any sort of reason why he would want to put her through this. He's never even told us the full reason why he wants us to spy on her and report everything back to him, to begin with."

"He has no reason to. It's not any of our business. It doesn't matter why he wants the information about her. All that matters is that he does, and he's having us get it for him," Marcus argued.

Hazel shook her head. "I just can't do this anymore. I don't want to keep sneaking around, spying on her."

"You're not going to mess this up for me," he growled. He started walking away from her.

"Where are you going?"

He didn't respond, and Dan immediately flew off to find Steve. After telling him what the two halflings had discussed, he sent Steve to follow Marcus while he went to talk to Mia. She needed to know what was going on.

Steve stayed high in the sky as he searched for Marcus, wanting to find him as quickly as possible without the halfling spotting him. By the time he caught up to him at the far edge of one of the campus fields, Marcus was already with José.

They stood close together as Marcus spoke quickly, his hands animated. "She is determined to stop helping you."

José didn't look concerned. "Don't worry. There's nothing she can do. No matter how much Hazel wants to, she can't break my enchantment. She is forever my slave. But if she is trying to resist, she may prove to be an obstacle. Keep an eye on her and make sure she doesn't get in the way."

With that, the vampire stalked away, leaving Marcus to walk back to the academy building alone.

CHAPTER FIFTY-TWO

Mia paced across her dorm room. Her hands tingled, and her head buzzed with anger. She couldn't believe what Dan told her the night before. She had decided not to approach the others so late, thinking if she had a night of sleep first, it would give her a chance to calm down and think through the situation rationally.

That's not what happened. Instead, she woke up angrier. Everything the gargoyle had told her sank in, and her fury split in two. She was livid for herself and with the threat against her. But now she was even angrier for Hazel.

Mia could take care of herself if she had to. She had already proved herself many times and was only becoming stronger, the more she practiced her skills. Hazel was different. The young halfling didn't have the same power Mia had, nor the amount of strength and support.

"He can't do this to her," she growled. "He can't keep her as his slave just because she isn't strong enough to fight him off. That's why he targeted her. He knew he could get control of her and use her against me."

"It isn't necessarily about strength. Marcus is a more powerful halfling than Hazel is in many ways, and Dan and Steve said he's in on it, too," Luna pointed out.

"But he's not bothered by it. He's happy to do the vampire's bidding if it means giving him a leg up on a better future. He'll gleefully toss me under a moving train if it's going to secure him a place at his college of choice and a good job. He doesn't want to escape José's control, so it doesn't matter. But Hazel does. She doesn't want him pushing her around anymore," Mia said. "So she shouldn't have to go through it."

"So, what are we going to do?" Luna asked. "How do we stop it?"

"If she's in a true thrall, it's not going to be easy," Vivi said. "Vampires aren't exactly known for their gentle persuasion. When Hazel says she is a slave to this guy, that's what she means."

"But there has to be some way to break the thrall. There has to be something we can do to get her away from him," Mia insisted.

"We'll find a way," Zander assured her.

"Why don't we go talk to her?" Mia suggested. "She might be able to tell us something that could help."

The five hurried from the dorm room and moved around campus searching for Hazel. They finally found her hunched in the library, reading the book the gargoyles had told them about.

"Hazel," Mia said.

Hazel glanced up and gave a slight gasp. "Mia," she said, trying to push the book out of sight. "What are you doing here?"

"You don't have to hide the book, Hazel. We know what's going on. That's why we came to talk to you."

Color splashed across the younger girl's cheeks, and she opened her mouth, about to say something, but no sound came out.

"Come on," Luna told her. "We don't know who might be listening. Let's go back to our room."

Hazel was still dumbstruck as she followed the five to the dorms. There, on the edge of Mia's bed, Hazel sat staring at them. "What is it you know about?" she asked hesitantly. There was almost a pleading sound to her voice, as though she desperately wanted to say something else, but needed those words to convey it for her.

"Dan and Steve overheard you talking to Marcus. So we know about José," Mia said. "We want to help you."

Hazel opened her mouth, and her eyes widened. She closed it and opened it again, but her eyes only grew wider. They were almost frantic.

"What?" Luna asked. "What's wrong?"

Hazel strained, her eyes filling with tears. She clawed at her throat.

"Is she all right? Is she choking?" Carson asked.

Hazel shook her head.

"No. That's not what's wrong. Ask her something else. Talk about something else," Mia said.

"What did you have for breakfast, Hazel?" Zander asked.

"French toast."

They all stared at the girl, and she exhaled slowly.

"She can't talk about José," Mia said. "She can't say anything about him."

"Write it down," Luna suggested. "Write down everything about him and how you got here."

They handed her a piece of paper and a pen, but her hand wouldn't move. Hazel stared at it, trying to force it to form words, but it shook and ached, not doing what she wanted it to.

"I can't," she said.

"We have to do something," Mia insisted. "This man is her jailer, and she can't even tell us what's going on so we can help her." She rested her hand on Hazel's shoulder. "I'm going to figure this out, Hazel. I'm going to find a way to break the spell binding you to this guy. You will be free."

The words were no sooner out of her mouth than a loud popping sounded, and Hazel cried out. Falling from the end of the bed, she landed on the floor and began to writhe, her body contorting and bending as she whimpered in pain. The agony was so extreme she couldn't even scream. She could only gag and fight to breathe.

Instantly terrified, Mia dropped to her knees and put her hands on Hazel. "Hazel! What's going on? What can I do?" she cried.

"I'm going to get Elmhurst," Luna said. She rushed from the room and along the hall. A communication sphere embedded in the wall would immediately connect to the headmistress and ensure she reached them as quickly as possible.

The room filled with the sound of Hazel's pain as the four halflings tried to figure out what was happening and what they could do. Their voices overlapped and blended, making it difficult to decipher any specific words.

Finally, Vivi held out her hands to stop them all. "This is because of the vampire," she said. "Mia removed the spell, but because José didn't do it, there was a price to pay. This is Hazel's price."

"So, we're just supposed to accept it?" Mia demanded. "We're supposed to just stand here and let her suffer until it's done because she deserves it for wanting to be free?"

"That's not what she said," Carson said, trying to calm Mia.

"It's not what I meant," Vivi said. "I— I'm worried about her, too."

It was a surprising revelation for all of them, but the way her eyebrows were knit together, and how much darker her eyes had grown had revealed how concerned she actually was.

"You are?" Zander asked.

"Yeah," Vivi spat. "I don't get it, either. Hazel was never a friend of mine. She's more of a nuisance, really. But now I'm worried about her. I don't understand why I would feel so bad for the girl, but there it is. Maybe it's part of the spell."

Mia shook her head. Vivi would never change. She couldn't even deal with a few minutes of normal compassionate emotion for another living being without being convinced something was wrong.

"Mia, try to make it go away," Zander said. "Like we talked about. Like slamball."

She didn't understand at first, but it sank in. Focusing on Hazel, she put all her energy and concentration into wishing for the pain to go away. She wanted it with everything in her and sent that thought out toward the girl. A few minutes into this, Elmhurst ran down the hallway and into the room.

"What's happening?" she asked. They explained it to her, and Mia looked up, eyes filled with pain. "I'm trying to make it stop," she said. "But it's not doing any good."

Hazel wasn't reacting as strongly, though, so some of the pain might have dissipated. But she was still writhing, still groaning. Elmhurst immediately dropped onto the floor and put her hand over Hazel's heart. She closed her eyes and whispered something Mia couldn't understand.

"Ancient tongue," Zander whispered to her. "Very few fae still know it."

When she finished, the headmistress glanced at Mia and nodded. Seconds later, Hazel's face relaxed and smoothed out. Her breathing calmed, and it was obvious she wasn't in pain anymore.

Relief washed over Mia, but seconds later it melted under a wave of grief and guilt. "I'm sorry," she whispered. "I'm so sorry."

"Why are you sorry?" Hazel asked. "You didn't do anything. This isn't your fault."

"But I couldn't stop it. I tried so hard. I did everything I could. Really, I did," Mia told her.

"Mia, what are you talking about?" Elmhurst asked.

"Like with the gargoyles and the snow falling on Narco. I wanted the pain to go away. I wanted Hazel to be all right, and I couldn't make it happen."

"That isn't your fault," the headmistress told her, taking hold of her shoulders and looking directly into her eyes. "You didn't do this, and it wasn't your responsibility to make the pain stop. You already did something incredible by breaking that spell. You can't expect yourself to do something some full fae struggle to master."

"If it wasn't for me..."

"No, Mia," Hazel said. "Don't think that way. This is José. Not you."

"Tell us everything," Elmhurst said. "We'll figure out what to do from there."

Hazel told them the entire story, explaining how she fell under the enslavement of the vampire José and what he wanted her and Marcus to do. The headmistress confirmed that Marcus was already gone, having disappeared off-campus, probably right after talking with José.

Elmhurst left with a warning that it was time to work harder, to push themselves further and build their skills, especially Mia. Something was coming, and they needed to be prepared.

For the next few weeks, Mia dove headlong into familiarizing herself with her powers, polishing her skills, and learning more about the world she belonged to. She worked as hard as she could, sometimes pushing herself into exhaustion so complete she could barely move. But it didn't discourage her. She wouldn't allow the difficulty of it to hold her back. This was what she was meant for, and she was going to do it.

She wasn't in it alone. It wasn't only the other four of the group of five or even Professor Elmhurst. Dan and Steve had dedicated themselves to being a part of the cause in every way they could. That meant the instant he was allowed off his pedestal at night, Dan came to Mia and stayed with her, and also sat outside her window while she slept. Steve spent every night flying over the campus and the nearby town, making sure there were no sightings of Narco or vampires nearby.

Everything was quiet. But that was the problem. It was far too quiet. Something was coming, and they all worried about what it might be.

CHAPTER FIFTY-THREE

It seemed as though it would take forever, but finally, spring came to Montana. Mia was beginning to think the snow would never go away, and she would always be stuck in a perpetual winter.

"I've seen that movie," Luna joked when Mia shared the thought. "It was cute."

"Maybe if you get to wear a fabulous dress and have magical powers that can control everything," Mia snapped.

Carson shot her a bemused look, and Mia realized what she had said.

"Yeah," Carson said. "It would be so strange and completely out of my frame of reference for you to have magical powers that can control things."

Mia kicked some of the sloshy, partially-melted snow from the sidewalk at him. He curved away, and it hit his shoulder with a wet plop. He gasped at the cold, and she snickered, but her laughter stopped when he leaned down to scoop up a handful of the slush. He turned to Mia, and she squealed.

She took off running away from him, heading for the field behind the academy building. It was still clean after being abandoned since before Christmas break. Now that the warmer spring sun was finally starting to melt the snow away, it was the perfect spot for a snowball battle to celebrate the last reminders of winter.

Mia managed to duck out of the way of the loose snowball that came flying at her but gasped when it stopped in midair and changed direction to come racing back toward her. It splattered in the middle of her chest, some of the bits of ice slipping down into her coat and making her shiver.

"No fair using magic snowballs!" she shouted.

"Why not?" Carson asked. "That was never a rule."

"Yeah, Mia." Vivi bent to grab her own handful of snow. "You're at Elmhurst Academy now. Everything has magic, even the snowball fights. It just makes everything so much better."

Mia held up a finger at the Unseelie girl. "Vivi," she said in warning, "we're supposed to be in this together."

Vivi grinned at her, lifting her hand to launch the snowball. At the last second, she turned and threw it at the back of Zander's head. The Seelie halfling shouted and whipped around, grabbing up more snow as he went. He threw the handful, and it broke into several small snowballs that showered down on the girls. Carson laughed loudly, and the fight was on. Vivi enchanted some of the snow to form itself into a fort, but it was melting so fast it couldn't stay solid, so she had to keep rebuilding.

Mia stared around her frantically. Luna stood several yards away in the middle of the field. "Luna!" she shouted. "What are you doing? We're getting pummeled over here."

"I'm making snowmen!" she yelled in reply.

"Snowmen?" Vivi demanded. "Why are you doing that?"

"Because they are fun." Mia smiled when Luna moved out of the way to present her snowman.

The two boys stopped their full-on snowball assault and turned to the snowman. As soon as they looked at it, the snowman melted into the ground. The snow spread out into a wide puddle, and from the pool of water, three snowmen emerged.

"That's a cute trick," Carson said.

"It's not done," Luna said.

On cue, the three snowmen melted, and the puddle grew wider. From it, six more snowmen appeared. Only this time, they were bigger, and each was holding an armful of snowballs. They each grabbed one and threw them in unison at the guys. All three girls released delighted screams as the guys thrashed about trying to dive out of the way of the sudden hail of snowballs.

"I want to play!"

Mia glanced up at the sound of the voice. Cinder was fluttering toward them. Instead of making her own snowball, she sent a blast of magic at some of the ones the guys were trying to form and send back toward the girls. They melted when she looked at them, creating little patches of grass where the remainder of the snow disappeared under the heated water.

The snowmen Luna made ran out of snowballs, and Mia enchanted them to start moving across the field toward the guys. Behind them, another row sprung up, then another, and another. Soon the ground was half-filled with melting soldiers advancing on Zander and Carson.

As they threw enchanted snowballs at them, they burst into flame from the magic of the little pixie giggling and flying around above them. They mostly evaporated before reaching the guys, but it was still fun for Mia to watch them scrambling and trying to fight back.

Mia held onto the memory of that fun early spring afternoon a few weeks later when all the snow was gone and the warmer season had officially set in. Their coats, gloves, hats, scarves, and boots finally put away for the year, the five halflings spent more time outside enjoying the sunlight on their skin.

As the days grew longer, a strange feeling settled over the campus. It wasn't the lack of clothing layers making Mia feel exposed. Everywhere she went, she felt eyes on her. She was being watched, her every move monitored, and it had her on edge.

She let it go on for almost two weeks before she finally went to

Elmhurst. The headmistress ushered the group of five halflings into her office and closed the door. Checking to make sure no one else was around to listen in, she sat at her desk and invited Mia to tell her what was happening. Mia explained the feeling and how many students she had noticed watching her.

"I think now that he's lost Hazel, José got himself new spies," she told the headmistress.

"That seems like a safe assumption," Elmhurst confirmed. "Do you have any guesses as to who it might be?"

Mia hesitated before she nodded. "I'm not sure, but I noticed something that might help lead us to who they are."

"What's that?"

"Earlier in the year, I noticed something odd about Hazel. I wasn't sure what it was, then I realized she had a slight aura. I don't know how else to describe it. But it was there. It went away after I broke the spell, getting her out from José's control. I've seen that same aura around some students on campus in the last few weeks. Only—"

She hesitated, and the headmistress made a gesture with her hand, trying to encourage the words to come from Mia's mouth. "Only what, Mia?"

Mia sighed in frustration. "Only Marcus didn't have one. Ever. So maybe it doesn't have anything to do with the vampire thrall, and it's just a halfling feature? That's why I never said anything before."

Elmhurst shook her head. "No. That's not something halflings usually have. I absolutely think the aura you're describing has something to do with José and his control. It's strange that Marcus didn't have one, but it could be because of his compliance. The aura could suggest a person forced into servitude rather than one who willingly accepts it."

"Then we start with them. If we learned anything from Hazel, it should be that those forced into following the vampire's control are the most likely to want to get away from it. We should talk to them and find out what we can," Mia said.

"Until the bonds have been broken and Narco is no longer a threat to you, Mia, you are not to be alone. There are to be at least two people with you at all times," Elmhurst said.

"Yes, Headmistress," Mia said.

"I heard from Cassia today. She will be coming back to campus for a brief visit this week. She wants to check in on you," Elmhurst said.

"What did you tell her?" Mia asked.

"I've kept her informed of all developments. I know you don't want to worry her, but she is your guardian and deserves to know. She is also the best bounty hunter in the fae world. If there is anyone who can track down Narco, it will be her."

Mia nodded. Cassia had been hunting Narco since she had left campus but hadn't found him yet. And Cassia was becoming frustrated, but she wouldn't stop until the threat against Mia was eliminated. It made the young halfling feel more secure and confident, knowing her guardian was putting so much effort into finding the man who wanted to destroy her.

That sense of confidence was shattered two weeks later when the gargoyles appeared as the five met with Elmhurst to discuss a project they were working on. They were frantic as they told her of a portal that opened right outside the campus. The headmistress immediately went into action.

"Gather all the students," she said to the gargoyles. "Get all of them in the dining hall. Mia, you stay with me. The rest of you, find the students Mia has labeled as having the auras and bring them to the Mathematics Building. There will be a professor waiting to help you."

As Mia followed Elmhurst to the dining hall, the reality of what was happening finally settled in. It was tonight. All their preparations, anxiety, and watching, had led them to this. Her initial fear faded as the sense of duty and responsibility filled her. She was ready to defend herself, her school, and her friends.

Once the students streamed into the dining hall from their dorms and the few spots on campus where they were allowed after class, Elmhurst created a portal. She ushered the students through as quickly as they would go, sending them to another school. The headmaster of that school was waiting, ready to accept and care for them until Elmhurst sent for them again. Several of the staff monitored the students as they departed, and when the last one had left, Elmhurst asked if any were missing.

The staff read off the names of those who did not go through, and Mia mentally ticked off the ones who had the auras and should be waiting in the other building.

"Thank you," Elmhurst said. "Mia, come on."

They headed quickly for the Mathematics Building, a small structure in a corner of the main portion of campus.

"There are people missing," she said. "Ones who don't have the aura didn't go through the portal."

Elmhurst nodded. "They must be the ones who willingly went into servitude. Or those who are exceptionally weak-minded and didn't need the blood curse to become slaves."

"We had planned to release them of their curse this weekend," Mia said.

The headmistress nodded again. "I know. Either someone knew and tipped them off, or it is very unfortunate timing." They arrived at the building, but they didn't go inside.

"What are we going to do about them?" Mia asked. "The missing ones?"

"We can't do anything about them now. We have to prepare ourselves."

The doors to the building opened, and a small group of students tried to exit. Elmhurst approached the entrance and performed an enchantment to seal them in so no one could get in or out without knowing the specific spell.

Mia saw Hazel coming toward her from another building. "Hazel, what are you doing? You should have gone through the portal to the other school."

"No, Mia." Hazel shook her head adamantly. "I'm not leaving you. I want to help."

"It's not safe," Mia argued.

"I don't care. You took care of me. You protected me, and you freed me. You were there for me when I needed you, and I'm doing the same."

"We all are."

Mia turned to Cinder, who had appeared from behind the legs of the Scooby Gang.

"All of us," Dan said as the gargoyles flew into place with them.

Mia's heart swelled as she looked at the group in front of her. There was no question in any of their eyes, no hesitation. They were going to stay and face this with her.

"Mia," Elmhurst said. Mia glanced at the headmistress, who was staring across the grounds. "They're here."

CHAPTER FIFTY-FOUR

The sheer size of the crowd crossing the grounds in their direction was dizzying. Mia had anticipated José and a few of his servants. She had thought she might have to face a few of the creatures she had encountered during her time in Shanghai. But she didn't expect the army coming her way.

A clan of a dozen wolf shifters walked beside several fae and two intense-looking witches. But it was the massive wall of vampires that took her breath away. Narco himself was leading the march.

"It's José's family," Hazel murmured. "His closest allies."

"He has dhampirs with him," Luna pointed out.

Mia noticed the five dhampirs interspersed among the true vampires. Even bolstered by the teachers and staff who weren't guarding the enthralled students, her group felt incredibly small. But that didn't lessen their strength. José's group had numbers and definite power, but they didn't know what they were coming up against. He didn't truly know what he was messing with when it came to Mia, or to the group of five. It was time for them to show him.

They rushed toward José, and his army advanced. The two groups clashed in the middle, and the battle began.

"Mia!" a voice shouted.

One of the professors stood a few feet away. He tossed her a set of weapons, and when it fell into her hands, she felt anchored. It was a pair of sai, a three-pronged weapon she had learned to use while training for Wushu. The blades were the ideal weapon for women, easy for her to control, and familiar in her hands.

She wielded them powerfully as she ran headlong toward a cluster of vampires. Sending up a temporary shield around herself to protect herself from their attacks, she swung each sai so they sliced right through the necks of the vampires. They paused, their eyes widening as they registered what she had done. Mia didn't hesitate. She cut through again, separating their heads from their shoulders. They bobbed for a moment, and toppled backward and onto the ground.

Mia didn't give herself the time to revel in the triumph. They were small, young, and weak. It wouldn't be so easy moving forward, and there was far more to be done. Around her, the grounds rang with the sounds of battle. Shouts and cries rose up into the night air, and the coppery smell of blood burned in her throat.

Ahead of Mia, a shifter leapt forward, transformed into a vicious wolf in midair, and bared his dripping fangs at her. She braced herself for the fight, but before the creature reached her, a large boulder fell from the sky and crushed it to the ground. The sound of bones cracking marked the shifter's immediate death.

Mia looked up at Dan, who hovered above. Steve floated behind him, holding another huge boulder, poised to drop it on a fae man below. Mia flashed him a grin and surged back into the fight.

One of the witches had Zander on the ground, and vines had come up from the soil to entangle him. They wrapped tightly around his body, held him to the ground, and wound around him to his throat. The witch laughed darkly as she controlled the vines. Zander managed to move his hand enough to send a blast of magic at her.

The witch stumbled away, but she stepped forward again and pointed at the ground near him. Another thicker vine burst from the ground, splitting the dirt and grass as it came. Covered in barbed thorns, it joined the other in encircling Zander's body. The Seelie boy gritted his teeth against the pain, refusing to give her the satisfaction of watching him scream, but Mia could see the blood.

The sight of her friend bleeding infuriated her. She lunged toward the witch just as Zander sent new magic through the vines that began to shrivel them. Before the witch could do anything, Mia thrust one sai through the woman's chest. The witch gagged and fell to the ground.

Mia wrenched the sai from her body and looked at the thick, dark blood running down the middle blade down toward the two smaller ones that came from either side. The grotesque woman groaned again before she sagged to the ground.

The instant she died, the shriveled vines pulled away from Zander. He fought the rest of the way out of them, and Mia reached for his hand to help him up.

"Thanks," he said.

"Of course. She doesn't know what she's dealing with," Mia said.

"Better believe it. I bet she had no idea I have previous experience fighting for my life against vines."

Mia stared at Zander strangely, but he lifted his sword to ready himself and shrugged. "Ask Vivi about it sometime."

He ran toward Carson, who was battling against two shifters, and Mia watched them combine their magic to kill both creatures in a single blast. Suddenly she felt a breath on the back of her neck, and she spun around.

One of the older, stronger vampires stood close behind her. She slashed her blade across his neck, but the weapon barely made a mark. The vampire laughed and stepped closer to her. He reached out, but before his hands could touch her, Mia slammed the sai blade into his chest.

It wouldn't kill him. But as she had hoped, the injury paralyzed him long enough for her to force him to the ground and pin him down to cut off his head. As soon as she moved away, Cinder came rushing from between the legs of a fae woman nearby and set the vampire's corpse aflame.

The longer they fought, the more brutal and intense the battle became. Blood ran down her arms, her vision blurred, and parts of her body were aching from injuries she didn't have time to check yet.

Mia blasted out her magic. She used every skill she could, putting every bit of focus and concentration on controlling what she was doing. A shockwave wiped out several vampires, and they tumbled to the ground at Carson's feet. He met her eyes.

"Maybe it's time for a little change of weather," he said with a wink.

She nodded, and they ran to find the rest of the Scooby Gang. All together, they made a plan and spread out. Conjuring a strong wind, Mia concentrated it into one strong ball and sent it across the battlefield to Zander. He spread it out a little and threw it through a group of fae to Carson. The fae were torn apart by the strength of the air and landed in a tangled mass on the ground. Mia and the two boys tossed the wind around, occasionally adding new magic and enchantments to further decimate the numbers standing against them.

They fought for what felt like hours, but finally, the enemy's numbers dwindled. Nearly all were dead. But not enough.

Mia turned from the final vampire she had killed and saw José right behind Hazel. She tried to pull Hazel away with her thoughts, but it didn't work. They were across the field from her, and Mia wondered if distance played a part, or if it was because she was so exhausted. Mia ran, wanting to snatch the girl away from him before he could bite her.

Bending her head back and to the side, exposing her neck, José sank his fangs into her and took deep gulps. Mia screamed out. Anger and hurt rushed through her as she realized that not being fully able to control her powers had cost Hazel her life. With the way José was drinking, Mia wasn't going to get there in time.

Her hands lifted, and glowing streams of magic burst from the six points of the sai weapons she held. Each burrowed into a fae or shifter nearby, instantly wiping out six of the few still remaining.

Narco stared at the carnage before he fled. The moment she'd killed half a dozen of his warriors, he knew he didn't stand a chance against Mia and her friends. None of the reports he'd received had said she'd possessed anywhere near this level of power. A strategic retreat was his only option at this point. It would make it possible for him to live to fight another day.

José didn't have the same compulsion. He wanted to stay and fight Mia, to be able to prove his bravery and his loyalty to Narco. Besides, he thought she would have used up too much of her power and be exhausted by this point. Killing her would be easy, and he could have his reward at last. It didn't matter what she tried with her blades. Lightning didn't kill vampires. It hurt a lot, but it didn't actually kill them.

The blood lust a vampire experienced in the middle of a large battle didn't help his sense of self-preservation, either.

And all that was left were vampires, José and his brother, Miguel. Mia cried out, channeling every bit of her anger and sadness at the vampires. Miguel instantly dropped to the ground, his head exploding. José came running at her, but Mia held up her hand, causing him to skid to a stop. It all came down to him. He was the last of his family left to fight. The field around them was littered with the bodies of the vampires and other species they had brought with them, but Mia also recognized the faces of a few fallen teachers from the academy.

Tears streamed down her face as she lifted her hand, pulling José from his feet with her magic so he hovered a couple inches off the ground. She clenched her hand, turning her grip into a magical vice that would slowly crush José to death.

Cassia ran to her side and put a hand on her shoulder. "Stop," she said. "Mia, stop. We need him for questioning. He'll be brought in and interrogated so we can find out as much about him and this operation as we can."

Elmhurst stepped forward and performed an enchantment. A jail cell appeared, and Mia forced José into it. When he was inside, she released the grip, and he fell to the ground in a heap. The headmistress went inside and checked him.

"He's not dead. At least, not for a vampire," she confirmed.

They brought him to an underground facility for interrogation, but they wouldn't allow Mia inside. She waited impatiently, and finally, Cassia emerged from the questioning to talk to her.

"What's going on?" Mia asked.

"The interrogation is over," Cassia said. "And it was interesting. It turns out that a certain fae believes you are a descendant of the royal line. It was once believed that this line of the family was extinct."

"Who? And what royal line?" Mia asked.

"José didn't know who Narco's working for," Headmistress Elmhurst answered.

"But, what about me being descended from royalty? How's that even possible?" Mia ran a hand through her messy hair and looked frantically between Cassia and Elmhurst.

Mia had zero desire to be royal. She'd seen how royals in Great Britain were treated, and she wanted none of it. Sure, in fairy tales, it always worked out in the end, but not in real life. And from what she knew about fae, it would be much worse for her than it ever was for the Duchess of Sussex, and she only married into a human royal family. Being a halfling descent of a fae princess had to be worse than an apocalypse.

Headmistress Elmhurst put her hands up in a placating gesture. "Don't worry, Mia. I doubt you are who they think you are."

"It must be possible if so many are after me." Mia began to pace the small room.

Cassia nodded. "While it is possible, it's not definite."

"At one time, the fae realm was controlled by one Court. The king and queen of the fae Court had three daughters. The two older princesses agreed to kill their parents and split the realm and share leadership thousands of years ago. Princess Violet, the youngest daughter, is dead. Not a lot is known about Princess Violet as her sisters tried to make everyone forget she was ever alive." The bounty hunter gave her charge a light hug.

Mia pulled herself from Cassia's embrace. "How does a dead princess from thousands of years ago affect me? If we are even related." She threw her hands in the air.

Cassia ran a hand down her face and sighed. "It's possible you're one of her descendants. You'd be a very long way down the family tree, of course, but that could explain what you are capable of doing. Even though you're a halfling, you have very powerful fae blood in you. That enables you to do things no one expects you to be able to do."

"Could I ever be a fae princess?" Mia asked.

Cassia shook her head. "No. Even if we believe what José said, it wouldn't be possible because you are a halfling. The fae would never accept you as royal or recognize your right to rule. Besides, neither of the queens would give up their throne. There are only two Courts, so there is no throne to be had."

"And if I disagree with that?" Mia asked.

"The queens are far too powerful for you to beat. And even if you did manage to beat one, there is still the other. She would come at you with absolutely everything and defeat you so she could be Queen of all Fae. The Courts would merge. Nobody wants that. There would be a war like nothing Earth has ever seen if the two Courts were forced to merge."

Mia nodded, her mind churning with questions and options. She didn't know how to move forward or what to do next. Should she try to take over one of the Courts and claim a throne? Perhaps try to take over both?

No. She didn't want to rule anything. That was far too much pressure and responsibility, not to mention the possibility of a civil war amongst the fae. Besides, she may not even be the descendant of Princess Violet. Although she doubted so many would be after her if she wasn't. Most likely, she was.

But that didn't change the fact that she couldn't simply accept people coming after her all the time. She had to keep herself and everyone around her safe. Perhaps she should go into hiding.

Whatever she was going to do, she needed to make a choice, and soon. The lives of so many depended on how she decided to move forward.

PART III

PROLOGUE

The noise inside the protective dome around the slamball field was almost deafening. Every single seat in the stadium was full, and the crowd was crushed together, trying to make room for others to squeeze in. No one should miss this kind of excitement. The World Slamball Championships only came along every four years, and members of the fae community eagerly anticipated the return of this storied event.

The locations hosting the games started preparing for the championships years in advance, often beginning before the last competition was over. They not only needed to make sure the stadium was ready for the players, but also for the fans. Huge crowds swarmed the host cities to attend the games, which meant the people of those cities needed to be prepared for the onslaught.

Hotels and temporary inns designed specifically to cater to the fae, would pop up and start taking reservations. Restaurants increased their seating and expanded their delivery options. Ambitious entrepreneurs designed clothing, signs, and other memorabilia to sell outside the arena.

It was a celebratory, thrilling time, and anyone within the dome could feel the energy rushing throughout. As freeing as it would be to not have the dome around the field, it simply wasn't an option.

The dome kept the players in line, and ensured fair play, but also concealed them from the humans who may be around. It didn't always work. There were times when wayward humans were drawn in by the spectators coming to the area and would wander into the dome. Since these protective features were designed to blend in with the surroundings and look like something expected in the area, the humans would simply join up with the crowd and walk in. Of course, that was always handled promptly, and the games would continue.

Today, the crowd was hungry for the game, and brimming with excitement to watch the match. Those with the most expensive and exclusive seats sat in their prime positions, peering out over the field. They were content to roam around in their private boxes, chatting with others, and buying refreshments. The rest of the crowd wasn't quite so lucky.

General admission meant getting a good seat was a fight of the fittest. Fans camped out for hours, sometimes a day or two, before the dome opened to allow the spectators in. When the stands opened, it was a mad rush, every fan for themselves, to find a prime spot.

Once there, no one moved. You stayed in your spot and protected it so nobody would come by and steal it. For some, that equated to hours of sitting in the same place, waiting for the game to start.

Now the time had finally arrived, and the anxious energy building in the stands was reaching a fever pitch. The cheering grew louder when the referee walked onto the field. Which was the first sign that the game was about to begin. He held up his hands to settle the crowd, but it took several seconds before the voices died down.

When it was quiet enough for him to speak and actually be heard, he used a spell to amplify his voice, so it went to every inch of the stadium. He didn't want to take the chance that any of the players or fans would miss what he had to say.

"Hello, fans. And thank you for joining us today. Welcome to the World Slamball Championships!" Another surge of raucous screaming filled the dome, and the referee let it go on for a few seconds before holding his hands up again.

"Before we introduce the teams and get the game started, I want to make the rules very clear. These apply to every single person in attendance today, players and fans alike. Listen closely. Claiming you didn't hear or understand the rules won't get you out of the consequences of not following them, should you make that choice."

Some of the cheering turned to boos, but he wasn't deterred. Presenting the rules at the beginning of the championships was essential. Perhaps more now than ever before. These games were coming at a harder time than any of the championships before, and he knew the risks were higher. It was a reality of the game. Everything was becoming more intense, and it seemed simple things like watching sports had turned into a potentially dangerous event.

"I want a clean game. No funny business. At the start of the game, an additional protective dome will be set up around the playing field itself. This will separate the stands from the players and ensure there is no interference. No magic from the outside of the dome will be able to get inside, and no magic being used within the dome for the game will be able to get outside. I don't want a repeat of what happened four years ago."

He didn't need to explain that any further. Everyone in attendance knew the incident he was referencing.

At the last World Slamball Championships, a particularly intense game had sent magic out into the stands. This, combined with illegal magic being used by a fan who had put down a very high bet on his favorite team and was going to do anything he could to make sure he made good on that bet. The result was devastating, with several spectators suffering serious injuries, and one had died.

The referee didn't want to go into detail about that now. It was important to lay out the rules and make sure everyone followed them, but he didn't want to ruin the fun of the beginning of the Championships by bringing down the energy and excitement.

He elevated his voice over the growing protests. "There will be no intentional harming of any of the players. This includes use of physical force as well as magic."

The booing grew louder, and some of the fans started hurling insults and derogatory slurs at the official.

"No throwing of curses of any kind. No mind-altering spells. Keep in mind there are referees and other officials positioned throughout the area of play as well as in the crowd. Some are in uniform, while others are not. They will be watching everyone carefully, and using spell detection techniques to identify anyone using forbidden magic during the course of the game."

The referee paused and looked around the stadium. Every single spectator felt chills down their spines, as though the ref was singling them out. "Any player caught using any form of prohibited spell or magic will be immediately ejected from the game, and will be considered for permanent expulsion from the games. Teams will not be permitted to call in further players or replace the ejected player with a player not already on their active roster."

"Any spectator caught using any form of prohibited magic on another spectator, player, or official will be removed from the game, all admission forfeited, and their rights to attend any future Games revoked." The referee's hand sliced through the air to punctuate his statement.

The insults became coarser, and the names more egregious. Someone threw an empty cup at him, starting a cascade of trash and balled-up programs tumbling down on him. A swipe of his hand created a barrier around him that prevented any of the debris from hitting him, and a young fae acting as the water boy for the players scrambled to start collecting everything that was thrown.

"Listen carefully," the head referee instructed. "If anyone is found to have used a death curse of any kind on any person within this stadium, they will find themselves being immediately tossed into the Dungeons of Forasaon. There will be no trial and no appeals. It will be up to the head jailer to determine the length of the sentence. His full discretion will be honored without question, and no relief of any kind will be offered. Let this be fully understood. There will be *no* exceptions. For anyone or any reason."

Loud laughter belted out from the crowd in several spots around the stadium, and spectators called to him.

"That may be the only way a halfling gets into Faerie!"

CHAPTER FIFTY-FIVE

The edges of the leaves were starting to change as the end of summer wound down on campus at the academy. The sun was still hot and dry and left Mia with little choice other than short sleeves as she strolled to the practice grounds.

She wished the weather would turn crisper, more fall-like, but only three weeks into her senior year, she knew that was a month or more away. Still, a jacket hung by her door, waiting for the first day that cool air would necessitate long sleeves and pumpkin-spiced coffee.

Mia flipped to a familiar song on her phone and lost herself in her thoughts and the music as she went down the path leading to the practice grounds behind the academy. Students were milling about, some finding sunny places to sit and study, others playing various forms of outside games, but nearly all of them wearing an insignia on their shirt or hat.

The logo of the Academy Slamball team shone from their gleaming gold pins. The World Championships were coming soon, and that meant more portals, more excitement, and more opportunities to lose herself in a shared experience, and not have the heavy thoughts of the summer weighing on her.

"Not doing this today," she muttered, calling out her brain for wanting to dive back into the mopey, homesick, and guilty part of her consciousness.

Spending a few weeks with her father had been wonderful, but not nearly long enough, though at the same time, it had seemed ages away from her friends and her new life. A new life her father still knew nothing about.

She had told him names of friends in passing and rewrote scenarios that happened on campus to fit the narrative, but her father still believed she was studying Wushu in China. He imagined her participating in tournaments, and learning more about the martial art she had dedicated so much of her life to before arriving at the academy.

Thankfully, she and Luna had spent time each week working on martial-arts training during her second semester at the academy. This year, Mia had plans to spend more time honing her skills and ensuring that she continued to learn more and more about her chosen art form.

Mia hated lying to her father, but it was essential, both to protect him and to protect herself. To make sure that no one in her outside world knew where she was. Even Becky didn't know the truth. And she shouldn't, she couldn't.

Returning to campus had been a difficult transition since part of her longed to be with her father. But still, she enjoyed learning about her powers, honing them, and spending time with her new set of friends. Even Vivi… Mostly.

Lost in her thoughts, Mia nearly missed the small dirt path leading into the heavily wooded area surrounding the practice fields. A solid, slightly shimmery dome rose in the middle, a sign of the group's increasing power and control. Now each of the five could hold the protection in place on their own without thinking about it. Their individual shields had a faint color tint and, if you knew what you were looking for, you could tell who was casting it. Today's had the slightest touch of periwinkle blue, and Mia smiled. Luna had the job.

"Mia, you made it," Carson called from across the field.

A floating purple orb hung in the center of the group's circle. Mia recognized it as a bender, a type of physical object that magic can manifest. When used correctly, it can literally bend reality, at least temporarily. Useful in fights with large groups, the bender can convince entire armies that not only are they naked and without their armor, but that their enemies are giant spider-creatures, or whatever else the casters decided to concentrate on. As usual, it wasn't something students of Mia's age ever did, but Zander was determined that perfecting this spell would be the key to acing their final scores.

"Sorry, guys, I thought you might want to see this." Mia held out the pamphlets that had been slipped under her door. Curious, the rest of the group allowed the bender to dissipate, and when it was well and gone, they crowded around her, each taking a copy.

"They're setting up new portals to get to Scotland for the Slamball Championships," Zander read.

"We don't need permission to go see other games," Carson noted.

"As long as we don't miss any classes." Vivi moaned. "How do they expect us to enjoy the tournament if we have to make sure we hit all our classes?"

"You just want to see the Highland team, don't you?" Carson teased. His voice held a trace of jealousy that Mia almost didn't pick up on.

"Angus McIntyre is a gift from the gods, and deserves to have his loyal and loving fans by his side," Vivi responded, deadpan. Mia tried to choke back a laugh, but the sound was audible enough that Vivi shot her a glare. "Like you don't want to see those vampire boys from Germany?" she teased.

"I have *one* poster, and it came free in a box of candy." Mia was trying not to laugh harder, or let on that Vivi might be right.

"We can take turns going to some of the non-school games, and take notes for each other," Zander interrupted, taking their attention off their petty bickering. "Vivi, you and Carson can go see the Highland teams, and I'll go with Mia to see the German team. I've been meaning to scout their forwards for a while, anyway."

"I'll tag along with Luna," a voice from behind Mia said, and she turned to see the small speck of a creature flying over her shoulder toward Luna. Cinder circled Luna a few times, and settled at eye-level, joining the group as though she were another student.

"Maybe we can see the Highland Games, as well?" Luna waggled her brows at Vivi, who didn't pay any attention to her.

Cinder laughed and nodded.

"You want to go with her?" Vivi said to Zander, and it was her turn to reveal a touch of jealousy in her voice.

Zander appeared to ignore her and walked to Mia. "Let's take a break for a while, guys. Good job today. I'll see you all at six," he said, referring to when their evening Human History class would start. Mia moved toward Luna, intending to ask if she wanted to walk with her back onto the campus grounds, but Zander interrupted. "Hey, Mia," he said.

"Yes?" Mia asked.

"Want to walk back with me? Since we have the same next class and all." Zander was referring to their Applied Mathematics class.

"Sure," she said, fighting the feeling that someone had turned the heat up from its already uncomfortable oppressiveness. She grabbed the bottled water from her bag and took a massive swig, hoping he didn't see the flushing of her cheeks.

Zander fell into step beside Mia as she walked toward the campus. In the distance, a few teachers were opening yet another portal on the grounds, this one closer to the athletic department buildings, and most likely for the exclusive use of their own Slamball teams. Mia watched them with interest for a few moments before Zander spoke.

"I feel like we haven't really talked much since you got back. How was your break?" he asked.

Mia paused before responding. Distilling all the emotions and deception, along with the comfortable and relaxing boredom of being at home with her father, plus considering the few weeks spent shad-owing Cassia on her assignments and hunting for Narco, was a chal-lenge. She exhaled slowly.

"It was good." For a moment, she thought about leaving it at that. An uninspiring and inadequate response.

"Just good?" Zander's hopeful expression turned to disappointment, as though he had hoped for more from her.

Mia couldn't just let him down, especially since it wasn't the whole truth. "Well, it was crazy, actually. I went home to see my dad and stayed there for a few weeks. It was like I never left. I was a little kid again, you know? Regular bedtime and family dinners at the table and all that. It was like none of this was real for a little while. I liked it, as a break, but after a while, I just wanted to come back. As much as I miss my Dad, I missed being here, learning my power, and all that too."

Zander nodded and fished a piece of gum from his pocket. He offered it to Mia, who shook her head, and he popped it into his mouth.

"What about Narco? Did Cassia find anything out?" he asked.

"No, not really. I actually went with her a couple of times. She thought it would be good for me to get used to the portal system, and hang out with her for a little while, so I went. It's like he disappeared off the face of the planet."

"Maybe he's dead," Zander said. When she didn't respond, he shrugged. "Hey, a guy can hope, right?"

"Cassia seems to think he's in Faerie, living like a hero."

Zander nodded and decided to move away from the depressing discussion and on to something different. "So, the German team?" A wry smile crossed his lips.

"No, not really. Like I said, it came in a box of candy. I'm still getting the hang of the professional leagues. I'm hoping our academy being in the Senior High competition will help me get to know the teams a bit more. I'm still not sure exactly how all this is working."

"Do you want to know? I don't want to bore you with details," he said, uncharacteristically reserved.

Zander was usually the first to go off on tangents about why things worked and how often, to the rapt attention of Mia and the general boredom of everyone else. Zander prided himself on learning how things worked, including people. Which made him such a strong leader for their group.

Mia nodded.

"Well, it's like the Olympics…in a way. The World Championships is only every four years, so it's a big deal when it happens. In order to get in, you have to be either first or second place in your league from the year before, and the eighteen teams in the tournament are from all over the world. This year, the first round will all take place in the Highlands of Scotland."

"Have you ever been there?" Mia asked.

"Only once, on a school trip. Apparently, they leveled out a bunch of land for the games. Scotland is full of history for fae, but it can be dangerous. Redcaps have a union house in Glasgow, and boggarts are all over the place, so security is usually tight for students. Even more so for the games. That's why Elmhurst is opening direct portals; she doesn't want people wandering off."

It made sense to Mia, especially since the history of the Isle of Raasay was of such importance to both the Seelie and Unseelie cCourts. The area was contested by both Courts and was the subject of various vicious battles throughout history. The patricide which had split the kingdom—creating the two Courts—still reverberated among fae today, even at the academy. Even among their group. She could only imagine that the area surrounding a place of such importance was bound to be rife with chaotic and unpredictable magic, and those who would want to harness it for their own purposes.

"Mia?" Zander asked.

It dawned on her that she had missed something. "Hmm?"

"I asked if you wanted to go to the German team's opening-round game. It's during a period when we don't have classes, and I'd love to check the game out with you."

The addendum of "with you" was not lost on Mia. "Sure, that sounds great." She was attempting to play it cool but was feeling miserable about it.

"Awesome. I'll meet you by the library around eight tomorrow morning, okay? And we'll see about getting tickets to the game."

"Eight then," Mia repeated, and Zander nodded.

It wasn't a date. Not really, anyway. But it also wasn't the first time

Zander had specifically asked her to spend time with him. Just the two of them. He told her he wanted to get to know her better, and she knew she wanted the same. It was hard to do much in the way of getting to know each other with their three friends around, so she always looked forward to the bits of time they had alone together.

CHAPTER FIFTY-SIX

Over the summer, Mia had become pretty good at going through portals, but that didn't stop a small, split-second of a stomach flip every time she went near one.

The memory of being so discombobulated last year was very present in her mind, even after going through dozens of portals with Cassia as she shadowed her. By now, it was old hat, and she shouldn't even blink at them, but there was always the slightest hitch of breath every time she stepped close to one before going through. And each time, there was that moment like when a rollercoaster has crested the first big hill, and though you know you are safe, everything in you screams to be let off the ride. That included going to see the games with her group.

"Do you know where this portal goes?" Mia said quietly to Luna as they stood in line. She figured if she didn't use her full voice, the hint of fear wouldn't be present.

"Scotland," Luna responded flatly.

"No, I know that. But where exactly? I know some of them drop off right outside the field, and others are farther out near the cities."

"Some are *in* the cities, actually." Luna turned to look at her. "As seniors, we are allowed to go to one or two of them, but the teachers are the only ones allowed to go to the others."

"Why only teachers?"

"Bars."

"Oh."

"This one lets us off on the Isle of Raasay." Luna appeared frustrated by the dreadfully slow pace of the line ahead of them.

Various security teams and professors were posted at each portal, checking with the students and making sure no weapons were leaving the school grounds. While that made sense, Mia was nervous about it. She always had her sai on her person, and not having them, heavy and cold, sitting in their holster on her back, was difficult for her to handle.

"We are going to meet Zander, Carson, and Vivi there," Luna added.

Since the other three had a different class than Mia and Luna, they had left for the portal earlier. Principal Elmhurst had moved the class schedule around for that one day so that they all had the afternoon off to go and watch their team's opening game.

"So, have you ever been there?" Mia asked as they took a small step forward. One of the students seemed to be in trouble for something in their backpack, and the audible groan from the line meant more waiting.

"A few times, actually. My grandfather owns part of a brewery in the Highlands. I hope I'll get a chance to see him while we're there. I've never been to any of the big cities, though. Too dangerous for fae to be out there with all the redcaps hanging around. At least in the Highlands, it's only boggarts and wood nymphs. And brownies, but they don't tend to bother anyone."

"Speaking of brownies, where's Cinder?" Mia asked.

"She went ahead with the rest of the group. As a faerie, she's allowed to go wherever she wants without anyone around and is pretty excited to go to the Isle of Skye."

"What's the Isle of Skye?" Mia asked, confused. She had heard a fair amount about the Isle of Raasay in the last few days, but this was new.

"It's where the faeries live. It's supposed to be gorgeous there, but no fae is allowed without an express invitation from the Faerie. Trust me, you do not want a faerie mad at you. But since the games are being held across the water from them, they have extended a blanket invitation to halfling students to come visit, provided they have someone escorting them. The only way a full fae is allowed at all is to escort the students, so there's been a lot of back and forth among the instructors as to who gets to do it. I know Elmhurst will be one of them."

"When you say faerie, do you mean pixies like Cinder? Or a different type of faerie?" The designations still confused Mia. They were all fae, but the word *faerie* seemed interchangeable at times.

Luna frowned and paused. "Yes, I can see how that would be confusing. A faerie is an adjective at times and used to describe most of the smaller creatures who are part of the larger fae group. But these faeries are cousins to pixies. Sometimes, they are even lumped into the same group. And, oddly enough, they look a lot alike."

Mia blinked a few times and processed what she just heard. "I don't think I'll ever get used to the fae and all of their weird names or designations. Why can't we all just be fae? Why do we have to have so many races?"

"Humph. I agree." Luna had always believed there was too much discrimination amongst the fae, but who was she to change up centuries of how they classified themselves?

"When I talked to Cassia, she said she would be attending some of the games. Maybe she could escort us?" Mia asked, not really trying to change the subject, but doing so anyway. Without her weapons, having Cassia around would cut down on a ton of the anxiety Mia was already feeling. Not that she didn't have a trick up her sleeve anyway, but it would still make her feel better.

"I don't think so. The faeries are pretty specific about this sort of thing. It's pretty rare they let anyone on their island at all, so I don't think Elmhurst or anyone else would risk it by letting Cassia in there," Luna said.

Mia frowned. "Looks like the line is finally moving," Mia said, her attention returning to the portal.

Students were now streaming through a bit faster, and Mia soon understood why. A second instructor, one she barely recognized from among the many faces she saw in the halls of the academy, had joined to check students through. In a matter of moments, Luna and Mia stood side-by-side, awaiting the go-ahead.

"No weapons or contraband of any type?" the male instructor asked, opening her bag and doing a cursory glance.

"No, I left the rocket launcher at home." Mia smiled wide. The instructor, who she now remembered was a law professor, did not seem pleased. He stood, stony-faced, looking at her in increasingly uncomfortable silence. Behind her, Mia heard Luna finish up and jump through the portal. "No, no weapons or contraband," Mia finally said.

"Go ahead," the humorless instructor said, and Mia snatched her bag and turned to the portal. A mild butterfly feeling ran through her stomach, and before she could let herself think about it any further, she jumped into the portal.

The best piece of advice Mia had received about portals was to close her eyes. It seemed simple enough, but something about the portals gave her a strange impulse to keep her eyes wide open, as though she might encounter an enemy in the vortex, and needed to see them to fight.

But in the split second it took to go from the grounds of the academy, just outside the cafeteria building, to the soft, cool grass of the Isle of Raasay, there were no enemies. No monsters. Only a blur of time and space and magic, like looking out from the inside of a blender. The sensation of moving very fast—like one of those roller coasters that went from stationary to a hundred miles an hour in seconds—then stopped, and she wavered on her feet for a moment before opening her eyes.

"Move out of the way," came an annoyed voice from behind her, and she realized she had been standing in front of the portal long enough for someone to come behind her and almost knock her over.

Mia spun around, muttering an apology, and stepped away. The Isle of Raasay was gorgeous, just like Luna had said. A lush green field of grass was broken in the middle by a gray winding road, weaving and turning toward the horizon.

On one side, the water sparkled in the sun, and when the light hit it at exactly the right angle, it looked like a sea of emeralds. Above it, wispy white clouds floated by in an endless blue sky, and the air was crisp, just the way Mia had wished for on campus. It was enough to make her pull her thin jacket around her tighter, and remind herself that next time, she needed something heavier.

Craggy rock formations grew from the ground at random, some rising many stories high, and formed shapes that resembled giants against the setting sun. There was magic here, not in the traditional sense of spells and curses, but the enchantment of the surroundings, which relaxed her, and piqued her interest in exploring it all at once.

"Mia, over here," Zander shouted from a few dozen yards away. Luna was nearly a third of the way there and turned to Mia, seemingly confused. She doubled back a few steps, and Mia met her halfway.

"I thought you were right behind me," Luna said, a slightly embarrassed smile on her face.

"Apparently." Mia smirked.

"Well, I was walking along, talking to nothing," Luna said, laughing. "Come on, the rest of the group is waiting for us."

As they reached the crew, Mia noticed Carson was decked out in full academy gear. His pants were school colors, and his sweater had ELMHURST emblazoned on the front, a pin just above the heart, and a big hat with ELMHURST across it as well. Of course, that was subdued compared to the neon, glowing and blinking fake glasses he was wearing.

"You look, uh...festive," Mia said.

"And you look boring," Carson responded. "It's called team spirit, Mia."

"It's called spending an hour in line because they have to check all those pockets and make sure your glasses aren't a bomb." Vivi pouted. "I wanted to be at the arena thirty minutes ago, but Mr. Showoff here had to put on every stupid thing in his closet."

"Well, it's a good thing, since we got held up as well," Luna said.

Vivi cracked a mirthless half-smile that said she likely would have pouted about that too but would have had no issue—zero—leaving Mia and Luna behind if possible.

"Well, we're all here now," Zander said, "so let's go get our tickets and get to the arena."

"Who has our tickets?" Mia asked.

"Elmhurst." Vivi's tone was gloomier. "It's like the world wants me to be miserable."

"She's just upset because she was hoping to squirrel away with one of those Highland team guys," Carson joked.

Vivi's glare spoke volumes about how realistic that scenario was. "She's going to be on top of us the entire time. I know it. Forget having fun, she'll shush us for cheering too hard," Vivi complained.

"Elmhurst will be fine. She's the one who insisted all the students get to go to our academy's games after all. If she didn't want us to have fun, she wouldn't have made it so easy to come." Zander was ever the voice of reason. Vivi seemed less than convinced.

As they walked toward the arena where the first game was set to begin, Mia took in the surroundings a little more. The peacefulness of the area was intoxicating, the type of peacefulness that didn't seem real. Certainly, the effect of magic was at work here, and she enjoyed the almost electric crackling in the air of so many beings capable of harnessing that elemental power all joining together in a place so full of it. Added to the picturesque view was the clean, crisp air tinged with salt from the sea, and Mia was certain this was the most perfect place she had ever been.

In the distance, the Isle of Skye called out to her, with its similar craggy shoreline and lush, green fields. Only the faerie went there unless expressly invited, Luna had said. Mia wanted to learn more, not just about the land but the people. The infamous story of the patricide that had created the Seelie and Unseelie intrigued her. So lost in her thoughts, Mia barely noticed a figure in the distance, watching her; unmoving, hands clasped behind her back. Until suddenly, recognition filled Mia's face.

It was Cassia. Beside her stood Elmhurst, and they were speaking to each other in low tones. When the group reached them, Cassia took Mia aside. Elmhurst motioned for the others to follow her, and Mia realized she would be playing catch up yet again.

"Hey, I just wanted to check in with you and let you know I was around," Cassia said.

"Thanks. Aren't you coming to the game?" Mia asked. Cassia looked around for a moment, appearing to be thinking about something.

"No, not today at least. I have some other things to take care of. Mia, just listen to me. Be careful out there. Stay with your group. And if you need me, I won't be too far away."

With that, Cassia left, and Mia returned to her friends, too excited to worry what Cassia's warning may have foretold.

CHAPTER FIFTY-SEVEN

Mia and her compatriots roamed around the dome in awe. The protective dome was erected over the area of the games to shield the events from humans, and to contain all the magic inside it. It was similar to the ones they had created on the academy campus when they had enjoyed the carnival celebration and the snowball fight, but much larger and more elaborate.

Those domes had only needed to shield the field behind the school building, or the field outside town when the Five used them to conceal their practice efforts. This dome was different. It had to contain the massive stadium structure which hosted the Slamball Championships as well as prevent passersby from noticing the major changes to the landscape in order to accommodate the Games.

Regulations regarding the stadiums used for the World Slamball Championships were very precise and had to be followed exactly. Much like the Olympics in the human world, cities vying to host the Games had to put in a bid many years before the championships. In that bid, they had to demonstrate they not only had a location with enough physical space to hold the stadium, but that any modifications necessary to fulfill the regulations could, and would, be made.

When it came to *this* arena, one of the major modifications needed to create the stadium was to level the ground. The natural rolling hills and moors of Scotland were not the right topography to build a Slamball stadium.

Fortunately, spells could perfectly level the ground to make it possible to build the stadium. After the conclusion of the games, The officials would put the land back the way it had been, and no one going past in the days to follow would be any the wiser.

But that did mean anyone familiar with the area would notice the major changes if there wasn't enough of a shielding precaution. Mia was surprised to learn, however, that all humans were not kept in the dark about the Games.

"Those people standing around at the edge of the grounds," she said casually, not wanting to sound confused or like she didn't know what was going on, even though that was exactly the case. "They didn't seem…"

She trailed off, and Zander looked at her with a smile. "Like us?" he offered.

Mia nodded. "Were they human?"

"Yep," Vivi answered, but didn't give any more explanation.

The dark-haired Unseelie reveled in the idea of knowing something Mia didn't. The stronger Mia became, and the more her powers revealed themselves, the more insecure and unsure of herself Vivi felt. She had worked her entire life to build her skills and become as strong as she was. Even with the uncomfortable reality of being forced to work alongside Seelie halflings, it was a tremendous honor to be chosen by Elmhurst.

Being part of the Scooby Gang was validation, confirmation that everything she did was worth it, and that her efforts would one day be rewarded. Then Mia had come along, unaware of who or what she was. She had no training and had instantly become the darling of the school. Even when she messed up, she was still adored and admired.

Gradually, Vivi was growing closer to Mia and didn't have quite the same level of disdain for her that she had when the red-headed halfling first appeared at the school. But that didn't mean she'd made a complete change. It still amused her and gave her a little extra boost when she knew something Mia didn't.

There was always that reminder that Vivi was born into the fae world and had spent her entire life knowing who she was. That gave her the connection to the culture, ways, and traditions which Mia was still trying to learn. This was one of those situations.

Mia stared at her, waiting for something more, but Vivi simply kept walking, pretending to be fully engrossed in the happenings all around them.

"Okay," Mia said after several seconds. "That was helpful. Thank you, Vivi."

Luna walked up beside Mia and shook her head. "Don't mind her. Yes, those are humans. They are the locals of the island who have lived here for generations. They all know what's going on."

"They know about the fae?" Mia asked, shocked.

"They do. Not only do they know about the fae, but they interact with them regularly. All of them come from families who have been serving the fae for many years. In fact, the first humans who ever came to the island were brought onto the island from the mainland, specifically for the purpose of serving the fae. Both sides have cooperated peacefully," Luna told her.

"So, they know about the Games?" Mia asked.

"Yes. That's why they're around. They know how important the championships are to us, and that we don't want to have any human interference. If it became a problem, or there were too many humans who caught wind of what was going on, there could be some very serious consequences. The Games might be discontinued. So, the locals on the island help every time there's a championship here. Their job is to stay near the edges of the grounds and keep the uninformed away. They come up with reasons why the area is being used and is inaccessible, and the humans trust them. They're very beneficial to us."

"And it's fun to do some human watching," Carson said. "You never know what they're going to do when they're around us."

It still struck Mia as strange to hear the other halflings talk about humans as if they were a somewhat foreign concept. Even the ones with close ties to the human sides of their families, or who were raised by their human parents, often talked about them as if they didn't fully understand them. But she supposed that was to be expected. They were raised in the ways of the fae and didn't have the same exposure to a fully human life that she'd had. For those who had spent most of their time with their fae parent, the world of the humans seemed odd.

"Can you believe this place?" Zander steered the conversation away from the humans as if he could tell it was making Mia uncomfortable. "They really went all out for the championships this year."

"It feels like it's been forever since the last one," Carson said.

"He only says that because his favorite team lost the last one, so he's decided to wipe it from his memory," Vivi quipped.

"I still say there were some funny dealings going on in that last game," Carson insisted. "That just didn't make any sense."

"They lost by fourteen points," Luna pointed out.

"Exactly! When does that ever happen?" Carson asked.

"When one team is nowhere near as good as the other," Zander said.

They all laughed and walked through the dome. The area where the games would be played was set up toward the back of the dome, with player dressing rooms and lounges behind it. The rest of the dome was filled with concession stands, merchandise booths, games, and vendors. All set up to appeal to the masses. Many of the spectators were already crushed into their seats in the stands.

Their general admission tickets meant they weren't going to risk ending up stuck in the top corners, or behind one of the advertising boards positioned strategically around the stadium. The students of the academy didn't have to worry about that.

Since their school had won the National Championships last year, they were considered VIPs. Each school had a specific section set aside for them in the stands. Almost as good as the exclusive boxes bought out by the wealthiest and most powerful families, these sections ensured the students had somewhere to sit to cheer on their classmates.

Elmhurst had used her name value to secure the most desirable spot for the Elmhurst students, and the Five were more than happy to take advantage of the privilege. It meant they didn't have to rush to their seats, and could enjoy the festivities before the game.

Carson eyed a giant inflatable set up nearby. People were climbing inside wearing harnesses and were attached to a large hook with a thick bungee cord. They could then run as fast as possible and see how far they could stretch before the cord won out and snapped them backward. His eyes widened, and he walked to it, waving to the others, telling them where he was going.

"I'll go with him," Vivi said in a resigned voice. "If he snaps himself in half, I'll let you know."

Luna laughed. "Let's all go watch."

Zander rested a hand on Mia's elbow. "You guys go ahead. I'm hungry. I want to check out what the concession booths have. Mia and I will bring back some snacks."

Luna and Vivi nodded, and they headed in opposite directions. Zander drew closer to Mia as they went to the long row of concession booths. He nudged against her slightly, and Mia smiled.

"Are you excited to finally be here?" he asked.

She nodded. "It's funny, I've never been here before or done anything like this. I never even heard of Slamball until coming to the academy and meeting you guys. But somehow, it feels like it's always been a part of my life. Like I've been waiting for these championships and have been excited along with the rest of you for all these years. Does that make sense?"

"I guess it's just a part of you. You're finally learning about where you come from and the types of things you should have been doing all your life. So, now you're excited to find out new things and feel like you're a part of it all," he told her.

Before Mia could answer, something caught her attention. "Well, *he* is certainly not feeling like he's a part of it all."

She pointed at a man wandering by, and Zander looked in his

direction. He was human and clearly *not* one of the locals in the know about what was happening. His wide eyes and an open mouth as he looked around said this man had no idea what was going on and was shocked by it all.

"How did he get in here?" Zander asked. "He must have wandered in with a group."

The man stopped in his tracks and stared at a group of vampires walking by. The dome protected them from the sunlight, which meant they could walk around without worrying. A few feet away, a tiny faerie spotted the man and the way he was looking at the groups around him. Knowing his presence could be a serious issue, she ran as fast as she could to talk to an official.

Hamish wasn't sure how to process everything going on around him. He was lured into the strange events happening and had followed a crowd into the carnival atmosphere. Around him, a variety of odd creatures roamed about. A gnome hurried past, carrying a massive container of popcorn. Pixies fluttered around his head, chattering to each other so fast he couldn't tell if they were speaking a different language or not. To one side, several people walked past, shifting into different forms as they went.

He was struggling to breathe and starting to feel dizzy. If he didn't know any better, he would have sworn he was living inside one of his video games.

"This can't be real. This can't be. But it is. They exist. They really do exist. All of them. They really do exist," he muttered to himself.

As he wandered and hyperventilated, the faerie reached one of the championship officials. "There's a situation," she told him. "A human is inside the dome. Not one of the locals."

"A human?" the official asked. "How did a human get inside? There are precautions set up."

"I know," the faerie said. "But something must have happened because he is inside. He's wandering around looking at the spectators."

"Something will need to be done about that."

CHAPTER FIFTY-EIGHT

Mia felt for the human man; he was so out of place and confused. He looked frightened as if he had no idea what he was supposed to do next. At one point, he turned toward the entrance to the dome but spotted a large group of vampires coming in, followed by a troll. Gasping, he backed up several steps and whipped around. He was obviously beginning to panic.

Mia felt terrible and wanted to reassure him. "I'll be right back," she said to Zander.

"Where are you going?"

Mia wasn't supposed to be alone at any point. The Games were crawling with security, but it wasn't enough for Elmhurst and Cassia. They wanted to make sure Mia was safe, and that meant keeping an eye on her every second. She couldn't be by herself at any time, even for an instant. It wouldn't take long for someone to snatch her and disappear through a portal where they wouldn't be able to find her.

"I want to go talk to him. He looks upset, and I may be able to help him." She headed for the man, and Zander jogged to catch up with her. "Hello," she said, approaching the human carefully.

Mia didn't want to startle him. He was already going through enough and looked as if even a little thing could spook him into total panic. She paused as he turned and slid his eyes over her, scrutinizing her.

With her red hair and friendly smile, she didn't look like anyone else around him, and he relaxed slightly. "Are you...human?" he asked.

"Um," she said. "Yes, I am of human descent."

It wasn't a lie. She was just glossing over the other half of her heritage. It would help to put him at ease if he didn't have to think of her as one of the strange, unexplainable creatures startling him.

"Okay," he said, but didn't seem confident.

Mia took another step toward him and extended her hand. "My name is Mia."

He took her hand, seemingly reassured by the recognizably human gesture of shaking hands when meeting someone. "I'm Hamish," he said.

"It's nice to meet you, Hamish."

He nodded. "You, too. Can I ask you something, Mia?"

"Of course."

"What is this place?" He lowered his voice and leaned slightly toward her when he asked the question, as though he was confiding in her and didn't want anyone else to hear him.

His gaze flickered over her head, and Mia glanced over her shoulder. Zander approached slowly, staring at Hamish. She recognized the look in his eyes. It was suspicious, gauging if he could be trusted to be that close to Mia.

She looked back at Hamish and gestured at Zander. "This is my friend Zander. We're here to watch the World Slamball Championships. That's what this is. The stadium itself is at the other end of the dome."

"So, all of you...you're here to watch a game?" Hamish asked.

"It's not just a game," Zander corrected him. "It's the World Championships. It only happens once every four years. That's why there are so many people here. And of so many different species."

"The dome was put into place as a precaution to prevent humans who don't know what's going on from coming here, and getting into the area," Mia added.

"Well, it doesn't seem like it did a terribly good job, now did it?" Hamish asked.

"It's not the dome's fault you came where you weren't supposed to," Zander said.

Mia looked at him and gave a subtle shake of her head, trying to stop him. It was flattering to have the smart, handsome Seelie halfling be so protective of her and want to make sure she was safe.

At that moment, though, she felt compelled to talk to this man and make sure he was all right. She understood that look of fear and uncertainty. It was so similar to what she had been through in Shanghai when she had first started noticing the unusual creatures she'd never seen before.

She highly doubted he was on the same sort of trajectory as hers. He was too old to suddenly be discovering he had a half-fae heritage, and there didn't seem to be anyone to guide him the way Cassia had done for her.

But that didn't lessen the fear he felt. If anything, wandering into this and having no one there to help would only make it worse. Maybe she could be there for him and help him deal with what he was going through.

It wasn't just curiosity about who this man was, or a desire to comfort him that led Mia to talk to Hamish. A part of her had reached a point where she questioned everything and everyone.

After uncovering the truth about Hazel, she was more aware than ever that the greatest dangers could be lurking right there in plain sight. As much as this man might seem like a hapless human who had somehow wandered his way into the Slamball Championships, he could also be a decoy. This could be the moment in which she was manipulated into being captured. She had to be on guard and stop that from happening.

"How did you get in here?" she asked. "Why did you come?"

Hamish shook his head. "I don't know. I just felt like I had to," he told her.

"What do you mean?" Mia asked.

"I can't really explain it. I just felt this pull to this part of the island, so I came here. It's like I just needed to be here," Hamish said.

At that moment, the faerie fluttered back, bringing three officials with her. Hamish's eyes widened as they faced him, and his body tensed defensively again.

"Sir, you're going to need to come with us," one of the officials said.

Hamish looked around him as though he was seeking out a way to escape. A second official held up a hand toward him.

"You don't have to be afraid. We aren't going to do anything to hurt you. We understand you came here by mistake and are out of your element, and just want to help you," he said.

Hamish hesitated for a few seconds, but he finally nodded. Mia watched as the officials and the faerie led him away. She turned to Zander. "What are they going to do to him?" she asked. "They aren't going to hurt him, are they?"

Zander shook his head reassuringly and steered her back toward the concession booths so they could complete the mission they had been on before her detour.

"No. They aren't going to hurt him. It's undesirable, and a little inconvenient, that he's here, but not criminal. And he didn't do anything threatening or damaging. They don't have any reason to hurt him. They'll just take him to the administration offices and wipe his memory. Then they'll send him home with the implanted idea that he wants to stay there for a few days. Hopefully, that will work, and he won't come back and wander into the Games again," he told her.

As they stood in line for nachos, Mia thought about what Hamish had said before the officials arrived. After a few moments, she realized Zander was staring at her. "Is everything okay?" she asked.

"I was about to ask you the same question. It looked like you were far away for a second there," he said.

Mia gave a short laugh. "I guess I was in a way."

"What do you mean?"

"I can't stop thinking about what Hamish said when I asked him how he got into the dome. He said he didn't know how he got in or why he came here. Just that he was drawn to this area and had to come. That's how I feel," she explained.

"Called to the Games?" Zander asked.

She shook her head. "No. Not to the Games. To the mainland. Something is calling me to Scotland, but I don't know where exactly. Not yet, anyway. I've never been before, and have always thought it was such a beautiful and fascinating place to read and learn about. Maybe that's it. I'm just drawn to explore the country."

"Or maybe you want to see the faerie pools," Zander suggested.

"What are faerie pools?" she asked.

Mia had heard several people whisper about them since their arrival, but didn't know what they were talking about. Before Zander could answer, the rest of the group showed up. They were laughing and bouncing off each other as they came, and when they got close, Carson's eyes grew huge.

"You should have seen it," he gushed. "I've never experienced anything like that. It was incredible."

Mia laughed and shook her head. "I love that you have had access to magic your entire life and have recently learned to manipulate it in some exceptional ways. Yet it's the power of a massive rubber band that really invigorates you."

"Come on," Vivi said. "We've got to get in there. I don't want to still be wandering around getting to our seats when it's about to start."

They headed to the stadium and went to the reserved section. As they were passing a row of students, Mia heard one whisper to the other. "I have to go see these mystical faerie pools. My grandmother used to tell me stories about them when I was little," he said.

Mia's ears perked up, and she zeroed in on the conversation.

"So did mine," another said. "I've been wanting to see them for as long as I can remember."

"What are they?" a third asked.

"They are pools in the domain of the faeries. But it's not just regular water. It's enchanted water. That water will cure you of anything you might have wrong with you. Even cancer. Just drinking the water, or swimming in it, will make you whole again," the first answered.

"I've heard if a human gets any on them, or drinks some, it will put them in a deep sleep for over a hundred years," the second said.

"No," another who hadn't spoken yet said. "That's not how the water in the faerie pools works. I've heard even the tiniest amount can lead a human, or even a halfling, to be under the thrall of the faeries for the rest of their lives."

Mia couldn't help but shudder. After seeing what Hazel had been through while under the thrall of Jose, the thought was horrifying. She hurried to catch up with the group and poked her head in between them. Sounding like she didn't know anything was wrong, as long as she could learn more about the famous pools everyone was talking about. "What are the faerie pools?" she asked.

Vivi gave a short laugh and shook her head. "Don't listen to them. They're all wrong. The water in the faerie pools won't do anything to a halfling."

They reached their seats and settled in. Luna looked at Mia.

"They were partially right. The water does affect humans. I obviously don't know for sure, but what I've heard is the water causes humans to fall into a deep sleep. It's short, though. Just long enough for the faeries to bring them to Faerie and force them to be their slaves. Sadly, humans don't last long in Faerie," she told her.

"Is it because of the food there? Someone told me the food in Faerie harms humans," Mia said.

"No," Vivi said. "It's the beasties. They will eat the humans." She said it matter-of-factly as if it was no big deal.

Beside her, Carson laughed. "You're all wrong."

"What do *you* know about it?" Zander asked.

Carson gave a smug grin and leaned back in his seat, looking out over the playing field. "You'll see when we go there."

CHAPTER FIFTY-NINE

"So, why do we call the Russian witch team the 'Wax Weirdos' again?" Mia asked in a rare lull in the action. The game had gone back and forth, a blur of passes and slam-dunks as Elmhurst Academy and the Russian Witch Academy team played a tough and physical game.

"Well, the person who founded the school was an old witch named Wetherwax. Nicknamed Wax for short. As for the weirdoes part, well, I think that's pretty self-explanatory," Carson said. "Even for witches, the Wax Weirdos are odd. They don't do a lot of the academy events where we all get together, and they seem pretty focused on staying at home and being, well...weird."

Time was ticking away in the game, and the score had stayed fairly even. The physical brutality of the two teams was somewhat alarming, considering it was only the first match of the tournament, but Carson and Zander seemed to think it could be rougher. At one point, Vivi lamented that the Elmhurst players had yet to seriously injure anyone, and Mia laughed before realizing the girl might have been serious. Slamball was a bit more intense than anything Mia had ever seen. Even the Wushu tournaments.

In the time since her first meet though, Mia had grown to quite like the game, and now nothing compared to being in an arena rooting for her school. For a few moments, everything else melted away. The studies, the tests, the looming danger of people like Narco, the guilt of lying to her father, everything else would disappear in a haze of adrenaline and euphoria when they won. And Elmhurst won a lot. The reason they were even in the tourney was they had won their division last year.

The clock was still moving, and it seemed to tick faster every time Elmhurst had the ball. Mia found herself biting her nails. It was a habit she thought she had grown out of as a child, but anticipation and anxiety over the score brought it back. Every time one team would take the lead, the other would thunder back and tie it up. When it seemed as if Elmhurst might take a commanding lead, a mysterious collision would happen, and only half the time would someone be penalized for it. As far as Luna was concerned, and very loudly so, the judges had it in for Elmhurst from the start.

A buzzing sound alerted the players that five minutes remained in the game, and the score was still tied. Mia caught herself whispering words of encouragement under her breath, words no one could possibly hear over the roar of the crowd, not to mention the various noisemakers some of them brought. How that didn't count as contraband, Mia was still trying to figure out. The time was slipping away, yet the score remained tied, and players from each side were becoming increasingly desperate. Only seconds remained.

One of the players for the Wax Witches had the ball and took a deep bounce on the trampoline to try to slam it in. An Elmhurst player soared up to meet them, in an attempt to block. The witch panicked and threw the ball in a high arc, directly into the hands of another Elmhurst player who was jumping into just the right spot.

But before the crowd could react, another witch player shot a weak spell at him, and the Elmhurst team-member crashed to the ground, narrowly missing the trampoline with the top half of his body before landing on the mat. Whistles blew the game to a stop for injury.

A gasp filled the stadium, and the group all stood on the benches to see what was happening. Unfortunately, the people in front of Mia were extraordinarily tall, so she tugged on Zander's arm until she got his attention. He looked at her briefly and then focused on the court.

"What's going on?" Mia asked.

"A foul. It has to be. If the refs can't see that, then someone needs to do a vision spell on them," Zander said.

From between the bodies of the two tall people in front of her, Mia could almost make out the head referee who held one hand up in the air to get everyone's attention, and then made a complicated motion with her hand near her mouth, which amplified it as if it were coming through a public address system.

"Personal foul on number twenty-two. That player has been eliminated from the game."

A roar of approval from the Elmhurst side of the arena rippled through the crowd and died when it got back to the witches' side. Mia watched as medics attended to the injured boy, who looked as if he was gingerly moving his arm due to a shoulder injury. The witch being escorted off the field, however, was laughing. Not only was she unremorseful, but she was also happy.

"Elmhurst will have the ball and a free throw," the referee announced.

A general settling down of the fans meant the line of sight opened again for Mia, so she sat. This shot was for the whole game. The time on the clock was almost up, and if the Elmhurst player scored, it was likely they would win. The player, who Mia recognized as a kid named Sam, bounced the ball a few times in preparation.

Sweat dripped from his matted hair, and he eyed the hoop. On one side of him stood an Elmhurst teammate, and on his other side, a Russian witch. When Sam took the shot, they would both bounce up there, ready to grab a rebound and take another crack at it before the buzzer meant the game was over.

Sam seemed to steady himself, and Mia focused on him. The stands grew warmer, and the sound died away. Everything blurred other than Sam, the ball and the basket, which were in hyper-focus.

Mia stared at the ball as Sam lifted it to take the shot. She focused hard on the ball, on the little circular dots texturing the ball. The lines that crossed it. The logo of the league. Then she felt something else. Eyes on her.

Everything faded back into reality and real-time all at once. She turned to see Zander staring at her. He knew what was going on, and he was hoping she would do it. Like the other time, where she helped Elmhurst win, Zander was watching her to see if she did it again. Her hand shot up to her mouth, and her eyes widened in shock as Sam made his move.

Zander slid over to her as the ball hit the rim and bounced up in the air. Both of the other players jumped to get near it, but the arc of the bounce took it straight up before it fell ever so slightly toward Mark, an Elmhurst team-member, who grabbed it and slammed it in with one mighty movement. Elmhurst had scored.

The roar of the crowd was deafening, and all around them, people were on their feet, high-fiving, and shouting. But Zander and Mia sat next to each other, his hand moving to touch her back.

"Are you all right?" he asked.

"Yes, I'm fine. I just realized what you meant last year."

"Shhh," Zander said. "Let's discuss all that later, okay?"

Mia nodded, and Zander offered her his hand. She took it and stood with him, just in time for Luna to turn around, a mask of excitement on her face and a squeal coming from deep within her.

"We did it," Luna shouted and wrapped Mia up in a tight hug.

"I know, it was so awesome," Mia responded. It was awesome. But something was bugging her.

"Now *that* was a pro-level move," exclaimed Carson. "But how in the hell did Mark and Sam pull that off? There's no way they could do that."

"Well, Sam missed the shot," Vivi said. "It was all Mark there. And Mark is better than you give him credit for."

"Please," Carson argued. "I've seen that kid miss dunks when he had no defenders. And that was the Weirdoes' best defender he dunked on. No way."

"Well, you saw it happen, Carson," Luna interrupted. "We won!"

Zander turned his head slightly to look at Mia. His eyebrow arched up questioningly. Mia shook her head firmly and smiled. It wasn't her.

"Well, either by luck or by talent, we won," Carson said. "And now we move on to the next game, and the Weirdo's are toast. I say we celebrate. Anybody else for a stroll through the faerie pools?"

"I don't think that's a good idea." Zander sounded disappointed as he looked at his watch. "It's getting late, and we still have class tonight."

"We could head over there this weekend, though," Luna suggested.

"Not a bad idea," Zander said. "Everybody in agreement?"

Nods of approval rounded the group, and they gathered their things for the trek back home. Once through the portal and back on campus, the group split off in different directions to prepare for their classes. Zander sidled up to Mia, though, and she slowed to give them a little space to talk alone.

"So that wasn't you?" Zander asked, his voice above a hoarse whisper.

"No, but you were right. I did manipulate the game last year. Not on purpose. It almost happened again tonight, but since I have a better handle on what magic feels like leaving my body, I was able to stop it. I could feel it building up when Sam was getting ready to toss the free throw. I wanted him to make the shot so badly. But I didn't know that other people could redirect the ball, and when he actually shot the ball, I had turned my attention to you."

"I saw," he said, with the hint of a smile. "But Carson has a point. That was a pro-level rebound and dunk by Mark. It was so smooth, so slick and perfectly timed, it just didn't feel like it was real."

Mia nodded.

"Hey, maybe they just worked on rebounds a lot this summer," Zander continued, his voice a little louder now, and seeming to break some of the tension in the conversation.

"Yeah, maybe," Mia said. "I saw them practicing an awful lot when we first got back to school."

"Maybe that's it, then," Zander said, his hands falling to his sides with a shrug.

"You don't seem so sure," Mia said.

"Well, let's suppose something *was* up. You didn't do it. And there are magical protections to keep players and fans from one side hexing the other. None of the other students can do it, for sure, so who does that leave? A fae in the audience? Or maybe a witch?"

"Why would a witch want their own team to lose?" Mia asked, confused.

"Exactly, it doesn't make sense. That brings us back to a fae. It had to be a fae, but who was it?"

Mia shook her head. With a shrug, Zander indicated he was as lost as she was. A few moments later, they said goodbye, and Mia stood alone under the setting sun, the oranges and reds painted across the sky calming her. She pulled her jacket around her tighter, noting with delight that some of the chill from Scotland had followed her home. Still, the pull to go back was strong, and she longed for tomorrow when there might be a chance to go again.

Zander was right. Something had happened tonight, and she didn't know what. But Mark making that play, so easily, and so perfectly timed, was a bit of a stretch. But who would have the motive, the ability, and the stealth, to pull it off? That was a mystery Mia couldn't figure out, but she did know Elmhurst was going to play at least one more game. And now, Mia knew what to look for.

CHAPTER SIXTY

Cassia sat back in the large leather chair in Elmhurst's office. It was stiff and hard, designed more for making students who had broken the rules feel even more anxious than it was for comfort, but she still tried to relax. She didn't give herself much time to sit anymore. If she wasn't eating or sleeping, she kept herself moving.

She had to keep looking, keep searching for the people who posed such a tremendous threat to her young halfling ward. Spending time with Mia over the summer had been wonderful, and had given them the chance to grow closer. It made the fae bounty hunter more devoted to ensuring Mia didn't fall into the wrong hands and get hurt. Cassia was exhausted and frustrated, but it wasn't stopping her.

"There's been no sign of him?" Elmhurst asked from her seat on the other side of the desk.

Cassia shook her head. "No. I haven't seen or heard anything from Narco in all the time I've been searching. It's worrying me."

"But, that's a good thing, isn't it?" the headmistress asked.

"It's good that he hasn't been around Mia, and hasn't tried to attack her. But it also means we haven't been able to stop him. If he's somewhere in hiding, staying away from her and from us, that's fine. The longer he stays away from her, the better. But if he is on the move, we may not see him coming. He has countless followers, and any of them could be helping to hide his tracks. They could be working to disguise what he's doing and where he is, so we don't know what to expect. How are we supposed to effectively protect Mia from an attack if we don't see it coming?" Cassia said.

"I don't think that's something you need to be worried about," Elmhurst assured her. "I know you're concerned about Mia, and you want to make sure she stays safe. That's the top priority for all of us, of course. But I have confidence in you and your associates. I know you'll be able to find Narco before he can get to Mia. And, besides that, I have full faith in Mia as well. I believe she and her friends can protect themselves. She is extraordinary, Cassia. Even more than you might understand. In the last few months, they have really devoted themselves to their work, and have come a long way. Their practice is paying off more every single day. It's becoming much easier for Mia to call on her powers, and to control them."

"Really?" Cassia asked.

"They haven't had a natural disaster since last semester. Not even a small windstorm. No fires. No floods. She hasn't accidentally hurt anyone. They have even managed to obtain the Power of 5 successfully on multiple occasions. They don't even have to do grade-school level spells anymore. Mia has not only managed to go from having no understanding of her powers and no skills to reach her grade-level abilities, to a place well beyond all expectations. I've even found her tutoring others in her grade to help them accomplish skills and spells they're struggling with. She will only keep growing stronger. I know she'll be able to handle herself," Elmhurst told her.

On the other side of campus, Mia, Zander, Luna, Carson, and Vivi, chatted as they walked to the library. The class they had inside the library was small and exclusive, one of the several invitation-only sessions designed for those in their senior year. The Five had been invited into one of these special classes solely for them to practice and study together.

As they approached the library, they heard Dan and Steve grumbling between themselves on their daytime perches. They fussed and groaned, lamenting at having to stay still all day long.

"It's not fair," Dan said. "The days are so much longer during the summer. We have to sit here all day, even when the sun is up for hours longer."

"I know," Steve agreed. "And that means the night hours are shorter, so we don't get as much time to be free. The rules should change with the time of year."

"But that would mean you would have to stay in place during the winter months when there are longer dark hours," Dan said. "We should be grateful that winter's coming, and the days are getting shorter."

"And what about cloudy weather and rain?" Steve demanded, ignoring Dan's comment.

"What about them?" Dan asked.

"They blot out a lot of the sunlight. They make it almost as dark as when it's nighttime. But do we get to get off our platforms when that's happening? No. We have to just stay here and get wet and be miserable," Steve snapped.

"The clouds aren't that bad. At least that means we don't have glare in our eyes," Dan tried to tell him.

"Look, I can resolve this for both of you." Vivi moved closer to both of them. "If you're tired of the weather, I can give Steve a burst of sunshine. And, Dan, I can make a cloud over just you. That way, both of you can have something different, and you won't have to complain."

Both gargoyles gasped. They turned their attention to her.

"Get bent!" Steve shouted.

"Yeah, Vivi, make like a tree and leave!" Dan joined in.

"Scram before I give you a knuckle sandwich!" Steve said.

"We don't need your kind of riffraff around here."

"You're nothing more than a dingleberry!" Steve shouted, and Dan burst into raucous laughter.

If he hadn't been attached to his pedestal, Dan would have tumbled backward with the intensity of his laughter. But Vivi merely stared at them in confusion. She was accustomed to them hurling insults and slang from the middle of the last century at them, but dingleberry was a new one. She glanced back at the group, but they shrugged. None of them had any answer for her.

"What are you talking about?" she asked. "What is a dingleberry?"

The gargoyles almost couldn't get themselves under control, but Dan finally managed to calm his laughter down enough to string words together. "You know those little poop balls that hang onto the hair around an animal's butthole?" he exclaimed. He barely got the words out of his mouth before bursting into laughter again.

Vivi's face grew hot and red, and she clenched her hands into tight fists at her sides. Anger and humiliation rushed up inside her, stinging the back of her neck.

"I really hope both of you are looking forward to a wet school year. I'm going to start a thunderstorm over both of you that no one can stop. As long as you're standing on those pedestals, it's going to be raining on you," she threatened.

Mia walked up beside her. "You know, Vivi, if you don't want the gargoyles mad at you, you really shouldn't tease them." She turned to the gargoyles. "You guys know she wouldn't actually do any of that to you, right?"

The stone statues blustered and stuttered, not ready to admit the Unseelie girl wouldn't carry out her threat.

"You've seen her," Dan said.

"You know the kinds of things she's done to us," Steve pointed out.

"Now, come on, guys. Vivi wouldn't do that to you without provocation," Mia added.

Behind her, Carson, Zander, and Luna laughed. Mia shot a glare over her shoulder. The three did their best to stifle their amusement and pull themselves together. Luna held her hand over her mouth, and Zander looked at his feet, but his shoulders were shaking.

Mia turned to the gargoyles. "Guys?" she asked.

"All right," Dan said grudgingly. "You're right."

"We'll just ignore her," Steve agreed.

Out of nowhere, Cinder zipped at Vivi's head. The little pixie was far from convinced of Vivi's innocence. "You better not hurt Dan and Steve!" she yelled, her voice a high-pitched screech

She zoomed around Vivi in a fast whirlwind, wagging one little finger at her. Just as she flew past her head again, Cinder sneezed. The tips of Vivi's hair caught fire. Luna gasped and ran to help before the other halfling went up in flames.

Before she could get there, Steve reached inside himself. Several weeks before, during one of the rare summer rains, he had opened his mouth—one of the few things he could still move while stuck on his pedestal—and had let it fill with water. He'd been holding it in case Vivi ever decided to play another practical joke on them again.

He hadn't planned on needing to use it to save her. But he did, dousing her with the water and putting out the sizzling flames. Vivi's hands balled up again, and she released an exasperated, infuriated sound, somewhere between a scream and a growl.

"How dare you?" she shouted, stomping her feet.

"Hey, I saved your hair by putting out the fire as quickly as I could," Steve pointed out. "You should be thanking me."

Vivi drew in a breath and stalked toward the dorms without saying another word. The other four exchanged glances. They knew she wouldn't be coming back any time soon. There was a brief moment when Mia and Luna considered following her, but it wouldn't do any good. Besides, they needed to go to class. Vivi brought these things on herself.

With as much as she messed with the gargoyles—and everyone else for that matter—eventually, it was going to come back on her. She should be happy it was something as simple as some water on her head.

They entered the class as the teacher was beginning her lecture. She looked at the four halflings. "Where's Vivi?"

"She had to go back to the dorm," Zander told her.

"There was an incident with Dan and Steve," Mia explained. "And Cinder."

The teacher looked at Luna for more information. "Cinder was worried about the gargoyles, and accidentally sneezed on Vivi's head, which set her hair on fire, so Steve dumped water on her head."

The teacher's gaze moved to Carson.

"Oh," he said, not expecting to need to add anything.

"It started because they called her a poop ball," Mia said.

The class erupted into laughter as they went to their seats. Carson leaned toward Mia.

"You should have made something up," he whispered. "This is going to make Vivi mad at you."

"Isn't she always mad at me, anyway?" Mia sighed.

"You're the one who told the class they called her a poop ball," Zander pointed out. "That probably isn't going to help."

Near the end of class, the teacher was still droning on about the same lecture she gave during the last session, trying to get some of the stragglers to understand. Luna moved closer to the group.

"I think we should start planning our trip to the Isle of Skye so we can learn more about the faeries and their pools," she whispered.

"I think we need to search the library for the truth about the water first," Zander suggested. "I want to know what we're getting ourselves into before we just go."

"I think that's a fantastic idea, Zander," the teacher said, over-hearing their conversation. "In keeping with the spirit of the Slamball Championships, I'm assigning all of you a report on Scotland. I want you to research how its history is intertwined with the fae and other supernatural elements. You're all dismissed."

Mia shrugged as she packed her bag. "I think the assignment is going to be interesting. We can find all the local lore and cross-reference those with the fae library. We can find out which stories are real. Or, at least as close to real as they get."

As they left the class area, she again felt the tug toward Scotland, and maybe even to the faerie pools.

CHAPTER SIXTY-ONE

"Fun assignment, huh?" Zander said, coming around the corner of a bookshelf and surprising Mia, who was deep into a chapter of a book.

She had grabbed the copy off the shelf at random, hoping anything with the words "Scotland" and "Faerie" in it might shed some light on both their assignment and the mysterious pool in Skye. A chapter had caught her attention, and she had been lost in a world of vampire lore when Zander's head popped into her peripheral vision, startling her so much she almost dropped the book.

"It is. It's complicated, though," she responded.

That analysis was growing more obvious the longer she worked on the project. The report they needed to do was on a broad subject. Researching the history of Scotland, and how it intertwined with the history of the fae and other supernatural creatures, was a long, long story, as she was finding out.

As interesting as it might be to read about the local lore with a thought to possibly exploring some of it during the Games, it still represented a challenge as a project. Especially since Vivi had checked out so far.

Usually, when Zander interrupted her thought process, Mia was all too willing to drop whatever it was and follow his lead. Yet, this time, her eyes returned to the page, as though magnetized. It was hard to let go of the world she was learning about, and the tug on her heartstrings to Scotland, and on her mind to the faerie pools, was strong.

Mia fought the urge to sit cross-legged in the aisle and read until the end of the class time. She shut the book a bit harder than she meant to and looked up at Zander, who was staring at her expectantly.

"Sorry," Mia said, shaking off the spell the book had put her under.

"So, Carson and Luna have wandered off into the lower level of the archives. We only have a few minutes left in class, so I was going to head down to them and see if they found anything. Want to come?"

"Sure." Mia tucked the book under her arm and picked up her bag.

They went deep into the library, which seemed to stretch on for miles. From what Mia understood, it actually did in a way. The building itself was so infused with magic that temporal holes in reality had been created in certain areas, allowing for exploitation by those who knew how to bend and shape forces in on themselves.

While on the outside, the library was only one large domed building, on the inside it was at least four times that size, and that was before counting the stairs leading underground to the second and third floors. The bottom floor was forbidden to anyone except teachers, professors, and visiting alumni, along with students who had a special pass.

Mia often wondered what magical texts were kept there. She had heard rumors of books that were sentient and needed to be caged since horrible creatures and terrible spells had been trapped inside them.

Though they were still on the first floor, Carson and Luna had gone deep into the stacks to a place Mia had never been before. Though she tried to keep up with the categories on the shelves, she was soon lost, and dependent on Zander to guide her.

He had spent far more time in the library than any of them. Thankfully, he seemed quite confident in where they were going.

They rounded a particularly odd sculpture, surrounded by old-looking books. Luna and Carson appeared in the distance, and Mia walked more confidently toward them. When they looked up and saw her, Carson's eyes shot to his watch, and panic crossed his face.

"Crickets! We only have five minutes left, and I have to get across campus for my next class. We've got to get out of here," Carson said.

Zander checked his watch too. Both he and Carson had the same class.

"Well, that was a waste of my time then," said a voice from behind Mia. She turned to Vivi, who looked less frazzled, her hair an inch or two shorter. "I'll just take this." She reached into the display with the statue and grabbed a particularly old book.

"Wait, what book is that?" Luna asked, suddenly intrigued. She went to Vivi, who held it out, turning it this way and that.

"I don't know, just something old as dirt. Probably boring too," Vivi said.

"That's bound with leather." Carson came up behind Luna.

They were all crowding around Vivi, staring down at the book. Even Vivi was starting to look more interested. Mia was close now, and she reached out to touch the cover.

The leather felt warm and smooth, like a high-backed chair in a fancy office. But old. She couldn't properly describe it, it just felt *old*. Older than old. Ancient. Like it was an artifact from another time.

"It looks like animal skin. They used to print them on animal skin centuries ago, but books that old are usually locked up in the special reference section. What is that doing out here?" said Luna, mesmerized.

"Maybe it's some kind of special edition reprint or something," Zander suggested.

"Yeah, because that's a thing," mocked Vivi. "I can't tell you about all those volumes of Ancient Texts of the Babylonian Fae that I got with special gold binding. My father joined one of those clubs where you can buy one for full price, and get a hundred others for a penny apiece."

"Then what in Faerie is it doing up here?" Carson asked.

"I don't know, but it's glowing," Zander said.

He was right. A small yellowish gleam had begun to emanate from the leather cover where Mia had placed her hand. The light was cold and silky, like putting on lotion, and when Vivi looked down, the glow had grown brighter and wider and was threatening to cover her hands.

She screamed and dropped the book. "What is that, what is that, what is that?"

Vivi ran for cover behind Carson, shaking her hands as if trying to get water off them. They all stared at the book where it now sat on the ground, unmoving. It was almost mocking in how normal it looked, lying there on the ground—as though the glowing had been an illusion.

"What do we do now?" Carson muttered.

Vivi was clutching the back of his shirt, peering over his shoulder, prepared to duck at the first sign of sentience displayed by the book.

"Someone has to pick it up," Zander said.

Various non-committal sounds came from Carson and Vivi. Luna, for her part, stood stock still. She was obviously interested in the book and was fighting the dual truths. A book that could harm her shouldn't possibly be where she could access it, and this book was most certainly not meant to be where she was.

"I'll do it." Mia had been expecting an outcry. When none came, she knelt to pick the book up, noting that, for what it was worth, *she* was being the brave one right now.

Or the stupid one. Most likely the stupid one.

As she wrapped her hands around the book, the glow returned, and she dropped it. She looked at the others and saw the curiosity mixed with mild panic on the faces of her friends.

On the one hand, the book had to be returned to where it belonged, and it certainly wasn't here. On the other, if this book belonged down on the third floor of the library, then it contained forbidden knowledge and was, therefore, what Mia wanted to see.

In spite of her own better judgment, she snatched the book up again and threw it open to a random page.

"Well?" said Vivi from just above Carson's shoulder.

"Is it full of ancient spells?" Zander asked.

"Or tales of the bloodlust of the Elder Ones?" Luna whispered. Zander, Vivi, and Carson all turned to her slowly, staring. "What? The Elder Ones were well known for having bloodlust. Do you guys not pay attention in class?"

But Mia didn't hear them. She was lost in the story, taking it in as if she were breathing in the words rather than reading them, and they became part of her, intertwining with her DNA with every letter. The story was intoxicating, and she stood transfixed until she felt Zander's hands on her shoulders as he was shaking her.

"Mmm-wha?" she said, coming out of her trance.

"Are you okay? What does the book say?" Zander asked.

Carson and Vivi had sat down at some point, Carson apparently forgoing his next class and risking punishment.

"I'm fine. Really." Mia paused and then looked at the book again. Just like the book about Scotland, this one had its own gravitational pull, and she had to force her eyes up to look into Zander's. "It's about a princess. A fae princess lost in the human realm. It's an ancient story, well before the last king and queen of faerie. Her name was Caledona. Princess Caledona."

She looked between the faces of the group and saw no recognition. No one had ever heard that name. Mia cleared her throat to go on, forcing herself not to look at the book again.

"She was brought up by the Picts. They thought she was the child of one of the local deities, but she wasn't. However, she helped them. Her powers let her make the crops grow, and the forests larger. She could help animals and bewitch men to do anything she wanted them to."

"Now we're talking. I could go for some men bewitching," Vivi said, snickering.

"She was most likely a fae child left behind," Zander suggested. "Maybe even a halfling. For a Pict, she would seem like a goddess. Especially considering that, to other species, fae all have an innate beauty. Even halflings."

CHAPTER SIXTY-TWO

"Will you shut up?" Vivi said, slapping Zander on the arm.

"Did you just hit me?" Zander asked incredulously.

"Yeah, and I'll do it again if you don't zip it. For once in her life, Mia has something interesting to say that has nothing to do with her setting everything on fire, or not being able to do a basic spell. So I, for one, would like to hear it."

"Thank you for that," Mia interrupted. Her stony expression toward Vivi was met with a similarly hard glare, and Mia decided to just move past it. Sitting in one of the ubiquitous chairs in the library, she thumbed through a couple of pages, her mouth moving with the words. "Okay, so this is interesting."

"Just get on with it, please," Vivi pleaded. Carson sat cross-legged in front of Mia, and Zander joined him. Luna followed suit, leaving only Vivi standing. She huffed loudly, looking at the rest of the group before plopping down herself. "Go on, tell us a story, you've got the spotlight, just like always."

Ignoring her, Mia cleared her throat.

"In the time of Princess Caledona, it was known there was no other creature like her under the stars," she read. "Thusly the natives of the land, the Picts, did worship her and made her their *bana-phri-*

onnsa, as the locals even now call her, a Gaelic word for 'princess.' There were many battles in which the Picts were dominant with her at their side. They held off more sophisticated and well-appointed armies twice their size, with their own simple archers and soldiers bearing only rocks and clubs. Stories remain of her ability to bend the sky and tame the land at will, to create light and fire from her hands. There was a battle the locals called 'The War of the Broken Water,' which solidified the legend near the beginning of her time.

"Though she was barely an adult, she came to the aid of her adopted people, joining them on the battle lines as an invader from the east raided them. The battlefield was littered with the bodies of many of the Picts, the broken and the dead, but with a movement of her hand, Princess Caledona brought forth the power of water in multiple forms. First, heavy snow fell, though it was the middle of the warm season, and it buried the enemy where they stood. Then she called upon the waters of the lakes, which filled the valley and became ice. The invaders were frozen in the water, and there perished of the cold. When all of the invaders, save two, had died, she unfroze the lake and allowed them to live if they would go back to their people with the warning that the Picts were under her protection. They did as she asked and were never seen there again.

"For every battle the Picts fought with her by their side, the Picts would find themselves victorious, against insurmountable odds. She could call down the rains and the fires of the Earth. Even the strong winds would bend to her will, and destroy the enemies of their tribe. Yet, with this power, they never tried to conquer more land or aggress against anyone else. They preferred to be left alone, to be left in the land their fathers settled. But the march of the Romans was soon at hand, and thus they faced enemies for many of their days.

"And so it went that Princess Caledona was laid to rest, having passed of nothing worse than the effect of age, the Roman armies were at their doorstep. Without her, the Picts fought to nearly the last man but succumbed to the armor and steel of the Roman armies. Within a matter of years, Romans, invaders from Ireland, and southern Scots claimed the land of the Picts and sent them away, most to the grave. Those who were left had to flee their land and live as wanderers. Yet, her story remains, and her name is

spoken of in many languages, but only in whispers, and by those who fear a return of the Princess of the Picts, and the revenge she could cast on the world.”

When the words stopped echoing in the chamber of the library, as one, the group felt the tension release. As Mia had read from the book, it was as though the room had grown smaller and warmer, and the outside world had lost focus.

Mia's voice grew in strength and tone, and she had commanded their attention. It was as if something within her had risen to the surface when the name of the Pict Princess was mentioned, and Vivi especially was intrigued. She eyed the book, watching intently as Mia closed it and lay it on her lap.

"Wow," Zander said, finally breaking the silence.

"Wow," Carson agreed.

"Do you think—" Mia began, then shrugged the thought away. But the question was too strong, the implication too large for her to ignore. "Do you think she could be an ancestor of mine?"

Mia looked at Zander, who gave a shrug and shook his head. Carson repeated the motion and brushed his hand through his hair. Vivi's eyes closed as she shook her head confidently. Only Luna didn't move. They all turned to her, and she shrugged, sighing.

"We don't know. We can't really. Not without knowing more about her heritage. I mean, you didn't even know you were a halfling, so we don't know that much about you. But most likely, Princess Caledona was the first-ever halfling," Luna said, finally.

"I need to know more about where I really come from," Mia said firmly. "I need to get to the bottom of this anyway, and this...something about this story, and the way I feel every time I think about Scotland—"

"You can't just go around telling people, though," Carson said. "Maybe you can talk to Cassia. Or Elmhurst. But nobody else. It's way too dangerous."

The group jumped to their feet and came closer to Mia. They were looking directly at her, but Vivi's eyes were somewhere else. They were on the book. Luna nudged her.

Vivi snapped her head toward Luna and glared at her. "What?" she asked.

"You haven't said anything about who Mia really is, have you?" Luna asked, a sharper tone than normal in her voice. "Not to anyone, right?"

"Ha!" Vivi exclaimed, moving back a half-step. "Why in the world would I do that? Not only would it get us *all* in hot water, but this is— I'll say it slowly, so you'll all understand—the single dumbest thing I have ever heard. I mean, look at her. It's Mia. Our darling, rather inept Mia, some sort of lost princess? Come on. Why would I spread gossip that makes someone else look good, if it has no benefit to me? It would make me look dumber than a box of rocks, anyway."

"True, you wouldn't want anyone else to be elevated above you, so I guess Mia's probably safe," Luna responded. This elicited a laugh from the boys and Mia, and finally, Vivi, who shook her head, smiling.

"Yeah, that's the problem. Me and my big ol' ego. Why would I say something to make Mia look good? Why wouldn't I just spread the rumor about myself? See? Dumb," Vivi replied.

Luna nodded and turned to Carson, who was muttering something about the class he was now hopelessly late for, and Vivi's attention left the conversation. Her eyes returned to the book, and they crawled over it hungrily. She needed that book, and she needed to see if her theory was right. Zander would never go for it, and neither would Carson, but if she could get the book back to her room, maybe, just maybe she could find out for herself.

"You should put that back," Zander said, breaking Vivi's concentration. She looked at him as he knelt and reached for the book. "May I?" he asked Mia, who nodded. He took the book and held it out to Vivi. "Since you're the one who found it, you should be able to figure out where it was placed and put it back there. Last thing we need is someone saying we broke into the archives and stole a restricted book. Here."

Vivi fought to keep her hands from shaking as she took the book from Zander. She wanted to snatch it and run back to her room. She wanted to find out right here, right now. She wanted to clear all this up before she drew another breath, but she had to play it cool. Zander was a good kid and was growing into a good man, but he was a stickler for rules. She needed to get him away before she could do anything.

"No problem," she said, blinking quite a few more times than necessary in an attempt to appeal with her feminine sensibilities.

"Do you have something stuck in your eye?" Zander asked quietly.

The smile, which had turned upward in an attempt to diffuse, now vanished from her face as she reeled from the insult. She turned her back on him and went to the display where she had found the book. The rest of the group joined her, and she feigned a critical examination of the arrangement, as though she were trying to figure out exactly how the book had been laid.

"We're going to head out. See you back at the room?" Luna asked.

"Yeah, I'll be right behind you. I just want to make sure this is perfect," Vivi said, placing the book on top of a stack of others, turning it a few times as if she was trying to get the angle right.

When the group was several steps away, she glanced at them to gauge the direction of their attention, and deciding they were all looking elsewhere, she stuffed the book in her bag and threw it over her shoulders. As soon as they rounded a large bookcase and could no longer see her, she rushed after them.

CHAPTER SIXTY-THREE

Mia was on edge throughout the walk from the library to the dorm. She had seen Vivi sneak the book into her bag, and was worried someone was going to catch the Five in the act.

Though there weren't any signs or anything that expressly said they weren't allowed to take the books out of that section of the library, she didn't think it took much of a stretch of the imagination to understand the point.

The books were kept in a section far away from everything else, and the barcode that should have been on the back of the book was missing. Mia had used the restricted-circulation research-books at the library in her human high school and knew how intense the librarians could be about those books staying safe. And those hadn't been bound in animal skin that glowed.

"Aren't you going to get into trouble if someone finds out you have that?" she asked, eyeing the book as Vivi curled up onto her bed to look at it.

The dark-haired girl was startled, then looked at Mia with an expression of false innocence. "Why would you think that? Would I ever do anything against the rules?" she asked.

Mia gave her an unconvinced glare. "Yes. Without thinking twice about it. But that's not the point. I'm thinking more along the lines of the fact that the book was in a hidden section of the library I didn't even know existed. And it doesn't exactly look like the rest of the books there. Besides, you didn't check it out. I wouldn't think you would need to smuggle a book out of the library if you were allowed to take it with you," Mia pointed out.

"All right. So I'm not technically allowed to have this book out of the non-circulating section of the library," Vivi said.

"I don't think that's a technicality. I think that's just a rule. What are you going to do if they figure out it was you?"

"How are they going to figure that out?" Vivi asked.

"I don't know. Magic detectors?"

Luna laughed. "They don't have magic detectors the way they have metal detectors in the human world."

"It's going to be fine," Vivi assured her. "No one is going to go looking for this musty old book. And even if they do, there's no way they are going to figure out I took it."

"And if they do?" Mia asked.

"I'll blame it on you," she said matter-of-factly, shrugging as she looked at the book again.

"What?" Mia snapped.

"I'll just tell them you were so enthusiastic about the project you wanted to do extra research. And since you are not as knowledgeable and well-versed about the school as we are, you didn't know you weren't allowed to take those books out. You put it in your backpack, and we didn't know you had it until we came back to the dorm and saw you with it," Vivi said.

Mia stared back at her for a few seconds and blinked. "You can't be serious."

"She's not," Luna said.

"But even if I was, it's not like you'd get in any trouble. You get away with everything around here," Vivi pointed out.

"That's not exactly true," Mia said.

"It doesn't matter. You're not going to get in any trouble because no one is going to find out."

"Why did you take it anyway?" Luna asked. "I thought you didn't believe Mia was descended from Princess Caledona."

"I don't. But I can't help but notice that this book seems to react to her." She held the book out toward Mia. "It illuminated when you touched it. Maybe there's a special message in it for you."

Mia took the book. Just as it did before, the book gave off a glow when she touched it. She didn't know what it meant, but it stirred something inside her.

"What kind of message could it have?" she asked. "No words are showing up on it, or anything. I don't think I see anything in it that you don't."

"Maybe it's not just that you touch it," Vivi said. "Maybe the illumination is just pointing out that there is something special about you and the book combined. We have to do something else to make it reveal itself."

"Like what?" Luna asked.

Vivi thought for a few seconds before her eyes widened. "Blood."

"Excuse me?" Mia asked.

"Blood," Vivi said again.

"I was afraid that's what you said," Mia said.

"What do you mean?" Luna asked. "Why are you talking about blood?"

"Maybe the book will respond to her blood. If there really is something special about Mia, if she really is royal, then it is literally in her blood. That could be what it takes to reveal the meaning of the book."

"And how exactly do you suggest we find something like that out?" Mia asked.

Vivi shrugged nonchalantly. "I have a knife. We can just cut your hand and collect some of the blood. We'll put it on the book and see what, if anything, it does to it."

Mia and Luna laughed, shaking their heads at the absurd suggestion. Vivi looked back at them with a blank look on her face, then crawled to the edge of her bed. She opened the drawer of her nightstand, reached in, and pulled out what looked like a dagger. The laughter instantly died, and a painful lump formed in Mia's throat when she realized Vivi was serious. She recoiled from Vivi and stared wide-eyed at Luna.

"Vivi, be serious," Luna said.

"I am." Vivi presented the knife. "Come on. It won't be deep. Just big enough to get some blood. I'm not asking for a full-on deluge or anything. A few drops should be enough for the book to reveal its secrets if there are any. I'll do it in the heel of your hand. You'll barely feel it." She waited for an acknowledgment. "Okay, you can do it yourself then. That might make it easier for you. Just a quick cut, and it will be over."

"Absolutely not," Mia said. "I don't care what your theory is. I'm not going to slice open my hand to test it out."

Vivi sighed. "Fine. It was just a thought." She put the knife back in the drawer and closed it.

"Thank you," Mia said.

"You know, using blood in a situation like this really isn't all that strange," Vivi said. "At least, it didn't used to be."

"You've got to be kidding me," Mia snapped. "I'm not going to change my mind, Vivi. You're not going to convince me."

"Actually, she's right," Luna offered. "Not that I condone her suggestion or anything, but the ancient fae were into a lot of really strange stuff. Blood spells weren't out of the question."

"See?" Vivi asked. "It's legitimate. Some magic is designed to only work for a very specific person. And the only way to prove you are that person is to offer some of your blood."

"Yes, Vivi, but that was more than two thousand years ago," Luna said. "I don't really think those kinds of things apply anymore. It could be really dangerous. Not just cutting Mia, which has its own problems, but what the blood might do to the book. We have no real idea why the book illuminates when she touches it, or what that might mean. We can't do something as drastic as put her blood on the book without having someone more knowledgeable and skilled with us. It could be really dangerous."

"Yeah, you said that," Vivi pointed out. "Come on, Mia. Aren't you just a little bit curious about what might happen?"

Mia shook her head. "I don't want to do it. I'm not familiar with anything like this, and I don't feel comfortable trying it."

She held the book out to Vivi, who sighed and took it. "All right. We won't," she said, putting the book away.

The three girls were so invested in their conversation that they didn't notice they weren't the only ones in their dorm room. A little creature flitted around, paying close attention to everything they were saying. She took it all in, listening to their words, watching the way they looked at each other.

Cinder listened carefully to the girls talking about the book, and to Vivi trying to convince them to do the blood spell. There was so much more to all of this than they knew. She knew more, but she wasn't going to say anything to them. She didn't want to come right out and reveal everything she knew. At the same time, Mia deserved to know.

The little pixie tossed the situation around in her head. She debated the importance of telling Mia and making sure she understood. Finally, she decided she would tell Mia, but not the others. They shouldn't know. At least, not yet.

That meant she needed to watch Mia and find a time when she wasn't surrounded by the other halflings so she could talk to her. Once it was just the two of them, Cinder would tell her what she knew.

CHAPTER SIXTY-FOUR

Classes always seemed to take longer on Fridays. By the time she had completed her third month at the academy, Mia was all but convinced that was by design. She figured the teachers sometimes didn't accomplish enough during the week and didn't want to drag their lesson plans and projects into the next week.

Rather than cutting the amount of work they had for the students short, they used magic to extend the lessons on Friday without the clock actually showing the minutes passing. Mia hadn't shared that particular theory with any of the others, but it came back to mind every single week of the school year.

This Friday seemed especially long and tiresome. It was as though the teacher knew they were all distracted by The Games and weren't going to be paying much attention to their schoolwork until the championships were over. She wanted to stuff as much information as she possibly could into this week of classes before releasing them into the weekend.

By the time the lesson ended, Mia felt like she had been sitting in that same class for days. She slung her backpack over her shoulder and dragged herself from the classroom to meet with the others.

Zander looked energetic and excited as he joined her.

"What are you so happy about?" she asked. "Weren't we in the same class?"

Zander laughed. "Yes. But I'm still in a good mood."

"You're always in a good mood," Carson said, sounding as exhausted as Mia felt when he walked up to them. "It's kind of disgusting."

Zander shot him a look of mock anger. "Be nice, or I won't take you with me," he said. His voice was almost sing-songy as if he was baiting them. But it worked.

"Take us where?" Vivi asked.

"It's Friday, isn't it?" Zander asked. "I think it's time for some fun. And it just so happens I made us reservations."

"Reservations?" Mia asked.

"On the Isle of Skye. I secured a site for us to camp for the weekend. That way, we don't have to come back here every night. It will save us a lot of hassle, and we'll be able to experience more of the fun. There are two tents there waiting for us, and I have all the rest of the gear we'll need in my dorm room. My father had it delivered to me today," Zander announced.

His extremely wealthy human father always ensured that Zander had what he wanted and needed. This was especially true when his son accomplished something impressive at school. Considering how rapidly Zander and the Five were progressing in their studies and their skills, this was frequent. He was very proud of his son, and with his tremendously powerful position working for the fae, he earned the money and privilege to provide for Zander.

It didn't surprise Mia that Zander would do everything he could to make sure their experience with The Games was the best it could be. But she also knew Zander still longed to know his mother, the fae woman who had abandoned him at birth. It was only natural that he would want to know why she didn't want to be a part of his life.

"Camping? You made us reservations to go camping at the games?" Mia asked.

"Count me in!" Cinder appeared unexpectedly and startled the group.

Zander smiled. "Of course, you're always included, squirt."

Cinder's eyes narrowed, and she clenched her fists against her sides. "I'm warning you."

"All right, knock it off, you two." Mia chuckled and looked at the expression on Carson's face, hoping he wasn't upset about Cinder tagging along. She liked having her pixie friend along with them. Plus, since she was related to the faeries who guarded the pools, Mia believed it would be helpful having her along.

Carson's mouth fell open. "Isn't that against the rules?"

Cinder crossed her arms over her chest and hmphed. "I'm allowed to go anywhere I want."

Mia thought Cinder's pouty face was cute and had to hold back a giggle. "Cinder, I think he's asking about us camping for the weekend."

"Oh, well. Yeah. I think that might be against the rules. You should probably get permission from Elmhurst first." Cinder nodded and flew away from the group in order to watch them all. She wasn't sure what they were up to, but she would keep an eye on them and do her best to protect Mia. Even if that meant she had to protect the girl from the stupidity of her friends.

Zander made a slight face and shrugged as they walked toward the dorms. "Technically speaking, I guess Elmhurst never actually said we were allowed to stay on the island during the weekend. What she did say was that we had to make sure we were in all of our classes during the week. There are no classes during the weekend, so we're not breaking those rules. She never mentioned anything about us having to sleep in our own beds every night, did she?"

"Nope. Not a word," Carson said with a wide grin. His exhaustion had vanished now that he was looking ahead to a weekend of camping at The Games. "She said we had permission to be in Scotland for the weekend so we could watch the Championships. I know I personally take that as meaning we can stay the night, as well."

"Are you sure about this?" Luna asked.

"Elmhurst didn't say we had to sleep at the academy," Vivi said. "And she said we could be in Scotland for the weekend."

"But you know she expects us to be in our rooms."

"Does she?" Zander asked.

He winked at Mia, and she blushed, looking away. "I think we should do it," she said. "It will be great to be there for the whole thing. And just think of how much research we're going to be able to do for our projects."

Luna finally relented. "All right. Let's pack."

They split up to get ready. They packed their clothes and toiletries quickly and met in front of the dorm building. Sleeping bags, blankets, lanterns, and cooking supplies, were piled at their feet. Mia didn't want anyone to see their gear. Although she had agreed to go and was excited about it, she had the nagging feeling in the back of her mind that they weren't supposed to be doing this.

It wasn't enough to stop her, though. She was too excited about going. The lure of Scotland was growing stronger, and she wanted to see what might be waiting for them there.

Their campsite was on the Isle of Skye, overlooking the Hebrides Sea. It was close to Glenbrittle, where the faerie pools were located. They dropped off their bags, and Mia turned to look at the ocean. The view was gorgeous, and she could see the Isle of Raasay, where they would go to watch The Games.

The two tents waiting for them were larger than Mia had expected and looked as comfortable as she could imagine tent-camping out here could be. But she braced for Vivi's evaluation of the sparse accommodations. There wasn't much by way of luxury going on, and while Mia thought of it as part of the experience, she didn't believe the Unseelie girl would be quite as understanding.

It seemed the others were expecting the same thing. Carson looked at her out of the corner of his eye as he unzipped the tent assigned to the boys, and tossed his bag inside, and Zander also watched her as he started building a rock circle for a fire pit.

But it turned out Vivi wasn't the one who complained about their situation. Instead, it was Luna. She stood back from the site and stared at the tents with distaste.

"What's wrong?" Mia asked.

"I just can't believe this is where we're staying for the whole weekend," Luna said.

"What's wrong with it?" Carson asked. "Look. The tents are even on platforms. We're going for the full pampering camping experience here."

"Yeah," Luna said. "The tents are fine, I guess. But I hate the thought of not having running water."

Carson scoffed. "We're not asking you to turn the woods into your own personal facilities, or to take a bath in the ocean, Luna. There are bathrooms with indoor plumbing, shower rooms, and everything."

Now it was time for Vivi to start voicing her opinion. "Shower rooms?" she said in disgust. "Ugh. I didn't think about us having to shower with other people. I really don't want to do that."

"You do it at school," Zander pointed out. "Why is it all right to do it there every day, but not here for a weekend?"

Vivi straightened and rolled her eyes at him as if she simply couldn't fathom why he didn't understand the issue. "That's not the same thing. There is a big difference between sharing a bathroom on a floor of halflings we know and go to school with, and showering in front of a bunch of women we've never even met."

Zander and Carson exchanged glances, unconvinced by the argument.

"Boys just don't get it," Luna said. "They probably would be perfectly fine with turning the woods into their own personal facilities and taking baths in the ocean."

Carson's words sounded more unpleasant coming out of her mouth. Zander sighed and looked at Mia. "You get it, don't you?" he asked.

Mia shrugged. "Sorry. I'm with the girls on this one. The tents are really nice, and I'm excited to be camping. But when it comes to showering with strangers, I'm siding with Vivi. But, I will say this is much better than having to trek back to the school every day."

The others nodded in agreement.

"Definitely," Zander said. "Especially since we aren't allowed to make our own portals anywhere on Earth. It would have been so much simpler if we could just get permission for you to make a portal to Scotland from your room. Then we could just go back and forth through it each day."

All five sighed, agreeing that would be so nice. Having their own personal portal would have made the travel so much easier, and they would get the benefit of being able to go whenever they wanted, and they wouldn't have to camp.

CHAPTER SIXTY-FIVE

Mia thought about the portals she had created when she hadn't meant to, well before she had fully understood what she was capable of. It had been such a shock at the time, and even now, she was still working on grasping the ability and creating portals reliably and effectively. This made her think of the others she created, and a blush came to her cheeks. She looked away to try to cover it, but Zander was watching her, and caught it.

"What is it, Mia?" he asked.

She sighed and shook her head. "It's really embarrassing."

"Tell us!" Vivi exclaimed. The others turned to stare at her, and she raised her shoulders. "What is camping for if not for sharing about ourselves and bonding?" she asked.

It was insincere, and so far out of Vivi's normal behavior that it was ludicrous, but they knew it was harmless and laughed.

"You don't have to tell us," Luna reassured her.

"But if you happen to have a good story and felt the need to divulge it, we wouldn't object," Carson said

Mia relented with a shake of her head and a smile. "All right. I'll tell you. I actually did make a portal over the summer."

"You're not supposed to do that," Luna pointed out. "Especially when you're not even on campus."

"I know. And after doing it, I think I probably know why. I figured since Elmhurst told us to do everything we could to practice our skills and strengthen our magic, it would be okay. Especially since I was with Cassia. She's a full fae and is trusted by Elmhurst. I thought it would be fine to get some practice in."

"Let me guess. It didn't go so well," Carson said.

"Not exactly. Well, not at first, anyway. The first couple of tries didn't go so great."

"You weren't able to make portals?" Vivi asked, clearly hoping Mia would admit she struggled. Somehow that would make it seem like Mia's strength and ability really did come from being on campus, or at least from being with the others.

"No. I was able to make them. That wasn't the problem. It was getting them to take me where I wanted to go that caused some issues," Mia said.

"Where did you end up?" Zander asked.

"In a creek," Mia admitted, hanging her head and covering her eyes. "One second, I was trying to send myself to the beach, and the next, I was on my back in a shallow creek. No injuries, thankfully." The other four giggled, and she smiled, feeling more relaxed now that she had admitted her struggles. "I don't know if that was better or worse than when I ended up in a cargo freighter."

"Did you see any pirates?" Carson asked.

They all stared at him, and his gaze flickered to each of them. "What? Pirates are cool."

They laughed, and Zander cocked his head a fraction. "What did you mean, that it didn't work out great *at first?*"

"Well, obviously, I was having a little bit of trouble to start with, but then I got hold of myself. I was able to create some that got me to just local places. Nothing too far away at first. Then I branched out some and was able to move a few states away at a time. But that was it. Nothing international worked for me."

"Where were you trying to go?" Vivi asked.

Mia didn't want to admit that she had been trying to return to Shanghai. She felt like she had unfinished business there and had wanted to see it again. "Just anywhere," she told Vivi.

"Well, if you were able to make all those portals during summer break, and Elmhurst didn't catch wind of it, you should be able to make some for us now," Carson said.

Mia shook her head. "No. Cassia was happy I was doing as well as I was. She agreed to talk to the headmistress about us being able to work together on making stronger, more effective portals during this semester, once the Narco situation is fully resolved. But until that happens, she agrees with Elmhurst. No portals. She gave me one stipulation. If there is mortal danger, and there's no other way out, I can try to make a portal. But that's a last-resort, a no-other-option thing."

"At least she's being reasonable." Vivi scoffed.

"Sort of. She went a little further. If I'm at school when it happens, I have to make a portal either to Elmhurst or to Cassia. I can't choose somewhere else," Mia added.

"What happens if both of them are in situations that put you in mortal danger too? Like, what if something happens to both Cassia and Elmhurst, and you're afraid for your life? It wouldn't make a whole lot of sense for you to portal yourself to the same place so you could be with them. And you shouldn't *not* get out of the danger because you wouldn't be headed to one of them. That seems a little counter-intuitive," Carson said.

"I don't think that was part of the planning," Mia said. "They probably figured if both of them were around me, I wasn't going to be in mortal danger. At least, that's what we're hoping."

"But it does still give you a loophole you could manipulate. What does serious danger mean, exactly? That could have all kinds of definitions," Carson pointed out.

"Absolutely not," Zander said. "We aren't going to have Mia make us a portal just because it would make things easier on us."

Carson made a face at him. "That's not what I meant. I'm just saying she probably shouldn't wait until the very second she feels like she is going to die and concentrate so much on making sure she gets to Elmhurst or Cassia."

"What do you mean?" Mia asked.

"No offense, Mia, but you aren't that great at making portals intentionally," Vivi said.

"I didn't hear you complaining about my portal-making skills when we were getting chased through the Louvre," Mia snapped. "They seemed to work out just fine for us then."

"Sort of. We traveled to different places in the museum, and still almost ended up getting killed. The point is, you can make a portal. I'll admit you are the only one of the five of us who can actually make one by yourself. But you're not great at doing it reliably, or at getting to a place you want to be."

"The five of us can do it together," Mia suggested. "If something dangerous happened and we needed to get away, we could combine our powers and make one to get us away to somewhere safer."

"With all of us concentrating on it, we could do it," Luna said.

"But it takes too long," Carson said. "Don't you remember how long it actually takes to make a usable portal when we merge our powers? If we're in danger, we're not going to want to stand around trying to achieve the Power of Five so we can portal our way to Elmhurst."

"Did you just argue against yourself?" Mia asked.

Carson paused. "I don't know."

"I think the point is if something happens and Mia is in serious danger, getting her out of the situation as fast as possible is going to be the top priority. She's proven her ability to use portals to get her out of danger when it's needed. But it's not something to play with," Zander said. "We don't want to try to use it just because she gets spooked, or wants a shower without thirty other people in the same room with her."

"So, we're in agreement," Mia said. "Portals are a last resort."

They all nodded, but she felt a heaviness hanging over them. She didn't want them thinking about the danger and the fear. She didn't want to think about Narco and all he had planned for her. They were in Scotland to have fun and to experience new things.

"Come on." Zander seemed to sense her discomfort. "Let's go to the faerie pools."

A short walk took them to the path that led to the pools. Mia was immediately in awe of the beauty surrounding her. The path wove gently into the distance, taking them through peat bogs and towering rocks. Waterfalls tumbled down some of the stones, sparkling in the sunlight and forming little pools in the crevices. It was all so beautiful, so mesmerizing, Mia almost wanted to stop and enjoy it. But every time she slowed down, Zander would gently pull on her hand, or Luna would laugh and coax her forward.

"Come on!" Luna said. "There's so much more."

"It's so amazing here," Mia said. "How could it be better?"

Zander tugged on her fingertips again. "Let's get to the actual pools and find out."

CHAPTER SIXTY-SIX

Something fluttered by at the edge of Mia's vision. It got her attention, and she tried to find it again, to no avail. It wasn't an insect or a bird, but something bright, small, and fluttery had zipped past her arm and disappeared into the woods just off the path. She strained her eyes to see, but it was either long gone or standing still, camouflaged by the trees, leaves, and tall grass.

"Mia?" Luna asked, stopping beside her on the path to scan her face with concern, trying to read her.

Mia shook her head and smiled, turning her attention away from the deep woods. "Hmm?"

"You were saying something," Luna said, still studying her face. She was looking at the spot Mia had been staring at. "Then you just stopped talking and started staring over there. Did you see something?"

"I don't think so," she said, and then something moved, zipping across the sky and down on the other side of the path. "Look!" she exclaimed, pointing.

The others, who were ahead of them, suddenly stopped in their tracks and tried to see what Mia was pointing at. Zander ran back to them, followed by Carson and Vivi, with Cinder zipping along over Carson's shoulder.

"Is that a faerie?" Vivi asked.

Ignoring her, Mia walked off the path toward the now stationary sprite, hovering above a patch of long weeds that covered the embankment of one of the pools.

"Hi there," she said, trying to sound as non-threatening as possible. "I'm a friend. Can you talk to us?"

The faerie, seemingly spooked, shot up in the air and dove again, corkscrewing into the pool and out of sight. Mia stared at the water for a moment and saw another faerie, or at least she assumed it was a different one, zipping out of the pool and flying off into the woods. No water came up with them. Not even a ripple in the stillness of the pool.

"I wonder if the pools are portals," said Mia, climbing back up onto the path,

"Duh, of course, they are," said Cinder, incredulously. "How do you think the faeries get from Faerie to Earth so fast all the time?"

There was a temporary silence as everyone turned to Cinder, and the attention made her cheeks flush. She folded her arms. "What?" Cinder exclaimed.

"Hold up one second..." Carson began to speak.

Mia took over when Carson failed to follow it up in his shock. "You mean to tell me that these faeries don't actually live on Earth? That they travel through these portals back and forth to where they live, in freaking Faerie?"

Now the red-faced Cinder turned her nose in the air and crossed her legs as her wings beat rapidly, keeping her floating in a position that made it look like she was sitting. "You really didn't know?" she asked huffily. "All this time you have known me, and all this studying you do, and you didn't know?"

"No, I did not," said Mia evenly.

"Neither did I." Zander backed her up.

"Even *I* didn't know that," muttered Luna.

"We all thought the fae who guarded the pools lived here and didn't go to Faerie," Vivi said.

Cinder looked at each of them, her tiny hand over her chest now, as if she was shocked. Then the shock turned to frustrated anger, and she gritted her teeth as she floated around them. Her voice, which was barely intelligible at the best of times, became a squeaking, high-pitched wall of noise as she dive-bombed between them, undoubtedly yelling at them all. But the more worked up she got, offended to the highest degree at their ignorance, she began to sneeze. Dust flew from her as she did so, and before long, the halflings' feet were leaving the ground.

"Uh, Cinder?" Carson called the pixie.

"Shh, let her figure it out," Vivi interrupted, and lay back, allowing the magic to float her in the air. "Just enjoy it."

"Hey, look at me. I'm Superman!" Zander shouted.

He was higher than the rest, faerie dust covering his hair where he had been the target of a direct sneeze. He was locked in a pose with one arm outstretched, hand balled in a fist, and his other cocked by his side. His legs were straight out, and he looked as though he was flying across the sky in one powerful motion.

"Yeah, well, I'm Peter Pan!" yelled Carson, suddenly getting into the spirit. "Thanks, Tink!" he shouted at Cinder, which only served to make her screeching even worse.

Luna and Mia floated lower than the others, having not been subjected to direct blasts of the pixie's dust. Still, it was enough to break the tension of the moment, and soon laughter filled the air and began to attract attention. Faeries began to close ranks around the pools, guarding them from the laughing, floating halflings wandering near them. They hadn't trusted them before, and now they had more reason not to.

Cinder, having yelled until her throat was hoarse, slowed down and slumped into a large open flower. She lay back for a moment before sitting up and waggling a finger at Carson one last time. She fell back again, exhausted. The group continued to enjoy the floating until the magic began to wear off, and when they all were on solid ground again, Zander went to Cinder and offered his hand.

"We're sorry, Cinder. Would you like to join us now?" he said.

Reluctantly, Cinder hopped into his hand, and he picked her up and placed her on his shoulder. This bit of respect seemed to appease her, and everyone returned to the path. Before long, faeries were popping up from the little pools and following them. Some hung back far away, watching with suspicious eyes, while others floated out of arm's reach.

As they neared the area outside the main pools, Vivi tugged at Mia's elbow. "Look, there's one of them over there behind that scrub brush between us and the stream. See it?"

"I do," Mia said.

"I'm going to try to catch it," Vivi said. "Watch."

"No, Vivi. I really don't think that's a good ide—" Mia was too late.

Vivi was already halfway down the path and almost at the spot where she had seen a faerie hiding. As she reached out to touch it, the faerie panicked, and a blast of dust filled the air. Unlike Cinder's dust, which either set something on fire or made things float, this was more explosive in nature. Vivi was flung backward fifteen feet and landed with a sound, not unlike a hammer being slammed into a custard pie.

Cinder began to laugh uproariously as everyone rushed to Vivi. She had been blown directly into a mud puddle in a bog and was now covered from head to toe in slick, brown goop. She was frantically trying to wipe it away with hands also covered in the stuff, which only served to remove some mud and replace it with more. A rather impressive series of expletives streamed from her mouth as she struggled to gain her footing, slipped, and fell back again.

"Will someone please help me?" she shouted, sitting there dejectedly.

Cinder was now laughing so hard, she was snorting, causing tiny bits of flame to shoot from her nose and land on dry leaves on the path. Tiny brush fires began to spring up, and within seconds, the group was shut off from returning to the path by a wall of yellow flame.

A sound like a hummingbird rattled and buzzed near Mia's ear as a faerie zipped by, casting some of her own dust on the flames and putting them out. A harsh, but unintelligible conversation was held between Cinder and the heroic faerie before it zipped along to Vivi in the mud while everyone else moved back onto the path.

"What did she say?" Carson whispered to Cinder.

"She scolded me for being careless," muttered Cinder, embarrassed.

The faerie helped Vivi out of the bog and back onto the path, and with a quick pass around her head, a spray of glittering dust fell on the girl that dissolved the mud in seconds. In the span of a few breaths, Vivi's clothes were dry, and only the faintest hint of her mud-scapade was visible underneath her fingernails.

"Thank you so much," Vivi said gratefully. "I really appreciate it, thank you."

It struck Mia how nice Vivi was being to the faerie. Sure, the faerie had just saved her more embarrassment, but still, Vivi being that nice to anyone was not to be expected. It was a remarkable transformation, and Mia wondered if, while Vivi may not be a friend yet, she could at least count on her now to be an ally, and the effect on her had been positive. Who knew, maybe by the end of the school year Vivi *could* be a friend after all.

CHAPTER SIXTY-SEVEN

The hike continued, and for the most part, the group was in high
spirits. All except for Cinder, that is. Most of the time, she sat
on Mia's shoulder, sulking, and when she didn't have her fist shoved
into her cheek, elbow resting on her thigh, she was sighing heavily
and crossing her arms over her chest.

Mia resisted the urge to talk to her and try to cheer her up. It
would only result in more huffing and puffing, and possibly a rant.
Not wanting her hair on fire, Mia opted for silence— better safe than
sorry.

Still, Mia wanted to find a way to get the pixie out of her funk, and
as the group walked closer to a large pool, Mia pushed ahead of them.
When she reached the very edge of the water, she looked down, seeing
her face reflected in the shimmering pale blue water. She watched
Cinder's reflection as the faerie took in her own image and smiled a
little. Mia suspected no matter how down Cinder was, she couldn't be
depressed around these pools.

"Cinder?" said someone from nearby. Both Mia and Cinder spun
toward the voice.

Cinder jumped up and stood on Mia's shoulders. She knew that
voice, but it had been a while since she had heard it. "Alania?" Cinder

exclaimed and took off from Mia's shoulders, diving toward the sound.

A bright purplish light rose from the high grass, and when she squinted, Mia could just make out the shape of another faerie. Cinder tackled her in mid-air, and they tumbled backward in an embrace, laughter filling the area and drawing the attention of the rest of the halflings, who were quickly approaching.

"What's going on?" Vivi asked.

"Beats me," Mia responded.

The two faeries shot back up into the air, chattering away at a speed and pitch that made it impossible for the halflings to understand. They stood in a slightly uncomfortable silence until Cinder realized she hadn't introduced them yet. Gliding down on gossamer wings, Cinder and Alania hovered between Mia and the crew.

"Everybody, this is Alania, my cousin!" Cinder exclaimed and wrapped her arms around Alania's neck in a tight hug.

"Shh, Cinder, you need to calm down. I am excited to see you too, but you know how the elders get," Alania responded.

"How do the elders get?" Zander asked, suddenly on the defensive.

"Oh, you're fine," Cinder said. "It's me they would be mad at. They would ask me to leave."

"Again," Alania added.

"Yes, again," grumbled Cinder. "Anyway, this is my cousin, and she's the best."

"We spent the first thirty years of our lives growing up together in Faerie. I got chosen to be a guardian in training and Cinder..." Alania's voice trailed away.

"I was punished for not having enough control of my powers and was sent to Elmhurst. So now you know the story, and if you say anything to anyone, I will light your nose-hairs on fire."

"That is an oddly specific, and wholly frightening threat," Carson said.

"There's a reason for that," Alania said.

The group waited for her to elaborate, but nothing followed, so Mia decided to move on. "Why Elmhurst?" Mia asked.

"Cinder has a knack, if you will, for cleaning. Her magic is especially suited to keeping things tidy, and they need all the help they can get in buildings filled with teenagers," Alania explained. "So, she was sent there as a favor to them, and as a sort of punishment for her."

"It worked out. I enjoy being there, and I got to meet you guys," Cinder said.

"Well, it's good to meet you, Alania. Any family of Cinder's is a friend to us," Zander said. "My name is Zander, and this is Carson, Vivi, Luna, and Mia."

Alania's eyes lingered a little longer on Mia, and it wasn't lost on her. It was as if the faerie saw something she didn't quite believe. She kept a close eye on Mia as she poked her cousin with her elbow and whispered to her.

"Hmm?" Cinder asked her as they glided back a few feet.

"Who is this Mia?" Alania asked in hushed tones.

"Oh, well, that's an interesting story," Cinder said, a bit louder than Alania had hoped for, and just loud enough for Mia to catch some of it. "It's a big secret. I'll tell you when nobody else is around."

Mia was about to ask Cinder what she had said and why she was being so secretive, but she was interrupted.

"Maybe you could help us," Luna said, getting the faerie's attention. "We are doing a class project on Scottish Fae lore. The faerie pools would make a really neat subject to do the paper on, and someone of your knowledge could really help get us the most comprehensive and accurate information about this wonderful place. I know as far as grades go, that would be an A for sure."

"Luna, do you have any idea how many students are going to be doing a paper on the pools?" Carson asked. "Like, everybody. All of the students are allowed to visit, which means *all of the students are going to visit*. They are all going to have the same idea. Even if none of them get the inside scoop from a real faerie, it's going to still end up being one of a million reports on the pools. We might bore our teacher to death."

"He has a point there," Vivi said. "We should try to find some other topic to write about."

A series of nods was enough to convince Luna. "Okay, fine. If not the pools, what else then?"

"Well," said Mia, after a moment or two of contemplative silence. "I would like to learn more about Princess Caledona."

At the mention of the princess, Alania's gaze snapped to Mia, and her jaw dropped. Mia didn't see it, but Cinder did, and she lifted her finger to shut her cousin's mouth. "What do you know about Princess Caledona?" Alania stammered at last, pushing Cinder's finger away.

"Not a whole lot, really. We found an ancient text in the school's library. One we thought was supposed to be in the restricted area, but it was out in plain sight. It was old, like really old, and seemed to be the writing of a historian from just after the time that the Romans conquered Scotland. It had one story about her in it, more of a small biography really. Just that she lived, was really powerful, and she helped the Picts, and that after she died, they were beaten back, and their land was conquered."

"Stolen," Alania muttered under her breath.

"What was that?" Vivi asked.

"Nothing. Go on."

"Well, that's it, really. There wasn't much else in the story, and we had never heard of her before then," Mia responded. "Is there something you know? It would really help us out for our project, and honestly, I'm just really intrigued."

For the first time since they had met the faerie, Alania was silent. It was odd, but the rest of the group was already deep in conversation, talking about how they would stretch out the story if they needed too, and who would be tasked with doing all the legwork to research the Roman Expansion. Which left Mia, Cinder, and Alania standing quietly together.

After a few moments, Cinder seemed to think of something. "So, how's the guardian thing going?"

"Great," Alania replied.

"Great? Just great? Nothing else?"

"What do you expect?" Alania said. "No one comes here except faerie. Until now, of course. I had yet to see any students before your friends showed up, but I've heard that others were filtering in and out. The boy is right though, most of them are trying to learn as much as possible about the pools. They all miss the magic stored in the forest trees. All they ever think of is the water."

"What about the trees?" Mia asked.

"The trees are of the Earth. They are concentrated with thousands of years of magic. The water just transfers energy, lets us make portals, and can be used for protection. But the trees are where the real magic lies. Without the trees, the pools become just simple water. The Picts knew that."

"Did Princess Caledona teach them?" Mia asked. Alania's lips pursed in a tight smile, and another moment of awkward silence followed.

Cinder patted Mia on the head in a way the little faerie probably intended as reassurance, but made the halfling feel like a puppy instead. Mia glared at her, but Cinder simply smiled.

"Don't worry about the princess," she said. "You have plenty of time. You'll find out more about the ancient girl, I promise."

Mia decided to let go of her frustration. "Do you think there's enough information out there for me to do a paper on Princess Caledona?" she asked.

Cinder nodded enthusiastically. "Definitely. You'll be able to find everything you need to write an amazing paper."

To the side, Alania's eyes widened, and one little hand slapped over her mouth to stop her from saying anything. She mumbled for a few seconds as if her voice was doing everything it could to push past her hand and get something out, but she was fighting to hold it back.

Cinder glanced at her, then looked back at Mia and smiled as she grabbed hold of Alania. She pulled her cousin back and dragged her away to a spot far enough from the group that they wouldn't be heard talking. Her gaze flickered back to the group, and she was relieved to see Mia already falling into a conversation with Luna rather than watching her.

"Be quiet!" she hissed at Alania.

"I didn't say anything," her cousin said.

"And you're not going to say anything. You can't. Nothing. Not a single word and not to anyone. Understand? Mia's life is already in danger," Cinder insisted.

"I'm not going to say anything," Alania agreed. "I won't tell anyone. And the faerie guardians will help protect her if Mia asks."

Cinder gave a slight sigh of relief. "Thank you. I appreciate your help."

CHAPTER SIXTY-EIGHT

The voice was almost like the shadows themselves. Narco watched the darkness around him shifting and morphing, moving with the wind and the will of the shadowy space around the trees. The branches reached out and clawed at each other, scraping and tangling as they moved and swayed with the rush of the air.

Fog swirled around them. It wove between the trees, climbing up higher into the top branches before sinking low where it crawled and slunk across the ground. It seemed to breathe, and if he listened closely, Narco could almost hear it whispering, but there were no words. It drew closer to him, pressing against his skin as though the forest drew in a breath. An instant later, it sank away again and dissipated into the trees.

The man in front of Narco moved slightly to one side, shifting his weight from one leg to the other. The shadows appeared to move with him. They combined with the shade cast from his hat to conceal his face. Narco couldn't see him fully, but it didn't matter. He knew who the man was, and he didn't need the confirmation of his eyes.

"What are you saying?" Narco growled.

"I can't just kill the girl without confirmation of her being a descendant of Princess Violet. Too many fae know about her. She is being talked about in circles all throughout Faerie," the man said.

"What do you mean she is being talked about?" Narco demanded.

"Some are curious about her abilities. They saw the video you posted and can't help but notice the types of things she was able to do. Things most halflings shouldn't be able to do at her point in their training. People are wondering about her," the man said.

"It will be fine," Narco replied. "It was only a video. There have been many more showing many other things."

"It wasn't just a video," the man snapped. "She is becoming too well-known. You should never have put that video up. Thank Faerie Elmhurst had it pulled down within just a few hours of it going up, but too many fae saw it. The reaction is spreading, and it isn't good. Some fae who saw it have stretched the truth on what she did, and people are believing them. Others are saying it was a hoax and don't think any of it really happened. But that doesn't matter. So many are gossiping about her, it's created a damaging situation. Your idiotic decision has made everything much more complicated. She can't just disappear or die. Not without good reason. Too many know of her and have questions about her abilities. They will notice, and it will come back."

"Then we have to make sure no one thinks anything strange. It can be done," Narco insisted.

"Remember, Narco, this is my assignment. You work for me. I control your destiny. Your future, or lack thereof, is in my hands. You don't want to disappoint me. With all you have done, and all the fae you have crossed, few would wonder what happened should something befall you," the man threatened.

His voice had lowered to an ominous, gravelly growl.

"It will all work out. It will be exactly as it is meant to be," Narco reassured him, almost stumbling over himself to try to appease the shadow man. "People can talk, but unless they have proof, they will soon forget what they thought they saw, or what it could mean. It will mean nothing when she's gone. People talk and make things up and try to find meaning in everything. There will be something else that comes along to distract them, and they won't give her another thought. So, when it is time for her to be eliminated, it won't be of any concern to any of them."

"I can only hope you're right," the shadow man said. "If you're not, there will be consequences."

"I understand," Narco said.

"And speaking of proof, I will need it from you. This is something that can't be taken lightly. It can't be guessed or estimated. I need you to bring me physical, irrefutable proof that this girl is a direct descendant of the royal line. I must have absolute proof that cannot be argued. Only then will I know for sure this girl is the one I have been looking for. Without that proof, I won't accept her. Do you understand?" the man asked.

"Yes. I understand," Narco told him. "I will get you proof. You will know she's the one. I'm sure of it."

The shadow man gave a slow nod, almost imperceptible within the movement of the darkness and fog around him. Narco only knew he was making the gesture by the slight tip of the dark edge of the hat toward him.

The nod wasn't fully a sign of confidence, or a show that the man believed in Narco and his assertions. It didn't mean he trusted Narco or thought he would come through and do what was expected of him. But it was an acknowledgment. It said he had heard what Narco had told him and was willing to at least give him the time and the opportunity to make it happen. It was all Narco could cling to for now.

Without another word, the man turned and walked away from him. Narco stayed in place, watching him as he disappeared into the trees and the shadows beyond. It almost looked as if the fog was reaching to take hold of him, pulling him in so the rest of the forest could swallow him whole. But Narco knew that couldn't be. The forest wouldn't want him.

"Proof," he muttered to himself when the man was out of sight. "He wants me to bring him physical proof. What does that even mean?"

He thought about it for a few seconds. His assignment was to bring the descendant of Princess Violet to his boss so she could be dealt with once and for all. But with all the mistakes and missteps along the way, the man had lost his confidence in Narco. He no longer trusted in Narco's skill or his reputation. He needed absolute proof that would ensure they had the right girl this time.

"The only thing that would truly prove lineage would be DNA. But would that really do anything? Do they have DNA on file for the last king and queen?" He considered his options for a moment. Maybe he could compare Mia's DNA to that of the Unseelie Queen?

He continued whispering to himself, trying to determine if going after Mia's DNA would have any real benefit. It would be definitive proof of her being a member of the royal family, but it wouldn't do any good if they didn't have any proven royal DNA to compare it to.

He thought about it for a few more minutes and didn't come up with any other idea for the type of proof the shadow man wanted. He wasn't exactly sure it was going to work, but it was all he could think of at the moment. He was going to get Mia's DNA.

All he had to do was come up with how he was going to get it. His mind drifted to that shock of strange red hair that set her so boldly apart from the other halflings. A few strands of that from her brush would be enough.

CHAPTER SIXTY-NINE

The walk along the path seemed to stretch out the longer they were on it. Mia wondered if that was the same type of effect as the classes on Fridays but in reverse. Their campsite didn't seem like it was far away from the faerie pools, but she was so excited to get to them and see what the fuss was all about, it seemed it took longer the closer they got. At least she had the fun of talking with her friends and looking at the lush surroundings as she went.

But finally, the path took a sharper slant upward, and they emerged from the tighter, peat-lined path to the open space of the pools. It was nothing short of breathtaking. Mia had seen beautiful things, and been amazed by the world around her before, but nothing like this.

Everything she had ever experienced, all she had ever seen, paled in comparison to the faerie pools. An array of pink, blue, and purple hues, filled the air, creating a shimmering mist around the large pools. Little waterfalls glinted in the sunlight and danced with reflections of the colors as they came down the side of the mountain, and poured into the pools. The sound around them was almost as entrancing as the sight. The water trickled along the rocks and bubbled into the pools, blending with the laughter of all the faeries playing among them.

They were everywhere. All around the water, perched on the rocks, flitting in the air, splashing in the pools, hundreds of little faeries with big eyes and swishing wings played. Some rode the waterfalls like slides, and others swirled in the spray that came off them. They giggled and whispered, all turning to watch the halflings as they came to the pools. Most of those big, wide eyes were focused directly on Mia. She felt like they knew something about her, almost as though they expected her to be there. And at the same time, there was an uncertainty about it, as if they weren't sure about her.

One flew up to them and bowed her head to Mia. The halfling was stunned by the little creature's appearance. Like with all faeries, she was beautiful, with a creamy complexion, and shimmery silver wings. But it wasn't her beauty that immediately caught Mia's attention. Instead, it was her hair. Flaming red, it tumbled down her shoulders and along her back. A bold reminder of Scotland, but also of Mia's own differences that made her stand out against the other halfling fae.

"Welcome, Mia and friends."

The greeting took Mia aback and she looked at the others around her. They stared back, as surprised as she was.

"Hello," Mia said. "How do you know my name?"

"I am Guardian Myla. I am the Head Guardian of the Faeries. It has been my responsibility, my duty, and my privilege, to guard the Faerie Pools against intruders for the last three thousand years."

"Three thousand years?" Mia asked, astonished by the incredible length of time.

"Yes. I became the head guardian just as the Romans invaded Caledonia."

Mia looked at Zander.

"Caledonia is the former name of Scotland," he whispered.

As soon as he said it, Mia remembered reading that in one of the books she was using for research. It was a brief mention, so short and inconsequential it hadn't even stuck with her as they continued their investigation. But now the memory made her think of something else.

"Was Princess Caledona named for the land?" she asked.

For several long seconds, the head guardian stared back at Mia. Mia felt scrutinized, as if in that stare, she was suddenly the only person who existed, and no one else mattered. The intentional focus in the faerie's eyes was almost too much, and Mia couldn't fathom what she might be thinking. Perhaps Mia had asked the wrong thing or brought up something she shouldn't have. But a huge grin broke out across Myla's lovely face, and she nodded happily.

"Yes," she said. "Yes, the land's first princess was named for the region. Princess Caledona. That's right. And now, welcome." She gestured to the water all around them. "Welcome to the faerie pools. I'm sure you have heard many stories about the amazing properties of the water. I cannot promise that what you have heard is true. I also cannot promise you that it is not. You are welcome to come closer and enjoy the waters. But be careful."

Her voice suddenly became more serious and intense. The five halflings had started walking toward the water but paused and looked at the head guardian.

"Be careful of what?" Zander asked.

"You must stay clear of certain pools. You cannot get anywhere near them, and should not touch the water. You shouldn't even let the spray from them touch your skin. The water is very powerful, and can be very dangerous to halflings," Myla cautioned them.

"Which pools?" Mia asked. "How will we know if we are getting near water that will hurt us?"

She wanted the guardian faerie to give them specific instructions, to point out the areas of the waters that weren't safe, but Myla didn't. Instead, she looked Mia directly in the eyes for another intense second, then glanced back at the faeries still playing in and around the pools.

"The faeries will tell you. Just pay attention to them, and they will let you know if you are getting too close to any of the dangerous areas."

"I'll keep an eye out for you, too," Carson said. "And make sure you're paying attention to what the faeries say."

"You're not getting in the water?" Vivi asked.

Carson shook his head. "No. I'm fine out here."

Zander eyed the water, his face uncertain. Mia moved closer to him. "Are you going to get in?" she asked hopefully.

"I want to," he acknowledged. "But I'm not sure about the cold."

"Oh, don't worry about that," Alania said, suddenly making herself known again after insisting on staying silent for the rest of the walk after her confrontation with Cinder. "The water is warm for those of fae descent. Even halflings. You should get in and enjoy it."

Luna and Vivi exchanged glances. Neither of them had made a move to get into the water. Mia suspected they were thinking about the halflings they had overheard talking in the stands at the slamball game, and the conflicting opinions they had all had on the effects of the water.

"What does the water do?" she asked. "Can it hurt us?"

"What do you mean?" Myla asked.

"We've heard a lot of things. Some people have told us the water can harm humans and even fae. You said that there are some pools that are dangerous to halflings, but are the other ones safe for us?" Vivi asked.

Around the halflings, the air filled with the tinkling, musical sound of hundreds of little faeries laughing at the question. One particularly young-looking faerie who was sitting on a rock laughed so hard she wrapped her arms around her stomach and toppled backward into the pool behind her. A spray of water came up after her, colored in hues of pink and purple, and filled with tiny specks of glitter.

"Those must have been some stories," Myla said. Then she smiled and gave them a conspiratorial, almost mischievous look. "Don't let it worry you. The faeries like to come up with those stories and spread them around for people to hear. We have to come up with some scary myths about the place, or too many fae would come in search of the mythic Water of Life."

That had all the halflings perking up. They looked at each other, their eyebrows raised as they silently asked each other if they knew what she was talking about.

When none of them volunteered any information to each other, Zander turned to Myla. "What is the Water of Life?"

The head guardian waved her graceful little hand dismissively.

"It's nothing. Only a myth. There is no true Water of Life. But it stems from the story of Princess Caledona, the first princess of the land Mia asked about. She was well-known and beloved in this region. She was unusual and alluring to all who knew her or even knew *of* her. There were many things about her that were truly amazing. Because she had so many powers and lived for hundreds of years, many people assumed she had found some way of extending her life. They thought perhaps she had been the one to discover the fountain of youth. But, alas, it didn't exist. There isn't any water source around here that will extend the life of a human. Not even one so wonderful as the Princess."

CHAPTER SEVENTY

The five halflings sagged, all a little deflated by the declaration from the head guardian.

"Well, that burst my bubble a little," Luna said. "It would have been fun to find out there really is a Fountain of Youth."

"You're still teenagers," Cinder pointed out. "Maybe you shouldn't start worrying about trying to figure out ways not to get older. At least, not yet."

The halflings laughed, and the girls again considered entering the water. But as soon as Luna and Vivi walked toward the nearest pool, Carson took several steps back. Mia saw the movement and the look of worry on his face. This was not like Carson at all. She had expected him to be the most enthusiastic about getting into the pools. In fact, she had been preparing herself to deal with him being ridiculous, to try to ride some of the waterfalls the way the faeries were.

She inched over to him. "What's wrong?" He shook his head, but she wasn't dissuaded. "Come on. Let's get in. I actually thought you were going to be the most troublesome of all of us. I figured it was a distinct possibility you were going to get yourself hurt messing around here, and we were going to have to explain it to Elmhurst."

"Thanks for your vote of confidence," Carson said flatly.

"What is it? What's wrong?" He shook his head again, easing farther away from the water. "You've been here before, haven't you?"

This time, Carson reacted. His eyes got slightly wider, and he gulped heavily. "As a small child."

Beside them, Myla suddenly laughed. She nodded. "Ah, yes. The boy who fell in." She laughed again, but Carson didn't seem to see any of the humor in the situation.

"What is that all about?" Zander asked. "What does she mean the boy who fell in?"

Carson didn't say anything, so Myla smiled at the group. "I thought I recognized Carson when I first saw him. Of course, it has been many years since I last saw him, and he has changed very much. But I will never forget when he was last here. He was a very small boy when he came here with his human family. The water has little meaning to humans, with the exception of some areas, but it is different for the halflings. Because Carson is a halfling, he was able to get close enough to the pools to find a portal. It fascinated him, of course, and he wanted to play. Before anyone was able to warn him or help him, he toppled off the rocks and into the water. The portal immediately took control of him and sent him to another place."

"Where did you go?" Mia asked Carson, but he shrugged and shook his head.

"I don't know," he said. "I know it was a portal and it took me somewhere, but I have no idea where. No one was able to tell me. I was terrified."

"One of the guardians was able to rescue him and bring him back. When he did, Carson told everyone wherever he had gone was full of monsters. Of course, none of them knew what he was talking about, and they figured he was just a frightened little boy trying to understand something he had never experienced before. But he was insistent. He described what he saw wherever the portal took him as monsters. His family took him and left," Myla said.

"And we never came back here," Carson said. "Can you blame me? They were monsters. At least, that's what they seemed like to me at the time. I don't know what they really were, but to my mind, when I was that little, they were monsters. It was the only way I could think of to describe them. They were absolutely horrible, and I was scared out of my mind. I think it might have scared my family even more. They knew what I was, of course, and that I was going to be different. I already knew of magic and had started playing with some silly little spells. But they didn't know what to think or do when that happened. It was the first time the fae half of me put me into a type of danger they weren't able to see or fend off for me."

"Do you think you went to Faerie?" Mia asked.

Myla's face became more serious, and she looked at the halflings pointedly. "There are portals here that go to very dangerous places. That is why we are here. It's not just to keep the visiting fae and humans from damaging the pools, or hurting themselves. They must be protected from the portals. We are here to guard the links. No one should go through them. Not ever. Those portals aren't safe for anyone and must be avoided. Carson was very fortunate that he was very young, and the guardians were watching him closely. The instant he fell, a guardian was already after him and was able to bring him back very quickly. He likely feels he was there for a long time, and it probably felt that way because of how frightening it was for him. But Carson was safe. He was brought back quickly, and couldn't be hurt. Others who have gone through were not that lucky."

She didn't expressly say Carson falling into the pool when he was young had sent him into a portal to Faerie, but all the halflings assumed that's what she meant. There were several seconds of tension before Carson took another step backward.

Mia knew it was best to let him be. Myla had started telling the story of his childhood visit as if it was a very funny event, but it had ended far more ominously. Carson wasn't going to go near the water, and Mia couldn't blame him. He was courageous enough to have come this far. He would be fine to sit on the rocks and watch his friends have fun.

Which was exactly what Zander wanted to do. He wasn't wasting any more time. He removed shoes and stepped into the water. He was cautious at first, not knowing how much he trusted Myla's assurance that the pools were warm. But when his toes touched the water, it was soothing, almost like bath-water. He sank the rest of his foot in and walked into the pool. The warmth enveloped him, and he sank down to his shoulders.

"Come on," he invited Mia. "It feels good."

She shook her head. "Not right now."

The story of the portal had been enough to take away her desire to enter the pools, at least for now, but she was enjoying watching Zander. Beside her, Luna appeared to have forgotten they were on a trip for the weekend and was back in school mode.

"What can you tell me about the history of the pools?" she asked a faerie who had come to settle on the rock beside Luna. "Did they always look like this? Have they changed much in the last three thousand years?"

"I thought we were here to enjoy the pools and have fun," Vivi pointed out.

"We agreed to stay for the weekend because it would give us so much time to explore and do research for our projects," Luna retorted.

Mia laughed. "Leave it to you to be very literal with that conversation."

"Covering all her bases," Zander said from the water.

"You'll all be jealous when we get back to school, and *I* have all the research," Luna teased. She turned her attention back to the faerie. "What about the rest of the area? What's the history of the island, and that area where we're camping? Did people used to live there?"

Mia chuckled and turned to watch Zander. He slid through the water slowly, appearing to revel in the feeling of it on his skin. Carson and Vivi were off somewhere together, and Mia continued to listen to Luna, and watch Zander for the next hour.

Suddenly, she sensed eyes on the back of her head. It felt like she was being watched. She assumed it was the faeries who had been fascinated by her since they had first arrived. They had been paying her a great deal of attention since the five had walked up to the pools. After a few seconds, she acknowledged it felt different. She wasn't just registering the little creatures' curiosity about her. The feeling was making the hair on her arms and the back of her neck stand on end.

It was a very strange sensation, different from the slight discomfort of having so many faeries watching her at once. She hated it. As much as she had wanted to see the pools when they had first arrived in Scotland, now all she wanted was to get away from them.

CHAPTER SEVENTY-ONE

"Hey, guys," Mia said. "I think maybe we should start heading back. It's getting dark."

Vivi and Carson appeared at her side. They had been walking around the pools, looking into the water, and talking with some of the faeries.

Luna stopped grilling the faerie sitting beside her, and looked around. "Wow. You're right. I didn't realize it was already getting so late," she said. "We should head back to our tents and get ready for bed."

"Yeah. We're getting up early for the games," Zander reminded them. "I forgot we already went to school all day today."

He climbed out of the pool and looked down at his soaked clothes. He shivered, suddenly cold now that he wasn't in the soothing heated water of the pool. One of the little faeries rushed up to him, and in a shower of sparkles, dried him off.

He smiled at her. "Thank you. That would have made for an unpleasant walk back to the campground."

"Speaking of which," Vivi said. "It's really dark. Did everybody bring a flashlight with them?"

Mia picked up her backpack, which was sitting at her feet, and unzipped it. She dug through the few things inside and found her flashlight at the bottom. She flipped it on and held it up for the others to see. "I've got mine," she said.

Zander checked up his bag and retrieved his own light. "I have mine, too," he announced.

Carson, Vivi, and Luna followed suit, and soon all five beams of light were shining up into the sky. As bright as the flashlights had seemed while they had still been surrounded by the colorful glows of the pools, it was quickly apparent they wouldn't be nearly as beneficial once they got onto the path leading back to the campsite.

"It won't be so long a walk this time," Myla reassured them. "When it gets dark, there is a small bus that comes to the bottom of this path to take visitors up the path to the campsites. It helps to keep visitors safe, and also prevents them from trying to remain here at the pools overnight."

"People aren't allowed at the pools at night?" Luna asked.

"It would not be safe." Myla didn't elaborate.

Several of the faeries gathered around them, and one fluttered closer. "We would be happy to guide you down the path," she offered.

"I will be with them as well," Cinder said.

Mia glanced at the pixie, realizing she had forgotten Cinder and her cousin Alania were there with them. They had been so quiet during the visit that they melded in with the rest of the faeries.

Myla smiled. "Thank you. Take them down and wait with them until the bus comes." She turned her attention to Mia again. "You are all welcome to visit again."

"Thank you," Mia said. "Perhaps we will."

With the faeries around them and the beams of their flashlights shining on the ground, the halflings walked back down the peat-lined path to the bus pickup point. Several yards along the path, Vivi gave the others a deliberate look. Her expression drew them closer so she could whisper without the faeries listening in.

"Did everyone else feel eyes on the backs of your heads while we were leaving?" she asked.

"I did," Mia admitted.

The others nodded, murmuring their own confirmations.

"It was really freaky," Carson said. "It was like someone was watching us. Someone other than the faeries."

Though the walk hadn't been very long to reach the pools in the first place, Mia found herself grateful for the idea of a ride back to the tents. She was tired and looked forward to settling in for the night. But, the way her mind was churning, she could only hope she would be able to relax.

Mia was relieved, almost two hours later, when they were changed, and tucked into their sleeping bags in the tent. She tried to push away the sensations of being watched, and the strange feelings of the pools, and concentrate on the next day. She was looking forward to seeing more of the sights of the Isle of Skye, and to go to the Isle of Raasay to watch the next phase of the competition.

As soon as the young halflings were far enough away from the pools that she could no longer see the beams of their flashlights shining through the darkness, Guardian Myla flew to the edge of the rocks. She burst to the front of a group of four fae to confront them. They had been watching Mia and her friends while they were at the pool.

"You are not welcome here," she said. "Leave now and never return."

The four didn't seem too concerned with her warning and only snickered at her. Alania and a small group of others flew up to Myla.

"Head Guardian, will you give us permission to remove them?" Alania requested.

Myla agreed with a nod. The other guardians soared over the fae males and sprinkled them with fine, shimmering dust. Immediately, they lifted off their feet and hovered in the air.

"What's happening?" one of them demanded. "What are you doing?"

"We were getting ready to leave," another said. "There's no need to play dirty."

The collection of faerie guardians didn't care about their protests. They giggled and flew higher over the floating men. They took delight in the confusion and fear the intruders showed as they looked around, trying to figure out what was happening. None of them had control over their bodies. They couldn't get themselves back to the ground or even move their arms enough to reach any of the tiny creatures above them. All they could do was continue to argue.

The faerie guardians sprinkled more of the dust over them, which put them completely under the faeries' control. The four fae could do nothing as the guardians flew toward one of the waterfalls, luring the floating men along with them with the enchantment of the spell. Once behind the waterfall, the faeries positioned themselves over a small pool. When the men looked down, all they saw were the rocks jutting out from the sides of the walls covering the water. They were terrified the faerie guardians were about to dash them against those stones.

Instead, the guardians flew sharply toward the water, taking the four fae along with them. At the last moment, they pulled up and used their combined magic to throw the men under the edge of the rocks, and into the water beneath. The fae broke through the surface and down into a very tight portal. Within seconds their screams were gone. The portal claimed them, and there was no one to save them. It took them down into a very dark, isolated place within Faerie.

Carson had been right; there were monsters in some of the portals.

Once the shadows found them, no one would ever see or hear from the four henchmen again.

When the sound of the screams was gone, and the guardians returned, Myla called out to a faerie who was standing at the edge of a pool, staring into the water. "Alania, may I have a word with you?"

The young faerie turned to her and nodded before coming over. "Yes, Head Guardian?" she asked.

"I think you should join your cousin Cinder, and keep an eye on the heir," Myla said. "But keep your reasons quiet. Don't give too much away."

"What should I tell Cinder?" Alania asked. "She knows I am

training to be a guardian. She will wonder what I'm doing so far away from the pools."

"Tell her you were granted leave to spend time with her, and to help keep them out of trouble during their time here in Scotland. Offer yourself as their tour guide. Your cousin doesn't spend much time here, does she?"

"No," Alania admitted. "She much prefers to be at the academy."

"Perfect. That means you know the island much better than she does, and certainly better than the halflings. Tell them you will be their tour guide and show them around the island. That one, Luna, seemed very interested in the history of the area. You can give them information and answer their questions. Just watch out for Mia and keep her safe."

Alania nodded and hurried off to join Cinder. Her cousin was staying in the tent with the girls and was surprised when Alania flew through the flap.

"Alania," Cinder said. "What are you doing here? Is everything all right?" Her eyes flashed to Mia and back to her cousin.

"Myla gave me leave from my guardian responsibilities and training so I can spend more time with you, Cinder. I thought you might like to have a tour guide." Alania smiled as she said it, hoping she was convincing. She thought they may be suspicious, but the girls were immediately excited.

"That would be fantastic!" Luna gushed.

"She could help us with our papers," Mia added.

"Oh, now you're excited about having someone help you with your work," Luna teased, and Mia tossed a pillow at her playfully.

"It could be really great," Vivi said. "She can show us things other people don't know about. Imagine all the possibilities."

Cinder looked at each of the girls, then back at her cousin. She nodded.

"Thanks. That could be fun."

CHAPTER SEVENTY-TWO

Narco stormed angrily through his study, his mind racing and his hands tingling with the fury rushing through him. He couldn't believe he hadn't heard anything yet. He had sent his henchmen out far too long ago to not have heard anything back from them. He had reached out to them, wanting an update on their patrols around the Slamball World Championships, searching for Mia and the others. But he'd heard nothing, and the longer he waited, the angrier he became.

He hated having to rely on other people while he sat around and waited for them to get back to him. It drove him to the edge of his sanity. There was nothing he could do about it right now. There was no way he could show himself at the games. Far too many people were looking for him. He would stand out and be captured. He had sent people he thought would provide him with information he could use.

"This is ridiculous!" he shouted, sweeping his arm across his desk to knock away the papers piled there. "How am I supposed to get anything done if they can't manage a simple task?"

Narco needed someone he trusted to be his eyes and ears at the games. They were swarming with students, and nothing would keep Mia away from them. If he could find out what she and her friends were doing and follow their patterns, he could finally capture and deliver her and complete the mission that had been hanging over him for so long.

But everyone he had sent kept failing him. None had been able to give him even the smallest bit of useful information, and every minute that ticked by reminded him of the meeting with the man in the shadows. The man's words kept repeating in Narco's mind, and he grew more anxious.

Finally, he couldn't take the waiting any longer. His henchmen weren't going to give him the update he needed and were doing him no good.

"If you want something done right, you have to do it yourself," he muttered.

He thought through the situation for several minutes, using what he knew about the championships and Mia to put together a glamour he thought might help him. It was compelling and made him look different at a glance.

But if anyone was to look too closely or know what they were looking for, they would see past it. The only thing he had going for him was that the weaker halflings couldn't see past glamours. As long as he could stay clear of officials, and any of the full fae who might be there, he would likely be fine.

It would at least give him some time to find her and put himself in a position to watch her. Once he found her, it would be a matter of not making himself obvious. There would be so many people at the games that he hoped to blend in with them and remain among the halflings who wouldn't recognize him.

If he stayed to the shadows and didn't draw too much attention to himself, he could keep an eye on Mia.

But he couldn't leave for the championships yet. Before he went to the games, he had something else to do. The need for proof for his boss hadn't left his mind. He still hadn't come up with any other means of proof besides DNA. Which meant he had to get Mia's hairbrush. He was going to take hair from it to use for her DNA. Once he had it, he could prove her heritage.

First, he wanted to make sure he was on the right track. Without the updates he had requested, he couldn't be sure the halflings were where he thought they were. He couldn't imagine Mia willingly giving up the chance to go to the World Slamball Championships with her friends.

Yet, when he thought about it longer, he realized that might be exactly why she wouldn't go. Anyone would know she was going to be there, and that's where she would be most easily found. Elmhurst had put extensive security on her already, and it wouldn't surprise Narco if he found out she forbade the girl from being there on the weekends when the chaos would make her the most vulnerable.

When last he knew of her whereabouts, she was in Scotland, but he needed to check again before he went to find her brush. He didn't want to arrive on campus at the academy and find that she was still there. Narco prepared all he needed and then returned to his study to create a portal. With a tap of his hand, it appeared on the wall. He needed little effort to create the portal and here, unlike near the campus, no one could monitor his movements.

Stepping through the portal brought him to Scotland. Once there, he used the skills that made him a formidable bounty hunter to track the group of halflings. The games hadn't yet started for the day, so he had to search the area. He finally found them in the small village of Portree on the Isle of Skye.

Narco watched them from a distance. He was very familiar with the small island, though he wasn't allowed to visit there. As a full fae, he wasn't permitted to set foot on the island when he wasn't in disguise. But he knew Portree well enough to know that the small village always drew the attention of those visiting.

The faeries were often stingy in their willingness to give permission to anyone wanting to come to their island, but occasionally they felt generous. Sometimes, when they were feeling celebratory or nostalgic, they would give more people permission to come. Those were the times when Narco had managed to sneak onto the island in disguise.

It never lasted for long. The faeries could recognize intruders, and he made it a point to spend only long enough on the island to experience bits of it, but not long enough to get onto the bad side of the guardians there.

Portree was quite small but had everything visitors wanted. Historical sites and stops set up purely for the entertainment of those passing through always brought in crowds. Dotted among them were tiny shops, bakeries, and booths, overflowing with delicious foods.

Narco heard Luna scolding Carson for eating so much, reminding him they were going to the games later, and he would be too full to enjoy it. The Unseelie boy assured her he would happily enjoy the games, and by then would have plenty of room to stuff himself with more of the snacks available there.

Seeing Mia so close, and not being able to grab her, was torturous. Narco was so near her that he could have snatched her, and taken her through a portal before anyone would have had the chance to react. It took all his control to stop himself. For so long, he had searched for her. So many times he had believed he had found and finished her. But every time he had been wrong. Now he couldn't just act. He had to wait for approval, for confirmation. She was right there, but he had to wait. At least now he knew for sure where she was, and that she wouldn't be on campus to thwart his plan.

Narco found a place where no one would notice him and created a portal to the academy campus. The restrictions on the school ensured that he was unable to simply appear within the building, as he would have preferred.

It would have been so much easier to create a portal directly to the dorm building and go up to her room. But there were enchantments and spells in place to stop that from happening. Instead, he had to use the same place he had used several times before, arriving on the edge of the grounds.

While the campus did have certain protections from anyone creating un-sanctioned portals, there wasn't anything to stop him from *walking* onto campus. As long as he entered with confidence, and acted as though he belonged there, no one would give him a second look.

He didn't bother to use a tremendous amount of caution. The chances of him being caught were slim to none. It was morning in Scotland, which meant that, with the time-zone difference, it was the middle of the night in Montana. Everything was quiet, and the very few students who weren't in Scotland were in bed asleep.

He was able to climb over the wall and onto the academy grounds easily. He was still using his glamour, which meant he could roam around as if he belonged, and the students would have no idea who he was. He strode right through the campus without a care and headed directly for the dorms.

CHAPTER SEVENTY-THREE

Morning would be coming in a few hours, but for now, the sun wasn't up. That meant Dan and Steve were still free from their pedestals and flying around campus, keeping an eye on things. These nightly outings had taken on more meaning for them when the championships started, and students were leaving the grounds in droves.

So many people were gone from the campus that it felt less secure and protected. They both believed there should be more security, ensuring the buildings and grounds were protected and guarded, even when there weren't as many students there.

"I don't understand why Elmhurst doesn't make sure there are guards in place during the night," Steve worried as they glided together over the library in a low loop. "So many students and teachers have left the grounds, it feels like it's leaving the academy wide open for anyone to come."

"There should definitely be more security," Dan said, swinging his head back and forth so he could scan as much of the surrounding area as possible as they flew. "I know it's Saturday night, but that doesn't matter. She should understand that is what's making the school vulnerable. While everyone is off enjoying the games in Scotland, the school is sitting here unprotected, and anything could happen."

"You're right. What if someone came in and stole from the library?" Steve asked. "There are some priceless books and artifacts in there. Someone could take something that couldn't ever be replaced. Or that has information in it no one wants in the wrong hands."

"Well, what if someone went into one of the school buildings, and broke all the equipment in the classrooms? Then when the students came back for class, they wouldn't have any way to do their lessons," Dan said.

"Without anybody around to watch the buildings and keep them secure, someone could sneak in and plant a bomb that blows up the whole building," Steve offered. "It could destroy part of the campus."

"What if they set a booby trap specifically for Mia and no one noticed, and she got hurt? Or snatched?" Dan asked.

They were building on each other, escalating to increasingly bigger and bigger problems the more they talked about what could possibly happen. Which made them more and more worried and anxious because they couldn't do much other than patrol the area and watch for anything happening. They both wished they could do more, and their conversation drifted back, as it often did, to their inability to leave their posts during the day. It would have been more beneficial if they could go out and provide additional surveillance when the students were more likely to be on campus.

Because of the time difference with Scotland, the students drifted on- and off-campus at all times. The rules mandated they were there for their classes during the week, but then they could go to the games in the evenings. When the weekends came, they could spend more time there. It made the gargoyles more nervous when it was a day without a senior high championship game. That meant the students were scattered across the country, making it harder to gather them and protect them if necessary.

On days when there was no high school match, there was usually a major league slamball game to attend. Unlike the high school games, tickets to the major-league meets weren't guaranteed and were harder to come by. Everyone wanted to watch the impressive spectacle of the professional players and cheer on their favorite team.

Tickets had to be distributed by lottery. Only those whose names were selected were given the opportunity to buy the tickets. Not only did that make the game exclusive and more desirable, but it meant those who didn't win had more free time. They weren't about to give up their chance to tour Scotland and connect with other fae students. Instead, they spread out through the country and its islands.

This was especially an issue today. The major league game taking place next to Arthur's Seat, on the edge of Edinburgh, was a heated rivalry. It wasn't only the students who swarmed to Scotland to see the game. The majority of the faculty had gone to watch their favorite league players battle each other to settle the bid for supremacy for another season.

For Dan and Steve, that just meant fewer people on campus to monitor things. They had to pick up the slack and keep watch over as much of the academy grounds and its surrounding areas as they possibly could.

CHAPTER SEVENTY-FOUR

Narco could see the dark shadows of the creatures flying overhead. He knew who they were and what they were doing. Having few people on campus was an advantage for him. It meant less chance to be seen. But the gargoyles could be a problem.

He couldn't let them see him. The bounty hunter measured his movements by the way the two flew around the sky. They could only cover a certain area at a time, which meant there were stretches when his way was clear. They hovered near the dorms for several long minutes, almost as though they sensed something was wrong, then parted ways to go to other points on the grounds.

As soon as both were out of sight, Narco rushed into the girls' dorm. It took little time or effort to find where Mia and the other two girls of the Five lived. Just as he expected, the three were given special treatment, with a more elaborate room than the standard ones. The smaller rooms only accommodated two girls. This room, with its prime position within the building and bigger space, ensured the three were forced into spending more time together. It was, by design, melding their lives together to increase their power.

Narco took a deep breath as he walked into the room and looked around. He pulled his magic forward, calling on his gift of bringing stories to life to conjure the image of the last person to use objects within the room. Going to each of the bedside tables, he focused on the brushes and combs sitting there.

The table next to the bed nearest the door held an assortment of four brushes arranged across it. For a moment, Narco thought maybe all the girls kept their things together, but then the image in his mind proved they all belonged to Vivi. He rolled his eyes at the vanity of the Unseelie girl. Next, he moved on to a table with one comb. The strand of hair tangled in it was lighter, and he envisioned Luna using it. That meant the last table had to belong to Mia.

Narco walked up to the table but didn't see a brush or comb lying there. He opened the drawer and found nothing helpful. She must have taken her only brush with her when she went to Scotland. He was feeling discouraged until he turned to her bed, and an idea came to mind. It was neatly made, the blankets and sheets tucked around the pillow and smoothed perfectly into place. He carefully loosened one corner and folded it away from the pillow. A smile slithered across his face when he saw the pillowcase. Just as he hoped, several strands of long red hair clung to the white fabric.

He reached into the inner pocket of his jacket and retrieved a small bag he had brought along for the occasion. Carefully picking up the hairs, he tucked them into the bag and returned it to his pocket. He took them all, knowing that not all hair came out with the follicles intact. With extra strands, he was confident there would be enough to extract DNA for his testing needs.

Then he put the blankets back in place and headed for the door. Feeling triumphant, he casually sauntered back outside and headed across the school grounds.

He was almost at the wall when Steve and Dan caught sight of him. They rushed across the sky but weren't in time to stop him. They watched as he created a portal beyond the grounds, and strode through it, disappearing in a flash. Eyes wide, they looked at each other.

"That was Narco," Steve said. "He's come back to the academy."

"What was he doing here?" Dan asked.

Steve shook his head. "I don't know, but we have to tell the head-mistress. Right now."

"We need to make sure that new wards go up to keep out evil fae." Steve always hated that anyone could walk on campus. That seemed dangerous, as well as stupid. He never understood why they controlled portal usage on-campus, but didn't control who came and went beyond the gates of the academy.

CHAPTER SEVENTY-FIVE

Trying as hard as they could to not panic, Dan and Steve flew to Elmhurst's office. They were in such a state of worry it didn't enter their minds that it was the middle of the night, and the headmistress wouldn't be sitting at her desk the way she often was after sunset most evenings. She loved her academy and was devoted to her position, but not enough to sleep in the big chair in the office. They reached the window where they often paused to talk to her and peered inside. Her office was dark, so they soared off to her private quarters.

Elmhurst lived in the same ancient impressive quarters as her ancestor, who had created the academy centuries ago. It looked like the interior of a castle, all heavy stone draped with tapestries. She had done a few things to add her own personality to the space and lighten it up, but for the most part, had left it as it was when she had moved in. It was tradition and part of the prestige of holding the position of headmistress.

Dan and Steve glided right to the large curved window of her bedroom and landed on the rounded stone edge of a small balcony. They looked in through the glass, but they didn't see anything. It was dark inside, and there were no candles or lights burning anywhere. It was only after they flew around the building, and looked into every window they could find, that they remembered she, too, was off-campus.

Elmhurst was a huge fan of Slamball, and her favorite team was playing in the major league game at Arthur's Seat. She had entered the lottery as soon as it was announced, and had been thrilled to be able to scoop up tickets.

But that meant she wasn't there for them to tell her about Narco. They rushed around campus, checking the buildings, looking into windows, trying to find someone they could notify about the intrusion. Not all the faculty and staff were viable options. Some only knew the most essential basics of the situation because of their limited abilities, or their connections and alliances outside the academy. It wasn't that Elmhurst didn't trust them, but for some, their families and friends in Faerie could become problematic if they revealed too much.

The gargoyles couldn't find anyone to tell, and the night was slipping away. It wouldn't be too much longer before the sun came up, and there would be nothing more they could do. They had no choice but to notify Elmhurst in Scotland.

She had given them a communication stone that allowed them to instantly connect to her. It was much more reliable than any other form of communication when she was at a distance, especially in another country. They activated the stone and waited.

The game was reaching a fever pitch, and Elmhurst was buzzing with excitement when the communication stone around her neck warmed against her skin. The feeling instantly dampened her spirits and tightened her muscles with concern. Steve and Dan knew using the stone was only for truly urgent situations. Especially today as she took an extremely rare break from campus and everything going on there to enjoy herself and watch her favorite team.

She reached under her jacket and pulled out the stone. It hung from a chain around her neck that was long enough for her to hold the stone in her palm and look at it. Pressing the glowing depression in the middle of the stone, she activated the message sent by the gargoyles. There was only one word. Narco.

Elmhurst scrambled to her feet, rushed from the stadium, and ran to a secure location to create a portal back to the academy. Watching carefully around her to ensure no one was about who might try to enter the portal with her, she jumped through to the school. Dan and Steve were waiting outside the window to her office, and she opened it to let them in.

"What happened?" she asked, worried.

Both statues burst into an elaborate story of what they saw.

"He had to be planting a bomb."

"He's going to sabotage the whole school."

"Maybe he took someone hostage and made them invisible."

"Narco is so dangerous, he probably rigged the entire school to trap Mia and all the other students as soon as they get back."

She held up her hands to silence them. "One at a time. Tell me what actually happened," she said. "Not what you *think* could happen. Not guesses. What actually happened?"

They described Narco crossing the school grounds, and then going through a portal. A chill ran along her spine. Elmhurst had hoped they were imagining things or were coming up with some wild idea, but now she knew it was serious.

"I'm going to recall all the faculty, and get Cassia here. We need to secure the campus," she announced. "There is still some time before the sun comes up here. Keep watch over the grounds, especially the borders. Tell me immediately if you see anything."

Dan and Steve nodded their acknowledgment and flew out of the window into the night. Seconds later, Cassia appeared at the door. She looked worried as she rushed up to the desk. "What happened?" she asked.

Elmhurst explained the situation. "Do you know where Mia is at this very moment?" she asked when she finished.

Cassia reached into the leather satchel she wore over her shoulder and pulled out a mirror. "I put a spell on this mirror to keep me connected to her," she explained. She activated the mirror and held it out to the headmistress. "Here."

Elmhurst took the mirror and looked at the glass. Color rippled across the surface for a second before clearing and showing an image. Mia walked along with Zander, Luna, Carson, and Vivi. They seemed happy and carefree as they strolled along a narrow road, eating ice cream. Mia looked at Zander and laughed before they went into one of the little shops lining the street.

"They're in Portree," Elmhurst said with a relieved sigh. "They're safe. Cinder is with them. And the faeries control the island. They wouldn't allow someone like Narco in their territory."

She relaxed slightly, relieved to see the five having fun and not concerned about anything.

"Good. I always liked the Isle of Skye faeries." She chuckled.

"What should we do now?" Cassia asked, taking the mirror back and looking down at the image.

"For right now, they don't know anything is amiss. There's no reason to worry them yet. It's best for them to stay where they are and continue enjoying themselves while we search the campus and make sure it's safe. Once we know more about what he was doing here, we can decide what needs to be done," Elmhurst said.

The faculty and staff Elmhurst recalled from Scotland filtered into the building, and she gathered them in one of the larger meeting rooms. They divided up the campus and planned out how they were to methodically search the grounds. It was critical no corner was missed, no detail overlooked. The smallest thing could be an indication of something much larger. Every single room needed to be checked, every inch of the grounds had to be searched. It was a massive undertaking, but with all of the faculty, staff, and extra security working together, they managed to do it.

Two hours later, they had found nothing out of the ordinary. While a few of the teams went over the outer sections of the grounds again, Elmhurst returned to her office to meet with Steve and Dan.

"Are you absolutely sure you saw Narco?" she asked. "You know it was him?"

"Yes," Dan insisted. "It was him."

"We swear. We wouldn't cause this much trouble if we didn't know for sure it was him," Steve added.

Elmhurst nodded. "I know. The only thing left to do is look at the security cameras. They don't have full coverage, but they might show us something. Of course, if he knew they were there, nothing is going to stop Narco from concealing himself, and his activities."

It was a last-resort effort. Searching the grounds to eliminate any immediate threat was the most important thing to do first. But since they hadn't found anything, it was time to dig deeper. She pulled up the footage from the camera and watched it closely. Several panels on the screen showed the feed from all the different cameras positioned around campus.

"I don't see him anywhere," she said a few minutes later.

Cassia leaned over her shoulder, and they watched the footage again. The bounty hunter suddenly pointed at the screen. "Look right there," she said. "That's a glamour."

Elmhurst couldn't believe she hadn't spotted it when she watched the video the first time. It was convincing, and glamours were much more difficult to see through over cameras than they were in person. Now that she knew what she was looking at, it was obvious. There he was.

They watched Narco move across the grounds and into the dorm. Elmhurst and Cassia looked at each other.

"Was the dorm searched?" Elmhurst asked.

"Yes, but only quickly," Cassia said. "Nothing seemed to be moved anywhere in the building, and the team didn't want to waste any time."

Elmhurst nodded, understanding the decision, but knowing they had less time to waste now. "We need to search it more deeply. He could have done something that isn't noticeable at just a glance."

CHAPTER SEVENTY-SIX

"I will put a protective spell on the dorm," Elmhurst said, standing. "It will prevent anyone from getting out, and anyone unauthorized from getting in."

"Good idea," Cassia said, "I'll take a couple of my friends, and we'll go search the dorm and see if we can see anything. They're bounty hunters, and can use their skills to help."

Elmhurst nodded and the two walked to the dorms, splitting up when they reached the main entrance. The principal stood stoically as she conjured the spell that would envelop the dorm in a protective bubble, impenetrable by anyone who wasn't expressly allowed in.

As powerful as she was, it only took total concentration for a few moments to conjure it, but Cassia knew she would want to be thorough. Elmhurst would likely go through a sealing process that would take a few more minutes to complete, giving her spell a sort of authentication double-check.

While the principal took care of the bubble, Cassia met with the three bounty-hunter friends she had called on for the job. Often, bounty hunters were distrustful of anyone and everyone, including other bounty hunters. If one day you ran afoul of someone powerful, your colleagues would likely be the ones sent to find you, so you kept mostly to yourself. But still, there was always a loose network of hunters who tended to remain friendly, if nothing else other than for the ability to call in help if a hunter realized they were in over their head. Considering Cassia wasn't entirely sure what she was up against, calling in these three made the most sense for her.

"Carl," said the lone woman of the three, a thin fae with sharp bone-structure, and a long nose that made her resemble a hawk. "She's here." The woman, Valerie, tapped her husband on the shoulder, and he turned to see Cassia coming.

"Ahh, Cassia," said the portly man.

Valerie's husband, Carl, was a legend in the bounty-hunting community, primarily for a string of jobs he had done in his youth that had nabbed him a great deal of fame and fortune. He was skilled and experienced, more so than most anyone else Cassia knew besides herself. Carl wasn't much of a field guy anymore, though, as evidenced by the belly now hanging over the belt of his pants, but Cassia had no doubt that in a moment of action, he would be ready.

Valerie, his wife and fellow bounty-hunter, was less famous, but perhaps better than he was. She was fast, athletic, and exceptionally smart. Cassia had met them when she had still been learning the ropes of bounty hunting, and they had become very close mentors for her.

"Are we ready?" asked the stick-figure of a man on the other side of Valerie.

If Valerie was a thin woman, Warren was nearly two-dimensional. His seemingly nervous disposition hid the fact that he was a brilliant detective. On more than one occasion, when Cassia lost track of a target, Warren had been the one to save her hide.

"We are. I'll pull up the last twenty-four hours and see if we can find out what happened before doing a deep search," Cassia said.

As the four bounty hunters walked into the main hall, Cassia began the motions required to use the spell. With it, Cassia could create an image of the last twenty-four hours of any space, and wind through it at will. Casting it around her would allow her and her associates to watch as the day unfolded around them, ghosts of the students and faculty going around and through them as they sped through time. If there was someone worth following, they could simply walk the path that the person trod and check what they did and where they went, provided it was within the space the spell was being cast.

"Who are we looking for?" Valerie asked, as the images popping up around them, mostly transparent people, came to a stop twenty-four hours earlier. They were standing in the main hall, which was crowded with apparitions.

"I am trying to find Mia and the rest of her little gang first," Cassia explained. "If I can find them, I can see if anything out of the ordinary was going on around them yesterday. Failing that, we are looking for Narco, who was using a pretty poor glamour. Should be easy enough to spot."

A few minutes passed as Cassia went around the room, looking into the transparent faces of all the students. When she couldn't find Mia or any of the others, she motioned for the bounty hunters to join her, and they walked up to the girls' rooms. With Warren and Carl remaining on the floor below, Cassia and Valerie went onto the next floor. Cassia checked the shower room first, and, finding it empty, moved down the hall.

"Her room is just ahead. At this time of the day, she should be in there asleep," Cassia said as if trying to convince herself Mia would be there. Something was nagging at her. She had a bad feeling about what she was going to find when the door opened. Sure enough, when Cassia turned the knob and went inside, the room was empty.

She knew the girls were in Portree, but that didn't mean she hadn't hoped they would have come home by now, and be safely tucked away in bed. "Let's just do the time-lapse to last night. I want to see what, if anything, Narco did in here."

The spell caught up to just a few hours before, and Cassia stopped as the doorknob turned. As they watched, the door swung open, and a shimmery, unconvincing glamor—hiding Narco underneath—entered the room. Cassia watched him in confusion as he went around the room, looking through drawers.

"Well, that's creepy," Valerie said, as he picked up a comb that lay on Luna's bedside table, and tossed it down. Narco went to Mia's bed, knelt on one knee, and pulled something from his pocket. It was a plastic bag. Cassia watched in horror as he picked up a few strands of hair and put them in the bag.

"Oh, that good-for-nothing roasted cricket," Cassia said under her breath.

"That can't be good," Valerie said.

They watched Narco leave the room and followed him down the stairs, walking past Carl and Warren.

"Is that the guy?" Warren asked as the glamour-bound spectral image passed him.

"Yes," Cassia said through gritted teeth. "And he took some of Mia's hair."

"What would he want that for? A spell?" Warren scratched his chin.

Cassia didn't answer. Of course, it could be for a spell. That was the easy option. The alternative was worse; That Narco had figured out who Mia was, and was aiming to prove it. Either way, Mia was in deep trouble.

The portal opened outside the coffee shop, and Cassia, Elmhurst, and the three other bounty hunters walked into Portree as the five halflings were exiting the cafe. They stumbled in surprise.

Without a moment's hesitation, Carson passed his cup to Luna, put his hands behind his back, and took a neutral pose. Taking his inspiration from Zander, lawyering Carson had turned the spotlight on himself, and Elmhurst was not amused.

"To what do we owe the pleasure of such a…well-attended visit?" Carson said, looking at the three bounty hunters and then at Mia, who shrugged.

"None of you slept in your dorm room last night. We checked. That's against school rules," Cassia said, her eyes stabbing into Mia, who winced.

"Well," Carson began, suddenly looking relaxed and argumentative at the same time. He was now embodying every slick lawyer in every crime-drama TV show in the history of time. "Technically speaking, we were given permission to be in Scotland for *the weekend*," he said, his fingers doing air quotes around the last two words. "As it is still the weekend, we are not due back yet. Nowhere was it said that we needed to sleep there. Arrangements were all set up here, and are on the up and up. The boys stayed in one tent and the girls in another. No harm, no foul."

"That is where you are seriously mistaken," Elmhurst told him.

CHAPTER SEVENTY-SEVEN

"You know very well you aren't allowed to sleep anywhere but your assigned dorm rooms without written permission," Elmhurst said firmly. "That is a rule of the academy you learn from the moment you are granted admission and is in force at all times. Luna, who lives nearby, can't just go home for the weekend with her mother without permission from the school. That is done for the safety and security of each of our students. I need to know where you are at all times. That rule does not change just because of the special circumstances of the World Slamball Championships. There are already many concessions being made, and special privileges being granted because of the games. But that is not one of them. You know that. All of you know that."

Cassia shook her head as she looked at Mia. Her eyes were heavy, and the halfling could see the dark emotion on her guardian's face.

"I am so disappointed in you, Mia," Cassia said. "You know the rules. We've talked about them. Just because you are allowed to go visit Scotland for the championships, doesn't mean you don't have to adhere to the rest of the rules of campus. That includes sleeping only in your assigned room each night."

Mia hung her head. She felt guilty for her part in the weekend. She had known she was agreeing to something that wasn't right when Zander had first suggested it. The time difference made it hard to keep up with a normal sleep-wake cycle between the two places, but she had known when they did sleep, it was supposed to be in their dorms.

"I'm sorry," she said. "I just got wrapped up in the excitement of going."

Elmhurst shook her head again. She caught sight of a small faerie hovering near the group. "You," she said, looking at the creature sternly. "You are a guardian-in-training for the faerie pools. What are you doing here?"

"Yes," Alania replied. "I am. My name is Alania. I was granted a break from my training and responsibilities at the pools to visit with my cousin, Cinder."

Elmhurst raised an eyebrow, not saying anything as she thought the response through. Then she gave a single nod. "Very good," she said. She turned to the group of halflings. "We are going back to the school. Immediately."

All five nodded solemnly, saddened to have lost the carefree fun of exploring the village together. They didn't want to be back on the academy campus, away from the games and the festivities. But in a situation like this, there wasn't going to be any leniency. Elmhurst escorted them to an isolated area behind a building and created a portal to the academy. It brought them directly into the girls' dorm room, so there would be no argument about where they needed to go.

When they arrived, the headmistress looked pointedly at each of the halflings. "Listen closely. Your rules have now changed. You are no longer permitted free access to Scotland and the Championships. You are to stay on campus unless you have an adult with you, and you must have that adult with you at all times."

The five sagged, exchanging pained looks, sulking over their lost freedom. They understood the gravity of the situation they were facing, but none of them wanted to. Going to the games and exploring Scotland was a way for them to not have to worry so much, and to relax and have fun. Now they had been forced back into being constantly monitored and controlled.

Alania saw how upset they were, and flitted a bit closer to Elmhurst. "Headmistress, if I may? Cinder and I are adults. We can supervise the children if they want to continue to spend their free time in Scotland," she offered.

The halflings couldn't help but laugh at the idea of the faeries being their chaperones, but Cassia gave them a sharp glare, instantly silencing them. Elmhurst studied the faerie, evaluating her words. Alania was not just a faerie making a generous offer to allow these students freedom from campus. There was more going on here than met the eye. But this wasn't the time to question it.

Elmhurst nodded. "If you can arrange for you and two of your guardian sisters to stay with the children the entire time they are in Scotland, that is acceptable." She turned to the students and pointed at them, making sure they were listening and would fully understand her. "But you must sleep in your own beds here at the academy, in your dorm rooms. And you will now have a curfew that must be met on all occasions, no exceptions. During the week, you have to be in all of your classes, do all your work, and attend all extracurricular activities, meetings, and events required of you. If you miss anything, you will not be permitted to go to Scotland that day. You will not be permitted to leave until all classes and activities for the day are done, even if you have met the requirements for the day. Every weekday, you will be back on campus no later than ten. That is still very early morning by Scotland time, so it will give you plenty of opportunity to sleep before the next events begin."

"We can accept that," Zander said, returning to his self-appointed post as the group's quasi-leader.

"You don't have any choice, Zander. This is not a negotiation, it is a declaration of terms. This is the only option you have. On weekends, you will have a bit more freedom. You can leave first thing in the morning, assuming there are no seminars or extended coursework assigned. Your curfew is midnight."

They nodded, and Elmhurst began to leave the room to return to her office. Before she went too far, she glanced over her shoulder at them. "All stated times are Montana time. I don't want to hear you thought the curfew was midnight, Scotland time."

It was the last little bit of hope a few of the five had been holding out. The headmistress hadn't been specific, which had meant they might get away with a little bit of wiggle room. With that stipulation, though, their hopes of stretching out their time in Scotland were dashed. Deflated, they all nodded again and mumbled their agreements.

Elmhurst took two steps before saying, "Alania, a word." She walked far enough away that the halflings wouldn't hear their conversation. Someone needed to know that Narco was around, and she wanted to know what Alania knew.

"I told you it wasn't going to work," Carson grumbled, kicking the floor.

"You did not," Mia corrected him. "You were just as enthusiastic about camping on the Isle of Skye as Zander was. Luna is the only one who was really resistant to it, and said we shouldn't do it."

"All of you should have known better," Cassia said. "And if one of you was arguing against it, you should have listened."

Luna sighed and threw her hands up in the air. "And yet, I did it anyway, and look where it got me. Why do I always go along with all of you?" she asked.

"You have to," Vivi teased. "It's the Power of Five, not four."

The joke helped to lighten the mood slightly, and they all laughed. They still felt discouraged. They had only gotten the chance to camp out in their tents for one night, and all of them had enjoyed it. Even the girls had relaxed and had started having fun.

There was something exhilarating about being in such a different environment, doing something out of their usual routine. They always slept in the same space, and the elevated tent had brought them into closer proximity with each other, but it still felt fun and exciting. They had enjoyed being around the other visitors, and feeling like they were a part of it all.

Being students from the number-one-rated school in the World Slamball Championships was a rare and special thing. Something they had had the opportunity to experience once, and this was it. Now, instead of being among all the other revelers, fully immersed in the thrill, they were stuck on campus, imagining everything they were missing out on.

But at least they had Alania, and her offer to supervise them when they wanted to go. They didn't have to ask one of the teachers to come with them or try to find a parent willing to do the traveling.

It was a kind and generous offer, but it also made Mia wonder. She waited for Alania to return to their room, and for Cassia to say goodbye and leave, before turning to the faerie, who stared back at her.

CHAPTER SEVENTY-EIGHT

"Alania, why would you offer to supervise us?" Mia asked. "You said you were given permission to take time away from your training and guardian duties to visit with Cinder, not to watch over us."

The faerie shrugged. She didn't want to tell them the truth and let them know what was actually going on. Head Guardian Myla had asked her, in confidence, to keep an eye on Mia. If Myla had wanted all of them to know about it, she would have asked Alania to do it in front of them. Alania wanted to protect that confidence, and not let them know she was actually there to watch over the heir.

"Guarding the pools, and training with the other guardians isn't a lot of fun sometimes. My friends and I would find it much more exciting to hang out with you guys, attend the games, and go sightseeing." Her tiny shoulders lifted, and she rolled her eyes. "Think of it as a human vacation."

That made sense to Mia. The faeries at the pools seemed to be having fun playing in the water, and the surroundings were beautiful and exciting when the halflings had first seen them. But it was probably different when those pools were a part of their everyday life, and they were tasked with protecting them.

Knowing they had hundreds, or even thousands, of years ahead of them at the pools every day, guarding them against people, and people from them, likely took some of the novelty away.

It would be like the time her human high school class went to a theme park for a field trip close to the end of the year. They had all believed it was going to be a fun day of riding rides and running around celebrating the end of the year together. But when they stepped off the bus at the front of the park, they were promptly met with thick packets of worksheets which they were expected to fill out during their time in the park. Having to analyze the rides, and answer seemingly endless questions about them, their themes, how they worked, what was good and what wasn't, had made the day seem much more like another boring school assignment than anything exciting.

The games were an infrequent event, even for the faeries, and would present an opportunity to see a lot of new things. It made sense that they would jump at the chance to change up their routine for a few days.

Mia and the Scooby Gang bought the explanation, but Cinder didn't. She had watched the interaction between Mia and Alania and knew something more was going on. She wanted to question her cousin, but before she could, Zander stood.

"I think we should go to the library," he announced.

Vivi groaned and toppled backward onto her bed. "I am so not in the mood to do more research."

"Not for research. I want to hear what Dan and Steve have to say about all this. All we know is what Elmhurst and Cassia told us. Maybe the gargoyles can give us a different perspective," he told them.

"Or at least a really entertaining story," Carson said.

The girls agreed, and Mia beckoned Alania. "Come on," she said. "We'll introduce you to Dan and Steve, the resident gargoyles."

"Where are they?" Alania asked, as they left the dorm room, and strolled across the grounds to the library.

"They are stationed outside the library," Mia explained. "They've been there since the academy was built more than one thousand years ago."

"If they are gargoyles, how did they manage to see anything?" the faerie asked. "Wouldn't they only be able to see what is immediately around them?"

"That's the way it used to be. Until Mia started feeling bad for them and managed to enchant them off their pedestals. Now they're able to fly around from sundown to sunup. They can go around and do pretty much whatever they like, but as soon as the sun comes up, they have to go back to their posts," Vivi told them.

"That doesn't sound like fun. At least there's nothing locking me to the pools," the faerie said.

"Yeah, they're pretty grumpy about it. It's like they forgot they didn't even know they could move for hundreds and hundreds of years. Now, all of a sudden, they get frustrated because they have to stay in place for a few hours at a time," the Unseelie halfling told them.

"But they make the most of the time they can be free," Mia said. "They like to keep watch over the campus and make sure everything is all right. They could go anywhere and do anything, but they still want to stay here and keep watch over the academy. And it's a good thing they do."

They reached the library, and Dan and Steve strained, as though trying to lean down toward the halflings.

"We're so glad to see you," Dan said.

"Tell us what happened. What's going on?" Zander asked.

The gargoyles burst into their hyped-up story and the halflings smiled at each other, ready to settle in and try to sift through the exaggerations to find what really happened.

Narco stood in the hidden room in front of a long table cluttered with chemistry equipment. He had gathered everything he needed to combine magic and science and draw the DNA from Mia's hair. If he could obtain a breakdown of it, he could then compare it to that of the royal line, and prove once and for all that she was the girl they were after. That is if his contact could procure a DNA sample from the Unseelie Queen.

He wasn't worried about that part. If his contact wanted proof, then Narco would give him the sample, and tell him he could compare it himself if proof was so important to him.

But Narco's efforts weren't going smoothly.

He picked up another piece of hair and slid it into a test tube. He poured in an enchanted solution and went through the process, which should have revealed all the secrets of who she was.

But within seconds of the solution touching the hair, the strand disintegrated with a *poof*. This was the third time it had happened. He picked up another strand and carefully went through the process again. And again, the hair disappeared. He was no scientist, and his understanding of exactly what he was doing was shaky at best, but Narco knew that wasn't right. He was down to his final strand of hair. If he lost this piece, he would have nothing left, and his chance at presenting proof would be gone.

He growled and felt like throwing the entire desk across the room. He barely managed to restrain himself, and he began to tell himself he could do this. He was Narco, the most revered bounty hunter ever. No one could best him.

He had killed that frustrating Flynn Terran who had believed *he* was the best bounty hunter in a hundred generations. If only Narco could tell all of Faerie that he was the one who killed their favorite hunter. Maybe, once this issue was done, he could let a few stories out about how he was instrumental in ensuring the two Courts were protected. Then he'd have the glory he was due.

Setting the hair on the counter far from the solution, he reached out to the associate who had walked him through the process, to begin with. Several minutes later, a portal appeared in the wall, and his colleague stepped out. A scientist with experience in this process, Orin, listened to Narco's description of what was happening to the hair when he had attempted to withdraw the DNA.

"I am doing what you told me to, just as you told me to do it,"

Narco insisted. "The same thing keeps happening. It can't be what I'm doing. I think there might be something wrong with the hair."

"You're right. That sounds like someone put a spell on the hair. It's rarely done, but there are enchantments that can be placed on living beings to make it so no DNA can be extracted from things that fall off them, like hair or skin cells. You won't be able to get any DNA from strands of hair, or anything that comes off her naturally," Orin told him.

"Then what am I supposed to do?" Narco asked.

"If this girl has been enchanted, the only way you're going to be able to get DNA is from her blood."

Narco liked where this was headed. He had long envisioned his opportunity to draw blood from Mia. But he had to calm himself down. He remembered what the shadow man had said. He was not permitted to harm her until he had obtained proof she was the girl they wanted.

"Is there a way I can do that without being obvious?" Narco asked.

"It's not difficult to get blood, especially from a halfling. I have worked with several bogans who can be discreet. Unlike the redcaps you prefer. They shouldn't have any trouble getting a sample of blood from Mia. I can reach out to them if you'd like me to," Orin said.

Narco met Orin's eyes, his expression serious and firm.

"Get it done."

CHAPTER SEVENTY-NINE

"Now that you've had a few days to think about your assignment, I want to check in with all of you, and find out what you're thinking about," the teacher said in class on Monday.

Some of the students shifted around in their seats uncomfortably. It was obvious they hadn't thought about the writing assignment since walking out of class at the end of the previous week. They'd been far too wrapped up in the Championships, and in exploring Scotland, to think about what they were going to do for their project. It seemed none of the others had thought about the fact that being able to go to Scotland was the perfect opportunity to find a topic, and do in-depth research. She turned her focus directly to the five.

"What about you, Luna? What did you come up with for your research project?" she asked.

"I want to research the faerie pools more. We went to visit them over the weekend, and I had the opportunity to talk to one of the guardians for a while. I got some interesting information about the pools and the history of the surrounding area. I'd like to look more into that," Luna responded.

"Very good. The pools are fascinating. There are a lot of myths and legends revolving around that area. I look forward to reading your insights into those legends and how they connect to the true history of Scotland and the pools." She smiled at Luna and looked at Mia. "How about you, Mia? Is there something in particular about Scotland that stood out to you?"

"Yes," Mia said, nodding. "I want to learn more about Princess Caledona. We found out she was named for the region, and that people thought she had found the Fountain of Youth because she was powerful, and had lived for so long. I'd like to find out more about where she came from, and what happened to her."

"Interesting," the teacher said with a smile. "And you, Vivi?"

Vivi shrugged. "I haven't made up my mind yet. But I wouldn't mind finding some handsome knights to study."

The class laughed, but the teacher wasn't quite as amused by the declaration. She scowled at Vivi, her arms crossed over her chest.

"I expect you to have a topic by the end of the week. A real topic, Vivi," she said.

She moved on to Zander, who was ready to gloss over the issue with Vivi for the teacher.

"I want to study the Roman-Pict battles," he announced.

The teacher looked intrigued. "That's an interesting idea. What about that particular topic got your attention?"

"There was no way the Picts back then could have stood up against the Roman soldiers and succeeded. There had to be fae intervention. I want to find out about that and see if I can trace some of the fae who were involved," he told her.

"That's ambitious. If you were able to accomplish that, the library might be interested in your findings. That could definitely be something that would make your application stand out to the universities."

She winked at him, knowing his ambitions and how hard he was working to get ahead. The competition for the most elite universities was always fierce each year. He wouldn't just be up against the other seniors from Elmhurst. He would also have to stand out from students from all the other schools as well. He needed to make himself as appealing as possible to be accepted, and start working toward his desired position after graduation.

When Zander had first come up with the project involving the fae interference in the Roman and Pict battles, he had secretly hoped it would be compelling enough to be impressive, but he hadn't wanted to say anything. Getting the validation from the teacher was encouraging and made him more excited to continue with the research.

"I know what I want to do," Carson said, raising his hand. "It actually kind of goes along with what Zander is doing."

"Okay, go ahead," the teacher said.

"I want to study *The Highlander*. He had to be fae, or at least a halfling. There is no way a human could survive the kinds of things that happened to him," Carson said.

The class laughed, and the teacher laughed right along with them, though she stopped herself quickly. She didn't want to embarrass Carson. He was a very good student, and it wasn't often he made a serious mistake. Which made this error particularly funny, but it could also make it more humiliating for him.

"Carson, I think you're confused. That's a movie. It wasn't based on a real person," she said gently.

Carson shook his head. "No," he said firmly. "That's not right. The movie was based on a real person. Just like that one about the guy who painted himself blue and ran up into the mountains. It's a real person, and he could only be killed if he was decapitated. That can't be human."

"Carson," Luna said, shaking her head. "It's not a real person."

"It's true, buddy," Zander said, patting Carson on the shoulder.

Carson looked at the two of them, then at the teacher. After a few seconds he suspended hope, and it puffed out of him in a gusting exhale.

"Well, I guess that means I'm going back to the drawing board for a topic," he said.

The class laughed again as he shrugged.

"We can both study the Roman-Pict battles," Zander suggested. "It's a really big topic. There has to be a lot of fae intervention, and if we're both working on it, we'll be able to find out even more about it."

"That sounds like a fantastic solution," the teacher said. "You two can work together to really dig into this idea and see what you can discover."

Zander and Carson were happy about the decision and immediately delved into talking over the ideas, planning how they were going to move ahead with their research.

When classes were over for the day, the five met up in front of the library. Alania appeared with two of the other guardians in training. Cinder hovered a little behind, seeming to watch her cousin and her friends carefully.

"Are you guys ready?" Alania asked.

The five agreed enthusiastically. They'd been waiting all day for the chance to go back to Scotland and couldn't wait to get there.

"We wish we could go," Steve grumbled.

"Yeah, it's not fair," Dan said. "Everybody else gets to go. We should, too."

"You know the rules," Vivi told them. "When the sun comes up, it's back to your pedestals."

"Exactly. Not fair. I wish Mia could fix it so we don't have to be stuck to the library during the day. We shouldn't have to sit around at all," Dan said.

Mia sighed, frustrated. They had had this exchange a few times already. "I'm sorry, guys. I can't."

"It's not like we want to do anything wrong," Steve told her. "We just want to stick with you and make sure you're safe. You know we won't fly away. We are loyal to the academy, and to you."

Mia felt tightness in her throat and shook her head. "I'm sorry. I don't know how to do it. I didn't know how to do it when it happened the first time. But I'm practicing with my powers. When I get better and learn more, I can try again. But now, I'm afraid if I try it and don't do it right, I might reverse what I did. And you will be stuck in place forever. Then you wouldn't be able to leave your pedestals at all, not even at night. That's why I want to wait until I have full use and understanding of my powers."

Dan nodded. "I understand. I appreciate you thinking about us."

Steve continued to grumble like a grumpy old man, but it was nice that at least one of them was understanding and appreciative.

"You know, I'd be happy to try," Vivi said, with an evil glint in her eyes.

That was enough to stop Steve's grumbling. "Nope. That's just fine. No worries. We are happy to wait for Mia to get better control," the gargoyles both scrambled to say.

Vivi winked at Mia. The gesture made Mia smile, confirming that the offer wasn't genuine, or even a way to torment the gargoyles more, but a way to back Mia up. It made the red-haired halfling reflect on the continued changes in Vivi. She was constantly growing, and Mia was happy to see how she was turning out.

As Vivi walked away, Zander sidled up to Mia. "What's going on with Vivi recently? Why is she becoming such a team player?"

Mia shrugged. "I don't know, but I'm happy about it."

Zander smiled as they went to the portal that would take them to Scotland. When they walked through, he turned to her again. "Um, I wanted to know if…I mean, later, well, if you're hungry, would you like to have dinner?" he asked.

Mia looked at him strangely. "Of course, we can all have dinner. There's a little restaurant we didn't get to try last time."

"Oh, yeah. That sounds great. But I was just thinking…I mean, not all of us," Zander tried again.

"Very smooth, Zander," Carson teased. "At this rate, you should be able to get a date with her by the time we graduate…from college."

Mia realized what was happening and blushed. She glanced away, then looked back at Zander and nodded. "I'd love to have dinner with you," she said with a smile.

CHAPTER EIGHTY

Mia spent the day looking forward to dinner. She went back and forth between being excited to spend time with Zander, and anxious that it was officially an actual date. It was different from the other times they had spent alone together. They would often receive curious looks from their friends, and from other students who saw them.

And Mia had always felt that the time she spent with Zander was special, more than if it was any of her other friends. But she and Zander had never talked about it. They had never confirmed they were anything more than just friends. This time was different. This time he had purposely asked her out on a date, and she was eager to see how that change was going to feel.

As the end of the day grew closer, Mia wished she had the chance to change clothes before dinner. It didn't feel as much like a date when she was going in what she had worn all day. But when it was finally time to leave, one smile from Zander made her not care what she was wearing. He looked so happy to see her that she couldn't wait for them to go off together.

If only they could actually be alone.

"Where do you want to go for dinner?" Alania asked as they walked away.

Zander and Mia turned and looked at her questioningly.

"We're going to dinner together," Zander said.

The faerie looked at him for a few seconds, as though waiting for him to remember something. When he didn't say anything else, she put one little hand to her chest.

"I'm your chaperone, remember? The other guardians and I were assigned to be with the five of you while you are not on campus. You two aren't allowed to go off by yourself together. I have to be with you. Elmhurst was very clear that you can't be without us," she told them.

Zander and Mia exchanged a disappointed look. Neither had thought of the restrictions when they made the date earlier, and they weren't looking forward to having the entire group tag along with them. But they also knew there was no way Elmhurst would give them any special consideration on their need for a chaperone simply to go to dinner together. They agreed and went to the small restaurant Mia had thought would be romantic. Which now seemed nothing but cramped.

The hostess guided Zander and Mia to their own table, but the rest of the group were seated a few feet away. It didn't give them any real privacy, and every few seconds Mia or Zander would look at the other table and see one of the halflings peeking at them or whispering as they stared.

What had begun as something they were both looking forward to, quickly turned into an awkward situation. They barely spoke, and instead gazed around the restaurant, and occasionally smiled at each other uncomfortably.

"Was your dinner good?" Zander asked after they finished their almost silent meal.

"It was delicious. Thank you. Did you enjoy yours?"

Zander nodded. "I've never seen a restaurant attempt a vegan Scotch Egg. That's hard to do when the entire dish is just a hard-boiled egg wrapped in sausage."

Mia laughed. "But it tasted good?"

"It really did. They managed to make the tofu in the center taste like an egg."

The waitress strolled up to the edge of the table and asked if they wanted dessert. They both said they did, and she handed them menus, waiting the few seconds it took for them to decide on lemon sorbet with raspberries.

When she walked away, Zander put his hands on the table. One twitched as though he was thinking about reaching for her hand. Mia wanted him to, but the others being so close stopped him. Alania fluttered past as though she was going to the restroom, but she was eyeing them, making it obvious she was checking in.

Mia wished they could be alone, even for a short time. A second later, the restaurant around them disappeared. They popped up on a distant part of the island at the edge of a cliff, still sitting at their table from the restaurant. Ahead of them, the Sea of Hebrides rolled and crashed against the rocks. It was beautiful, and Mia knew exactly what had happened. Her wish had been enough to accidentally create a portal that sucked them through it and away from the others right to this spot.

Several yards away, Alania kept her distance from the couple. When the portal had appeared, she had been close enough to get sucked through with them. At first, she was shocked, but she remembered what Cinder had told her about Mia and her skills.

She couldn't really be aggravated about it. She knew of Mia's abilities, and the portal appearing that way only meant the halfling had deeply wanted the time with Zander. Besides, they were still on the island, and they were in a safe place. Cinder and two other faerie guardians were with the other three, so Alania decided to give them a few moments to themselves. It was cute watching them together, and she knew when the time came, she would easily create a portal to bring them back.

The only problem would be if humans saw the creation of the portal in the restaurant. But she'd deal with that when they returned.

The sky was clear, and the moon was bright enough in the darkness for Zander and Mia to see each other clearly. Happy to be alone with Mia no matter what the circumstance, Zander stood from the table and walked around to Mia. He finally took her hand in his, pulling her up to stand next to him.

"It's a good thing Dan and Steve aren't here with us. They would have told Elmhurst on us for sure," he said.

"They really don't seem to be able to keep a secret from her," Mia agreed.

They laughed, and Zander brushed his fingers along the side of her face. He leaned in to kiss her. Just before their lips touched, they tumbled backward through a portal that formed directly behind them. They landed in a heap at Cassia's feet, and when they looked around, they saw the rest of the Scooby Gang gathered nearby.

Cassia glared at them angrily. "What do you think you're doing?"

Alania moved forward to defend them. "I was with them the entire time, and they were safe."

"It doesn't matter. Mia shouldn't be creating portals. She knows the rules, and how dangerous it could be for her to just travel around on a whim," Cassia argued.

"How did you know where we were?" Mia asked. "Or that I created the portal that got us there?"

"I will always know when you are in trouble," Cassia replied.

It wasn't really an answer, but the cryptic message made Mia stay silent.

"That's not exactly true. You didn't know we were in the Louvre until after the fact," Carson quipped.

Cassia turned an angry scowl on him, and Luna tugged him back by his elbow.

"You aren't helping matters," Luna said.

"I didn't create the portal on purpose," Mia insisted. "It just sort of appeared. It's not like I asked for it."

Cassia turned to Alania. "Where did they go?"

"Just to the cliffs across the island," the faerie told her.

Cassia nodded, her expression relaxing slightly. "Well, at least you didn't go too far. I'm glad for that. But you better not do it again. Do you understand me?"

"I didn't do it on purpose," Mia said again, her voice growing louder and higher with frustration.

"Are you going to rat on her to Elmhurst?" Luna asked.

The other halflings looked at her in surprise, shocked Luna would ask something like that.

Cassia seemed to think about the options for a few seconds, then finally shook her head. "No. Mia insists she didn't do it on purpose—"

"I didn't!"

"And as I was going to say, I believe her. And since Alania was along, and no one was hurt, I don't see the need," Cassia finished.

Mia nodded in acknowledgment, but couldn't bring herself to thank Cassia. She didn't feel like she had done anything wrong, and it would have been needlessly harsh of her guardian to report her to the headmistress for something she hadn't intended to do.

"Good. Can we get back to our food now?" Carson asked. "I'm really looking forward to dessert."

Cassia nodded and turned to leave. She took a few steps, then paused and looked over her shoulder at Zander and Mia. "He is pretty cute," she said and winked at Mia.

Carson, Vivi, Luna, and the faeries, burst into laughter as Zander and Mia hung their heads in embarrassment, their cheeks flushing. This wasn't the way they had expected their first date would go. But at least they'd had those few seconds together, and they weren't in trouble.

CHAPTER EIGHTY-ONE

In the shadows outside the restaurant, hiding in an alley between the building and the bicycle shop next door, stood a short, squat figure, watching the door intently. Beady eyes scanned the street over and over as it waited for the target to exit. Every time the door opened, the bogan would prepare to follow her, to isolate her, but each time it was someone else.

Growing tired of the wait, his rat-like nose twitched. He stroked his long beard and pulled his long brown cape around himself. The night was getting cold, and though the temperature didn't necessarily bother the bogan if he kept moving, standing still presented a bit more of a challenge. Sitting still too long for a bogan was a boredom that could barely be withstood.

The bogan hopped from one foot to the other to keep himself entertained and watched as the door opened once again, and a fae creature stepped outside. This excited him because he knew this particular creature. It was the one they called Cassia, and she was here with the target. If she was leaving, it was either with his assignment, or she was leaving it unprotected. Either scenario satisfied him.

Cassia stepped out into the night and instinctively knew something was up. Keeping her cool, she took a few steps, allowing her senses to take control, and finding herself drawn to a dark corner in an alley beside the building. Something was there, though she couldn't be sure what, and she had to find somewhere to observe it. It came as no surprise that things would be following Mia, especially now, and especially here in Scotland, where there were so many creatures.

Cassia didn't let on that anything was wrong, and went down the sidewalk, away from the restaurant and rounded a corner. As soon as she was past it, and out of sight, she pulled a small makeup mirror, opened it, aiming it behind her and around the building.

She angled it at the shadowy corner and watched as first, a nose poked out from the darkness, followed by the head. She exhaled in relief when she figured out it was just a bogan. As ugly and mischievous as they were, they often weren't capable of much violence, and with the faeries inside with the kids, she was confident that an army of bogans would be no match for them. Not with someone as powerful as Mia was becoming, at any rate.

Something ahead of her drew her attention off the bogan, and she slammed the mirror closed. The thing she saw was unmistakable and far more dangerous than a mere bogan. It crept down another alley, away from the restaurant on the next street, hunting something.

Whatever it was hunting was in danger, and since it was a redcap, its victim was likely a child. One last time, Cassia glanced around the corner at the alley where the bogan was hiding and sprinted toward the redcap.

She stopped at the corner of the alley the redcap had entered and popped her head around it. The alley was dark, though not pitch black. A lone light shone over a door near the end of the alley, above a fire-exit for one of the buildings.

In the distance, between the redcap and the light, was a small child, no more than eight years old, lost, scared, and running. Suddenly the redcap stopped sneaking and hauled off after the child, its mouth opening wide, saliva trailing on the ground behind it.

Cassia burst into a run, pushing herself to make it to the redcap before it did any damage. Its wiry arms reached out, and its long brown beard flowed behind it. She heard the cry of the child as the redcap's hands grabbed him, pulling him closer.

The child tried to scream, but nothing came out as the image of such a horrible creature struck him so full of fear that all sound refused to leave his throat. Terrified, he struggled against the grip of the redcap as its long fingernails dug painfully into his arms, and he lost control of his bladder. His face was disappearing inside the terrible creature's mouth, and soon all the child could see was the horrible sharp teeth, dripping with wet, sticky spit.

With a crack, Cassia's foot connected with the side of the redcap's head, forcing the neck to snap to the side. Its hands opened, releasing the child. The boy tumbled to the ground and rolled to safety in a dark corner.

He pulled a trash can lid close to him like a shield, watching as Cassia landed gracefully on her feet and charged after the thing on the ground. It hopped up on its feet and spun into a kick that landed hard in her stomach. She doubled over and stumbled into the wall of the alley.

The redcap dove at her, gnashing its terrible teeth and swinging its nails at her like blades. She recovered in time to knock the hands away and shove her elbow into its jaw. A punch to its nose sent it backward, and she leaned into a thrust-kick that sent it barreling backward against the other wall.

A flurry of punches to its side weakened the redcap, and she knew she was gaining the upper hand. Cassia was pulling her arm back for a knockout blow when she was suddenly stopped by a cry from the boy in the shadows.

He was peering over the trashcan lid, his eyes wide and terrified, and his mouth open in a full scream. The terror locking up his voice before it could be released, and now he was wailing for help and for his mother. It was mostly unintelligible cries, but the cry for his mother was piercing and loud, and Cassia felt for him.

With her attention diverted for a split second too long, the redcap escaped her grip. It started to run for freedom to the open end of the alley, and she dove after it, barely grasping its leg with her hand.

"Let go," the thing hissed and kicked at her.

"Not a chance." Cassia yanked the leg back toward her, grabbing at the foot to put it in an ankle lock.

The redcap rolled with the momentum, swung its other foot into her jaw, knocking her loose, and making purple spots appear on the edge of her vision. She grasped again for the thing, but missed and, though still woozy, had to get to her feet to chase it. The screams of the child were echoing through the alley as she grabbed the redcap just before he pulled free. Cassia tugged him into a headlock. He struggled against her and then bit her forearm hard. She screamed in pain.

"Stop biting me!" she shouted to no avail. It gnawed at her, trying to bite through the thick leather she wore, and undoubtedly would try to eat her arm clean off in an effort to escape.

Cassia had to think fast, and the sounds of feet pounding on the sidewalk outside the alley meant someone was coming to help the child. But worse, it meant they would see both her and the redcap. She focused as fast as she could, opened a portal to Forasaon against the wall of the building, and yanked on the redcap's head to shove it toward the prison. It tried to fight her, but she dragged it a few feet closer. If she could get him through, she could take him to prison, and allow her to get back to keeping an eye on Mia.

It sank its nails into her sides and thrashed wildly in her grip, but she was too strong. She could feel blood beginning to slide down her sides as the creature dug into her, desperate not to go through the portal.

Voices were coming from outside the alley, meaning she only had seconds. She lurched with the redcap in her arm, popped her hip to one side, and threw herself and the creature through the portal and into darkness.

CHAPTER EIGHTY-TWO

Usually, Cassia's arrivals at the prison were smooth and controlled. She moved through portals as though walking through a door, and could easily enter the prison without bringing much attention to herself. Not so this time. Rather than guiding herself through the portal with ease, and walking comfortably into the prison, she tumbled through like a child learning to create their first portal.

The pair flailed and fell through, and the redcap wrenched himself free of Cassia's hand. The instant they hit the ground in the prison, he got to his feet and tried to flee. One of the ogres standing guard laughed when he saw the redcap, and he reached for it. Cassia watched the ogre snatch the redcap by the scruff of his collar, and pick him up as if he was nothing more than a stray cat getting in the way.

"Well, that was quite the entrance," Fan said, laughing. "What is going on here? Cassia, I've never seen you go through a portal like that. What happened?"

Cassia sighed, exasperated as she waved his words off, and got to her feet. She pointed angrily at the redcap. "This creature was caught trying to eat a small boy in Scotland during the games."

The amusement disappeared from Fan's eyes, and his expression turned serious. He released a sigh that said he was very unhappy to hear about the incident. "That's really too bad. The Fae Council put out an edict ahead of the games this year. Anyone caught messing with the humans in Scotland during the games is to immediately get the ax."

"She's lying," the redcap cried, trying to lunge for Fan in desperation. "I would never try to eat a child!"

"I saw you," Cassia insisted.

"That's preposterous. A child is far too easy prey. No self-respecting redcap would bother with kids, especially not when there were so many halflings around that would taste so much better," the redcap said, his pleading fading to mocking as his mouth curled into a grotesque smile.

Fan scoffed and looked at the ogre, still holding the redcap. "See that it's done."

"On it," the ogre said, dragging the redcap away.

Fan turned to Cassia with a smirk. "I guess you'll be wanting the bounty for that one?"

Cassia nodded. "If there is a bounty, I want it. I got him here. Maybe not in the smoothest way I've ever brought somebody in, but I got him here, and the kid didn't get turned into a midnight snack. I think that warrants the reward."

"I agree, and as it turns out, there is a bounty on his head. He was telling the truth, though. This redcap is not in the habit of going after little kids. Not to say the games didn't inspire him to try something new and go for a quick refreshment in the form of a kid, but that's not his usual thing. He tends to favor the halflings. Which means the bounty isn't too high."

"Halfling murderers don't bring in high bounties anymore?" Cassia asked. "Nobody's worried about the halflings?"

"Not as much during the games. The Fae Council is putting a lot more attention on the humans right now. They are much more worried about them," Fan answered.

"Why? What's going on?" Cassia asked.

"There has been a lot of activity in the human realm lately, and they are worried the humans are going to catch on soon. Too many of them are beginning to see things they shouldn't and are asking too many questions," Fan explained.

That wasn't what Cassia wanted to hear. She was already worried enough about Mia. Now this news merely put more pressure on her. "Great," she said. "That's all I need. More humans learning the truth and forming their own bounty-hunter parties."

Her frustration was obvious as she planted her hands on her hips and paced across the dimly lit chamber. Human interaction with the fae world was almost never a good thing. Of course, there were exceptions.

The locals on the Isle of Raasay who served the fae and ensured events happened smoothly were very helpful. Humans working in the corporations and in conjunction with fae also helped to protect the fae and the security of their world.

But these were very limited exceptions. Most of the time, when humans interacted with the fae, it created serious problems that had ripple effects for the entire world. The worst were the ones who thought they were helping by going after criminals. All too often, they ended up in danger, or they hurt innocent fae.

"Speaking of bounty hunters, the Fae Council wants to bump up efforts to limit the criminal activity, and reduce the danger for the humans who are around. There are so many more criminals here because of the games, and the Council wants to make sure there aren't any issues with multiple deaths, or with humans making connections with the criminals," Fan said.

"That sounds like a fun adventure," Cassia said sarcastically.

"It's good to hear you say that," Fan said, deciding to skip over her sarcasm and pretend she was being sincere. "It just so happens you stumbled into my neck of the woods right at the perfect time. I was about to call you with a special assignment."

That didn't sound appealing to Cassia. She shook her head. "Nope, not happening," she said.

"You didn't even hear what the special assignment was. How are you going to refuse to help?" Fan asked.

"It doesn't matter what it is. I'm not doing it. I'm helping the Elmhurst Academy right now, and trust me, there is plenty for me to be doing there. I don't need to stack anything else on top of it. It's all I can do to make sure they have the extra protection they need with the games going on," Cassia told him.

The jailer stared at her, his expression stern and unchanging. She knew what he was thinking. "You know the council doesn't care much for halflings," he said darkly.

Cassia stiffened at the sentiment. She'd always had a problem with the way the fae council looked at halflings, and with the prejudiced manner in which they handled protecting or defending them. It was worse now that she had Mia in her life. She hated the thought of Mia being overlooked or mistreated, simply because of her halfling parentage.

"I know," she said flatly. "That's why I'm helping the academy. The Council doesn't care to. The way they see the halflings, and how little they seem to care about them is baffling. Some of them have their own halfling children. They should be worried."

Cassia and Fan looked at each other. Behind them, the ogre guard who had remained struggled to hold back a laugh. Cassia's lips tingled. Fan was fighting his own laugh. Finally, they gave in, and both broke into a cascade of laughter.

"The Council? Worried?" the ogre said through his laughs. "About their own children? Listen close, and you might be able to hear the redcaps in hell strapping on their skis."

This made Fan laugh harder. "If the members of the Fae Council ever actually started caring about their own halfling children, I think it would be too cold in hell to even go skiing," he said.

"They'd all be frozen solid," Cassia agreed.

They all knew the Fae Council couldn't care less about their own halfling children. Most of them wouldn't even acknowledge they existed. They were the result of flings with humans and were simply cast aside. Many never met their halfling children, and those who did barely behaved like the kids were alive, much less like they mattered to them at all.

If the Council didn't care about their own children because they were halflings, nothing was going to make a whole academy full of unrelated halflings mean anything to them.

CHAPTER EIGHTY-THREE

The restaurant where the kids were eating, along with Cinder and Alania, was in an area where humans were quite used to seeing fae. However, that didn't stop Sam from crying out in surprise when the flame from the match lighting his cigarette illuminated the bogan a few feet away. He released another short, high-pitched cry as the bogan slammed his head into the wall, knocking him unconscious. It had a plan, and it needed the body alive.

The bogan stood over the fallen waiter and cast the spell to take the waiter's form, using it as a glamour. It would be a convincing glamour, one that would allow him to move through the restaurant. He was glad it only needed the illusion to last for a very short amount of time. This man wasn't something he wanted to look like for long. The creature opened the door to the back of the restaurant and kicked aside the wooden block holding it open, in case the waiter regained consciousness and tried to come inside to warn people.

The kitchen was chaotic. The games provided a huge surge of business and kept the cooks and servers hopping almost from the minute they opened until closing very early in the morning. This would help to keep the bogan under the radar. Most of the young people in the restaurant wouldn't see through the glamour, but the full fae would if they looked long enough. The busy atmosphere would make it easier for him to blend in and go unnoticed.

It didn't take as long as he had expected. Within moments of stepping into the dining room, the bogan saw the perfect opportunity to fulfill his mission. His eyes locked on a waitress carrying a tray of fragile glasses. She was balancing far too many of them to remain steady if she happened to trip on something. And she was heading directly for the girl the bogan had been told to target. He needed blood, and shattered glass was great for that.

The bogan crossed the room and placed himself between the oncoming waitress and the table of kids. At the right moment, he stuck out a foot, tripping the woman. It wasn't elegant, but it worked. Glasses tumbled and crashed into the halflings' table, shattering on impact. The bogan, not leaving anything to chance, snatched a shard and feigned a stumble backward into Mia, aiming at her hand in the chaos.

"What the heck," Zander exclaimed as he jumped up, wine now drenching his shirt.

"Oh, I'm so sorry," the waitress stammered. "Let me get something to help you clean up."

"You're bleeding," the bogan told Mia, feigning shock. "Here, put this on it until she gets back." He handed her a white cloth, which she put over the wound to soak up the small stream of blood.

Mia inspected the cut. "Thanks. It's not bad, actually. Just a little slice. My shirt is ruined, though," she said, looking down at the giant green stain from something sticky that had landed on her in the fall.

The waitress returned quickly with napkins and a first-aid kit. As soon as the bandages were brought out, Mia dropped the white cloth, and the bogan picked it up, stuffing it in his pocket as he shoveled glass into a dustpan. He walked away, snickering at how easy it had been. He tossed the entire dustpan in the trash and headed for the back door. No one saw a thing.

Or so he thought.

Inside the restaurant, Alania pursed her lips. The waitress tripping as she walked by Mia could have been an accident. Things like that happened all the time in restaurants, especially when they were as busy as this one. But she couldn't help but notice when the waiter took the cloth stained with Mia's blood and slipped it into his pocket as he walked by. There was something strange about him. She watched him hurry across the room and saw the tell-tale shimmer around him.

She fluttered up from her place at the table and motioned for Lily to join her. "I think that waiter was actually a glamour. Go follow him," she said, pointing to the kitchen door. Lily nodded and took off without a word.

"We should get back to campus," Carson said. "I know you don't think the cut is that bad, but you should still see the campus nurse. Last thing we want is Elmhurst getting upset that we didn't follow protocol again."

"Carson's right," Zander said. "Besides, I need to get out of this shirt. I smell like alcohol, and I can only guess what Elmhurst would say about that."

The owner of the restaurant waved them off when they asked for the check, insisting that the whole incident was reason enough to comp the meal, and the Five went to the portal to campus. Most of the gang returned to their rooms for the night, but Luna, Alania, Cinder, and Mia, went to the nurse for Mia's cut.

A few hours later, Mia was settled in her room, and Cinder accompanied Alania back to the lounge on the bottom floor. Most of the students were already gone, leaving the two faeries alone in a corner by the fire.

Cinder scooted close to Alania and whispered, "What's going on? You've barely said a word since we got back."

"Someone used a glamour to cut Mia on purpose," Alania said flatly.

"What? It was an accident. She was cut by glass," Cinder argued.

"No, she wasn't. I think it was a bogan. I can't be sure, though. I sent Lily to check it out," Alania explained.

"Speaking of," Cinder said, glancing over Alania's shoulder. "Here she comes."

Alania rose to greet her, and Lily sat next to Cinder. She seemed upset, which Cinder took to mean bad news. "What did you find out?" Alania said, not wasting any time.

"Yeah, tell us what happened," said Cinder. In spite of the worrisome charge Alania had just mentioned, she was excited to be working with her cousin on something that might be important.

"Well, it was definitely a bogan."

"Knew it," Alania said under her breath, shaking her head.

"Yeah, he had cast a glamour of some poor waiter who was knocked out outside in the alley," Lily said. "I checked to make sure he was alive, but he looked like he got his clock cleaned pretty good. Then I noticed a bogan running away from the restaurant with the white cloth the waiter had in his pocket. So, I followed him around the corner and through a portal."

"And?" Cinder asked.

"It's not good."

"How not good?" Alania asked.

"When I came out, I saw him go into a house. I stayed around in the shadows a while until I noticed a light on in his basement. He has a lab down there, and he was doing something with the cloth. It looked like he was testing it. For what I don't know."

"DNA," Alania shrieked. "He got her DNA. Crickets!"

"What should I do now?" Lily asked.

Alania thought for a moment before answering. There were a lot of moving parts now, and things had to be done in a certain way to keep everyone safe. "Go back to Guardian Myla and tell her what you told me. Now. Quickly."

Lily nodded, and left immediately, leaving Alania and Cinder alone once again. Cinder was fuming, but Alania was trying to keep calm.

"We should tell Mia," Cinder said. "She deserves to know."

"We can't. Not yet," Alania insisted.

"Why? She might be in terrible danger, and she deserves to know she might need to look over her shoulder."

"*We're* supposed to be looking over her shoulder. That's our job. And tonight, we failed, and let a bogan get her blood. If she knew, who knows what she would try to do. She might do something stupid, and we wouldn't be able to help her. If she is who we think she is, we need to keep her safe at all costs, including not letting her know what she doesn't need to know yet."

"Cassia. We should tell Cassia then," Cinder said, frustrated. "She's the girl's protector and fae guardian. If no one else, *she* needs to know."

Alania took this under consideration for a moment. Despite the embarrassment of having allowed something to happen to Mia, she knew Cassia was the best person to handle the information, and she definitely needed to know. She nodded.

"Tomorrow. When we see her tomorrow, we will tell her. But for now, we should go back to the dorm room, and try to get some rest."

CHAPTER EIGHTY-FOUR

Mia had expected Cassia to be there when she got up the next day. The bounty hunter had been so angry and worried that Mia was all but positive she was going to wake up to her guardian sitting there in her room, making sure she was where she was supposed to be.

When no Cassia appeared, Mia couldn't help but feel relieved. Her guardian must be on assignment somewhere and didn't have the time to come check in on her. Or ask her a bunch of embarrassing questions about her date with Zander. Not having Cassia there to bug her or spy on her was exactly what she needed.

Down at breakfast, Cinder was worried, too. "You were supposed to be watching her," she hissed at Alania. "You were given an important responsibility. Don't you understand that?"

"Of course, I understand that. I might be younger than you, but that doesn't mean I'm stupid. I know what I'm supposed to be doing," Alania retorted.

"Then why aren't you doing it? You were right there, and look what happened!"

"It was just an accident. Nobody knew that was going to happen."

"Do you have any idea what could happen if there's another accident like that again?" Cinder asked. Cinder had stewed all night over the incident, and how they had allowed the bogan to get away with Mia's DNA. She was as angry as a dragon whose lair had been raided. If she could control her fire, she'd probably spit fire at that bogan right then and there.

Zander overheard the conversation between the faeries and moved along the table toward them. "What's going on?" he asked.

Cinder looked at him and promptly sneezed. The spark hit the hem of Zander's shirt and set the fabric on fire. He swatted at it a few times, hopping up from his seat to shake the shirt and make the flames die down. It only took a few seconds for the fire to go out, but he glared at the little faerie, frustrated that she couldn't control her sneezes better.

"Don't aim at me next time," he said. He looked at the damage to his shirt and released an exasperated sigh. "Great. Now I'm going to have to go back to the dorm and change shirts before I can go to class. I guess there won't be any breakfast for me today."

He stormed off, and Cinder watched him for a few seconds before turning back to Alania. That was what she had intended to happen. She needed him to leave the conversation and not overhear more. Hopefully, the brief little fire would quickly leave his mind, and he wouldn't hold it against her.

That didn't work out. Cinder didn't see him again until later in the day after all his classes were over. She smiled at him pleasantly, but he stalked to her with a glare.

"Cinder, what is going on?" he demanded.

She widened her eyes and looked at him with the most innocent expression she could manage. "What? What are you talking about? Did something happen?"

Zander wasn't impressed. He knew something was up, and he wasn't going to let her off the hook no matter how cute she tried to be. "Don't try that with me. I know something's going on, and you need to tell me what it is. I can't help protect Mia if I don't know what I'm supposed to be protecting her from. I need all the information," he said.

Alania shook her head, but Cinder knew she wasn't going to get by with any more diversion. "Mia is in danger," Cinder said.

"I already know that," he said. "That's why everyone needs to be working together to protect her as much as we can."

"It's a lot more than you and the others know," she added.

Alania shook her head again, pressing her lips together to stop herself from saying anything. She swatted at her cousin, trying to make her be quiet.

"What do you mean?" Zander asked.

"Shhhh," Alania said harshly, trying to keep Cinder from going any further without saying anything herself.

"No," Cinder said, shaking her head. "I'm done. I'm tired of keeping secrets, and I don't want to do it anymore. If there's anyone who is going to be able to help Mia, it's Zander. He cares about her and won't let her get hurt. But he has to know what's really going on if he's going to be able to help her."

Zander's worry immediately skyrocketed. His eyes snapped back and forth between the faeries and finally landed on Alania. "If you don't stop trying to keep secrets about Mia from me, I will glue your wings together," he threatened.

This ticked the little faerie off. She was trying to do her job and didn't appreciate him being so aggressive with her. She wriggled a little closer and sneezed on him. Zander was accustomed to Cinder sneezing and lighting things on fire, but he wasn't prepared for Alania's sneezing abilities.

As soon as the little faerie sneezed in his direction, Zander's feet left the ground, and he was floating in the air. With a single flick of her hand, ropes appeared out of nowhere. The long lengths wrapped around Zander, tying him up so he wasn't able to move. He struggled against them, trying to escape, but it was of no use.

"You're not going to get out of those ropes," Alania told him. "They were made out of the vines around the faerie pools. They were enchanted specifically to hold fae in place. You can't get out of them."

"Alania doesn't like to be insulted," Cinder said.

"I'm sorry," Zander said. He gritted his teeth to prevent any more words from coming out. He was smart enough to keep quiet while she still had him subdued and floating around in the air.

"Listen to me carefully. I am the guardian. I will be the one protecting the princess, not you," Alania said firmly.

Zander's eyes widened, and his mouth fell open, but he stopped himself before he said anything. However, in his silence, he swore he would do anything he had to in order to protect Mia.

What Alania had said was the confirmation he needed. He knew for sure now that Mia was the missing heir. They had all suspected that she was. As soon as they started learning more about Princess Violet, they had come to the conclusion that Mia must be descended from her. But Princess Violet died almost two thousand years ago. At least, that was what everyone assumed. That meant Mia couldn't be very closely related to her, and why they had all said she couldn't be related. But Zander knew everyone, well, everyone except for Vivi, still considered it a possibility.

The human blood that made her a halfling only tainted her lineage further. It complicated things. Mia had already said she didn't want to claim her heritage, which meant no one should be worried about her. That would be the only reason anyone should want to be after her. But it was obvious someone was concerned about the possibility of her deciding she wanted to claim her right to the throne.

Even though she had too much human blood in her to truly take the throne, someone was upset by the possibility, enough to want to kill her. He was extremely confused by it all, but that didn't do anything to change how he felt. He still wanted to do anything he could to protect her.

"I care about Mia very much," he finally said to Alania. "I would do anything to protect her, and would never want anything to happen to her."

The faerie flew up to look him straight in the eye. She pointed at him firmly. "I am swearing you to absolute secrecy. You can't say anything about any of this to anyone," she said.

"I won't," he promised.

"Not even Mia. She doesn't need to be worried about it all," she added.

Zander nodded his agreement, and Alania let him float back to the ground. The rope disappeared in a sudden poof. He hurried away from them, wanting to find Mia as much as he wanted to be away from them.

As soon as he was gone, Cinder looked at her cousin. "He already suspected her lineage. We found out last semester that she is most likely a descendant of Princess Violet, but very far down the line. It has been too long since her death for them to be closely related," she said.

"Suspecting is one thing. Knowing is another," Alania said. "He needs to keep his mouth shut."

Around the corner, Vivi leaned against the building, listening to the conversation. She had watched the entire interaction with Zander, and now her eyes sparkled with an evil glint. She gathered her books and rushed off to the dorm, where she knew she would find Mia.

CHAPTER EIGHTY-FIVE

Vivi returned to the dorm room, and burst inside, eager to tell Mia what she had heard so she could watch her reaction. But when she entered, she saw Elmhurst had arrived. Luna and Mia were both sitting on the edge of Luna's bed, and they turned to look at Vivi when she came in.

"Is everything all right?" Vivi asked.

Having the headmistress in their room wasn't something that happened often. She highly doubted Elmhurst would just come by to say hello and check in on them. Something had to have brought her to see them.

"I was just telling them that Cassia has been called away on Council business," Elmhurst said.

Vivi nodded as she went to her bed. She decided to keep what she had heard to herself, at least for now. As much as she had wanted to be the one to tell Mia, and to be there to see her response, she wasn't going to do it while Elmhurst was standing there. She didn't want the headmistress to know and take drastic actions.

As upset as Vivi had been when they had first learned they had to take Mia into their group, she had since seen the benefits. In the short time they had worked together, the group had managed to achieve the

Power of Five on several occasions and were growing stronger. They would be able to do so much more as time went on. It would help all of them accomplish their goals, and put Vivi in a stronger position to earn the accolades and attention from the prestigious schools and roles she wanted to attract.

She didn't want the headmistress to take Mia away. Not yet, anyway. Maybe after graduation, but that thought made her pause. If they kept working together after graduation, they could achieve more. Suddenly, it hit Vivi. Did she really want to keep Mia around? She could barely believe it herself.

"Oh, and Vivi," Elmhurst said a few moments later. Vivi looked up from folding the clothes she had dug through that morning to choose her outfit as she contemplated what to do with her juicy news. Elmhurst was holding a piece of paper out to her. "This came in from your father earlier. He asked that I give it to you."

The sound of the principal's voice didn't give Vivi a lot of hope that the message contained in the note was a good one. She took it and sat on her bed, holding the folded paper in her lap while the headmistress said her goodbyes and left. When she was gone, Vivi opened the note and stared down at it.

"Are you okay?" Luna asked several seconds later when Vivi hadn't looked up from the paper again.

"What does it say?" Mia asked.

Vivi shook her head and balled up the paper. She hopped off the bed and left the room without answering. This was something she didn't want to tell them. Her father had yet again canceled plans with her. This time they had arranged to attend a game together.

He had told her to return the ticket he had bought for her to attend the major league game that upcoming weekend. Instead of going with her, he was planning to use her ticket to schmooze a fae who had offices in Europe. It was an important business contract, he explained, as though that was all she needed to hear to be understanding. It was an important business contract, so the promise he had made to his daughter didn't matter. It was expected that she should accept and be fine with it.

At least he had given some sort of concession to the idea of her feelings. According to him, since both of the Slamball Major League teams competing at the event on Saturday were from Europe, he figured she wouldn't care about seeing them. Using the tickets for his European business contact would be a more advantageous use of it.

Of course, that didn't matter to her. She didn't care why he believed the ticket would be better used by someone else. She only cared that he had given it to her and had planned on seeing a game with her, then he had gone back on his word. As usual.

She was hurt, and seriously ticked off. There was a time when her initial reaction would have been to put someone else down or cause problems for someone else, likely Mia. This time, instead of being a bully, she decided to make herself feel better by going out and having fun. That's why she was on her way to find Carson. He would be up for anything.

She was right that he would be up for some fun, but it wasn't going to be just the two of them. After she explained what had happened, Carson pointed out that it would do her good to be around the entire group.

No matter what she said or what she wanted people to think, she got a lot of comfort and support from the five. They worked hard together, but they also managed to have a lot of fun. Vivi reluctantly agreed, and they made plans to go into Edinburgh and sightsee, foregoing anything to do with Slamball, and instead, experiencing new things, and having fun together.

In his hidden lair, Narco was far from having fun. The test result came back on the blood the bogan had managed to harvest from Mia, but it was confusing. The blood had ruined the test, leaving a mess instead of true results. He realized by looking at it that even her blood had been touched by the spell meant to keep prying eyes away from the girl's genetic secrets. He was furious.

At this rate, he wouldn't have anything to compare to the royal

DNA, should he even be able to get a sample from his shadow contact. Without a clean DNA strand from the girl, Narco's contact wouldn't attempt to get something from one of the queens.

"Try again," Narco demanded. "Obviously there's something wrong with the test. You have to try again. You said blood wouldn't be impacted by a spell."

Orin shook his head. "Trying again won't do any good, Narco. The same thing would happen. It is extremely rare, and only someone of the highest levels of power can do it, but some are capable of putting a genetic cloaking-spell on blood. I told you that you would need some of Mia's blood if you wanted to test her because I didn't think she would be affected by that kind of enchantment. I've never seen it myself."

"Then how could it have happened? If it is so rare, how could this be?" Narco asked.

"Princess Violet must have cast a generational spell," Orin suggested.

"Generational spells are from ancient times. Even before Princess Violet," Narco pointed out. "Fae haven't messed with them in a long time."

"She must have learned the details of it before she left the fae realm. Perhaps she took a book or two of ancient spells with her and learned about it from them. I've heard that some ancient texts went missing when the kingdom split. She must have wanted to mask herself and any offspring she had," Orin told him.

Narco shook his head, not convinced by the idea. "I can't believe it would still be in effect all these years later. It's been over two millennia, for crickets' sake!"

"Rumor has it, the third princess was just as powerful as her two sisters," Orin told him.

Narco thought about Queen Mab and her incredible power, then about Queen Tatiana and how powerful she was. He scowled.

"Mia can't be as powerful as Mab and Tatiana. She's a halfling. It's just not possible. There has to be a way to remove the spell protecting her DNA," he said.

Orin nodded, relenting to his associate's intense refusals. "Fine. I will work on it. But we'll need more blood. We don't have enough left to run an effective test," he said.

"That's not a problem," Narco agreed. "I could send a redcap in to get at least a finger."

Orin shook his head firmly. "No. That will cause too much attention. She's already been injured. I will send another associate to the school to get her bandages. There will be enough within the bandages to work on the spell. Then once I've figured that out, if we need more, we can contemplate doing something more severe."

"All right," Narco said. "But we need to move quickly. There isn't any time to spare. We need her DNA."

CHAPTER EIGHTY-SIX

"Do you think we stayed in our dorm rooms long enough to qualify as having slept here?" Luna asked as the group gathered together in the predawn darkness.

It was four in the morning on Saturday, and they were getting an early start to make sure they could fit as much in their day as they possibly could before having to obey the curfew Elmhurst had set. With Scotland so many hours ahead of them, starting this early in the morning meant they had already missed a few hours of the day there. The group didn't want to miss anything else.

"We were in our rooms, weren't we?" Carson asked. "And we definitely slept after midnight."

"And Elmhurst didn't say anything about how long we had to be in bed. She didn't make any specifications about leaving before the crack of dawn. Just that we had to be in our rooms, and sleep in our beds," Vivi said.

"I'm really not interested in any more arguments about technicalities," Luna said. "That run-in with Elmhurst was enough for me."

"It's not a technicality," Zander reassured her. "It is morning."

"And think about it," Mia added. "We've gotten this early of a start before, like on days when we were practicing our spells. There were times when we left even earlier than this, and she never said anything about it."

"That's true," Luna said.

"Great," Vivi said. "I already know where I want to go first. I read about Merlin in the library this week. He had to be fae. It's so obvious. I want to check out this place called Arthur's Seat, and see if there's anything left over that might give me some good gossip for my paper."

Mia and Luna laughed.

"The papers aren't supposed to be gossip, Vivi," Mia said. "They're supposed to be actual facts."

"Remember, how did the fae and the humans in Scotland interact over the centuries?" Luna asked, lifting her voice into a shrill impression of the teacher's voice.

She didn't sound anything like the teacher, but it made the group laugh. Vivi nodded. "I know that. But it could still be good. Let's get going," Vivi said.

The Unseelie girl's chirpy good mood didn't last long once they reached Scotland. She'd had visions of Arthur's Seat being a palace or a hidden sanctuary of some kind, brimming with ancient knowledge and signs of fae doings she would be able to uncover. Instead, she learned it was a mountain located on an ancient volcano, to which they would have to hike. They stood at the bottom and stared at the mountain.

Carson turned to her after several long, silent moments. "You know, this could actually be a good thing," he said.

"How exactly do you figure that?" Vivi asked.

"Well, we're supposed to be finding all the ways the fae and humans interacted in Scotland. Ancient fae used to hide out near volcanos. The humans worshipped them and their volcanos. We should at least try to see it," Carson said.

"It will be good for you," Luna said, slinging her arm around Vivi's shoulders. "People say good exercise can clear your mind and help you think better."

"I don't need my mind cleared," Vivi said.

"But it will be a great story," Carson pointed out. "How often do you get a chance to say you climbed a volcano?"

She finally relented, and they headed for the path that led up the mountain. The hike wasn't easy, but halfway up, the challenge became invigorating. Reaching the top of the mountain gave them their reward. At the summit, they could see all the way across the city of Edinburgh. It was stunning, even according to Vivi. They stood there looking out over the city, appreciating the view for a while. Until Vivi stepped back.

"Let's keep exploring," she said.

"What are you looking for?" Carson asked.

"I don't know. But there has to be something. This place wouldn't just be called Arthur's Seat for no reason. There has to be more to it than just a volcano."

They agreed, and roamed around the area, seeing what they could find. After several minutes, they discovered the remains of what looked like an ancient tower.

"Well, there's your castle, Vivi," Mia teased.

"It does look like it was once part of a castle," Vivi agreed. "I wonder what it was."

They went farther and wandered around the base of the crumbling structure. There was nothing to indicate what it was or what significance it had.

"Vivi, can you read the history?" Zander asked. "Is there enough?"

Vivi concentrated on the area for a moment, then nodded. "There's plenty."

Using a similar ability to what she had used with the book from the library, she called up an image of the history of the tower. The first thing they saw was a bunch of teenagers. They danced around the tower and knocked back beers, throwing the bottles into a fire they had built nearby. Some chanted and yelled, while others exchanged sloppy kisses, and tumbled on the ground, drunk.

"That's charming," Mia muttered.

Vivi nodded. "Let me rewind a bit." She rewound the image as far as it would go.

When the image returned, they saw a very old man, hunched over as he put a spell on his home. They couldn't hear what he said or see what he was doing exactly. All they saw was a large bubble forming over it. The dome covered him and his small castle, leaving only the tower where they stood exposed. He wore a blue cloak, held a large walking stick with a gem at the top of it, and had a very long white beard that hung to his waist.

"It's Merlin," Mia said.

The other four looked at her quizzically.

"It could be anybody. We have no idea when this even is," Vivi told her.

"Trust me. I've seen *The Sword in the Stone*, and that is Merlin," she insisted.

They continued to stare at her.

"What?" Carson asked.

"Seriously?" Mia asked, shocked by their seeming lack of knowledge of the movie. "You guys are halflings. There's human in there somewhere. You're telling me you've never seen it?" They just kept staring at her. "I don't have a phone, or I would show you a picture. But trust me. That man is Merlin."

"Okay," Vivi said. "We'll just shelve that one and consider it a possibility. With a whole lot of question marks beside it."

She turned to the image and saw that the man was now looking at her. She admonished herself. He wasn't looking at her. He wasn't really there. This was the history of the area. Whatever was going on in that moment so long ago, he just happened to be looking in the direction she was now standing.

A second later, the man winked at her. Startled by the action so clearly directed at her, Vivi gasped and backed away a few steps. The vision faded, and the other four halflings groaned and shouted their protests.

"Hey!" Carson said. "Where did it go?"

"Bring it back," Zander said. "We didn't even get to see what he was doing."

"I want to know why he was protecting his house," Luna said. "There had to be something interesting going on."

"Bring it back, Vivi," Mia insisted.

Vivi tried to bring the image back, but she couldn't. She was too shaken by the wink to fully concentrate. Instead, she walked around the remains of the castle again, this time in search of signs of the spell shielding the structure. It was possible the spell was still in place, and they might find more of the building.

"Look at this," she said, a while later.

The other four halflings, and the faeries tasked with protecting them, gathered around her.

"What is it?" Zander asked.

Vivi pointed. "Right there. It looks like a cave leading into the volcano."

Curiosity drew them to the mouth of the cave, and into the volcano, almost breathless with anticipation at what they might find when they got inside. None knew what to think when they found nothing but a book.

"It's like the one Vivi found in the library," Mia pointed out.

"Touch it," Vivi said. "See if it reacts to you the way that one did."

Mia marched up to the book and lay her fingertips on the cover. It immediately illuminated, and she pulled her hand away. Vivi and Carson joined her, and each took turns touching the book. It didn't react. Alania and Cinder each tried, followed by the other guardians, Lily and Dalia. None of them changed the book when they touched it. Mia tried again, and again, it glowed brightly.

From the corner of her eye, Vivi spotted something shiny in a far corner of the chamber. She went to it and bent to look. A sudden gust of dust blew up on her, and she sneezed, stumbling backward and landing on her butt. She almost swore, but she bit the words back. "Stupid crickets," she said instead. She got up and brushed herself off. "I'm hungry. Come on. Let's get some lunch."

Mia scooped up the book and put it in her backpack as they left the cave.

"How about afternoon tea at the Holyrood Palace?" Luna suggested.

"That sounds perfect. We are, after all, in the presence of royalty," Vivi teased.

Alania cut her eyes at Vivi, worried about what she might know. She couldn't tell if Vivi was teasing about something she knew was the truth, or if she was just speculating.

CHAPTER EIGHTY-SEVEN

"I don't want the championship to end," Mia said, as they returned to the portal after their day in Edinburgh.

"I knew you would become a big slamball fan," Carson said. "As soon as you started watching, I knew you were going to get hooked."

Mia laughed. "I do like slamball, but that's not what I'm talking about. I'll miss the games, of course, but I'm going to miss exploring Scotland even more. This has been so amazing."

Zander moved closer beside her, and their fingers linked together lightly between them. They exchanged a smile but didn't let it linger too long. The whole day had been filled with ribbing and teasing from the halflings, and even the faeries had joined in. Any time the two of them looked at each other for too long or touched, someone made a comment or a silly sound. It wasn't making her angry, but she'd already had enough for the day.

"We can still go exploring even after the championships are over," Carson pointed out.

"I think she means she's going to miss being able to do it without risking getting in trouble," Luna said. "After the championships are over, I really doubt Elmhurst is going to keep up her blanket permission to go visit Scotland."

"And, no, I'm not going to make portals for us to go whenever we want and pretend it's because we're practicing our Power of Five," Mia said with a laugh.

"Well, you are just going to have to be more specific now, aren't you?" he asked.

They all laughed and went through the portal together. Mia checked the clock on the wall overhead as they all came through. They wanted to make sure they were back for their midnight curfew. Not only did they not want to get in any trouble, but they also didn't want their guardian faeries to be on Elmhurst's bad side for letting them stray from the rules again.

"Perfect," she said with a grin. "Look at that. We're not just on time, we have a whole minute to spare."

"We could have lingered on that walk back to the portal," Vivi said with a roll of her eyes, but nobody missed the smile on her lips.

They took a few steps and noticed dark little figures standing in the shadows. Dan and Steve walked toward them, and held up their left arms, looking at their wrists as if they were checking their watches.

"Guys, you don't wear watches," Carson pointed out. "You're not finding out anything new from staring at your stony little arms. If you want to know what time it is, there's a clock right up on the wall there."

"What are you doing here?" Zander asked.

"Isn't it obvious? They're spying on us for Elmhurst," Vivi snapped.

"We are not!" Dan immediately protested.

"Why would you suggest such a thing?" Steve asked, offended at the accusation.

"Because you've done it ever since we've known you," Luna replied.

"And you're here making sure we're back on time," Mia added.

Both gargoyles opened their mouths as if they were going to try to argue again, but no sound came out. The halflings and the faeries moved around them and headed toward the dorm. They slipped inside and immediately closed the door, locking it.

No one ever came into their room unannounced, except for Elmhurst. But they didn't want to take any chances. Not only would they find the boys in the room, but they'd also catch the five looking at the book they'd been waiting to dig into since finding it in the cave.

Mia eagerly pulled the book from her bag and set it in the middle of the bed. She stared at it for a few seconds before resting her hand on it. It instantly began to glow, and Luna gasped.

"Look," Luna said.

They looked at the first book, which had begun to glow as well. A second later, the book shone brighter, and a scene appeared above it.

"Vivi, are you doing that?" Mia asked.

The Unseelie halfling shook her head. "No. I'm not doing anything."

The book was revealing its secrets without any of them having to call them forward. It was as if the books had been waiting for Mia to put them together. It had to be her. The others knew they weren't the ones who made this happen. Only Mia's touch on the books made them glow. She had initiated something amazing with that touch, and the halflings and faeries fell into a hushed silence to watch.

An image of a beautiful girl appeared in front of them.

"Hello," she said. "I am Princess Caledona."

The girls gasped and exchanged glances.

"The books belonged to the princess," Vivi whispered.

"Which means that couldn't have been Merlin's castle. These books are much older than him," Luna said.

"Unless he was holding one of the books for Caledona," Mia pointed out. "That could explain why he had one. But why would he have anything belonging to her?"

The image of the princess turned and looked directly at Mia. This startled the halfling. She didn't realize such a thing as an interactive vision existed.

"Merlin was a fae mystic who loved humans, especially King Arthur," Princess Caledona explained. "He was also my half-brother."

"Merlin was your brother?" Mia asked, stunned by the revelation.

"Yes. He was born to my father, a fae, and his wife. We don't share a mother," the princess told them.

"Who is your mother?" Carson asked.

"A Pictish woman who caught the attention of my father Callum."

"When was Merlin alive?" Luna asked. "You said he loved King Arthur."

"Merlin died about one hundred years after King Arthur," the princess answered.

"How do you know all this?" Mia asked. "You died well before Merlin was even born."

Princess Caledona smiled. "My spirit lives on between the two books. I am not really gone."

"Why is this all tied to me?" Mia asked. "What do I have to do with any of it? These books respond to me, but I don't understand."

"You are the one who will save the fae from destruction. You must take your rightful place. Along the way, there will be those who will want to kill you. And there will be those who will give their lives for you. You will have many around you who will fiercely protect you from anyone wanting to do you harm. But in the end, it is up to you. You must make the right choices, and you are the only one who can do that. You may have a destiny, but it will only come to fruition if you choose it and follow the right path."

Alania watched, startled by what she saw. She knew they couldn't handle this completely on their own. Without anyone noticing, she slipped out of the room and returned through the portal to the Isle of Skye. She went directly to the pools to get Guardian Myla. Alania knew giving her too many details or trying to explain what was happening without her actually seeing it, would be confusing and take too much time, so she asked the Head Guardian to simply come with her.

Myla followed her, and when she entered the girls' dorm room, she paused. Her eyes fell on the image hovering above the books and tears welled up in them.

"My old friend," she whispered. "I can't believe it's you."

Princess Caledona's eyes filled with tears as she gazed back at the faerie guardian. "I've missed you so much, my dear friend. I'm very happy you've done so well. There are many who want to steal the pools, and you have done an incredible job protecting them. It is very important for you to continue your work. You have a long way to go."

Before anyone could ask any more questions, the image of Princess Caledona disappeared. The halflings protested, demanding that Mia try to bring her back, but Myla held up her hands to quiet them.

"She will not come back until she wants to," Guardian Myla told them. "You must all keep this quiet. Do you understand? It would be best if I take the books with me."

"We found them," Mia pointed out. "And they respond to me. Why should you have them?"

"You may visit the books any time you want, but you have to understand. These books would be extremely dangerous if the wrong fae found them. It would put an even bigger target on Mia, and we can't risk that. If I have the books with me, they are secure and will be guarded with the same power as the pools. No one will be able to get to them and use them for their own purposes. Mia will be safer."

The five looked at each other, silently communicating through their eyes. Finally, they all nodded.

"You can take them," Mia said.

Myla thanked her and took the books into her arms. As the faerie guardian flitted away, Mia thought about Cassia. She wanted to tell her about all this, but she didn't know when she would see her guardian again. This was not something she could say over a phone call.

CHAPTER EIGHTY-EIGHT

"Something has to be done. It is simply not possible she is so thoroughly enchanted that there is no way to get her DNA," Narco said.

"I'm sorry, Narco. So far, none of the tests we've done have been successful, and my previous attempts have used up all the samples of Mia's blood we had available to us," Orin told him.

"Then we need to get more blood," Narco insisted. "I have to have the proof, although in a way, not being able to get the DNA from her blood is proof in and of itself."

"What do you mean?"

"I already had the strongest suspicion that Mia is the girl I have been looking for. Now that you've proven her hair and her blood are under a spell to prevent anyone from extracting genetic material, I am positive of it. There's no other explanation. Why would a normal halfling need to have those types of protections?"

"That makes sense," Orin told him. "The type of spell needed to veil her DNA this way is extremely hard to do and can be very dangerous. It wouldn't be used for no reason. The only people who would go to the effort and risk of putting on this type of spell are those with very strong motivations for protecting heritage. This isn't just about privacy."

"I want to know more about her," Narco said. "No one seems to know all the details of her life. If I can find out more about her, I can convince my boss of what I already know."

"What do you want to know?"

"I want to know where she comes from and who her parents are on Earth. Is it possible she was staying with foster parents the entire time? Both humans who have no idea who and what she is? Or fae who would be able to protect her as she grew up, and not let the truth of her magic abilities come to the surface when she was young?" Narco suggested. A thought suddenly came to mind. "Or maybe…"

His voice trailed off, and Orin looked at him questioningly. "Or maybe what?"

"We're assuming she was raised by both parents. It's possible she was raised just by her father. And if she was, she could be the child of the woman I killed in Boston seventeen years ago."

"We can find out," Orin said. "Someone can check her school records for any indication of family or friends in the human world. Elmhurst is very strict about records."

"How do you know about what goes on at the academy?" Narco asked.

"I have associates with children at the school. They've told me about how extensive the headmistress is with her record-keeping for each student. Apparently, there have been instances in the past with students disappearing. In some situations, it was magic gone awry, and they were able to find them fairly easily. In others, it wasn't so straightforward. They had to dig through everything they could find about the students, their families, all their associates. Everyone on Earth, and in faerie. Over time, the school made it a requirement to have deeply thorough records, so if anything like that ever happens again, they can more easily search for them," Orin explained.

"So the school will have detailed records of her family and any contacts," Narco said.

Orin nodded. "Yes."

"Then we need to get inside. We need her school records and her computer. You said you know people who have children who go to the academy. Ask if one of them can arrange for you to have a tour."

"A tour?"

"Yes. Pretend you're considering it for a future child or a nephew, or whatever. Come up with something. While Elmhurst is giving you the tour, I will have one of my men go into the office and look through her records."

Three days later, Narco paced through his house while he waited to hear from the man he sent onto the campus behind Orin. It was taking too long. If the records were as thorough as Orin said, Narco should have heard something by now. Finally, a message appeared on his computer. He released a sound of angry exasperation and slammed his hands on the table.

"How could he find nothing?" he shouted.

He couldn't wait any longer. People were on high alert at the campus, watching for him, but it didn't matter. He would have to take the risk.

He created a portal and walked out onto the road leading up to the school. This time, he decided to arrive farther away from campus, in case they had any alarms set up for portals opening near the academy grounds.

Narco put on a different glamour from last time. Since the blasted gargoyles had seen him, he had to create a new persona. This time he used a wig. The Unseelie fae walked across campus as though he belonged there and knew exactly where to go.

Without any issues, other than one halfling looking at him strangely, he went into Mia's dorm room. He could still smell Luna's perfume and knew he had arrived with only seconds to spare. Mia's computer was sitting in the middle of her bed, and he snatched it.

He'd have to give his academy contact a bonus for figuring out a way to get him entry into the dorm after Elmhurst had put a spell on the building barring him. Those halfling fae kids were too easy to bribe. All it took was the promise of getting them into the best college, and they were his to command. The glint in his eyes was evil, and he was almost giddy.

He left the dorm, retraced his steps, and returned through a different portal outside the fence lines. Moments later, he was back at his house, the computer on a table in front of him as he tried to access it. It was protected by far more than just a password. The spell locking it was designed to keep out prying eyes and was far too strong for any halfling to bypass. It took Narco half an hour, but finally, he managed to break through the enchantment and open the laptop.

He sifted through the homework and projects, silly poems and seemingly meaningless lists, everything he thought he'd find in a teenage girl's computer. Finally, he located what he had been looking for. Hidden in a folder filled with pictures was the virtual paper trail of Mia's old life. And in an instant, Narco knew exactly who her father was.

Cassia couldn't ignore the tugging feeling that came with the alert. The small stone, which she had woven into a leather bracelet so it wouldn't stand out to anyone, now glowed a vibrant shade of blue, telling her something was wrong. It had happened before, but each time it had been brief. Now it had been going on for most of the day, and she was getting worried.

Mia's father was missing. The spell she had put on him right after she brought Mia to the academy was meant to trace him in a distant way. It ensured that Cassia would know where he was and if he was following the regular patterns of his life. If he deviated too far, the stone alerted her so she could check in on him. Every other time, it had been something as simple as taking a long weekend, or an assignment at work that took him somewhere he hadn't been before. This time, it wasn't so easy.

Later that day, she sat with Mia, holding her hands as she stared into the young halfling's face. Mia looked shocked, pale, and drawn as she processed what her guardian had told her.

"Are you sure?" she asked.

"Yes," Cassia told her. "I went to check on him, but no one has seen him. He didn't show up for work, and his car is still in the driveway at the house, but he isn't there. He's missing."

Mia jumped up. "We have to go search for him," she said desperately. "We have to find my dad. He's an innocent in all this. He has no clue what's going on, or who I really am."

Cassia shook her head. This was a moment she hadn't prepared for. She had known it would come to this eventually, but she hadn't let herself think about it, not yet. Now, there was no way to avoid it.

"He did know, Mia," she said.

"What?" Mia asked.

"Your father did know who your mother was. Not that she was royalty, but that she was fae, and was in hiding from some very bad people. That was really all he knew. He suspected you were important, but he had no idea how important."

Far away from campus, Narco had just learned the same information. James writhed and gritted his teeth against the pain as the bounty hunter's magic tore through his body without causing any visible injuries. The fae was drawing information from James, forcing his mind and soul to give up the truth because he couldn't trust what the man's tongue might say.

"What's this?" Narco asked, pondering a new piece of information he had just gotten. "You're still hiding secrets."

The interrogation had already revealed that James knew about Mia and had raised her without ever telling her. He had kept her from her heritage and birthright, and also kept everyone searching for her at bay. Now Narco had a new detail that surprised him.

"What?" James asked through gritted teeth, staring defiantly at

Narco.

"It seems Mia isn't really a halfling at all. She's not full fae, of course, but to be a halfling, she would have to have one full human parent, and she doesn't."

"What are you talking about?" James asked.

"You don't know?" Narco asked. He used his magic to force out the truth, drawing a growl of pain from the man. "Oh, you didn't. How interesting. I guess I should be the one to tell you that you also have a fae heritage."

"That isn't true," James said.

"You want proof? I can arrange for that."

He called in Orin. When the scientist came in, Narco took a knife and gathered blood from a long slice down James's arm. Orin brought the sample to the table where they had the equipment set up and ran tests. Moments later, he turned to Narco.

"The results are inconclusive," he said.

"What?" Narco snapped.

"I can't get any information from this blood. His DNA must be under the same spell as Mia's. All I can tell you is that he's part-human. That element of his genetic profile is coming up clearly," Orin told him, offering him the sheet of results.

Narco looked at them and gave a mirthless laugh. "It's a shame, really. Your human part shows you are very healthy and would probably have lived a very long life if you had never met Mia's mother. Unfortunately for you, you did. I guess DNA can't predict everything," he said.

"Narco, you have to keep James alive for now," Orin told him.

"Why? He hasn't given me anything valuable."

"We might need him as leverage against Mia," Orin pointed out.

Narco was disappointed. "I was really looking forward to the kill. It's been so long, and I've missed the feeling," he said.

"You will need to learn to control those impulses. They're going to get you in trouble one day," Orin said, shaking his head.

Narco smirked. "No one will ever catch me. I'm far too smart for that."

CHAPTER EIGHTY-NINE

Mia paced the room, her arms crossed over her chest as she tried to cope with the news and the limitations she was under. No one wanted her to go search for her father, and somewhere in her mind, Mia knew it wouldn't help. She would be a liability, at best. At worst, kidnapping her father was only to draw Mia out, and she would fall directly into the trap.

She knew she was too emotional to focus on it, but she was also a complete wreck not doing anything about it either. Mia needed to stay somewhere safe and protected and allow Cassia to do her job.

The door opened, and everyone turned to see Elmhurst on the threshold. She looked somber and reserved as she strode into the room, walking directly to Mia and placing a hand on her shoulder. Her face was a mask of swirling emotions, but she remained tightly controlled.

"Mia, I am so sorry this is happening. You should know that I have some of the best investigators working on it," Elmhurst said, stepping back.

"As do I," Cassia said. "It's Narco. We all know it's Narco. It's just a matter of finding him."

"But what if Narco kills my father before they find him?" Mia asked, tears streaming down her face. Luna stood to comfort her, and Mia leaned into her, though her eyes remained on Cassia.

Cassia cleared her throat. "Frankly, if Narco wanted to kill him, he would have done it already, and made a big show of it," Cassia responded. "He wants to use him for something. Either bait, to get you to reveal yourself where he can catch you, or eventually to use him to trade for you. He might be ruthless, but he's not stupid. Narco will keep your father alive out of a need to use him, and we will catch him before anything else happens. You need to believe that."

"As hard as it may be, Mia, you need to try to continue on as if nothing has happened," Elmhurst added.

Mia looked at Elmhurst as if that was the craziest thing anyone had ever said to her. How could she act like nothing had happened when her father was missing? Elmhurst didn't flinch, though, stoically standing by the door.

"As best you can," said Cassia. "You have to act as normally as you can under the circumstances. Everyone here in this room knows what's going on, and I am sure Elmhurst will alert your teachers to let them know as much as she can about the situation as well."

Elmhurst nodded in confirmation. "I will. We will all wait to see what our contacts can find out, and for Narco to make his next move. It won't be long. As for the rest of you, classes have already begun. I will escort you to your current classes and explain to your instructor what has happened. Mia, you may be excused for the day if you need time to get your emotions under control."

Mia shook her head. "No. I don't want to be alone. I'll go to class."

"Very well," said Elmhurst, looking over her shoulder. "Follow me."

The five students followed her to class. The rest of the day was a blur to Mia, as she floated in and out of being able to focus on her surroundings. At times, she felt disassociated from the school and numb. No anger, no sadness, just an empty well of nothingness.

Then the nothingness would be filled by sadness, or terror, or frustration, or white-hot rage. She was coming out of one of her empty stages when the group shuffled off to their normal practice area. As Vivi put up the protective bubble, Zander collected them to work on the Power of Five.

But as the spell began, Mia's mind drifted away again, and rage filled her heart. She could feel her body shaking with it, and her vision went blurry. Her eyes closed.

"Um, Zander?" asked Carson. "Do you hear—"

The sentence couldn't be finished as the rumble he was drawing attention to turned into an explosion of flame, dirt, and grass. A tree at the side of the bubble was aflame, its branches sparking and shooting orange light high, licking the edge of the protective dome. Vivi closed her eyes as she tried to focus on keeping the shield in place.

"Mia, please, calm down," Zander said, rushing to her.

Another explosion rocked the ground nearby, and everyone but Mia dropped to their bellies. A large oak crashed into the center of what had been their circle. It, too, was ablaze, and Mia's eyes were open, staring deeply into it. The tree went up in flames fast, leaves crackling in the intense heat.

Smoke was filling the bubble, and Vivi was struggling to hold it together. It was risky, though, and she debated dropping it. If she let it down, Mia might start exploding trees where innocent people were. But if Vivi kept the dome in place, they all could all die of smoke inhalation.

Before Vivi made a choice, Elmhurst appeared at the edge of the bubble. She raised her hands, released the protective spell, and Vivi fell over in exhaustion. Striding up to Mia, Elmhurst commanded her attention, and the pressure in the air dissipated.

"All five of you, back to your dorm," she said, her voice rising above her almost-legendary even tone. "Mia, you must learn to control your powers. This is far too dangerous. I know you're worried about your father, but you must get your emotions under control before you hurt someone else...or yourself."

A few days passed, and at the behest of Cassia, the group decided to take a much more controlled Mia to the Slamball World Championship Finals. The Elmhurst Academy had made it into the finals, and the entire school would be there to cheer them on against a halfling academy from France.

After the incident on the practice field, Elmhurst needed a little convincing to let Mia off the campus. Cassia was still working on Elmhurst to reluctantly give permission as they walked the grounds of the school, the gang trailing behind them.

"Seriously, what can happen at a game filled with fae who are specifically on the lookout for something happening in the stands? Mia needs some time to do something other than worry," Cassia argued.

"Fine," Elmhurst said, as they walked past the library. She addressed the group. "You may go to the games, but you must return immediately after."

"I wish I could go," said a voice behind Cassia. She turned to see a dejected Dan on his pedestal.

"It sounds like so much fun," said Steve, pouting.

"I wish you could too," said Mia, her head bowed. "I would feel better if you could."

Dan shifted his weight, and his eyes bulged. "Steve?" he asked beneath his breath.

"Yeah?"

"I just moved my leg," Dan said, sounding confused.

"Hey, I just moved mine," Steve said in surprise.

"No," Elmhurst objected. "Not those two."

Without waiting for permission, Dan and Steve took to the sky, soaring around delightedly in broad daylight. After a few moments of flight, and a heavy sigh from Elmhurst, they returned to the ground beside Mia.

"Thank you, Mia," Steve exclaimed. "Can we go with you now?"

"I hardly see the point in drawing that much attention," Elmhurst said. "You are needed to protect the campus."

"Who's going to mess with a girl who has two gargoyles, though?" Cassia asked, smirking.

Elmhurst sighed heavily again. "Fine," she said. "But when the game is over, you two will return to your normal schedule. Or rather, your *new* normal schedule."

The game was tight, and the score was close. Elmhurst was playing exceptionally well, but the French Cantrell Academy was an even match for them. Mia sat nervously in the stands. With everything going on, the excitement of the game was overwhelming, and she felt like thousands of eyes were watching her and not the game. The blue uniforms of the Cantrell team blurred with the green of the Elmhurst players, and she tried to shake off the tension, and focus on the game.

The third quarter was winding down, and Cantrell had the ball. A quick pass underneath a leaping defender got to an open shooter. He bounced off a trampoline, flipped over the outstretched arms of one of Elmhurst's defenders, and slammed the ball in for the lead. The Cantrell side of the audience went wild, and sudden desperation filled the Elmhurst supporters. Taking the ball on their side of the court, the Elmhurst forwards tried to make a shot, but Cantrell stole the ball and began making their way back down the court.

"You should do something," Zander said, elbowing Mia lightly on the arm.

"Hmm?" Mia responded, having again lost focus.

"We're going to lose," Zander pointed at the court.

Mia gave a short laugh. "I thought you looked down on interference."

"This is the World Championships!" he exclaimed. Mia wondered if that meant when the stakes were high enough that his morality about cheating went out the window.

"No," she responded. "Cheating is cheating. Even in World Championships."

Off in a corner, not too far away, Narco, Orin, and the rest of his team sat in the stands, disguised. They were watching Mia with great interest, but the roar in the stadium was far too loud to hear what they were saying. Narco tried a spell that grew a small weed at their feet to act as a receiver to spy on them, but the crowd was too loud to identify anything other than the occasional word. He swore under his breath and turned to the bogan he had brought as part of his team.

"I need to know what's going on," he muttered. "I need her to get up and leave the stands. When she does, I'll cut her off."

Orin tried to object, to argue that perhaps blowing their cover wasn't the most strategic move, but Mia was standing, and Narco stood with her. He was already walking down the aisle, getting into position to wait for her. Orin shuffled from his seat to join him as they went to a mostly empty stairwell, across from where Mia was standing. She began to leave the stands, with Cinder, Vivi, and Luna joining her. Narco swore again.

"Why does she always have a posse around her?" he spat.

High above him, Dan and Steve were soaring over the stadium, watching the game below. Their attention was fully on the match as they believed Narco couldn't possibly be stupid enough to go after Mia where so many fae were looking for him. They swooped low for a better view of the play on the court, and their shadows passed over Narco, stopping him in his tracks. He looked up and saw something flying overhead.

CHAPTER NINETY

Narco watched the dark figures flying overhead and looked away dismissively. Just a bunch of flying monkeys making trouble. His face contorted in distaste, disgusted the league would allow them to attend the games. There should be some sort of screening process, some guidelines creatures had to follow in order to qualify to attend the events. Other, more appropriate beings shouldn't have to be subjected to them.

When he pulled his attention from looking around for an official intending to have the flying monkeys removed, Narco realized that Mia was on the move. Luna, Cinder, and Vivi in tow, she had left her seat, and was headed out of the stands. Narco pulled a folded note from his pocket and pressed it into Orin's palm.

"Take this to Mia, and be sure she reads it," he instructed.

He couldn't take the note up to the halfling himself. The instant he stepped out of the hiding place to approach her, he would be detained. Though he didn't see any security near her, and there wasn't anyone very obviously watching her closely, he knew the measures were there.

Especially now that it was well-known that her father was missing, Elmhurst would ensure there were plenty of adults on high alert around her. Orin was a different situation. No one knew who he was, nor would anyone have any reason to think he was a threat to Mia in any way. He could walk up to her, hand her the note, and be gone before there was any indication that anything was amiss.

Even if someone did have suspicions, it didn't matter. Narco didn't care if Orin was detained. At this point, his skill set wasn't needed any longer. It wouldn't be much of a loss for Narco if the other man was taken in. As long as Orin kept his mouth shut.

"What do I do if someone asks why I'm giving it to her?" Orin asked.

"Play dumb. Don't give any indication you even know what's inside. When you go up to her, say someone bumped into you in the crowd and asked you to give the note to her. Hand it to her and walk away. Just go somewhere like that's where you were headed in the first place, and like you have no idea that anything else is going on," Narco told him.

Orin nodded and walked toward the halflings.

***

"Excuse me."

Mia looked away from Vivi to the owner of the deep voice who was standing beside her. A man she didn't recognize held a folded piece of paper out to her.

"Someone in the crowd asked me to give this to you," he said.

She looked at the paper quizzically, then stared back at the man. "Who?"

He shrugged. "Just some guy." He waved it closer, and Mia took it. As soon as the paper left his hand, the man smiled and wandered away, quickly disappearing amongst the other spectators.

"Who was that?" Luna asked.

Mia shook her head. "I don't know. I didn't recognize him."

She didn't think anything of the man, but the paper in her hand intrigued her. She wondered what it could be, and why someone would want it given to her. She opened it. The words written inside the note made her head swim.

"It says I have to meet with Narco, alone, or my father will die. He says to meet him in one hour on the south side of the island," she told the others.

Alania hung back from the three halflings, watching as they moved through the crowd, and saw the strange messenger. He seemed casual and unaffected by the interaction, but his presence bothered her.

She flew higher to watch where he was going. The man strolled through the crowd, and made a few turns and twists, not going to any specific place. Soon, he looped around and walked a wide arc to avoid the halflings, before meeting up with Narco.

As soon as she saw the bounty hunter, Alania shot off toward the stands. Elmhurst and Cassia were sitting there among the others, watching the game. The championship was coming to an end, and despite all they were facing, they had wanted to take some time to experience this together. But they were all on edge, and as soon as Cassia saw the little faerie coming to her, she got to her feet.

"What is it?" she asked.

"Where are the others? Where are Zander and Carson?" Alania asked.

"They went to look for Mia. What's going on?" Elmhurst asked.

"Narco is here," the faerie announced.

Back near the concession stands, Mia felt as though her feet were rooted to the ground. She stared at the note, trying to process the words and decide what she was going to do. She was shaken out of the trance-like state by Cassia's voice.

"Mia, Narco has been spotted. The man who handed you that note is working with him," she announced.

Elmhurst moved slightly away from the group, standing with Mia at her back, and created a shield around them in case Narco was watching. Alania, Lily, Dalia, and Cinder knew he was watching them because *they* were keeping their eyes on him. But the shield would guard them, keeping Mia away from Narco if he did try to come for her.

"What are we going to do?" Cassia asked. "We can't just let him be here and do something like this without stopping him. We've been waiting for him to make himself obvious, and now he has."

"He's not going to go down easily," Elmhurst told her. "It would be too dangerous to go after him now. With this many people around, a confrontation could be disastrous. We need to limit the danger as much as possible."

"I'll go meet him," Mia said.

"What? No. You can't do that," Zander argued.

"Yes, I can. Look, he wants me. That's obvious. He has my father. He's hurt other people. It's all because of me. He's willing to get away from all these other people and not cause any trouble if I'll meet him alone. So, that's what I'll do. I'll go to the south side of the island, and he'll see me there, by myself," she said.

"But she won't be," Cinder added. "She won't be alone. I will be there with the other guardian faeries. We can protect her without Narco knowing we're even there."

"And Dan and Steve will be there as well," Elmhurst offered.

"We will stay in a central spot, and I'll create a pinhole portal," Cassia offered. "My team and I will watch, and as soon as Narco shows up with Mia's father, we will come through."

"Not until you know he's safe," Mia instructed.

Cassia agreed, but the other halflings surged forward.

"You can't do this," Vivi said. "Not alone."

"Mia, it's too dangerous," Luna said. "Even with Cassia and her team watching, something could happen before they even have a chance to get to you."

"Let us go with you. We have been in this together from the beginning. We want to be there and protect you. Remember what Princess Caledona said. You have people who will fiercely protect your safety and not let any harm come to you." Zander reached for her hand.

She held his hand for only a second before letting go, shaking her head as she stepped back from him. "No, Zander. She also said I would have friends along my path that will die for me. I won't let that happen to you. I can't let any of you come with me. You have to stay here," Mia demanded. She turned to Elmhurst. "Headmistress, you have to keep them here."

"I will," Elmhurst said. "It's not an option. None of the rest of you will be allowed to go. I understand your concern and that you believe you could help her. But it is far too dangerous for everyone involved."

"It's already too dangerous for her," Zander pointed out angrily. "This man has been trying to get to her since before she arrived at the academy, and you're just going to serve her up to him on a silver platter."

"If there was a way to get Narco there without Mia, I would do it in a heartbeat. But there isn't. He would see through glamours or spells to create a stand-in for her. He would know if we were trying to deceive him. Mia's father would be killed without question. Mia's own powers, along with the protections of the faeries and gargoyles...this is the best way." Elmhurst's sour face was the only outward indication of her hatred for this plan.

But internally, she was stewing. If there was time to get more trusted fae in place, she would do it. Sadly, this was the only way she could think of to capture Narco and end his pursuit of Mia.

CHAPTER NINETY-ONE

Mia didn't allow herself to feel afraid as she stood in the meeting spot, waiting for Narco. He might be able to sense her fear, and she wasn't going to give him the satisfaction of knowing he affected her in that way. She stood firm, looking around so she would see him coming. It felt like she had been waiting for hours when he finally arrived. But her father wasn't with him. Only the man who had come up to her at the game to hand her the note stood by his side.

Mia took an aggressive step toward him. "Where's my father?" she demanded.

Narco didn't respond immediately. He was scrutinizing their surroundings. He scanned the shadows and hiding places around them. When he was satisfied they were alone, he stepped closer.

Mia kept her eyes locked on him. She wouldn't allow herself to glance up at the faeries he hadn't noticed hiding among the branches of the trees, or the gargoyles flying high enough overhead to not be recognizable.

Narco looked at the man. "All right, ,."

Hearing some meaning Mia didn't understand, the man he called Orin turned away. He walked a few feet, opened a portal, and disappeared through it. Moments later, he returned, this time pulling James along with him.

The sight of Mia filled James with even more worry and he lunged toward her, wanting to comfort her. Orin tightened his grip on him, holding him back from going to his daughter.

"Let him go!" Mia shouted angrily. She stared Narco fiercely in the face, refusing to show fear, wanting him to see the threat in her eyes. "Let my father go now. He is human. He has nothing to do with this."

Narco sneered at her and made no move to have James released. "You don't know your father like you think you do," he said.

"What do you mean?" Mia asked through gritted teeth.

"Your father is more than human," Narco sniggered.

"I'm not falling for some stupid trick. Let him go," Mia exclaimed.

"You don't believe me? Why don't you ask him yourself?"

Mia turned to her father, who stared back with wide, sad eyes. But his lips didn't move. Eventually, he looked at his shoes, and Mia's breath hitched. Something more was going on than she knew, but she didn't have time for that now.

"I don't care," she said, at last. She faced Narco. "Let him go. That was the deal."

"New deal," Narco said giddily. "I'll let James go, but only if you go with me without a fuss."

"Mia, no," shouted James, and Orin shook him hard.

"Fine," Mia said, without missing a beat. "But only *after* you let him go. I need to know he is safe before I come with you."

Narco thought about it for a second, rubbing his chin before nodding at Orin. The scientist released James from his grip, and he ran to his daughter, embracing her. Mia embraced him tightly and felt him move his head so he could speak into her ear.

"They are going to double-cross you," he whispered.

"I know," she replied. "I have a plan."

But the portal should have opened by now, and Cassia should have come through. That was the plan. But nothing had happened. Moments ticked by as Mia waited, staring into her father's eyes. Behind him, Narco cleared his throat loudly.

"I really am getting impatient, Mia. We had a deal," he sneered.

"I am saying goodbye to my father," she shouted, hoping to stall for a few more seconds.

"No, you aren't," Narco said, stuffing his hands into his pockets as if he didn't have a care in the world. "You are waiting for your friends to show up. Unfortunately for you, they won't be coming. I saw to it they were distracted."

Mia swallowed hard and winced. So much for that part of the plan. Yet the fear she expected to grip her heart wasn't there. She wasn't afraid, nor was she worried. She was angry.

Exceptionally, extremely angry.

She could feel the anger taking complete control of her, and where she normally stopped it from engulfing her in a flame of hatred, this time she let it pass through, filling her with an energy she had never felt before.

"Mia, what's going on? Why are your hands glowing?" James said, taking a small step away from his daughter. Her eyes rose to his, brimming with tears, and the fire of vengeance beyond them.

"Run," she whispered in a hoarse voice. "Get away."

Before he had a chance to react, her body stiffened, her hands shot out by her sides, and electric sparks flew from her fingertips. A spark struck James, and he fell. The air crackled with sulfur and sparks, and she looked down at him, curled on the ground. He was okay but stunned. It was the only confirmation she needed.

Mia turned to Orin and held out her hand, fingers splayed. Clenching them into a fist, she shot a bolt of electricity that hit the fae in the center of his chest, knocking him several feet back and into unconsciousness. She stepped in front of her father, and faced off with Narco, her eyes narrowed and her jaw set. Mia raised her arm to point at Narco and sent a bolt of electricity at him.

Narco ducked, rolling to the side, and threw up a small blocking shield. The electric bolt bounced off and flew away, and Narco stood there, grinning. He had pulled his hand back, conjuring an attack spell of his own, when a shadow soared over him, low and foreboding. He looked up to see Dan flying at close range, and Steve just behind him.

Narco ducked in time to escape the reach of Steve's grasping fingers. From the trees came a warrior band of faeries, and Narco spun to see them. They were coming from every direction.

"What the crickets?" he exclaimed, not knowing which way to turn first.

"Dan, Steve," called Mia. "Take my dad and get him away somewhere safe!"

The gargoyles nodded, and grabbed an arm and a leg, carrying him safely away. Narco was still searching for a way out, and he spotted Orin sprawled on the ground. He elected to save himself. Opening a portal a foot away, he tried to jump through, but he bounced off. The portal closed, and he cast it open again. Before he could move, it was closed once more.

The faeries were now surrounding him, waiting. Outside the protective bubble, Cassia and the gang were shouting to be let in. He was surrounded, with no means of escape. Mia stepped closer and saw her friends, but she didn't drop the shield. She wanted to take care of this on her own.

"Why are you after me?" she shouted, getting his attention. Narco turned to her slowly, an evil, malevolent smile on his face. He laughed.

"I am far from the only one. You can do what you like with me, but there will always be someone after you, Mia. The queens cannot have you left alive. You will suffer death by someone's hands, sooner rather than later."

"Why?" Mia demanded. "Why me? I'm only a halfling, and I am still learning what that even means. There's no way anyone would follow me."

"You are much more than a halfling. And you know it."

Narco rushed at her, firing a ball of energy that missed wildly above her. It was meant to miss, to cause a distraction so he could hit her hard with his fists, but she was ready. Not fooled by the missed shot, Mia side-stepped, sweeping her leg out to kick him in the jaw.

He stumbled away, and charged again, swinging his fists lamely at her. He was no match for her years of Wushu training, and with little difficulty, Mia found an opening and smashed her fist into his face, sending him sprawling backward to land hard on his bottom.

Roaring, he stood again, and Mia shot an electrical ball at him. He ducked out of the way, but she pulled her hand back, casting a spell to bring the bolt curving around like a boomerang. It hit Narco in the back of the head, and then enveloped him. He fell to the ground, motionless, encased in what looked like a small, personal electric storm.

After he stopped twitching and was no longer a danger to anyone, Mia dropped the protective bubble. Cassia and the group rushed in, and they crowded around Narco's body.

CHAPTER NINETY-TWO

Elmhurst couldn't believe what she was seeing as she stood over Narco. The makeshift sarcophagus surrounding him was unlike anything she had ever seen a halfling create. It was truly incredible, and she couldn't help but be impressed at the sight.

"If this were a test, you would have gotten an A-plus, Mia," she said. She looked at the halfling, who still appeared shaken by her experience.

Mia's eyes narrowed slightly. "Um. Thanks," she said.

"No, you don't understand," the headmistress told her. "What you just did is something very rare. I have never seen a halfling accomplish anything even close to it. Most full fae can't even do it. Almost anyone who tried would end up killing the prisoner."

Mia shook her head. "I don't understand. What did I do?" She was confused and slightly disoriented. She didn't even know what had happened or why. Only that as soon as it did, the danger was over.

Cassia smiled at her. "Fan would be so jealous," she commented. Everyone looked at her with confusion, and the smile faded. She stared at each of them in turn. "What? Fan. You know, Fan, the head jailer?" None of them responded, and she shook her head. "Never mind. Anyway, Mia, you created a prison of sorts. When you sent out

665

that blast of electricity, you encapsulated Narco in an inescapable bubble. He won't be able to move, or leave it, for as long as he's trapped within it."

"But he doesn't have anything in there with him. No food or water. He won't be able to survive long," Mia said. "What good is it as a prison?"

"That's the thing. He doesn't need anything else in there with him. The bubble will keep him alive. He can survive in there for up to twenty-three years," Cassia told her.

"Twenty-three years?" Mia asked.

"Give or take, depending on how strong you are," the bounty hunter guardian clarified.

"Then it will probably be closer to fifty years," Zander said.

They all laughed, and Mia looked between Cassia and Elmhurst.

"I still don't think I understand. What does this all mean?" she asked. "What happens to Orin?"

She gestured at the fae still sprawled on the ground. His silver hair clung to his face, and his body looked broken.

Cassia shook her head dismissively. "Don't worry about Orin. I'll take care of him. He won't see the light of day for a very long time. Attacking a halfling at the Slamball World Championships will bring a very long prison sentence, with no chance of a hearing."

"What if he tells people who I am? Narco said he isn't the only one who is after me. He's working for someone else, which means there are other people out there determined to take me out. If they toss him into prison, Orin might start rambling about me to anyone who will listen. If he thinks having information about me could protect him, or get him any sort of better treatment or privileges, he's going to do it. I'll still be in danger."

"I'll see to it he can't say anything about you," Cassia reassured her.

The tone of her voice said she was serious, but Mia still didn't feel secure. "What about Narco? What will happen to him? He's stuck in that bubble for now, but what happens when he gets out? I can't imagine he's going to look at being stuck in an electrical bubble for that long as a time out that has mended his ways and changed his views. He's going to be mad as…crickets," she said.

"Try not to worry about Narco for now," Elmhurst told her. "I will take care of him. You've done everything you needed to. Far more, in fact. We have at least twenty-three years to figure out what to do with him."

Vivi shook her head. "Why should we bother leaving him in the bubble? We should just kill him. He's not going to do anyone any good, and Mia shouldn't have to live the rest of her life afraid because he's still out there."

"I agree," James said. He walked into their circle after the gargoyles released him. "There's no point in keeping him prisoner. He needs to be eliminated. He wasn't just looking for her so he could confirm who she was, and he didn't just have me in order to lure her out. I heard them say as soon as they had Mia, they were going to kill me. Then once they were able to conclusively confirm her identity, they would kill her as well." James put his arm around his daughter's shoulders.

"Killing him now would be too easy," Luna argued. "He has put Mia through so much. Just killing him wouldn't be justice. She deserves to know he's suffering."

"It isn't just that," Carson said. "Like Mia said, Narco was working for somebody, and that means there are other people out there who are a danger to her. Keeping him alive could give us access to information about them. He might not be willing to talk now but give him some time in the bubble, and he could start singing."

The group argued back and forth for several minutes before Elmhurst held up her hands to silence them.

"We have adequate time to consider all of the available options. We don't need to come to a conclusion today. For now, I'll lock him up in the basement of the library where he will be out of the way," she said.

"We'll keep an eye on him," Steve offered.

"Thank you. And now, it's time to go back to the academy. Dan and Steve will need to take their places again," the headmistress told them. "And I'm sure we all need some rest."

When they returned to the school, the group discovered a dejected campus. Dan and Steve had been drawn back to their pedestals and hadn't had the chance to discover that the Elmhurst Academy Slamball team had lost to the French team by one point.

Mia sighed. "At least we beat Narco." She glanced at her father. "What are you going to do now that you know everything?"

"You should stick close to the school," Elmhurst suggested before he had a chance to answer. "You can learn more, and the time near Mia will do you good."

Alania rushed forward. "Guardian Myla wants James to come to the pools to be trained."

The group looked at her strangely. They didn't understand why Myla would be insistent about something like that. The faerie shared a conspiratorial look with Cinder.

"If James is to survive, he needs to learn how to protect himself," Alania explained. "Who better than guardians to train him?"

Mia felt uncomfortable about the suggestion. This was all so much, happening so fast. She didn't understand what Narco had meant when he had said her father was more than human. She'd never seen any signs he wasn't human, but he had kept her background a secret from her. So maybe he also hid his own from her? *What did any of it mean?*

"I don't know if that's a good idea. I'm afraid for his safety. Wouldn't it be dangerous for him to be around the water of the pools considering how it is supposed to affect humans?" she asked.

Alania waved her hands in the air between them as though brushing away the idea. "That's all a myth. He will be perfectly safe. Besides, your father is not fully human, remember?"

"What does that even mean?" Mia had been wanting to ask about it ever since Narco had mentioned it, but now was the first chance, and she simply couldn't wrap her mind around it all.

Alania stared at James for a few moments, then looked at Mia. "I'm not sure. We should ask Orin about that. But, I can sense something fae about him. It's not much, but there is something inside him." She flittered around his head and sprinkled him with faerie dust.

Instead of floating in the air, she kept him firmly on the ground as she looked inside his aura. What she saw surprised her, but she didn't trust her sight. Alania was going to have to ask the Head Guardian if it was true. Only she would know.

When Alania pulled back, she released the dust that encased James and said, "Yes, he needs to come back with me."

"If that is what will be best for me, I'll do it," James agreed.

"And you will have permission to visit him," Elmhurst assured Mia. "Now that we don't have to hide anything, there's no need for you to be apart like you were. It will be better for both of you if you see each other frequently."

Mia and her father had agreed enthusiastically, relieved to not have to live in separate worlds any longer. Mia was thrilled to have her father back in her life and to be free to share everything with him again. The long months that had stretched between the times they had seen each other had made her feel as though everything wasn't quite real.

Now he would get to know her friends, Zander, and everything she was learning and experiencing because of the fae part of her. She was going to have her dad back in her life again, and she was thrilled.

The only thing missing now was Becky. She adored her friends here, but a part of her still missed her human best friend every day.

James spent the next several days at the academy with Mia, catching up on everything and getting his first taste of a world he never realized was his. Then it was time for Alania, Dalia, and Lily to take him back to Scotland and the faerie pools to begin his training.

Once James left, Mia went to the edge of campus alone. She knew better than to leave the school grounds without permission, but she wanted time to process everything. Her father wasn't human...well, not fully human. What did any of that even mean? She had talked with him about it, but they didn't know. Her father had suggested that he might be able to learn more from the faeries.

She had to discover more about her own powers, just like he had to learn what he was capable of, if anything. Alania had assured them James could be taught to tap into his inner strength. And if nothing else, he would learn how to fight the fae. For surely, this wasn't over with.

After stewing for a few minutes and crying for a few more, Mia wiped the tears from her eyes and turned to find she had company.

"What are you doing here?" She hiccupped and felt her cheeks heat up with embarrassment.

Zander rubbed the back of his neck and smiled wryly. "I thought you might want some company." He shrugged. "And...um...well, we never did get our date to see the German Vampire team compete."

Mia smirked. "Yeah, turned out those were some of the hardest tickets to get. Who knew, right?" She had known when he had originally asked that they wouldn't be able to get the tickets, but she didn't care. All she had wanted was to spend time with him alone.

Almost from the beginning of the World Championships, they had never been left alone. Even on their one date, they couldn't be alone. But now...

Zander dropped his hand when he realized his palms were wet. He didn't like the idea of spreading sweat all along the back of his neck. Hoping she didn't see it, he wiped his hands along the sides of his slacks.

"I thought maybe we could do something closer to home?" He didn't sound as confident as he normally was, and Zander mentally berated himself. He was the leader of their team, and she liked him, didn't she? So, why was he so dang nervous?

A slow smile spread across Mia's face, and she looked at her feet. "Yes, that would be nice."

Though her answer was more of a whisper, Zander still heard it, and his heart skipped a few beats. "How about dinner in town tomorrow night?"

Mia bit her lip and nodded.

EPILOGUE

The next time James returned to Elmhurst Academy, it was graduation day. He found it hard to believe the day had actually come, and Mia, along with the other halflings, would be graduating from high school. This wasn't the type of graduation he had expected to attend with his daughter when she was young.

Even two years before, he'd had a different vision of what it would be like to watch her graduate from high school and look ahead to what the future held for her. He had believed he would be sitting in the cramped stands around the football field of her high school in Pasadena, looking down at the folding chairs lined up on the grass. The large class of seniors would walk up to a stage built in the same place as for homecoming, pep rallies, and the annual senior picnic.

Instead, he now sat in the luxurious theater of the academy building to watch a group of impressive halfling students accept their diplomas. Of them, a small number stood to be acknowledged with special accolades.

He could barely contain his pride at seeing his daughter standing there among them. She beamed, the traditional fae cloak she wore sparkling with the pins and ribbons she had earned through her studies and exceptional accomplishments.

Though others had been training in their skills and magic throughout their entire lives, she still stood high above them in her capabilities. It had been born into her, a gift from the incredibly powerful princess far back in her bloodline.

For she had to be a descendant of Princess Violet. While he had learned about himself at the faerie pools, he had also learned more about his wife and daughter. Although he didn't know how many generations separated Princess Violet and his wife, Lilliana, one thing was sure—his daughter was a princess.

James knew that power came with risk. It put her in the crosshairs of people who didn't want her to exist. But he didn't want to think about that. Not today. Today was for celebration.

After the graduation ceremony, Elmhurst invited the families to a lavish banquet in the formal hall. Both human and fae came together to eat a decadent feast, enjoy entertainment, and meet each other. The five flitted around together, introducing each other to their families, and then their parents to each other.

Now it was Vivi's turn. She led them up to a stark-looking man James had seen watching Mia throughout the graduation ceremony. Vivi gestured at him. "Father, this is the group I have told you about. This is Luna, Carson, Zander, and Mia. Everyone, this is my father."

He looked less than impressed with them, not bothering to offer an insincere smile. His eyes locked on Mia for a long moment, as though he was contemplating something about her. But he didn't say anything. The group moved on, hurrying to Nicoletta, who stood at a dessert table set to the far side of the room.

"Mom, you don't have to stand with the desserts," Luna told her.

"Principal Elmhurst specifically asked me to make these for the celebration," Nicoletta argued. "She could have had anyone else make desserts. I'm sure the kitchen here at the school is more than capable."

"Not like you," Luna said. "No one can make the decadent creations you do." She scooped up one of the tiny individual cheesecakes her mother had presented on a cut-glass plate and ate it in one bite.

"I just want to make sure everything is all right," Nicoletta said.

"And we want you to enjoy yourself," Luna said.

"She's right. Come on," Carson said, taking Nicoletta's arm and tugging her toward the banquet table. "You deserve this celebration as much as any of us. Without your diner, and all the food you made for us, we wouldn't have made it through. I know I'm going to miss your veggie meatloaf."

Nicoletta laughed and allowed them to take her into the party. The group ate and danced, they sang and enjoyed magical drinks that sparkled and changed colors and flavors as they drank them. The party continued for hours, but finally, the families started drifting away, and soon it was only the Five, Cassia, James, and the faeries that remained. Elmhurst came up to them and gave a satisfied sigh.

"Now that it's just us, I wanted to let you know that Narco is gone," she announced.

Cassia's eyes widened, and she surged to her feet. "Gone? He's gone? He got out of his bubble?" she asked, her voice heavy with worry.

Elmhurst shook her head. "No. All I meant is that I had him moved into a room in the basement and the door concealed with a spell to ensure he's not messed with. Remember, it was Mia who put him in that prison. It will hold him for at least twenty-three years."

"Thank goodness," Cassia said, dropping back in her seat as the others laughed.

"And those years will give us time for Mia to train and learn as much as possible about who she is and what she can do. But that is for another time. For now, the five of you need to focus on college," the headmistress said.

Carson released a celebratory whoop. "I can't wait. I can't believe we all made it into the University of the Northwest."

It was the most prestigious university in the supernatural world, and only the best of the best were accepted there. For most halflings, going to UTN was a dream—something they all aspired to but few considered a possibility.

It would be a tremendous change for the halflings who had never attended anything but fae-based schools. Humans also attended the university and knew nothing of the supernatural programs. The halflings and fae who attended had to be extremely careful not to let the truth about themselves come out. If a human found out about a fae, the human's memory was wiped, and the fae was immediately kicked out of the school.

"What about you, Mia?" Zander asked.

"It will be amazing," she answered, but college wasn't what was on her mind.

"What are you actually thinking about?" Cassia asked.

Mia looked at each of them and released her breath.

"I have twenty-three years to claim my birthright. I'm not going to back down. I know who I am and what I need to do. It's just going to happen about a hundred years sooner than I expected."

AUTHOR NOTES J.L. HENDRICKS

MAY 11, 2020

WOW, first off, thank you so much for picking up this book and reading alllllllll the way back here! LOL This is one long book!

I am so excited that this series has finally launched! I approached Michael Anderle about doing this together back in October of 2018! He agreed right away, but it took me a little while to finish a project I had started and then once we began this one, it took longer to get right than I expected. The first book had three different iterations before we were finally happy. Then we sent it to the Beta Readers and had a lot of work to do. But I know it's a much richer story because of the fantastic people who volunteer to read LMBPN stories and offer their opinion on them.

So, I have to give a huge shout out to those on the LMBPN beta reading, editing, and JIT teams! And especially a huge thank you to Lynne and Kelly for managing the process on their ends.

But most importantly, I have to thank Mike. I wouldn't even be a writer if it weren't for him. Way back, during Christmas of 2015 I was out of work and wanted to read more before I went back to work in the corporate world. Turns out, I didn't have to thanks to a little-known indie author named Michael Anderle. When I reached out to ask if he needed help with beta readers, something I had done before, he said yes. There were four of us who ended up being talked into writing books of our own and publishing. Three of us are still working in this industry today.

Along the way Michael has helped me to improve my skills at writing, and he's introduced me to other authors who've helped my career in ways I could have never done on my own. He's my mentor and friend. Now, after two shelved attempts at writing together, we are finally collaborators as well.

If you've read any of his books before, then you'll know this one was a little bit different from what he normally does. Did you notice there weren't any cusswords? That was something he and I discussed at length. And laugh over all the time. While I prefer making up my own expletives, like stink and crickets, he enjoys putting together long sentences that would make a sailor blush while laughing so hard they spit their beer out. LOL But he has no problems leaving them out of a book when a collaborator doesn't want them. Thank you, Mike!

I can't wait to see what we can come up with together next! I know it will be exciting and unique. Hopefully, it will also include a halfling, or a little faerie who sneezes magic.

All my best,

Jen

AUTHOR NOTES MICHAEL ANDERLE

MAY 13, 2020

THANK YOU for reading our story!

We have a few of these planned, but we don't know if we should continue writing and publishing without your input.

Options include leaving a review, reaching out on Facebook to let us know and smoke signals.

Frankly, smoke signals might get misconstrued as low hanging clouds so you might want to nix that idea...

Cursing

Jen and I met as she was reading the first set of stories I ever wrote called The Kurtherian Gambit where I would write these little notes to the fans I called Author Notes.

Now, doing author notes is a common practice.

In these author notes, or at the end of the book I would mention our Kurtherian Gambit Facebook page where the fans and I would socialize and chat. During one of these discussions I was answering questions about being a new Indie Author and what I liked about it.

Feeling I needed to get the conversation about writing off of a page about the stories, I created a Facebook group and named it 20Booksto50k® and she was one of the first fans to move to this page.

I continued to share my thoughts on this opportunity (writing) as a business on that page.

(Just a note we are about to celebrate the 40,000th member joining the 20Booksto50K® group. If you are considering taking up writing and working to sell your stories, come join us – it's free.)

It's about this time in talking with those first four that I learned Jen actually didn't find the main character's cursing to be nearly as hilarious as I did. While there is a group of readers who love literary fiction (and the turn of phrase associated with the prose) I'm not one of them.

Give me a good turn of phrase with cursing? I seem to admire it.

Having admitted all of that I will suggest that maybe I am not so quick to throw in cursing after writing so many books. Even the best turn of phrase can get old and stale after writing and editing it a few hundred times over the course of so many books released.

Jen's first story released as we all talked about being an author and it broke the top 10,000 on Amazon back in 2016. Her results with book 01 (along with the other three authors results) got the attention of many other struggling indie authors. She will forever be known as 'One of the Four'.

She did a .…. *Great* Job!

(*No cursing...NO CURSING!*)

Diary for May 10th to May 16th

So last week, I blamed Ramy Vance for messing up my office in the virtual world with a bunch of gnome "stuff."

Unfortunately, I blamed the wrong person! Not only did I blame the wrong person, but I also got the right person upset by not giving her credit in the first place.

I can't make this up, people. (Well, ok, I could, but it wouldn't normally come to mind.) It seems that Elaine Bateman, and more importantly, Sarah Noffke, were the people responsible for putting up all the gnome stuff around my office.

It seems that Sarah was cheerleading Elaine the whole time. So, between the two of them, my virtual office was essentially TP'd.

Thinking that Ramy Vance, who had been talking to me about samurai and vampires, was responsible, I gave him credit last week.

FOR THE RECORD, it was Sarah and Elaine. Ramy has been exonerated, but I'm still not doing the Samurai / Vampire effort. But, you know it's "never say never."

(Editor's Note: If you do it, make sure you get the samurai armor right. Editors know these things. No pressure.)

VEGAS IS OPENING BACK UP SLOWLY

A couple of days ago, I was able to have a dining experience with Mike Bray of Wolfpack Publishing. On Saturdays, we normally eat at the Las Vegas golf club and enjoying chicken fried steak and hash browns. Little did I know this restaurant was the *only one* that had their dining room open at the moment.

It seems most of the other restaurants I enjoy don't have dining in yet.

I'm still starving for Chinese food, but the best Chinese restaurant I know of around Vegas is still closed. Ping Pang Pong is inside the Gold Coast Casino and won't be available for at least another five weeks.

Minimum

Do any of you remember when folks would pop up tents outside of Apple stores to get the latest iPhone when they went on sale? That might be my plan for when Ping Pang Pong opens again.

Did I mention I am still hungry for Chinese?

Oh, and chili. Maybe once the hotels/motels re-open, I can rent one with a kitchenette and make chili properly (which requires time, proper ventilation, and me not being at home where my wife smells it cooking.

(Editor's note: We are here for you any time, big guy, have fabulous ventilation, and we have Mexican Cokes. Plus, Marc loves chili! Bring Mike Bray! Only a short, scenic drive from Vegas.)

THE KURTHERIAN GAMBIT

On the Author side of things, I have great news for people who enjoy audiobooks. We signed a contract last week to publish the

Kurtherian Gambit first twenty-one books and the four books from the *Dark Messiah* series with RB Media, a multi-cast audio publisher.

I remember driving back and forth to work, listening to a couple of my favorite stories on Audible with multi-cast narration. To this day, I still hear the sound effects in the ships when opening doors inside, or the blast of their engines as the spaceships rose out of the water, heading to the deep dark of space.

To know that my own *Kurtherian Gambit* series is heading for multi-cast is a really cool feeling.

That's it for the diary entry for this week. I hope you have a fantastic week and weekend coming up!

Ad Aeternitatem,

Michael Anderle

ABOUT J.L. HENDRICKS

J.L. Hendricks is a USA Today Bestselling independent author who enjoys many genres, as evidenced by her catalogue of available books. She is currently focused on Clean & Wholesome Romance and Urban Fantasy, but has also written Space Opera, LitRPG, Paranormal, and Christmas books.

This past year has been spent researching the Clean & Wholesome genre for her new pen name, Jenna Hendricks. She also just finished writing an Academy Urban Fantasy series with a very exciting name in the Indie Publishing world.

One thing she learned early on is to accept help from others in the Indie world, and she is very grateful to those who have helped her along the way! The Indie publishing world is full of extremely nice and helpful authors, which is what makes this the best job she's ever had.

In early 2016 she decided to finally write, and finish a book, because of a few friends who encouraged her to do so. She hopes her stories entertain you and can bring a laugh on occasion.

Actually, it was her roommate's cat who talked her into staying at home to be her minion all day long! Pyper truly believes that J.L. is here to serve her alone.

Come and chat with J.L. on Facebook at:
https://www.facebook.com/JLHendricksAuthor/

But don't forget her website and blog at:
https://jlhendricksauthor.com/

OTHER BOOKS BY J.L. HENDRICKS

The Voodoo Dolls

Book 0: Magic's Not Real
Book 1: New Orleans Magic
Book 2: Hurricane of Magic
Book 3: Council of Magic

Worlds Away Series

Book 0: Worlds Revealed (join my Newsletter to get this exclusive freebie)
Book 1: Worlds Away
Book 2: Worlds Collide
Book 2.5: Worlds Explode
Book 3: Worlds Entwined

A Shifter Christmas Romance Series

Book 0: Santa Meets Mrs. Claus
Book 1: Miss Claus and the Secret Santa
Book 2: Miss Claus under the Mistletoe
Book 3: Miss Claus and the Christmas Wedding

Book 4: Miss Claus and Her Polar Opposite

The FBI Dragon Chronicles
Book 1: A Ritual of Fire
Book 2: A Ritual of Death
Book 3: A Ritual of Conquest

See these titles and more at https://www.jlhendricksauthor.com/

BOOKS BY MICHAEL ANDERLE

For a complete list of books by Michael Anderle, please visit:

www.lmbpn.com/ma-books/

All LMBPN Audiobooks are Available at Audible.com and iTunes

To see all LMBPN audiobooks, including those written by Michael Anderle
please visit:

www.lmbpn.com/audible

CONNECT WITH THE AUTHORS

Connect with J.L. Hendricks

Facebook:
https://www.facebook.com/JLHendricksAuthor/

Website:
https://jlhendricksauthor.com/

Connect with Michael Anderle

Website: http://www.lmbpn.com

Email List: http://lmbpn.com/email/

Facebook
https://www.facebook.com/LMBPNPublishing/